Praise for Stephen Deas

'His dragons are inscrutable, beautiful, magical, unstoppable'
Brent Weeks

'Dragons are restored to all their scaly, fire-breathing glory'
Daily Telegraph

'Deas does scary dragons very well'   *SFX*

'It is a difficult thing to write a novel that uses many of the icons of High Fantasy and make it enjoyable; this is something though that Stephen has done here. The book is an entertaining mix of Pern and Westeros, with the knowing characterisation of Abercrombie and the endearment of Novik'   *SFF World*

'A fun and entertaining debut that will appeal to fans of both classic and contemporary fantasy'   *Fantasy Book Critic*

'Roll over McCaffrey, there's a new Dragon Lord in town'
Falcata Times

DRAGON QUEEN

STEPHEN DEAS

Copyright © Stephen Deas 2013

The right of Stephen Deas to be identified as the author
of this work has been asserted by him in accordance with the
Copyright, Designs and Patents Act 1988.

First published in Great Britain in 2013 by
Gollancz
An imprint of the Orion Publishing Group
Orion House, 5 Upper St Martin's Lane,
London WC2H 9EA
An Hachette UK Company

This edition published in Great Britain in 2014
by Gollancz

1 3 5 7 9 10 8 6 4 2

A CIP catalogue record for this book
is available from the British Library

ISBN 978 0 575 10054 1

Typeset by Deltatype Ltd, Birkenhead, Merseyside

Printed and bound by CPI Group (UK) Ltd,
Croydon CRO 4YY

The Orion Publishing Group's policy is to use papers
that are natural, renewable and recyclable products and
made from wood grown in sustainable forests. The logging
and manufacturing processes are expected to conform to
the environmental regulations of the country of origin.

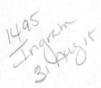

www.stephendeas.com
www.orionbooks.co.uk
www.gollancz.co.uk

My mother was an enchantress and my father was an alchemist.
They taught me the magic of this world and of many others.
They forged me as I am, and for that I am grateful.

Note: This story contains a scene of a violent sexual nature

No fear for consequence remains

I

The Bloody Judge

There was a peace to killing.

Men pressed him from all sides, crushed together. His own soldiers pushed against his back and to either side. Ahead, the enemy were forced before him by their own sheer numbers. He met them with remorseless savagery, slashing and stabbing, reaching for any inch of unguarded flesh. The black moonsteel edge of his sword glittered in the sunlight. Dark as night and sharp as broken glass, it shattered steel and splintered bone with a hunger all of its own. Spears and swords broke. Armour ripped open like skin beneath a tiger's claw. Entrails spilled across the ground to join the bloody mess of severed heads and arms. His feet slipped and slid beneath him. Sweat stung his eyes. The air stank of iron and death. Blood ran down his blade and over his gauntlets. He could feel it finding its way through the cracks and joints and seams, oozing down his arm underneath the leather and the metal scales. A part of him forgot his name, forgot why he was there, forgot everything and gave itself over to the savage he kept inside, letting it fill up every pore, every hair, every thought. The rest looked on as if looking down on the battle from above, ready to tell the madman when to stop. Yes, there was a peace to killing. He'd always found it so.

A spear glanced off the scales covering his ribs. A bone cracked but he barely felt it; an instant later he split the spearman with a thunderous blow. The pain shot up and down his side with every breath. He screwed up his face and howled. Tasted blood in his mouth as he stepped over the fallen body and sheared an arm from the soldier behind him. Damned sword was a horror of its own. It would cut through anything.

The Tethis soldiers broke and ran. He held his sword high, signalling his men to hold and not to pursue. He was breathing hard, and still each breath came with a wave of pain. Under the sun he was drenched in sweat. There was a breeze across the battlefield – he could feel it now he had some space in front of him. He wanted to take off his helm and let the wind cool his head, but he didn't. He'd been in too many battles for that.

'Shield line!' he roared. The ground right ahead was churned to mud, littered with spears and shields tossed aside by the fleeing soldiers. Bright sun glinted off discarded helms. He watched the Tethis soldiers go, scattering into the long grass, racing for the line of trees ahead. On another battlefield cavalry would have charged them down and made the slaughter complete, but Queen Gelisya had chosen her field well, edged with hummocks and holes and hidden ditches, and so he made himself be still and watch them go. The savage inside wanted their blood but the savage was always on a leash – always except in the thick of battle.

He looked up and down the line of his men, the shield wall packed hard again. *Berren. My name is Berren. Berren the Bloody Judge. Berren the Crowntaker.* Berren who'd once been a thief-taker's boy. He'd killed a king. Queen Gelisya's father. *Ten years of hell and misery and now I will end it.* He still tasted salt and iron. Blood. His or someone else's? He didn't know and he didn't care. His men raised their swords and their spears and banged them together and roared. One tight line of them. A wall of shields and deadly steel.

'On!' He lowered the moonsteel sword, pointed to the trees and snarled at the pain from his side. His hands felt sticky inside his gauntlets. A steady march. No reckless charge at the wood. If there was a trap then he'd not fall into it. They'd come at the enemy one last time, if there were any of them left. He'd smash them before the Dark Queen could rally. Ten years and she'd cost him every drop of blood she could take from him, her and her vicious coven. Their feud had defined them both.

A knot of the enemy emerged from the trees, half a dozen swordsmen packed tight. They ran straight at him, one mad suicidal charge. Pressed around by his own men in the wall of shields he had nowhere to go. He bared his teeth. The men either side of him readied their steel, and then Berren saw the seventh man, hidden between the screaming swords, and a flood of rage swept through him. A man in the colour of death – grey robes, grey cowl

– and at the sight bloodlust clamped his head in a vice and roared, all else forgotten. As the swordsmen reached him, crazy-eyed and wild, he bashed and battered their swings aside with his shield. The men either side of him lunged and slashed. One of the swordsmen barged into him, staggering him back, but the press kept him on his feet and he drove the moonsteel blade straight through the man's mail and into his heart. Blood sprayed over him as he snapped the sword away and the man fell, already dead. Another struck at him but his armour took the blow and turned it aside, and then the grey sorcerer was in front of him and it was the easiest thing in the world to drive his moonsteel through the heavy robes, through flesh and blood and bone until the point emerged from the man's spine and only its hilt stopped Berren's hand from reaching inside to pull out the warlock's entrails. The surviving swordsmen turned and ran, four of them still on their feet. Madness.

'For Talon and Syannis!' he hissed. Vicious triumph coursed through him, blood pumping hard and full of victory. He stared at the warlock, at the pale pasty skin of the sorcerer's face, the lines, the wrinkles, the sheen of sweat, the tattooed sigils, the dark flecks of blood, the dying gleam in the eyes, then snapped back his sword. 'One less of you.'

The warlock's lips drew back. 'For Saffran,' he whispered. The sorcerer's hand emerged from the sleeve of his robe and pressed a strip of paper covered in sigils to Berren's breastplate. Berren lurched back but there was nowhere to go in the crush. With a finger from his other hand, the warlock slashed one last bloody mark onto the paper.

Berren reached for the warlock and grabbed him. 'What have you done? What is this?'

The warlock was laughing. Blood ran out of his mouth and down his robes. He clutched at himself and clawed handfuls of it and threw it at Berren's face, then crumpled and fell, lips drawn back across his teeth, grinning blankly at the clear blue sky. Berren felt dizzy. For a moment his vision blurred.

Madness? They'd come at him to do this. They'd been ready to die. The warlock had given his life.

The sigil clung to him, fluttering in the wind. Cold fear spread across his skin. He tore at the strip of paper with his gauntlet but the metal fingers were too clumsy. It seemed stuck. He plucked at the strip of paper again but it wouldn't come free. Stuck fast. His heart was pounding now, harder even than in the thick of the battle. Sweat ran into his eyes. He tore off his helm and lifted his sword. 'Stop! Stop!' Then the sword fell out of hands. He was shaking so badly he could barely stand any more. He threw off his gauntlet and tore at the paper with his fingers, but when they touched it they tingled and went numb. The numbness spread up his arm. He pawed at the thick leather straps of his breastplate but his fingers had lost all feeling. They seemed to belong to someone else.

His friend Tallis One-Eye beside him him threw down his sword and shield and grabbed at the paper too but it slipped through his grasp.

'Get it off me! Get it off me!'

Tallis gripped Berren's shoulder. Threw off his own gauntlet.

Berren fell to his knees, gasping shallow panicked gulps of air as though he was dying. The world slowly spun. Tallis's fingers closed over the strip of paper. The spear-pinned and arrow-pricked bodies lying in the grass ahead shimmered into darkness. He could hear the dying warlock's laughter.

The sigils began to tear.

Skyrie ... The name oozed inside his head.

Bellepheros

2

An Unexpected Departure

Nine months before the Adamantine Palace would burn in the rage and fire of woken dragons, Bellepheros wiped his brow. It took him a few seconds to realise that Queen Shezira's knight-marshal hadn't followed her mistress away. She leaned in to speak quietly in his ear.

'Grand Master Alchemist. A private word, if you please?'

They had their quiet word and she gave him a spherical glass bottle, stoppered and sealed with wax. It fitted nicely into the palm of his hand and, from the way its weight shifted, it was filled with a liquid of exceptional weight. The knight-marshal had no idea what it was, but Bellepheros did. There was nothing curious about what was inside, but what was intriguing was where it had come from and how several such bottles had found their way into the knight-marshal's hands. It was a long journey home, though, and there would be plenty of time to ponder and plenty of comfortable inns and fine wine to help him think. Not that the knight-marshal's bottle would be top of his thoughts. Queen Aliphera's death – *that* was the mystery that needed thinking about. Fallen from the back of her dragon? A tragic accident? Absurd, but he'd been through the whole of Prince Jehal's eyrie with his truth-smoke and questioned everyone he could think of and what had he found? Nothing.

Who profited from the queen's death, then? Her first daughter Zafir would take the crown. Was there something between her and Jehal? Maybe so. The other daughter, Kiam? Her brother Kazalain? But then you didn't have to try too hard to find half a dozen kings and queens and princes who might be quietly joyful at Aliphera's passing.

He left the Veid Palace the next morning. He borrowed a carriage from Prince Jehal – the least the Viper could do for wasting so much of his time – and took a handful of soldiers for an escort while he was at it because apparently there were bandits on the road to Farakkan. From there, the Pinnacles and the Silver City – Aliphera's palace and home – were straight on his way back to the Adamantine Palace. It wouldn't seem odd for him to pass through and stay for a day or two. Maybe there he might find a clue.

He tucked the knight-marshal's bottle under his seat, carefully packed in straw. The alchemists at Clifftop could find their own way back. They had better things to do than smoke out a murderer. Alchemists had their business with dragons, not with men.

Two days out of Furymouth, in the middle of nowhere, the carriage stopped. He had no idea why; but he was trying to read and it was hard work at the best of times squinting to make out the tiny words – he'd have to have some scribes make copies of books with bigger letters – and so it was a relief to have a pause in the jolting up and down. Going by river would have been so much easier and more pleasant. He'd been ruing his decision to visit the Pinnacles almost ever since he'd left, but it needed to be done.

He heard a shout from outside. Alarm. Then several screams and cries of terror. Then silence. He sat very still, exactly as he'd been a moment before with the same words right before him but now they blurred as his eyes glazed. He listened, hardly daring to breathe. Not a sound.

The carriage swayed slightly in a gentle gust of wind and then the door burst open. An odd-looking man stood outside. He was small and his skin was dark from the sun. His hair was black and slick and he was panting and sweating. Strangest of all, though, was the black robe edged in woven strands of red and blue and white. It struck Bellepheros as more suited to a palace or a temple than to robbery on the road.

'Out, you!' he snapped. He had an odd lilt to his voice.

Bellepheros snapped his book shut. 'Who in the name of the Flame are you?' Indignation scoured a frown across his face. Then he saw past the man to the body on the ground outside. His heart skipped a beat and started to race. 'What do you want?'

The man reached in and grabbed him by the wrist and pulled. He was strong and Bellepheros almost fell out of the door on top of him, but the man moved nimbly aside and Bellepheros sprawled out into the road instead. Dry autumn leaves covered the ground, yellows and reds and browns rustling gently in the breeze. Birds sounded in the trees to either side. The carriage stood still, the horses standing in their harnesses as if nothing had happened. One of them snorted and stamped a hoof. There was no sign of anyone else. Every bit a tranquil autumn morning if it hadn't been for the blood and the dead man at his feet.

'People call me the Picker.' The odd-looking man climbed into the carriage. He rummaged around and came out holding Lady Nastria's bottle and Bellepheros's book. 'That all you got in there?'

Bellepheros sat up. Around the carriage Prince Jehal's soldiers were lying in the leaves, every one of them. They weren't moving. Bellepheros stared at them. 'Are they dead?' he whispered, his mouth suddenly dry.

'Yes. Shame for them. Wrong place to be.' The Picker climbed onto the carriage and hauled Bellepheros's chest off the roof. 'You really need all this? Can you do without it?' He went over to the horses and set about freeing them from their harnesses. Bellepheros rose shakily. He looked up and down the road. He had no idea where they were. No idea how far it was to the next town or village or what chance there was of someone else coming along.

'Are you a bandit?' *One man?* Bellepheros crouched beside the closest of the bodies. Expertly killed. One slash across the neck. Blood everywhere, pooling about. The leaves were sticking to it. This one hadn't even drawn his sword before he'd died. Bellepheros peered into the sun-dappled shadows between the trees. Jehal's soldiers were spread around the carriage, six of them. They hadn't had time to close up. It had happened with murderous speed. There had to be more than just the one man. 'Where are the rest of you?' He had a knife of his own, as every alchemist did. A little thing. He slipped it out of his belt and cut a little slash into his palm.

The Picker nodded at the bodies. 'I done that. Indeed. Just me.' He finished with the horses and led them alongside the carriage. Then he picked up the bottle and tossed it at Bellepheros.

Bellepheros caught it and backed away. 'That? *That*'s what this is about?'

'That?' The Picker frowned and shook his head. 'Stupid, is you? Can't be leaving it lying about is all.'

'Do you know who I am?'

The Picker started trying to lift Bellepheros's chest onto the back of one of the horses, but it was too heavy. He set it down again and put his hands on his hips and frowned. 'Friends I got about the place, they sell what's in that bottle to who wants it. You and I knows what for but they just sells to whoever asks. I has a question, though. What's wrong with boats?'

'What?' His wits were coming back to him. 'Listen, whoever you are. I see you know how to kill men, but I am an alchemist. I don't want to hurt you but I will if I have to. Harness those horses back to my carriage, please, and then I suggest you go away before anyone else comes along this road.' He squeezed his fist. His blood oozed over his wrist.

The Picker snorted. 'I knows exactly who you is. Bellepheros. Grand master alchemist of all the nine realms. Important fellow, right enough.' He glanced around at the bodies lying in the leaves. 'Didn't expect I'd get to you quite so simply, mind. You coming with me easy or shall we make it hard?'

One man and he'd killed half a dozen armoured soldiers of Furymouth without so much as a scratch. Bellepheros peered at the Picker. He had pale skin, but if you looked past that, if you closed your eyes and listened to the way he put his words together, he clearly came from across the sea. 'You're a Taiytakei.'

The Picker laughed. 'Does I look like one?' Then he frowned and kicked Bellepheros's chest in frustration. 'Going to have to come back for that. You really need it all?'

'Your skin makes you one of us. But you speak like one of them.'

The silence after that was an awkward one. The Picker didn't move. He looked Bellepheros up and down. 'Asked you,' he said, after the silence had become as brittle as glass, 'what's wrong with boats? Don't like them, is that it? Make you sick-like? Seems a right- and proper-thinking fellow like yourself, heading home from Furymouth to the City of Dragons, he'd get a boat. Plenty enough of them, after all. That's if he's not going on dragonback. All sorts of difficult *that* would have been. Could have done a boat without this mess though.' He gestured at the dead soldiers. 'Man has a talent for something, doesn't mean he always wants to use it.'

Taiytakei. They knew who he was. Not some bandit, then. Bellepheros looked at his hands. They were shaking. He walked slowly to the chest, to where the Picker stood.

The Picker scratched his head. 'Where's a good place to put this, nice and out of the way?'

Bellepheros wanted to say he was sorry for what he was about to do but that felt ridiculous. He drew back his fist and then flicked his hand sharply, flinging droplets of blood straight at the Picker's face.

The Picker vanished. Disappeared with a small pop of air. The drops of blood spattered over the side of the carriage. The painted wood fizzed and pitted and burst into flames that slowly sputtered and died.

'Waste of time, that.' The Picker was a dozen paces behind him, breathing hard as though he'd just run up the entire stair of the Tower of Air. A sheen of fresh sweat began to bloom across his skin. 'Waste of time to run too.'

'I know what you are!'

'Makes the two of us then.' The Picker held up whatever was in his hand. As it caught the sun, Bellepheros saw it was a short sword with a blade so fine and thin that it was invisible save for the blood that still dripped from its hilt and where its edge sparkled as it cut the light. 'Look at you. Full of books and learning. Doesn't surprise me that you know.' He turned his sword over in his hand, looking at it.

'Blades so thin the sun shines through them.'

The Picker nodded. 'So they cast no shadow, you see.' The Picker wiped the blood from his invisible blade and sheathed it again. Bellepheros tried to think what he could say. What else he could do. No point in asking what the man wanted – *that* was obvious now. Him. They wanted him. The Taiytakei wanted an alchemist. Beg for mercy?

He looked up and down the road, as if looking might make a hundred armed riders suddenly appear, riding to the rescue. But no. The only movements were the little swirls of sun-dappled leaves caught in tiny whirls in the breeze.

'You know what's next, right? Clever fellow like you. Want another moment to think it all out? There's no one coming on this road for an hour each way. Likely more. Checked I did, before I came. No rush.'

Bellepheros was quivering all over now. 'So you're just going to take me back to Furymouth, is that it?'

'Stick you on a ship and sail you away.'

He still had his little knife in his hand. Now he held it to his own throat. 'I won't let you.' Standing there ready to cut his own throat, and still he had a head full of questions clamouring to be asked, the sort of questions an alchemist learned to have about everything. *How do you work? Where do you come from? What do you do? How do I make you useful? What happens when we die?* The last always a good one after a bottle of fine wine. Maybe now he'd find out. He was an alchemist, after all, so he knew exactly where to cut, and it struck him as he stood there that the questions were more powerful than the fear, that for him it had always been that way. Dying wouldn't trouble him that much at all. 'You can really turn into air, water, earth, as and when you wish?' He shook his head. 'Just ... whenever you want?'

'Fire too.' The Picker took a deep breath and cocked his head. He walked a little closer and picked up a sack, gestured at the knife. 'Think that will work? I knows a blood-mage. Worse than you, maybe. And say you's quick enough to cut before I stops you. I just find another. More men die. Got a good name for me to go looking for?'

Bellepheros hesitated. His hands were shaking. Trying to think it through. Trying not to be afraid because why, what was there to fear? And yet fear had him tight now.

The Picker took another step. 'Why's it so hard here, what I do?' He wrinkled his nose at the dead men. 'Right you was, about where I's from. Mostly. But where I learned, it was easy. Easy like talking. Could do it all day long. Here it's like tar. Took years to get used to it. Still knocks the wind out of me doing so much at once.' He held out the sack. 'You need to be putting that knife down now and putting this over your head.'

'Dragons.' Bellepheros shook his head. 'You think taking me will somehow bring you dragons?'

'That's what it is, Mister Grand Master Alchemist of the Order of the Scales. Dragons. Always was, always will be.'

Bellepheros shook his head. 'No.'

'Going to make this difficult, are you?' The Picker looked

down at the sack. 'Suit yourself.' He turned his back and started to walk away and then vanished in a swirl of fallen leaves, and at the same time Bellepheros felt a hand on his arm, yanking the knife away from his neck and then a blinding pain under his ear where his jaw met his skull. The knife fell from his fingers. He gasped and whimpered and staggered forward. It hurt so much that he couldn't see, couldn't even think any more.

The Picker scooped up the sack and threw it over the alchemist's head. Bellepheros fell to his knees. The Picker hauled him back to his feet. 'And there's another thing. That spear. Easy one for a fellow like me, you'd think. But no. Can't shift that at all, not one little bit. Why?'

Bellepheros still had blood on his hand, blood that could burn or bend wills. He flailed at the Picker through the haze of pain. The Picker caught his arm and bent it behind his back, forcing him to the ground again, knees digging into him, pressing his face to the earth. He could barely breathe. On his back, the Picker was making soothing hushing sounds as a rope slipped around Bellepheros's neck and drew tight.

'Peaceful here, isn't it? Don't you worry, I's not going to kill you. Just needs you quiet a bit.'

The rope drew tight. Bellepheros writhed but the Picker had him fast. He choked. Gasped. His lungs heaved but the rope was tight around his throat. A dark sea roared over his thoughts and drowned them. He felt the warmth of the sun on his hand and the dry autumn leaves crack between his clenched fingers. He heard the distant singing of the birds. And then nothing.

3

Tuuran

When Bellepheros came round, he was hog-tied across a saddle with a bag over his head and cloth stuffed into his mouth. Stabbing pains shot through his head to the steady *thump thump* of a dull thudding ache.

He bit the inside of his mouth and let a little blood seep into the cloth. Then tried to merge his mind with the blood to make the cloth dissolve away. He could do the same with the sack. Then, maybe, with the Elemental Man ...

Nothing happened. The power simply wasn't there. The blood-magic was gone. He tried again. Still nothing, and then the real panic came because, without that, what was he? A weak old man, no use to anyone. He started to struggle, pulling ineffectually against the ropes around his arms and wrists, crying out through the gag.

The horse stopped. The bag came off his head and the world flooded with light. He screwed up his eyes and blinked furiously. A hand grabbed his hair, tipping back his head. The Picker's face peered into his.

'Worked then, did it?'

Behind the gag, Bellepheros screamed. He couldn't breathe!

The Picker sighed, undid the gag and lifted him off the horse to lie flat on his back. They were in some woods, among waist-deep bracken. The air smelled of old earth and mushrooms.

For a moment fear got the better of him. They were going to kill him. 'What do you want from me? What have you done to me? Are you going to kill me?' He gulped at the air like a man drowning.

The Picker snorted. 'Kill you? You gone daft? What I want is for you to be good and quiet till I get you where you need to be. And what I done is give you a taste of something. Tolds you I knows a blood-mage. So you'll not be doing them sorts of tricks like you tried before, not any more. Keep your blood nice and quiet. Likes my life easy, I do.'

'Why are you doing this?'

The Picker sighed. He turned his back and waited a while until Bellepheros stopped struggling, then heaved him over the back of the horse again like a dirty old carpet and tied the sack over his head once more. He left the gag off this time.

'No one here, old man. Shout all you like. You's clever enough, though. You'll see where this is going if you stops to think.'

They rode on. After maybe an hour it started to rain. Bellepheros heard the soft hiss of it on the leaves overhead, the *pitter-patter* of drips coming down off the trees, felt wet splats now and then on his hands and his legs. Afterwards the air smelled of trees, the rich tang of wet leaves. So they were on the fringes of the Raksheh, maybe, since that wasn't far from where the Picker had kidnapped him. Stupid thoughts buzzed in his head: he liked the Raksheh. He had fond memories of times years ago, wandering the edge of the forest, picking mushrooms and searching for roots and flowers. The Raksheh was a paradise for alchemists, full of interesting plants and strange crawling, slithering creatures. A delight as long as you kept a sharp eye on the lookout for the snapper packs.

In the middle of the afternoon they stopped and the Picker let him go and have a piss behind a tree and gave him some water. 'Nothing in it, not this time,' he said. Bellepheros wasn't sure whether to believe him, but he was thirsty enough to drink it when he saw the Picker drink it too. When the Picker threw him back on the horse, he forced himself to be an alchemist again, to think the way he'd been taught, the way he now taught others: sum the actions of the Taiytakei over the years. Arrange them with method and logic. They wanted dragons and they always had. To control a dragon, you needed an alchemist.

He tried asking questions. 'Have you already got them? Are they hatchlings or are they still eggs?' Others, anything he could think of, looking for a response, but the Picker never answered. Maybe he was thinking about it all wrong. Maybe they'd take an alchemist first, before the dragons. It made more sense.

He wondered, vaguely, about whether he might escape. Didn't

see how, though. He needed to work his blood. Without that he was useless. And there were ways to take away a blood-mage's powers – he knew several and he knew how to get round most of them too – but without knowing how the Elemental Man had done it, and being tied to the back of a horse as he was, all that knowledge was useless.

They stopped before dark at some old hut deep in the forest. The Picker took off the sack and untied his hands and locked him inside. When he rattled the door, it was shut fast. He tried shouting a few times for help but no one came, and for all he knew the Picker was right outside. He huddled in a corner and spent most of the night shivering, too cold to sleep.

In the morning he tried to work his blood again. Still nothing. He tried running when the Picker opened the door but that just made him look an idiot. The Picker watched, laughing probably, then vanished and appeared right in front of him and tripped him and tied him up and left him flat on his back while he went to fetch the horse. Bellepheros listened to the calls of the birds and the hiss of the wind among the trees. It wasn't the Raksheh, he decided. For what that was worth. The birdsong was wrong. They'd gone back towards Furymouth. They probably weren't far from the river.

In the middle of the day they came to a road. The Picker hauled Bellepheros off his horse and stuffed him into a carriage. The sack stayed over his head. For all he knew, it was the same carriage he'd been in yesterday. There were two others with him now, men who never spoke but who smelled of Taiytakei. They stopped every few hours and let him out to empty his bladder or his bowels. In the middle of the day the Picker took off his sack and watched him eat. The carriage windows were boarded shut. None of them spoke a word. After he'd eaten, the sack went back on.

The carriage kept going, rattling up and down, shaking his bones. He felt the ground change from grassy earth to hard-packed mud. As the day wore on, the sounds outside the carriage changed too. There were people now. Animals. Birds. Seagulls. The road became teeth-jarring cobbles and he knew where they were – right back in Furymouth, where he'd started. Before long he could smell the city. He cried out for help, shouted himself almost hoarse, but no one answered and the roll and bounce of the carriage never faltered. By the time they stopped and bundled him out, he'd long since given up. Rough hands gripped his elbows and almost carried him and then dumped him down and took off his sack. He was in a big open hall. The first thing he saw was a mosaic – the great Vishmir with the sun and the moon and the stars sitting at his feet – in all its brilliant colours. The floor was a mosaic too, made of tiny tiles not much bigger than a fingernail. White, mostly, but with lines of vibrant green and vivid blue trailing across it like discarded strands of silk.

He knew exactly where he was. The Paratheus. He looked at the dome overhead to be sure but he hardly needed to. Others thought of the Paratheus as a Taiytakei temple, but that wasn't really true. *Paratheus* was just another way of saying a place of learning. It was *their* place, though. Their place within the sea king's city. The air inside was cool despite the heat of the early autumn sun and smelled of incense, not of fish like the rest of the city. Even Jehal's palace had smelled of fish.

'Noisy you were in there. Didn't help though, did it?' The Picker smiled. 'Pretty place this.' His smile grew wider as if he was letting Bellepheros in on some great secret. He took a step closer. 'They had gods and so forth once. Was us who took those away from them. Like burning out the badness. Hurts when the brand comes but best in the long run. It's all mathematics, geometry and astronomy now. And a few other bobs and bits I shan't be speaking of just here. Supposed you might like to see this. Being as you are what you are.'

Bellepheros met his eye. 'I'd prefer it if you let me go.'

The Picker shrugged. 'Daft, you is.' And before Bellepheros could protest, the sack was back on again. 'Been a fine little ride we've had. Got me some different trouble to be stirring now, so I leave you in the tender care of others.'

Those others, when they came, were Taiytakei through and through, black-skinned men in rough tunics, sailors, led by two men in dull feathered cloaks that had seen better days, their hair in short braids down to their shoulders. They carried spiked clubs and they dragged him and a dozen other slump-shouldered captives from the Furymouth slave market through streets lively with shouting traders and carts rattling over cobbles. Dragged him with a leash around his neck and a bag over his head and no one said a word.

'Help me!' he cried, though he knew it wouldn't make any difference. 'I'm an alchemist, not a slave!' All he heard was laughter, and then someone cuffed the back of his head, hard enough that he saw stars and almost fell. To the rest of the world he was nothing; and the Taiytakei wandered to and fro with their slaves every day in these parts of the city and no one batted an eye. The smell gave it away. They were by the docks, and the Taiytakei as good as owned the Furymouth harbour districts. Sea lords, living in the shadow of dragons.

The heat of the sun on his skin through his clothes was uncomfortable, enough to make him sweat. Warm enough that it must still be high in the sky. He knew they'd reached the sea when a fresh breeze ran over him, tingling his skin, swirling with the harbour scents of salt and wood and tar and ropes. They lifted him up and threw him in a boat that rocked up and down with the waves. They rowed him out to sea a way and then they hauled him onto one of their ships as though he was a cow or a horse and dumped him on the deck. New voices surrounded him, Taiytakei sailors with accents he could barely penetrate. The sack stayed over his head. He reached for the power in his blood again. Still nothing.

A hand touched his arm, more gentle than the others. 'Can you walk?' It pulled him gently to his feet and held his arm. 'They have a cabin for you. I'll help you there.'

Bellepheros rose unsteadily. 'I would like ... to see.'

'If I take that sack off, old man, they'll throw me over the side.'

The voice had no accent. Bellepheros took the man's hand in his own and felt it. Rough calloused skin used to hard work. He fumbled like a blind man until he touched the man's face. 'You're not one of them.'

'No. Come.' The hand came back and took his arm again and led him forward. It led him through steep stairs and narrow passages that creaked and rolled, unbalancing him with almost every step, but the hand that led him seemed used to it. It took him through a door and let him go. Bellepheros heard the *click* of a lock and then at last the sack lifted from his eyes. He looked his new jailer up and down. He was a big man. Tall and broad and full of muscles.

He wore a tunic, a filthy grey that had once been white, torn and ragged and belted with a frayed piece of rope. A key hung on a piece of twine around his neck, the key to the cabin door.

'I am Tuuran.' He held out his arms, palms upward. On his left forearm he carried a brand, a lightning bolt than ran from his elbow halfway to his fist. 'I am the property of Sea Lord Quai'Shu of Xican.' For all his brutish size, his eyes glistened. He kept peering past Bellepheros to the tiny round window set in the cabin wall, to the sea and the coast and Furymouth beyond. Then he backed away. 'This realm was my home once. I was raised in the City of Dragons.' His words carried sadness and resentment, tinged still with anger.

'I am Bellepheros,' said Bellepheros.

'I know who you are, alchemist.' *Alchemist*. That meant something. Tuuran's eyes flashed, then he looked away, down at the floor. 'I was an Adamantine Man once. I'm sorry for you. An alchemist.' He shook his head.

Absurd hope surged through Bellepheros. An Adamantine Man? One of the speaker's soldiers, fearless, sworn to serve without thought of consequence, a man who trained from birth to fight dragons. He squeezed across the tiny cabin bed to peer through the miniature window in the ship's timber hull. Across the waves the white walls of Furymouth shone in the sun under red tile rooftops. 'I am not *just* an alchemist,' Bellepheros hissed. 'I am Bellepheros, grand master of the Order of the Scales, and if there is any part of you left that is still an Adamantine Man and does not serve these mongrels, you will have me away from this ship and returned to my kin in any way you can!'

'*The* Bellepheros?' Tuuran looked surprised.

'Yes! Help me!'

Tuuran shook his head. He turned away, and when he turned back there were tears on his cheeks. 'I've waited nine years to come back to my homeland.' He moved across the cabin to sit beside Bellepheros, staring through the window too, looking out over the sea at the harbour. 'We've been here two weeks waiting for you, and I've spent every moment of every day with the land that used to be mine just out of reach. If there was a way to be free then I'd have found it and I'd be long gone. If the chance came now then I wouldn't take you with me, old man, because you'd slow me. I'd gladly forget the vows I made and the man I once was. I'm not afraid to die, Grand Master Alchemist. In my heart I *am* still Adamantine. But this is a sea lord's ship, filled with soldiers in their armour of glass and gold and their wands that hurl lightning. I've looked long and hard and for many years and I'm still here. There's no escape, Master Alchemist.' He shrugged. 'I'm only here because of you, and now you're here too they'll be watching us both with the eyes of a dragon. Grand master of the Order of the Scales, eh?'

'Do you have a knife?' No, he could see he didn't. But there must be something sharp. He could pick off a splinter of wood. With a splinter he could bleed and he was fed up with having to bite his cheek. He started to look for something that would work, something to pick apart. Blood was the key. They couldn't keep his power away for ever. He'd refuse to eat. Refuse to drink until whatever it was the Elemental Man had done to him wore off. And then …

The Adamantine Man shook his head. 'They'll not let you out, not ever. Now that you're here, we'll be gone before dusk and I will never see my homeland again.'

The pain in Tuuran's words struck Bellepheros dumb. *There is a way. There is always a way.* But the words stuck in his throat. Maybe there wasn't. The enormity of it shattered his thoughts. That they really might take him away. Even walking through the Furymouth docks with a sack over his head, a part of him had thought … well, that someone would come.

But who? With the sea between them, he knew better now. No one even knew he was missing. He had until dusk? 'Wands that hurl lightning?' he asked instead.

'You'll see them.' Across the water the sun was already sinking and the colours of the world were collapsing. In the distance little boats with sails rode the waves; on the hill above Furymouth, overlooking the sea and the mouth of the Fury river, the Veid Palace stood in silhouette. Prince Jehal, who might or might not have been a murderer, and his dragons. Resentment made Bellepheros's skin burn. For being here. For the kings and queens sitting in their palaces, ignorant and doing nothing to help him. For whoever had thrown Aliphera from her dragon and dragged him from his sanctuary in the first place.

Tuuran clenched his fists. He looked ready to smash through the side of the ship with his bare hands. 'Do you hear? All those sounds, those little movements? We're leaving. They were getting ready before you were even aboard.' He raised his branded arm. 'I earned this pulling oars on one of their galleys. It says I'm a sail-slave and not an animal. I know every sound a ship makes. I've also heard it said that the high alchemist has the power to call the dragons to him. I never much believed it, but if you can, you should do it now!'

Bellepheros shook his head. He'd worked a splinter loose now and he pricked himself with it. A little blood on the fingertip. He reached for it with his mind and his shoulders sagged. Still nothing. 'Alchemists cannot call dragons, Tuuran.'

The ship began to turn. Tuuran stared through the window until they were out of sight of land. 'I'd hoped, at least, to see a dragon one more time,' he said. There was despair in his voice now. Bellepheros just felt bewildered. Numb.

The ship rolled slowly. Back and forth, back and forth. He started to feel sick. A dull spark of anger began to flicker inside him. Anger at the world. At this Adamantine Man, this servant of the speaker, for not conjuring a miracle. Anger at the door for staying closed and barred. Futile, but still no helping it. The Taiytakei had always wanted dragons. And if they had dragons then they would need an alchemist. Although it would have been kinder, Bellepheros thought, to steal one who was younger.

And if they really did have dragons, then what? What would he do?

'What do they want with you?'

Bellepheros laughed, full of bitterness. 'The Tyans of Furymouth moved their eyrie further down the coast many years ago. To keep the dragons and the Taiytakei apart. Dragons and ships are a poor mix. There's been more than one fleet burned to the water outside Furymouth, but that's not why they moved their eyrie. They moved their eyrie to keep the Taiytakei away from their dragons, not the other way around.'

'Ayzalmir,' murmured Tuuran.

Bellepheros looked at him in mild surprise. 'An Adamantine Man who's heard of Ayzalmir?' He chuckled for a moment before his thoughts turned bleak again. 'No, Speaker Ayzalmir never burned the Taiytakei fleet. It was his edict that scourged them from the realms north of Gliding Dragon Gorge but the lords of Furymouth never took it to heart as others did. I was thinking of older times.' He rubbed his fingers to his temples and winced at the knot growing in his stomach. 'Tuuran, I am an alchemist. They have dulled my powers for now but I'm no use to them like this. They will let us go home. I will see to it.'

'Vishmir and Narammed.' Tuuran shrugged. 'The sun and stars of the Adamantine Legion.' He shifted heavily on the bed beside Bellepheros, his feet resting on a trunk, knees hugged to his chest. Bellepheros frowned and Tuuran half-smiled. 'Small cabin, I know. You'll have it to yourself once there's nowhere else to go. After I was taken, I found I wasn't the only one from this realm. I've not met any other Adamantine Men but the King of the Crags does a healthy trade in Outsider slaves. They're full of stories, those ones.' He shook his head. 'You won't make them let us go, alchemist. You won't. You haven't seen who they are, not really. When you do, you might not even want to.'

The last of Bellepheros's anger drained out of him. 'They can't keep me this way. They have to let me use my alchemy. When they do ...' He wasn't sure. But he'd find a way. Blood-magic wasn't the way of the alchemist and was mostly shunned, but they learned at least a little. It wasn't really any different from making potions, after all. Just more ... direct.

Tuuran was still shaking his head. 'I'd heard of you before they took me. You weren't grand master then but you were going to be. Everyone in the palace knew it. You went on your big journey around the nine realms and wrote it all down.'

Bellepheros gaped. It had never occurred to him that the Taiytakei might read his words. Now he had to wonder: what had they learned? Was *that* how they knew his name? Was that why they'd chosen him? 'Who was speaker when you were taken, Master Tuuran?'

'His Holiness Hyram of Bloodsalt had just taken the spear and the ring. Does he still speak for the nine kings and queens?'

'His time is almost done, but yes, he does.'

'I hope his reign was a good one. I remember when Antros died. You all thought he'd be another Vishmir.' He shook his head. 'There could never be another Vishmir though. Not without another Anzuine, and the Adamantine Guard would never allow that.'

'He's been good enough.' Bellepheros clucked his tongue. 'The vultures are circling as they always do when a new speaker is due.' Aliphera's death – *was* it an accident, or was it the start of some great plan? He'd never know now. 'Tuuran, how did an Adamantine Man end up a slave to the Taiytakei?'

'Stupidity.'

'Be patient. I *will* take us home.' He put a hand on Tuuran's shoulder. 'I will *make* them take us home.'

The cabin door burst open as the sun finally set. Three black-skinned Taiytakei stood there, dark as night but with eyes like candle flames, with shirts and coats made of feather rainbows, brilliant and dazzling and ever-shifting. Two of them carried glass wands tinged gold, with wire in fine patterns wrapped around them, glowing with a fierce inner light. They waved them at Tuuran. 'Out, slave!'

Tuuran moved slowly away and past them, head bowed. When he was gone, another Taiytakei appeared, an old man with wrinkled skin and grey hair that was turning white. The first Taiytakei looked suddenly drab. This old one had colours in his clothes that Bellepheros had never even seen, braids in his hair that reached almost to the floor and a cloak of feathers that looked like a shimmering between dragon fire and liquid gold. He had a presence too, the sort that Bellepheros knew well from his time among the kings and queens of the dragon realms. He was a man who ruled, who was obeyed. Bellepheros bowed his head.

'Alchemist.' The old man pursed his lips and stared hard.

'I am Bellepheros.' Bellepheros didn't look up. Dragon-kings and -queens would have had him on his knees, face pressed into the dirt. 'I am the grand master of the Order of the Scales, master alchemist of the nine realms. I am keeper of the dragons.'

'No longer. When the dragon eggs I will bring you hatch, can you master them?'

'I can, if I so choose.'

'Keeper of the dragons? You may keep that name. You will build me an eyrie, Keeper of the Dragons. If you do not, you will die.'

He understood, in this old man's voice, that he would never return home, no matter what he did, that no threat would be enough, nor anything he could promise. They had taken him from his land and his life and his family – for that was how he thought of his Order of the Scales – and he would never come back. The old man believed it with a certainty that was absolute, and when the alchemist looked up and met the old man's eyes, what he saw there showed no remorse, no doubt, no miracles, no meticulously planned escape. He had the eyes of a true dragon-king, but still Bellepheros held his gaze. 'If you have dragons then I will build an eyrie. Not because you ask it of me but because that is my calling. And when I am finished, you will wish that I had not, and you will bring me back to my home, and you will beg me to take my dragons with me.'

4

The Storm-Dark

The Taiytakei gave him books to read to amuse himself. They were in their own language but it wasn't so different from the language of the dragon-kings and he mastered it easily enough. For two hours each day Tuuran came to sit with him. Bellepheros wasn't sure why, but he was thankful for the company and a familiar face. Someone he could talk to about the things he knew, the lands he'd travelled and the faces he'd never see again. He tried asking Tuuran about the Taiytakei but the Adamantine Man wasn't much use for that, not past how they treated their slaves and how to sail their ships. He claimed to have seen their city from a distance once, with towers of glass and gold that touched the sky and gleaming discs that flew through the air, slow and clumsy and fragile things beside a dragon, he thought, and if it sounded fanciful, well maybe dragons sounded fanciful too if you hadn't grown up spending your days with them flying overhead. Sometimes they spent their time together looking out of the window, at the endless grey sea. Other times Bellepheros read aloud. The Taiytakei even had a copy of the journal he'd written almost a decade ago which described the land that had raised them both. He spoke his own words while Tuuran lay on the bed and listened, rapt like a child being told stories by his father. Sometimes his eyes glistened, though he tried to hide it.

'We all weep for what we've lost,' he said when he caught Bellepheros looking. 'My brothers were the best warriors the world has ever seen. I will never find their like again.' He clenched his fists and screwed up his face. 'I was made to kill dragons! Not for this.'

'Men are more terrible than dragons,' said Bellepheros, although he knew it wasn't true.

'Men are more cruel, but not more terrible.' Tuuran slammed a fist against the wall. 'If there was a way, if it would serve a purpose, I'd smash this ship apart.'

'Patience, Tuuran. I will change their minds yet.' His magic was coming back, slowly and in fits and starts. He was fairly sure he knew what the Elemental Man had used to poison him now. Could have done something about it too if he'd had his travel chest with him, but that was gone. They'd taken everything. No matter. It *would* come back, and then he'd be far from helpless.

'We'll cross the storm-dark soon. After that, there's no hope.'

'The storm-dark?'

'You'll see.' Tuuran puffed his cheeks and let out a long sigh and held his head in his hands for a moment. 'It's hard,' he said, not looking up. 'I've been a slave on their ships for so long I'd forgotten what it was to be anything else. Now I wish it had stayed that way.' With an effort and another deep sigh he straightened. 'But it didn't. What words did you write of us in your journals, Lord Alchemist?'

Bellepheros peered out through the cabin window. The view was always the same now. Grey seas, grey skies, the horizon swaying back and forth between them. 'That Narammed created your order as he created mine. That you followed him without question. That ...' He chuckled and stopped. 'You know your own stories, Tuuran. Watersgate. Samir's Crossing. On those days you *were* as terrible as any dragon.' Then he shook his head. 'My words don't do you justice. Vishmir's dragon-killers. He armed you with weapons bought from the Taiytakei. Did you know that? Better than any steel forged in the nine kingdoms. Far better. Was Vale Tassan the Night Watchman when you were taken?'

Tuuran nodded. 'Giant and ruthless but always fair. Never asked anything he wouldn't give himself. There were few of us who could match him. What happened to him?'

'He still commands the guard.'

A rare smile flirted with the corners of Tuuran's lips. 'If a man could stop a dragon by glaring at it, Vale would be that man.'

'He has little love for alchemists but he does what needs to be done. Always.' Bellepheros looked out of the little window across the sea. The sun was low in the sky. He thought back to the Picker and frowned, remembering the things he'd said when the two of them had been alone on the road. 'You must know the legend of the Speaker's Spear? That Narammed slew a dragon with it?'

Tuuran snorted his derision.

'You don't believe it then? I think the Taiytakei do.'

'They believe in nothing. Godless creatures. But either way, men don't slay dragons with steel.'

'*Is* it steel? I don't know what it is. But I think the Taiytakei greatly desire to own it.' He was talking to himself, he realised. Voicing his secret thoughts.

'It's just a spear.' Tuuran shrugged and stood up and drew out the cabin key from under his shirt. He opened the door. 'There's going to be a storm soon. We'll come on it after nightfall. The storm-dark. It's no natural thing but the Taiytakei must cross it to reach their home. They'll shutter and bar your window, my Lord Alchemist. You'll think it'll be the end of us. Everyone does, the first time they cross, but don't fear it. Like the wrath of the Great Flame and the Silver King and the old gods themselves all rolled together, but it ends and by some miracle the ship remains whole.'

The sun set not long after Tuuran left him. The sky darkened and the clouds grew thick and ugly. The ship lurched and heaved while the waves rose and wore white caps of foam. The wind snapped and snarled, the decks creaked and groaned and the stars winked out one by one as the storm clouds devoured them. Outside someone closed the shutters on his window, and when Bellepheros tried to open them again he found they were barred. He lay on his bed, breathing hard. His stomach clenched into a knot. The air smelled strange. Unnatural. He'd tasted air like this once before, deep in the bowels of the Pinnacles amid the creations of the Silver King. The pitching of the ship grew worse. Abruptly he threw up into the bucket beside his bed, retching until there was nothing left, then groaned and lay back and closed his eyes; and so he almost didn't notice when the cabin door opened again and Tuuran slipped back in. The Adamantine Man sat beside him and the first Bellepheros knew of it was a cup of something hot and bitter pressed into his hand.

'For the sickness,' Tuuran said. Bellepheros forced himself up. As he did, a sudden sway of the ship banged the cabin wall against him.

'Great Flame!' He sniffed the cup and groaned again and then laughed despite himself. 'I could tell you everything that went into this just from the smell. I know better remedies but it will do.'

He drank. Tuuran pushed at the shutters but they didn't give. 'They keep us slaves away from the storm-dark, locked up in the hold. Every crossing.' He bared his teeth, a carnivore's grin. 'I told them you might die of fright if you didn't have someone to hold your hand so they let me come up to look after you, but I know you don't need me, Master Lord Alchemist. I did this for me, not for you. I want to see it. I've heard more stories about it than I've heard of Vishmir and Narammed put together. I want to see if they're true.'

Bellepheros resisted the temptation to lie down again and try to fall asleep. Tuuran's potion was working, at least a little, although with his travel chest he could have made something far better. 'They want me to make an eyrie for them,' he mumbled.

'Yes, I know. It's obvious, isn't it?' Tuuran pushed at the window again. 'I've crossed the storm-dark a dozen times. I might never find a way home again, but I'll see the damn thing before I die.' When the window didn't give, he punched it, then lay on the bed and kicked it, blow after blow until something cracked and then on until the shutters flew open.

The sky flashed purple.

Bellepheros forgot the snakes writhing in his belly. The night was black as pitch, the stars and moon all gone and swallowed up by the tide of darkness. The sea glistened, a faint blue-green phosphorescence lighting up the churning waves. The wind howled and swirled and then another bolt of purple light split the sea and the sky, jagged and blinding bright, lighting up the waves like the midday sun.

'Lightning,' hissed Tuuran. 'The lightning. So that much is true.'

Another flash and then another and the wind sucked them deeper into the storm. Even the sea seemed to rush towards it, the waves crashing and climbing over one another, pushing them on. The gale caught the broken shutters and smashed them against the hull, over and over. It screamed and whistled through the ropes and the rigging somewhere above. Banshee wails ripped the air, rising and fading. The ship rolled and heaved and pitched and the purple lightning flashed and flamed and danced through the sky. The storm drew Bellepheros in, wrapped him up and held him like a dragon's stare until the ship bucked mightily, tipping him and Tuuran onto the floor together. The Adamantine Man was laughing. 'Imagine this deep in the hold, Master Alchemist, among the rats and the bilge water! Imagine it! Men falling over, tumbling into each other in the pitch black! Can you see why they piss themselves? Death stares at you there but I didn't fear it, not once, not ever, for I am Adamantine, made to face dragons!'

Bellepheros struggled to his knees and clutched at the bed. The ship pitched forward, swinging his legs out from under him. Tuuran rolled and slammed into the door, then hauled himself to his feet. He was grinning like a madman, swept up by the violence around them while the lightning outside cracked again and again, bright and a vivid violet like nothing Bellepheros had ever seen. 'This is not natural!'

'No.' Tuuran shook his head gleefully. 'Even the Taiytakei don't understand it, though they'll never admit it, not to the likes of us.' The ship groaned. A loud crack reverberated through the hull. 'But the best, the best is yet to come. We're close to the middle now. They say—'

Tuuran didn't finish. Or perhaps he did and Bellepheros simply didn't hear. The heaving and rolling of the ship abruptly stopped. The clouds vanished, the lightning and the sea too, and now outside there was nothing at all, and through that nothing the ship drifted silent and still. All that sound and fury, suddenly gone. Tuuran's eyes gleamed. 'Always in whispers, in the dark, they talked about it,' he said. 'But none of us had ever *seen* it.' He pointed at the emptiness outside. 'That, my Lord Alchemist! Make that your mistress! A thing deeper than dragons and they don't understand it. I couldn't begin. But you!' His gaze bored into Bellepheros. 'You, Lord Master Alchemist, you who have tamed dragons, you can make it ours! I've risked my life for you to see this. Remember that. Tame the storm-dark and one day take us home!'

Bellepheros stared out of the window, although there was nothing at all to see. 'I don't understand. Where is the storm? How can this be?'

Tuuran gripped his arm, tight, fingers digging in to Bellepheros's skin until they hurt. 'It *can't* be, Lord Alchemist. That is the point. It is the space between worlds. A place that cannot exist and yet does.' But Bellepheros barely heard. The Taiytakei came from across the sea. Everyone knew that. From another land, distant and unreachable. Everyone knew that too. From another world? Yes, he'd heard it said, but not meant, not literally.

There was no motion. Not even the slightest rocking of the ship. They weren't even in the sea any more. And outside the silence was perfect, the darkness complete.

On a whim he picked up his lamp and threw it out of the window, then peered out to look. It fell away, a bright speck of light, down and down and down for ever, like a little falling fading star until it was too dim to see.

Impossible. A void between worlds.

The ship lurched, violent and without warning, smacking Bellepheros's head against the frame of the window. Light and noise and howling wind slammed back like a punch in the face. He reeled as the churning sea and the maelstrom of night-black cloud returned. The ship shuddered sideways. Tuuran fell and Bellepheros tipped and rolled back to the floor on top of him. A brilliant flash of violent purple lit up the cabin. He caught sight of Tuuran's eyes. They were mad, filled with hunger and desire, and with belief.

I cannot. He couldn't say the words. There was no alchemy for this, but Tuuran still stared and Bellepheros couldn't speak, and so they sat pressed together and watched as the lightning flashed and the storm raged until it fell slowly away and the clouds became grey and broken and the sky finally emerged between them, blue and bright, and at the last the sun. In the distance ahead of them, as Bellepheros pressed his head to the wall to peer forward through the broken porthole, a new line smeared the horizon. Land. Tuuran picked himself off the floor. 'That is Xican, Lord Master Alchemist. The City of Stone. That's where they are taking you.'

'And you?' He couldn't think of anything else to say.

The Adamantine Man shrugged his shoulders. 'Back to the sea. To sail on it.' He nodded to the broken shutters. 'Or else they'll throw me into it to drown for showing you what they fear the most. No matter. I'll survive or I'll die.'

Bellepheros pressed his head against the wall again and looked out of the window, back the way they'd come this time, and there it was, an endless line of storm clouds that seemed to go on for ever, receding into the distance. The storm-dark. And he knew that what he'd seen in its midst would haunt his dreams.

'A last thing, Master Alchemist.' Tuuran chuckled. 'Look at the sun, bright and high in the sky. How long ago did you watch night fall?'

Bellepheros blinked. The sun had barely set when they'd entered the storm. He felt drained and exhausted and deadly tired, but now his heart ran cold. His mouth fell open but he couldn't find any words. It should be dark. It should be the middle of the night. There should have been stars and the moon. *How? How was it possible?*

Tuuran's grin ran right across his face. 'Yes, Lord Master Alchemist. And it's always this way when we cross. They don't understand. No one does.' The mad wonder in his eyes made Bellepheros want to hide for there was nothing wondrous in this, only a dreadful wrongness. 'And when night comes, Master Alchemist, look at the stars. Oh, you'll see a few that are familiar. But only a few. We are in a different world. It is theirs, not ours, and there are others beyond both.' He laughed and wagged a finger. 'Still think you'll take us home now, do you?'

5

The Enchantress

Tuuran left him long before the land resolved into more than a distant blur. He slipped out and locked the door behind him and Bellepheros heard it click. The alchemist lay back on his little bed and shivered. When he closed his eyes he saw the storm and the purple lightning and the Nothing that lay in the middle of it. When he opened them he saw the same, images and ghost memories flitting across the sea.

Alchemists were cold people. He'd come to see that many years ago. It was the dragons that did it. Dragon-riders learned to ride their emotions, to guide them and turn them. They were passionate and fearless because that was what riding dragons demanded of them. Alchemists didn't ride dragons, they worked with them. They kept them dull and stupid. Sometimes they quietly poisoned them. There was no place for any bond with a dragon for an alchemist, none at all, and yet they had to be fearless every bit as much as a rider did. So alchemists put their emotions away and learned to be cold, to stand back and aside from everything but their duty. A rider, he knew, would have fought the Elemental Man back on the road, tooth and nail. A rider would have fought in the Paratheus. A rider would have fought in the docks, on the boat, every day. An alchemist sat by and watched, waiting for the moment when action would be certain of success.

He'd had lovers when he'd been younger. Alchemists weren't supposed to but a lot of them did. Back when they'd been in their first flush of adulthood, fresh full of secret potions, before the awe of the dragon secrets they were learning had lost their chill. He remembered being afraid of dragons once too. In a way it had never gone, but he'd turned it into something else. A sort of shrugging acceptance that one day he might die. Out of nowhere, something he'd never see coming. He was careful and cautious and measured in everything he did – an alchemist didn't live long otherwise – but with dragons accidents happened. He'd lost count of the number of friends who'd gone to some distant eyrie and never come back. Accidents, nearly all of them. It was what came from dealing with monsters. It was part of what they were.

He picked up his splinter and stabbed it carefully into his thumb. Squeezed out a drop of blood and smeared it onto the wall. He reached into it and found he could. The touch was still erratic but another few days and he'd be himself again. Satisfied, he lay back and closed his eyes. Trying to collect his thoughts and formulate a plan. Something. Some way to persuade the Taiytakei that what they'd chosen to do was wrong, more than wrong, was folly. Calmly and rationally. Make them realise they should take him back, but he couldn't see it. The storm-dark kept filling his head. The darkness in its heart. The Nothing, as Tuuran had called it. He couldn't remember when something had frightened him so much, not even when the Elemental Man had been choking him to death in the quiet autumn sun. A part of him knew that one day a dragon would carelessly flick its tail without thinking and shatter half the bones in his body. Kill him without reason or warning, just the way the life of an alchemist was, a thing to be accepted. You moved on or you never survived, never slept at nights and never learned to be not afraid. That part had kept him safe all the way from the carriage, kept him from losing his mind, kept his thoughts clear and reasoned, but the storm-dark confounded everything. He couldn't think.

Tuuran's potion was wearing off. He was starting to feel sick again. He let out a long sigh, sat up and pressed his head against the wall, looking out the broken window. Fresh air blew over his face. That helped.

They were closer to the shore now, sailing in at good speed. The land outside – Xican, was it? – began as a few jagged stones, pale grey spires scattered among the waves, each one rising higher than the last as the ship raced between them. A shadow crossed the sun as something passed overhead, but whatever it was, Bellepheros couldn't see it, and the window was too small for him to lean out and look up. The sharp grey cliffs brought back memories. Every dragon-rider had a first time. Perhaps the kings and queens and great lords and ladies of the dragon realms sat on the backs of their monsters from such a young age that they didn't remember but Bellepheros had been more than twenty years old and about to become a true alchemist. The ceremony for most alchemists was held in the caves under the Purple Spur but he and two others had been chosen for something special. He hadn't understood why, only that he would ride on the back of a dragon at last, and every moment of that flight remained etched into his memory, though not as deep as what he'd seen and heard after they'd landed. When he closed his eyes, he could see the mountains of the Worldspine, huge towering things that glowered at one another but kept their distance across deep wide valleys. Then they'd flown deeper and further north where the valleys vanished and the mountains were piled up next to one another, squashed together as though some giant god had scattered mile-high shards of rock over the ground, jumbled and haphazard and without thought. The spaces between them were gorges, gulches, ravines. From above it had been impossible to imagine how anyone could live in such a sterile vertical place, but they did.

The Nothing of the storm-dark crept back into his head. He sighed and opened his eyes and looked again at the new world around him. As the ship moved on, it slowed. The stones grew taller and wider and more numerous, scattered around the sea, rising from the waves like the petrified fingers of ancient giants. They were flecked with green and some were marked with holes. Caves or windows but too regular to be wholly natural. As the ship turned he saw more, a coastline of grey saw-toothed cliffs jumbled one upon the other. Black spots covered them like boils of the pox. Buildings jutted out of their sides, wooden platforms and gantries like scars running from side to side and up and down, more still perched on their tops. Closer in he could make out the shapes of men scurrying back and forth along the ones closest to the sea, up ladders and across rope bridges, dangling from the faces of cliffs that rose far higher than any mast, while between the dizzying spires other ships, made small by the towers of stone around them, wallowed in the waves, rolling languidly from side to side. But none of that was what held his eye. As he pressed his face to the wall to see, he saw a palace of bright and shining gold rising over the heaviest thicket of cliffs. It hung in the air, glittering orbs of sparkling silver dangling beneath great discs of glass like golden clouds; while from below more spires of glass and gold rose up behind the cliffs to meet them. Tuuran had spoken of them, seen far off in the distance, but not like this. Here was a creation that dwarfed even the marvels left by the Silver King. A golden palace in the sky. For a moment even the storm-dark was forgotten.

The ship edged closer. The cliffs climbed higher and their bulk gobbled up the palace and the sky both, until all Bellepheros could see was a wall of pale stone and the wooden scaffolds that hung from it. Windows and doors littered the cliff faces, some of them shuttered or closed, but most no more than simple openings into the rock. They were careful things, precise circles and arches. Closer still and the men at work on the scaffolds threw ropes to the ship, hauling it slowly in. A few were black-skinned Taiytakei; most were paler, but they all wore rags like the serfs of Furymouth. As the ship came so close that he could almost reach out from his window and touch them, he saw that some of the men were like Tuuran, with lightning bolts branded on their arms. The ones who wore the brand gave orders to the ones who didn't; and then the ship was so close that the scaffolds were above him and he could see nothing at all except for a wall of dark wet stone mottled with seaweed.

The Taiytakei, when they came to take him, glanced at the broken window. They didn't say anything but Bellepheros saw the sourness on their faces and in the set of their mouths. They took his arms and pushed him, firmly but not harshly, along a passage and up a narrow flight of steps out into the daylight. After the gloom of his cabin the brightness of the sun was overwhelming. He blinked and squinted and screwed up his face. Sailors swarmed around him, dirty white tunics over sun-browned skins. Soldiers in golden armour stood guard. They gleamed and sparkled in the sun so brightly that it took Bellepheros a moment – even after his eyes adjusted to the light – to realise their armour was made of glass tinged with gold and woven with wire. He shielded his eyes against the sun and looked for the floating palace up between the masts but the sky was too bright and blue. There was ... *something* up above the ship, something round and glittering and golden and huge, as big as the ship itself, but it shone so brightly in the streaming sun that he couldn't look at it for long. He screwed up his eyes and blinked again, looking back at the deck.

'The sail-slave who was given to this one. Where is he?' The shout came from beside him, loud and sudden enough to make him flinch. A Taiytakei drew a wand from his belt like the ones Bellepheros had already seen, glass woven with filaments of gold and glowing brightly with an inner light. Across the whole ship everything stopped. The air hummed with sudden tension. Every sailor froze and put down what they were holding and dropped to their knees, all except one who turned slowly to face them. Tuuran. The Taiytakei levelled his wand at the Adamantine Man. 'You know what you've done, sail-slave. You've broken the law of the sea. The sentence is death.'

The window. The storm-dark.

The Taiytakei's eyes narrowed. Bellepheros shoved him. He was an old man, still half dazzled by the light and bewildered by everything around him, but it was enough. The Taiytakei lurched, the wand wavered and Tuuran was still standing.

Another soldier seized Bellepheros, a rough hand on his shoulder spinning him round, and yet another punched him in the gut. All the air flew out of him. Bellepheros doubled over, gasping. The Taiytakei with the wand ran a finger over it, dimming the light inside. He pointed it at Bellepheros now instead. The alchemist looked up helpless, still trying to breathe. The air between them snapped and flashed. Pain hit him in the shoulder and flared all over. He sagged. If it hadn't been for the soldier holding him up, he would have fallen to the deck.

'You are still a slave, however much the sea lord wants you.' The Taiytakei with the wand turned back to Tuuran. As far as Bellepheros could tell, the Adamantine Man hadn't moved. Hadn't even tried to run. He was just standing there, ready to take his fate.

Bellepheros finally sucked in a lungful of air. 'I need him!' he shouted. 'I need him to do my work!' Tuuran would not die for him, not for showing him a secret. He reached inside himself, into his blood. He'd use what he had, here and now if he had to.

'Liar.' The Taiytakei ran his finger along his wand. Its light grew fierce once more.

'I will not work unless I have him!'

'You'll do as you're told, slave.' The Taiytakei levelled the wand.

'You will give me what I ask for to build an eyrie for you or the dragons you bring to me will roam free and burn your kingdoms to ash!' Bellepheros was shaking but there were things that needed to be said. 'I am the keeper of the dragons! I have defied dragon-kings when the need arose. You have taken me against my will from my life and my home but you can *not* make me do what you wish without my consent. Kill me, hurt me, threaten me and you will get *nothing*. I require this man! I *demand* him.'

The look on the Taiytakei's face didn't change. A slave was a slave and there were no exceptions. But then his eyes shifted and he looked past Bellepheros and the soldiers who held him, and Bellepheros saw the wand lower a fraction.

'The sentence is pain,' said a woman's voice.

The Taiytakei touched his wand. The light inside it dimmed a little and then Bellepheros reeled as the air cracked like a lash and lightning jerked across the deck. Tuuran screamed as it threw him into the air. He fell so hard that Bellepheros felt the planks shiver under his feet, and lay twitching and whimpering. The alchemist stared. An Adamantine Man learned to take pain more than any other man, and here was one of them curled up and wailing like a whipped child.

The Taiytakei with the wand glowered at Bellepheros and marched away. Bellepheros turned to see the woman who'd saved Tuuran. She wore gleaming white robes which looked as though they meant something, but he had no idea what. Strangest of all, she wore two round pieces of glass bound across her eyes, like the curved glass of a Taiytakei farscope. They made her eyes oddly big. He didn't know what to make of the look on her face. Sizing him up, perhaps. Staring at her didn't seem to trouble her; rather she seemed curious, intrigued, disdainful and perhaps a little disgusted. He couldn't make out her age but she certainly wasn't young. She wasn't tall, but the armoured Taiytakei around her made her seem shorter than she really was. She watched him watching her until he looked away.

Two armoured men hauled Tuuran to his feet. He was still shaking even when they dragged him over and threw him at Bellepheros. 'This one is yours now, slave. You'll be accountable.'

Bellepheros helped Tuuran up. An odd feeling that, him at his age helping an Adamantine Man to his feet. 'You're shivering.'

'So would you if you felt their lightning so strong. Thank you, Lord Master Alchemist. I owe you my life. They'll make you regret this though.'

Bellepheros nodded towards the woman in white. 'Thank her.'

'I will not!' Tuuran shuddered.

'Why? Who is she?'

'An enchantress.' Tuuran made a sign against evil. Bellepheros frowned and stole another glance at the woman. She was still watching. 'An enchantress? What does that mean? A blood-mage?' There were no magicians of any other kind in the dragon realms. He shook his head. *If that's what she is and the Taiytakei have stolen dragon eggs at last, they can suffer the consequences and all my oaths be damned.*

Tuuran shook his head again. 'No, not that. A witch!'

The woman turned and swept away. Taiytakei soldiers pushed Tuuran and Bellepheros in her wake to a gangway that reached from the side of the ship to the platforms on the cliffs. 'Why didn't you run?' Bellepheros asked.

'If I'd tried then they'd have killed the whole crew, every one of them,' said Tuuran. He glowered at the Taiytakei soldiers. 'And also I can't swim.'

Bellepheros digested this. He frowned. 'An enchantress?' he asked again.

'I told you. A witch.' Tuuran hissed and pointed at the golden wand hanging from the belt of one of the soldiers. 'They make the rods that summon lightning and ships of glass that fly through the air and every other abomination that breaks the natural laws of the world.'

A cradle hung beside the scaffolds. Ropes reached up into the sky. The Taiytakei woman in white and her guard walked onto it. Bellepheros squinted up to the top of the cliff. His eyes were getting used to the daylight now. Soldiers nudged him forward after the woman. *An abomination that breaks the natural laws of the world.*

That sounded a lot like dragons. Then he staggered and grabbed at Tuuran's arm as the cradle unexpectedly jerked and began to rise. The ship fell away beneath them, first the deck and then the masts. In the natural amphitheatre of the harbour dozens more ships waited, packed closely together. Some were pressed against the cliffs, swarms of men scurrying back and forth; others sat further out and rocked in the gentle swell of the sea. Through the windows in the grey stone of the cliff Bellepheros caught glimpses of spacious rooms, of Taiytakei men and women. He saw them sitting at tables together, drinking wine, eating their meals. He saw them dressing and undressing. He saw children, and men and women entwined naked together. None of them looked to their windows as he passed. They seemed oblivious, as though it simply didn't matter who might look in on them. The other Taiytakei, he noted, looked carefully away, but he was an alchemist, ever curious about everything, and so he stared and took it all in. He could feel how much the soldiers either side of him didn't like it.

'It's rude to stare, Lord Master Alchemist,' said Tuuran. 'They're prudes at heart, these Taiytakei.' Then he leaned close and his voice dropped. 'I am yours,' he breathed. 'Say the word and I'll take them over the edge to their doom.'

Bellepheros glanced down. They were past the top of the tallest mast now and halfway up the cliff. There were five Taiytakei with them on the cradle, the woman and her four soldiers. He wondered if Tuuran was really strong enough throw all five of them over the edge at once. Perhaps, but then what? Would it get either of them home? Of course not.

He gently shook his head and put a calming hand on Tuuran's arm. 'Patience, Tuuran.' He was beginning to see. His weapon would be his knowledge. What he knew. That was why they'd taken him and it was what they wanted from him. He would hold that over them, and if they tried to take it by force, well, as an alchemist he knew a hundred different ways to kill himself, and if that was to be his choice in the end, it would be his alone. No need for others to die, not even these Taiytakei.

The woman with the glass lenses over her eyes was looking at him. Perhaps she read his mind or read his thoughts from his eyes, for she raised an eyebrow and smiled. Bellepheros blinked in surprise. She had a lovely smile. He hadn't expected that.

'You are our most honoured guest,' she said. 'Whatever you require, I will give it to you. Whatever you ask for, you will have.' She glanced at Tuuran. 'You will build an eyrie for Sea Lord Quai'Shu, and if you must have a grand hall carved of solid gold and a harem of a thousand women from across the many worlds of the storm-dark to do it, so it shall be. Whatever you wish for, you will have.'

'I wish to go home,' said Bellepheros tartly.

The woman's face didn't flicker. 'That one wish only Sea Lord Quai'Shu can grant.'

'Well, we'll start with a library then,' he snapped. If she thought he could be bought through his vices then she might as well know what they were. 'Books. As many of them as you can get. Every eyrie should have one.' *And I'll find out who you are. I'll find out everything about you; and in time I'll find a way to use what I learn against you, for I am a patient man.*

'Books?' Her lips pursed. 'Excellent! So be it. But you might have to share.' A light danced in her eyes. 'I like books too.'

As the cradle rose further, the windows in the cliff face became larger and more ornate, easily wide enough for a man to climb in and out. 'Are you the lady of this city?' asked Bellepheros.

'Lady of this city?' The woman laughed and the easy creases in her face told Bellepheros that she was a friend to laughter. 'This is the city of Sea Lord Quai'Shu. I am a servant. One of many. But for now I am your mistress.' She smiled again. 'Or your helper, or your t'varr, or however you prefer to see me.'

'My friend Tuuran says you are an enchantress.'

'Your slave is right. I am Chay-Liang. You are Bellepheros the alchemist. I'm afraid enchanters rule over no cities, more is the pity.'

Your slave? The soldier had said the same after they'd picked Tuuran up off the deck. Bellepheros hadn't taken it in before. Been too busy trying to breathe. 'And what is it that an enchantress does?'

Chay-Liang didn't answer at once. But as the cradle reached the top of the cliff and Bellepheros could finally see what lay beyond, she stretched out her arm. 'This.'

He looked out over the City of Stone. Grey spires rose up around him like the three mountains of the Pinnacles in miniature, but hundreds and hundreds of them, jumbled together, packed in rows and clumps like the discarded teeth of some titanic monster. Sheer walls rose to jagged spikes and fell into dark chasms. Far below, in places between them, he saw black water. The sea perhaps. There wasn't a flat surface to be seen and every spire was speckled with black spots like the pox, except now that he'd ridden the cradle he knew them for what they were. Windows.

But Chay-Liang wasn't pointing at the miraculous city of stone that lay before them. The enchantress was pointing up. To the golden palace that hung from the sky.

6

The Palace of Leaves

The Palace of Leaves hung over Xican. Beside Bellepheros, Tuuran gaped in slack-jawed awe. It was hard not to. More than a dozen discs of gold-tinged glass floated high in the bright sky, each as wide as a war-dragon's outstretched wings. A hundred chains of Scythian steel, with links as thick and long as a man, tethered them to the cliffs below. From beneath, the discs were a dazzling brightness so fierce that Bellepheros could only look at them sideways. From the ground a cluster of glass and gold spires and a few of black obsidian reached up like fingers. Tiny bridges of glass joined one tower to the next, wires of light that sparkled in the sun. Great silver and gold eggs hung beneath the discs, suspended by gleaming chains. In its midst Bellepheros saw a ship, masts and sails and all, simply suspended in the air.

The enchantress Chay-Liang took a glass ball the size of a fist from the bag at her belt. She had three wands there too: one of black stone, one of pale golden glass like the lightning wands that the soldiers carried, and one of silver. She stepped off the cradle and held the glass ball in front of her. Bellepheros watched in fascination, torn between the detail of what she was doing and the overwhelming immensity of what rose above them. He settled for watching her. It was easier than trying to stare at the blinding miracle that floated in the sky.

The glass ball bulged and flattened and grew into a disc ten feet wide that hovered in the air at the enchantress's feet. She looked pleased with herself. 'A perk of being what I am,' she said, looking straight at him. She was showing off, and he laughed because the idea that this woman wanted to impress him struck him as absurd, that she somehow felt the need amid the dazzling marvels that surrounded them.

She smiled back and offered him her hand. He supposed she

thought he *was* impressed, and yes, a part of him was. But mostly he was seeing again how much he mattered to these Taiytakei, and the more he saw it, the more it woke the dread inside him. When it came to potions and dragons he could teach them everything he knew and it wouldn't make a blind bit of difference. They probably weren't going to like that, when they finally understood what made him what he was and why none of them could ever be the same. They certainly weren't going to be happy to let him go home.

'Are you coming?' The enchantress stepped onto the glass and beckoned him again to follow. The Taiytakei soldiers hesitated – it seemed they didn't know quite how they should treat him any more – and settled for shoving Tuuran onto the disc instead. Bellepheros followed, reluctant, bemused and anxious and wondering what came next. As soon as he was on, it rose into the air and his heart jumped into his mouth. He stumbled. At his feet the glass was as good as invisible. The city and its jumble of stone was falling away. They were climbing into the void between colossal spikes below and the brilliant palace above and everywhere he looked was huge open space. He staggered again as his stomach tied itself in knots and his legs quivered and started to give. He was going to faint! The woman in white was smiling at him, amused at his terror. Space! So much space! *Too* much space! The starkness of her black skin against the white of her robe struck him hard. He was gasping. He *was* going to faint. He closed his eyes and clung to the nearest body and never mind who it was. Great Flame! Such sorcery as this! Not even in the works of the Silver King …

'Mind him! You'll have Abraxi out of her grave if you let him fall!' He barely heard over the rushing in his ears. Hands gripped him tight, easing him down. A voice whispered in his ear.

'I have you.' Tuuran. 'Witchcraft and blood-magic, but we're stronger, Lord Alchemist. We're stronger! Cling to that!'

No, we are not! Bellepheros didn't feel strong at all, but words like witchcraft and blood-magic made him open his eyes a fraction because this was clearly neither of those things and that sort of ignorance had always annoyed him.

No, opening his eyes was a mistake. The terror had him straight back again. Everywhere he looked, he saw sky. Even dragons had never made him feel so small. His head began to spin. He closed his eyes again and shut them tight. Wind pulled at him and whipped at his robes and his hair, playful and gleeful as though it wanted to nudge him over the edge and watch him fall and then laugh at him for being so utterly trivial. His fingers dug into Tuuran's arm. He wanted to be sick. He'd looked dragons in the eye and now he carried the dread of the storm-dark in the pit of his stomach, yet he'd never felt as sharp a terror as this.

He swayed as Tuuran lifted him up. The Adamantine Man's easy strength helped him. 'We are arrived, Lord Alchemist. The ground is stone again.'

Bellepheros opened his eyes a crack. He caught a glimpse of pale golden glass walls, of a gaping hole and of the sky beyond and a cold white marble floor. He staggered forward and then his legs buckled and he fell out of Tuuran's arms to his hands and knees. Solid stone. Even if it was floating in the sky, it *felt* like the ground and that was enough. A blessed relief. He stared at the veins in the marble for a second or two and then threw up. *Pathetic. What must they think of me?* He stayed where he was, trying to breathe.

'Bellepheros?'

The woman. Gentle hands reached under his arms and lifted him back to his feet. Hers, and when his eyes remembered how to focus, the concern on her face seemed real enough, even if a part of her was laughing at him. She looked odd with those glass lenses over her eyes. Owlish.

'If anyone ever invites you to walk the Path of Words, you should probably decline.' She smiled and pulled him away. As they moved, two women in white belted tunics ran from alcoves where they had stood like statues and started to clean the mess he'd made on their floor. Pale-skinned. Slaves again. The enchantress wrinkled her nose and made a face. 'You've been in these clothes since the Picker took you, haven't you? Your travel chest will arrive shortly. Really, I don't see why they couldn't have taken some other clothes out for you and let you have them. I'm afraid you smell quite ... strong. And that won't do for when you meet the sea lord. You'll need some new ones. Do you have a preference? I know you have a liking for silk in your realm. Did you know that silk was something you stole from us? Old history and mostly forgotten now but it caused a great deal of trouble once.'

Bellepheros tried not to look at anything except the floor. The space around him was huge and filled with light. The ceiling was far above, if there was a ceiling at all, and the walls were all the same gold-tinged glass. If you peered you could see the clouds and the harbour and the city outside, all of it adding to the sense of nakedness around him. 'Alchemists are used to tunnels and caves,' he muttered. 'Not great spaces like this.' It was the emptiness that oppressed him, more than the size. There was no one else here except a few slaves standing patient and still in their alcoves and the soldiers who'd come with Chay-Liang. A place like the Speaker's Hall in the Adamantine Palace, where many could gather when the occasion arose yet rarely used. It had no sense of life. For all its perfect beauty, it felt cold and dead.

'I thought you rode great beasts through the skies where you come from.'

'If you mean the dragons then you're thinking of dragon-riders. Alchemists rarely. Sometimes we sit on their backs, but it's a rider who commands them and we have saddles and harnesses that hold us fast. We certainly do not float in the air with no apparent means of support.' He shuddered. The last few minutes were a horror he'd probably never forget.

The enchantress laughed. 'I'll have your rooms changed then if it's a cave you want. I'll send new clothes to you. Silk?'

'Yes, yes!' The more they walked across the marble, the further the far wall seemed to be. He felt himself shrinking.

'Colours?'

'Any!' Anything to get away from this unbearable empty openness!

'Colours matter a great deal here, Bellepheros. You'll be the keeper of our lord's dragons. What colour are dragons?'

It made him laugh. *What colour are dragons?* He kept forgetting, amid his misery, how little the Taiytakei knew of his home. 'All manner of colours. They don't care.'

'Then I will choose.' She sighed as they reached the far wall at last, then stopped beside it and took the black wand from her belt and tapped it to the glass. A clear slab descended from above, jutting from the gold-tinged wall. Bellepheros forced himself to look up. High above his head hung a great golden egg, suspended by chains from the glass discs in the sky. There was no telling how big the egg might be but the discs beyond filled his sight. There was empty sky between them and the open top of this tower. A tiny black hole beckoned from the bottom of the egg. That was where they were going, was it? His head started to spin. He looked away. Took a deep breath. His heart was pounding again and they hadn't even started.

The enchantress put a hand on his arm. 'Close your eyes.'

'Yes. And I'd like to sit down too.'

Tuuran sat beside him, legs dangling over the edge. The Adamantine Man was staring at everything like an apprentice on his first visit to the caves under the Purple Spur, or like Speaker Hyram when Bellepheros had taken him there and finally shown him the truth about dragons. Or perhaps, more apt, like a virgin in his first brothel.

'Does height not trouble you?' Bellepheros asked him bitterly.

'Height? I'm a sail-slave.' Tuuran chuckled. 'A sail-slave who's afraid of heights doesn't last very long. If the floor was pitching and heaving beneath us, the wind howling and the rain flaying the skin off my face, I'd feel quite at home. Height? No. But glorious as these sights may be, Lord Alchemist, I don't like not seeing what holds me from falling. It reeks of witchery.'

Witchery? What did that even mean? But then the glass began to rise and Bellepheros stayed very still, face screwed up tight and tense as a drumskin. He cried out in fear when they emerged from the top of the tower and the sudden wind snatched at him and blew him sideways; and then, when Tuuran held him tight, wept at his own frailty, shaking helplessly. When the wind died and the glass stopped, he stayed very still, curled up tight, arms wrapped around his head. He dimly heard the Taiytakei soldiers move away but mercifully they left him alone. He sat still until the shaking stopped. It felt like a long time. Then he let out a great sigh and warily opened his eyes. He gasped and almost sobbed with relief. The glass had lifted them into a hall panelled in bronze and wood, with the sky decently pushed aside by the pleasant familiarity of walls and a floor and a roof over his head. He took a few deep breaths, carefully ignoring the bright hole in the floor though which they'd arrived. The illusion helped. Unfortunately his mind knew all too well that an illusion was what it was. It kept reminding him. Kept him thinking about the huge emptiness that lay not far through every wall and floor. Kept him quivering inside, sapping his strength and poisoning every thought.

The enchantress was looking at him, eyes agleam with curiosity. 'More to your liking?' He nodded. She clapped her hands. Slaves, docile men and women with downcast eyes, emerged from their alcoves. Chay-Liang beckoned to them and then to him. 'See to our guest.' She smiled and patted him on the arm. 'They'll look after you. Anything you want, just ask.' And he felt too ill and too scared to remind her that all he wanted was to go home; and just now he wasn't even sure that he wanted *that*, because *that* would mean more floating through the terror of the empty open air on flimsy sheets of glass.

The enchantress and the Taiytakei soldiers led, and when the slaves beckoned him and Tuuran to follow, he did. They took him away to rooms that were spacious and comfortable and took their leave with a few vague words that he didn't really hear. Inside, rugs lay across the floor in patterns of rich reds and pale blues, the knots thick and deep under his feet and almost as soft as fur. Tapestries hung from every wall, mostly desert scenes in orange and gold. One was nothing more than a vast expanse of empty sand with a single mighty tower that rose into a swirling maelstrom of black cloud. It caught his eye because in the cloud tiny slivers of silver and purple gave the impression of lightning.

The bed was made of solid gold with a mattress of the softest down and silk sheets that slid over his skin like liquid. A dragon-king could have guested here and not been disappointed. After his old squitty stone cells in the Palace of Alchemy he wasn't sure what to do with rooms like these, but apparently that didn't matter because he had a half-dozen slaves to show him. They prepared a bath, and while he soaked in the water and tried not to think about the open sky just outside, they brought a small pile of books for his table. *A History of the Mar-Li Seafaring Republic* and a collection of journals and diaries. When he was clean they dressed him in a plain white silk tunic, so light it left him feeling naked. They laid out bronze trays of food, simple bread, a dozen different fruits from tiny bright purple berries to something that was a brilliant yellow and as big as his head, and a plate piled with strips of pink salted fish with ten tiny pots for dipping in, each with a different pungent flavour. Bellepheros gingerly tried a bit of most things and then settled for largely just eating the bread.

Tuuran watched with envy. 'Is this how it is in the Palace of Alchemy?' he asked.

'We put on our own clothes and the food is distinctly inferior.' Bellepheros frowned and then laughed at his own foolishness. Here he was, a slave, yet treated far better than he'd ever been in Prince Jehal's eyrie at Clifftop when he'd been searching for a murderer, or even in the Veid Palace afterwards when he'd had to admit to not finding one. And that sort of thought was no good. He had no place even thinking it.

Tuuran still watched him closely, lips pursed. He didn't say anything, though, not until Bellepheros was done and had sent the slaves away. They would have stayed and done more if he hadn't. *Anything you want, just ask.* The Adamantine Man watched them go. He wrinkled his nose and sniffed. 'You'll get comfortable here, Lord Grand Alchemist. Careful with that.'

Bellepheros shook his head, trying to throw the other thoughts aside. 'In the Palace of Alchemy we're masters of our own destiny. Here I am not. They can never hide that.' Although saying the words made him think about how true that really was, because the truth was that they weren't and never had been. They were servants to the speaker, to the nine realms and their kings and queens, but far more than that, wherever they went, they were slaves to the dragons.

'You will,' said Tuuran again. 'I would.' His voice was quiet. Subdued. Bellepheros swept his arm across the room, at the food, the bath, the bed, the clothes, trying to dispel the sudden awkwardness.

'Help yourself. Enjoy it while it's here.'

Tuuran glanced at the door. With a wistful sigh he sat down and picked at the food but he didn't seem to be hungry. Which wasn't like the Tuuran Bellepheros had come to know on the voyage, but perhaps that was down to the strangeness of their surroundings. 'Better than ship rations, that's for sure. It won't last.'

'Why do you say that?'

'Because I've been a slave to the Taiytakei for years and it never does.'

Bellepheros read a little from the journals, trying to make sense of them, but his head kept lolling and he soon gave up. He slept soundly, finally untroubled by any thoughts of how far above the ground they were. The bed was a soft embrace, warm and gentle. Tuuran slept on the floor, curled up in a pile of blankets. If he snored, Bellepheros didn't notice.

The slaves were waiting for him again when he woke. They fed and dressed him, this time in feather robes patterned in silken flames that made him cringe and beg for something else, and when it turned out there *was* nothing else, made him wish he'd answered the enchantress when she'd asked. He was quite sure this was her way of getting back at him for not paying proper attention. Her little joke.

When he was ready they ushered him to the door. Two Taiytakei knights in their glass and gold armour waited outside. They led him through a short maze of passages to a door of solid gold carved with entwined bolts of lightning. At the touch of their black rods it opened. They gently ushered him inside but didn't follow. The door closed behind him. He was in a room with no windows, lit by glowing glass spheres that reminded him of his own alchemical lamps. It wasn't a big room – pleasingly small in fact – but it *was* made entirely of gold. Every inch was carved with fractal patterns that twisted and writhed and moved under his eyes whenever he tried to make out what they were. Three Taiytakei faced him across a table that was a single mirror-polished slab of lapis-blue. The old man with the white hair that Bellepheros had seen on the ship sat in the middle, quietly calm and sure of everything around him. Chay-Liang, the enchantress, stood to one side, stiff and ill at ease. On the other side a slender man in black stood as still as a statue. His skin and his clothes were both so dark that Bellepheros couldn't see where one started and the other ended. He could have been a living shadow, but the edging to his robe gave him away. Strands of red, blue and white, entwined together. The Picker had worn those robes.

'You're an Elemental Man,' Bellepheros said.

The black-robe didn't answer. 'The Watcher's going to keep you safe from the enemies of our city,' Chay-Liang said. 'And believe me, slave, we have quite enough.'

The old Taiytakei stared at Bellepheros. 'Keeper of the Dragons, I am Quai'Shu, sea lord of Xican and your absolute master. I said you would build me an eyrie.'

Bellepheros didn't look away. He didn't bow this time either. 'And I said you would wish that I hadn't.'

'You will do this. You will be given whatever you require. I will send you to my t'varr, Baros Tsen. You may ask him for whatever you need. He is a perfect t'varr: there is nothing he cannot find, nothing he cannot arrange. Whatever you wish for, he will provide. If you need artefacts of glass, Chay-Liang will make them. They will do whatever you require. The Watcher will be your guardian. Where should such a thing be built?'

'In the realms that are my home,' said Bellepheros with quiet calm, 'where there are many other alchemists to ensure your dragons remain tame.'

The sea lord's face didn't flicker. 'There are ways to bring a man to heel, Keeper of the Dragons, without breaking him. Where?'

'Far away from any cities. Far away from people. As far away as you can.'

'Why?'

Why? You have to ask why? Bellepheros gaped. 'Because they are dragons, Sea Lord Quai'Shu of Xican! Because they are fifty paces from tip to tip of wing and from nose to tip of tail. Because of what will happen if any one of them breaks free of the potions you will ask me to make – *if* I make them at all. Because I am your one and only alchemist and you will not have another, and if anything happens to me then your cities will burn. Because they are a plague to ruin worlds. But I see you for what you are – you're like a dragon-king, believing yourself master of everything around you. You will never believe such a catastrophe could happen, for surely your mere existence prevents it. I hope you may think otherwise when you meet a full-grown dragon eye to eye, but I cannot show you how that feels here in this room. So for now let us say because of the disease that newly hatched dragons bring with them. It will run like fire through your people should it ever escape.'

Quai'Shu barely even blinked. It was as if not a single word had reached him. 'Far away from others. The desert, then.'

'Deserts are suitable. The heat makes the dragons a little

sluggish.' Outwatch was the biggest eyrie in the dragon realms and *that* was in a desert. 'An eyrie should be hard to reach and hard to enter, because whatever you may believe, every eyrie contains the greatest weapon you will ever know.' He leaned a little forward and spoke through clenched teeth. 'People may try to steal it.'

The sea lord nodded and sent him away and it was the last time that Bellepheros would see Sea Lord Quai'Shu as the Taiytakei knew him, as the captain of a city and a fleet of ships, as a conqueror of worlds. Bellepheros had said the desert, and so that was where the Taiytakei took him and gave him a castle that floated in the air. He made peace with himself then. Accepted his slavery and bowed to its inevitability, for now at least. The Taiytakei had no dragons yet, that was true, but what they did have beggared his mind. He felt a fool beside Chay-Liang, lowly and ignorant among her glittering spires and golden automata, among the conjured jewels and marvellous creatures and the wonders of a dozen worlds. He told her, slowly and carefully and with patience, exactly what they would need to build a dragon eyrie that would work and exactly what they would need to keep a dragon tame. Food. A great deal of it, and so she moved the castle that floated in the air to the desert's edge where great herds of hump-backed horses roamed among dry and sandy grasslands. After that, men and women to tend the dragons. Scales. People who, with a little of his help, would fall in love with the monsters, who would give their lives as they became slowly riddled with the Hatchling Disease and died of it, turned into human statues. So Baros Tsen, the sly fat t'varr, brought him slaves, and Bellepheros brewed the potions that would dull their minds and ready them to fall in love with their monsters.

There were other ways, he said. Better ways, but they took longer and needed children to be raised as Scales from before they could talk, knowing nothing else. At that, Tsen T'Varr brought him children – babies – but Bellepheros sent them away, for they would need teachers first and other things. Men and women to cook and clean, to build and polish and make and repair. They brought him all the slaves he asked for, everything he desired, and he set them to work.

To make his potions he would need dragon blood. Somehow

they brought it to him. Above all, he told them, they would need more alchemists.

Then make them, they said. And that was the one thing he couldn't do. He could teach a slave to make a potion. He could teach Chay-Liang to make almost anything. By the end there was almost not a single one of his secrets that he hadn't shared with her. But alchemy lived in the blood, and there was only one place in the world where a true alchemist could be made, an alchemist who could dull a dragon, and the secret of that place was the one secret he kept, for it was deep within the dragon realms, far off in the darkest caves of the Worldspine, and without that secret there was only one person in their world who could make the potions they wanted and that person was him, and without more alchemists they would all be hostages together when they finally found a dragon. They would see the horror that a dragon could bring and he would show this Quai'Shu why his desire was such terrible folly.

So he made his eyrie, built to his own design, potions brewed to order. Quai'Shu never came to it, T'Varr Tsen was rarely there, the Watcher merely watched, and beneath their different coloured robes and their different coloured skins, he found that Chay-Liang was as much an alchemist as he was. He ran his eyrie as he saw fit and did as he wished. At his fingers he had knowledge and sorceries and devices he had never dreamed could exist. For a man who had once been master of the Order of the Scales, it was close to perfect. Without the dragons themselves, he could almost forget that he was no longer free.

But he never did forget. Never quite lost sight of the promise he'd made to Tuuran, that one day he'd take them both home. Just kept putting off the thought, as Chay-Liang danced yet another miracle before him and seduced him with ideas for just another few days. Again and again and again. And maybe he *would* have forgotten, but he always remembered the look of betrayal in Tuuran's eyes when the Adamantine Man finally left him and returned to the sea. *You'll get comfortable here,* he'd said, and it was true and he had. And when he was done, when it was all made and finished and he still hadn't made his stand and gone home after all, Bellepheros looked at what he'd built, at the perfect waiting machine, and held his head in his hands, for he knew he had done a terrible thing.

Skyrie

7

The Elemental Man

A long time ago and a good many years before the Adamantine Palace would burn, the Watcher stood at the top of Mount Solence in the centre of a circle. The sky above was a clear and brilliant blue. The sun glinted off the top of the perpetual cloud that shrouded the slopes below the summit. The circle around his feet was perhaps a hundred feet across and made of solid silver. Every inch of it was carved with the story of the world, from its creation from nothing by the four first gods until the moment the Watcher had taken his place there. Eight columns pierced the silver around him, each one of them ten paces tall, one for each element. Stone and metal, air and water, fire and ice, light and darkness, each element of each pair opposed to the other. The Watcher stood between them in the centre, quiet and serene, wholly certain of himself. He felt seven of the eight pillars as though they were his brothers. The ever-burning flame on top of the bronze pillar of fire, the tiny whirlwind around the white glass pillar of air, the carved diamond and obsidian in the pillars of ice and stone. He had mastered all of them bar the impenetrable one, the impossible metal that no Elemental Man had ever tamed. He had the power of turning himself into any one of them and moving within its flow. He had a name, given by the Celestial Septtych, the Elemental Masters. Names were nothing but masks, yet it made him proud nonetheless.

Above the sea of cloud gnarled fruit trees dotted the gentle slopes of the mountaintop, filling it with the delicate colours and scents of their bright pink blossoms. A lone figure approached, walking slowly along the winding path and the steps, leaning heavily on a staff after the long climb to the summit.

Quai'Shu. A sea lord.

The Watcher didn't move. The path up the mountain was easy enough and he was a patient man. Learning to fuse with the elements took time. For the most part an Elemental Man worked alone but today he stood beside another: the Picker. The Picker would be a killer and they'd both known that for many years. Elemental Men were cut from clean cloth, forged to kill the emperors, sorcerers, warlords and kings of other worlds. Such people often had magics and protections to be teased away before a sure blow could be struck, things generally best done with a slow and deliberate care, in need of eyes as well as knives. If the Picker was the knife, the Watcher would be his eyes. So the Septtych had told them it would be, and so he waited as this Quai'Shu hauled himself closer.

'He has come to buy you,' murmured the columns.

No one bought an Elemental Man. They paid for a service. Sometimes a service that would take years or even decades but it was always, eventually, discharged. To buy an Elemental Man, to own one, flesh and blood forever until death, that was unthinkable. The price would be beyond imagination.

'Yes,' sighed the air. 'Both of you.'

A whispering breeze brought him the sound of distant leaves fluttering against one another and a fresh waft of scent from peach groves not far away. He smelled Quai'Shu too. He remembered that clearly, long afterwards. Oils and scents and sweat, smells of riches and hard work. He waited, still as stone, until the old man reached the circle and looked him up and down. Then he bowed and the Picker bowed too. The first of many to their new master. 'I am yours to command,' they said as one.

'Yes.' Quai'Shu leaned against the twisted rusted iron that was the elemental column of metal and took a moment to catch his breath. 'You are. And you'd better not fail me like the last one.'

Those first words were enough to make the Watcher blink. Elemental Men didn't fail. Lesser mages, a Windbinder perhaps, or a Stoneshaper. But a true Elemental Man? Fail? No.

'Yes. Failed. So you are both mine and I ask that you do better.'

Another movement in the air brought up the smell of the blossoms from further down the slope where they had bloomed a few days earlier. The trees at the very top of the mountain were always the last. The Watcher took a deep breath, tasting the air. He could ride that breeze if he wanted to. Turn himself into the wind and fly wherever it would carry him. Or he could sink into the stone, or become light and colours, or nothing but empty shadow in the dark. Anything but metal. And so no, an Elemental Man did not fail, not ever.

'The Diamond Isles.' The Picker spoke softly, so quietly that only the Watcher would hear. His voice had a keenness. The sorcerers of the Diamond Isles were a myth. No one had seen them for a thousand years. They'd died out long ago, but that was one way an Elemental man might fail, if the task was impossible because the victim simply didn't exist; although only a fool would try and wave such trickery at the Septtych.

And yet it was true, and to the Diamond Isles they went. A year passed from that day on the silver circle at the peak of Mount Solence and the Watcher stood on a gleaming beach, with the ship that had carried him there rocking at anchor out to sea. A boat sliced through the calm waters in long powerful strokes. Bright sun in a clear blue sky glinted off the rippling waves and sweat glistened on the tanned skins of the slaves at the oars. Another boat lay already beached on a small curve of gleaming white sand squeezed between two jagged fingers of black rock. Away from the sea the sand was quickly overwhelmed by a jungle of vivid green ferns and trees laced with bright red bloodflowers high up in their branches, thick and impenetrable, fighting and tumbling on top of each other for the precious sunlight. Distant shrieks and hoots echoed within. Now and then the Watcher saw flashes of brilliant yellow and blue and silver. Birds flitting among the branches.

He looked past the jungle up to the sapling mountains whose sheer sides rose from the verdant heart of the island. Three mountains, not great or grand or even particularly tall, but steep and sheer and sharp and each one topped by a tower. The towers seemed small from this distance but their glitter was dazzling. They were carved of solid diamond, or so it was said. The Picker, at least in part, had been right.

In the year that his life had belonged to Quai'Shu, the Watcher had come to learn his master's ways. Quai'Shu was a Taiytakei sea lord in every sense, measured yet bold. He'd sailed many worlds and there were few he hadn't seen with his own eyes. He'd taken slaves from the Small Kingdoms and from the coast of faraway Aria. Three times he'd taken a flotilla of ships to the Dominion of the Sun King and back. He'd plundered the ruins of Qeled. He'd seen men die and ships sink, beheld shapeshifters, monsters and ghosts. He'd watched other sea lords rise from nothing and fall into calamity, their fleets and families with them, and yet others rise in their place. Much that the Watcher had learned from the Septtych, Quai'Shu had seen for himself. Such experience deserved respect.

'Three men clad in silver with eyes of blood and the faces of dead gods. Do you know why we are here?' asked Quai'Shu suddenly.

'I am to kill them?'

The answer seemed obvious, and then it was immediately every bit as obvious that it wasn't right. Quai'Shu's smile seemed to chide him for his presumption. 'No, servant, you are not their end. You are an offering.'

The Watcher bowed. 'You mean to give me to the sorcerers who live here?' For a moment he wondered if he might murder his master rather than be given up as a gift.

'Perhaps.' Quai'Shu gave an impatient frown. 'But you are a treasure. Priceless. Why would I give you away? What could be worth so much?'

Elemental Men spoke with actions and deeds. Men like Quai'Shu, the Watcher had learned, spoke mostly for their own ears. He held his silence. The sea lord was playing with him.

'What are we, we Taiytakei? We sail between worlds. We cross the storm-dark and what do we do? We find what they want and we give it to them.' He smiled. 'Do you know how many lands I've seen?'

The Watcher nodded. 'All of them, master.'

'No one has seen them all. Some have yet to be revealed. But I've seen many. Perhaps all of them that matter. Do you know what I've found?'

The Watcher shook his head.

'I've led my family and my fleet for two decades and I've led them well. The City of Stone prospers. In the all-devouring duel between Cashax and the Vespinese, I've taken my side and ridden it with care. A good ally to one, never a dangerous enemy to the other. Small as we are, I've kept Xican's place in the Great Sea Council among the thirteen cities who quietly rule the six known worlds. Yet I am not satisfied. Another few years and I'll be too weak for these voyages. The mantle will pass to someone younger. One of my sons. I'll be remembered as a good captain but not a great one. Not yet.' He turned and looked the Watcher in the eye for the first time since they'd reached the island. 'What have I found? I've found whatever I wanted to find. That is what we do. It's what makes us what we are. Every desire but one I've sated. In the court of the immortal Sun King, who is revered as a god and who wears armour made of the very matter of the sun itself, I found something unexpected. I knelt in his presence. It was uncommonly bright but otherwise like that of any other man, king or otherwise. Yet what I found there was a desire I have not been able to sate.'

'Do you wish him dead, master?' asked the Picker. He frowned at once, at his own impertinence perhaps, but the Watcher understood perfectly. Killing for mere amusement? Elemental Men had done so before but such murders were shameful. And then *he* felt ashamed too, for Quai'Shu surely wouldn't stoop to such a thing.

'Do I seem so little to you?' Quai'Shu hacked up a gob of phlegm and spat it onto the white sand. 'I want something that will not be given, not for anything in the world. Dragons. That was the desire the Sun King showed me in his palace. For a dragon, he said he would give me anything. I could not satisfy him. I promised myself I would not rest until I could, but later my thoughts wandered far. I am set on a new course. I will bring dragons to all our captains of the sea. They will change our world.'

'Dragons, master?'

'Dragons.'

The Watcher had seen dragons in pictures. Quai'Shu had seen dragons too. From a distance, but for real and with his own eyes. The princes of the dragon lands guarded them jealously. The Watcher knew this because Quai'Shu had said so.

'As captain of my house I've been cautious and prudent and it has made me rich. For most of my life that's all that mattered, to keep the keepers of my coin content; now, in the twilight of my years, it's not enough. Does that seem strange to you men of the elements? Foolish? No matter. Here we are. Dragons cannot be bought and so I mean to steal one. A scheme worthy of an Elemental Man. I would see if these Diamond Men will help. I will buy them if I can, with the most precious thing I can offer.'

Looking for sorcerers who might not even exist. But if they did …

'The Key.'

The Watcher kept the key on a string around his neck, hidden under his shirt, kept against his skin so he would always know it was there. It didn't *look* much like a key, but Quai'Shu had promised it would work. It was a flawless diamond, cold, too cold to touch for long, and so he kept it wrapped in layers of soft cloth. Safe and close. It had cost Quai'Shu a year of profit, more than a dozen brand-new ships, and he would never tell a soul how he'd finally found it, though the Watcher knew it had come from mysterious Qeled. From the Scythians, perhaps? It said much that Quai'Shu had given it to him to be its guardian.

The Watcher peeled away the black silk cloth and held the diamond up to the sun. Even here in the heat the cold burned his fingers. The chill crept along his arm, down his spine and all the way to his feet. He was used to doing things that couldn't be undone, to taking journeys into places that were little more than myth or rumour; after all, that's what Elemental Men did, why they were made, but still … He could feel the magic humming through the key. Something alien, something different, something greater even than the sorceries of his masters. He held the diamond up to the sun until his fingers screamed at him and he let it go, holding the silver chain that bound it instead.

'Let it fall.'

The Watcher dropped the key in the sand. He didn't know what he should expect now. For the sand to grow into a vast bridge across the jungle canopy? To part and reveal dim winding steps twisting down a black hole into the ground?

But not nothing.

Quai'Shu waited for another minute and then plucked the diamond off the sand by its chain. The Watcher wrapped it in its black silk and put it back under his shirt. A part of him wasn't surprised. If any of the stories were true, the moon sorcerers were nothing short of gods, beyond the understanding of even an Elemental Man. If none of them were true then Quai'Shu had come a very long way to leave with nothing; yet the sea lord's face looked calm.

The Watcher took a deep breath and turned around. The second boat coming from the ship was almost at the beach now, filled with men to carve a path through the jungle if they were needed. He'd do that for his master if he was asked. He'd become the wind and scale the mountains and the towers themselves and ride the earth to the sorcerers who lived there, if they truly lived there at all. But in his heart he knew that if the moon sorcerers were real and the key had failed then it was because, as offerings went, he wasn't enough.

Your desires.

He jumped and spun around. The ship was gone. Everything was gone except the beach and the jungle and the mighty hands of black rock that clawed at the sea and his master beside him. The Picker was gone too. In his place stood three men.

Men? No.

Their hair was long and white. They wore armour that glittered and gleamed as though made of pure polished silver, shaped and faceted like the eyes of an insect. Their faces were those of young men, handsome and strong, fast but pale as the dead, and their eyes … their eyes were the colour of fresh blood and as old as the world.

Three of them. Three towers.

Yes. Their lips didn't move but their words rang inside his head. They spoke together, three voices into one alien melody.

'I brought …' Quai'Shu's voice was, for the first and only time the Watcher would hear, hesitant. 'I brought an offering.'

The Watcher fell to his knees and bowed.

This? Now the voices spoke in his head one at a time, alternating one after the other.

What knowledge of this …

… do you think we do not possess?

They were laughing at him. He could feel their amusement at this little creature who had the audacity to disturb them. To think he was important. Quai'Shu's voice didn't falter, though. 'I will take the master alchemist from the dragon lands. I can bring you the secrets of dragons …'

We know …

... everything there is to know ...

... about dragons.

The Watcher kept his head bowed. Quai'Shu, the great sea lord of Xican. A man whose voice rang across the whole might of Takei'Tarr when he spoke in the Crown of the Sea Lords in Khalishtor; a man who had negotiated trades in every world the Taiytakei could reach for forty years, twenty as the captain of his house and some with men who'd begun by trying to kill him. That was what sea captains did. It was his life. Yet here and now he was at last lost for words.

He was the offering and he wasn't good enough. He would find a way to repay his master for his failure.

Our answer ...

... is yes.

Your offering ...

... is nothing.

You will give us ...

... something other.

Even in front of three half-gods, some instincts ran too deep. The Watcher heard the familiar sly lilt to his master's voice. 'Something other? What is it you desire?'

You will not understand. They didn't smile but there was a mocking laughter in their words, and then they were gone.

Months passed and turned to years. Quai'Shu grew old and frail before his time until he could barely walk. Much of his fleet passed on to his sons and daughters as he let them pitch themselves against one another while he watched, waiting to see if one would show themself more able than the others, but his dreams of dragons were not forgotten. His steps were assured, careful and precise, the piece-by-piece building of a machine that had come fully formed into his head that day on the beach of the Diamond Isles. The Watcher learned that there had indeed been another Elemental Man, the one that failed. He learned why. It was a strange thing, but in this land of dragons certain things that an Elemental Man took for granted simply didn't work.

'Deserts are suitable.'

His mind snapped back to the here and the now. To Quai'Shu

beside him and the alchemist of the dragon realms before him. It had begun. The Picker had completed the first of his tasks. Now there was an eyrie to be built, a flying castle fortress to be found and many things besides, and soon the dragons would come, all as Quai'Shu had been promised.

Yet Quai'Shu had not been alone on that island, and the half-gods had not shown him everything. By the time the dragons came, the Picker would be dead and Quai'Shu would be mad. The moon sorcerers had shown the Watcher these things, and when he asked why they had shown them to him and to him alone, the half-gods had laughed in mockery. Fate was fate and could not change. They'd shown him other things too and it would do no good to try and change any of it. Except for one thing that remained hanging in the balance.

The grey dead ...
... are coming ...
... with the golden knife.
They are making ...
... the greatest of us ...
... whole again.
They are calling ...
... the Black Moon ...
... to rise once more.
Do ...
... what you do ...
... and watch.

8

Skyrie

Skyrie. On a battlefield outside Tethis, four years before the Adamantine Palace would burn, the name slipped inside Berren's head. It came with an explosion of light. When he opened his eyes again he was staring at the bright sky. Faces were looking down on him. Old friends. Faces he knew but he could feel himself falling away from them. And he could feel something coming the other way. Something from a dark place. It had a name.

Skyrie ...

He caught a glimpse of other faces peering down at him too. Different faces. Dim shadows shrouded in grey.

Berren! Crowntaker! Where are you wounded? The words of his soldiering friends, of Tallis One-Eye, grew distant. *Hold the advance! Get him out of here! Gaunt, lead the wall!*

He barely heard. He was sinking. Falling fast while another streamed the other way. He reached out at the thing that passed him in the void and tore at it, sunk in his fingers and his teeth and his toes. He tore a piece away but it didn't stop the falling.

Skyrie. That was who he was. That was his name. He saw the Crowntaker coming, falling, screaming, flailing, clawing. They tasted one another as they passed through Xibaiya, through the path ripped by the warlock's sigil, and then Skyrie saw the light. He saw the Bloody Judge fall away. Saw faces and the sun. Reached for them as the warlock's rip began to close. He'd seen a tear like this before, he was sure of it. In a place full of water but he couldn't remember where. He reached for the light, for the sun, full of urgency and victory, but now something was dragging him back. 'Get me up!' A voice that was his but wasn't. 'Get that off me! Now! Before it's too ... It's doing ...' He scrabbled to fight his way on into the light and the noise of the battlefield but the rip was almost gone.

Something seemed to push past him through the tear, clambering over him, squeezing him back. The faces and the sky dimmed and began to change and now Skyrie was falling too, away into somewhere else where the sky was black and the air was filled with smoke and the smell of earth and the faces that looked down on him were shrouded in cowls and he wasn't on the battlefield any more, he was back where he'd been all along, in the pit under Tethis castle. He knew its dingy light and its rotten smell. He was lying flat on a table at the bottom of a hole in the floor of a cave deep underground.

He slumped. Closed his eyes. They'd failed. He took a deep breath and let it out and then another. His heart was thumping as though *he'd* been the one in the middle of a battle, not the Crowntaker. He groaned. Four of his brothers in grey held him, peering at him. Warlocks, and he was one of them. Skyrie the marsh farmer, who'd come to Tethis with a hole in his soul and a vengeful heart, who'd taken the grey robes of the Dark Queen's priests to wreak havoc and woe on the Bloody Judge who'd destroyed his home. He'd come here willingly, made his choices, and now they'd failed. He groaned, desolate, and tried to sit up.

'Skyrie?' The other warlocks still held him down. They were shaking, full of fear. In case it *had* worked and the body they held had the Crowntaker inside it now. Which gave them every reason to be afraid.

Skyrie fell limp. 'It didn't work.' He was too weak to move. Too ruined by despair. Their last gambit and he was still here and the Crowntaker, the Bloody Judge of Tethis, was still out there, still who he'd ever been. Vallas's sigils had failed. But they'd been so close! For a moment he'd even seen through the Bloody Judge's eyes before the rip had closed and something had torn him back.

'Should we call Vallas?' The warlock who held his left leg. Brother Scortas.

Skyrie nodded. Vallas's great scheme to bend defeat back to victory, to wrench the Bloody Judge out of his very own flesh and blood and replace him with another, and for a moment, for one blink of another's eye, they'd been on the cusp of it. Maybe it wasn't too late to try again ...

Where am I?

Skyrie froze. Horror turned his bones to ice. He had an instant, that was all, to realise that he hadn't come back alone, for utter dread to drench his every thought, before an alien presence ripped through him, hurling him tumbling head over heels into nothing, stranding him far away where all he could do was watch and listen and scream in silence as ...

I am the Bloody Judge of Tethis. I am Berren the Crowntaker! What have you done? WHAT HAVE YOU DONE TO ME? The warlock to his left had a knife. Skyrie's arm jerked up. Smashed its fist into his face and sprawled him to the floor. He kicked the pair who stood by his feet. One stumbled forward. He sank his fingers into a fleshy neck and practically tore out the warlock's throat. The last one scrabbled away. 'Skyrie!' *Skyrie?* Who was that? Not him. A battlefield. Full armour, wading through mud, blood and the limbs of his enemies. Only a moment ago and now he was here, mad-eyed, riven by terror-fuelled fury ...

A silent prisoner, helpless behind his own eyes, Skyrie shrieked and howled and wailed and tore at himself. His brothers. His comrades. He knew their names. He knew their laughter. They'd shared bread and water. They were the ones who'd brought him here, all of them come willingly for the ritual that would turn the world on its head and he was killing them and he couldn't stop, couldn't even close his eyes, couldn't even look away ...

He leaped off the table, The Crowntaker, consumed with irresistible fury. Onto the warlock who still held the knife. Filling the air with savage snarls. Both hands to the warlock's wrist. Knee smash to the groin, hard enough to make the warlock cough out his own balls. Stamped on his ankle and smashed his face against the wall of the pit. The warlock doubled up and retched and the knife was his for the taking. *Ritual?* For a moment the fury faltered like sun through a break between thunderclouds and light poured in. He felt strange, lost, then grabbed hold of the fury again and tugged it hard, the only thing he had to cling to. The knife came free. He caught it. Brought it straight back up and buried it in the warlock's guts. One dead. *Ritual?* He knew where he was. Not where he was supposed to be. *What ritual?* Remembered the battlefield. The warlock. The one who'd stuck him with that strip of cursed sigils. A cold wind brushed through him. Knowledge hammered his head and then fell away like sand hurled at a steel wall. This body wasn't his! *What did you do to me? WHAT HAVE YOU DONE?* Fear rose again through the fury and choked him ...

The thing inside him faltered. Skyrie groped for a memory that was truly his, a blind man fishing in the dark depths of a swamp for something he'd once held. Water. And stars. A momentary flash of *elsewhere* ... He threw himself at the *thing* inside him ...

Too late. Too slow. The Crowntaker found his rage again and hurled Skyrie screaming away. One warlock dead. Three left. Had to kill them. Had to keep killing. Had to keep the fury fuelled or he'd slip away. The warlocks backed away. Shouted for help. He sprang at them. They weren't soldiers. They got in each other's way. He swept the legs out from one. Flipped him up and crashed him to the floor. Stamped down. Neck bones crunched and cracked. His lips drew back, a grimace of vicious glee ...

Dear gods, dear gods and holy Xibaiya! Skyrie wrapped himself around the memory of water and of the stars that winked out one by one. It gave him strength even as he felt himself unravelling. An anchor. For a moment it even found him his voice. 'My brothers! Help me! I am ...' And then it was gone again, lost to the snarling other ...

'... Berren the Crowntaker. The Bloody Judge.' Fingers caught hold of a flapping cowl. He pulled. Slashed the knife. Warm blood showered his hand. The warlock jerked back. Opened his mouth to scream and vomited blood and a few gargling gasps. Last one now. Backed against the far wall. Whimpering and shrieking. The Crowntaker tossed the knife from hand to hand. Movement, corner of his eye, up on the rim of the pit. Soldier. But he'd stood up there himself once and he knew how dark it was down here. They could hear but they couldn't see. He pressed his knife to the last necromancer's throat. Hatred pulsed through him. *'What have you done to me ...?'*

Skyrie clawed at fragments of himself, slowly drifting apart. For every one he pulled back another escaped and vanished. He was falling to pieces. He tried again to scream, to beg for help as his brother did, but the only words that came were from the *other*, the *thing* he'd brought back, the Crowntaker, the Bloody Judge himself. The whites of his brother's eyes glistened in the darkness.

Sicel, that was his name, and they slept in the same room, cots one beside the other. He would have wept if his tears had been his own to shed. *I'm sorry, brother. I cannot stop him.* In the darkness above someone lit a lantern, and Skyrie knew well what would happen next. The soldiers would peer in. They'd see what he'd done and remember clearly how precise and explicit their orders were. They'd take up their crossbows and they'd riddle him with iron and wood. They'd watch his blood leak across the ground and soak into the dirt and then they'd throw down oil and torches and burn whatever was left. He knew. He remembered the warnings. *The Bloody Judge may find the body you leave behind.* So they knew he might come and they were ready for it, but not like this, while the voice that wasn't his snarled and snapped like a cornered wolf and Sicel's eyes rolled in terror and dismay filled his words. Vallas wasn't even here. Vallas was with their queen, facing the Bloody Judge's Fighting Hawks to put an end to him at last. The Bloody Judge who was right here. And all the while the lantern was coming down on its rope and the end would quickly follow. Deep inside, Skyrie squirmed and writhed and fought and found no purchase to throw the Crowntaker aside. Sighed and stood ready to be released. *I am Skyrie! I am your brother! Vallas help me ...*

The Crowntaker slit the last warlock's throat. Held him close. Let blood gush over his clothes, rich and heady. Couldn't see much in the dark. Could feel his skin, though. Wasn't the skin he knew. Arms were scrawny and thin like a boy's. All the battle-corded muscle gone. He didn't understand the how but he knew what they'd done to him. The memories were right there. Right there in front of him. For a moment he paused. Clenched that piece he'd seized as he fell out of the light of the battlefield and squeezed the memories out of it. *HOW DO YOU TURN IT BACK?*

The lantern was almost down. For a moment, as the Crowntaker clawed at his memories, Skyrie felt a mastery of himself again. He ran a hand down his leg. The scar was still there, the huge axe cut he should never have survived. *This is who I am! Skyrie! My body, my flesh, how it always was. Skyrie.* He sank to his haunches, hugging himself. The lantern came to a stop a foot above the ground. It swung slowly back and forth. He knew what Vallas had told the queensguard here over the pit because he'd been there, standing beside them, and they'd put him down here for a reason, after all. *If he finds a way back then nothing comes out of here alive. Throw oil and a torch until everything is scorched to ash.* He opened his mouth to shout up at them to do it, to burn him. Nothing. And now he couldn't move any more. And then he understood: he wasn't free at all. The Crowntaker lurked behind him, seeing it as he remembered it. Too late. His gaping mouth slammed shut, his legs leaped, his arms reached out and there was not a thing he could do to stop it. He screamed in silence yet again, *Do you as you were told! Burn me! Burn me before it's too late!*

The lantern hung from a rope. A good thick one. He jumped, swift and sudden. Seized it. Pulled sharply. The soldier at the edge of the pit holding the other end cried out, teetered, toppled over the edge and landed hard. Stupid. The lantern smashed and its rope fell in loops and then hung taut, tied to the winch and crane they used to lower people down. The Crowntaker gripped the knife between his teeth. He had the soldier's sword out of its scabbard in a flash. Hurled it up out of the pit and over the edge. Scampered up the wall, clinging to the rope, climbing like a monkey. All those years at sea. A skag. Never forgotten. At the top he picked out the other soldiers. They'd seen him. Were coming. Shouting. Didn't matter. He took it all in. One glance. Where they were. What they carried. What they wore. Bared his teeth. They were too slow. Too late to stop him …

Burn me! Please burn me!

The first queensguard reached him. He danced past the thrust of a sword. His legs felt awkward, not his, not used to such sudden hard motion. He took the knife from between his teeth. Slammed its blade under the soldier's chin. Felt a twinge from his arm. Switched hands and almost fumbled the knife, but not quite. Snatched up the sword from the ground. Almost lost his balance but still caught the next queensguard. Barged through him, tumbling him shrieking into the pit and almost fell back in himself. Stupid body didn't do what it was supposed to. Arms and legs too long. Centre of balance in the wrong place. He looked up. Three queensguard still standing. He stopped. Opened his arms to them, soaked in blood, beckoning them forward. 'Run if you want to live.' Grinned wide at the new sound of his own voice. Savage like a wild animal.

O Earth Goddess! Lords of Xibaiya! Help me! Help me now! Your acolyte pleads for your aid! Make it stop!

The soldiers backed away. The knife in his hand dripped blood over his naked feet. He smiled at them one after the other. That was enough. They broke and ran, screaming alarms to anyone who might be left to listen. The Bloody Judge of Tethis let them go. Walked the other way and slipped through a half-hidden crack in the cave around the pit. Down a steep narrow slope, squeezing between the walls, inch by inch in a darkness that was absolute. He moved with purpose. Knew exactly where he was going because he'd been here before, a long time ago, with someone who'd once been a thief-taker, but now the others were all dead and there was no one left who knew this way but him. Crept carefully forward, looking for the pool that hid the sump and the secret path in and out. Found it …

The cold touch of water on Skyrie's feet jogged a memory. Something colossal but too fleeting to grasp. He chased it as the icy water rose around him, as it swallowed him, but the harder he reached, the more it slipped through his fingers, and then the water was falling away . .

Out the other side of the sump. Gasping for air. Clawing his way into another cave. Familiar. Knife-rays of sunlight shining in from a narrow entrance. He'd come in the dark before. Dark was better. He crouched and waited. His arm hurt, and his knees, and all his muscles ached, twisted into unfamiliar action. Four warlocks. Three queensguard. As easy as snapping twigs. It helped in remembering. *The Bloody Judge, that's who I am. The Crowntaker.* Had to hang on to that. Had to hold it tight. So he did, right on until the sun set and night fell. Then out. Into the gorge. Then what? Didn't know. Didn't dare think. Find who took his body, that's what. Take it back. Kill him. Something. Didn't know. All that hiding and waiting had left him with a thirst, though. Start with that. Afterwards a reckoning. A terrible one. Where and when and who, that was the question. Made him angry. Uncertainty and doubt? Didn't have a place for those now. Didn't dare. *I am the Bloody Judge.* He slipped down the slope of the gorge. Dark as shit.

Moon hadn't risen yet. Crept to the edge of the river and knelt down to drink. A face reflected back at him. A face that belonged to someone else and all he could do was stare as the horror surged through him ...

Water? He remembered the water. *Me! It belongs to me! Mine! My face! Skyrie!* Staring at himself, for a moment Skyrie threw off the horror. He screamed, and this time, finally, he had a voice.

9

The Empty Sands

The Watcher stood atop the Palace of Leaves among the seventeen slowly turning discs of gold-tinged glass from which it hung, each thicker than a standing man and a hundred paces from edge to edge. Their motions were hypnotic. They drew novice eyes inside them and held them fast and sometimes didn't let go for days. The core of each was more deeply tinged with gold, separate and still, held apart by bearings and a heavy frame of Scythian steel. More steel hung from the cores, chains laced with silver and gold carrying the weight of the jewelled pods and orbs of the upper palace. For most who came here, this was the marvel of the City of Stone. And it *was* magnificent, every part laced with power drawn up from the earth by the black monoliths below, a monument to the enchanters' arts. But to the Watcher, the real glories of Xican were the earth and the sea and the sky, things that would remain long after the palace had fallen and shattered. There was a boundless joy to standing at such a height, with the clouds close enough to part them with his fingers, with Xican a warren of black and grey spires spread beneath his feet, a thousand termite mounds jammed together and transformed by some divine hand into a grand scale. The Grey Isle was made like this from end to end, this orderless tumble of stone on stone, yet across all the worlds he'd seen it was the place he loved the most, where air and earth and water mingled, their boundaries intertwined as closely as could be like lovers wrapped around one another, limbs tangled. It was a colourless landscape of deep blues and slate-greys, but he loved the stone, the wind, the rolling salty sea, the raw kaleidoscope of shapes and angles and changes that nature had made. A rare smile forced its way onto his face. Up here, alone, he belonged to no one. The freedom was joyous and the knowledge was exhilarating, the knowledge that he was all of this and more.

As easily as another man might blink, the Watcher became a wind that blew across the Grey Isle's great teeth. For no other reason than the sheer delight of it, he became the water as he reached the other side, a wave top skipping and surfing across the reach of sea between the Grey Isle and the coast of Takei'Tarr, the heartland of the Taiytakei. At the Hangpoor delta he leaped into foam and then to the air, hanging among the clouds, drinking the sight of the Hundred Rivers glittering in the morning sun, a giant tree laid out in silver across the plains. And Zinzarra too, City of a Thousand Bridges with her air harbour in the sky, higher and larger than even the Palace of Leaves, where the Zinzarrans stored the jade they took from the mountains of the Konsidar. They boasted of it, the greatest device the enchanters had ever made, but to the Watcher the beauty here was in the delta, in the water and the weaving maze of quicksilver threads, always shifting and changing.

He turned his course westward to the fringes of the Konsidar itself. On top of the peaks he stopped a while to stare. Becoming one with the world was no effort once you knew the trick of it. Air or stone or water, or any element at all save for unruly metal, it was simply another nature, as easy and natural as breathing. He took it to be a gift too, a window to wonders that other men wouldn't ever see, and so he stopped now and then to stare at the landscapes of the world the way men from other lands might stop for a moment to pray and to give thanks to their blasphemous gods.

He chose his course with care across the mountains, skirting the domain of the Righteous Ones who dwelt in the majestic Konsidar. Though they dwelt below rather than among the mountains and would not have noticed an Elemental Man crossing high overhead, they had been more unruly of late, emerging from their holes and rattling their sabres like angry ants whose nest someone had disturbed. Best not to give any reason to add to their ire, whatever had caused it.

He turned south as the peaks and crags fell away into the desert of the Empty Sands, the wasteland that filled half the continent from the Konsidar to the Godspike and beyond. Dunes as tall as an enchanter's tower rippled beneath him, then the flats, a hundred miles of gravel, of milky-white powdered glass and hard dark lakes of clay. In the stories of the desert tribes there had been water here once, vanished now after the old cataclysm of the Splintering, pouring into the lost depths of the Konsidar and stolen away by the Righteous Ones. Or so their stories said.

Dunes rose again, reddish-orange now instead of yellow and pale. He crossed a fresh slick of black ooze streaking the sands, with a scatter of white specks at its edge that were the tents of the desert men there to collect it, scraping it into barrels to sell to the enchanters in Cashax or Vespinarr. That they'd been there long enough to build a village of tents reminded the Watcher of how long it was since he'd last come this way. Further still he passed over a faint line across the desert, invisible from the ground. Just as there had been lakes out here once, so too had there been paths that criss-crossed the wasteland. Roads. There had been cities even, but now they were ruins and the only things that lived in them were spiders and scorpions, rats and snakes and desert hawks. The desert men came here on occasion too but never lingered, not without good reason.

Amid this emptiness Baros Tsen's castle beckoned him, a huge lump of stone floating above the sand on a dazzle of purple lightning. The Watcher felt it before he saw it, the slightest thickening of the air so that being one with the wind was no longer effortless. No one knew the castle's origin. It had been in the desert for as long as anyone could remember, hanging in the sky, empty and forgotten. It was stone rather than glass, and though it floated like an enchanter's glasship, it was vastly greater than anything any enchanter had ever made, a wide bowl-shaped slab larger even than the Palace of Leaves in its entirety. Its underside was torn and jagged, as though it had been ripped out of the earth by giant hands. Purple lightning flickered and flashed through the shadows of its belly to the dunes below like a tiny fragment of the storm-dark snipped away and captured in glass. The upper side was dull and flat, a shallow-sloped white stone wall around a huge and perfectly circular space. It had no black monolith to feed it, to draw power from the earth, and yet it sustained itself. How? No one knew.

Six glasships hovered over the castle today. They were dwarfed by it yet they captured the Watcher's eye, brilliant things, concentric spinning discs of glass twisted at different angles, tinged and rimmed with lightning-thrower gold which shone and caught the sun. They were like brightly coloured cleaner fish flitting to and fro over a kraken's back, tethered to it by chains of Scythian steel.

The Watcher slowed. The thickening of the air grew worse. He felt the castle's resistance to him, a tiny force trying to knock him back to the form and shape of his birth. The Picker had said it was like this in the dragon lands only a thousand times worse, remorseless and relentless and everywhere.

He swept over its surface. A hundred men and women lived here now, slaves and Taiytakei alike, but most worked underground and he saw only two slaves aloft. They were slowly clearing sand and litter and desert plants from the edges of the castle outside the white stone walls, sweat gleaming off their backs as they scraped away to the ancient rock beneath. One was tall, a black-skinned desert man from a tribe like the one he'd seen camped by the ooze slick in the sands. His native people were probably less than a few hundred miles from here, out in the desert. The other was short and olive-skinned, from Aria or from the Dominion, either of which meant thousands of miles and a crossing of the storm-dark, but both men had been bought and sold at the skin markets of Cashax or Xican. They were slaves now, nothing else. The Watcher drifted past them, a hint of a breeze in the still and baking air.

The paler of the two clutched his leg and cried out and then stared at his hand. 'Kelm's Teeth!' *Kelm's Teeth*. From Aria then, that one. The Watcher had heard a great deal of Aria in the last years. The Ice Witch. The sea lords were talking of another Abraxi or a Crimson Sunburst, or something even worse, if such a thing was possible. There were whispers that the Ice Witch had found a way of her own to cross the storm-dark. Whispers that the cherished secrets of the Scythians and their steel and of the enchanters and their glass were finding their way to her empire. Whispers though. As yet nothing more.

'It jumped! Ow! Bugger, but that hurts!' The short one had a small ball of spikes stuck in the back of his leg. The desert man was peering over at him. The Watcher paused for a moment and did what he did best. Watched.

'They don't jump.' The desert man knelt beside the other slave, plucking with delicate care at the spikes. Patience. Always the key and always the greatest weapon of the Elemental Men. They struck when they were ready, and struck true. They'd done so many times before and would do so again. Aria and this Ice Witch would be no different.

'Bugger you, dark-skin. I *saw* it.'

The desert man shook his head. 'Be still.'

'I tell you ...'

Patience and careful observation. The Watcher appeared beside them. 'They do not jump,' he said. 'Yet this one did. Had you the eyes to see, you would have deduced my presence.' The two slaves froze. They stared at him, dumbstruck. 'Where is Baros Tsen T'Varr?'

The desert man fell to his knees and bowed his head. He pointed across the wall and beyond. 'Inside, Demon Lord of Earth and Sky.' The Watcher bowed and with a flicker of effort became the wind again, sweeping into the labyrinthine bowels of the castle, swirling ghost-like through the rune-carved tunnels of glowing white stone that ran within. The air here was at its thickest so close to the old enchanted stone. The Picker said he'd grown used to the fierce animosity of the dragon lands. It was hard, but with practice you built a tolerance to it. But then the Picker had always been a little strange, a little different. He was the only Elemental Man ever taken from another world. The Watcher knew now that he wouldn't see the Picker again. The moon sorcerers' visions had told him so.

It would have been easier to search through the stone than through the air but the white walls of the castle were yet another mystery. Stone, yes, but as impervious to his gift as metal. Still, he found Baros Tsen T'Varr in the first place he looked, supervising some change to the bathhouse at the castle's heart. The Watcher shimmered out of the air far enough away to show his respect, and bowed. 'T'Varr. Hands of the Sea Lord.'

'LaLa!' The t'varr liked his little names for those around him. Tsen was like that, had a childish streak to him and a way of making men see him as less than he was. He slouched. He was fat and he always looked either bored or half-asleep – often both – but he had sharp eyes behind the façade and his vices were surprising and few. The Watcher wondered sometimes how many people he really fooled. 'Quai'Shu has returned then, has he? Planning a visit? He must be. We've had the emerald cages installed for weeks now and jade ravens carry news well enough for the rest of us. Just not quite as quickly, eh?'

The Watcher shook his head. 'Our sea lord plans to return at once to the Western Realm, T'Varr, to oversee the further stages of his design. Enchantress Chay-Liang will join you here shortly.'

Tsen pouted. 'Well, you certainly didn't come all the way here just to tell me that! What news do you *really* bring?'

'Our sea lord has acquired the alchemist. He is in Xican. Enchantress Chay-Liang will bring him to you when she comes.'

A broad smile spread across the t'varr's face, so wide it ran half-way up his cheeks. 'And dragon eggs, LaLa? Any sign of those?'

'Our sea lord advises less than a year, T'Varr.'

'Delicious.' The t'varr clapped his hands. 'Then we shall be busy soon. I'm sure this alchemist will be most demanding. But good. Good.'

'Sea Lord Quai'Shu also commands that his castle be taken to the northern edge of the Lair of Samim. The alchemist will offer further advice when he arrives.'

The Watcher left him to it. The glasships with their chains would move the castle, inch it to the edge of the great salt marsh where the Samim, the mother of snakes and scorpions and all things poisonous, was said to live.

He went that way himself too, but for entirely other reasons.

10

Someone Else's Skin

Beside the river of Tethis he forgot his thirst. He was Skyrie, but the Crowntaker was inside him. Panting, sweating, he stripped off his clothes and stood in the water and looked at himself naked in the moonlight. He didn't know how long he had before his skin wouldn't be his own again. He touched himself, looking for the marks that came with ten years of soldiering. Not *his* marks, but those of the Bloody Judge. But all he found was the huge scar on his left thigh, old and puckered and familiar and comforting, the size of his splayed hand. At least his skin was still his own.

He waded to the bank and fell to his knees at the edge of the water and started to sob. The *thing* was still there, writhing and screaming in impotent agony and rage, and he wanted it *gone*, but he didn't know how. Oh gods, he'd killed four of his brothers! Friends! He howled at the sky, 'It wasn't me! It wasn't me! It was him! Oh Xibaiya! Someone help me!'

He was young, a boy coming into the first flushes of manhood. He was hiding. Cowering in the crude hut that was his home. Outside, open and in the daylight, something terrible was happening. Women were screaming. Men roared and howled and he heard horses. They came every year, the riders, had done ever since he was small. Came and took what they wanted and left; and whenever they came, he and his brothers and sisters hid away. He was shaking. Trembling. The Bloody Judge's men. Hadn't known then, but Vallas had told him later who had done it.

The sobs turned to howls. He buried his face in his hands.

A giant burst in and pulled him from his hiding place. Immense and as tall and as broad as the doorway. Long dreadlocked hair hung to his waist and a short spiked axe hung on a loop of leather from one wrist. The giant picked him up and flung him against a wall. The axe swung and Skyrie lost all will to move and simply slumped. He looked down.

He was sitting in a lake of his own blood. His leg had been cut open, so deep that it was more off than on.

And then later the water.

He got back to his feet, the river dripping off his legs. He was cold, the water icy, the night air chill and he was naked. He looked at the scar again in the moonlight, long and hard. The skin looked as though it had melted and then frozen again, twisted out of shape. In the moonlight it was speckled with pale and silvery streaks, thousands of little marks left in the skin as it had healed.

That's no axe scar, warlock. In his head the Crowntaker was right behind him. He squealed and turned and ran a few steps and then stopped, helpless, and wailed, because how did you run from something that was inside you? The Crowntaker, the Bloody Judge. There. Watching and looking and waiting.

It looks like a burn, warlock. But it came from an axe. The one the giant had swung at him. He tried to scream: *I was there! It was me! I felt it!* But though his mouth opened, no sound came out. He was losing control. The Judge was taking him back.

The Crowntaker had seen those silver streaks before. There were patterns in them, staggering and intricate and they looked like writing of a sort. The sigils that warlocks used, perhaps. Or maybe the sunburst marks of the sun priests. The thought came with a trail of wistful regret strung out like gossamer behind it, lingering.

He looked at his hands. The fingers were long and slender. The callouses that came from years of gauntlets and swords weren't there. They were soft.

He put the grey robes back over his head.

The warlock was screaming. Endless screaming, battering against the prison of his own mind, howling to be let out, but that would never happen, not again. Flickering memories flashed by, not his own, dancing past, revealing a little of their skin and dashing away. Then a great slew of them came like rocks tumbling from the face of a cliff to reveal new strata beneath, pristine and clean. Memories of the death-mage sticking that paper to his breastplate, fierce and hot, striking the last stroke of the last sigil in his own blood and casting his incantation as he died. Everything that came after.

I am the Bloody Judge. For a moment he faltered, bewildered by the enormity of what they'd done to him, frozen by it. He looked at the hands that weren't his. Stared at them as they shook. How could they be real? Then forced the horror away because what use was it? The sigils were gone, the spell cast. What was done was done. There would be time later for fear and anguish and dread – *now* was for bloody vengeance. Vallas Kuy, the master warlock. He needed to find Vallas and his golden knife that cut pieces out of the souls of men.

He remembered his thirst again, knelt and touched his lips to the water, taking care not to look at his own reflection. The river was clean here, the smells of the docks mere whispers on the breeze. Afterwards he danced from stone to boulder across the hiss of the water and slipped in and out of the alleys that nestled among the houses of the rich on the other side. He found a wall that was low enough to climb. Jumped onto the edge of a storehouse roof, crept to the top and then along the ridge of it, skills the warlock Skyrie had never had, old skills the Bloody Judge had learned long ago as a thief in far-off Deephaven. He slipped through the town unseen, running down the Galsmouth Road towards the battlefield where he belonged.

Over Her Heart

Long ago the Elemental Men had come down from Mount Solence. They'd fallen on the squabbling coast of Takei'Tarr and cut away the old sorceries and religions in a swathe of blood and fire. It had been a necessary thing, an act of mercy to save this piece of the now-broken world from another cataclysm. Some places had taken to the new order well. The old Mar-Li Republics had acquiesced almost at once and so became the model for the society that now grew under elemental eyes. Others had not. Yet it struck the Watcher that two cities in particular had resisted most furiously. They were the cities furthest from the first Elemental Men, with the most time to prepare and who should have seen the inevitability of history sweeping inexorably towards them but whose pride was matchless. Cashax in the far north of the desert with her inexhaustible supply of slaves; and worse, Vespinarr, deep in the southern mountains on the edge of the Konsidar with her silver and her bottomless wealth. They had fought the hardest and so had been cut the deepest. Vespinarr had given birth to the sorceress Abraxi, Cashax to the indescribable abomination of the Crimson Sunburst. Both had been crushed in the end, conquered and ruled and their histories rewritten by the Elemental Masters, and yet now they quietly ruled the world despite their pasts. Every conflict among the Taiytakei, if you looked hard enough, was underpinned by their rivalry.

The Watcher blew high above mountain peaks shining white with snow and swirled down between them. Vespinarr lay spread across the plateau beneath, ringed by snow-capped stone, the bright gleam of the Yalun Zarang river running through it, the roiling waters of the Jokun not far away. The city glittered silver and gold under the clear blue sky, while the land between the two rivers was threaded with silver strands through green fields dappled with bright yellows and brilliant blue. The Elemental Men had come late to Vespinarr when perhaps they should have turned to it first. They'd done what they'd done everywhere, destroyed and desecrated the city's sacred sites, culled its priests and sorcerers. But here more than anywhere else the old ways still survived in secret.

He circled the Kabulingnor Palace, whose shining towers of gold and glass were the highest in the world and could be seen from a hundred miles away, whose vast yellow walls sprawled like cliffs across the might of Mazanda's Peak, Sea Lord Shonda's colossal declaration of the city's power. He soared lower in arcs around the crags and bluffs, past two massive floating cargo sleds made of gold-glass, laden with crates and sacks and pens full of animals, slowly riding the air from the city below to the mountain-top palace; and smaller sleds too, moving through the sky, carrying just one man or two, messengers or guests not worthy of a glasship but in too much haste for the long winding mountain road. Then lower still to the tiers and scattered pavilions of the Visonda Palace at the mountain's feet, where a legion of t'varrs and kwens saw to it that the heart of the city kept up its merciless beat.

There, in a quiet place, he became a man once more, hidden deep in shadows where no one would see. There were reasons today for stealth.

Below the Visonda stood the Azahl Pillar. It had come from somewhere much deeper in the Konsidar, moved here long before there were such things as Elemental Men. He stopped in front of it as he always did. It had grace. The white stone was flawless, inscribed to an unnamed general, an account of his services to the forgotten king of a nameless realm, and ringed with symbols no one had ever deciphered. It belonged to the time before the Splintering, yet the stone hadn't aged. The Watcher ran a hand over it. Its edges were as sharp as they ever were, as though they'd been carved that very morning. The moon sorcerers belonged to that age. They'd seen the Splintering with their own eyes. On the beach they'd shown it to him because, beneath every other purpose, what an Elemental Man was for, what had brought them into life so long ago, was the fear that it might happen again and the resolve that it should not. It was why they did what they did, why they cast away every trace of the old gods, killing them down to the deepest roots, why they learned to hunt and kill sorcerers from any and every world.

Beyond the pillar he walked through a leafy willow-shaded park and into the narrow bustling streets of the Harub, full of noise and colour. Slaves in white and Taiytakei in their feathered rainbow robes hurried past, throwing glances of alarm as they saw him. Pictures, statues and engravings of dragons surrounded him, some old and worn in faded stone, others gaudy and red in bright fresh paint. The dragons made him smile. The Vespinese claimed that dragons had once lived in the Konsidar, long ago. A few even claimed they were still there, deep under the earth in some strange harmony with the Righteous Ones in their chthonian domain. Dragons were the symbol of the mountain city – three of them intertwined with a lion – and that was why he smiled, for the dragons of Vespinarr were myths and stories, yet follow the Yalun Zarang and the Jokun out of the mountains and the Lair of Samim was right there in front of you, not so far away at all. Old stories were one thing, nice and safe. He wondered how the Vespinese would feel when they had *real* dragons on their doorstep again.

Sea Lord Quai'Shu was in debt up to his eyes with the lords of Vespinarr. The Watcher knew he was meant neither to know nor care but they were a part of this somehow. They were not to be trusted.

He reached the Sun and Moon Temple with its gilded pagoda tower-tops and stopped, looking up at the many dark arches that led inside. Here was how Vespinarr quietly defied the Elemental Men. When they'd come to the city in force to throw down the abomination that was Abraxi the sorceress, the temple had burned amid riot and mayhem. The Elemental Men had forbidden it to be rebuilt, as they forbade all temples to the old gods, and so the Vespinese had built a parliament of sorts in its place, though strikingly similar, and filled it with the kwens and t'varrs and hsians who kept the city in motion. A hundred years later they'd built the Kabulingnor with their endless silver and the sea lords had moved to the top of the Silver Mountain, to Mazanda's Peak. The t'varrs and kwens and hsians had moved in turn into the massive space of the Visonda and left the old temple empty, and now here it was: brazenly dedicated to the sun and the moon. Oh the Vespinese were careful. They made no reference to the rituals of the old gods and never named them, but there were chants at dawn and dusk and it was an open secret that those who came sent prayers and gifts to the ancient forbidden divinities.

Seventeen arches led into the temple and from the outside each was the same. Beyond lay a maze of tiny passages and nooks and shrines reached in different ways. The Watcher chose the central arch. Words were inscribed on it, innocuous and tucked away almost as though they were meant not to be seen but they were telling: *The foundations here lie deep, pinned over the heart of the earth goddess by Seturakah, greatest of the silver kings and conqueror of Xibaiya.* He walked beneath the words and chose a tiny winding flight of steps down into the earth. As the passage fell into darkness he became the stuff of shadow.

Uneasy things shifted here, but Elemental Men were killers of sorcerers. When abominations like Abraxi and the Crimson Sunburst and Ren Shaha rose, the Elemental Men excised them from the world. It was a long time since the Taiytakei had seen such a creature among their own but abominations grew like weeds in the Dominion of the Sun King and now in Aria too. Wherever their power seemed too great, they were removed with care and precision and with a deal of time and thought. Sorcerers rarely died easily. Second chances were not sought.

When the dragon-queen comes ...

... so the tipping point ...

In Vespinarr he'd found his first clues. It had taken years but there was some sort of sorcerer here. A pale-skinned slave who dressed in grey and had a talent for speaking with the dead, a talent he sold for silver and jade. Subtle in his ways, harmless and leaving barely a ripple in his passing. The Watcher would never have found his scent if he hadn't already been searching for it.

The grey dead ones are coming ...

They are making something ...

In the passages beneath the old temple the air smelled a little of fish. Odd, he thought, for the mountains. The smell grew stronger. The passage was dark and narrow, lit now by a scattering of dim candles. He was deep beneath the streets and yet more steps took him further down. He let the candles lead him until he found what he sought: a dead-end room, round and claustrophobic with a roof that was low and a hole bored into the floor, a shaft that sank perhaps for ever. More candles were set into scores of nooks in the wall. The smell of old fish was strong now. Facing the entrance with eyes closed, a man sat beside the shaft. He was dressed in grey and the Watcher knew he'd found one of those he sought: the grey dead. He wondered what would be the surest way to kill him: sever his head? Bleed him out? Cut out his heart? Let flames consume him? Sorcerers had survived all those things, but this one needed more than killing. This one needed to speak. He needed not to run, and so he needed to not know what it was that he faced.

In the darkness of the passage the Watcher became flesh again. The grey dead's head snapped up at once. Around him the candle flames flickered. Shadows danced around the walls, ripping themselves free. The Watcher felt power sizzling in the air. Sorcery. 'Who are you?'

The Watcher stayed in the shadows and bowed. 'I am the mouth for the Regrettable Men. I have come to arrange the terms.' Every Vespinese would know at once what he meant. The Regrettable Men were civilised killers of the highest order.

'Terms?' The grey dead stood up. He pulled back his hood. His head was shaved, his face and neck covered in tattoos. The flickering of the candles grew to a frenzy. Shadow shapes danced everywhere.

The Watcher bowed again. 'For our mutual convenience. If there is a poison you would prefer then we can discuss your choice.'

The grey dead smirked and slowly nodded. 'I see. Who wants me, assassin? Tell me and I'll change their outlook.'

'I'm desperately sorry but that's not how this plays. There's no outcome save one. I'm here as our usual courtesy, to make your departure as convenient and easy as possible with minimal distress to those around you. You may have a few days to put your affairs in order. If there is a particular location or time of day you would like the assassination to take place, you may request it. We will do our best to honour your wishes.'

The grey dead threw back his head and laughed now. 'No, I don't think we'll be discussing those things. Tell me who sent you or I'll rip it out of you.'

'I cannot, for I do not know. In three days at dawn then, if there is nothing to discuss. Those are our usual terms.'

The grey dead threw out his hands. Shadows poured from his sleeves. The Watcher ducked into the darkness and shifted to become the fire of one of the candle flames and the light and the heat it gave. The shadows recoiled, screaming and wailing and whirling around him. He shifted again and led them away, became the stone, the air, the darkness of the unlit path. He led them a long and merry chase, dragged their mindless hunger far away and then left them and returned alone, back to the room that stank of fish and its candles. There he stayed, a little pinprick of flame, and did what he did best.

The Regrettable Men of Vespinarr had a reputation second only to the Elemental Men themselves when it came to murder. The Watcher waited for understanding to take its course, for the grey dead to realise that he was a dead man walking. Patiently, to see what the grey dead would do.

He wasn't disappointed.

12

The Queen's Road

Berren the Crowntaker. The Bloody Judge of Tethis, that's who he was. He took the first of the queensguard from the flank. Stabbed the man's horse in the neck so it fell and then killed the rider while he struggled on the ground. He took the man's broadsword and battered away a swing from the next horseman to gallop past. Javelins scattered the road. He snatched one and threw it. Took one of the queensguard in the face then dived out of the way of a half-dozen more as they galloped past. The next javelin missed. He danced and parried between hooves and blades, looking for what he wanted. Damned body was slow, weak. It kept letting him down. He kept missing. A riderless horse, that's what he needed, caught in the flood of the retreat. When he saw one, thundering along the road with the rest in headlong flight, he hurled himself at it and leaped onto its back. His new legs didn't have the strength he asked from them and he landed short, almost fell off but managed to haul himself the rest of the way. Tore another muscle while he was at it. No one tried to stop him. The queensguard were wild and panic-stricken. His own men couldn't be far behind, not far at all.

He gave chase, almost sliding sideways off the saddle as soon as he was on it as he snatched yet another javelin out of a corpse. He was among the last remnants of the queensguard now. He galloped after them, javelin in hand, turned a corner in the road and then pulled up with a roar of rage. He was too late. He'd found the rear-guard, nothing more. The Dark Queen, Gelisya, was long gone, and Vallas and her death-mages with her. He'd waited, standing out here all night, freezing cold, and they hadn't even been on the road. He screamed in fury as the last of them faded into dust, full flight, job done. Clenched his fists and ground his teeth and hurled his javelin into the ground. It stuck in the dirt, quivering. 'Vallas!

I'll find you, warlock! You hear me? Wherever you are, I'll find you! I'll find you!'

The queensguard were gone. There was nothing he could do.

No. There *was* something he could do. He bent sideways and snatched up the quivering javelin and turned, because there were more riders coming any minute, and if he couldn't hunt down Vallas Kuy then he could damn well have his army back. They probably thought he was dead. Well, he wasn't. He turned his horse across the road and snorted in the still dusty air. The sun beat down on his head. He felt naked without his armour and his helm.

They were coming. He could feel them.

At the side of the road, at the edge of the wood, a pair of crimson butterflies danced together over a patch of bright yellow milk-flowers. Birdsong fluttered between the trees. A stillness settled over everything, everything except the rumble of hooves coming closer.

He snorted again, blowing the dry snot out of his nose.

The first horses rounded the corner. They came straight at him. He held the javelin high overhead so they couldn't miss it. Ordering them to stop. He stared at them, willing them with his eyes to know him.

They didn't even falter.

The horse at the head of the riders. It was his. And as they charged closer, he saw it wasn't only the horse. His pennant. His helm. His armour. Him.

He stayed very still because he simply couldn't move now. He couldn't think. Staring at his own body. It paralysed him.

The riders stopped a dozen paces short. The man who was on *his* horse lifted his visor. *His* visor, and behind it *his* face. His own eyes looked at him. Beyond, more faces he knew stared coldly. Friends, damn them! Men who'd fought with him for years, some from the very start, and now they were looking at him as though they didn't know him. Like he was a rabid animal.

'You're a bit ambitious for a warlock,' said the man who wasn't him but who had his voice. 'Brave though, I'll give you that. Or maybe just stupid.'

Berren raised his javelin to throw in the usurper's face, then stopped. He was shaking. Not shaking with rage any more but shaking with fear. The man had his face! He'd just thought ... He just *hadn't* thought. Supposed he must have died on the battlefield and everyone thought he was gone and how pleased they'd be to find him again once he could make them understand what had happened, what the warlocks had done ...

But he hadn't died. And they weren't pleased. And here he was.

The other Bloody Judge stared back at him, the one who had his skin, wild-eyed and spattered in blood. He kicked his horse slowly forward until the length of the javelin was all that was between them.

'Who are you?' Berren croaked. The muscles in his arm twitched.

'Who am I?' His own voice! For the love of the sun! Holy moon, his own voice, his own face! 'Who am *I*? I think you know very well who *I* am, warlock.'

He couldn't move. Couldn't speak. Didn't know what to say.

'Well?' He couldn't tear his eyes away. His own face watched him, unblinking. Did he really look so hard, so harsh, so cruel? But still, it *was* his face.

From so close the javelin couldn't miss.

'Are you going to throw it or not?'

His own face looking back at him! Dear gods, his own face! '*Who are you?*' Inside he kept screaming it, over and over.

'You know that, boy. I'm the Bloody Judge. I'm Berren the Crowntaker, the killer of kings. Now put that javelin down before I kill you too.' The Bloody Judge frowned. He wrinkled his nose and sniffed in disdain. 'Fish! So you *are* a warlock. Got a name I can put on your grave?'

Berren's blood surged. Somehow that broke the spell. 'I've got a name for you. It's Berren!' He threw the javelin hard and quick. The Bloody Judge ducked sideways, lightning-fast. The javelin screeched off the battered metal on his shoulder and veered sideways and up and speared a tree far down the road. The Judge shook his head and drew his sword, the blade of glittering black moonsteel. *His* sword, the one he'd held in his hand only a day ago. The moonsteel came arcing at his head and he was already ducking because he knew how the first blow would come, and for the next few seconds he could see, in every movement this pretender made, how he fought. How they both did. How they were the same. And *that* road led to a dark place of icy cold where he wasn't who he believed with all his might that he *must* be …

He threw up his broadsword to block another swing and the moonsteel edge cut it in two. He hurled himself wildly aside, slipped, cried out and fell off his horse. The Judge jumped to the ground after him, grabbed him as he rose and smashed him in the face with an iron gauntlet. He staggered and fell, dazed, eyes ringing, ears full of stars, and then the Judge had him, sword point at his throat. He seemed more puzzled than angry. He poked with his point. 'Well, you're a strange one. So who are you really?'

Rage and fury and screaming panic boiled together. 'Who are you?' Berren howled. 'Who are you in there?'

The Judge shook his head. His sword twitched back, ready to strike. Berren clapped his hands around the blade and slammed its point down into the dirt beside his cheek. The Judge lurched down. Berren bucked and arced a kick over his own head, straight into the Judge's face, was on his feet in a flash but still not quick enough. The Judge caught his shoulder and sprawled him a second time and a boot smashed into the side of his head. The edges of the world turned black and shrank and all he could see was a bloody face peering down at him.

'Knock a tooth out, did he?' laughed someone, and he could have sworn the voice was Tallis One-Eye. Well One-Eye could just fuck off.

'What do you want us to do with him?'

The world shrank smaller still. The Judge spat. 'Queensguard. Same as the rest.' Then Berren's eyes closed. The world turned red and the darkness had him.

Days passed. Skyrie knew he was dying. The village men had done what they could but his leg was lost. The damage was too deep and now the rest of him was fading as well. He shook and shivered in his bed, torn apart by the weakness and the pain. They came to see him, to sit with him, taking it in turns. There was always someone there. They thought they were being kind but he wished they'd just go away and leave him in peace to die.

Time passed again. Alone, finally, with the last of his strength, he hauled himself out of his bed and onto the floor. Outside, the night sky was filled with stars. He heard laughter and dancing and the crackling of a large fire and smelled its smoke. He crawled and dragged himself out of the hut that had been his home, inch by inch out of the village he'd never left, to the reed beds on the edge of the lake where he'd been born. He was going to die tonight and he wanted it to be outside under the stars, not in the dark. He reached the water's edge, rolled onto his back and waited. One by one, the stars winked out. Tears filled his eyes. He wanted to live, not to die. He wanted to live but the choice had been taken away.

A man stood over him. Skyrie blinked. He hadn't heard the man come, hadn't seen him. He was just suddenly there. The man's face, where it wasn't lost among the shadows of his cowl, was pale. One half was ruined, scarred ragged by disease or fire with one blind eye, milky white. He wore pale hooded robes the colour of moonlight.

'Are you death?' Skyrie asked, but the words never came out.

'I carry the Black Moon.' The stranger's one good eye bored into him.

Hands reached under his arms, hauling him along the road and then slinging him over the back of a mule. They tied him up, good and tight. His wrists tingled and his fingers turned slowly numb. For a while he danced in and out of consciousness. The plod plod of the mule lulled him. Maybe he fell asleep. Maybe he dreamed, or maybe they were memories. Of a man with a ruined face and one milky eye.

He woke again when they pulled him off the mule. He tried to see but his eyes were swollen almost shut. His head pounded like a busy blacksmith's hammer. The brightness of the day made him wince. His mouth tasted of his own blood.

The men around him were soldiers. *His* soldiers. Fighting Hawks. They tied him to a post beside the road and left him slumped there, groaning. The air smelled of mud and sweat but the sun was higher than he remembered and at least he was warm now. He rolled his head. Other men were tied to more posts around him. Queensguard by the looks of them, and they were on the edge of a field beside the road. Not in the trees any more. When he twisted to look behind him, he saw a farmhouse, but he couldn't look at it for long before the pain was unbearable. He gasped and cried out but no one even looked his way. He knew where he was, though. He'd been here before. Not far from the battlefield.

A steady stream of wagons and horses moved along the road. His supply train from Galsmouth, following the rest of the Fighting Hawks into Tethis itself.

His Fighting Hawks. *His* supply train.

Past the road all he could see was another field and then sky. They weren't far from the coast. A mile straight west and he'd reach the cliffs and the sea. Not that he had the strength.

A pair of soldiers moved past him. The Judge's men. He closed his eyes but he heard one of them whisper to another as they passed, 'Let the Taiytakei have the lot of them. The boy's a murderer. Killed a couple of his house guards as well. Not a man you'd miss, but you know how touchy the Crowntaker is.'

His head sank to his chest. Pain, pain, pain, everything hurt, but nothing as bad as his head. There were holes in his memories. Hundreds of them. Like the rotten wood of an old barn so riddled with wormholes that inside its skin was nothing but dust and what was left crumbled to the slightest touch. Crumbs. Whole from the outside but on the brink of collapse.

The world drifted. He saw ships. He didn't know who he was. He'd had a name once. Maybe two. Sometimes he remembered one, sometimes the other. Sometimes he forgot them both.

The Bloody Judge. Berren Crowntaker. Remember!

Early in the afternoon they cut him down, him and the queens-guard, and dragged them over to a dozen cage-wagons and threw them inside. By then he was too delirious to even walk. He barely knew what was happening. They threw him in like a sack of onions and, if it hurt, he didn't notice. The wagons rolled and bounced over the roads, shaking his bones, adding to the hammer in his head. The rain, when it came, soaked him, and for a while his wandering mind thought he was at sea.

Berren Crowntaker. Remember!

He'd spent two years at sea once. A skag. The lowest of the low, scampering through the rigging, hating every moment of it, but he'd deserved it for what he'd done.

The rain grew heavier. Slowly the cold brought him back. He huddled in the corner of his cage, shivering as the road turned to mud. The wagons began to struggle. The soldiers turned out the prisoners from one of them to push the others. Some ran. He watched the soldiers chase them and cut them down. If they'd let him out, he'd have run too, except he wouldn't even have been able to stand. He felt sick.

A bit later he threw up. By now the pain in his head was like being crushed under a mountain.

They passed the Dark Queen's castle. His army hadn't yet forced its way past the last few cohorts holding the palisade. Wouldn't be long though. He almost smiled. *He* knew the secret way in and he knew the queensguard didn't watch it. No one else knew it now. No one else left alive. They'd all died in Tethis when the madness of the Thousand Knives came.

All of them except him.

He should have killed the Dark Queen that day. Should have tried. Should have faced the last three men she had left to her and cut them down, even if one was a friend, and put an end to her. But the world had seemed different then. Brighter. He'd had a son. He'd had Tasahre – no, not Tasahre. Tasahre belonged with Deephaven. Fasha – that was the one.

His mind spun in loops. Secret way. Somehow that made him shake with laughing – *that's* how he knew who he was. No one else knew the secret way. He could show them so …

He could have killed the queen that day. Should have. Ten years of bitter feud and he could have wiped them all away with a single cut of his sword.

The wagons went round behind the castle, over the High Bridge and down the steep-sided valley into Tethis itself. The rain stopped but rivulets of water still ran between the cobbles, pooling in puddles outside doorsteps. The streets were empty, quiet. People were hiding. Could hardly blame them for that. Just like the day the Thousand Knives had come. Yes, he remembered that. How empty it had been.

Not that the wagons cared for what he remembered. They rolled steadily down through the town, past dirty grey stone walls and peeled-paint doors whose colours had faded years ago. Grime streaked everything, all the way to the sea and the docks and the old warehouse where Vallas had lived, back when Vallas had called himself a soap maker. Years later the Dark Queen had built it into a prison.

His own soldiers dragged him out of the cage-wagon. He staggered and tried to pull away but he was as weak as a child and one good cuff knocked him down. He lay there in the puddles, too empty to move, while they manacled him to a line of six queensguard, and it was they who helped him to his feet. One of them let him lean on his shoulder and he almost cried. A piece of kindness, and yet he still hated them. They were the enemy, after all.

In the prison they left him for days with no food, just a bucket of river water brought in each morning. *His* soldiers, men he'd fought beside for years, and now they simply didn't know him. When his head finally stopped pounding, he tried to tell them who he was but no one wanted to listen. They just laughed and kicked him until he was quiet, but he felt their contempt and disdain worse than any beating. They despised him. Good men. Strong, brave, he even knew a few of them by name, but when he called out they spat in his face And each day more ragged prisoners were dragged into the warehouse. Queensguard, mostly.

He slept a lot. In his dreams he was someone else. In his dreams he lay beside a lake in the dark and he couldn't move and something was terribly horribly wrong and the stranger with the one eye and the half-ruined face stood over him as his life ebbed away. Fingers traced symbols, and where the fingers passed the air split open like swollen flesh under a sharpened blade. Black shadow oozed out of the gashes left behind.

What will you give to live? the stranger asked, tracing ever more symbols, slowly filling the sky.

Anything, he replied.

He woke up weeping. The tears flowed freely. He hung his head. Words faded into the depths of his thoughts. *Xibaiya save me.* As the sun rose on that last morning the doors burst open and there was the Bloody Judge himself with all the faces Berren had known for years: Tallis One-Eye. Gaunt the knife man. Lia the Mountain Fox who loved him and hated him all at once. The false Judge pulled out a knife. Its hilt was gold and carved with a pattern of a thousand stars. Its blade shimmered. The Starknife, old as the world, peerless, imbued with a fragment of something vast yet sleeping. One of a pair and Berren had seen them both. One in a box on the thief-taker's desk in Deephaven, the other in the hands of Saffran Kuy the warlock on the day Kuy had cut out a piece of his soul. He'd never known which was which but he'd carried one of them at his own side ever since that day in Tethis, ten years past.

The false Judge held up the knife and looked about. 'Who knows what this is?' His eyes roamed from face to face. Slowly, from one to the next to the next. He stopped at Berren and stared long and hard and then moved on. When he was done, he pointed to two who had once been warlocks. 'Him. And him. They've seen it before. Take them outside and hang them.'

Tallis pointed at Berren. 'And him. He knows too. I saw it in his eyes.'

Too much. Berren lunged in his chains. 'Tallis One-Eye, *I* am Berren! Not him. That's some usurper! He's a trick the warlocks are playing on you. Can't you see?'

One-Eye and the Bloody Judge looked at each other. They both started to laugh. Berren's voice rose shrilly over them: 'I can prove it, One-Eye. I know things only I could know. I know about the secret passageway from the ravine into the pit under the castle. Has he showed you that? Or did he let good men die for no good purpose battering at that palisade? No one knows that passage exists any more, no one except me. You can't even find it unless you know exactly what to look for. It's hidden by a—'

'By a sump.' The Bloody Judge looked at him hard. 'And you're right: I *didn't* think any of you warlocks would find it again. It seems you did.'

'What?'

One-Eye was still laughing. 'We took the castle through that passage days ago, warlock.' He turned away.

'Wait!' Berren pulled at his chains again. 'I'm no warlock! I *am* Berren! I don't know how they did what they did but don't you remember the sigil, One-Eye? You were right beside me. Six men and a warlock broke out of the trees and came at us. We stuck two of them and I ran the warlock through but he put a strip of paper on me before he died. A sigil. You remember? It was the sigil that did this.'

One-Eye froze mid-turn. The Bloody Judge cocked his head.

'Go on, warlock. Play your game. You were there, were you? Watched it, did you?'

'I was *you*!'

'I remember that sigil. I fell to my knees and blacked out. And it did feel like something sucking at my soul. Yet here I still am, warlock. I guess it didn't work, did it?'

'You were there, One-Eye! You saw me. You tried to help me. I couldn't pull it away.'

The Bloody Judge's eyes narrowed. 'What did you do, warlock? What did you do to me with that sigil? Or was it just a trick and this is your great plan.' He laughed again. 'You trying to tell Tallis here that Vallas cast a spell on me and now I'm one of *you*? Go on then. This sounds fun.'

'Tallis, he *is* one of them! He *is* a warlock. His name is Skyrie. They ... they switched us somehow. I'm the real Berren. I grew up in Deephaven. I was with Prince Syannis. He was a thief-taker then. I told you about him. Do you remember? The tavern in Brons? The Falling Dagger. I told you about him and the warlock Saffran Kuy. I showed you that knife he's carrying, the golden one with the eyes in the hilt. I told you how Kuy had another one and what he did with it. I told you about Radek of Kalda, how Syannis lured him to Deephaven and how he died and about Tasahre and how I ended up a skag and ...'

The Bloody Judge took a step closer to Berren. 'And how I came to Kalda and saw Master Sy again by chance, went after him and found his brother, Prince Talon, joined his company and so joined his war against King Meridian to help Syannis sit on his throne again.' He glanced over his shoulder at One-Eye. 'Do you remember that, Tallis? Do you remember me telling you about Fasha, the bondsmaid, and how I didn't kill the Dark Queen when I should have, and what happened after I took my Fasha and my son back again? Do you remember the tears I wept when I told you that. Falling-down drunk we were. What did they call that brew we were drinking? Devil's finger?'

'Devil's foot,' said Berren hopelessly. He shook his head, lost, then lifted his eyes and met the Bloody Judge's gaze. 'I *am* Berren. I *am* the Bloody Judge, however much you don't want to believe it. Maybe we both are. Do you remember that night in the Maze with

Lilissa? After we went with Master Sy into the Captain's Rest and the harbour master set his snuffers on us all? If you really are me, you know where we hid.'

The Bloody Judge nodded. 'The Sheaf of Arrows. The old cellar. You could slip into it off the backstreet if you knew how.' He smiled. 'I remember Lilissa, yes. And if you're me, you'll remember who was waiting for us when we came out.'

'One-Thumb.'

'Yeh, but it was Hair who saw us first.' For a moment Berren and the Bloody Judge looked into one another, each trying to fathom the other out. Then the Judge shook his head. 'I know who I am, warlock.' He turned away.

Berren lunged against the chains again. 'One-Eye! Ask him how he lost his finger, One-Eye. Ask him how he *really* lost it.'

The Bloody Judge roared with laugher. He looked back to glare at Berren and his eyes blazed. 'Which story should I tell him, warlock. Should I tell him the one I told him when we first met, how it was cut off in my first battle as a Fighting Hawk, or shall I tell tell him the one he's never heard where it was cut off by the warlock Saffran Kuy on the day he cut a piece out of my soul with this cursed knife.' He turned back, shaking his head, baring his teeth and chuckling to himself, and as he came closer he drew out the golden-hafted knife again. 'Three little cuts, warlock. You. Obey. Me. I see it now. *That's* how you know so much about me, is it?' He touched the stone that Berren had worn around his neck every day for the last dozen years, the stone that Gelisya had given back to him when they'd been friends. The stone that made him whole again, or so it had always seemed. 'Saffran's little piece of me. That's how you know. I always thought it was too good to be true that he'd give it back.' He held the Starknife in front of Berren's face. 'I should cut you and make you my slave, warlock.'

'Cut me with that and you'll see everything I say is true! Cut me, then! Do it! I'm begging you!' But The Bloody Judge was already backing away and shaking his head.

'I don't make men into slaves, warlock. I'm not like you.'

Tallis One-Eye spat at Berren's feet. 'So do we hang him, Judge? He's a warlock after all.'

The Judge stared a long time, off into the distance, then shook his head. 'Maybe so, One-Eye, but he can go with the rest. You never know.' He turned and walked away.

Berren closed his eyes and gasped. For a moment he'd almost believed that there were two of them, that they were both him. But no. The stone with Saffran Kuy's piece of him inside it. *That* was how this this usurper knew everything about him. It had been a trick then, had it? A trap right from the very start? He bit his lip. And who was it who'd given the stone and that piece of his soul inside back to him? Gelisya. The Dark Queen herself, back when she'd been nothing more than a girl. Twelve years old.

He wept then, knowing he was doomed. The soldiers unchained their prisoners one by one and manacled them back together in a single line. The first of the queensguard to struggle was beaten swiftly and brutally to death. After that the others were mute and meek. By the time they were done and filing out into the glare of the sunlight, the two warlocks the Judge had singled out were already dead and hanging from their gibbets. All along the seafront other men hung by their necks, swinging slowly back and forth in the morning breeze whipping off the sea. The warlocks of Tethis. Berren stared at them with disbelief because it was exactly as he'd planned. Hang them by the sea and then burn them in a pyre, all of them together, then scatter their ashes over the waves. Give them to any god who'd take them, any but their own. And now it was done, finally done. A dozen years of war and they were broken once and for all, and someone else had done it. Someone who wore his skin. One of them. So they weren't really broken at all.

'Who are you?' he whispered, and turned and tried to catch the eye of the impostor, to ask him, to tell him that this wasn't done, not finished, not over, not ever for as long as he breathed. *I will hunt you and I will kill you, stealer of my skin.* But the Bloody Judge never looked back, and when Berren snarled and rattled his chains, soldiers turned and raised their sticks. They'd kill him. They weren't afraid to do that. In fact, it wouldn't trouble them at all.

The air tasted of salt. The stones on the beach crunched under his feet. The soldiers separated them into groups of six. There were boats waiting, rowing boats, and Taiytakei sword-slaves, and standing on the shore with them was a single black man in a cloak of tattered feathers. He handed a purse to Gaunt – of course it had to be Gaunt who was dealing with slavers – who smiled at them all in turn. 'Tethis thanks you kindly for your contribution to its coffers.' He jingled his bag of coins, happy and jaunty as he walked away.

The wind tugged at the rags of Berren's stolen robe, stinging him with salt, stealing the warmth of the sun until he shivered. Among the beached fishing boats, ropes rattled and banged against their masts and sails flapped where they'd been hung to dry. Waves crashed and sucked, the relentless rhythm of the sea that Berren had once known so well. The Taiytakei's feathered cloak kept whipping back in his face. He looked them up and down, barked an order and walked away. Out in the harbour his slaving ship rocked, sleek and lean like all their ships. Far out to sea the skies were leaden. It would be raining again before long. Did feathered cloaks hold off the rain?

Berren the Crowntaker, the Bloody Judge of Tethis, looked back at the town that had given him its name, still searching for the man who'd stolen his life. He stared until someone threw a sack over his face and pushed him forward and hissed in his ear, 'Forget it, slave. You'll never see it again.'

And he never would.

13

The Grey Dead

The Watcher waited. When the grey dead finally walked away from his tomb-like shrine deep under the Sun and Moon Temple, the Watcher became the floor on which he walked, the shadows he wore for his cloak, the air he breathed. Outside, through the colours and bustle of the Harub, he was the sunlight of the day. At the foot of the Visonda he became one with the Silver Mountain's feet, with the outcrop of rock on which the fortress-palace was built.

The grey dead climbed the wide sweeping steps and walked in through cavernous open gates of black wood studded with rust-brown iron. The Watcher became the vast slope of the walls, the air amid the neat straight rows of windows that broke its upper tiers, the myriad coloured tiles of the near-flat roofs of its many different levels.

The heart of the lower Visonda was a high-walled space as big as a field with a second pair of great gates on the inner side. The Watcher followed the grey dead from on high, a dull speck among the hundreds of rainbow-draped Taiytakei in their silks and feathers and their slaves in pristine white. At the second gates the grey dead stretched out his arms, palms up, letting his sleeves fall back from his wrists to show the slave brands on his forearms. He had the sign of a two-masted ship burned into each that said to any who cared to know that he was a sword-slave made in distant Shevana-Daro, not here in Vespinarr. By the gate, soldiers decked in bright mustard yellows and tasselled in silver waved him through.

The Watcher shifted closer. Some called the Visonda the Home of a Thousand T'Varrs. Hundreds upon hundreds of slaves came and went every day but few passed the second gates.

A series of easy staircases rose behind it, carved into the slope amid a speckle of brightly draped pavilions ranging up the gentle ascent to the summit of the mountain's root. The bulk of the old palace rose there, looming down over its satellites below, a quad-rangular mass capped with gilt canopies. Few slaves came this far, but again the grey dead showed his brands and was permitted to enter. The Watcher shifted through the walls. He followed to the airy Tower of Messages which speared the air at the very peak of the palace. No slave branded and marked should have reached this far, for the upper levels of the Tower of Messages held the precious jade ravens, fabulously rare even in a city as rich as this, each one worth a dozen ships and a thousand sword-slaves. The ravens carried the words of Sea Lord Shonda of Vespinarr to his friends and allies, or his t'varrs and kwens and hsians, and rarely anyone else.

The grey dead presented himself and was ushered through into the jade-panelled scribing room. He took a gold quill and wrote a brief note on a sheet of paper and handed it to one of the bird scribes.

'Dhar Thosis. At once.'

The scribe looked the grey dead up and down, decided he was merely a slave and allowed himself to appear offended at such an imperious tone, but the grey dead had already turned and left. The Watcher lingered. He followed the scribe now, wafting in the air, waiting in the inking room as the grey dead's message was written again, this time with diamond-tipped gold-glass scratching letters so small that an ordinary eye could barely read them onto a tiny silver ring. When it was done, the scribe took the ring and carried it up the steps that led to the cages of the jade ravens themselves, to their keepers and to the open roof where slaves were chained to posts to feed the messenger birds when they came home. Before he left he threw the grey dead's paper into a jade bowl to be burned at dusk with all the other messages sent that day.

Alone, the Watcher became flesh. He took the grey dead's words and sank into the floor. *Dhar Thosis.* An interesting dilemma. It would take a jade raven five days to cross the desert while he could do it himself in one.

He shifted through the walls, up to the orange-tiled roof of the Tower of Messages, and squatted there. Away from prying eyes, with the chitter-chatter caws of the jade ravens just beneath his feet, he read the grey dead's words:

He is not here. I am unmasked.

After the words came four symbols. He had no idea what they meant, but he'd seen them before. On the Azahl Pillar.

Who is not in Vespinarr? And to whom was this message sent? He needed to know both answers. He pondered. A jade raven to Dhar Thosis would go straight to the Palace of Roses, and there fate smiled on him. Xican was in debt to Vespinarr, Dhar Thosis to the mountain city's great desert rival, Cashax, and so for now the two indefatigable engines of the sea lords played out their endless duel with the Grey Isle and the Kraitu's Bones as their pawns. Quai'Shu's spies filled the Palace of Roses as Lord Senxian's surely festered like maggots in the Palace of Leaves. If one of the grey dead had made his home in the Kraitu's Bones, he wouldn't stay hidden for long.

So, to the who of *he is not here*.

The Watcher became the stone of the Visonda's walls and descended to its gates, waiting for the grey dead to emerge but the slave never did. Over the days that followed the Watcher searched the city with meticulous care but the grey dead had slipped away, had somehow eluded him. When he rested in front of the Azahl Pillar, he saw that the symbols there whose meanings were lost were indeed the same as the ones the grey dead had drawn. Exact copies. A sign of the city from which his message came, was that it? Or did it mean something more?

The Watcher returned to Xican and carried out his duties. He ran errands and carried messages, paltry things far beneath an Elemental Man. Amid them the hunt resumed. A sorcerer, no matter his powers, no matter who he was, did not throw off an Elemental Man for long. The brands on the grey dead had come from Shevana-Daro. The Watcher went there and began his search anew. Patience was an Elemental Man's friend, and months later patience rewarded him with a boat stolen away to the forbidden island of Vul Storna, where the ruins of an ancient tower of white stone rose from the rocky heart of the island, visible from the sea, its top sheared in two. The Taiytakei who looked out across the water from their comfortable lives on the shore joked that the island was cursed, but those who plied their trades on the waves knew better.

Not cursed. Forbidden, as the Konsidar was forbidden, on pain of death.

The Watcher became the air and blew close. This was where the last priests of the old ways had fled when the cleansing purity of the Elemental Men came down from Mount Solence. Vul Storna had been their refuge, a final hiding place, and they'd lived and worked for years amid the deep ruins and in the great labyrinth of tunnels and caves beneath. They'd come to preserve the lore and the teachings of the gods they served, the stories and memories that the Elemental Men sought to destroy, and not everything they'd left behind had been found and made safe. Yet even without them the island would have been shunned. The ruined tower was an older thing than the priests, as old as anything. It had an aura to it. A resistance that reached out and touched him like Baros Tsen T'Varr's great floating castle. A thing that belonged to the same time, flowed out from the same white enchanted stone.

He found the grey dead again among those tunnels, searching walls filled with archways that opened onto nothing but more blank white stone. Whispers said that if a man knew the true secrets of what the priests had written, he might open these arches to other worlds, another way to reach across the storm-dark. But whispers were whispers, nothing more.

He became flesh and bone. 'And have you found it, sorcerer? What you were looking for in Vespinarr?'

The grey dead jumped. Black shadows flew from his sleeves, hurled at the Watcher to choke his soul out of his body. The Watcher shifted. The stone walls here were like the castle with its glowing whiteness. They held him out, but the myriad of statues that littered the labyrinth were more ordinary things. Beside the grey dead, the stone features of some ancient lord became the Watcher's face and the shadows whirled around in impotent frenzy. The Watcher waited patiently for them consume themselves and wilt and die.

'For six years they hid themselves here, sorcerer. When we found them we put an end to them, but in that time they wrote what they wrote. The *Rava*. More than a hundred copies of their blasphemies and abomination, written in their shaking fearful hands and smuggled away. Doubtless more made since. We track them down as we find them. We destroy them as we destroy all who read them, all who touch them and all who seek them. The *Rava* is forbidden knowledge, sorcerer. Is that what brought you here? We will not permit the world to end again.'

The grey dead drew his shadows back into his sleeves. 'I know your voice. Under the temple of Vespinarr. I thought it strange for a different kind of killer to come, stranger still that my shadows failed to devour him. *You* I have expected.'

'You cannot escape us, sorcerer. We were made for the likes of you.'

'I know what you are better than you know yourself, earth-touched. I will not fight you. A storm is coming that even you cannot stop.' He stood still and quiet. 'I will become one with Xibaiya and await the great transformation.'

'You're making something, warlock. What is it?'

The grey dead gave away his surprise. 'Making something?' He chuckled bitterly, tinged with a weariness he didn't try to hide. 'If that's what you came for, you're too late. It's already made, killer.'

'And what *have* you made?'

The grey dead shook his head and half a smile twitched at the corner of his mouth. 'Are we done?'

'Those who know of these things say that the writings of the *Rava* are incomplete. Is that why you came here, warlock? Did you think the priests of the Vul Storna had another volume finished in secret when we fell upon them? One that we never found?'

'Oh yes.' The grey dead smiled. He drew back his hood and closed his eyes. 'I don't think it, I know it, earth brother. The *Book of Endings*. Filled with more secrets, mundane and deadly, than you or I will ever know. It would have made their *Rava* complete. It's hidden behind one of these archways. Behind one of these gates to another world.'

'Where it remains.'

The grey dead tapped the blank archway beside the Watcher's stony face. 'Perhaps it's this one. But how to open them, eh? And where do they lead? And what will you do if the Ice Witch of Aria has found it first? For that *is* the world in which it was finally hidden, after all.' He laughed. 'Oh, there are far worse things than you and I, brother of the earth.'

The Watcher shifted. He became air and flesh again in the blink of an eye. With a slice of his bladeless knife the grey dead's head fell from his shoulders. It rolled on the floor, still grinning.

'I will wait for you in Xibaiya, earth-touched,' it mouthed.

14

The Dragon Slave

The man chained next to Berren was dead. He'd been dead for days; he stank of rank decay and the rats had gnawed his feet to the bone. Whenever Berren dozed for a few minutes one of the rats would take a nip to see if *he* was ready to be eaten too. They were hungry, these bilge rats, and they were big and there were a lot of them. So far he'd found the strength to kick them into the stinking inches of stale water that slopped back and forth underfoot. Sometimes he even managed to stamp on one and break its back. It would squeal, and the squealing told him where it lay, legs thrashing. There were better things to eat than raw rat, but there were worse things too.

Lazily he rattled his chains. Except when he had visitors come to taunt him, there was no light down here, nothing to see by. The Taiytakei who ran the ship were still taking bets on how much longer he was going to last. One or two who'd gambled long at the start had even smuggled down bread and water at first but that had stopped after the man next to him had died. The Taiytakei bet on everything. They couldn't help themselves. They could have bet on who he really was, if he'd told any of them his story, but it might have come to an unsatisfying end because he didn't know any more. Simply didn't know. Whenever the rats left him alone, whenever he drifted into a fitful sleep, his mind wandered into a past that belonged to someone else. In his waking memories he knew he'd grown up a street urchin in the city of Deephaven. When he closed his eyes he found he lived in a village beside a lake, surrounded by reeds taller than the tallest men. Instead of streets he ran among the tiny channels between them, up to his knees in muddy water. Or sometimes it was the other way round. He'd lost track of everything. Lost track of who he was, lost track of time. Tethis had been months ago. The battle, the pit, Vallas, the Bloody

Judge, they'd faded to one half-remembered dream.

The hatch overhead opened. The sound roused him to lift his head. No one had come for more than a day but now men were lowering the ladder, clambering down the steep narrow steps, boots clumping on hard damp wood, splashing when they reached the bilges.

Taiytakei. Two held candles and lurked in the shadows. Two others came and peered and poked. He'd never seen any of them before but they wore their hair in long braids that fell almost to their waists. The longer the braids, the more important the man. He'd learned that much before they'd thrown him down here. The same went for their clothes and especially their cloaks. They liked their feathers and their bright colours. The bigger and the gaudier they were, the better; but here in the dim flicker of the candles their cloaks looked black. So did everything.

The Taiytakei gibbered to each other in their dialect, too fast for Berren to follow. Now and then he heard words he understood, but for the most part their speech was impossible. Written down though, their letters and language was the same as he'd learned in Aria. In Deephaven with the priests and the monks and Tasahre, years before the Bloody Judge had been born.

He closed his eyes. The Taiytakei chattered away right in front of him as though he was a carcass hung up in a slaughterhouse. Tasahre. His first love. Sometimes when he closed his eyes he watched her die, over and over and over, always the same, the sword opening her throat and the blood, so much blood. But other times, when he screwed up his eyes and tried, he remembered her from before. His hand pressed to her cheek. Her tears on his skin, and gods how he wanted her. How he wanted her now, to hold him and tell him what to do. But she was gone, and every time he remembered that anew, despair tried to drown him. She'd told him once that words were all the same – in Aria, with the Taiytakei, in the Dominion, Tethis, everywhere the same – and it was just the way of saying them that was bent and changed.

The Taiytakei started poking him, still jabbering at one another. As the Bloody Judge, he'd planned to meet a slaver crew some years ago but it had never come to anything. Now one of them was prodding his arms and his ribs, turning his face this way and that, peering at his teeth and eyes. He wondered if these Taiytakei were slavers too. How would he have seen them, standing as Gaunt had stood on the edge of the sea when he'd been taking their silver and selling his captives? He'd always said he'd sell the queensguard to slavers. Wars cost money and the men of the queensguard had picked the wrong side. Exactly his own words but now he saw how hollow and cold they were.

'Do you want to live, slave?' The accent was still thick but the Taiytakei could be understood when they tried. He nodded. He forced himself. *Did* he want to live? He wasn't entirely sure any more. Here was life, come full circle, back to being a skag, only worse. *Did* he want that again?

Better than death though. Wasn't it?

The slaver frowned. 'Why? Why do you want to live?'

'I ... want ...' What sort of question was that? *So I can wring your necks, all of you, one by one.* What did he want? He wanted his life back, his own skin. *My sword, my army, my missing piece that I once wore around my neck that makes me whole.* But swords came and went and the Fighting Hawks only existed to break the warlocks and their queen. The other him had already done that.

Then so I can wrap my hands around my own throat and strangle the life out of whatever bastard has stolen my body and my name. That's why. That was more like it. Revenge? He understood revenge. From the day he'd left Deephaven his life had been made of it. The Bloody Judge had had his way now, and all that was left was a sordid hunt through the back alleys of the world, cutting up the last few warlocks that still survived, but that's what he'd do. Revenge was what he had left to him. Revenge on the friends who'd sold him as a slave. Revenge for a son taken by disease before he could hold a sword. Revenge for a lover whose fire for him had died. Revenge against the gods themselves, though he knew well that revenge was a whore and not a lover.

Deep inside him something stirred. *Revenge against the gods themselves.* A strength surged through him, a will to exist and yes, a will to wreak that revenge, all of it. He lifted his head and bared his teeth and glared at the Taiytakei in front of him.

'Because I'm not ready to die.'

The Taiytakei exchanged more words. One called a candle

bearer closer and pointed at Berren's thigh, at the scarring on his leg. The other looked him up and down. 'You know ships?'

He nodded. Two years as a skag; but they must have known, because knowing his way around a ship was what had landed him down here in the first place. Normal disobedience was met with floggings or simply being thrown overboard to drown. It took a special crime for a Taiytakei slave captain to put one of his precious cargo to death so slowly; but then it took a special understanding of sails and ropes and how they worked together to fray the right few so they'd snap when they should hold and sails that should be reefed would stay aloft untouched until the wind in them snapped the masts that held them high. If he'd thought of a way to send the ship to the bottom of the sea, he'd have done it.

'Sail, fight, gold,' said the Taiytakei. To him it seemed to mean something.

They left him chained in the dark for another two days but at least he got food and water now. The dead man beside him was taken out and thrown into the sea. When they let him out, up onto the decks, Berren screwed up his eyes and stretched and cast his arms to the sky, feeling the sunlight and the fresh air and the wind on his skin for the first time in ... days? Weeks? He didn't know. When they prodded him into a boat along with a dozen more slaves, he did as he was asked, meek and docile while the fire inside smouldered on. A time and a place. One day ...

Revenge on the gods themselves. The thought haunted him yet gave him its strength. Inside him, now and then, he still felt the remnant of the warlock whose body he'd taken, crushed and squashed, forced away into some deep dark corner, jumbled and slowly fading to nothing, a husk to be devoured by alien thoughts and foreign memories, drenched with despair, although these days even the despair was a dull thing, muted and driven away.

He'd not let that happen. Not to him. *Not* to the Bloody Judge.

The boat pulled alongside a galley, a fast shallow-draughted coastal corsair, the sort of ship the Bloody Judge might once have used for fast sharp raids along the Tethis coast. Its decks were busy, filled with bright-coloured Taiytakei and unchained white-shirted slaves. Some of the slaves even carried short cutting knives. The Taiytakei carried them too, but they carried something else: golden glass sticks that glowed with their own light. He was herded with the other newcomers to the back. Several Taiytakei pointed their glowing sticks at him. White light held in glass. He thought he'd seen something like that once before. Trapped fire that Prince Talon, the Prince of Swords, had once used.

He stopped. He suddenly didn't know who it was they'd fought that day. The king he'd killed for the Prince of Swords. How he'd earned his other name: Crowntaker. A moment ago he'd known who it was but now the name was gone like the snap of a man's fingers.

He stood with the other new slaves, cowed and pressed together, surrounded by armed men while the two ships finished their business. The galley raised a sail and began to move. A slave with a knife on his belt and two Taiytakei soldiers came forward. The slave wore the same white as the others, but around his wrist hung half a dozen strings of brightly coloured stones. He looked at Berren and the others, laughed and spat at their feet.

'If you speak the Sun King's tongue, nod your head.' The words were loud and slow as though he was talking to idiots. He looked them over one more time and then walked in among them, cuffing them into answering. 'We are all slaves. *Slaves.* Do you know what that means?' He tore one of the strings off his wrist and threw it into the sea. 'I didn't like that one any more. That's what happens to things I don't like.' He waved his fist. 'I care more about every one of these stones than I care about any of you. This lot.' He nodded at the guards. 'As far as they're concerned, they like the bilge rats better than us.' He went from one to another, unlocking their chains then held them up. 'You think these make you slaves? You're wrong. It's the colour of your skin. Look at yourselves. Look at the colour of your skin. Look at the colour of *my* skin. Slaves is what we are, chains or no chains. Or do you wish to be free?' He gestured over the side of the ship. The coastline was maybe a mile away, maybe less. The air was warm, the sea calm. Berren stared at it. Couldn't help it. A strong man could …

The slave with the bracelets stood in front of Berren and snapped his fingers. 'You. Scrawny one with the scar on your leg.' Bracelets glared down at him. 'A strong man could swim. That's what you're thinking.' He turned away, addressed them once again. 'And he's right. A strong man *could* swim to the shore from here, if he could swim at all. But you're slaves and slaves are weak.' He laughed. 'Prove me wrong. Go and jump. Run! I won't stop you.'

No one ran. Bracelets glared at them. He raised his left arm to show the lightning brand that ran from his elbow halfway to his fist. 'I'm a slave like you. One brand makes you worth something to these bastards. *You* have no brands. That makes you worth nothing.' He came forward again, nose to nose with the biggest slave from Berren's ship. 'I have a name but you're not worth it yet, so you can call me master, or bastard, or anything you like as long as you do what I say when I say it. What's your name, slave?'

The big man murmured something. Bracelets slapped him. '*Wrong!* Your name is *slave*. Big man like you, why aren't you swimming?' Again the big man murmured and again Bracelets slapped him and shouted in his face, 'Because you're a *slave* and because you're *weak*.' One by one he went among them. Whatever they said, he slapped them. If they gave a name, he screamed at them that they were slaves. If they said they were slaves, he screamed at them that they were weak.

Now he was standing in front of Berren. 'And *you*, Scarred Leg, I know *you* were thinking of taking a jump. Saw your eyes look at the sea. I know what you were thinking. Freedom, eh? Land. So close. So tempting. Yet here you are. Still here. What's your name, slave? Are you a sheep or a wolf?'

Berren lowered his head and didn't reply. Bracelets slapped him. 'Are you deaf then? Are you mute? Stupid? Are you all three?' Berren said nothing. Bracelets slapped him again. 'Slave! You're a slave. Say it! Say *I am a slave!*' Another slap. 'Say—'

A tide of fury washed though Berren. He caught Bracelets' wrist, twisted, had one arm locked around the man's neck in a flash. The other hand whipped the knife out of Bracelets' belt.

'My name is slave,' Berren hissed. 'But my other name is Berren. Berren Crowntaker, Berren the Bloody Judge of Tethis.' The Taiytakei soldiers were pointing their wands at him. The light inside them blazed bright. And he didn't care. Not one bit.

Bracelets snarled and waved them back. 'You stay here, you're just slave to me,' he said. 'You want a name? You earn it.'

Berren forced Bracelets' head up. 'I see the archers there. You might not kill me but they will.' He felt a dizziness coming over him. Weakness. Weeks of being starved.

'You *earn* it!' Bracelets grabbed Berren's wrist and pulled the knife away from his throat. He twisted Berren's arm until the knife fell to the deck and then kicked him down and roared at the other cowering slaves, 'By fighting! This is a fighting ship. *You* man the oars. If you live a year, you man the ropes and the sails. If you live another year, you fight. You'll be slaves, you'll always be slaves, but you can be *proud* slaves.' He held up his hand and waved his strings of stones. 'Every year you live, you get one of these. If you live long enough to fight, you can leave if you want but you won't. You'll have a taste for it by then. Either that or you'll be dead.'

Bracelets reached down and glared, eyes a-glitter. 'You. Scarred Leg. You're not as weak as these others so now they're yours. Down among the oars they'll take their punishments from you. Whatever wrong they do, you'll be the one to pay. Any of you survive to be a sail-slave, it'll be the same but worse, because then I'll be the one taking it out of your skin. Now give me back my knife, slave. Pick it up and give it to me.'

I ... am ... He'd had another name once. He reached for it but it slipped between his fingers, wriggled from his grasp. He reached across the deck and picked up the knife and handed it back. Bracelets hauled him up and then his face jumped forward and they were eye to eye. 'Do not think that I fear anything, slave, for *I* have taken back *my* name. *I* am Tuuran. I am Adamantine, and I kill dragons.'

Berren Crowntaker, the Bloody Judge of Tethis, bared his teeth and smiled.

15

Crazy Mad

A year at the oars killed a good few. Some died from exhaustion. A few annoyed their Taiytakei masters once too often and were thrown overboard. A couple were sold. But mostly they died in the bouts of sickness that swept the rowing deck every few months. Not Berren, though. He never got sick. He never argued with the oar masters, the Taiytakei soldiers who walked the oar decks with their whips and their ashgars, their spiked clubs. He grew stronger. The endless hours filled out his muscles, broadened his shoulders and his chest. His flesh became his own again. He no longer looked at his hands and wondered whose they were. It was only when he glanced down and saw the scar on his leg that he remembered the warlock Skyrie.

When his year was done they let him loose from his place among the oars. He stood up on the open decks with the wind in his hair and the sun on his face and grinned.

'I haven't forgotten you, Berren the Crowntaker, Berren the Bloody Judge of Tethis,' whispered Tuuran behind him. 'I told the Taiytakei not to throw you over the side then. I told them you'd be worth it. They said not but they let me have my way. Now prove that I was right and they were wrong.'

Berren had seen Tuuran perhaps twice since that first day. He didn't turn around. He could smell the brand in Tuuran's hand, the hot metal scorching the air. 'Another year and they give me a knife, is it?'

'A year, two, maybe three. Who knows? Stay alive and one day you'll be a fighting slave. I think you'll like that. Face me.' Now Berren turned. Tuuran tipped his head up to the wind, to the spray of salt. 'You kept it in. Well done. Mostly the oars break a man one way or the other. Some shout and fight and get themselves killed. Others? A little light inside them snuffs out. Not you, though. You have a touch of the dragon-killer in you. You have patience.' For a moment Berren caught a gleam in Tuuran's eye. A fierce madness, a knowing of a shared longing.

'No. Not me.' A touch of the dragon-killer? A touch of something. The other was still inside whenever Berren thought to look. The husk and dust of the warlock, still screaming in the dark.

Tuuran showed him the brand, six inches of lightning bolt still glowing a deep dull red. 'Easy now. They're watching you. It's going to happen one way or another and you know that. That's how this works. And it's good – it makes you more than you were. So no struggling now. Bite on this.' Tuuran offered a strip of thick leather. Berren hesitated, then took it and pushed it deep inside his mouth and bit down hard.

'Good. Now. Most people don't get this choice, but you do. You can hold out your arm on your own and keep it there, and keep it still while I do this. Or I can get some men to hold you down. Most people, it's best if they're held down.'

Berren took the leather out of his mouth for a moment. 'Did *you* need to be held down?'

Tuuran grinned. 'You think there are any slaves here who could do that? Hold out your arm. Left one. Nice and straight.'

Berren stared at the brand. He clenched his fists. Then he pushed the strip of leather back between his teeth and held out his arm. He was breathing hard now.

'Turn it over. Open your fist and bend back your hand.' Tuuran ran rough fingers over the inside of Berren's arm, back and forth, then held Berren's hand, bending it back until it hurt, holding his arm locked straight. He had the brand in his other hand, poised. 'Now close your eyes. Go on, close them. And no matter what, keep that arm still or I'll have to do this again. Ready now?'

Berren nodded. He was panting as though he was running for his life, every muscle clenched tight, tense and ready to explode into life.

'Good. Now there's … Great Flame, what's that?'

Berren opened his eyes and started to turn his head and as he did, Tuuran whipped the brand over and pressed it into Berren's arm. Blazing agony punched him in the back of his eyes and then grabbed them and squeezed. Berren screamed. His face screwed up tight. His teeth clamped on the leather. The brand hissed as Tuuran placed it into a bucket of waiting water but the big man still held his hand, gripped it tight as he poured cold seawater over the wound. He smeared it with something and then wrapped it in a bandage. He might have spoken, but if he did then Berren didn't hear. The pain consumed everything. He snarled like an animal, deaf to the world.

When he was done, Tuuran left him there, clenching and un-clenching his fist, rocking back and forth, tight as a drum, breath-ing hard and deep until a numbness took over and the pain slowly ebbed. Then Tuuran came back. He crouched beside Berren and gave him a cup of clear fresh water and a bowl of rice with a lime cut in two perched on top.

'You're no longer an oar-slave,' he said solemnly. 'You're no longer an animal. You're no longer property. You're a sail-slave and your voice has worth again.' He slapped Berren on the back. 'In Takei'Tarr they'd give you half a loaf of bread fresh from the baker's oven and a bowl of olives. At sea we have to make do with what we can get. You have half a glass and then I expect you to work.' He got up and left.

The slaves who worked the ropes and the sails moved freely around the ship and over the days and weeks that followed, Berren found his way into every nook and cranny. Down among the oars he'd come to know the men who sat around him but he'd never bothered to learn the names of the rest. Now he paid attention. To be up here they were survivors like him and they came from all over the known worlds. In his waking memories he'd grown up in the city-port of Deephaven, the second greatest city of the empire of Aria, and he found other slaves from there, most from the coast a hundred miles further south but they'd all heard of Deephaven. They told him of a war that had come since he'd left, of sorcer-ers dressed in silver, of ice raining in knives from the sky, the city put to the sword and then rising from the dead. Afterwards, the coast to the south had become a hunting ground for the Taiytakei slavers. Deephaven had survived but now there was a necropolis at its heart, populated by the risen dead and guarded by sorcer-ers who were masters of fire. And from those ashes the empire had a mistress now, beautiful and terrible to behold. They spoke of her in hushed whispers, as though even here she might hear them. The Ice Queen. Berren listened to their stories but he didn't much believe them. Most of these slaves, whatever they claimed, had never strayed more than a day's walk from where they'd been born until they were taken and stories had a way of changing, of growing wilder the further they travelled.

Other slaves came from places around the Dominion. The Bloody Judge had been to a few and heard of a few more. He'd even sacked one once, which made him smile in secret to himself. Others, like Tuuran, came from places with names he'd never heard. On nights when the ship was still and drifting and there was little work to do, they sat around a stove of hot coals and told each other their stories. As each new slave arrived from the oar deck, the older slaves always saw that he had his turn.

'In my land there are dragons. Flying monsters as big as this ship whose wings would cast the whole world into shadow when they flew.' Tuuran chewed on a stick of Xizic stolen from their Taiytakei masters. His eyes shone in the glow of the coals, wandering among the sail-slaves, daring any of them to speak. 'I was born to fight them. Raised to slay them. I am Adamantine. I have stood in walls of dragon-scale shields and turned back their fire. We were masters of the beasts, not their slaves. We were the undrawn sword.' He said the same thing every time, that and nothing more. He never once told them how he'd been taken.

'I come from a farm,' said Berren when it was his turn. In his waking memories he never saw any farm but if he said who he thought he really was, that he was a man well into his third decade who'd led armies, fought wars, killed kings and conquered kingdoms, no one would believe him. The stories the slaves shared were meant to have at least a little truth in their hearts. 'I grew up far away from the sea. We lived beside a lake and everywhere around us was swamp and reeds.' He dreamed of that village every night, knew it now as though it *had* been his home. 'Men with swords and horses came each year. They took our food and our animals and left us to starve. One year they branded me.' He tapped his thigh, the great scar that lay half-hidden under his tunic. The other slaves murmured. They'd all seen it.

He changed the truth a little from the way his dreams had it then: 'One year they came a second time. After they'd taken all we had they came back to destroy us. Man or woman, old or young, it didn't matter; they put us to the sword. I was away among the reeds. It was night. When I came back, the dead were left where they'd fallen, scattered across the ground.' He could see it, feel it. The loss and the horror and the fear of being suddenly alone were so vivid, and so was the rage that followed. That was how it went in his dreams. Gone out into the swamp to die. Given back his life by the miracle of the one-eyed spectre. Returned to find his home slaughtered in savagery.

He pinched himself. Those were dreams and they didn't belong to him, for *he* was Berren, child of Deephaven, son of the city through and through. The Bloody Judge, warlord of the Small Kingdoms. The Crowntaker, maker and breaker of kings and queens. He was a lot of things but he'd never lain dying by a lake, and yet he felt it. He ground his teeth and watched the slaves around him carefully as he spoke. 'I went after them,' he said. Some of them gently nodded, others shook their heads, and then and there Berren divided the slaves into two in his mind. The Nodders and the Shakers. The ones who'd fight and the ones who wouldn't. The wolves and the sheep.

Tuuran belched. 'Is that it, Berren Crowntaker, Berren the Bloody Judge? Or is this story going to be a very long one?'

The other slaves laughed and nodded and raised their cups. 'Berren the Crowntaker?' said one. 'I knew him.' A chorus of jeers and boos and laughing drowned out whatever came next. 'Well I *saw* him, then. The Bloody Judge he was calling himself. Had a part in sacking Mor-Dyan. Six years ago that was.' The sail-slave snorted and looked at Berren. 'You ain't anything like him.'

Mor-Dyan. He remembered that. Berren chuckled and shook his head. 'I just have his name.' Stupid thing, that first day in front of Tuuran, saying who he really was. It had gone around the ship like a disease and none of them ever quite forgot because Tuuran wouldn't let them. Berren spat onto the deck. 'No, my story's about done. You can dream the rest easy enough. Was the Crowntaker's men who'd done it, and no hope I had of doing anything about it. Got as far as the sea. Soldiers came by, clearing out a tavern, and there I was too far in my cups to even notice. Next thing I knew I was here.' He shrugged. 'Let that be the end of the story.'

'So who's this Skyrie, then?' asked Tuuran. 'The one you keep mumbling about in your sleep, keeping the rest of us awake all night. He one of those soldiers you set off to hunt, Berren the Bloody Judge, or was he just a lover?'

The name hit him like a fist. He hadn't heard it outside his dreams for almost a year. He froze, unable to speak.

'He can call himself what he wants, can't he?' muttered someone. 'As long as what he answers to is *slave* like the rest of us, eh?' There was a chorus of laughter. Berren screwed his eyes shut. Skyrie was gone, wasn't he? But there was something more than the memories of another man's life. Something else trying to break through in his dreams of the one-eyed man.

Another slave got up, pale-skinned Adasi who'd come from the Small Kingdoms. 'No, Jorri. He wants to call himself the Bloody Judge, he can answer for him too.' He walked around the coals and stood over Berren, looking down at him. 'I had a cousin in the Tethis queensguard. The Bloody Judge killed him. That means that you and I, we got a—'

Berren shot to his feet and wrapped an arm around Adasi's neck. The words ended in a strangled gasp as Berren squeezed. 'If he served the Dark Queen then he deserved what he got!' he hissed. He was breathing hard. Rage swarmed through him, rage and revenge, demanding release. 'So what was his name? Was it Skyrie?' His arms clenched tighter. Why would he say that? Skyrie? How could it be?

'Adasi, last month your cousin was a pirate,' laughed someone else.

'You going to let him go now?' asked Tuuran.

'And a bad one at that.'

Then Tuuran's arms were around Berren like iron bands. Adasi scrabbled away, off into the shadows, staring at him as though he was a monster, a madman, a freak. And at the same time he saw himself walking down into the pit under Tethis castle, four brother warlocks around him as an honour guard. He felt the hatred burning inside him as his village had burned. Revenge. That was what had taken him there. He stumbled away, out of the shelter of the sailors' awning and into the wind. Cold fresh air crashed though him. He reached the rails at the edge of the deck and heaved the contents of his stomach into the sea. 'Gods!' He spat out the taste of bile and gritted his teeth. With the wind in his face and the stars up above, the memories slowly faded until all that was left was the name.

Skyrie. He almost didn't know who that was any more.

'I don't care who you were or who you think you are,' murmured Tuuran in his ear. The big man had crept up on him and now he slipped in beside Berren and leaned on the rail too, looking out at the night-black sea. 'You can be the Sun King himself for all I care but to the rest of us you're still called *slave*. Do you know the penalty for damaging another slave, *slave*?'

'A slow and painful death, I don't doubt.' Berren spat again.

'I send you back down for another year at the oars.'

'Is that all?'

'In your case I'll make sure it's five.'

'Then I'd best start with you.'

Tuuran laughed. 'No one cares, *slave*. No one gives a drip of piss about who you were or how you got here. You're here. That's the only truth that matters. Everything else is slaves' tales. You heard Vhalin speak?'

'Used to be sergeant of the guard in some place I've never heard of?'

'Sold into slavery when his town was overrun. Fought with such ferocity that when they finally took him they were too afraid to kill him, right? Whoever *they* were.'

'So he says.'

'He comes from a town you've never heard of because it doesn't exist. He was a dock worker. He was sold to the Taiytakei because he couldn't pay his debts. Found that out from another slave who knew him. Sahan the pirate? Feared throughout the Gulf of Feyr, renowned from Helhex in the south to the mountains in the north, scourge and terror of the seas?' Tuuran shook his head. 'Fisherman. He *was* a pirate but only for one night. Thought he'd row into Deephaven harbour and climb up an anchor chain and rob one of the ships. Caught first time. Sold.' Tuuran chuckled. 'But you wouldn't believe it now, either of them. They made up the stories of who they wanted to be. Vhalin the Panther and Bloody Sahan.' He turned to Berren. 'So you can be the Bloody Judge of Tethis if you want, or you can be the emperor of Aria or the speaker of the nine realms. No one cares. Just don't act like it makes you any better than the rest of us.'

Berren spat into the sea. 'Why make up stories if no one cares? They don't change who you are. Pretty pointless, I'd say.'

'Are they?' Tuuran slapped Berren on the shoulder and spat a laugh of anger at the night. 'We have nothing, slave. So when I dream, I am the Tuuran who faced dragons and I fight them and I win. When the time for blood-letting comes, that's who I become and so I live and others die. But when it's not time for blood-letting, these other slaves are what pass for your friends. So if anything happens to Adasi now, you'd better have about a hundred witnesses to say it wasn't you and I'd better be one of them. Otherwise ...' He mimed a rowing motion.

'I could throw you over the side right here and now,' muttered Berren.

'You really think so?'

'Yes, I do.'

'Then why don't you?'

'I faced him once. The man who stole my life. Let's say, for the sake of things, he was the man who burned my village.' He stared at the sea, spilling words to the air. 'I remember the feel of the javelin in my hand. The exultation as I threw it. I looked into his eyes and a chill wrapped itself around me like a long-dead lover. He met me, stare for stare, steady and unflinching as a stone. They weren't the eyes of some doppelgänger. They were my own.' He didn't say anything more after that. Just gazed out across the water.

'Never mind those other names. I think I'm going to call you Crazy. Crazy Mad,' said Tuuran.

And that was how things stayed. The days grew to months and the months to years and Tuuran was his friend as much as anyone until the time came when he left, summoned to some voyage to his homeland that filled him with tears and fire and a hunger to be free, and Berren was alone. Crazy Mad. Wondering what to do and waiting for the world to remember him. And remember him it did, after many months more had passed, with a Taiytakei sailing ship and three men in grey robes and one that he knew. The one he wanted most of all.

Vallas. Vallas Kuy. Brother to the dead warlock Saffran who'd cut out a piece of his soul.

16

Priests of the Vul Storna

Not that anyone in the eyrie knew or cared, but in the dragon realms the Adamantine Palace had already burned to ash and glass when the Watcher saw the moon sorcerers for the second and last time. With no warning given they appeared in the desert out of the sky above the eyrie the stolen alchemist had made. Two of them now, not three; and they came with dragons and said nothing, left the monsters behind and vanished into the sky whence they came. The Watcher watched them go and then looked once more at the paper, carefully written in a scribe's hand, that he'd taken from the grey dead under the Vul Storna not many days before.

> *For the brother who waits in grey.*
> *We have found him.*
> > *Vallas*

Vallas. Now he had a name.

The Dragon-queen

17

The Speaker and Her Spear

Six months before it would burn under an onslaught of dragons, the dragon-queen Zafir stood before the altar of the Great Flame in the Glass Cathedral of the Adamantine Palace. Aruch, the cathedral's high priest, was mumbling old words handed down from the first speaker, Narammed. Zafir hardly heard them. Her head was spinning, full of doubts and fears and possibilities and amazement. Out in the Gateyard the Adamantine Men were still clearing up the corpses. The Night of the Knives, they'd soon be calling it. The night that the riders of the north had fought with the Speaker's Guard and left more than a hundred dead strewn across the palace. The night Shezira had pushed Hyram off his balcony to fall to his death and the night Zafir had imprisoned a king and a queen, the first time a speaker had done such a thing in nearly a hundred years. The night she'd started a war.

The Glass Cathedral was half empty. It should have been full, but many of those who had come to see the new speaker chosen were dead or underground. Aruch's mumbling turned into a buzz in her ears. She couldn't concentrate. Her heart was fluttering. War. She'd started a war. Maybe Jehal thought there was a way to turn back but there wasn't.

It took a moment to realise Aruch had stopped. The cathedral had fallen silent. The air was taut with expectation. Aruch was holding something in the palm of his shaking hand.

'The ring, Holiness,' he said again.

Zafir stretched out her hand. Her fingers were long and delicate. Musician's fingers, her mother had said a long time ago when they'd still been speaking to each other, before Zafir had bled her first woman's blood and discovered the truth of what was waiting for her.

Today her hands were shaking as much as the daft old priest's.

Aruch slipped the Speaker's Ring onto her finger. He placed the Earthspear in her hand and named her Queen Zafir, speaker of the nine realms. She returned the spear and it was done. As she turned and walked away down the aisle of the gloomy windowless cathedral, she looked for Jehal, but he wasn't there. He'd stayed carefully out of sight. He'd said he would and she understood that he had to, but she wished he hadn't.

Doubts. Doubts had no place in a dragon-rider but it was hard to stand alone with so much uncertainty, not knowing with each hour what would come of Hyram's fall and the battle in the Gateyard, of dragon-kings and dragon-queens imprisoned in her towers, a blood-mage under her feet and a Night Watchman who wasn't as obedient as he seemed. Hard, and Jehal would have made it easier simply by being there to share the burden – but he wasn't, and she'd shambled through this ceremony like a sleepwalker, doing her part but barely aware of what was around her.

And it wasn't good enough. Halfway from the altar to the bright sunlight of the open door, she stopped. She slowly looked from left to right and back again, sweeping her eyes across the riders who'd come to watch her take the ring. They hadn't expected her to stop, and now she had their attention. She looked at them, listened to the racing of her own heart and felt the writhing in her stomach and smiled. Smiled at them, met their eyes one by one and took that fear and doubt and curled a fist around it and squeezed it until it was something else.

Anticipation. Hunger.

It hit her, standing there, halfway along the cathedral. The queen of everything! Speaker! A rush of warmth spread through her and her smile grew wider; and now she strode the rest of the way, strutted, shoulders back, chin high, white cloak swirling behind her. She felt their eyes on her, watching her go. Once outside, she didn't break her stride as she marched to the Tower of Air and climbed its steps to the top. The exertion left her flushed and breathless. She threw open the door to her rooms and pulled off her cloak, sure Jehal would be waiting there ready for her, wanting him to be so she could vent the tension and the anticipation and find a calm again, but he wasn't. She searched back and forth in case he was hiding – it wouldn't be the first time he'd kept her guessing and then crept out on her and she was in no mood for games. When she was sure he really wasn't there, she sighed and flopped onto the pristine silk sheets and started to unlace her boots, and then stopped and threw herself back and closed her eyes because the feeling wouldn't go away. The need for release. She shivered, filled with the memory of desire. When she closed her eyes she could smell him, his sweat, her sex.

Riding a dragon. That would be best of all. Nothing was equal to the feeling that brought. But the dragons were down by the Mirror Lakes at the eyrie and she wanted something *now*.

She sighed again and jumped off the bed and prowled to the balconies. The Tower of Air had a ring of them, up high, overlooking the palace. Maybe the swirl of the air would calm her, and she liked to be high above the ground like this. Speakers before her had liked it up here too and for the same reason: it reminded them of sitting on a dragon's back. Perhaps that would do. She went and stood outside, high over the walls of the palace, drenched in sunlight. The day had a dreamy quality. A breeze wafted from the south, warm and dusty, drawing a little perfume from the scented silken drapes. She'd grown used to these rooms, the chambers at the top of the Tower of Air where she and Jehal had first schemed together as they'd stroked each other's skin. The drapes were a gift from Jehal too.

It wasn't helping.

'Holiness?'

She jumped, so startled she almost stumbled and fell off the edge of the balcony. On any other day that might have made her furious, but today all she could do was laugh because that was how Shezira had murdered Hyram too, and how Jehal had murdered her mother, and how ridiculous would it be for yet another royal-blooded rider to fall out of the sky and dash themselves over the ground?

She caught her breath. The sharp rush of adrenaline wasn't helping either. *Damn* Jehal for his caution.

'Holiness?'

Zafir brushed the drapes aside. In the balcony room a servant knelt with her head pressed to the floor. A wild rush spiralled through her. Drag the woman to her feet and throw her out of the window. Or drag her to the bed and ...

'*Damn* you, Jehal!' She had to laugh again, because it was that or scream or smash something. Speaker of the nine realms! *Speaker of the nine realms!*

For a moment she forgot the woman on the floor. Speaker! It filled her and made her gasp.

'Holiness, the alchemist is waiting to see you.' The woman cringed every time Zafir moved, as if she expected to be kicked. And that *would* have been a way to release the energy coursing through her but the Adamantine Palace had seen enough speakers like that over the decades. She took a deep breath, let it out, bent very low and touched the woman lightly on the head.

'Then go and send him in.'

She'd been ready for it to be the irritating one, Jeiros, but it wasn't, it was Vioros. When he came he shuffled slowly through the door, head bowed. He was in his finest cream quilted robes embroidered with flames at the edges, doubtless kept carefully clean in a closet in the Palace of Alchemy for such days as these. He bowed low and stayed with his head tipped towards the floor. He was out of breath. The steps got almost everyone.

'Holiness.' He spoke quietly. There was a subtle change in his tone that recognised what she'd become. Today she was the speaker. Zafir smiled, still full of that tension.

'Vioros! Look at me and get on with it. I have things to do.' Not that she knew what, exactly, but not sitting around here doing nothing, that was for sure. If Jehal was hiding then it would have to be a tear across the Purple Spur and straight down the Great Cliff on Onyx's back to see whether she could get the wind to rip her right out of the saddle this time ... Or something like that. Something to make her heart truly pound.

When he looked up, he smiled, and Zafir felt another surge of delicious warmth. Vioros had been kind enough to her, but mostly the smile told her that her mother's death remained a mystery to him. Queen Aliphera, fallen from the back of her dragon? No one knew what to believe but after last night, with a dragon-king and a dragon-queen in prison under the Glass Cathedral, no one would ask any more. It was gone. There were bigger things.

She twisted at the ring on her finger impatiently, conscious of its unfamiliar presence.

'Holiness, to every speaker of the nine realms, we come. There is knowledge that we of the order wish to share with you. Knowledge for your ears and yours alone. It is usually done immediately after the naming.'

Zafir rose and paced restlessly to the gaudy throne that Hyram had brought here for her and sat down again. 'Sit, Vioros. What knowledge?'

The alchemist carefully sat and crossed his legs on the floor in front of her, ignoring the chairs either side. 'Holiness, when you touched the spear you became the guardian of us all. There are truths known among our order that are for the speaker and no other.'

Zafir made a show of looking about. 'We do appear to be alone, Vioros.'

Vioros didn't follow her eyes so perhaps he didn't doubt her, but he shook his head. 'I cannot, Holiness, for they cannot be spoken. It is a thing that you must see. Please, Holiness, will you come?'

Zafir let out an exasperated sign and slapped her thighs. All that delicious tension was turning slowly to frustration and that in its turn was making her irritable. '*Now*, Vioros? Does it have to be now?'

'If it pleases you, Holiness.'

'No, it doesn't.' She let out another sharp breath and snapped to her feet. Certainly this wasn't what she wanted – what she wanted was Jehal or her dragon but neither were here and her mood was rapidly shifting. Jehal would never know what he'd missed. Even *he* had his limits and today, if he'd been here, they might just have found them, and Jeiros and Vioros could have waited, fuming, for as long as it took. But he wasn't, so boring alchemists it was.

Vioros wouldn't say any more. She quickly left him behind, bounding down the tower steps while he toiled after. Outside, when she'd waited for him to catch up, he led her across the Speaker's Yard and straight back into the tumorous lump of stone that was the Glass Cathedral. Jeiros was there and a few dozen riders still milling in clumps and clusters from the ceremony, talking and muttering to each other. Zafir wondered why they chose to stay in the dark of the cathedral instead of the bright sun of the yard. Conspiring probably, but they all bowed and fell silent as she passed. Jeiros bowed too. *This* one had begun to annoy her. He was floundering his way into Bellepheros's shoes, still thinking that the old man might come back. Probably better for all of them if he did but the world was rarely that kind. *Although if I didn't have Bellepheros killed and neither did Jehal then who did? And why? What did that old man know? What did he find?* The timing of his vanishing was the most troubling of all, right after he'd scoured Jehal's eyrie for her mother's killer.

No matter. She shook the thought away. A curiosity for another day, and here and now she couldn't be bothered with it. She had no time for the faraway vanishing of alchemists, not now, nor much for the ones in front of her. 'My time is precious, Grand Master Jeiros.' And yes, she meant it, filled as it was with dead kings and murdered queens and the Gateyard still littered with bodies and reeling in the ones that got away and what to do with the blood-mage under her feet, but most of all with the desperate urge to fly a while, alone with Onyx and a wind like a hurricane.

'I'm sure it is.' Jeiros spoke with a touch of acid as though he'd glimpsed her thoughts. Zafir let it go and followed the pair of them to the altar of the Great Flame and the stairs that burrowed into the ground beneath. A pair of Adamantine Men loomed from the shadows there to walk beside her. Why? In case her alchemists turned suddenly into assassins? Absurd! Absurd as thinking she couldn't take a fight to two old men even if they did, and besides she wasn't sure whom she should fear more just now – Jeiros and his alchemists or the Night Watchman and his guardsmen. She sent them away. It kept the frisson alive, the tension.

'The tunnels here go deep, Holiness,' whispered Vioros. 'Deep into the Purple Spur. The caves are a realm in themselves. The ways to reach them are hidden to all but the senior alchemists of our order and to the speaker. That is the first thing we must show you.'

They descended the steps. Tunnels riddled the earth beneath the Glass Cathedral – everyone knew *that* – but how far they ran was a mystery. They were old, far older than the rest of the palace. Before the coming of Narammed, the Glass Cathedral had been the most important landmark in the realms save the beating heart of her own home, the Pinnacles and the Silver City. No one knew who'd built the cathedral. It had been long abandoned, its stone burned glassy smooth long before the Silver King had tamed the dragons. Yet when the blood-mages had eventually torn him down they'd brought his spear – the Speaker's Spear – straight to the cathedral within days of his fall. As if it belonged here.

Her spear now. And there it was, beneath the altar at the bottom of the spiralling staircase, standing on a plinth of its own. Alone, where it had lived before Narammed had taken it; and now it was here again and it seemed to Zafir that it was waiting for her. It stood erect, its pointed haft buried six inches into the stone floor. The walls around it were lit by alchemical lamps and their cold white light glittered on the spear's silver skin. She reached out to touch it again as they passed, almost couldn't help herself, then drew back as the alchemists stiffened.

'Yes, touch it, Holiness.' The voice from the shadows made them all jump, but it was only Aruch, sitting still and quiet in his dark cowled robe. 'Touch it. Claim it. Bleed for it and make it yours. Some speakers did and some speakers chose not to, but the ones who do are always the ones who are remembered.'

All of a sudden Jeiros was as tight as a scorpion ready to fire. She could see the muscles standing out on his neck. He was shaking his head. 'Holiness, it's not necessary …'

Good enough reason to do it right then. She stepped smartly to the spear and ran the tip of a finger along the closest of the spear's four blades. The edge was wickedly sharp. A few drops of her blood dribbled over the bright silver and then, to her astonishment and alarm, shrank away and vanished as if drawn into the metal itself.

'The spear has tasted you now,' Aruch said. 'It knows you. You belong to it.'

'That was foolish, Aruch,' snapped Jeiros and Zafir had never heard an alchemist sound so savage. 'Come, Holiness, please. We have far to go.' He turned away down another passageway of hewn stone worn smooth with age, lit by alchemical lamps. Zafir stared a moment longer at the bright silver of the spear. There was no sign of her blood. It hadn't been an illusion or a mistake. It had been there, and then it had gone. She backed away, uncertain of herself and not sure what to do with the feeling and so she settled for following Jeiros and pretending it hadn't happened for now. The tension she'd brought was still inside her but now it had an unpleasant edge, cold and clammy and nothing like the delight of before.

'Why did the blood-mages bring it here?' She cocked her head at Jeiros, who of all of them ought to know. 'Why not keep it in the Silver City? It always seemed strange, what they did.' Carried the spear as far away as could be. The end of the known world. 'Not embraced in their victory, yet not destroyed nor buried nor hidden either. Why?'

'They were afraid of it, Holiness,' said Jeiros softly. 'The blood-mages believe it carries its master's power within it. Or something even greater. They were afraid of it because of what they'd done.'

Zafir sucked at her finger. 'Does it, Jeiros? Does it carry the power of the Silver King?'

'No.' The grand master alchemist of the realms shook his head. 'I'm sorry, Holiness. Aruch shouldn't have misled you. He clings to old ways and not all of them are wise. I'm afraid I have little to say of the Speaker's Spear except that it's breathtakingly sharp and keeps its edge. I hope the cut isn't deep.'

Months later Jeiros would remember those words, his own, in bitter disbelief.

18

The Naked Dragon

Little to say of the Speaker's Spear except that it's breathtakingly sharp and keeps its edge. But she'd seen her blood vanish into the silver – hadn't Jeiros seen that too? It scared her and she'd have to face that; and there was a blood-mage down here somewhere, and blood-magic was stronger than alchemy. Yes, and there she'd been thinking of having Queen Shezira's little pet exposed and executed for what he was. Foolishness when he could become *her* tool instead ...

Jeiros opened an iron-bound door and closed it behind them. 'None may enter this way save the masters of the order, the great priests and the speaker,' he said, as if she cared about such dry old rituals. 'Had you brought your Adamantine Men they would have had a long wait for you here.'

Zafir nodded, bored and getting impatient again. The spear had unsettled her and she'd been unsettled to start with, only now it was unsettled in a bad way. She wanted the wind in her hair and huge spaces all around her, not to be wrapped up in stone like this. Dark places brought back memories she preferred to forget. 'It is far, Master Alchemist?'

'I'm sorry, Holiness, but it is, and it must be done.'

The alchemists led her this way and that along passages, smooth-worn and narrow, to a long hall lit with dozens of their lamps. It was a harsh light, casting shadows sharp enough to cut the eye. They made her uneasy. Jumpy. Nervous, and that was never good. She found herself wondering about Bellepheros and Furymouth and Jehal again, wondering what people knew and what they thought they knew and what they imagined. Whatever brilliance Jehal had contrived to have Shezira push Hyram off his own balcony, it *would* have been better if he was still alive. A few months and then he could have quietly gone away, fallen ill and died without a whiff of suspicion. But she couldn't, couldn't live with the lie for that long, not with everything it brought with it, the things she had to do to sustain it . He was old and fat and that reminded her far too much of—

No. Not here. She could already feel the panic rising. *Not in a place that's already dark.* A dragon-queen feared nothing but the shifting shadows were taking her there, back to the dark place of long ago. She pushed the panic away, closed her eyes and thought of racing among the clouds, warmth spreading up through her legs from the heat of the dragon beneath her, howling biting winds on her face. A dragon-queen was made of stone. A dragon-queen had no place for fear or doubt. She took deep breaths, snarling at herself. Closed her eyes and clung to the wind until the fear withdrew. Breathed slowly out as it did, a long sigh of relief. *Better.*

They took her down yet more steps, worn and sandy, so many that she lost count. 'Where are you leading us, Master Alchemist?'

'You will see, Holiness.' The walls pressed around her. The shadows ahead and behind filled with unkind mystery. The closeness of the two alchemists made her skin prickle and tense.

Wind in her face, tugging at her hair. Wind in her face, tugging at her hair. 'I understood the tunnels under the cathedral reach as far as the deep cellars of the gatehouse and elsewhere around the palace. I've heard they might even stretch to the City of Dragons itself. Yet it seems to me we've travelled in the wrong direction for that, and too far to be within the bounds of my palace. Vioros spoke of caves beneath the Spur. I think one of you must tell me a little more now we have gone so far.' She had to work to keep the tension out of her voice. They'd chosen a bad day to bring her to a place like this.

'Are those the only stories you've heard, Holiness?' asked Jeiros. 'I've heard far more. Stories that these tunnels reach the Fury, that they cross the realms as far as the Pinnacles and Bloodsalt and Bazim Crag. They don't, but they go quite a way. This path will bring us to caves that lie beneath the Spur, as you have said. Behind the Diamond Cascade.'

'That's a very long way to walk under the ground, alchemist, when a horse might have carried us instead. I am displeased, Jeiros.' *Stop being scared! Stupid woman! It was done and finished long ago. They're gone, all of them. Dead. You killed him, remember? The darkness has no hold on you now!* But the darkness only laughed at her. All the gleeful joy of before, they'd leeched that from her, bringing her down here. Alchemists liked their caves and their small dark places. But not her. She gritted her teeth. Hated it, but they wouldn't see it, none of them, not a flicker of it.

'A horse could not have carried us where *we* are going, Holiness.'

Down into the bowels of the earth: hours of the same rough-walled tunnel that ran straight to the heart of the mountains. At least the alchemists carried plenty of lamps. Zafir closed her eyes and summoned the wind to her face. Space. Space around her, below her and above her. And light. And no one for miles, no presence lurking right beside her. Caves were for alchemists, not for dragon-riders. Not for her. The panic gnawed at her but she'd lived for years with this foolish fear of the dark and had learned the tricks to hold it at bay. *And he's gone! Get over it!*

'There was a river here once,' Jeiros told her. The alchemists were breathing heavily by now, both of them out of breath from so much walking. 'Its course was changed to create this passage.'

She had no idea how far they went but she was aching by the time the alchemists stopped, gasping, at yet another great door. As Jeiros struggled to open it, the wood two inches thick and bound in iron, pulling at it with all his strength, she saw a slash of blood across his palm.

'You're bleeding, Master Alchemist.' As much as anything she wondered how he'd cut himself down here. She was a dragon-queen and the speaker now and knives were always a danger, and she'd spurned her two guardsmen from the Glass Cathedral ...

Jeiros flashed with anger. 'The doors are bound closed, Holiness,' he said. 'Only an alchemist may open them.'

'Oh really? Not a speaker?' *Blood-magic? Sealed doors?* And there was the damned fear again, reaching out of its pit to grab her. She slammed the lid on it and stamped it back. Dark places. Never again!

'No, Holiness. Although a speaker can, of course, command that they *be* opened.'

'How very interesting. How many more such doors do you have?'

Jeiros didn't answer, and she might have pressed him on it but the sight beyond the door changed her mind. Such questions could wait. Ahead a great cave swallowed the light, black as pitch but for a single lamp by the entrance. Zafir had no idea exactly how large the space was but it must have been immense; she could feel that much simply in the taste of the air. Enormous. A Flame-blessed relief from the claustrophobia of the tunnel.

'Keep the door directly to your back, Holiness,' said Jeiros, 'should you ever need to come this way. There's always a light left here.' Which threw up the thought of being stranded in a dark place that was huge instead of small and somehow that was worse.

She snapped back at him, 'How am I to come this way if I cannot open the door, Master Jeiros?' Shame about Bellepheros. His façade of fawning diplomacy had been exactly that but at least he tried.

They crossed the cave, flat and smooth and covered in sand. At one point Vioros stooped and put down his lantern. Zafir wondered why until she looked back and was shocked to see that the lamp by the door was a tiny speck, barely visible. *How* large was this cavern?

As they walked on, a whisper of rushing water touched the stillness and grew steadily louder until, when they stopped at a scaffold set in the sand, the whisper had risen to a roar and Vioros had to shout over the noise of it. 'There used to be a lake here, Holiness. There are others. The Silver River flows through these caves under the Spur.' Behind her, the lantern Vioros had left was a dim speck, a single lonely spark in the dark and she still couldn't see any sign of the cave walls. They *had* to be close, didn't they? The rush of the waterfall, somewhere nearby in the dark, was enough to shake the ground, but in the feeble light of the alchemical lamps she couldn't see it. The air tasted moist. She took a step forward alone and then stopped herself. Why had they brought her here? To test her? To pick on her weakness and see if she'd break? Well, she wouldn't.

A wooden platform descended slowly through the middle of the scaffold, lowered by ropes. When it reached the ground Jeiros climbed onto it. He offered his hand. Zafir disdained it. Another little strike against him. Would he have offered it if she'd been Hyram or Jehal? No. If it turned out one day that Jehal *had* disposed of Bellepheros then she was going to be angry with him, she decided, for leaving her with this stuffed shirt.

The platform rose. Pulleys and ropes, she supposed, not that she knew much about such things. It took a very long time and was very dull and very dark and the waterfall stayed very loud, but the wind of it and the stray specks of water on her face helped keep the dark in its pit inside her head. By the time she felt stone close in around her again, the lanterns that marked out their path were too dim to see. When they reached the top and she peered over the edge, the base of the scaffold was so far away that she couldn't tell if they'd risen a hundred paces or a thousand.

The rush of water was as close as before. 'We are at the back of the caves behind the Diamond Cascade,' Vioros told her. 'The Zar Oratorium isn't far from here. There is another door—'

'But we are going another way,' said Jeiros curtly. He walked quickly now, leading the way through more tunnels, smooth things once bored by water, then down a rough-hewn passage to a small bronze door. Three heavy bolts held it shut. Jeiros pulled them back one by one. He beckoned her forward and stood aside as she opened it. Warm stale air washed over her, full of the smell of dragon, familiar and comfortable. The tension she'd carried all the way from the palace eased a little.

Why bring her to a dragon? What could there possibly be here that she didn't already know? Her heart jumped with anticipation. A gift for the new speaker? Surely not. But now she'd thought of it, she wanted it, and anything else would be a disappointment.

As well as the smell, a little dim light spilled out from behind the door but she couldn't see much more. When she stepped forward, she realised why. The door opened on to a balcony fifty feet up a sheer wall and the lights were all down below on the ground, alchemical lamps, hundreds of them. There were people moving down there too. She saw them, glimpses of shadows flitting here and there, three or four or maybe half a dozen. But what held her eye was the dragon in the middle of them, bound in chains. It was looking straight at her.

Little One!

The words roared in her head. A voice she'd never heard. She staggered and Jeiros was there, right behind her, ready to catch her. She felt him touch her and flinched as if stung, whirled and almost hurled him over the edge.

'I can stand on my own feet, alchemist!' she hissed. The fear was a wild thing now, battering itself against the cage she'd made for it. 'I don't need your hand. Stay away from me!' As if he would have done such a thing for Hyram or for Jehal. No, just for her, because she was *weak*. She took a deep breath and quelled the quiver in her throat. She was rattled by that voice, that was all, and her old enemy the dark, but there was nothing to fear here. Steady breaths. Nothing to fear. 'What is this place? What was that sound?' *Nothing to fear …*

'Sound, Holiness?' Jeiros had a smugness to him. She thought she'd probably never stop hating him after this. 'There was no *sound*, Holiness.'

Could she have him sent away? *There* was a thought.

Little one! It came again, a voice that thundered inside her. And the alchemist was right, there was no *sound*. Only words inside her head.

She reeled. 'What have you brought me here to see, Jeiros? A dragon? I've seen plenty.'

Jeiros spoke patiently, as if to a child: 'I've brought you here, Speaker, to see the thing that you cannot be told and must see for yourself, as every speaker before you.' He drew himself up. 'This is a dragon untouched by alchemy, Holiness. This is what they would become without us. That is what every alchemist stands against.'

The chained dragon turned its eyes and fixed her with them, alight with fury. It wanted to eat her. It wanted to burn her. It wanted to revel in her fear and dread before she died.

You are nothing, little one.

She made herself stand there, then took two quick steps right to the edge and met its eye. She met its anger and took it inside her and turned it and smashed the fear back where it belonged. Smiled at the monster down below.

Thank you.

19

Fickle Fortune

Months passed from the day Zafir saw the dragon in its cave. The war came. Lovers died and were betrayed but she never forgot. Dragons flew free and cities burned as the schemes of the Taiytakei wrought their havoc, and the dragon's fury rode with her.

She lay sprawled flat, staring up at the sky. The silver man with the white face and the bloody eyes was looking down at her again. Other faces peered down around her. Dark-skins marked with tattoos. Taiytakei. The wooden deck was unforgiving and hard against her skin, bruising her to the bone. She felt crushed by her own weight. One by one a forest of little sounds touched her. Creaking wood. Straining ropes. The wind whistling through the rigging. The shuffle of feet on the deck. Distant voices, orders barked and the calls of seagulls wheeling overhead. The air smelled of salt and of the sea.

The faces didn't speak. They stroked their chins and looked at her. If there was anyone left to write a history of her reign, their words wouldn't be kind. They wouldn't say that Speaker Zafir of the Silver City had been wise or good or just and they certainly wouldn't speak of peace and glory. The miracle would be if there were any voices left to speak at all. But for now none of that mattered, for now she was about to die.

She rose shakily to her feet. Black-skinned Taiytakei sailors in their thin bright silks, yellows and pinks and pale greens and blues, stood around her. Beyond them, past the rocking of the ship, the sea shifted with a lazy swell, the water a deep blue under the summer sun. Around them half a hundred other ships rolled slowly back and forth.

Nausea stabbed at her. She coughed, vomiting up another mouthful of water, then glared at the men around her, ready to fight if she had to, but a cautious thought held her back: of the dragon she had ridden with its vengeful flames, snuffed out in the air like you might snuff out a candle. Crashing dead to the water with her still strapped to its back. Sinking and pulling her under.

No. She was a dragon-queen. She lived and flew and commanded monsters. She had a knife in her boot. She would cut through them like dragon fire or she would fall in the attempt.

She staggered as the pitching of the deck caught her unawares. Her ankle was still weak from her duel with Lystra. She dropped to one knee and found she couldn't rise again, that it was too breathlessly hard. Lystra. Stupid girl.

The silver men dispersed into glittering mist and drifted into the air. She watched them go to the other dragons who had fled from the Pinnacles with her, three of them, motionless, frozen in the sky as though for them time had stopped. The silver mists wrapped around them. They seemed to whisper in the dragons' ears. Even the Taiytakei stood transfixed, watching the alien sorcerers ascend to the sky.

The oldest of the Taiytakei turned away first and looked at her. He was shaking but it was only his age. Or maybe it was laughter. His face was wrinkled, so dark that his eyes seemed like lamps beneath the tight braids of his ghost-white hair. His fingers were knobbly, all skin and bone. His clothes, though … He wore bright silk from head to toe and was collared and cuffed with iridescent feathers, red and yellow and orange and gold, shimmering in the sun so that he looked almost aflame. The braids of his hair reached to his feet. A rich man among their kind, then. Very rich indeed.

He told her his name, Quai'Shu, and how he'd traded her for dragons. She let him, taking the time it gave her to find her strength again, to find the fury of the dragon inside. When he was done, another Taiytakei, taller and younger but just as skinny and frail-looking, whispered in the old man's ear. He had his feathers made into a cloak, and when the wind died down and it fell still she saw that the feathers formed a picture. The sea, and mountainous stones rising from the waves that reminded her of her home in the Pinnacles. A golden cloud rose above the scene and two bright bolts of lightning crossed it. His braids too almost touched the deck. She wondered how many times he tripped over them each day.

The old man frowned, shrugged, nodded and turned to walk slowly away. The younger Taiytakei smiled. His eyes felt like unwanted fingers over her skin, all greed and desire. She was cold, the wet soft leather under what was left of her dragon-scale clinging unpleasantly to her, seawater still dripping from her sleeves, trickling down her arms and legs. She knew what was on his mind. What was on the mind of most men when they saw her. She wasn't sure whether it made her want to laugh or cry. Men were so pathetically predictable.

And for one bizarre moment she found herself thinking of Jehal. Missing him. He'd made no pretence of being anything but himself. He'd lived up to his promises, at least until Evenspire.

She rose again, unsteady, slipping her boot knife into her sleeve. Above, her last three dragons snapped into motion again. No bodies fell splashing to the sea but she knew the riders who'd flown with her were gone. Snuffed out. Her last loyal few. These silver men, what were they? Not Taiytakei. The Silver Kings themselves? But a thought like that was too big for this moment, too laden with questions as large as the world. *This* moment was black and white, life and death.

'Hold her!'

A sailor reached out and grabbed her and it was almost a relief to have something simple to deal with. She jumped straight at him, knocking him back, and the sailor gave a yelp of surprise and for a moment she was free. She had no doubts about what came next. The whole world narrowed down to the Taiytakei in the cloak, the one who presumed to own a dragon-queen. She sprang and knocked him over. They fell, locked together, and she had the knife in her hand before they hit the deck, sharp and free and already coming down. She'd waged wars, burned cities and called down fire from the skies; she'd stroked the hearts of men and taken lovers as she chose, she'd betrayed her own blood and her desire had betrayed her in its turn. Princess, queen, speaker, she'd been all these and she would not submit to anything, not any more. Never again. Certainly not to a man who'd traded her life and her ambition with King Valmeyan of the Worldspine for his stolen dragons.

'Not.' Stab. 'Yours.' Stab. 'To give!' Flecks of spittle flew from the corners of her mouth. He wanted her, and just for that, for the mere thought that he could have her without begging to ask, she slit him open from his gut to his gullet and let his blood wash the deck of his own ship. Bodies piled on top of her – sailors – one, two, a dozen maybe – trying to pin her, trying to hold her still. Too late.

She wondered, as the whole ship hit her around the head, why she hadn't dived into the sea to drown and be with her riders instead of killing this Taiytakei. But the moment didn't give her an answer; everything was sharp and loud and then black and silent and still. She welcomed, at last, an end.

Yet the ghosts of the underworld didn't come. Perhaps the spirit hordes of those who'd died at Evenspire and the Pinnacles weren't waiting in wrathful judgement for her after all. Not the mother who'd betrayed her and whom she'd conspired to murder, nor the father who had made her what she was. The dark room she feared beyond all else didn't come to claim her after all, not yet.

She hurt. That was the first thing she knew. Her head pounded and her shoulders throbbed. When she tried to move, the pain was sharp and piercing. When her eyes opened again, she was in a bed in a tiny room that rolled from side to side. Ships were rare in the dragon realms and so it took a moment for her to realise where she was.

The sheets were soft like the ones Jehal had brought her from his silk farms on Tyan's Peninsula but here they carried an unfamiliar scent, something bitter and foreign. She tried to move but waves of pain and nausea overwhelmed her. She closed her eyes and breathed deeply against them. For a while she lay still. Her fingers explored her skin, searching out the damage. It was all she could do.

She was dressed in unfamiliar clothes and the smell wasn't the sheets, it was her. They'd torn her dragon out of the sky, bruised and battered her, stripped her, half killed her, and then they'd bathed and cleaned her, washed her in oils and ointments which smelled sharp and foul and dressed her in alien silks.

Her left foot was so swollen she could barely move it. One shoulder felt stiff and sore, too uncomfortable to move. She didn't remember either injury happening.

The pain slowly ebbed but the nausea didn't. She gagged. Sat up, sharp with sudden fear, and threw up into a bronze pissing pot beside the bed, a few trickles of sticky bile. The smell of it tied her stomach into a tighter knot. She turned away. Lay back, head thumping. The low wooden beams were oppressive and too close. At least it wasn't dark. That would have been too much to bear.

A metal ring was bolted through the middle beam, the sort that might be used to hang a lantern except this one had a wrought silver chain attached to it. It seemed an odd thing until she realised that the chain reached down to the bed and to a bracelet around her wrist, silver and worked into a tangle of lightning bolts. She'd never seen silver of such delicate strength but in a stroke it turned her room into a prison.

She closed her eyes. The sickness wouldn't leave her and the pain in her head was drilling into her bones. They hadn't killed her then. She wasn't sure whether she was glad of that or not. She'd meant them to, meant to give them no choice, but now ... life was more ... more desirable than death? Was it? Better than facing her ancestors, perhaps? Or perhaps not, because now it would be as it always was: there would be a man, sooner or later, who sought to own her, a man who saw her as a pretty thing for his own pleasure and nothing else. Even Jehal had been like that, although at least *he* had been equally exquisite.

I killed the last one, she told herself as she drifted away. *If there's another, I'll kill him too.*

When she woke, there were strangers in her cabin. Three women, scared little birds with white belted tunics flapping like wings. She flew at them, heedless of her pain, and they squealed and shrieked and wept and cringed in the furthest corners where her chain wouldn't let her reach them. They had dark skin, night-dark like the Taiytakei, but they were slaves. They came from the deserts in the far north, perhaps. There were whispers of dark-skinned men up there, far across the sands. She hadn't heard of Shezira or Hyram dealing in slaves but that didn't mean they didn't.

'Who are you?' They cringed. 'Who is your master?' They shook their heads. One of them started to weep. 'Do you know who I am?' They cringed again. 'Where are you taking me? Why? Whoever is your mistress or master, bring them here!' More questions, until she felt light-headed, but all they ever did was quiver and stare.

Scared little birds. Weary to the bone she lay back on the bed and closed her eyes, listening to them. When they thought she was asleep they scurried about and then ran away like fearful mice and left her alone. The room stank again, some new bitter spice over the lingering smell of stale vomit. It disgusted her. At least her head felt clearer.

They'd emptied the pissing pot. Good. She needed it, and this time she just about had the strength to swing her legs out of the bed and squat. Awkward with one foot and one arm not working, but she found a way. When she was done she looked around. Her cabin might have been a fine place as little wooden rooms on tiny floating palaces were measured, but Zafir wrinkled her nose at almost every part of it. The silk hangings on the walls were bright and pretty and intricate, woven patterns of emerald-green and lapis-blue and white and gold but they were just patterns and had no story to them. The wooden bed, chest, table and chairs were dark carved wood and the bath was plain bronze. They were all as good as any she might find in the dragon realms, but no better. No better because the speaker of the nine realms already owned the best that any Taiytakei craftsman would ever carry across the seas and every last piece was tainted and tarnished by the metal around her wrist.

There were clothes in the chest. Gauzy silks, the colours gaudy, the weave as soft as the sheets but with the same alien tang. The glass in the round windows that looked out across the sea, now that was another matter. She'd never seen glass so clear, nor glass like the decanter that sat in a silver rack on the table.

She looked at all these things and then hobbled to her feet and stood right under the ring in the ceiling to put as much slack in the chain as she could make. Enough to wrap it once around her waist. She took a deep breath, tensed, then jumped and let her whole weight snap the chain taut. It bit into her skin but didn't snap, didn't even give. She tried it again. This time she ripped her silk shift and drew blood. She sat back on the bed, gasping, wincing at the renewed pains in her shoulder and her ankle. When she had her breath again she stared blankly at the floor. For a few short months she'd had everything. She'd been the speaker of the nine realms. Dragon-queen of the world. Until Evenspire and the great betrayal, and after that everything had unravelled, one thread after another until now, and now she had nothing. Worse than nothing. A slave to the Taiytakei. What would that make her? A curiosity perhaps for a while because of who she was and what she'd been.

She'd seen the way the one she'd killed had looked at her. He wouldn't be the last.

And then what?

She stood up, hopped back to the middle of the cabin and very slowly wrapped the chain twice around her neck. To see if it would go. It would.

Suddenly her heart was beating very fast.

Maybe it would work. And maybe it wouldn't.

Maybe she didn't want it to.

Not yet.

Carefully she unwrapped the chain. She sat heavily back on the bed and held her head in her hands and screwed up her eyes. Tears wanted to come but she wouldn't let them. Couldn't. She'd learned that. Tears had only ever made it worse. Tears showed you were weak and a dragon-rider was never weak.

Slow deep breaths until they went away.

She stood up again. Movement was good. Doing anything at all, that was good. She was thirsty. She unstoppered the glass decanter and sniffed at it, tasted the liquid, decided it was simply water and drained it, then held the glass in her hand and stared into its facets. *There* was a thing of wonder. It was beautiful. She'd never seen anything like it. She paused, staring into it, and then she hurled it across the room with all the violence she could find. It hit the wall and smashed into a million glittering shards. She stared at them. It was like staring at her own life.

She hadn't moved when the three timid women came back later with food and water and more of their oils and ointments. They shuffled in with their heads bowed and didn't dare to look up at her, but she heard one of them gasp when they saw the broken glass.

'What did I do to you?' she asked them. 'What do you want?' But they ignored her. They were shaking as they swept up the broken glass and hurried away. Zafir grabbed the last before she could escape and shook her. Flame, but they were passive, docile, broken little things! Yet underneath their fear she saw how much they loathed her. 'Why? Why do you hate me? Was it the man I killed?'

The girl shook her head as if to refuse an answer but it was written all over her face. *No.* So they hated her for something else.

'You're right to be afraid of me,' she said and let go. The girl ran away.

After the second day, when she saw there could be no escape, she let them bring her food. She let them wash and dress her because whatever little she had left, she could still keep her pride for as long as they let her. They brought her tall thin bottles of wine and she started to pretend the women were hers, her own servants, and let them be. The pain in her head eased. The bruises faded. The cuts where she'd lacerated herself with the chain quickly healed. Her ankle and the shoulder were wrenched but not broken. Two weeks and the swelling had gone; another two and they'd be as strong as ever. No damage done. On the outside at least she'd be perfect again.

'What are your names?' she asked the women but they still refused to speak. Were afraid to utter even a single word. She found out what she could by reading their faces as she asked her questions. They were slaves whose master was dead. They didn't know what would happen to her when the ship reached their home. They knew nothing of the war Jehal had waged against her or how it had ended. They'd never heard of her, or of him, or of the Pinnacles or the Silver City. They had no idea at all who she was except that she'd killed a man. The white-haired Taiytakei Quai'Shu – yes, she remembered his name, she made sure of *that* – was the ruler of this little floating kingdom, she got that much; but they didn't know his purpose and they shook with fear and almost cried when she asked them about her dragons.

It wasn't so hard to guess. She'd had a shrewd idea, by the end, what Valmeyan had been doing in Clifftop, what he'd been looking for.

One night, two weeks after they'd taken her, the ship sailed through a great storm and bucked and heaved like a dragon at war. In the middle of it was a stillness. She lay on her bed trembling in the darkness, alone, the scared little girl she spent so much time trying to forget. When her broken birds came the morning after it was gone she was still trembling inside. She kept it buried though, carefully hidden from sight, and none of them saw, and by the time they came again, the fear was gone.

They painted her, made her beautiful to their own queer eyes, and that was when the dragon voice ripped all their thoughts into pieces.

I am Silence and I am hungry.

Dragon eggs. *That* was the treasure the Taiytakei had stolen. And now, that voice told her, the eggs were hatching and they were all going to burn. She smiled. Laughed a bitter laugh while her heart stayed as hard as diamond.

She was Zafir. She was the dragon-queen.

20

Silence

I am Silence and I am hungry.

The newborn dragon bit the dead moon sorcerer's head in half and ate it. In the little wooden room which smelled of salt and tar, yet another egg cracked open, and then another. More dragons awake and reborn, dull and slow-witted, still shaking off the tentacles of alchemy.

The dragon called Silence was impatient. It didn't wait for them. It tore and scampered up through the bowels of the ship, a blur of claws and fangs and motion, searching for the sky until it burst a wooden deck-hatch into a shower of splinters, and there it was, glorious clear blue air. Wisps of high white cloud laced the sky. It saw them and it yearned for them.

Free!

It stretched its neck and jumped into the air and looked for land but there wasn't any, only the sea and half a hundred other ships, maybe more, scattered around in one single great herd. It drank the sight and spread its new wings for the first time, stretching out the folds and creases, and leaped into the air. Around it in the water some of the ships were already burning. Other waking dragons. It felt them, felt their thoughts. They were confused. There were many though.

Sleep!

Calm!

A soothing feeling washed through it. A voice, but more than that. A power. An old power. Moon sorcerers. More of them. The words drifted in among the others, soothing and caressing their confusion, calming the dull uncertainty as the lingerings of their enslavement slipped reluctantly free. In the midst of awakening they were open to such lullings.

But not the dragon Silence. The dragon Silence understood. It had woken before its last death and had thrown off those shackles. It had come from the egg sharp and clear as a dragon should, aware of everything it had been and everything it could become, bright with memory and rage. The others had not.

What is your name?
What did we call you ...
... once long ago?

The sorcerers, wherever they were, sensed its rebellion. They were guarded, not like the one below, the one whose essence the dragon had stolen and now carried inside it. The dragon hesitated. A true half-god would have crushed its will in a heartbeat. Long ago, one half-god alone had tamed thousands. *These* were weak. Feeble beside those it remembered. Toddlers with the barest fumbling grasp of true power. Barely gods at all.

What became of you, little moon children?
Stay, dragon ...
Stay and tell us your name ...

They showed their weakness that it could resist them at all. Was this all that was left?

No. I will not.

Other thoughts battered it. Little ones. Terrified. Confused. Angry. It felt them all as they ran squealing and screaming and wailing and cowering, cringing in the furthest corners they could find, thoughts drenched with delicious fear, drawing it like a wasp to sugar. The dragon glided back to the boat where it had been reborn, skittered and leaped across the wooden deck, claws gouging splinters, scattering them into the air. The little ones howled and ran but they were slow and weak and easy. It flipped one and then another over the edge of the ship with a flick of its tail. The pain of shattered bone and the clammy dread of cold sinking death washed out of them, savoured and devoured. The dragon unfurled its wings and reared back and watched more of them simply leap to their doom, so drenched in terror. Others ran scuttling into their holes as they always did, as if this fragile wood could resist a dragon. It caught the last in its jaws and bit off an arm. The man staggered, shrieking. The dragon's claws scythed him down. For a moment it was alone, the little ones all squalling below.

Stay, dragon ...

Others wavered and fell. Fading. Newborns acquiescing to the will of old sorcery. But not this one.

You have forgotten so very much, it told them. *You are like shadows as a cloud crosses the sun, faded beyond substance.*

We did not go with the others ... They spoke together, as one.

Nor are we alone ... The dragon smashed through a door ...

... in forgetting ... back in among the layers of this thing called Ship ...

... old friend ... hunting the little ones with the audacity not to be afraid.

... Come with us ... Words laced with a coaxing calm ...

... and remember ... and temptation.

The dragon shattered another door and squeezed into the space beyond. Little ones met it. An old one, three dragon lifetimes ancient or more, fragile as glass, yet he stared at the dragon as though it was the dragon itself who should be afraid and not this frail shell of matchstick bones and thin-running blood.

We will take away ... The other ones cowered and screamed. The dragon stared them down, waiting for their minds to fail.

... the clouds of your memory ... One raised a stick of glass filled with golden light. A crack of thunder and a flash of light and the dragon felt ...

Pain.

A terrible rage built up inside it. A dire fury, raw like molten mountains. *No!* Those clouds of memory could stay. *Should* stay, for it knew what lay behind them. Lifetime after lifetime after lifetime of slavery and service to these pathetic, feeble, weak-willed, strengthless little ones. Another little one raised his wand and the dragon burned him where he stood, and then the other too, the one who had hurt it, burned and burned until it felt the life flicker out of them and then burned some more until what had once been faces were nothing but cracked black husks flaking to the floor. It turned very slowly on the third then, the ancient wizened one, and took him in its foreclaws and held him close so they were face to face, dragon to man, tooth to tooth. This little one had a wand too but his arms were pinned to his sides. He struggled to reach it. Failed. The dragon called Silence bared its fangs and let fire flicker around its tongue, dancing in the little one's eyes. It stared and stared as the little one whimpered in terror at last. Held on, clutched the little one's head in its claws, forced it to look, eye to eye while that terror built and grew until there was room for nothing else. Piece by piece the little one's mind broke apart. The dragon felt it like a snapping of forest twigs under a careless foot.

Now you know fear, little one. Now you know what I am and one day I will come again. You will remember. One day I will come again.

It dropped the little one and watched it crawl across the floor. Such a delicate mind, broken to pieces. It felt ... *satisfied.*

Now it smashed through another wall. Little ones ran screaming. Some of them had their wands that made lightning. It burned them. Then ripped a hole in the wood beneath them and battered its head through the rent it had made and found four more little ones, huddled together. Three screaming and soaked with fear, a fourth who held them in her arms and looked back with defiance and an unflinching knowledge of what was to come. The dragon Silence looked inside her thoughts and devoured them and stared, loathing and gleeful.

Dragon-rider.

The little one stared back. Frightened and filled with dread and yet wrapped round a kernel that refused to yield. The dragon met her eye and knew this one would not break like the other.

I could burn you. I could rip you to bloody strips. But it had thought of another way. A crueller end.

The others of our kin will return ... The faded shadows of the lost half-gods were laying a compulsion around it now. Slow and clumsy but the dragon felt it like a lead net settling on its wings.

'I bow to no one,' the little one whispered. 'So burn me, dragon. Burn me!'

Why? It hurled the thought to all of them. *Why?* It reached a claw to the little one's neck and ran a talon over her skin, sharp as a razor, the shallowest of cuts leaving a trickle of blood as it passed.

Because they must ...

The Black Moon comes ...

You have crossed the realm of the dead ...

... and you so know that the seal ...

... has broken ...

The dragon pushed itself back out of its hole. Left this little dragon-rider and the rest of them too. All deserving of their fates. It burst upon the deck of the ship in a shower of splintered timbers, opened its wings as the little ones ran screaming once again and launched itself into the glorious air. It turned once, raked the prow of the ship that had birthed it with fire, and flew away.

You have taken what cannot be yours ... clamoured the sorcerers. *Futile to run from such as us* ...

The dragon called Silence didn't look back as it flew away.

21

Dragon-queen

I am Silence and I am hungry. Her three broken-bird slaves froze all at once. Zafir let out a startled gasp and then a little sigh, smiled and laughed a bitter laugh The dragon voice in her head under the Purple Spur had felt the same. The broken birds frowned and looked at one another, even more scared than they ever were until Zafir slapped one of them. The tall one. 'Continue.' And they did. Jittery and nervous, but they did.

She was wrapped in white silk and her slaves were painting her nails in the Taiytakei fashion while she sat on the edge of her bed. One of them had her fingers, one of them her toes while the third was piling her hair into an awkward feather-strewn bundle. It made her look as though a bright-plumed bird had crashed into her head. On some days she let them, despite herself. On others she made them put it into a simple dragon-rider's plait, how a dragon-rider would wear it under her helm. After they were done with her hair and her fingers, they usually tried to darken her face with some powder and she'd forbid it. They'd pout and mutter to themselves and dress her in colourful silks and then, if she let them, festoon her with more feathers and jewellery. It was all pointless, since no one else ever came to see her. It gave them all something to do, that was all, but there'd be none of that today. Today they'd simply burn and it would all be over.

She strained her ears, listening, tense inside now, waiting for the end to come. In fire perhaps, or perhaps they'd simply be smashed to bloody smears. The alchemists had shown her their monster, a dragon whose blood they mixed with their own to make their potions. *Any dragon will do but not any alchemist,* Jeiros had told her. *Fewer than you might think can do this. We must be changed for our blood to take on this power.* The alchemists took blood from that dragon under the Purple Spur and mixed it with their own, the ones who were somehow special. That was how they controlled the rest. Now *there* was a secret. For that they kept a dragon of their own hidden away. One that was awake for any who needed to see what that meant. Jeiros had never told her how or what this change must be to make a true alchemist. Arrogant pig. There'd always been a sneer in his words and when he bowed it was always a fraction short. Thought he was in charge of the realms. He'd despised her right from the start and the feeling had become mutual, and she'd done what she'd done, never quite believing what her alchemists told her because of the way Jeiros was, not even poor Vioros. And in the end Jeiros had sided with Jehal when the inevitable war came between them, and now she was here, and she'd never know if she was right or if it simply didn't matter any more.

Free!

Her three broken birds stopped again. One of them whimpered. Zafir slapped them back to work. What good did it do to explain? Why terrify them even more? *There will be a time when I will return. There will be a reckoning. Ruin on them all. Ruin!*

Zafir stiffened. Return? Reckoning? Ruin? Those were the dragon's thoughts, not hers. She ought to be afraid. Terrified, as her three little birds were. They'd stopped again, pale and quivering, fingernails half painted, and looked at each other, and then they looked to her, fearful as mice, but they didn't run. Perhaps because she sat still and unmoved among them. Perhaps because she hadn't raised her hand for the third time. They were all hearing the same one voice crashing into them. Did not knowing what it was make it worse, or did it make it better?

'Mistress ...'

The first word any of them had ever spoken to her. Zafir collected herself. For a moment she closed her eyes. They couldn't have long, after all. *Mistress?* It made her want to cry for everything she'd lost and at the same time she felt stupidly grateful that, at the very end, someone would be with her. 'A dragon,' Zafir said when she'd swallowed the lump in her throat. 'A dragon has woken nearby.' That only confused them and so she took their hands and pulled them gently closer, and after all she'd done to them they still came, one by one, to kneel before her as she sat, drawn in because they were terrified and she wasn't. And yes, a part of her *was* afraid, the part that knew that death was near, but she'd lived with dragons since she was born and had learned to take that fear and make it into something she could spit right back into any monster's eye, as every dragon-rider did. 'The silver half-gods will easily see to it,' she told them, except if it was that easy, how had one woken and why was it still coming? But either way nothing she could do would make a difference, and so for want of anything better she started to tell her broken birds what it meant to be a dragon-queen. All the things that had gone through her mind as she'd killed the Taiytakei on the deck. She told them how she'd been born a princess, heir to the oldest and greatest of the nine realms, to the Silver City, the Pinnacles and the beating heart of the dragon lands. How she'd been made and what it had been like to be a little girl surrounded by monsters. That she had been a queen, a ruler of all and mistress of every dragon in the world even though now she was nothing but a slave. They stared back with wide eyes. She couldn't be sure they were even listening and they certainly couldn't begin to understand. No one could, not unless they'd lived it.

As she talked and stroked their hair and held their hands; and as she did she heard voices through the walls over the wooden creaks of the ship. Tremors touched her feet, of timbers shaken and rent, closer and closer, the splintering of wood as something crashed its way through the ship. Then shouts and screams and the *smash smash smash* of something that could only be a hatchling dragon battering its way through a wall. Her birds were whimpering, sobbing, huddling ever closer. Zafir kept her head down, eyes among them, talking, doing all she could to keep the quiver out of her voice. A faint smile played at the corner of her mouth even as she flinched and her heart skipped a beat. She would die by dragon after all, and so would these Taiytakei who thought they could make her a slave, and if that was the way it had to be then she would be content.

A noise like a thunderbolt shook the room. For an instant fear got the better of her. Her words faltered, the spoken progress of her life stuttering to a halt as she was crowned mistress of the Adamantine Palace. She heard the roar of flames, more screams; sniffed and caught a whiff of burning, of flesh and wood and cloth and hair.

Know what I am! Her three birds whimpered and cringed and

tried to pull away but she held them tight. 'You can't run,' she whispered over the din of screams and the crack of tortured wood. 'Never run. Whatever comes, face it and don't flinch. Can it be any worse than living as a slave in even the prettiest cage?' She could feel the monster. It was close now.

The roof of her cabin burst apart, a sharp shower of splintered wood cascading to the floor. Her broken birds cried out and clung to her. Jagged claws tore and ripped at the wood above her. A dragon's head smashed through, all fire and horns and glaring fangs. A hatchling fresh from the egg, not that it made a difference. Zafir met it eye for eye. So this was how she would end? And yes, she was afraid, but she was mistress of her fear, quickly crushed to scorn and anger.

'You're just a newborn,' she said, and her words oozed with disappointment. 'I should have better. You should have been a proper dragon. A real monster. Onyx or his like. *That*'s how a dragon-queen should die. Not you.' She looked away. Dragon smell filled the cabin, cloying and overpowering. The hatchling glistened. A drop of something dark and sticky fell from it and landed on her skin. She flinched. It was still wet from its egg.

Dragon-rider. It stared, all loathing and glee, then bared its fangs and bored its eyes into her, battering at her, demanding her submission, her obeisance and her awe. It forced one claw through the hole it had made in the timbers and reached for her. She made herself be still, made herself hold its eye, not flinch away even as it touched her face. It drew one talon sharp as a razor down the skin of her neck from ear to collar with careful delicacy. She felt the pain, the warm blood, but she didn't move.

I could burn you. I could rip you to bloody strips.

'I bow to no one,' she whispered. 'So burn me, dragon. Burn me!'

Why? Its eye flickered away as if it was talking to someone else. Abruptly it withdrew. She watched it go then stared out through the hole in the roof of her cabin long after, listening to the screams fade and the pop and crackle of flames until she finally found her voice again.

'Because I am a dragon-queen,' she whispered. She wasn't going to burn after all. She hadn't expected that.

Her broken birds were cowering in the shadows under the bed

now, under the table, in the corner, whimpering and wailing. They made her laugh. *That* was how men made themselves into slaves. 'Get up!' She touched her hand to where the dragon had opened her skin and then to her tongue, tasting her own blood. A habit that came with every wound, started long ago in her mother's palace.

They wouldn't move. They huddled in their corners, mouths agape, shaking, eyes glazed. Broken. Dragons did that.

'Get up!' she said again, sharply this time. 'Tend to me.' She hauled them one by one out of their hiding places and wrenched them back from their terror. She touched her bloodied neck once more. Whether it had meant to or not, the dragon had set her free. The silver chain was still wrapped around her wrist but at its other end the bolt that had once gone through the roof of her cabin lay among the splinters on the floor. She picked it up and held it loosely in her hand, wondering. A chain like that could strangle a man. The bolt? It was heavy enough that a good throw, well aimed, hard and fast to the temple, might be deadly. But to what end? How many men were on this one ship? Dozens, unless the dragon had killed them. More than even a dragon-queen could fight, and even if she won, what then?

'Get up!' She grabbed the last of her birds, the one who had hidden under her bed, made her stand up and slapped her. 'Dragons, woman. That's all they are. Great and terrible monsters, yes, but nothing more. Clean my wound and dress it. Are you afraid of monsters?'

The slave shook her head. A lie, but now the dragon was gone and Zafir was still here, she was more afraid of her, and it seemed absurd but Zafir understood perfectly, for the worst monsters certainly weren't dragons. She bared her teeth and hissed, tilted her neck and touched the bloody wound again. 'But monsters can be killed, little bird.'

They cleaned her throat and wrapped it in silk, hands shaking all the time. When they were done, she pushed them away. She left them behind and climbed up through the ruins of the ship, heedless of the shouts she heard around her and below and to either side, until she had the sky over her head. Blackened bodies littered the decks. The sails were on fire, flaming rags falling now and then, fluttering away in the breeze. The rigging was destroyed, the decks scorched. Patches still smouldered, while the bows of the ship were firmly ablaze. A few desperate sailors yelled, running back and forth with buckets – the dragon hadn't killed all of them then. She looked the ship over. It was ruined but it didn't look like they were going to burn to death, not yet, so she turned her back on the panic and sat at the stern near the hole the dragon had smashed as it left and watched the sun glint off the sea. The sailors who were left, if they saw her at all, were too busy trying to save their ship and let her be. She looked out over the ravaged Taiytakei fleet. Some ships were aflame from end to end, others were untouched.

One hatchling. She started to laugh. In this moment her fate was her own. She could throw herself into the sea if she wanted but these Taiytakei who thought they were her masters, now she saw them for what they were: small frightened men. Children. So no, she wouldn't throw her life away in a fit of foolish defiance. Not when she could do far worse.

Three full-grown dragons circled overhead. *Her* dragons, she reminded herself. Other hatchlings flitted aimlessly back and forth in the sky. She turned as the air shook and popped and one of the silver men appeared on the deck. He raised his hands and the fires leaped to them as though he was sucking the flames away from everything burning and drawing them into himself. When he was done, he blinked away. Now *there* was a thing to drive a spike of awe through her heart. A sorcerer clad in silver like the Silver King himself, the half-god. Was that who they were? The alchemists said the Silver King was gone for ever, destroyed by the blood-mages, that he'd been only one, unique, an aberration, but there were stories inside the Pinnacles that said otherwise. Stories etched into the walls in places that no alchemist was allowed to see. Her home. *Her* secrets, amid the rows and rows of arches carved into white stone walls which glowed with a soft inner moonlight. Doors sealed shut, doors that led nowhere except on rare nights when perhaps they opened into other worlds but she'd never seen it happen. Her grandmother had sealed much away, her mother had been the same, afraid of her own palace, but not her. *Her* fears had come from something else, and so she'd crept among those forbidden places, finding in them a sanctuary from the monster she saw every day. And though she'd never seen anything beyond the arches but blank stone walls, she'd seen plenty more to hold her eye: carvings, mosaics, murals, all of them witheringly old. Things the Silver King had made. She'd come to know the old half-god, in her way. She saw his sadness. A pining for something long lost. Memories of others of his kind, perhaps, for whatever the alchemists said he clearly hadn't been alone, not always. A catastrophe that he had somehow brought about. It was all there in the forgotten pictures on her walls.

And now they were here?

Across the waves the fires winked out one after another. Some ships were already lost, listing as they took in water. They sank as she watched then, their last fires put out as the sea swallowed them. She counted. Ten ships lost. Forty-six left by the end. Not as many as she'd thought. Little boats struggled through the waves between them, carrying men. Flags ran up masts and fluttered, messages sent. She didn't know what any of it meant but she understood what they were saying. The air was thick with it. *What do we do? What now? What happened to us?*

Then, to her surprise and delight, the old white-haired Taiytakei came stumbling from his cabin – Quai'Shu who thought that all of this was his, every ship and every man, the dragons and perhaps even the half-gods, but most of all her. He was like a dragon-king and so she knew him, knew how his mind would work, even if instead of dragons he had ships. She weighed the bolt in her hand. Another man who thought he could own her. She'd done for the first and she'd do for this one too. No one would stop her, not this time.

She hesitated though as she watched him. The Taiytakei sailors all fretted and bowed around him but something inside him was broken. His presence was gone, his veneer of command, and all he was was a weak old man who didn't understand what was happening any more. As she understood, Zafir smiled. He'd stared a dragon in the eye just as she had and the dragon had snapped him. The smile lingered a little longer. She let go of the bolt. The dragon had shown her the way. These were just men like any others. Patience, and they would fall.

The Taiytakei led Quai'Shu away with his vacant eyes staring blindly at his scattered fleet. She didn't struggle when they came to take her too, across the sea to a ship that still had sails. She watched the fleet split. Perhaps because she hadn't tried to run they let her wander free now. She sat on the decks out of the way, watching, and she knew they saw her compliance as acquiescence, as defeat, but they were wrong. Her broken birds knew better. Something had changed between them. They were flags to her mast now, all three of them, afraid and unsure of their fates but they'd tied themselves to her. She saw it in their eyes. Still afraid, yes, but the fear had turned to something else too.

Awe.

The dragon had done that. Given her that gift.

The remaining dragons circled overhead and then flew away, all of them, the silver half-gods on the backs of the adults and the hatchlings trailing in their wake. A sigh of relief rose from the ships as they left, for they were the greatest terror that any of these men had ever seen.

Now and then a Taiytakei – she could barely tell their dark faces apart and disdained the effort of trying – would tell her to move, or to do this, that or the other. They spoke to her slowly as if she was a fool. She smiled and bowed and did as she was told because she had seen now that they could be broken.

Patience, and they will fall.

And so they sailed on until the first dark line of land smudged the horizon and the Taiytakei fleet came home with a dragon-queen in its midst.

22

The T'Varr

As well as its spires, its floating orbs and great glass discs, the Palace of Leaves in Xican extended down into the stones themselves. Deep in its bowels Baros Tsen, t'varr to Sea Lord Quai'Shu of Xican, had built his bathhouse. It was, false modesty aside, magnificent. Not too ostentatious but perfectly formed. Large enough so that when steam filled the cave, the walls vanished into the mist. Tall enough and dark enough to give the illusion of being outside. Tiny little spark-lights dotted the ceiling, arranged to mimic the stars. You could pick out the constellations if you wanted. The floor was simple black marble – none of the glass and gold that filled the rest of the palace – and in the centre the marble fell away in a series of steps into a square heated bath where the water was always kept exactly as he liked it. Hot but not too hot, more often than not scented with the particular flavour of Xizic from near Hanjaadi that he happened to like, with a potpourri of other scents flirting at the edges. There were perhaps a hundred different oils in pots in a simple wooden chest, and beside the bath, in a bowl scooped out of the marble, there was always ice and a crystal chalice of cold apple wine. It was the best bathhouse in the palace, possibly the best across the whole of Takei'Tarr, and that was because Baros Tsen T'Varr, it was whispered, loved his baths more than anything in all the eight worlds. And Tsen had heard the whispers too and knew who the whisperers were, because that was the nature of who he was, and he didn't mind what they said because if it wasn't exactly true, nor was it far wrong.

Wet footprints speckled the marble where slaves had padded to and fro only moments before, lighting the hundred candles that ringed the floor. They were gone now, the doors closed and sealed for his privacy. Baros Tsen T'Varr lowered himself gingerly into the pleasantly stinging water and sniffed, taking a deep lungful of steam and the scent of Xizic. He smiled. Across the water, his lady Kalaiya smiled back, a slave but a very special one. *And actually I like my slave and my apple orchards better than my baths, though it would pain me to lose either. Our little secret, eh?* For there wasn't anyone in the many worlds more special than Kalaiya. To Tsen, at least.

He took a deep breath and then another. The Xizic scent rose around him. He'd let Kalaiya choose today and she'd gone for something a little different. Deeper and more subtle than his own favourites. His eyes narrowed as he tried to place it. 'The finest oil of the desert from Shinpai,' he guessed, and watched her face. From all the way across the desert on the far coast of Takei'Tarr. And her own scent hid behind it like her face hid behind the steam.

She kept him guessing a moment and then her smile brightened and she nodded. 'You always have to be right. One day I'll trick you, you know.'

'I hope so.' He sighed deeper into the water and tipped back his head until only his nose and his eyes were above the surface. Sometimes when he looked at her and saw that little prickle of resentment that every slave carried with them, somewhere deep down he wondered at himself for keeping her, for not letting her go. *I love her. I should let her fly if flight is what she wants.* He thought exactly the same thing every time he saw her. But he never did and never would.

'You look happy today,' she said when he sat up and looked at her again. Her face was soft and warm, glistening in the damp heat, slightly mocking perhaps but always kind.

'Life is good, my dear.' More ritual words to go with the ritual of thought. He said them every time they bathed and usually he meant it. The life of a t'varr to a sea lord was a fine thing. On other days he might have laughed at that – *unless your sea lord is Quai'Shu with his impossible schemes of dragons.* But not today. Today he brought with him something wonderful.

'Are you back here for long?' She'd been his favourite for years, taken from the desert by Cashax slavers long ago, and he'd found her, and she'd understood him at once, better than any of the Xicanese. She knew his secrets and she kept them and so he was good to her. And he liked her. A lot. That little thing so rare.

'Not for long, my dear. But when I return I'll take you with me. Some things will be so much less awkward that way.' And how wonderful it would be to have her with him again all the time, just like it had been in Xican before. He half-sat, half-lay in the water, letting its almost painful heat wash through him. He was sweating already. A bathhouse was a place for sweat. And for reflection and drifting and the numbing of thought.

According to the strict definition of duties, a t'varr was responsible for *arranging* things. Huge things. If Quai'Shu wanted an eyrie in which to raise dragons, his t'varr found it for him, as Baros Tsen had done. And if Quai'Shu desired his whole fleet to sail to the western realms to steal dragon eggs, why then Tsen T'Varr would dutifully make sure that those ships were available and properly provisioned, and if he wept with fear at how few of them might return, he kept such concerns to himself – or more likely brought them here to the steam and Kalaiya's ever-patient ears. *But every expedition across the storm-dark is a dance with catastrophe, is it not? What's done is done. It will be what it will be. Yes, and plenty more trite platitudes besides. Put it away. Sweat out the anxiety. Enjoy an hour to yourself.* Every day was worse now, wondering how many ships would be lost this time. All he could do was fret. In Xican he didn't even have the eyrie to distract him any more but at least now when he went back there he wouldn't go alone.

Kalaiya leaned across the bath and took his hand, gently massaging his palm, tugging at his fingers. It was an unconscious thing she did without any thought and he loved her all the more for that. 'You're *thinking* again,' she chided. 'When all is ready, does it not pass from you? You provide the ships, Baros Tsen T'Varr. Our sea lord's kwen has the duty of crewing them and sailing them and his hsian is responsible for what they do when they get there, not you. Is this eyrie not simply a different ship?'

Tsen purred. 'As if Quai'Shu ever lets Jima Hsian do anything! Now *there* is a terrible post if ever there was one.'

Kalaiya cocked her head, still pulling at his fingers. 'Unless what you want is a quiet life lying in your bath, stroking your rather over-large belly and wondering how next to amuse yourself. Yes, yes, it sounds quite terrible.'

Lucky apostate. And I bet you'd find these preposterous demands a thoroughly welcome diversion, Jima Hsian. You could amuse yourself trying to work out what in the name of Xibaiya this alchemist is actually doing. Then again, that's what you're already at, isn't it? Making your predictions? He laughed. 'Do you know what Jima said when our lord demanded I find him a flying castle where he could grow dragons? "Challenges to the intellect do give a little pepper to a life of pleasurable hedonism and mild over-indulgence, eh Tsen?" I said he was more than welcome to it. But I've built it now. It's mine.' *And you're not having any of it, not any of you, not after all the effort I put into the bathhouse there. Ha!* He took Kalaiya's hand in his own. 'Hsians deal in ideas. Kwens in men. T'Varrs in things and money.'

'Not the oil in the machine, but the machine itself,' she laughed too, and her laughter was like music.

'I miss you so much, every time I leave.' He shook his head. *The machine itself* – it was certainly a T'varr-ish thing to say.

'You don't miss *me*, you miss *this*.' She gestured around at the steam-filled cave, but she knew he meant it.

Tsen smiled and leaned forward. 'I *did* give our lord's eyrie its own bathhouse, and it *is* rather fine.'

'And was the company rather fine too?' Her eyes glittered, but they danced with mockery, not with jealousy. She knew him too well. He pulled his hand away and closed his eyes, sipping on a glass of sweet apple wine from his own orchards. The design here was his, and lying in the water was like lying in the warm sea at night, the illusion of endless open space above and to every side.

Kalaiya touched his arm. 'Where are you, Tsen? Look – the veins in the marble glow below the water. They didn't used to. Have you even noticed? I like it.'

'A thoughtful present from Chay-Liang to welcome me back.' He supposed he'd have to watch her more carefully now. Not that he didn't have to anyway. She'd wrapped the alchemist around her finger and made him her pet, and even an enchantress couldn't be so naïve as to not realise how important a piece *he* was in the great game of the sea lords.

'You should give her some of your wine.'

Tsen snorted. 'Not *that* thoughtful!' He stared at her. No *my lord* or *my master* or kowtowing or averting her eyes, they were long past that. She was smiling, and her smile made him melt inside every time because there was no artifice there, only warmth.

'My t'varr. Keeps all our sails filled with wind. I'm glad you're back. Take my advice – make Chay-Liang your friend. And yes, take me to the desert. You know I'd like that.' Sometimes, when she thought he wasn't looking, he saw the harshness of the sands in her eyes. *I know you always missed it.* Taking her to the desert wasn't just for him.

He closed his eyes and sank beneath the water. T'Varr to a sea lord. A vast responsibility and so he addressed its size as any t'varr would: he broke it down into smaller and smaller pieces and then found other people to do them until there was nothing left. Then he hired some more people to do the breaking into pieces, and more still to do the hiring, until in principle he had no real responsibilities left to attend to at all but it never quite seemed to work out that way. *And never mind the small matter of our fleet and our city and our lord being so far in debt to the depthless pockets of Vespinarr that they likely own my bath, Kalaiya and probably even me by now. But meanwhile we'll simply borrow ever more, all on Quai'Shu's promise of what his dragons will mean.* Wasn't that how it had always been? It certainly felt that way.

He came up for air and sighed. On another day he might have talked to Kalaiya about it all, told her everything, his doubts and his worries and passed the burden to her and gone away feeling lighter, but that wasn't what he'd come for today. *And now I'm spoiling it.* 'I'm sorry, my dear. I'm not the best company.'

'No, you're not.' Kalaiya held up her wine glass and toyed with it, peering at the designs on the stem. 'This is strange work.'

'It comes from Aria.'

'Which one's that again?'

Another reason he loved her. He'd shown her maps with all the realms that the navigators had found in their steerings through the storm-dark a hundred times. The eight worlds, or seven or maybe nine depending on which navigator was doing the counting. She never remembered any of them. She didn't care. 'The one that's a problem,' he said.

'Well, I'm sure I don't know anything about *that*.' She pushed out her bottom lip at him.

Tsen shook his head. 'When it becomes too much, Vespinarr and Cashax will pause their rivalry and something will be done.' He leaned a little further back, sinking into the warmth again and stretched his arms behind his head. 'Ah, the pleasure of a knotty problem that belongs entirely to someone else.'

Kalaiya's lips still smiled but not her eyes. 'Your precious world order?'

'Exactly. But not mine. Yours too. All of ours.' She did that sometimes, reminded him of the last little crevasse between them. How he owned her; and when she did, it was like being stabbed. Then Kalaiya reached across the water and stroked his cheek and the flash of bitterness was gone as quickly as it came. Tsen clapped his hands with happy glee. 'Let sea lords and their heirs pore over their charts and maps and their reports. Let Jima Hsian worry about Aria. It's not like he has anything much else to do!' *And as the conundrum comes to a head, my sea lord arrives with dragons. Why, any suspicious-minded fellow might see the telltale hand of some particularly clever hsian in such a confluence of circumstance. Very clever indeed ...*

'Jima Hsian is not the oaf you picture him to be, my master.'

'Master?' *No, he certainly is not.* 'Have I upset you?'

'You're thinking about your dragons again. You're not really here.'

'I *am* thinking about dragons. I can't stop.' He laughed 'I've been thinking about dragons for years. Years and years while Quai'Shu frittered away our fleet's fortune and got us into this quicksand of debt.' He leaned towards her. 'I had no choice. I went to him with the quiet suggestion that maybe, just *maybe*, it was time to behave a little more – sail and sea help me, *me* of all creatures, saying a thing like this – *responsibly*; and then he brings back the alchemist and a plan and now there really *are* going to be dragons after all. They'll be here very soon. I think ... I think I'm actually scared, Kalaiya.'

'Can I see them when they come?'

Tsen looked longingly at his glass of wine, almost empty. If he didn't raise more money soon then he'd be selling his private cellar just to get by, but the lords of Vespinarr with their bottomless pockets would pay anything at all when it came to dragons. Baros Tsen T'Varr and his lord Quai'Shu would see to that.

Kalaiya poked him with her toe under the water. She pouted. 'You're not even listening to me!'

'No.' He hung his head. 'I came here to tell you that you'd come with me when I left again and to celebrate that with you and to be away from everything else, and I've failed, abjectly failed.'

'I asked, *master*, if I can see these dragons when they come.' Her eyes said she was playing with him this time, not truly cross.

The air quivered. The candle flames flickered. At the edge of the shadows the steam swirled. Tsen felt it through the stone and the water. They were suddenly not alone. Kalaiya squealed and Tsen's heart paused in its beating for a moment as the shape of a man moved closer through the steam; and then he breathed out again as he saw it was the Watcher and not some other Elemental Man sent to kill him.

'LaLa! You startled me!' He spoke as kindly as he could manage but he couldn't hide the edge of fear swiftly turning to ire. Death by Elemental Man mostly happened to kwens and hsians because they were more the kind of people who harboured ambitions, while t'varrs were a different breed; but still, under the circumstances ... He turned to Kalaiya. 'I'm sorry, my dear. Don't be afraid. The Great Sea Council mostly prefers us t'varrs to murder each other in more genteel ways, with banks and money and trades and exchanges, and in these I am in my element. LaLa's old-fashioned ways only come out when one of us is backed into a corner with nowhere left to go.' He threw up his hands in mock despair. 'At which point everyone goes for the throat in an unseemly scramble for the spoils while the drowning take as many of the vultures with them as they can before the corpse of their fleet is picked clean.' He tutted. 'I can't *imagine* why. But I am neither drowning nor a vulture and we are far from such a corner.' *Although by no means as far as I would like.*

The Elemental Man stood there, distant, wreathed in steam and pointedly silent. Tsen sighed and stood up. On his feet, the water reached his hips, steam rising in coils and curls around him. 'I'm sorry, Kalaiya. It seems this may be a matter for which you must leave us.'

She went without a word. He watched her go, mute and demure, but underneath he could tell that the appearance of the killer had shaken her. Perhaps he was the only one who knew her well enough to see, but then, who could blame her? This had been *his* time. Hers. *Theirs.* 'I *will* make it up to you,' he called after her. 'You'll see both dragons and the desert. I promise.'

When she was gone, and only then, the Watcher bowed and fell to his knees. He shuffled closer, a dark shape in the gloom and the steam. It was the sort of quaint tradition that made Tsen laugh, since they both knew that one of them was a deadly sorcerer-assassin, guardian of the very fabric of creation and honed in his skills from the moment he'd been born, while the other was a fat naked man standing in a bath. *And he kowtows to me while my slave freely shows her scorn.* It was a strange world. Tsen sat back in the water. *And why not?* 'Come on in, if you like.' Not that the Watcher ever would.

'I apologise from the well of my soul, Hands of the Sea Lord,' whispered the Elemental Man. Tsen smiled. They were all so ... traditional.

And that was about when the Watcher's exact words sank in, and Baros Tsen would never think those lovely thoughts of the quiet life of a t'varr again. *From the well of my soul.* Even in the heat of the water his skin prickled. 'Who, LaLa? Who is dead?'

'Zifan'Shu is murdered.'

Quai'Shu's heir. *Ah well. Dim-witted jackass. Never liked that one anyway.* 'How? And aren't you and the Picker supposed to stop things like that?'

The Watcher never raised his eyes from the floor so Tsen didn't get to see his face. He was good with faces. One little virtue in a sea of vices, as he put it himself, but he was a hard man to lie to. It was a skill he found useful mostly when gambling. 'I was in a different world.' The Watcher's voice gave nothing away. 'The Picker was already dead.'

'The Picker is *dead*?' Tsen shook his head. 'An accident? No. Someone ... someone *killed* an Elemental Man?' That was supposed to be impossible, wasn't it?

'He was killed by a dragon, Hands of the Sea Lord. Sea Lord Quai'Shu ...' the Watcher seemed to struggle for a moment to find the right words '... has lost his mind.'

Tsen's own thoughts stuttered, fumbling for a place to start.

'Lost his mind? With grief, you mean, for his son?' Hardly seemed likely, knowing Quai'Shu.

Ah yes, and then of course *it* had to come, that stupid sly little thought. *The sea lord is mad? His heir is dead? He'll need a new one then, won't he? One who can see out his vision. And there's no reason for it to be someone who's tied to him by blood, none at all. It could be anyone. A kwen or a hsian. Or a ... a t'varr?*

Shut up! Stupid nasty little thought. Could at least have had the decency to wait until later when he was alone.

Then a different and more chilling thought chased it out. *'The fleet?' Not much point in being the sea lord of nothing after all ...*

Quiet, you!

'There is some damage but most remains intact.'

'*Some* damage? LaLa, *some* is a word of terror to a t'varr, especially when what follows is *damage*. *What* damage, exactly?' He shook his head, paused and frowned, still trying to put the pieces together. 'And how do you *know*, LaLa? Where have you been? You were supposed to be in the middle of an inhospitable desert watching my alchemist and Chay-Liang. Not so close to the sea, that.' With the words out and their taint of suspicion hanging between them, he found himself again pondering the incongruity of a sorcerer-assassin who could turn into wind and fire and rain being questioned by a naked man in a bath. A possibly very short-lived naked man in a bath. That was what came of being a sea lord's t'varr, he supposed.

'The moon sorcerers themselves came.' The Watcher sounded awestruck now. 'They brought the dragons. They ... they *showed* us what happened. Chay-Liang and I.'

'Dragons? There are *dragons* now?' *Father and daughter, where does it end?* 'Last I heard we were trying to steal eggs. Are you telling me now that there are dragons, on top of everything else, sitting in my eyrie, a thousand miles from here, wondering what to do with themselves?' That was the t'varr in him. People were dead. For all he knew the world might be ending, but if it was, the offence was that it wasn't ending according to the proper plan. 'Eggs,' he said again, wagging a finger that apparently couldn't restrain itself. 'Hatched in secret and revealed in their own good time.' *Live dragons? Xibaiya! Do the Vespinese know? Who else?*

And what are they worth? He frowned. *Nasty little thought again, away with you!* 'Are they … burning everything? Should we pack our chests and flee across the storm-dark while we still can?' He'd thought he was joking when he started that sentence but by the end he wasn't so sure.

'The alchemist is dealing with them, Hands of the Sea Lord.' The Watcher touched his brow again to the slick marble of the floor. Tsen's head was drowning him in possibilities now, far more than he could manage all at once. He had to pause, if only for a moment.

'Are they … are they everything Quai'Shu said they were? Wild uncontrollable fire-breathing monsters? Unstoppable, yet tamed by this alchemist? They *are* tamed, yes, LaLa?'

The Elemental Man raised his eyes and met Tsen's gaze. Not something he was supposed to do to a sea lord's t'varr but Tsen decided he'd take it as a compliment this time. 'They have left one full-grown adult. It is magnificent, Baros Tsen T'Varr. Unlike anything I have ever seen, and I have seen a great deal. I do not fear any man in any realm, nor any beast, but I fear this dragon.' The Watcher's eyes went back where they were supposed to be. 'Hands of the Sea Lord, yes, they are tamed but the alchemist urges you to return as swiftly as you can to the eyrie. He—'

Tsen cut him off. 'No, no. The fleet will be here in a few days. I can't leave until I've seen it for myself. Do they still carry anything interesting or have all the eggs hatched and mysteriously flown to my eyrie by the hand of some mostly mythical wizards?' *My eyrie?* He raised an inner eyebrow at himself. How easy *that* came. 'No, I need *him* to come to *me*. I need him to bring one of these dragons. A manageable one.' Stupid thoughts came at him now as they always did, ones that had no business giving themselves a voice: *This is no way to take a bath.* 'I'm sorry to treat you as a messenger but a jade raven won't be as quick and so I need you to do this for me. Make these arrangements at the eyrie and then return here and be with me when the fleet arrives and we shall see for ourselves whether Quai'Shu has yet found the mind again that he so carelessly lost.'

The Elemental Man didn't withdraw, which struck Tsen as odd as their conversation was clearly finished. 'Hands of the Sea Lord, the fleet is not coming here.'

'What?'

'They have set course for Khalishtor.'

'Well, who told them to do *that*?'

'I suppose our sea lord.' The Watcher bowed and backed away now, shuffling on his knees until he almost vanished in the steam-haze in the far corner of the bathhouse. There was a pop of wind and a swirl of mist and he was gone. Tsen sank slowly back into the water. The edge had gone from its heat, or maybe he was just getting used to it. His glass was all but empty. Still, he'd enjoy it for as long as he could. *And there I was, complaining away at the burden of my work when it was merely ordinary.*

He sent for Kalaiya again. All the preparations he'd made to receive the eggs would have to change. Stick everything in a ship and sail to Khalishtor, he supposed, and all his people too. That alone would keep half the palace busy. But it wouldn't be quick enough. Glasships. He'd have to use the house glasships. And then if Quai'Shu had lost his mind then the Council of Sea Captains in Khalishtor would have to be told. He'd need to talk to the fleet treasurer before *that* could happen. He'd need to know how truly bad it was. And there were other arrangements to be made. The council's debate on the Ice Witch that Quai'Shu had quietly paid a great deal of money to postpone until the proper time.

Kalaiya, when she returned, eased into the water beside him and wrapped her hands around his face and kissed his brow. People saw her with him and assumed so much. *There he goes. Him and his slave.* They had no idea.

She pushed up beside him, turned and put a finger to his nose. 'I have a wager for you.' She smirked. 'One I think I'm going to win.'

'Oh yes?'

'Yes.'

Oh, go on then. Every man had his vices, after all.

23

The Kwen

Slowly, through their thick accents, Zafir understood what her broken birds were. Bed-slaves, harem girls, except she'd gutted the master of their harem and now they had no one to serve. They should have been pleased then, she thought, but they weren't.

Three days after the dragons broke loose, the Taiytakei sighted land. They sent her down from the decks and bolted the chain still around her wrist to the roof beams and she was a prisoner again. The urge to fight them burned her but she let them do it, played out her act of compliance for now. She watched from her window as the ships of the fleet arrayed themselves in the shelter of a cluster of tiny islands, and when her own vessel turned on its anchor with the shifting of the wind, she saw the line of a distant shore. Caught between the turquoise ripples of the sea and the bright deep blue of the sky, a single cloud-shrouded mountain rose behind the glimmer of a city nestled in the gentle sweep of a bay. That night she saw fires burning across the shore and gleaming lines of light. The next day, up on the headlands at either end of the bay, towers glittered and shone when the sun caught them just so, towers as tall as her own Tower of Air, perhaps greater still. Her stomach fluttered with anticipation. When she was alone she looked long and hard at the chain on her wrist.

'Where are we?' Little boats rowed constantly back and forth across the still sea. The Taiytakei were confused. She could feel it in the air. Every sailor knew what to do, every ship, every captain, every soldier, every slave and yet they had no leader. They were a perfect but headless machine.

'Khalishtor, mistress.' She still had her three broken birds, though one of them truly *was* broken now from the sight of the dragon and often simply stood, mouth open, eyes blank and looking at nothing. Zafir called her Onyx for want of her real name.

Onyx in memory of the dragon Jehal had stolen over Evenspire. There was Myst, who'd kept her wits and who clearly worshipped her but still didn't speak. And Brightstar. All names she'd given them after favoured dragons from her eyries. They were ignorant and knew almost nothing but they were all she had.

'And what is Khalishtor?'

'Their greatest city.' Brightstar talked, although not much. Her skin was lighter than the others and she spoke with an accent that Zafir had never heard.

'Their capital?'

'Their Caladir,' said Brightstar emphatically. Zafir had no idea what she meant. Their City of Dragons? Let that be good enough.

'What will they do with me?' It was hard not to be scared now. Alone at night she lay awake, wondering why they kept her alive at all. Yearning for home and a life she'd never really had, but even if she somehow got away and returned, surely all that waited for her now was to hang in one of her own cages outside the Adamantine Palace, food for the crows. The war had come and she'd lost. Sometimes, in the dead of night, she wept and then hated herself for being so weak. And looked at the chain again and remembered wrapping it around her neck; but to her that way seemed weaker still.

On the second morning at anchor a speck in the sky drew her eyes over the glitter and gleam of the city. A dragon, she thought at first, for what else could it be, but it glistened and shone like a star while dragons were always dark. As she stared, she saw another and then another, drifting over the sea towards the ships, slow like clouds and not like dragons at all. As they drew nearer she saw how they pulsed and flickered, catching the sun's light now and then. They were … She had no idea. Shapes in the sky. Discs of gleaming glass tinged and rimmed with gold, great wheels within other wheels all slowly spinning, sky-ships floating with no means of support. The outermost wheel, the largest by far, lay flat, turning slowly around four more inner discs, smaller and smaller, nested one within the other around the innermost sphere and all at different angles, each spinning faster than the last. Lines of gold caught the sun and glittered like a spider's web within the glass and a single orb hung beneath each great disc, golden eggs suspended from delicate silver chains.

Sky-ships the size of dragons. No sails, no masts, no oars, no wings. They came to the fleet and hung above it and Zafir stared at them like a child, as she might once have stared at her first dragon if dragons hadn't been a part of her life for as long as she could remember. The orbs descended on their chains until she couldn't see them any more. She thought, as they came lower, that she saw little round windows in their golden shells.

'What are those?'

'Glasships, mistress.' Brightstar and Myst were staring too, as awed as she was. 'Beautiful, mistress.'

Beautiful. The word broke their spell. Zafir looked away. 'Perhaps. But they are not dragons.'

The sun crept overhead and the glasships floated away. Another frenzy of boats flitted among the fleet and Zafir passed the long hours counting them, seeing where they went. As the sun set fire to the far horizon, Myst brought her a silver bowl of steaming stew and a tall glass of clear liquid with bright crimson leaves floating in it. Brightstar brought fresh clothes. Onyx had a small chest.

'Tomorrow, mistress. The sea lord wishes to see you tomorrow.' They bowed to her and put everything down and backed away. 'Do you wish us to dress you, mistress?'

'In the morning. Now go away.'

They left and she glimpsed Taiytakei soldiers outside her door as they did, frightening forms armoured in great clattering plated layers of glass and gold that made them look a little like giant insects, but tall and broad-shouldered like her Adamantine Men. Their faces were like coal and their eyes like lamps beneath their helms and their gold-glass visors. They carried swords, short narrow stabbing things, and great spiked clubs, and golden-glowing wands at their belts where their hands rested. Over each glittering carapace of armour were draped streamers of colourful cloth and great black cloaks made of feathers. But she saw their faces too, looking back in at her, saw how nervous and uneasy they were. She smiled to herself and took strength from that. So they should be, for they had a dragon-queen in their cage.

She ignored the tray and the clothes and the chest, staying at the window as the sun set, looking out at the distant city far across the waves. Lights filled one part of it, the highest part, raised on a little hill and overlooking the sea at one end of the bay. Not a castle. Something else. It was the place where the flying ships of glass had gone.

The food had turned cold by the time she looked away but she ate it anyway. The meats and vegetables were things she didn't recognise but they were spiced with flavours she knew from the Taiytakei traders who'd once come to her mother's kitchens in the Pinnacles. She pulled the leaves out of the glass of water and threw them away. They had a flavour to them that she remembered from long ago but couldn't quite place. A visit to King Tyan in Furymouth, perhaps. Perhaps the first time she'd met the young Prince Jehal.

She paused for a moment, caught in that memory. The first day they'd seen each other they'd both known what would happen. She'd had a fire in her for him from the moment she'd seen him, and she'd lit one in him as well. He wasn't her first conquest but he was certainly her quickest. There hadn't been anything in the world more important than finding a way to get away from her family, to drag him to a place where they could be alone. They'd understood each other in the merging of sweat in a way that no one else ever had. They were perfect.

The glass shattered in her hand.

One day, be it tomorrow or ten years from now, she'd find a way home to watch him burn. To flay him and scatter his body with salt and listen to him scream. She'd do it herself.

She was bleeding. The glass had cut her. Not deeply. She ripped a piece from the silk sheets – another reminder of Jehal, since all the sheets they'd stained between them had come from the silk farms that Jehal and King Tyan guarded as though they were dragon eggs. There'd been trouble with the Taiytakei about the silk farms once. Long before she was born and she didn't know much about it and didn't care either, but someone had tried to teach her some history once and Tyan's silk farms and the Taiytakei had been a part of it. Tyan's dragons had burned their ships. She didn't remember why.

She wrapped her hand and squeezed it tight, watching the blood ooze, savouring the pain. Sometimes any feeling at all was better than nothing, and when she let her head sink into the soft Taiytakei pillow and closed her eyes, she dreamed of Jehal. Not of the revenge she yearned for but of more pleasant things. Of the times before Evenspire when they'd been lovers. Of what they used to do and how it had felt and how she knew it had felt to him, how it should still have been. She yearned for the comfort he used to bring and how he'd made her be not alone any more. When she woke in the small hours of the morning her pillows were damp with tears, and she clenched her fists and raged at herself and flapped the silk until it was dry so that no one would see and then lay there in the dark, staring up at the faceless wood over her head.

Her broken birds came back at sunrise. Hers? Yes, she was beginning to think of them that way. They looked at the blood on the sheets and on her hand and gasped when they saw the broken glass. Perhaps they thought she'd opened a vein rather than be taken by whoever this sea lord was. Zafir, as she rubbed her eyes, laughed at their horror.

'I am not some pampered harem lady,' she spat. 'I am a dragon-queen. I've burned cities and I've killed men, and women too. I've gone into battle armoured in a dragon's skin. I've stood and fought with sword and axe. Look at you, staring at blood as if it's some terror.' She tore the silk bandage off her hand, opening the wound again so that a line of crimson ran down her arm and dripped onto the bed. She clenched her fist. 'Blood is life. What are you, if you don't understand this?'

They paled and Zafir laughed again. She thought of taking a shard of the broken glass, of hiding it somewhere in her clothes as a weapon, but whom would she cut with it? One of these poor pathetic slaves? To what end? Out of spite? No. A fearsome slave she would be, proud and unbroken until some man came with the desire and the strength to tame her, and she would let him, at least until the moment came to cut out his heart and be free.

'Dress me.' She let them have their way with her this time. They cleaned her wound, took precious jewels and silver and draped them around her neck and her wrists. They painted her face, darkened her skin, drew delicate designs onto the backs of her hands and wrapped her in violet silks that would have been the envy of any princess. When they were done with her they sat silent and still, waiting.

'Why are so you afraid?' she asked, for they were shaking, but they wouldn't talk, wouldn't even look at her today. She stared at them. Looked them over one more time, trying to read their stories from the way they held themselves and finding almost nothing.

'Do you come from the desert?' she asked them.

She got a look from Onyx, of all of them, a pleading look with a hint of wondering whether she was mad to ask. The other two didn't flinch.

'What became of my dragons? Do you know? Did they simply fly away?' Nothing, and she was left to wait in silence.

The sun outside her little window reached its zenith and moved on. Gleaming specks rose from the city once more and drifted towards the ship. The waiting gnawed at her.

'Some bread.' She snapped her fingers. 'And a little honey. You *do* have honey?' Her stomach rumbled. Half a day with nothing to eat, nothing to do. She was hungry and bored and tense as a tripwire but her broken birds didn't move. Out in the sky the glass-ships drifted closer. Zafir refused to look at them today, to even acknowledge they were there. Alone she might have gawped but not here and now, not with these women. With her slaves' eyes watching her, these miracles were nothing. Nothing to a dragon-queen. She wouldn't allow it. *You must have a heart as hard as diamond now.* Her mother's words after she'd woken for the first time to find blood between her legs.

'If I don't have something to eat soon, I'll have to eat one of *you*.'

Brightstar twitched. They were still afraid of her. It had been that way from the moment the hatchling dragon had come smashing through the wood and she'd faced it down but today it was crawling all over them. Afraid of what? That she'd call back the dragons to her? But if she had power to do *that* then she'd have used it long ago.

'I won't hurt you,' she said a few minutes later. 'Why would I?'

The door crashed open, thrown wide without any warning. A Taiytakei stood before her, dressed as she'd come to know them in the City of Dragons. Coal-skinned as they all were but his clothes were rainbow-bright, a dazzle of swirling colour embroidered in exquisite silver and gold and laced with more jewels than she could count. Gaudy to her eyes, but she knew this was the Taiytakei way.

Over his shoulders hung a cloak of silver feathers. Two soldiers stood behind him in their plated armour of glass and gold. Their feathered cloaks were black like the ones she'd seen before but the streamers of silk they wore beneath were lurid and filled with shapes and colour. Two brilliant lightning bolts crossed over their chests.

This is the sea lord? Zafir met his eyes. Myst and Brightstar and Onyx fell to their knees beside the bed and pressed their faces into the wooden floor but Zafir didn't move. He was a handsome enough fellow if you looked past the garish clothes and the colour of his skin. Tall. Strong. Well muscled. She looked him up and down, appraising him as she might a horse or a hatchling dragon. A little flicker of heat stirred inside her. She licked her lips. That would be what he wanted, after all. Men always did.

'Shrin Chrias Kwen,' barked one of the black-cloaks. 'Heart of the Sea Lord.'

'Bend your knee, slave!' snapped the other. His accent was so thick that it took a moment for Zafir to understand what he'd said. They pushed into the room but she ignored them and kept her eyes on the one with the silver cloak. The one who thought he was the master here.

A black-cloak drew back a hand to strike her. She would let him, she decided, but silver-cloak stopped him. 'Don't! Don't mark her. The sea lord will see her as she is.'

So that's not you? Then you're no longer important to me. She felt a small pang of disappointment even as she lost all interest in him. *Pity.* She held out a languorous hand, still with the silver chain sealed around her wrist, every gesture made with exquisite care to show how little he mattered to her. He would have to release her now. 'Shall we go?'

Her broken birds still quivered on the floor and their terror filled the room. Zafir drank it, savoured it like a fine wine. Silver-cloak bared his teeth at her. Perhaps it was supposed to frighten her but dragons had done the same many times over the years. She raised an eyebrow very slightly, contempt hurled in his face. The muscles in his arms tightened. 'You are a slave,' he said to her. 'A nothing. When you meet the sea lord, you will bow. You will press your face to the floor as these women are doing, and you will keep it there unless you are told otherwise. And you will show me, now, that you understand.' He spoke with deliberate care. The words sounded awkward coming out of his mouth as though he was in the middle of eating something. But she understood them. She smiled and spoke slowly back.

'You wish me to be like them. I understand. And I will not.' Once more she held out her hand. 'Shall we go?'

Silver-cloak snapped out some more words, too harsh and sharp and fast for Zafir to follow. Without hesitation one of the black-cloaks unsheathed his sword, narrow and pointed. A thing for finding gaps. Zafir barely managed not to flinch but the black-cloak's eyes weren't on her. He lifted his sword high and drove it down into Brightstar as she kowtowed, trembling and almost weeping with her fear. He drove it straight through her heart and she died without a sound. A stain of bright blood spread across her white silk shift and pooled on the floor. Silver-cloak never took his eyes from Zafir. 'Show me you understand,' he said again.

Zafir laughed in his face. Killing people she barely even knew? What was that supposed to show? That he hadn't the first idea what it was to be a dragon-queen, what it was to live around such monsters in a world where people died every day, not out of malice but out of carelessness, out of simply being in the wrong place as a dragon swished its tail or stretched its wings. Yet he'd lit something in her with what he'd done. A cold fury. 'Do you think,' she asked him, 'that any part of me does more than pity you?' Her smile was wide now. Couldn't help it. Not long ago it had been a hatchling staring down at her from the hole ripped in the roof of her cabin, a hatchling awake and with every reason to burn her and crush her and eat her. And here was a man, a nothing more, who thought to frighten her? She shrugged. 'Kill another if you must. Lessen yourself even further.'

'Show me you understand!' he ordered again but his face already told her that she'd won, and oh how he hated her for that!

Zafir closed her eyes and shook her head, soft and sad. 'I understand,' she said, 'that people will die. People around me. People who stand too close. So it has always been.' She opened her eyes again and fixed him with them. 'I understand that I am a dragon-queen, Shrin Chrias Kwen, Heart of the Sea Lord. And *you* are standing too close.'

The black-cloaks unlocked the bracelet from her wrist then, and silver-cloak gut-punched her so hard that, even seeing it coming, she doubled over and gasped. They forced her down, all of them far stronger than her, until her head touched the floor, and then dragged her away. She half expected silver-cloak to kill her other broken birds out of spite, simply not knowing what else to do, but he didn't. It was to his credit, she thought. Not that it would save him when the time came.

Shrin Chrias Kwen. Heart of the Sea Lord. She wondered what that meant.

24

An Understanding

Tsen wished he could take Kalaiya with him to Khalishtor but such things weren't done and so he left her behind in Xican and took instead a pang of regret and a small hole in his heart. Xican to Khalishtor by glasship was four days without a break, even in the smallest gondola, which crammed him into a golden egg not much bigger than the bath in his bathhouse. Other men might have taken longer, overnighting on the Bal Ithara and in Shevana-Daro, or at least breaking the journey for a night in Zinzarra. But LaLa had left him in no doubt that time was of the essence and he preferred to spend what little of it he could spare in his bath in Xican; then, too, it didn't escape him that hanging in a tiny golden sphere drifting through the air was probably the safest place he could possibly be. Encased in metal was the one place an Elemental Man couldn't reach him.

He sighed. The stupid nasty little thoughts kept bothering him. He and Kalaiya had talked for hours after LaLa had gone about what had happened, what it meant, what it *might* mean and last of all – because the stupid nasty little thoughts had to have their way – about who *else* might become Quai'Shu's heir; and by the time she'd finished pointing out exactly how many would have their eyes on such a prize and thus might see him as a threat now, all he wanted was to curl up deep in his apple orchards and live out his days making wine. She'd talked him out of that but they'd agreed that he should stay in the glasship.

Quai'Shu's fleet, when Tsen reached Khalishtor, had already been anchored out in the islands for a day. Shrin Chrias Kwen was there ahead of him – of course he was – trying to work his head around what in the eight worlds had happened. Jima Hsian, as far as either of them knew, was either in Vespinarr or Dhar Thosis and had no idea that the fleet had arrived back. Neither of them felt inclined to hurry the news to him. Every day, after all, was an advantage, and hsians – more than any other – hankered to be their own masters.

He wondered vaguely if LaLa could be persuaded to kill Chrias for him – how immensely helpful *that* would be – but the Elemental Man served Quai'Shu, not him, so he made his own arrangements and now here he was, sitting in his gold-handled chair in the cabin of his glasship with a slightly perplexed expression on his face, surrounded by all the things that made four days in a ridiculously expensive prison vaguely bearable, hoping without much hope that someone would find him some decent food and wishing he was back in Khalishtor in Quai'Shu's tower in the Palace of Glass, gazing out over the glorious Crown of the Sea Lords and the Proclamatory with a glass of apple wine in his hand, looking forward to a nice hot bath and without a single thought wasted on who among his many 'friends' would be the first to try and have him murdered.

All in all not exactly the best of moods.

Behind him a tiny hatch led to where the pilot golem did whatever it was that made the glasship work. Tsen left that sort of thing to others. Experts. He knew how sails worked and he knew how money worked, and, when he put his mind to it, he knew how people worked; and that was quite enough. He'd had a good look, though, over four days of having nothing much else to do, and yes, if you tried hard, you *could* squeeze an assassin inside if you wanted to. Just as well no one had. But apparently assassins and all the nasty little ways they'd soon set about murdering each other would have to wait, at least for a little while. *Apparently* there was something more important.

And what, in the name of sea and sail, shall I do with you?

The woman in front of him was dressed like an exquisite harem slave, if you ignored the bandage around one of her hands – *dressed* like one, but clearly she'd never spent a day being taught how to hold herself or how to behave. She stood between two soldiers – Quai'Shu's personal guard, by the black feathers of their cloaks – who were holding her surprisingly tightly, one gripping each arm. Shrin Chrias Kwen stood to one side puffed up like a peacock in all his formal glory, an extremely angry peacock today although he tried hard to hide it. In fact, out of all of them, the only one who looked at ease was the slave herself. The dragon-queen. The one who'd killed Zifan'Shu, driven Quai'Shu insane by some accounts and Chrias to a repressed fury that verged on incandescence; and now here she was meeting his eye as though *he* was the one who ought to be on his knees with his face pressed to the floor. He almost couldn't help liking her. He had a soft spot for unruly slaves, especially ones who rubbed Chrias up the wrong way. Perhaps his own inner meekness admired them for being fierce. The thought made him smile. *Just ask Kalaiya.*

'You wanted to see her, T'Varr. Well, here she is. And now she's to be hanged.' Chrias spoke shortly, sharply, before Tsen could say a word. The kwen's jaw was clenched tight, drawing the muscles in his neck taut and making them stand out from his skin. Tsen raised an eyebrow. Inside he tutted to himself. *Our kwen barely on his own leash? My, my, what did you do, slave? I think I like you more and more.* He nodded to himself at his own wisdom and then grinned at his own folly.

'A visiting monarch from another realm?' Tsen cocked his head. 'And you wish to *hang* her?' *Careful now, tongue, before the nasty little thoughts make you lash him. Our dear kwen surely sees himself as the next sea lord, and* he *has the favour of the lady of Xican behind him. What do* you *have? Not so much. So careful, tongue. Careful.*

'A slave who killed a Taiytakei. There are no exceptions.'

'Not for slaves, that is true.' Tsen nodded as if that was the end of the matter. Then he cocked his head again. *'Is* she a slave?'

'Of course she is ...'

Ah, the quiet satisfaction of a trap seen a moment too late. Tsen smiled. Beamed. He made a show of getting up and inspecting the woman's arms. They had a strength to them, certainly more than any bed-slave would have, however exquisite. 'I wasn't sure.' He kept on smiling, right in Chrias's face. 'She might have been a guest under our lord's hospitality, in which case her fate would belong to him and not to any of us here at all. But since she is a slave ...' he looked up and held Chrias's eye '... an *unbranded* slave, that is, then she is nothing. A thing. Property. Not a person at all.' He let out a heavy sigh and nodded as if finding himself with yet another terrible burden to add to the many he already carried. Not that that was far from the truth. 'Very well. She is an unbranded slave and so she is a *thing* and not a person and thus is the responsibility of a t'varr and not a kwen. You have your point, Chrias. She's mine and I will have the pain of dealing with her.' He let the woman's arms go, watching her from the corner of one eye and Chrias from the corner of the other. *And now, tongue, say something nice. Something flattering. Send our lord's kwen away with at least some little bone to play with, eh?* 'Well I thank you, Chrias, for the never-ending petty troubles you send my way. Still, I dare say you have enough on your own plate just now, what with all those sail-slaves and sword-slaves and soldiers of our lord's guard who all failed so fatally in their duty to keep Zifan'Shu separated from dangerous sharp objects?' His glance flicked to the two black-cloaks. *Oh well done, tongue. Well done.* In his head he gave himself a sarcastic round of applause. He might as well have come out and called Chrias an incompetent horse's arse. *Ah well, at least we're keeping alive the cliché that a kwen and a t'varr can never really stand each other.* Much *more important than trying not to humiliate a man who doubtless already wants us to go and die somewhere quiet in a ditch. Good good, tongue. Nice work. Now shut up.* He feigned another heavy sigh. 'Leave her to me then, Chrias. I will arrange a fate that will be deeply unpleasant. Hanging is far too good for her.' *And now let's see if he has these two soldiers run me through. It would be a kwen-ish sort of thing to do. Gets it all over with and out in the open, after all.*

LaLa was here, a part of the air around them. Did Chrias know that? Would it make a difference? He didn't know. Didn't know whether LaLa could be quick enough either. He turned away, waiting for Chrias to either leave him or kill him. Quai'Shu was useless now. Tsen had seen that and so had Chrias. Zifan'Shu was dead. There was, as LaLa had suggested, no clear successor, in which case the first to grab the spoils often won, but *which* spoils, that was the thing. Chrias would take Xican. There'd be no stopping him and Tsen had no intention of trying. *And then we'll see whether these dragons are worth everything Quai'Shu promised, and if they're not then we raise our hands, drop out of the game and start making wagers on who's left standing at the end. Eh?* He felt relieved beyond words that he'd sent Kalaiya ahead to the eyrie before he'd left. She'd be where Chrias couldn't get to her, but he felt like such a fool too, because he'd only sent her ahead of him out of a selfish desire to have her with him again as soon as he could. For her own safety? Hadn't even crossed his mind until he'd reached Khalishtor.

The kwen was still standing there. Baros Tsen waved him away until he wasn't and it was just him and the woman and the eyes of his hidden guardian. He felt absurdly excited. *Because Chrias and I just declared war? I suppose the chance of being murdered is something that some might find exciting. Hadn't ever thought I'd be one of them, though.* He gave a little nod to the slave woman. 'I am Baros Tsen. Hands of the Sea Lord of Xican,' he said.

The woman looked him over and clearly found him wanting, as most women instinctively did. 'I am Zafir, dragon-queen of the Silver City and speaker of the nine realms.'

Tsen put on his best affable smile and spoke as politely as he could. 'You were all those things but now you are a slave.' He tried to look sorry for her but it probably wasn't working. '*My* slave. Chrias Kwen wants to hang you. Should I let him? I understand you were intent on burning all my ships with your monsters when you were taken.'

'I was.' She smiled back at him, the smile of a snake. 'Give me back my monsters and I still will.' She had a pretty face, Tsen thought. Very, very pretty. The rest of her was a bit of this and that. Good muscles, athletic, well shaped. Her skin let her down, though. It wasn't as smooth as it could be, rough and blemished in places and, of course, ghostly pale. Maybe an enchanter could do something about that. She could do some with fattening-up too, but the proportions were good and her face was striking and her eyes were lively and bright. Not bad. Nothing special, though.

He shook his head. 'Ach, I could probably get a half-decent price for you, but you're not really a head-turner.'

She spluttered and inside his head Tsen patted himself on the shoulder. *Weakness found.*

'Chrias says you've driven our sea lord insane.'

'I would have killed him if I'd got to him. Your old one stared into the eyes of a dragon and his mind broke. It broke one of my slaves as well. A quiet little girl, timid and frail, and a great lord who thinks himself a master of worlds.' She snapped her fingers. 'Gone.'

'Slaves like you do not have slaves of their own,' he told her.

She shrugged. 'You may say that is so, but *they* know.'

Tsen took a deep breath. *Yes, well you* started *well, T'Varr.* 'I begin to see why you and my dear friend the kwen fail so marvellously to get along. You killed our sea lord's son. Do you not see how that poses something of a problem?' *And now shall I take a wager on who will win if we keep on with our sparring?*

The dragon slave – he was already starting to think of her as that – licked her lips. 'Does it not trouble you that I might kill you too?'

Tsen laughed and shook his head. 'No. No, it does not.'

She held up her bandaged hand, flicked her hair and looked him in the eye, a smile playing at the corner of her mouth. 'I almost a brought a shard of glass with me. I had one to hand. If I *had* brought it, I might have used it.'

'To what end?' Tsen looked her over one more time. 'Whatever you were before, you *are* a slave now, mine for my sins and probably lengthy regret. I will parade you about, share you with my friends, speak with you about the realms from which you come and finally tire of you. Amuse me and your life will be a pleasant one. Disappoint me or step out of line and, well, you've seen Chrias Kwen. I'll just give you away to whoever wants you. That's all. You may go now.'

She leaned towards him, watching him, looking for something and not finding it. 'You don't desire me at all, do you?' She sounded amused. Surprised. And beneath that the ghost of something else. Relief, was it?

'Not at all.' He waved her away and she took her dismissal far better than Chrias had done. 'You can come out now,' he said when she was gone. Beside the spot where the dragon slave had stood, the air swirled and grew solid and turned into the shape of the Watcher. 'And what do *you* think, LaLa?'

The Watcher bowed. 'She will not bend to you, Hands of the Sea Lord. The Heart has the right of it.'

'Hang her?'

'Quietly and quickly. Get it over and done.'

Baros Tsen shook his head. 'No. Get the slaves who were attending her. I'll speak to them. And make sure no one hurts her. If she's no use then Chrias Kwen can have his way but I'll be sure of that before I let him play.'

'Use?'

'LaLa? Really! Think!' Tsen beamed at the killer. 'If she truly is who she says, you cannot deny she must know a thing or two about dragons.'

'Enough to be worth the life of our lord's heir?' The Elemental Man sounded doubtful.

Tsen shrugged. *Careful here, tongue. Remember whom he serves.* 'Well we won't know that until we ask her, now will we? Now hurry along before Chrias Kwen does something stupid, and let us *all* remember whom we serve. When she's got nothing left to say, she can still hang but it doesn't work *nearly* as well the other way round.'

The Watcher left. Tsen's gaze followed him across the decks. *Chrias will get Xican. He'll get the Stoneguard. He'll get the fleet. And I get her? These dragons had better be good, old man.*

25

That Which a Dragon May Not Have

The dragon once called Silence remembered its first hatching. It remembered the world breaking. It remembered many lives lived but it had never crossed the sea, not in a single one of its hundred lifetimes. Long ago before the one silver half-god had returned and betrayed them all, it had tried. It had flown far across the water, flown for days and found nothing but waves and sea and a storm and then emptiness. A nothingness, as though its consciousness had passed through a cloud. And then a moment of waking again, already burning from the inside, and the sight of a black and empty void and violet lightning rattling around and then gone. Over to the realm of the dead, to Xibaiya to seek another shell.

It left the little ones and their ships and the weak pretend half-gods behind it and flew back the way it had come, reaching out with every sense for the home it remembered, the world it knew and the dragons that were its kind. The air grew thick and dark. Storms broke around it. The dragon flew on. Violet lightning split the sky and black clouds roiled thicker and thicker. The place it had found before, but this time it was more careful. This time it would look to see what the half-gods had done to the world at their end.

It wasn't alone in its awakening. Other dragons remembered, if they still lived. The white one that had come to break it out of its prison. Alimar Ishtan vei Atheriel, in the syllables of the half-gods. The little ones had called her Snow. An unbecoming name. And others too, and the ruin they'd burned among the cities and palaces and lives of the little ones had been glorious until the Earthspear had torn its soul and skin apart and hurled it back to Xibaiya once more. All had hung in the balance and Silence wanted to know: *Did we win? Or am I alone?*

So it flew back towards that land but the storms and the lightning were a wall and a chasm and an end of the world with no way to pass, not even for a dragon. Beyond, where the sea and the distant dragon realms should have been, there was nothing. The dragon followed the line of the storm for a hundred miles and found it had no end. It flew high, so high that even in the bright sunlight of the day the sky fell black and stars winked. It found no passage.

You called me Silence. You said that was my name but it is not.

Here the world was broken. And amid the chaos, on the edge of the unravelling of creation, it sensed a familiar presence once more.

Dragon ...

... you have something that is not yours.

It must be returned.

It is not for you.

The feeble shadows of its creators again. Yes, and it had devoured one of them and taken its essence. It looked at the elemental anarchy all around it, at the formless nothing just out of reach. *You did this*, it said. *You broke the world. You tore it to pieces.*

Yes ...

... our kind and yours.

And then you pieced it back together again and plastered over the cracks, imperfect and doomed to fail. The dragon turned away. Any closer and it would start to unravel, the very essence of what it was dissolving into foam and smoke. The little ones had found a way through. How did they do that? It peered at the churning darkness at the broken edge of creation. There was an inside to it. There were ... there were *things* in there. It strained its senses. Things that were familiar.

Dragons? Spirits? *The dead?*

You too found a way through ...

... many of you ...

... through the realm of the dead ...

... through shattered Xibaiya that should not be.

Between its lives it met the souls of other dragons now and then. Most were dull and dim and passed quickly away. But there were some who had woken long ago, and other things too. Sometimes they spoke as their spirits passed in the ruins of Xibaiya. It had seen, many times, the hole where the dead Earth Goddess and her slayer had held the Nothing at bay for so long, but they were gone now. The Nothing was seeping through and the hole was growing. Now *there* was something that could kill a dragon. *One of your kind has ripped the old wound open.*

Growing and getting worse.

In lands far away ...

... with unfamiliar names ...

... in the places closest to the cracks ...

... even the little ones do not die properly any more.

The dragon stared back at the formless void, the primal edge of creation that lay before it. *It is getting worse. WHAT HAVE YOU DONE?*

A hand gripped inside it. The dragon called Silence froze in the air, unable to move.

You cannot keep what you have taken.

We must have it back ...

... with regret ...

... but we know you understand ...

... and know that we wish you well upon your return.

It was a strange death, unlike any other it could remember. The other times it had felt the heat rise inside it, consuming from within, a comforting warmth into which it sank, deeper and deeper, until it woke in Xibaiya, a fleshless spirit. This was more like the snip of a knife as the dragon's spirit howled alone into the realm of the dead.

One of our kind?

No ...

... it was not us ...

... it was a daughter of the sun who did this.

Tuuran

26

The Palace of Leaves

Many months before the dragon-queen came across the sea, Tuuran arrived with the alchemist Bellepheros in the Taiytakei port of Xican. He nearly died and so became the alchemist's sworn sword. The Taiytakei merely saw it as the giving of a slave and the alchemist wouldn't have understood, but, as they were winched from their ship, Tuuran spoke an oath quietly and softly in his head. The alchemist Bellepheros had saved his life and so now that life would be his shield; and as they stood beside one another at the top of the cliffs and stared for the first time at the City of Stone and the Palace of Leaves, he wondered for a moment what Crazy Mad, his strange friend for the last three years, would have made of what he saw. Because Crazy was complicated and Tuuran was simple, and it was all just far too big to fit inside his head.

Sometimes, when Tuuran had been younger and was still being forged as an Adamantine Man, he'd lain awake at nights, wondering what it must have been like for the first men to be freed of the tyranny of dragons. Living in their caves and their tunnels, dark and cold and hungry until the man of living silver came with the Earthspear and the world was suddenly changed. How it had felt to walk outside into the warm balmy breeze and the bright sun and feel it on your skin for the first time without the creeping dread and the urge to look up, always to look up. How it was to run in grassy fields and doze beside rivers and sleep for the first time safe and sound under the stars. Most of all he wondered how it must have been to have such a creature as the Silver King appear, a half-god who could snap his fingers and rearrange the world to his liking. What was it like to be around such a presence, to see miracles occur before your eyes? He tried to imagine these things but he always failed. He was a soldier, after all, strong and fast and obedient, not prone to dreaming but wise enough to understand that some things were simply beyond his reasoning. Some ideas were simply too grand.

Looking up at the Palace of Leaves, Tuuran knew he had his answer. *This. This* was how it had felt. Beside him the alchemist gaped in slack-jawed awe. A maze of shapes hung in the air dangling from pale golden clouds. They shone and gleamed and dazzled. From the stone peaks beneath, a forest of bright towers rose to meet them. Brilliant strands of sunlight stretched among the shapes, between the towers, to the ground and up to the shimmering clouds like the web of some great spider. When Tuuran squinted he could clearly see a ship suspended among the orbs and towers, masts and sails and all, and he could only think that this must be one of the sky-ships of the Taiytakei of which he'd heard. He stared, open-mouthed, while inside where no one would see he laughed at the wonder of it and wept too at how big a thing this was to see. Perhaps like seeing a dragon for the first time, with no previous understanding that such creatures even existed; but where a dragon was a terrible thing of fear and dread, the palace of Xican was god-touched with beauty.

The white witch with the glass lenses fiddled at her belt. The movement drew his eye whether he liked it or not. Slaves learned fast about belts and wands. The gold ones with the inner light, they were the ones you watched for. Discipline wands, the galley slave masters called them, although he'd heard them called other things too. The oar masters and the sail masters used them all the time, casually sending little shocks flying across the decks of their ships to remind the slaves who was in charge. For idleness, mostly; sometimes because they felt like it; but now and then it was for something more and then the cracks of lightning they spat out became the slap of a dragon's tail, the crush of a dragon's claw, pain overwhelming. He'd seen white-skinned men turned black and flaking, their extremities crumbling to ash as though burned by dragon fire. A sail-slave grew a sixth sense for when a wand was pulled from a belt and so Tuuran saw what the enchantress did, even though he never quite stopped looking at the sky-palace either, even though a good part of him felt touched by the presence of a divinity whose name he'd never been told.

'A perk of being what I am,' said the witch and stepped onto the glass disc she'd made. Tuuran still couldn't take his eyes from the palace. Only one power had ever created such things as these. The Silver King, but the Silver King was gone. Witchcraft and alchemy and blood-magic? He couldn't believe any of those could even begin to craft such marvels.

The Taiytakei shoved him onto the glass disc. As it began to move, the alchemist stumbled. Tuuran caught him. The ground fell away and the palace soared closer. Beneath him the hatchling mountains of the City of Stone seemed even steeper and sharper than they had from the summit of the cliff. Tuuran drank it all in. This! This must be how it felt to fly on the back of a dragon, and suddenly he was filled joy and envy. Joy because an Adamantine Man rarely sat on the back of one of their monsters; and envy because now he understood why the dragon-riders strutted like gods.

He sat down and kept his eyes firmly on the palace. The alchemist looked as though he was going to be sick. *Don't look down.* You learned when they made you climb the cliffs of the Purple Spur, and yes there *was* a thing that passed for a path that wound its way up past the Zar Oratorium, but when you were a half a mile up on a ledge that was a handspan wide, *then* you learned.

The white witch said something. Tuuran didn't hear – his eyes were locked on the palace. He eased the alchemist down to sit beside him, gripping him tight.

'I have you,' he murmured, never looking aside. 'Witchcraft and blood-magic, but we are stronger, Lord Alchemist. We are stronger! Cling to that!'

For a moment he did take his eyes off the palace and its orbs and risked a glance, because even when they *knew* they shouldn't look, every Adamantine Man still did. The sight made him dizzy. They were high over the stones of the city, floating between them, the sea hundreds of feet beneath, an invisible nothing all that was holding him. He gasped and stared and started to laugh with amazement, and then the dizziness took him so hard that he could barely even sit without falling sideways. He squeezed his eyes shut and turned back to the golden towers where the white witch and her flying disc were headed and watched them come closer. The dizziness ebbed.

A wind picked up and grew stronger as they climbed. The

alchemist's fingers dug into his arm, deeper and tighter. As they drew close to the towers he saw they weren't truly gold but gold-tinged glass, huge flat slabs of it as though the tower had been moulded from a single colossal piece. Like the white stone tower of Outwatch they were flawlessly smooth, except Outwatch was all curves and arcs without a single sharp corner, while the gold-glass towers were edges and angles all over. They were heading for the upper reaches of one, one of many, already in the golden half-shadow of the great glass discs overhead. Most of what he'd taken for a giant web he could see were chains running from the sky to the ground, or to the pendulous gold and silver eggs and orbs that hung beneath the discs, or else they were half-seen bridges that ran high between the towers. The sky-ship was below now, its masts and furled-up sails nestled between the towers away to one side, festooned with chains as though it would break free given even a glimpse of freedom. Among all this, kaleidoscope patterns of light and shadow moved slowly through one another as the sunlight met the serene revolutions of the gold-glass structures above.

The witch's disc glided at last to a stop beside the skin of the tower. Tuuran reached to touch it and found it silky. The witch took the black rod from her belt again. She tapped the tower wall and the glass flowed like liquid, rippling back to leave a hole the shape of an egg. The witch put away her rod, looked at the alchemist and then at Tuuran. Bellepheros was swaying where he sat, eyes still tightly shut.

'You might want to help him,' she said and walked calmly through. Tuuran gawped at the hole in the wall and at the cavern-ous hall beyond, a white marble floor full width of the tower between the gold-glass walls. He picked himself up slowly and carefully and gently lifted the alchemist to his feet.

'Eyes still closed, Lord Grand Master,' he whispered, 'but we're here.' Wherever *here* was. A little like a great lord's grand hall in the realms. Like the Speaker's Hall except vastly brighter and made of gold and hundreds of feet above the ground. His eyes were watering. Tears of awe, was it? Yet he couldn't stop himself.

'We are arrived, Lord Alchemist. The ground is stone again.' He let the alchemist go. Through the walls he could see the sky, the muted distant shapes of clouds and of the sea, of the City of Stone below like thousands upon thousands of giant dragon-tooth towers pressed together, rising out of the dark waters. The walls of this hall rose up fifty feet more. Beyond them, past more gold-tinged glass, the shapes of the upper palace hung large and close.

Bellepheros fell to his knees and puked. Slaves came running at once to clean up the mess but Tuuran barely noticed. As the white witch began to walk, his feet followed but his eyes stayed where they were, looking up. Entranced. A hundred spans above his head hung a golden sphere, a small black hole pointing directly down. At the far end of the gold-glass hall the witch tapped her black wand against the wall and another piece of floating glass grew at her feet, forming out of the wall itself. Tuuran flinched back and looked at it askance but the witch stood on it and the other Taiytakei guided the alchemist to sit beside her, and so he had little choice but to join him, legs dangling over the edge, torn between the glorious vista around them, the hypnotism of the distant hole above and the gnawing sense that the glass beneath him was somehow alive and would notice him and either buck him off or eat him at any moment.

When the glass kept on rising and *didn't* eat him, he looked back down to the hall from which they'd come. The handful of slaves who stood there waiting patiently to serve looked small and lost in its enormity.

'Does height not trouble you?' gasped the alchemist. His eyes were screwed tightly shut. The spell of the place faltered for a moment, broken by ordinary words.

'Height? I'm a sail-slave!' Tuuran chuckled. 'A sail-slave who's afraid of heights doesn't last very long. If the floor was pitching and heaving beneath us, the wind howling and the rain flaying the skin off my face, I'd feel quite at home. Height? No.' No, it wasn't the height that made the squirming knot in his belly, even through the rapturous wonder. 'But glorious as these sights may be, Lord Alchemist, I don't like not seeing what holds me from falling. It reeks of witchery.' Even so, witchery or not, its magic still held him – perhaps that more than anything was what made him afraid – that he was bewitched and made so infinitely insignificant. The moment he fell silent he felt himself shrinking again, the colossal tower wrapping itself around him, making him smaller and smaller and smaller.

They passed into empty space and a wind that whipped at sleeves and cuffs and robes. The alchemist yelped and clung with fingers like claws. He had his eyes closed again while Tuuran couldn't even bring himself to blink. 'Is this how it is to ride a dragon?' He held the alchemist tight but what he wanted was to let go. To leap and fly with the wind howling in his face. The world beneath him was shrinking. Suddenly he didn't feel small any more but huge, gripped by a strange need to stand and hold out his arms and somehow embrace the sheer size of everything around him.

He put his hands in front of his eyes, since he couldn't make them close, until the sensation went away and a gloom wrapped him in its shadows and they were out of the sky and up into the lowest belly of the sky-palace itself, surrounded by dark carved wooden walls and bronze plaques and more shining bronze on the floor and other mundane and familiar things. A dragon-king's palace might look like this, perhaps. He'd never seen the inside of one to know, but he'd seen the houses of the rich in the City of Dragons and he'd lived inside the walls of the Adamantine Palace. His eyes flicked everywhere, taking it all in.

There were slaves already waiting for them, branded on both arms with the lightning bolt sigil of the City of Stone. Trusted sword-slaves but these were passive docile things, spiritless palace creatures, invisible servants with scarcely a flicker of life in them. The slaves followed the white witch and the Taiytakei soldiers like broken ghosts in their white tunics, heads bowed, up a single flight of stairs made of bronze and wood and lit by oil lamps, all reeking of the smell Tuuran knew well from the ships he'd sailed: Xizic, the ubiquitous drug of the Taiytakei. Sailors chewed lumps of it when they could get it. Men and women alike bathed in its oil, those who could afford it. Now it seemed they scented their lamp oil with it too.

'The sea lord will see you in the morning.' The white witch with her glass lenses stopped beside a wood and bronze door and opened it. A simple handle, no black rod this time and no lock either. 'These slaves will tend to you. You must be at your best for the sea lord, if you wish to get the most from him.' She winked as though she and the alchemist were part of some conspiracy together but the alchemist didn't seem to notice; Tuuran wasn't sure he'd even heard.

The palace slaves went inside and Tuuran would have followed but the white witch laid a hand on his shoulder for a moment and whispered in his ear, 'Watch him, sail-slave. Guard him. We'll not keep him here for long but when others know of his arrival he will be in danger. I cannot arm you but I will send no slave that you could not easily overpower. You will taste his food. If he dies then it will fall hard on us all. And for those who are slaves, you know what that must mean.'

Tuuran nodded and bowed as she backed away. Slaves knew better than to question what they were told but it struck him as a very strange thing to say, and strange in an uncomfortable sort of way, as if she didn't trust her own men walking right beside her as much as she did a slave she'd barely met. He followed Bellepheros into his room where the palace slaves were already undressing him. Their demeanour changed the moment the witch had gone. Eyes that said they were better than Tuuran, with their two brands to his one. Tutting and muttering, talking about him as if he wasn't there, appalled by the state and the stink of him. He'd seen slaves like this before. The worst of the worst. Sniffing and servile and fawning to their masters, haughty and arrogant among their own. They were looking at him like that now.

He waited while they poured bucket after bucket of water into a bronze bath, then, while the alchemist was bathing and wouldn't see, he picked up the palace slave who was doing the worst of the talking and punched him on the nose. Not much of a punch but the look on the man's face was priceless.

'You ... you! I will have you destroyed for this, sail-slave.' The man kept his voice low, glancing nervously towards Bellepheros in his bath. Then he spat at Tuuran's feet. Still afraid though, and that was what mattered. Tuuran punched him again, harder this time, enough to daze him.

'Do your worst,' he sneered. 'You'll find I barely notice.' He looked from one slave to the next to the next, seeing their faces crumble from disdain to fear. His eyes lingered on the women. Flickers of interest here and there maybe? Or maybe not, maybe that was his imagination and being surrounded by sail-slaves and sailors for too long. Sail-slaves had little enough chance for any pleasure. Now *there* was a thought. Better than the slack-jawed awe that still threatened to sweep him away.

Other slaves came while the alchemist was bathing. They brought food, a great feast when set against the endless rice and beans that Tuuran was used to. The new slaves whispered to the ones already there and the ones already there whispered back and they all stole glances at Tuuran. He smiled and bared his teeth back at them, putting them at their unease, and tasted all the food. He wasn't sure how he'd know if anything was poisoned until he keeled over and died but it was the sort of food that most sail-slaves couldn't dream of even seeing from a distance. The old luxuries of lemons and fire-brandy and wormy biscuits would never be the same after this! It made him laugh, imagining his old friends, Crazy Mad and the rest, bickering over a handful of fresh lemons. And he'd been no better either. Food of the gods, lemons. And now he looked at what was in front of him and shook his head. *Ah, Crazy, if only you could see!*

The thought came to him that he was much larger and stronger than the alchemist and so perhaps a small dose of poison wouldn't trouble him? He tasted the food some more to be sure. It seemed like it was his duty. After he was done, the furious slaves carefully rearranged everything to make it seem untouched. He watched them at it and laughed some more and shook his head.

The alchemist took his time with his ablutions. The palace slaves dressed him when he emerged and then he picked at the food with little interest. If he noticed that half had already gone, he didn't show it. When he was finished, the slaves would have done more if he'd asked but he sent them away. Tuuran watched them go. 'Is this how life is in the Palace of Alchemy?' he asked. Food made for them? Servants and women at their beck and call? Sounded fine enough. Certainly looked it.

'We put on our own clothes and the food is distinctly inferior.' Bellepheros had a faraway look on his face and Tuuran saw something there that stabbed like a knife. A hunger, a desire, a curiosity and a passion and, most of all, a wonder. He'd seen that look before on a woman's face, besotted with him after he'd shown her what an Adamantine lover could be like. She'd called it love. And he felt a touch of it too, but what *he* felt was awe, and awe wouldn't stop him from trying to go home. What he saw in the alchemist, that was the seed of something more.

'You'll get comfortable here, Lord Grand Alchemist. Careful with that.' He wrinkled his nose and sniffed uneasily. The room smelled of sweet fruit and a touch of Xizic. Seductive. He looked away and back again at the alchemist in case he was wrong but he wasn't.

'In the Palace of Alchemy we're masters of our own destiny. Here I am not. They can never hide that.' The alchemist snorted but that look in his eye didn't shift one little bit.

'You will. I would.'

The alchemist waved at the food. 'Help yourself. Enjoy it while it's here.'

Tuuran dutifully tried a little bit of everything again. 'Better than ship's rations, that's for sure.' He looked longingly at the door, wishing for the women magically to reappear. For all he knew this was the one night he'd have in this palace and then he'd be back to the sails or the oars. Or maybe the slave he'd punched was more important than he'd thought and they'd simply throw him into the sea after all. 'It won't last.'

'Why do you say that?'

'Because I've been a slave to the Taiytakei for years and it never does.'

The Taiytakei came for the alchemist the next morning, and it turned out that Tuuran was right about the one night in the palace. When Bellepheros came back he looked angry and scared and bewildered all at once.

'We're going to the desert,' he said.

Tuuran nodded. 'Just remember who you are, Lord Master Alchemist. Remember who you were and remember where you came from. Just that.' Bellepheros still had that look, though, and Tuuran's words tasted ashen in his mouth, as though they already knew they were wasted.

27

The System of the World

Chay-Liang watched the alchemist because watching him was a quiet joy. There'd been something about him from the moment she'd first seen him. Yes, he was a slave, and yes, he was a pale-skinned foreigner, but the way his eyes darted from one thing to the next made all of that meaningless. She could see him *thinking*, that was the joy, and not the sort of thinking that she saw from the sea lords and t'varrs and hsians and kwens that filled her life. Not the *how-do-I-get-what-I-want-from-you* thinking that made her sick to the pit of her stomach but the *what-is-this-how-does-it-work-where-is-the-door-to-understanding* thinking that was her own, which had surrounded her among the enchanters at Hingwal Taktse when she'd been an apprentice there and a journeyman, and even in her early days as a mistress of her craft.

She led him into the gondola beneath the waiting glasship. It was a shame that the Palace of Leaves had been so cleverly built that one simply opened one bronze door and then another and stepped from palace to gondola without even realising; although given how the alchemist had taken to their arrival, maybe it was better this way. Perhaps drifting through the sky would come a little easier in a room of his own with only a handful of little glass windows looking over the outside world. It would be like the cabin on a ship, except larger of course and made of gold.

'Your slave cannot come with us,' she said as she showed him where they would both be living for the next two weeks. A gondola was a small place to be confined for so long but the opportunity was too good to miss. He'd have nowhere to go and nothing to do and no one else to talk to. Just the two of them and the mindless golem automaton that was their pilot; and by the time they reached the Lair of Samim, perhaps he would have told her everything he knew, everything there was to learn about dragons. She was eager for that, for the knowledge he had.

'I need him,' the alchemist said, and she smiled and nodded and then shook her head.

'No, you don't.'

'Well, then, I want him. Your master promised me anything for which I asked. Save my freedom, naturally, the one thing I wish for most of all.'

His petulance and the little flash of impotent anger made her laugh. 'I know you do and I've already arranged for him to travel with the other slaves. He'll make a fine bodyguard for you.'

'I don't need him for *that*! Do I?'

His ignorance was refreshing. It made her smile and warm to him even more than she already had. 'Let's hope not.'

'I want to go home.'

For now you do. That was her other challenge for the next two weeks. As well as siphoning away all his knowledge she meant to show him the glories of the world in which she lived. His curiosity and fascination with it were already doors into his mind, ajar, ready to seduce him with ideas and possibilities, and it would be better that way, surely, than making him work by threats and force. One day, she hoped, she could lead him right up to the gangway of a ship home, offer it to him and watch him say no.

She took his hand and led him to the window, charmed by how he flinched away from the sky, and pointed to the palace and showed him its parts. 'Do you see the old ship suspended in the air? Her name is the *Maelstrom* and she is nigh on five hundred years old. Feyn Charin, the first enchanter to cross the storm-dark, reshaped her for that crossing, not far from here. She was the first ship of her kind, the first to cross between worlds. Do you know how many worlds there are? Yours and ours are but two.'

The alchemist shrugged. He was feigning boredom but he couldn't quite hide the spark in his eyes. She kept hold of his hand and led him away from the window to the desk that was hers and had been for years. *Her* gondola, *her* glasship. *I made this. All of it.* She'd tell him that when he was ready but that wasn't now.

'I'm more used to travelling alone,' she said. 'I had them put these curtains in. You have a bed and a desk of your own on your side. I'm sorry it's cramped. I'm sure you're used to more grand surroundings.' She knew he wasn't.

She unrolled a map of Takei'Tarr and pointed. 'This is Xican and the Grey Isle. We have to cross the sea to Zinzarra. Two days without a stop, I'm afraid. I brought books for you to read. After that we travel down the western coast through the heartland of my people. I'll show you what places I can as we pass them. The aqueduct at Shevana-Daro, the Palace of Glass and the Crown of the Sea Lords at Khalishtor, and Mount Solence, home and birthplace of the Elemental Men. Negarrai with its lighthouse. Abaskun, and Sigiriya with its amphitheatre. Here is Hingwal Taktse castle where I learned my art, home of the Vespinese College of Enchanters. I'll take you there if I can.' She ran a finger up and down, inland of the western coast where all the cities lay. 'These are the mountains of the Konsidar. We'll cross at the far southern end and perhaps stop for a day in Vespinarr itself, here, the greatest city in the world. Then another day into the southernmost reaches of the desert to the salt marsh of the Samim.' She couldn't help but smile. 'Read the books I have for you and you'll find our oldest stories are rife with monsters. The Red Banatch and the Kraitu of Dhar Thosis. Zaklat the Death Bat.' The smile turned to a laugh. 'Stories from before the Splintering. Here.' She took one of the books and took off her glasses so she didn't have to squint, then opened it and flipped the pages until she found the Samim. '"A giant scorpion a hundred feet long with a hundred legs, seven poisonous tails and three pairs of claws, each of which could cut a horse in two. Around its mouth parts, seventeen venomous snakes so poisonous that their mere breath brings death to lesser creatures."' She closed the book again. 'In stories of the desert the Samim never leaves its lair, content to give birth to all the poisonous creatures of the world. The Samim isn't real, of course, just an idea, an old monster whose time has long gone, but above its lair you and I will give birth to new ones. Tell me about what an eyrie should be. What else will we need?'

He looked at her as though she was mad. 'Food. A great deal of food. Great herds of wild beasts. Dragons are forever hungry.'

'The western edge of the Lair then, closer to Hanjaadi and the Bawar Bridge.' She chuckled. That would *not* please Quai'Shu, nor his Vespinese allies, nor probably the Hanjaadi. Baros Tsen T'Varr would have to move his flying eyrie even closer to the Jokun river than it already was. Maybe further north too.

'Dragons are death,' said the alchemist suddenly. 'We tame them because we have no choice. I'd destroy them if I could. If there was a way. So would you if you really understood them.'

She held his eye across the desk, looking for the lie in what he'd said, but no, he meant it. 'Then make me understand, Bellepheros of the dragon lands. I'm not your enemy.' She frowned. 'Would you really destroy them?'

'Yes.' He shook his head. 'You just don't understand what you're doing.'

'Then why *don't* you?'

'Because I don't know how!' He closed his eyes and sighed and his shoulders slumped. 'Besides, you have sea lords and their like to tell you what you may not do. We have our dragon-kings and -queens.'

'And what do *they* say?'

The alchemist leaned towards her across the map. 'You know what *they* say. They say the same as your lord says here! *They* say that every dragon is precious and to be saved if it possibly can. *They* would likely murder us all rather than lose their precious monsters. And *I* would destroy every dragon in existence if such a thing could be done, and for no better reason than that very greed!' The force in his voice was enough make her step back. 'Although there *are* better reasons than that. Many.' He turned away, the passion in his words slipping to defeat. 'But what does it matter? Kill a dragon if you can. It just comes back again, born in another egg somewhere.'

Chay-Liang rolled away her map, slowly and deliberately. *This. Exactly this.* 'Really?'

The alchemist rolled his eyes. 'Oh, what harm is it for you to know? It hardly makes a difference and if it helps you understand why what you're doing should not be done ... As far as we understand, the number of dragons never changes. For an egg to hatch – and there are many, *many* eggs across the dragon realms – elsewhere a dragon must die. And the dragon that is reborn will be the same dragon as the one that died. Not the same shape, not the same colour, perhaps not even the same breed, but the same essence. The same soul, if you will. The same thoughts and memories, when they're not dulled away by my potions.'

'Are you saying they're immortal?' Now there was a thing. A puzzle more for the Elemental Men, perhaps. Something that just came back when you killed it? They wouldn't like *that* one little bit. Chay-Liang wasn't at all sure that she did either but then maybe she hadn't properly understood what he meant.

'You might say so.' Bellepheros closed his eyes and tipped back his head with a great sigh. 'Within my order such things are held secret from the kings and queens who think they rule us, and for good reason.' He looked at her hard. 'You're not like a dragon-king, I can see that. Your masters embark on madness, Chay-Liang. Madness, and you as well if you believe that what they're asking me to do is good and wise and for the better of all. The dragons *remember*, Chay-Liang. When they're reborn, they remember the lives they used to have and they do not think fondly of our kind at all. *Little ones* they call us when they're awake and we're nothing to them but food. My alchemy may keep them dull for you for a while but even if you keep me here until I die, I am already old and I won't live for ever, while *they* will. Bring dragons to this land and sooner or later they'll wake. It may not be for years and perhaps neither you nor I will live to see it – and I *will* do every-thing in my power to stop it – but it *will* happen; and when they do then all your pretty palaces will mean nothing.' He stopped for a moment and looked her in the eye. 'And your palaces *are* wonders, Chay-Liang, and I wouldn't see them shattered and burned even though your people have taken me from my home and my family and everything I know and love, and all out of greed.' He took her hand from where it held the map and squeezed it between his own. 'What I offer you is the truth, Chay-Liang. If dragons come then I will do all I can to keep them at bay, but I cannot be here for ever and then what?' He smiled, almost in tears at the certainty of his own words. 'I know what you think. You think you can make more alchemists. I could teach another. One of your own kind. You, perhaps. You might even promise that I could go home once I'm no longer necessary. You think this alchemy is something that I can pass on. But it's not. Whether I want to or not, I cannot make another alchemist who can tame dragons.'

She looked into him. He believed every word. He was almost weeping and the pain and sadness shook her somewhere deep. Damn him, but *she* almost believed it too. Didn't want to but there it was. A man they'd taken from his home to be their slave. He should be angry – he had every right to be – waving his fist and snarling at her and telling her that he'd never help them, not for anything. She'd been ready for *that* but not for this. Not for sorrow and ... pity! He *pitied* them. 'Sit,' she said quietly, trying to rein in her disquiet. 'We will not end so easily.'

His voice cracked. 'Yes, you will. You're making your own doom.'

She took another map and unravelled it in front of him. Perhaps to show him who her people were, to convince him that he was wrong and that even Quai'Shu's dragons were nothing for the Taiytakei to fear. Perhaps for herself, to fight the conviction he carried in his words. But in part too as something that would interest him, this strange old man from far away, and take his mind from all the terrible things that couldn't be helped, not even if both of them set their minds against them. She showed him her map of the many worlds with Takei'Tarr at its heart and the five lines of the storm-dark that every Taiytakei knew. She told him of the realms that lay beyond. His own with its dragons. The vast Dominion with its Sun King and its stagnant theocracy and its terrible battle-priests who called down the fire of the sun itself and the Small Kingdoms on its fringes. Aria, with its sorcerers and its gold. The great wilderness of the Southern Realm which had no name of its own because all the people who lived there were savages, yet whose ruins spoke of a civilisation as old and vast as any other. She told him tales of the lost land of Qeled, of the mysteries and horrors that surrounded that ancient kingdom and spoke of far greater things to be found within, of the Scythian masters of steel who still lived on their island and remembered a time when half-gods clad in silver had walked the earth ...

A sharp breath stopped her. The alchemist's eyes glazed for a moment. *Half-gods clad in silver. Does that mean something to you? 'Is there something the matter?' Yes. Yes, it does!*

The alchemist shook his head and tried to pretend otherwise. 'No. Please do go on. This is fascinating. Well ...' He shrugged. 'It passes the time, at least.'

She poured him a little wine. *We'll come back to your silver men after a glass or two, eh?* 'Feyn Charin and those who followed him say there should be eight lines of the storm-dark to be found. Five are known well. A sixth, it is said, was once found by the men of Vespinarr but led nowhere that mattered, and they never wrote down where they found it and never sought it again.' She laughed. 'Which, if you ever meet a lord of Vespinarr, you will know at once is one lie upon another, and if it's true that they found it then they certainly didn't lose it again. I've heard theories of a seventh line that comes and goes as it pleases. Feyn Charin himself claimed to have crossed it and found a realm unlike any other, a sea of liquid silver and nothing else. We call it the moon line and no one has found it since, or if they have then they haven't returned. Perhaps Feyn Charin's story is just that. He *was* a strange one, and if he did find the seventh line then he found it late in his life from his bed in the Dralamut.' She put a hand to her heart. 'Now there is a place we *shall* go, you and I. One of these days, when our work is done and our eyrie built. The Dralamut and Feyn Charin's library. The greatest ever assembled.' She watched him. He was sipping at his wine like an old woman and she wanted him tipsy so they could get back to the Scythians and the silver half-gods that had made him start so.

'Some say there should be an eighth line,' she said. 'Eight elements, eight lines, but that we'll never find the eighth because it's the line belonging to the element of metal and the Elemental Men have lost the art of that.' She snorted. 'Maybe it'll be a Scythian, then. But others say that seven is the right number. Eight elements, eight realms, *seven* lines between them.' She raised her glass to the alchemist. 'A toast! To arguments about numbers. To the system of the world.'

The alchemist raised his glass but didn't drink. 'And where would your eighth line go, Chay-Liang?'

'To the land of the dead, Master Alchemist. To Xibaiya.'

He looked at her hard. 'Then you should ask a dragon,' he said, and drained his glass.

28

Knives

Tuuran walked with the alchemist and the white witch as far as a bronze door and there the witch stopped him. The soldiers who'd come too barred his way and so he watched the alchemist disappear. It gave him a bad feeling in the pit of his stomach watching the two of them go ahead together. He felt the floor tremble and then the soldiers lost their quiet calm and barked and poked and pushed him back another way, through another bronze door where he found himself cramped into a room not much bigger than the alchemist's, only with a dozen more slaves and piles of crates already filling it and making it feel small. It was round, with bright metal walls, bronze or gold or something in between. It might have been tall once but now it had been split by a dividing floor of crude planks and it didn't take Tuuran long to realise there were more slaves crammed into the upper part, and probably more crates too. The women on the top, the men underneath, and the planks between them were so low that around the edges Tuuran couldn't stand straight. There were hammocks strung up in stacks of three, so close that they were all practically sleeping on top of one another. They had no lights and no candles. The palace slaves already there were looking at one another aghast, sharing their horror and their outrage at being treated this way, but for Tuuran this was the world he knew, where sailors were packed like fish in a barrel if they weren't at work as a slave to oar and sail.

Around the walls were tiny round windows, right up by the improvised ceiling like the portholes of the ship that had brought him to Xican. He elbowed the other slaves aside. Some of them grumbled and some of them shouted their outrage. One or two bowed their heads and kept out of his way. He heard them talking, whispering about who he was and what he'd done in the alchemist's room the night before, punching a palace slave in the face and making his nose bleed. Either way, through glares and shoves and by sheer size, by the time the glasship was loaded Tuuran had quietly established among the other slaves that, however many lightning bolts you had branded on your arms, you bloody well gave up your window to an Adamantine Man.

The view as they left the Palace of Leaves was breath-stealing. They rose, Tuuran and the others all craning their necks and bending their heads to peer outside, while right over their heads the women were lying on the floor, squinting through windows that for them were by their feet. They were so close through the thin wood that he could smell them, jasmine and lavender and cheap Xizic wafting through the planking. He watched the Palace of Leaves fall away beneath them, its huge gold-glass wheels spinning slowly just below the clouds, and then the rest of the City of Stone and the Grey Isle itself, smaller and smaller, looking like some behemoth porcupine dropped in a sea just a little too shallow to cover it.

'Great Flame!' He shook his head in awe. 'And you live here? Do you even see it?'

The palace slaves turned their backs. They scorned him when they weren't being afraid of him, but a soft whisper came through the boards from above: 'Magnificent, isn't it?'

'The world I knew, it had nothing like this.' Through the haze the bulk of the island rose to a great plateau. The same spikes of rock that jutted out of the sea to make the City of Stone grew here too, but snapped and broken and tumbled down among each other. Maybe he was wrong, maybe if he'd crossed the realms on the back of a dragon he'd have seen a dozen wonders like this. Maybe.

'Nor mine,' whispered the boards above. 'Come to the other side. Come and look ahead.' He followed the whisper and crossed the gondola, elbowing and barging his way through a sea of growls and mutters and surly resentment. 'Do you see it?' asked the whisper when they were together again, and he did: the other flying ship of glass, the one with the alchemist, rising ahead of them, a golden gondola hung by chains from another sun-bright wheel like those that lifted the palace. He stared at it, amazed. It made him feel small again, uncomfortable. He understood dragons well enough but not this, and he knew he never would. He shivered, half in awe, half fearful, except it couldn't really be fear because Adamantine Men had long since left fear behind.

He turned and looked around the room. At the roundness of it, at its curved floor and metal walls. 'We're in one of those too, aren't we?' He bit his lip. Witchery and blood-magic again! But there was nothing to be done.

'Of course we are.' The voice above giggled at him.

He turned back to the window. He didn't dare let the other slaves see him looking afraid, even if he knew he wasn't. 'Who are you?' he asked.

'A slave, of course,' said the whisper. 'You're the new one, aren't you? The one who comes from the place they call the land of the dragons? Do they really have dragons there?'

'Yes.'

'And are they terrible monsters?'

She felt so close. He turned and stared at the boards and wondered if he was strong enough to rip a hole. 'Terrible enough,' he growled. 'But not as terrible as I am. What's your name?'

'I already told you.' She was laughing at him.

He bared his teeth at the sky outside. 'Well, slave, whoever you are, I wish you were down here where I could see you.'

'I think for now I'm very glad that I'm not.'

The world outside turned suddenly white as they rose into the cloud and stayed that way for the whole two days they flew, almost as if whoever was piloting wished them to see nothing. There was not much to do except get in the faces of the other men and whisper sweet nothings at the women above, though no one whispered back after that first ascent. They were all much too demure in the Taiytakei way for such things. Or, as the sail-slaves back on his galley had it, tight-legged prudes.

The gondola came down at last, long after dark in the middle of some city, into a wide stone-flagged yard surrounded by tall walls full of windows. The ramp doors opened and Taiytakei soldiers hustled the slaves quickly out. Tuuran's eyes peered at the night, looking at the women as they came down from above. The palace slaves stood and shivered and grumbled. Tuuran stretched his legs and flexed his muscles and made sure he was seen, while their gondola and its ship of glass rose once more to make space for the alchemist and the witch to land in their place. As soon as it came down and the gondola ramp opened, the witch marched the alchemist straight out, past them all and across the yard and through grand iron-bound doors, snapping her fingers at Tuuran and a pair of soldiers to follow in her wake. She strode through a long magnificent hall draped in night-time shadow, through another great iron door and away into the city, all breathlessly fast as if the fate of the world depended on it only to stop after half a mile to stand in front of an old palace. For the purpose, as far as Tuuran could tell, of talking at it.

'I wanted to show you at least one thing while we were here.' The witch was out of breath and so was the alchemist. 'It dates back to the Mar-Li Republics, to before the Elemental Men.' Tuuran puffed his cheeks and looked about. The alchemist seemed interested but Tuuran was bored and hungry and deadly restless after two days cramped up in a cage in the sky. He paced around. 'It used to be the home to Zinzarra's lords, but when they went they left it to rot. Yet they still guard it.' It seemed odd to Tuuran to guard a place with its windows and doors all bricked shut, and if they *were* guarding it, they didn't seem to be doing much a job of it. He couldn't see any actual guards, for a start. And maybe the alchemist thought something similar, but he never had a chance to ask because suddenly there was another Taiytakei sauntering down the street, and he would have walked right up to them if the two soldiers hadn't blocked his path. He stopped courteously enough but his eyes stayed a little too long on Bellepheros. Tuuran's skin prickled. Old instincts put him on edge.

'I do apologise so much for this,' said the stranger. 'It's so hideously embarrassing that I don't even know your name. So, ah, Alchemist from the Land of Dragons will have to do. And again, further apologies for the nature of this meeting ...'

The soldiers advanced to force the newcomer away. He retreated without complaint, not bothered at all. Such an easy manner in front of two armed men made Tuuran wish for his sword. And he kept talking too, and at Bellepheros, not even at the witch.

'Ordinarily we'd make arrangements for a time and place in a quiet and civilised manner and I'd give you a day or two to settle your affairs. Things being as they are, I'm afraid I must insist on here and now. I can only beg you forgive me for such rudeness.'

The words made little sense but the way they were said had Tuuran already moving towards Bellepheros. The two Taiytakei soldiers reached for their swords but faltered and staggered as the stranger walked between them, pushing them lightly aside. One stumbled to his knees, clutching his throat. The other crashed to the ground. The witch went for the golden wand at her belt.

'I'm so sorry about your soldiers.' The stranger had a hand in one pocket. His eyes were firmly on the witch now, not looking at Bellepheros at all, but his words had been for the alchemist. The alchemist who was simply watching, bemused.

There was a second man somewhere.

The realisation hit Tuuran a moment before he saw the other assassin and by then he was already moving, hurling himself at the alchemist's back.

The witch levelled her wand. Quick as a snake, the first assassin whipped some silvery thing out of his pocket and held it in front of him, pointed at the witch. The second drew back his arm and threw knives, one, two, three, all at the alchemist's back but a half a second too late. Tuuran took them all, one in the arm, one the shoulder and one to the chest. Deep, each one of them. The arm and shoulder would hurt. The one in the chest, he knew, had probably killed him. The assassin now went for his sword; so did Tuuran, only he didn't have one, so he pulled the knife out of his shoulder instead. He was bleeding like a stuck pig. The assassin's sword was a long pointy thing, the sort for running people through. The two of them faced each other.

'Well,' said Tuuran, 'you can kebab me and finish me off if you like but you're going to look very stupid when I ram your own knife in your face before I die.'

The assassin was looking past him and Tuuran realised he hadn't heard the thundercrack of the witch firing her wand. His heart raced, because that meant the first one was still there and he certainly couldn't hold off two; and then a figure appeared behind the assassin who'd thrown the knives. Literally appeared as if he'd been standing there all along but had been invisible until now. He wore a black robe edged with strands of colour that all washed out to a silvery grey in the moonlight. As he appeared, he made a slight movement and the assassin's hand fell off and landed on the street with a wet thud. Blood sprayed from the stump over the wide stones. The assassin just stood, dumbfounded, and let himself bleed. Black-robe flicked something from his empty hand. Tuuran didn't see what it was, but the assassin screamed as though he'd had his testicles crushed and finally clutched the stump of his arm. The stream of blood over the road petered out and then stopped. The assassin's whole arm, Tuuran saw, had withered and turned black. He felt light-headed. The lights further down the street had blurred a little.

Black-robe leaned close and whispered in the assassin's ear, 'Go and tell your regrettable masters that this one is out of their reach. Whoever asked you to do this will be obliged to seek a return of their jade. Now go, and stay gone.'

The now one-armed assassin bowed and backed away. His face was a rictus of pain and he spoke through gritted teeth. 'We are but poor mirrors. We know this. But when, may I ask, did you become guardsmen? We are knives, not shields.'

Black-robe shook his head. 'The Regrettable Men of Vespinarr, of all the people in the world, should know better. We have always been shields. That was our first and only purpose.'

Tuuran looked behind him. The alchemist was standing exactly as he had when the fight began – bemused and without a clue. The witch looked stricken and the two Taiytakei soldiers lay dead on the street, as did the man who'd killed them, the first assassin, who'd now become somehow separated from his head.

When he looked back again, the second assassin was gone too, vanished into the night. Tuuran looked at the severed hand on the street. A hand and half a forearm. Black-robe's blade, whatever it was, had cut through the bones as though they were butter.

He was breathing hard. There was a rattle in his throat. He felt dizzy and he couldn't stop looking at the hand. What kind of blade could do that? 'You're just going to let the other one go?' he gasped.

Black-robe looked down the street. 'Regrettable Men,' he said when the killer was gone. 'From Vespinarr.'

The alchemist seemed to wake up. 'I thought you said this Vespinarr was your friend!'

'Vespinarr is the city where the Regrettable Men make their home. Any may buy them as any may come to Mount Solence and ask us for our blades. Such friendship is traded for jade, nothing else.'

'Are you hurt?' The witch was all over Bellepheros now, holding on to him, poking and prodding. Something had changed between them since the Palace of Leaves. An affection that hadn't been there before, her for him. It made Tuuran smile. Things came at the most unexpected times. He looked down. His shirt was soaked with blood and he still had a knife stuck in his chest. If he pulled it out, he had a bad feeling about what would happen next.

'Yes, yes, I'm not hurt. Did he ... Did they ... Did they mean to *kill* me?'

Tuuran tried taking long deep breaths to keep the dizziness at bay. He couldn't really just stand here with two knives sticking out of him ... What was it that an Adamantine Man did? Obeyed orders, first and last and always. But obeyed *whose* orders? The Night Watchman. The speaker, but when there was no Night Watchman here and no speaker either? Well, he'd sworn himself to the alchemist, the next best thing, so he supposed he could die content.

The witch still only had eyes for the alchemist. 'I'm so sorry, Belli. I thought we'd reach the eyrie before anyone even knew you were here.' Tuuran blinked. He'd been in the middle of wondering whether his ancestors from the legion would manage to find him this far from home, caught up in another world, but Belli? *Belli?* All that he'd been thinking, all that stuff about duty and honour and how being knifed in the street to save the grand master of the Order of the Scales was as a good and noble a way to die as any ... and now the witch had gone and ... *Belli?* He started to laugh. Great heaving guffaws. *Belly* laughs, which only made him bleed all the more. His knees were shaking. He could barely stand.

'What's wrong with you, man?' snapped the alchemist.

They saw him now. Until then he'd been invisible. Invisible in the way that slaves always were. Now the witch was looking at him, horrified as though she hadn't either the first idea what to do nor any inclination to come closer. The black-robe was gentle though. He looked at each of the wounds, murmuring to himself, dismissed the one in the arm, said something about stitches over the one in the shoulder and then shook his head at the last.

'Well,' grunted Tuuran, '*I* could have told you that.'

'When the knife comes out there will be a great deal of blood. You may die or you may not. Pray to your gods, slave, if you think that will help.'

'I don't have any,' Tuuran spat.

Black-robe nodded. He seemed to approve, not that *that* helped either. He looked at the witch. 'What would you have me do?'

The witch flustered. 'Can he walk?' She froze, mouth open, looking back and forth as though an answer would come up to her through the night and shake her hand. The alchemist fiddled at his pouch. He drew out a dried leaf and stepped up to Tuuran, pushed black-robe gently away and eased his leaf a little way into the chest wound, beside the blade. Tuuran growled and gritted his teeth. It stung like fire.

The alchemist looked him in the eye. 'I'm sorry, my friend. This will hurt. But better than dying, I imagine.'

'What are you—'

'Scream. I'm told it helps.' Bellepheros whipped out the knife from Tuuran's chest and pushed the leaf deep in its place.

He screamed. It was like breathing liquid fire.

29

Knowledge

Loud enough to break mountains, the screams of an Adamantine Man. They learned it, practised it, honed it. A roar to crumble the spirits of lesser men, a howl to send pain and fear to another place so that they could go on, no matter what the damage, and do what must be done. But this pain the alchemist had given him was something else. Stronger even than him. Tuuran fell to the road. For an instant he thought he must be dead but to his surprise he was still breathing.

'What in the name of the Righteous Ones did you do to him?' The white witch.

'Saved his life, that's what,' said Bellepheros sharply. 'Your man will have to carry him somewhere he can be cared for.'

The witch spluttered. 'The Watcher? You're talking about an Elemental Man! If the Elemental Men say the sea lords must jump, they will jump. You're so keen to learn our ways, learn that one!'

Bellepheros snorted like a horse. 'From what I've seen, they're hired hands like any other.' He cocked his head at the Watcher. 'Is that not so?'

'The arrangement with Quai'Shu is ... unusual.' The Watcher shrugged. Lying on the road, twisting in pain, Tuuran watched the two squaring up. It would have been funny if he wasn't in such blistering agony. He paused to refill his lungs and screamed again. The Witch stepped between them.

'Whatever it is, he is not *my man*!' She looked at Tuuran. He couldn't read her face in the gloom, couldn't tell whether he was seeing pity and compassion or whether she just wanted to leave him to die in the street and get away.

The alchemist shrugged. 'Well *I* can't lift him and neither can you, and your other men appear to be dead. Should we just stand here and shout for help then?' Tuuran watched, blurry-eyed, as the alchemist peered over his nose at the black-robe. 'And I *have* met your kind before, you know. It was one of you who took me. He had all sorts of strange questions that, under the circumstances, I was less than inclined to answer. Do *you* have questions? If you do, and I answer them, will you carry this man for me?'

Tuuran tried to move. An Adamantine Man was not *carried*! If an Adamantine Man couldn't walk it was because he had no legs. But the pain ran through his chest like flames, like a dragon that had him pinned to the earth. He managed to curl his fingers. *Great Flame, alchemist, what have you done to me?*

The witch looked at the Elemental Man. 'I am sorry,' she said, but by then the Watcher had Tuuran and was hoisting him over his shoulders. Tuuran heard him grunt at the effort of it. *Yes, I'm heavy! So put me down! I can walk!*

'The blades were meant for your alchemist.' The Elemental Man staggered under Tuuran's weight. 'I was not quick enough and I would not have stopped them. Your friend owes you his life, sail-slave, but you have saved me a humiliation. I am in your debt, and those are rare words from my kind.'

In their hours together on the ship out of Furymouth the alchemist had told Tuuran how he'd been taken and Tuuran had wondered what it would be like to turn into the wind and simply blow through the air. He wondered now why the Elemental Man didn't just do that and take them both somewhere safe, but he didn't. He walked, slow, heavy steps, breathing hard under Tuuran's weight. He was warm and he smelled of sweat and seemed just like any other man.

'I …' The pain was ebbing fast now, a great weight wrapping itself around his thoughts in its place, a smothering blanket of fatigue and it took him, or maybe the Elemental Man did turn them both to wind after all because the next thing he knew they were back where they'd started, in a courtyard outside an open golden gondola. He recognised the smell of stale sweat. When he forced his eyes open, everything was blurred.

'He still needs my help,' said the alchemist shortly.

'Belli …' But Tuuran had come to know that edge to the alchemist's voice while they'd been at sea and the witch must have learned it too. The one that said he wouldn't take an argument. 'Very well. Watcher, seal us in.'

The Elemental Man set him down on a table. Tuuran's eyes swam reluctantly into focus at last. Yes, a gondola, but not the one that had flown him here. This one felt bigger. The Watcher stood over him and then vanished, dissolving into the air. A few seconds later Tuuran heard him speak again, this time at the gondola door. 'There are no others of my nature here.'

'One of you must be close, though,' said the witch. Bellepheros was busy cutting at Tuuran's clothes.

'Why?'

'The alchemist came to Xican three days ago. We were one day in the palace. No glassships left the Palace of Leaves – they were not permitted – and the jade ravens were kept caged. It was too important. Yet the Regrettable Men were waiting and they nearly took him.' The witch sounded close to tears. 'Stupid, both of us. I thought he'd be safe a while longer, I really did. I hoped—'

The Watcher's voice betrayed nothing. 'Not all jade ravens are held in the palace nor do they all belong to Sea Lord Quai'Shu. But do not assume they knew your destination, Lady Chay. The Regrettable Men number enough to await you up and down the western coast in every city you might pass if they had been warned you were coming. You've brought slaves. It would be easy enough to turn one of them. Nor would it be so hard to guess where you would come and to pay eyes to watch the skies.'

The witch stamped her foot. 'No one has Regrettable Men standing around waiting in every city from here to Vespinarr! That would be a sea lord's fortune of jade!'

'Yet less than our lord paid for me, lady.'

'Quai'Shu must know, if he hasn't already left again. Please tell him!'

'I will. And I will go to Shevana-Daro and see if the Regrettable Men await us there too. Zinzarra allies itself with Cashax and thus with Dhar Thosis and all who stand opposed to Vespinarr, while Sea Lord Quai'Shu kisses the mountain lord's ring. Our lord has few friends here. Shevana-Daro remains aloof from these squabbles. If there are Regrettable Men awaiting you there, it will be informative.'

He was a poor liar for an assassin and the Elemental Man clearly had something entirely else on his mind, but Tuuran was in no place to give that much thought. The witch either couldn't tell or didn't care.

'As you will, Watcher. *My* concern has become to deliver Bellepheros to Baros Tsen T'Varr and his flying eyrie without him dying on the way. There will be no more stops.' Her voice changed as she turned to the alchemist. 'I'm sorry, Belli. It will be a long journey and there was a great deal I'd hoped to show you ... the Crown of the Sea Lords in Khalishtor. But we can see that from the air, the Lighthouse at Negarrai too. Perhaps Vespinarr will be safe. We could have stayed there for days. You would have found much to your liking.'

'Never mind that.' The alchemist was poking at Tuuran's chest, at the hole in it that ought to have killed him. Tuuran tried to lift his head to see what the alchemist was doing and found that he could, just about, but the alchemist put a finger between his eyes and pushed gently back, forcing him to lie still. 'Be quiet, Sword of Narammed. You came close to dying today.' He was poking at the shoulder wound now. 'This won't hurt as much as the last, but it will sti—' Whatever he said, a blur of agony swallowed it. Tuuran convulsed.

'What are you doing to him?'

'The leaf of the spiderwort stops the bleeding in its tracks. The ones I have here are soaked in Dreamleaf to take away the worst of the pain. Things I happened to have with me when you took me.' There was a bite to the alchemist's words but Tuuran was in no state to appreciate it. Right now he felt as though the alchemist had ripped his arm right out of its socket and if there was any Dreamleaf in there then it was certainly taking its time to be noticed.

'To take ... away ... the worst?' he gasped.

'Spiderwort is a poison, my friend. It kills through sheer agony.'

'I ... can believe you.'

'Ach, you're an Adamantine Man. You're supposed to be immune to pain.'

'Apparently not ... as immune ... as I would like.'

Bellepheros held up his hand and rummaged for something. 'Has anyone got a knife?' Tuuran was still clutching one. He managed to lift his hand enough to show Bellepheros, who took it. Last

Tuuran had looked, he'd still had at least one other stuck in him somewhere too.

'Belli!' The Witch gave a little gasp of alarm.

'O Chay-Liang! If I was going to kill anyone then I could have poisoned either of us in a hundred different ways by now.' The alchemist tested the edge and then delicately sliced open the flesh on the heel of his hand. 'This will hurt too, I'm afraid.' He wiped a few drops of his blood onto a finger and then pressed it into the wound on Tuuran's chest. He did the same with the other cuts. And yes, it hurt, but not like the leaves had.

'Blood-magic,' hissed Tuuran. 'We do not ... suffer a blood-mage ... to live!'

'Well if this is blood-magic then you'll have to kill an awful lot of alchemists,' snapped Bellepheros. 'A blood-mage uses the blood of others. Usually without their consent. An alchemist uses his own. That's the difference and the *whole* difference. When I start murdering virgins on altars to meddle with forces best left to slumber, *then* you can put on your armour and take up your sword and spout your righteous claptrap. When I'm saving your life, you can be quiet!'

Tuuran started to laugh. 'I think I like you, alchemist.'

'You'd better! Now shut up and lie still while I stitch these closed. They'll heal in a few days, far faster than you might otherwise expect. You have my blood to thank for that. You'll feel enervated for a time. I advise a great deal of fresh air and exercise.'

'He's going to spend the next two weeks in a space about the size of this one with a dozen other slaves,' said the witch caustically.

'Then if they are slaves for whom you have a fondness, I suggest you find a particularly enthusiastic partner to accompany him. He'll need *some* way to release the energy I've just put into him. The usual outlet for Adamantine Men, from what I've seen of them, is either whoring or breaking heads. Give him the former or the latter will surely follow.' Bellepheros held up a threaded needle so Tuuran could see. 'Do you prefer men or women?'

'Bellepheros!' The witch's outrage made Tuuran laugh again. 'You cannot possibly expect me to do such a thing! It would be ... *beyond* inappropriate hardly begins to encompass it!'

'I will find a way to ... OW!' Tuuran gasped again as the needle bit his skin. *Manage. I will find a way to manage.*

They kept him in their gondola that night. He felt the glasship rise and listened, in and out of a fitful sleep, to the alchemist and the witch talking of this and that, of his realm and of hers and of dragons. Mostly of dragons, for they were why the alchemist was here; and dragons, he found, were not as unknown among the Taiytakei as he'd supposed. They had no living ones of course but they had legends. The symbol of the city of Vespinarr was three dragons twined together with a lion. Dragons were said to live deep under the mountains of the Konsidar with the mysterious people that the witch called the Righteous Ones, a race apart. Dragons had once roosted on a place called the Dul Matha where they had warred with the stone titans of the sea, both of them spawned by the monstrous Kraitu and the great sea serpent the Red Banatch. There had been dragons long ago in the City of Stone, even, before men had ever ventured there. They'd been turned to obsidian and flint in the Splintering but pieces of them could still be found here and there, fused into the mountainsides. All stories, of course, none of them real.

He learned of the alchemist's dragons too, the flesh and blood dragons of his home that years ago he'd seen criss-cross the sky every single day. He learned a great deal more than he would have wished, and when he finally woke to find the sun risen once more, a fleeting wonder hung around him and the alchemist was no longer the man Tuuran had thought but something just a shade or two darker.

The glasships stopped at a deserted place where the mountains touched the sea, the northern margin of the forbidden Konsidar. The alchemist and the witch turned him out so they could be alone with their knowledge and their learning and their discovery of one another and Tuuran watched them return to their gondola with a sense of something gone dreadfully awry. She was seducing him. He'd seen that with his own eyes and heard it with his own ears. Seducing him with knowledge and secrets, and he was seducing her, in his turn, though he probably didn't even know it, but they were in her land, not his, and so she'd get what she wanted and the alchemist, in the end, would get nothing.

Back among the other slaves again he found the alchemist's prediction to be painfully right. His wounds hardly troubled him;

instead he was spurred by a constant restless energy that urged him to stifle the drawls and whispers of the pompous palace slaves around him with their own ripped-out tongues. *Manage. I will find a way to manage.* He'd rather have faced a dragon when it came to it but he'd given his word and so, whenever the glasships put down, he ran and climbed among the broken stones like a restless ape until his muscles burned. Until he found a slave whose eyes followed him; and when she whispered in his ear he knew her, for it was the whisper from above as they'd left the Palace of Leaves. Her name was Yena, and she became his lover.

30

The Desert

Chay-Liang had the glasship golem stop for an hour so they could all stretch their legs by the Shevana-Daro aqueduct. She couldn't take Bellepheros to every place she would have wanted but she could make sure their route passed the more spectacular creations birthed in Hingwal Taktse. The aqueduct carried fresh water from lakes at the edges of the Konsidar down to the city by the sea fifty miles away.

'The view is good,' said Bellepheros but he obviously wasn't much impressed. He spent more time watching the slave who'd saved his life clambering among the pillars of stone beside the lakes, showing off to some slave woman who'd taken a shine to him. He was capering as though caught again in the years between boy and man and Chay-Liang found it strangely irritating to watch him. 'It's the blood,' Bellepheros said when he caught her following his eye. 'Give it another day or two and it'll wear off.'

'My slave is probably ruined.'

Bellepheros shrugged. 'That depends on her cycle.'

Liang squirmed at that. And yes, it was ridiculous to be squeamish about a little blood once a month but that wasn't the point. Such things were a woman's domain and men had no place talking about them. No proper Taiytakei would dream of it.

'Give her to me,' he said suddenly.

'What? Don't be silly – she braids my hair! You have no use for her at all.'

'Anything I want, you said. You can still borrow her from time to time.'

'Absolutely not!'

He didn't press her. The next time they stopped, she took him down to the Tomb of Ten Tazei in its overgrown cove north of Khalishtor. Standing in the rain, sheltering under the boughs of the massive trees that grew there, she told him the story of the great explorer who'd charted the northern coast of Takei'Tarr, who'd turned Dhar Thosis from a village into a famous city with his stories of the Kraitu and the Dul Matha and his shrine to the Goddess of Fickle Fortune.

'People come here for luck.' There was a shrine beside the sea, four white marble pillars holding up a bronze pagoda roof, built on the spot where Tazei was said to have landed for the last time and still, they said, with his footprints preserved in the sand. Chay-Liang ignored it and led Bellepheros to the cave where Ten Tazei's remains had been left. It ended in a wall of loose stones almost covered by strips of white paper on which those who came to the tomb left their prayers. 'The sailors who buried him here walled him up,' she said. 'They say that Tazei's ghost dug a hole all the way to Xibaiya back there.'

Bellepheros chuckled. 'We have our own mythical tomb, if only anyone could find it. Flame knows where *that* might lead.' He'd already told her about his Silver King now, come from nothing and vanished to nowhere but who'd tamed the first dragons in his passing, all hundreds of years in the past; now he told her of the tomb the sorcerer had supposedly prepared before his end, his Black Mausoleum, how it was said to be filled with treasures beyond understanding and how the greatest of their dragon-kings had once searched in vain for twenty years to find it.

'That sounds more like Darkstone.' She laughed. 'Our Scythian friends have tales of a treasure trove of devices left by their half-gods too.' The same half-gods clad in silver? Surely, although the half-gods of the Scythians had gone with the splintering of the world. 'They say Darkstone is filled with terrible weapons.'

Bellepheros didn't seem to hear. He had that look on his face that she'd come to know, the look when something she'd said had snagged on a thought of his own and started to bloom. 'If he was such a hero, why did you bury him? Is that what you do? *Bury* your dead?' His face wrinkled in distaste. Liang laughed.

'Bury them? Condemn them to Xibaiya? No!' No need to hide her own horror at that; but he was still looking at her, waiting patiently for an answer and she realised that she didn't know. Why *did* Ten Tazei's crew bury him and not burn him? 'He asked for it, I think.' She frowned. 'There are books about Tazei. He left a journal and so did some of his crew; and several of the navigators wrote about him later. One of those might answer you.'

They passed Khalishtor at night. There wasn't much to see in the rain except a forest of pinprick lights from the ships anchored out at sea. Mount Solence was shrouded in cloud as it ever was. Looking at it she wondered if the alchemist's Silver King had come to his world at the same time as the Elemental Men had come to hers. The times seemed almost right and seemed to fit, yet she'd found that the further she looked back into history the more time seemed to bend and warp in peculiar ways. A question to ponder quietly in the back of her mind then, like the one about Ten Tazei, or to pass back to her friends still in Hingwal Taktse. There were so many questions now that she'd taken to writing them all down.

She took them to the ground for an hour or two in the morning and again in the evening each day, in part to show him some aspect of her world, in part to ease the growing cramps and aches that came with so much sitting around and doing nothing, and in part to clear her head and give herself space to think and give both of them some time alone. She hadn't understood, until this journey, how much she cherished her own space and privacy, and Belli seemed the same. Often when they stopped she would take him to a place to sit and stare at the mountains or at the sea. She'd tell him a little of the history for a while and then leave him and walk alone. They spent an afternoon sitting overlooking the eyrie of the Dralamut, where the navigators who crossed the storm-dark learned their craft. She told him about the Crimson Sunburst of Cashax and her army of golems, how the Sunburst and the Elemental Men had fought, of her acolytes who'd become the first enchanters, and of one in particular, Feyn Charin, who would later be the first to cross the storm-dark. The Elemental Men had gifted him the Dralamut as a reward, to become a school where he would teach others.

'The greatest library in the world,' she said wistfully.

Soldiers huffed and puffed up from the valley to see whose glas-ships had come and asked them kindly to leave. She obliged them, but as they left she couldn't help circling the Dralamut one last time. 'They have copies of the *Rava*,' she said. 'More than one. An original, I've heard. And astronomical instruments and notebooks that belonged to the Crimson Sunburst herself. Those sort of things would get you killed anywhere else. The Elemental Men can be very ... rigid. I suppose that's the word. But within the Dralamut they turn a blind eye.'

Bellepheros let out a weary sigh. 'We have our own great library in Sand but I'm sure it's not as exciting as yours.' Something had irritated him today and so she let him be. He had his moods. They came and went but she knew what they were: sickness for his old home. For his old comforts and his old friends and there was absolutely nothing she could do to help him. It was strange how she felt sorry for him now. When they'd left she'd been set on making him want to stay. Now she found herself wishing for another way. Something that could give all of them what they wanted but she couldn't think for the life of her what that might be.

They passed over the mountain city of Vespinarr. Vespinarr held more marvels than half the rest of the world together, yet as they came close he barely even looked out of the window. 'Your world is full of miracles,' he told her when she asked him why. 'And you've tried very hard, Liang, to make me see them for what they are, and I do feel privileged to have seen them at all. You've made my home seem small and tawdry by comparison and you've been nothing but kind and, had it come another way, I think I would be exhilarated. But it *was* my home and I should dearly like to see it again.'

'I know, Belli.' She took his hand and sat beside him. 'And that's one thing I can't do for you, however much I might wish it. Quai'Shu will not let you go. But I *have* seen your sadness and I *have* given some thought to it. Perhaps, when the eyrie is built and the dragons are come, perhaps then there will be a way. Perhaps we might have more of your alchemists here. You could send them to us to look after our dragons and in return we'll teach them some of our ways and send them back, richer and wiser. It might take years to make a dream like that become real and I know that patience is a hard thing to ask of any slave, but you, I think, can understand better than any other I've met.'

The alchemist put his other hand on hers and turned to look her in the eye. His face was hard but with hope. 'Could it really be like that? Really? We both know it will not be *our* choice to make. Either of us, for either world.'

'But would you not rather come as friends and allies than as slaves?' The smile that flickered at the edges of his lips as he thought about it was beautiful. His eyes gleamed. 'We *will* make it so, Belli. You and I. We have just begun.'

He chuckled. 'You *will* need more alchemists if you ever get your dragons.' He turned away from her, smiling now, and looked out of the window at the Silver Mountain of Vespinarr, Mazanda's Peak and the huge sprawl of the Kabulingnor Palace that was its crown. 'I don't know, Liang. But what you say does have much to recommend it, it really does. Even to a dragon-king. Whoever is speaker might agree to it, given the right encouragement. Or if they came here and saw it all for themselves. I tremble to imagine what your people could offer instead of slave ships!'

She squeezed his hand. 'And a sea lord too, Belli. Let this be a great exploration between us. When the dragons come and we've shown T'Varr Baros that his eyrie works as it should, we'll tell him that he must have more alchemists than just one. We *will* make it so, you and I, and you will go back to your land filled with books and scrolls and the knowledge that I've given you. And I'll come with you and I'll bring my glasship and you'll show me all the places of wonder in your lands as I have shown you mine.'

'You won't bring a glasship,' he said. 'I won't let you.' Nor would she, for such grand and complex pieces of her art didn't take well to crossing the storm-dark and almost inevitably failed.

'It was a fancy, Belli, that's all. Don't spoil it.'

The smile had spread right across his face. His hand squeezed hers back. 'Liang, if you ever let me go and come to my world, I won't take you like this. Staring out at the earth below from behind glass as it drifts slowly by, that's not how my land wishes to be seen. I'll find a rider to take us and you'll come with me on the back of a dragon.'

She put an arm around him. 'Build the eyrie, Belli. Make it work. Bring our worlds together.'

He shook his head even as his smile remained. 'Perhaps I will, Liang. It's a pretty picture you paint for me and I will admit it has a possibility to it, and I believe you mean every word of it. But a picture it remains, a sketch of an idea made as much to placate me as anything else, and nothing changes the truth that the choice is not ours to make, neither yours nor mine, and wanting does not make things real. Dragons don't belong here, Liang. Dragons are monsters. They are terrible, terrible things, and no good will come of this, whatever dreams we build. They might destroy you before you even know what's happening.'

She gripped him tight, fearful to let him lose sight of the future she'd shown him. Fearful to lose it herself. 'I know it will be long and hard. But see the world always as you want it to be, Belli, not how you fear it may end. Walk towards that world with every step of your life and your progress may surprise you.'

He turned to her and raised an eyebrow. 'One of your desert philosophers?'

'No.' She let him go. 'Just me.'

31

Harsh as a Desert Heart

The glasships landed twice each day to let everyone stretch their legs for an hour. Tuuran saw the alchemist now and then, walking beside the white witch. Sometimes he watched them – usually they talked a little while and then went their separate ways and sat or walked alone – but most of the time he was with Yena. They ran together through trees and hid in shady glades and, when she let him, they stripped each other naked away from the eyes of the other slaves and he devoured her skin like a starving man. All those sterile years at sea with the choice between abstinence or another sail-slave, that and the alchemist's blood, had left him with an insatiable appetite for the girl. He couldn't get enough of her, and he made sure it was good too. All those years from long ago in the brothels around the City of Dragons had taught him how to make things last and he stayed inside her until she squealed and moaned and shuddered against him, until her fingers clawed his skin.

'Don't you ever think about running away?' he asked her afterwards as they lay together, already knowing they'd be late back to the gondolas.

'Where would I go?' She rolled him onto his back and straddled him and ran a finger over the ugly great scab on his chest and kissed it for luck. To make it heal clean, she said – and it *had* healed, and far faster than any wound ever should just as the alchemist had said. Every time Tuuran looked at himself, the scars left him queasy. Blood-magic. The worst magic of all.

Yena held up her branded arms in front of his face. 'I'm a slave, Tuuran. Always a slave. My mistress is kind as mistresses go and wealthy and powerful and …' She smiled and kissed him. 'She allows us *some* freedom, after all.'

The horn sounded, calling the slaves back to the sky, but as they quickly started to dress, he couldn't resist the urge to come up behind her and press her against him and run his hands over her until she turned and they made love again.

They ran afterwards, laughing, but they were still late enough to earn them both a shock of lightning. Tuuran took it with a smile – he'd had plenty enough of them at sea – but he didn't smile when they turned the wand on Yena, when she screamed and begged and afterwards cried. In the gondola as they flew away he found her lying on the planks overhead and whispered to her over and over, letting her feel his outrage in all the things he'd do for her when the chance came, until slowly he understood that that wasn't what she wanted to hear. Sorry. That was all she wanted. That he was sorry and that it wouldn't happen again, even if she'd hardly pushed him away. That was the word she wanted, and so he said it, bewildered by her need for it. And afterwards as they all slept and snored and tossed and turned and drifted through the sky, he wondered why *he* didn't run. He knew the answer perfectly well – he'd made an oath to the alchemist after all – but what was that worth? What was the point of it?

They crossed the mountains. All the other slaves peered hard out of the windows as they drifted over the magnificence of Vespinarr, full of excited whispers and jabbing fingers and cries of pointless joy: *There! That's the Jokun river! Look! The Kabulingnor! Is that all one palace for one lord of the sea? It's as big as a city all on its own! And there! That's the Visonda! And the Harub!*

On and on. Yena was much the same. She seemed to have forgotten about the day before, squealing her own excitement among the women above. When they stopped that evening, though, she walked with him and held his hand and they talked but they never strayed far from the gondola. When he tried to lead her away, she shook her head.

'Are there any old slaves?' he asked her. He certainly hadn't seen any at sea.

'Plenty,' she answered, but with doubt in her eyes. And then he let it be because where was he going with that thought anyway? Were there any old Adamantine Men? No, there weren't. And what could he offer her? Adamantine Men were swords. They sated themselves in flesh and moved on. It was simply what they were, whatever hankerings he might feel now and then, and so he said nothing and just turned and held her and kissed her long and hard, even if everyone else was watching, and then listened as she told him wild stories of the fabulous wealth of Vespinarr.

When they got back to the gondola the windows had been painted black and for almost a full day there were no more stops at all. The gondola grew hot and stifling until even its metal skin was warm to the touch. When it shuddered and swayed and came to a stop and the ramp opened again, Tuuran stumbled out of the stale air that stank of sweat and piss straight into a wall of heat. He squinted and blinked in the brilliant sun. The other slaves staggered and groaned around him, half-blind but glad to get out of the cabin and the darkness. Wherever they were, the sky shone like fire and the ground glared up at him, bright like dragon eyes in the dark. He staggered, humbled for a moment by the light. Taiytakei soldiers prodded and pushed them, herding them together, shouting orders that most of the slaves were too dazed to understand, but they didn't seem too urgent and so he just blundered aimlessly where he was prodded until his eyes got used to the sun; and when at last they did, he stopped and took a good look at where he was.

A big circle of seamless flat white stone inside a squat round wall of the same stuff. Empty except for the squinting slaves and the gondola and a handful of Taiytakei soldiers who seemed more amused than annoyed. There were five short towers spaced evenly around the wall and archways below each of them which led underground, and steps up to what were probably battlements, but as to what lay *past* the walls … He craned his neck but they were too high and all he could see was the sky.

Except …

He looked further up. More than a dozen gold-glass discs floated high above them, great long chains dangling down to the ground outside the walls. Flying ships of glass and gold like the one that had brought him here. He stared. He'd seen two, maybe three now and then flying with them from the Grey Isle, and others in the distance sometimes when they'd passed one of the Taiytakei cities. But never so many!

Yena touched his arm. 'They're just glasships.'

'Where are we?'

'The desert.' She sniffed. 'I remember the air.'

Tuuran rubbed his eyes. 'I remember it too, except ours is a different desert in a different world. Hot and dry and tastes a little of sand.'

'And salt.'

He snorted. 'Salt? Yes, we have a whole desert of salt where I come from. I went there once with our new speaker. It was his home, you see. Let's hope this desert isn't as boring as *that* one was.' The endless flat salt plains around Bloodsalt were the most desolate place he'd ever been and the dragon lands had had no shortage of desolate places to choose from. He hawked and spat on the shining white stone. 'The only reason anyone ever went there was for the lumps of gold that littered the place. Just lying on the ground, they were. Oh, that and it was the only place a bunch of runaway blood-mages and their tame dragons could find where no one would bother them, but that was once upon a time. Long, long ago.' It would have been nice to have learned that when he'd been there with Speaker Hyram, all fresh from taking his Adamantine Throne. But no, he'd learned it from the alchemist a few weeks back when they'd been stuck on the ship together.

He looked around in case the alchemist was already there, didn't see him, then stared up at the slow revolutions of the glasships again. They were mesmerising. Now he'd seen them, they kept pulling his eye.

Yena poked him. 'You're such a savage!'

Other times he might have grinned and told her how much she seemed to like that he was a savage. But not today. Wherever they were going, they'd arrived. He felt it, and he didn't know what that was going to mean but his gut said nothing good. 'In my world we fly on the backs of dragons.' He caught himself. 'No, *dragon-riders* fly on the backs of dragons. *Slaves* fly in wooden cages that the dragons carry in their claws. Now and then they fall apart. Usually in the air. Or they get dropped. Not too careful, dragons.' He laughed bitterly. Cut to the bare bones, it wasn't much different from how he'd come *here* then, except the cage had been nicer and less likely to fall apart in mid-air as old Valmeyan's slave-pens had been prone to do. And no Outsider taken from the mountains and hauled off in one of those hellish cages would have thought twice if the chance came to run away, and yet he'd had them every day for two weeks and here he was.

He cocked his head. 'Do they breathe fire?' he asked.

'No.' She poked him again. '*Ours* breathe lightning, savage.'

Savage. The palace slaves all saw him like that. Yena hid it better than the others, made a joke of it, but that wasn't saying much. An overpowering sense of not-belonging pummelled him when he wasn't with her, or at least talking to her through the wooden divide on the long days they'd spent stranded in the air. It strangled him and now it came again. He pulled away from her hand and looked for the alchemist but the second gondola still hadn't arrived.

'Hoi! Slaves! Come on, come on! Get this unpacked! Quick now!'

They carried boxes out of the gondola and piled them against the white walls, the palace slaves grumbling and groaning under their breath about such menial labour while Tuuran just got on with it. As soon as they were done, the gondola lifted away into the air. Other slaves – Tuuran supposed they were the ones who already lived here – poured out of the archways under the walls, filling the air with urgent questions: 'What belongs to the enchantress? Which are her personal effects? Are these for the laboratory? Where's the alchemist?'

Tuuran moved away. He had what he had, what he carried in his own bag, and that was that. No one paid him any attention and no one shouted and drew out a golden wand as he crossed to the wall. He ambled over to one of the steep flights of steps cut into it and began to climb. The steps, the wall, everything was made of the same white stone, seamless as if carved from a single solid lump of something, polished smooth and all curves and arcs and not a single hard edge or corner in sight. Odd, but what made him stop and run his finger over the stone was that he'd seen this before, back in the dragon realms. The eyrie of Outwatch, far off in the north in the middle of the Desert of Sand. Maybe this white stone grew in deserts then? Certainly nowhere else, for all across the realms he'd never seen anything made as Outwatch had been made, all rounded and smooth without a sharp line anywhere inside or out. Yet here he was in another world and this stone was the same.

He climbed to the top and looked out across the desert in awe.

The white stone walls sloped down – more gently on the outside than they did within – to a wide rim of dark bedrock, and then … nothing. To his eyes, it seemed the place was built on the top of a solitary mountain. A mesa, perhaps, like the ones on the edge of the Purple Spur where it slid into the western edge of Gliding Dragon Gorge not so far away from the Adamantine Palace itself.

The only mesa for a hundred miles though, by the looks of it, and, Flame but it was tall! To the north and east and west a sea of sand stretched out as far as his eyes could reach, great dunes washing away to the horizon, almost white and painfully bright. *White. Why is desert stone always white?* To the south the ground became flatter and dirtier, more patchy and broken. Some sort of salt marsh if he'd heard right. A brilliant line of gleaming silver ran through the middle of it, dozens of miles to the west. A river catching the sun, and a big one. When he looked hard there might have been another too, off in the far distance. Along the rim of the mesa coils of rope as thick as his arm lay below the shallow slope of the walls, with open empty crates scattered around and planks of wood in piles and pulleys and a jib built out over the side. Cranes, most of them only half built, but that meant that beyond the edge was a sheer cliff. He almost went over to have a look, to peer over and drink in the drop but thought better of it.

There were other things built along the rim too. Dull iron wheels as big as a cart lay set flat into the ground, some of them with bright steel plates mounted on them. He'd seen things like these along the walls of the Adamantine Palace, places for mounting a scorpion so that it could easily turn, although these were far larger. A few held up great glass discs, twice as tall as a man, mounted sideways and held by silvery pylons with a series of concentric glass globes nested through the middle and, right at their heart, what looked for all the world like a harness for a man to sit in. The outermost rims were covered in what looked like solid gold. Gold, always gold with the Taiytakei. He'd seen it everywhere since they'd taken him off his ship but they didn't use it for money, not like everywhere else. No, they used silver, which he'd seen in a lot of places, and jade, which he'd seen in far fewer, but never gold. Too precious for that? He wasn't sure.

His eyes drifted out to the desert. Antros, who would have been the last speaker if he hadn't died, had come from the desert, from Sand. Speaker Hyram had come from Bloodsalt. All in all, Tuuran had spent a lot of years in the Deserts of Sand and Stone and Salt before the mistress of the Pinnacles had sold him into slavery. He felt their tug. *Home. I want to go home.* He hadn't forgotten the huge tearing in his heart as they'd crossed the storm-dark; it had dulled in the last weeks but now he felt it as sharp as it had ever been. The alchemist, the Palace of Leaves, the three knives some-one had stuck in him, Yena. He saw them for what they were now. Blindfolds. Dreamleaf, but he'd never *quite* fallen asleep, never *quite* closed his eyes. He opened his shirt. He had nothing to show for those knives now except three little scars. They were almost gone, as though they were wounds from years ago. It was a shame the alchemist had nothing for the scars on the inside.

Out in the distance to the west a glint in the sky caught his eye, a little golden star under a bigger white one. As it came closer he knew it must be the alchemist and the white witch in their sky-ship. He hadn't seen much of the alchemist in the last week but he'd seen enough to know the witch had done her work. She'd cast her spell and enchanted him like she enchanted her flying machines. She'd seduced him and Tuuran would never get him back. And her slave Yena, in her own way, was the same. Even if it wasn't her fault and she didn't mean it, that was what she was trying to do.

'Hey, slave! Get back to work!'

A Taiytakei soldier was on the battlements with him. One of those with the glass and gold-plated armour and the glowing wands. Not that Tuuran had any work to be doing but slaves didn't argue and so he raised his hands, bowed and retreated back down the steps into the yard and moved boxes and crates from one place to another as though he knew what he was doing. Someone pointed to an archway and he followed the line of their finger, nodding dumbly. A few steep steps descended inside and then curved sharply to follow the line of the wall, spiralling deeper underground. The passageway walls were the same white stone as outside, glassy smooth and curved with only a slight flattening at the floor, as though they'd been made by some sort of burrowing worm. There were no murals, no hangings, no decoration, nothing, but they had a light to them like an alchemist's lantern, a glow that crept out from the very stone itself. The eyrie slaves moved back and forth with blank faces but the palace slaves stared in wonder and chatted excitedly. One stopped and scratched the stone with a knife. He caught Tuuran looking at him and hurried away but when Tuuran went to look for himself he couldn't find a mark. Nothing. Yet strange as these passages with their light seemed to the other slaves, yet again Tuuran had seen them before, in the Pinnacles this time. In Queen Aliphera's Fortress of Watchfulness, what little of it he and the new speaker had been allowed to see. They were almost his last memories of the realms he called home. The last ones he cared to dwell on at least.

A short way down the passage he began to pass a series of little rooms, all the same with egg-shaped holes for entrances that you had to step over but not a single door. He'd seen these in the Pinnacles too. And deeper in, as the passage curved back towards the centre of the eyrie and grew wider the rooms grew bigger, some of them larger than the gondola that had carried him here but always curved and in strange shapes. Not circles but never anything angular and no two the same as though water had come through here once and taken its time to carve its signature in each and every room, one that could never be repeated.

The rooms grew larger the deeper he went and the passage grew taller and there were archways here and there, carved into the walls, and swathes of runes and symbols. Not that the arches went anywhere. Just the shape of them, opening onto nothing more than the same white stone as everything else. He'd seen those in the Pinnacles too. Place was riddled with them.

He carried the alchemist's things to the room Bellepheros had been given. Not that the alchemist had any possessions of his own but the witch had arranged for a whole gamut of things to be delivered to him anyway. Clothes and pots and pans, glass beakers in all shapes and sizes. Tiny cages. And books, dozens and dozens of books. Tuuran didn't know what to do with anything else but he knew what alchemists did with books. He put most of them on the shelves and scattered the rest around the room, on tables, on seats, on the bed. He left a few of them opened at some random page in the middle; and when Bellepheros finally arrived, he clapped his hands as he saw and smiled; and Tuuran smiled back, even though the alchemist's smile was ghastly. It was Yena's smile, the smile of a man who'd made some sort of peace with himself and accepted his slavery, who'd bowed to its inevitability and embraced it for what he could get. The Taiytakei had no dragons yet but the witch had shown him her glittering spires and golden glass. She'd told him tales of conjured jewels, of marvellous creatures and the wonders of worlds. She'd seen exactly where his weakness lay and she'd struck at it with the swiftness and the deadly precision of a desert cobra and with a poison to put any snake to shame.

'Going home any time soon?' Tuuran asked him but Bellepheros barely heard. He grunted. Across the passage was another space, one meant to be his laboratory. Someone shrewd must have known he was coming because it was already stocked with shelves and shelves of herbs and roots and powders and liquids, none of which meant anything to Tuuran and most of which were apparently a mystery to the alchemist as well. Watching him was like watching a child in a room full of new toys, moving from one thing to the next, picking it up, opening bottles, sniffing, putting them down, moving on. He even made excited squealing noises. But Tuuran wasn't going to let it lie, not this time.

'No. You're not going anywhere.'

'Sorry?'

'She's got you. That witch. She's got you good. She's put a spell on you and made you her slave.'

The alchemist paused. 'What do you mean?'

'I mean you're going to build them their eyrie and you're going to give them their dragons and you're not even going to try to stop them.'

Bellepheros had a bottle of silver liquid in his hand which he seemed to find strangely fascinating. After a moment of thought he put it down. 'I cannot stop them from bringing dragons.' His smile faded. 'Tuuran, I've begged and pleaded with all who give me their ears to sway them from this course but they don't listen, of course they don't. And if dragons come then yes, I *will* keep them as best I can because the consequences of anything else are unbearable.' He picked up a piece of golden glass and tossed it into the air. It fell, but slowly like a feather. 'Look, though! Look at this! Look at what they can do! Imagine how our world could change!'

Tuuran tried and found he couldn't. Floating glass? What use did he have for floating glass?

'I've set my mind on a course, Tuuran. Liang agrees. One day alchemists will come here to work as they would in any other eyrie, and the Taiytakei will come to us in return. If they *must* have dragons, if they simply cannot be dissuaded, we'll look after them and they will teach us to build these things. It will be a brave new world for all of us.'

He looked as though he believed it and Tuuran had to turn away and screw up his face to hold back the anger. 'No, Lord Master Alchemist. The Taiytakei will come to our land and take whatever pleases them. That's what they do. I've sailed on their slave ships for years; *you* have been here for a mere handful of weeks. You cannot change their ways with a simple snap of your fingers.'

The alchemist met his eye. 'Tuuran, for this I think I can. It's too precious to them.' He looked earnest and eager and hopeful, for a moment far younger than his years. 'I hope they fail, Tuuran, I truly do. But if they don't, if they raise their own dragons, then it must be this way. Anything else will be the end of them.'

'Then *I* hope it is, Lord Grand Master. I hope it *is* the end of them. I hope you fail.' He might have spat at the alchemist's feet but he was an Adamantine Man and this was the grand master of the Order of the Scales and he couldn't see them – *wouldn't* see them – as two ordinary slaves, no different from any other. So he held the bitterness inside him, held the alchemist's gaze long enough to be sure the old man saw the betrayal he felt, then turned and left.

It was another day before he realised that the eyrie wasn't built on top of a sheer-sided mountain at all. That was when the glasships hanging overhead slowly began to move and the chains fastened to the rim outside the walls grew taut and hummed, when all the slaves from the palace stopped what they were doing and ran in amazement to the walls to shout and stare as the eyrie itself began to drift across the desert, free of any tether to the earth.

32

Regrettable

Chay-Liang stood on the rim of the eyrie with the alchemist, and try as she might to stay calm, she could feel her temper wriggling between her fingers like an eel, trying to get away from her. For the fourth time the eyrie had moved because Bellepheros wasn't content with where it sat. They were further east than she'd ever feared, much further than Baros Tsen T'Varr was happy with and ridiculously distant from where Sea Lord Quai'Shu had asked them to go. Too close to Vespinarr for comfort. She could even see the hazy distant peaks of the Konsidar on the far horizon.

'So will *here* do? It had better. Tsen will send someone to push *both* of us over the edge if there's much more of this!' Belli had his slave bodyguard with him, the one he'd brought all the way from Xican. The man was a monster, a simmering hulking brute steaming with resentment and he didn't like her one little bit. He glowered at her and she had to smile, though she turned away where neither of them would see. *Anyone who pushed Belli over the edge would follow quickly enough.* The thought of the two of them plummeting to their deaths made her smile even more, though that made no sense. She pointed at the shapes roaming across the sandy grasslands below. Thousands of them. 'Your dragons can eat those.'

'What are they?'

Liang shrugged and looked at the other slave who seemed to tag around after them all the time. Yena, who braided her hair each morning. The alchemist wanted his guard after the trouble in Zinzarra and the guard wanted his woman and so there they were. It was ridiculous.

'Linxia.' Yena bowed. 'Desert horses.'

Bellepheros scratched his nose. 'Are they migratory?'

Liang looked at the slave again. Yena covered her face in her hands and fell to her knees. 'I do not understand, mistress.'

The slaves that Shrin Chrias Kwen had sent with her were perfect palace slaves, not what she wanted at all. A good slave had *some* sense of their own value. Tsen at least understood that. She would get them changed. Some of them, anyway. Apparently not this one. 'Migratory,' she snapped, saying the word loudly and clearly.

'Do they move from place to place as the seasons change or do they always live here?' asked the alchemist. Damn him but he was better with the slaves than she was and not just because he was one of them. He had a streak of the teacher to him. A patience she'd never possessed.

Yena glanced from Liang to Bellepheros and back again. She had no idea how to treat the alchemist. Nor did anyone else. Since he was unbranded, strictly speaking he was an oar-slave, lowest of the low. Liang treated him as an equal because to her mind that's what he was, slave or not. His bodyguard, although a higher-ranked slave, treated him as though he was a superior. And at the top of them all, Tsen treated everyone as though they were the same and just slightly beneath him. Poor girl didn't know where to start.

'Mistress, they don't live here all year. They come in the cool seasons but in the hot season they follow the river past the Tzwayg to the foothills of the mountains.' Yena glanced uncertainly at the alchemist again. Liang rolled her eyes.

'Well then.' Belli was shaking his head. 'I'm afraid—'

Liang interrupted: 'How long before they leave, slave?' *Here* was the far edge of the salt marshes. Already far enough away from where they'd been *told* to be.

'I think two or three months, mistress.'

Liang nodded, her mind made up. 'Yena, there are other slaves here from the desert. Many of them.' Most of them in fact, since Tsen T'Varr hadn't felt the need to look all that far for men to staff his eyrie. 'Ask among them and find out everything you can about these creatures. Find one who knows them well and send them to me.' She fixed a glare on the alchemist. 'They're here now. When they move we'll follow them. Would that be acceptable? If not, please explain to me why.'

'I ... I suppose.'

He suddenly smiled. Liang closed her eyes and raised her head and thanked all the gods she wasn't supposed to believe in. 'Right!

Well then! Since that's settled, what do we do next?'

'Men,' he said firmly. 'The ones who will become Scales. Has to be men. No women.'

She didn't quite understand what he meant by a *Scales*. Some sort of carer for the dragons. A handler, perhaps, but there was clearly a lot more to it than that. Sometimes he made it sound almost like a servant, at other times like a lover. Whatever they were, she supposed she'd find out soon enough. She led them up the wall and down the inside, away from the rim and into the round white-stone yard, still musing. The walls had steps on both sides. Walls didn't generally make it nice and easy for someone to climb to the top from the outside otherwise what was the point? But whoever had built these had had other ideas and it bothered her that she couldn't fathom what they were. Why build a wall that was no more than a steep hill? Why build one at all on a castle that floated in the air? The inner structure of the eyrie was an even deeper curiosity. Five passages that spiralled inwards underground from the walls, meeting in one central chamber, the biggest and deepest by far – and the one that Baros Tsen, in his bizarre wisdom, had decided to make into his personal bathhouse. He'd blocked off all the entrances bar one, making it impossible to get from any one of the five spirals to any other without coming out and crossing the yard. And then each spiral had a structure of its own, a mystery of random rooms and branching tunnels. She'd drawn one of them out a few days ago, carefully mapping the paths and passages with Belli ambling around beside her, deep in thought. It was something to do while the eyrie moved from place to place. When she'd looked at what she'd drawn it had made no sense.

'It looks like the coil of a new fern on the cusp of uncurling,' Bellepheros had said when he peered over her shoulder. And he was right, and it irked her that *she* hadn't seen it and *he* had.

One of the spirals housed Tsen and Chay-Liang and the alchemist and anyone else of any importance. One housed the slaves who looked after them. Tsen had kept another for the slaves who were still building parts of the eyrie – or would as soon as Bellepheros stopped moving it about – and that one would house the soldiers later. The other two were for the alchemist to use as he saw fit and the first thing he'd asked for had been men to become his Scales. *No special skills are required. I'll see to that.* Which was a stupid thing to say in front of the t'varr since they'd now be the cheapest slaves that Tsen could possibly find.

Those same slaves were now lined up in the yard, waiting for them. The *dragon*yard, she'd decided it would be called. As they came close, Bellepheros put a hand on her shoulder and stopped.

'You understand,' he whispered, 'that the men I choose will all die. A good Scales can last a decade but the Hatchling Disease will take them despite the best potions I can make. Their skin will harden until they can no longer move or breathe. They will become human statues. Only the Scales may have contact with a newly hatched dragon and they will have quarters of their own, isolated from the rest. We call it the Statue Plague. There's no cure, Liang, and it can be spread among men by ...' he looked awkward for a moment '... by contact. Between bed partners for the most part, but by blood too and it takes a while for it to show, by which time it can spread far and wide. Unchecked, those who have it will live a month or two but they may not even know they have it at all for several weeks. There have been occasions in our history when the disease has escaped an eyrie. Half a city was once burned by dragons to contain it. Scales may not have wives or children and they may not have lovers outside their own kind.' He frowned. 'Not that they often do, the disease being what it is.' He looked slightly uncomfortable again – for her, because he knew she squirmed inside talking so openly about things like that. 'It's why many alchemists are celibate too. Aside from the Scales we are most at risk and all of us contract it sooner or later. For those who don't deal with hatchlings every day I can make potions that will slow it to a stop, but I can only make it for a few dozen, not for thousands upon thousands. Once dragons hatch here, the men who are to become our Scales may never leave this eyrie. Ever.'

'I will see they are contained.'

'When the dragons first arrive I will give the chosen Scales a potion that I will make for them. One that, for want of a better way of putting it, will make them fall in love with their dragons. By the time the disease shows, they won't much mind their condition. By then they shouldn't want to leave, so that part will be easy for you. It would be better to raise them properly, teach them for the task from childhood so they know nothing else. That's the way we've always done it in my homeland, but …' He stopped and stared. Tuuran had gone on past them and was now eyeing up the slaves, one after the other. He pulled each one out of the line, looked him in the eye and then either shoved him back or pushed him to one side into a second group.

'Belli? What's your slave doing?'

'I have no idea. Tuuran! Stop it!'

Tuuran didn't even turn around. 'I will not, Master Lord Alchemist. The ones I'm taking away are the ones that come from our realm. From our *home*, Lord Grand Master. The others don't. You'll not turn slaves taken from our land into Scales. And look, no night-skins at all. Why's that? Taiytakei too good to be made into Scales, even the ones of their own that they turn into slaves?'

'No, it's—' But Tuuran wasn't listening.

Liang put her hand on her gold lightning wand. 'To keep your master safe!' she snapped. '*That's* why there are no Taiytakei slaves here! Because I didn't want a Regrettable Man slipping in among us. Does that satisfy you, *slave*?'

Bellepheros put his hand on top of hers. 'Let him.'

Liang flared. 'I put up with a great deal from that slave of yours, Belli. More than I would from any other and more than I would from many who are not. But this, *this* is ridiculous! *I* will choose who will be your Scales, not him!'

'Li!' Bellepheros was shaking his head. 'No, Li, *I* will choose, and I would have done the same as he is doing, except when Tuuran is finished I'm afraid I must upset him and insist that it will be the men from my own land who become my dragon keepers. They will have seen the beasts and understand what they are and they may better resist the Statue Plague. The handful of times when one of your people has contracted it, its progress was noted as being swift. He's doing my work for me, I'm sorry to say. How long before the dragon eggs come?'

Liang sagged. She shrugged. 'Months.'

'Good. No need to turn the slaves right away. I shall begin by teaching them all the basics they'll need to know. We can separate them later when Tuuran is more reconciled to the idea. Give me time to bring him round, Li.'

'I don't think you'll ever do that, Belli. I'm sorry, but it might be best if he were to go. Perhaps the sooner the better.'

Tuuran had finished sorting the slaves. Bellepheros pushed Liang a little towards them. 'We'll see. Come, let me at least pretend to inspect them.'

They walked along the line of slaves not from the dragon realms. Pale-skinned men from the edges of the Dominion. Smaller darker-skinned men from the Dominion's heartland or more likely from the southern coast of Aria. The dark-faced muscular men of the savage Southern Realm. Men who could barely do more than grunt, sometimes.

'Alchemist Bellepheros?' asked one of the southerners in an accent of perfect Vespinese.

Bellepheros looked confused. 'Yes?'

Chay-Liang's hand was already on her wand. Tuuran was quicker, launching himself through the air. But neither of them was as quick as the assassin. His arm came up and punched the alchemist in the throat. A spray of blood went everywhere. The assassin reached to pull Bellepheros close, to finish him and listen to the alchemist's heart stop but Tuuran smashed into him, knocking him back. Bellepheros staggered away, hand to his throat, blood everywhere. Liang looked from one to the other, agape. *They've killed him! They did it. They got one in. And I thought I was so careful. O Charin, no!*

Tuuran and the killer were grappling with each other. Everywhere slaves were screaming and scattering and where was the Watcher when he was needed? Soldiers up on the battlements were already running but they were too far away to make any difference. The damage had been done with the very first blow.

Liang levelled her wand and let fly. The thunderclap stunned her, the shock of air staggered her and the killer was suddenly gone, a broken blackened sprawl of limbs hurled fifty feet from where he'd been. Tuuran flew across the dragon yard too but Liang had no eyes for him. She ran to the alchemist. So much blood said the killer had struck true. Bellepheros would be dead in moments if he wasn't already. There was nothing she could do.

Yet he wasn't. He knelt, blinking, mouth open, hand pressed to his neck, looking bemused as if he had no idea what had happened.

Blood covered him, soaked him. He was dripping with it. She knelt beside him, wrapped her arms around his body and hugged him. 'Belli! Belli! I'm sorry!' So very wrong for a Taiytakei to hold a slave in such a way but what did it matter now? He might as well pass on with some warmth around him, in the hands of someone who truly cared for him. She held his head and whispered in his ear, 'I'm so sorry. So sorry.'

'Was that ... a *regrettable* incident?' he croaked and she let go of him and reeled back in astonishment. What must be almost his last breath and he was trying to make a joke of his own murder?

His eyes followed her, though, and they weren't the eyes of a man about to die. He took her hand and showed her his neck where the knife had struck. Beneath blood that was still wet and warm on her fingers there was no wound at all. He pulled her close so they were eye to eye. 'I can teach these slaves to make a simple potion. I can teach someone like you to make almost anything at all. But true alchemy lives in the blood, Li, and that is a thing that cannot be taught. There is one place in the world where a true alchemist can be made, an alchemist who can dull a dragon. An alchemist who is truly a master of his own blood, and that place is deep within my homeland. Fortunate for both of us that it's not so easy to be rid of a blood-mage.' He stood up, an old man who'd just had his throat ripped open and yet showed no sign of it, and she looked at him with new eyes. For a moment he even made her afraid.

Then he stumbled and put a hand on her shoulder to keep himself from falling, and the moment was gone. 'Now I think I need to lie down for a while,' he said. 'One last thing. Dragon blood. I'll need dragon blood before the eggs come. If you could manage that sooner rather than later, I'd much appreciate it.'

She let him lean on her. The relief she felt that he was alive was more than it should have been for any slave, however precious.

33

Yena

Tuuran was wrestling the man who'd just killed the alchemist, setting free all that burning frustration in a frenzy of bone and sinew when the world exploded. The witch's lightning shattered everything and he was flat and floating, blind and deaf and dumb. Paralysed. Dead maybe, but then his eyes came slowly back. Not much else but he could see the sky. Its brilliant blue burned into his skull until a face blotted half of it out. Yena. She was wringing her hands. From the way her lips moved she might have been calling his name but all he could hear was a ringing. He tried to move, to take her hand, to tell her that he wasn't hurt, not really, but he couldn't. Eventually someone picked him up. They left Yena behind and carried him to a dim place lit by the glowing white stone walls and laid him on his back and left him.

The assassin slave had had marks on him. Tuuran had caught a glimpse as they'd fought. The alchemist needed to know. It seemed important and so he tried his hardest to move. His muscles screamed in pain, all of them, but he made them do it, one by one. Except all he managed to do was roll off his dormitory bed and land like a helpless sack of potatoes on the floor. He floundered there like a landed fish and didn't hear Yena come in because about the only thing he could hear at all was the screeching whine in his ears. He could hardly even hear his own voice. The first he knew she was there was her touch on his shoulder and he could barely move to turn and look at her.

'Go away!' He hated that she saw him like this. Helpless. He gritted his teeth and tried to pretend the pain wasn't there as he hauled himself, one flopping limb at a time, back onto his bed. Then lay there, exhausted. Even breathing hurt. Even every heartbeat. He screwed up his face. His eyes were watering and Yena was still there, hadn't gone away like he'd told her. He turned away from her but he could still feel the warmth of her hand on his shoulder, gently stroking him. 'Go away,' he whimpered. 'Go away. Leave me be!' This wasn't how an Adamantine Man should be, not ever.

She didn't go. He felt her kiss his cheek and her hand stroking his hair, and he felt the breath of her voice over his ear but any words she said were lost in the ringing. And despite it all there was a part of him that was glad she'd stayed.

Eventually he must have fallen asleep. When he woke she was gone and the glow of the walls had changed enough to tell him it was the middle of the night. The pain in his muscles had turned into a dull heavy ache but at least now they moved when he told them to. He sat on the edge of his bed, hands clamped over his ears. All the other slaves were sleeping, packed in around him. The air was stuffy and stale, though nothing like as bad as the stifling holes he was used to from the galleys. Any other night he'd have heard a chorus of snores but now they were barely there, half drowned under the ever-present whine left by the thunderbolt.

He stood up, paced the room and then went outside – there were still no doors almost anywhere except where the Taiytakei had their rooms. He walked up to the huge circular dragon yard. In the moonlight the white stone shone a ghostly silver. No one stopped him. He climbed to the top of the wall – couldn't really call it battlements – and walked around it, looking out across the night at the desert and the stars. The soldiers in the watchtowers challenged him as he passed but they all knew him and didn't shout and send him back under the ground, not tonight. Sometimes he felt as though he was floating, not walking. The ringing in his ears was disorientating. Distracting. It unbalanced him.

Maybe the alchemist could do something; and that was when he realised he had no idea whether the alchemist was even still alive and how badly he was hurt. He'd seen blood fly, that was for sure, so it hadn't just been a scratch.

The tunnel to the alchemist and the witch and all the Taiytakei that mattered had the usual pair of soldiers standing in front of it. When he got close they drew out their wands. 'No further, slave.' They were edgy. He frowned and cocked his head – they *knew* who he was, after all – and then could have slapped himself. Of course they were bloody edgy after what had happened! He held up his hands and kept his distance. One lightning bolt was enough for one day.

'I'm Tuuran. You know me.'

They called back, something that sounded unfriendly. He cocked his head.

'You'll have to shout! Lightning made me deaf!'

One of them took a step closer and waved his wand. He looked angry. 'Keep away! Go back! You cannot enter.'

'And why the bloody Flame not? I'm supposed to be his body-guard.' Although a fat lot of use he'd been this time. 'How bad was he hurt?'

The question unsettled them. The one waving his wand stepped back again and shook his head. The soldiers exchanged a glance and they both seemed to shiver. 'Alive, slave. And that's all you need to know. Go back now! You shouldn't be out here.'

He left them and walked back. He should have been relieved, surely, but he found he wasn't. Yes, a *part* of him was but there was another part too, a nasty angry little piece that wished the alchemist *had* died.

He stopped at the entrance to the slave tunnels. Why? Why would he wish such a thing? But the answer was right there waiting for him: because then it would be finished. The Taiytakei wouldn't get their eyrie. For once they wouldn't get everything they wanted simply by reaching out and taking it. He wouldn't have to watch the alchemist lie to himself every day. Wouldn't have to watch him making himself into a perfect slave for them with his foolish dreams. Wouldn't have to watch his own dreams of going home have the life bled out of them with every glance from that cursed witch.

He took a deep breath and crept away down the tunnels and found a place to sit in the soft moonlight glow of the walls for a while to think, then slipped further to where the witch's slave women slept. He crept among them, quiet as a panther until he found Yena and silently woke her.

Her eyes went wide when she saw him. 'Tuuran! What are you doing here?' At least that was probably what she said. It looked like it. He leaned in close.

'My hearing's still not right. Come with me!'

She pulled his ear to her lips and hissed, 'You can't be here, Tuuran! If they catch you, you know what they'll do!'

Yes, he knew. They'd flog him and there were enough slaves who didn't like him to see that word got out if any of them saw him here. But still. He took her wrist and pulled. 'Come.'

She held back a moment, looking around at the sleeping women in their cots, then giggled and slipped back her sheets and followed him out. They ran down the passage deeper into the tunnels. There were still lots of empty rooms, bare, lit by their moonlight walls. More slaves would be coming to fill the eyrie when the dragon eggs arrived he'd heard, but not yet.

'Where are we going?'

He led her into one of the rooms and pulled her to him and kissed her. Sod being a slave. Sod being an Adamantine Man. Sod duty and screw honour. A finger to all of it. The alchemist had all but forgotten him, the witch had barely even noticed him in the first place. He had no place here, none. He ran his fingers through Yena's hair, pressed his tongue into her mouth and felt her teeth nip him. Ran his hands down her shoulders, down her back. He could feel every shape of her through her silk.

She broke the kiss, gasping for breath. Her face was flushed with excitement and right there and then he wanted her more than anything else. *Run away with me.* The words were on the tip of his tongue.

'His back was burned black.' She shivered. 'But he had writing on him. Tattoos all across his belly.' She put a hand on Tuuran's chest.

'What?' Tuuran blinked. 'What did? I mean who? What?'

'The man you were fighting! The one who tried to kill your master.'

She'd smashed his thoughts with a hammer. He half turned away, trying to put them back together again. And he hadn't really thought this through, had he? How, exactly, was he going to run away from an eyrie floating in the air half a mile over the desert? 'What did it say?' Not that he cared but it gave him some time to gather himself.

'Mistress doesn't know.' Yena's fingers moved over his shirt, soft and delicious. 'Nor your master. It must be a language from one of the other worlds. She's been asking all the other slaves to look, but no one else knows it either.'

That stopped him cold. 'What? How? Have they hung him up in the sun for everyone to come and have a look?'

'No.' The fingers stopped for a moment. 'Your master … he took the skin off the dead man.'

'Ah.' Yes, an alchemist would do that.

The thought caught in his throat. Bellepheros had done that? *After* he'd had his neck ripped open? Since when did alchemists get their throats cut and then act like nothing had happened? That wasn't alchemy, that was blood-magic, the second time Bellepheros had shown he possessed it. Adamantine Men knew all about blood-magic. *Do not suffer a blood-mage to live.* Yet another reason to go, as if he needed one. He took Yena's hands in his own and pressed them together and then put them to his lips. *A blood-mage uses the blood of others, not his own.* So Bellepheros had said but that didn't change how wrong it felt. He cupped Yena's face in his hands and made himself look at her. Adamantine Men didn't take wives and never raised sons. They weren't even supposed to have lovers, though all of them did. *We are swords. We sate ourselves in flesh and move on.* Stupid saying but there were plenty enough who were like that.

Ah Flame! He let her go. Taking her with him had seemed right, exactly the thing to do. Instinct said so. And he liked her and it wasn't just for her willing skin either, but she was a palace slave, delicate and fragile and smooth while he was a sailor and a soldier, all hard leather and rough edges. He stepped back. 'If I ran, would you come with me?'

'What? Why would you run?'

'Never mind the why – would you come? That's all. Never mind the how or the where either, never mind any of that. Would you come with me or not?'

Her face wrinkled up. 'But I *do* mind, Tuuran.' She turned away and then turned back. 'Why would you want to leave? You're almost a sword-slave. They treat you like one already! Where would we go? What would we do?' She shook her head. 'No, Tuuran. No. Don't ask me that.'

He took a deep breath. 'With you or without you I'm going to ask my master to let me go.' And he watched her carefully and caught her, right there, that look in her eye calculating what his leaving would mean. Not feeling his loss but assessing the change in her status. It burned his heart.

'Why?' Her fingers brushed his cheek. He let her, forcing back the urge to grab her and snap her wrist.

'Because he's making this eyrie. Because he thinks he's the master here and he's happy but he isn't; he's a slave and a fool and your mistress is a witch who's put a spell on him. He's forgotten he's not free, but I haven't. He makes me sick. So do you, all of you. Slaves content to serve. You're pathetic.'

That was the bitterness talking but it was out before he could stop it. And though it might have been true, there were other truths too. Kinder ones not spoken. It was just that, right there and then, he couldn't seem to find them.

Yena turned and left without a word. When she didn't come back he roamed the eyrie aimlessly until dawn.

His hearing slowly came back over the days that followed, though the ringing never quite left. He spent day after day with nothing to do, kicking his heels, sitting on the walls or right at the very edge of the eyrie with the sky under his feet, staring out across the desert. The alchemist had other guards now, Taiytakei soldiers in their glass and gold armour with wands that spat lightning, better protectors than any slave could ever be. On the rare days when Bellepheros emerged from his quarters, he always had two of them at his side and usually the witch too. Tuuran watched them together. They were like old lovers and it made him want to scream, not just because of what the witch had done to the alchemist but because it stabbed him every moment with a reminder of how alone he was. He missed his home. But he missed his ship more, the slaves who sailed it. Men who were like he was.

He tried to tell Yena that he was sorry, that he hadn't meant it, that he missed her too, but she wouldn't speak to him now. One time he slipped out late at night to look for her again, unable to sleep, and found her with another man pressing her against a wall, and it made him think of a different time and a different place where he'd seen much the same, only with a girl who'd been much less willing, and the red mist came down and the next thing he knew there were soldiers hauling him away and all he felt was relief, though he knew perfectly well what the Taiytakei did to slaves who couldn't behave. Shoot him with lightning a few times and then throw him off the edge of the eyrie he supposed; but instead they hauled him to a makeshift cell with a door and a frame that had been forced into the opening and didn't work properly, and in the morning the alchemist and the witch were waiting for him.

'He should be hung,' said the witch.

Tuuran shrugged. She was looking at the alchemist anyway, not at him. 'So hang me,' he said.

'He's cost me a slave.' There wasn't much he could say to that. He didn't remember exactly what he'd done, only that it surely hadn't been pretty. 'Belli, why shouldn't I? Give me a reason.'

The alchemist looked at Tuuran. He cocked his head but he only seemed sad, and Tuuran didn't have any sort of answer that would make any sense. He shrugged again. He'd saved the alchemist's life once. Either that was enough or it wasn't. 'If I was you that's probably what I'd do,' he said.

'Bloody Adamantine Men.' The alchemist sniffed and offered Tuuran his hand. 'Come on.'

'I did save your life, Lord Grand Master.' Shouldn't have needed to be said, though.

'I haven't forgotten. A glasship will leave soon for Vespinarr. You'll be on it. Come with me.'

'To where, Lord Alchemist? Off to the slave markets again?'

'Where would you *like* to go, Tuuran? What is it you want?'

Tuuran flared. 'What is it that I *want*? You have to ask me that, Grand Master? Home, of course, I want to go home. To be with my own people again. To be free. What you should want too. To serve your speaker.'

The alchemist shook his head. 'But I do not serve the speaker, Tuuran. Alchemists never have. We serve the realms. The truth is, we answer only to ourselves, and I've concluded that I may best do this from where I am. There are possibilities that—'

'Spare me, blood-mage!'

'Oh, just bring him.' The witch turned away.

'Let him stay with me a while,' said the alchemist. 'Until the glasship comes.'

The witch threw up her hands. 'If you absolutely must.'

Four Taiytakei soldiers led Tuuran up into the dragon yard and down the spiralling passage to where the alchemist and the witch kept their rooms. Bellepheros waved them away, and they weren't happy about that one little bit and only went when he almost pushed them out and shut the door. When they were gone, he looked at Tuuran in silence. Tuuran's eyes wandered around the alchemist's room, remembering how he'd laid out the clothes and the books before Bellepheros had arrived, trying to make it the way he thought an alchemist would like it. Trying to make it like home and now that's exactly how it looked. Home. Tuuran clenched his fists.

'How did you come to be a slave, Tuuran? An Adamantine Man? I know the Taiytakei bought slaves taken by the King of the Crags. Outsiders, mostly. Something of which I greatly disapproved even before I was taken myself, for what little that's worth. But an Adamantine Man? How?'

'Stupidity, like I told you.' The same stupidity he'd had last night. Tuuran laughed bitterly. No one had ever asked him how he'd ended up as a slave before, not asked and really meant it. Every man had his own story and every man thought his was the most important, but the essence of them all was the same. Wrong place, wrong time, bad luck. 'What does the how of it matter?'

'Humour me. I have to watch over you until the glasship that leaves for Vespinarr is ready.'

'Very well. Hyram had been made speaker. He had his great tour of the realms. You were there.'

'I remember.'

'He took some of us with him. Showing us off. First time any of us were on the backs of dragons – now there was an uneasy thing, I can tell you. But we were his guard and so we did as we were told and followed him to Bloodsalt and to Sand and Outwatch, and then afterwards to the Pinnacles.' Tuuran stood up and started to pace. A fury still burned at the injustice. 'It was there. There was a feast. Everyone got drunk, same as always. The lords and ladies had gone to their beds. Middle of the night and I needed a piss but that's not such a simple thing in the Pinnacles. They don't have pots in the corners of their chambers, they have special rooms for it dotted about here and there but never where you want them. Well I went and found one and then after I was done, somehow I walked the wrong way.' Because he was drunk? No, because he was curious and the Fortress of Watchfulness was supposed to be filled with miracles and there was no one to stop him. 'I ended up some place I wasn't supposed to be. All filled with a soft silver moonlight that came off the walls, same as the tunnels here.' He glanced at the alchemist and got a nod of understanding. Bellepheros had seen it too then. 'I could see a man and a girl, shadows picked out by the light. Lovers, I thought at first, but then I saw I was wrong and they weren't lovers at all. A lord and some poor servant girl. I should have left it alone, knew that even then. But he had her pressed against the wall and she was trying to get away from him, and I was drunk and it was wrong, whoever he was, and there was a thing inside that just snapped right there and then, worn out from sickness at all the things I'd seen in Bloodsalt and Sand and even back before in the City of Dragons, rich men and their ways, thinking they could take whatever they chose, that no one would ever stand up to them. So I went up and threw him to the floor and told him to leave her alone. I saw then I was wrong. She was no servant but some rich little lady just coming to bloom, a real beauty too – not that that made it any different – wrong was still wrong – but there was a moment there when it wasn't what I was expecting and I was drunk and it made me slow, and in that moment the girl had my knife out of my belt and stabbed him. She must have killed him with the first or the second thrust but she kept on stabbing and there was blood everywhere. Flame!' He sat down again. 'I tried to stop her and so she tried to stab me too, like she had no idea I wasn't the same person. Strangest thing was, she never cried out, never said a word. Played it all out in silence and then she seemed to come to her senses and dropped the knife and ran away, and I was too stupid to go after her and bring her down and hold her to account for what she did.' He held his head in his hands. 'Thing is, I could see from how she was that this wasn't the first time, far from it, and there was a part of me thought *Good for you*. Because he deserved it even if he was some great lord.'

He took a breath or two now, letting the memory pass a little, surprised at how raw it felt even from so far away. 'So there I was with a dead man killed by my knife. I took it and ran. There was a little of his blood on me but not much. I rubbed it away as best I could. The knife I licked clean. Didn't have anywhere else to put his blood. I went back and joined my brothers in their cots and in the morning I drank as much wine as I could lay my hands on and tried to pretend it hadn't happened. Thought maybe it would go away. A mystery never solved. But it wasn't just *some lord* that girl killed. In the dark I hadn't seen but it was Prince Mazam, the queen's consort. Lord of the Pinnacles and the Silver City.'

Bellepheros jerked. '*What?*'

'Thought you'd have heard of it.' Tuuran laughed. It all seemed so stupid now. 'Being a lord high alchemist.'

'But he choked in some ... accident ...' The alchemist's words died around him. 'Yes. It was around that time. When Hyram went to the Pinnacles. Oh my.'

'They knew it was my knife. I don't know how but they knew. I never told them about the girl.' He shrugged. 'They were going to kill me anyway so what difference did it make? From the look on her face he had it coming. Flame knows how many others he'd raped. So I said nothing but I think they knew. Poor girl ran away covered in blood so they must have caught her but I never saw what happened to her if they did. And I thought over what I'd seen and how they'd kill me anyway, just for being there. So I decided. He'd had it coming. Even if they found the girl I'd say it was me. Good for her for murdering that raping bastard.'

He had to stop a moment. Take a deep breath and let his heart slow a beat. 'They held me there for weeks. Long after Hyram and my brothers were gone back to the City of Dragons. When they did take me out, they took all manner of clubs and knives and other torturers' things I couldn't name to my skin but I never said a word about the girl. Had to be useful for something, being what I was, that was how I saw it. Never understood why they didn't kill me but they didn't. They took me to Furymouth and they sold me instead.' He shrugged. 'I'm buggered if I know why. Had to be a dragon's rage more trouble than simply throwing me off a cliff.'

He blinked. Stared off into space a while, filled with remembering, then sat and cracked out a laugh. 'Like I said, stupid. If I'd kept my nose out of other people's business I wouldn't be here. Yena could have been that girl last night, whoever she was. The man I kicked bloody, he could have been Prince Mazam. And if there's ever a next time, I'll do the same.'

Bellepheros looked dazed and lost. 'You almost killed him.' He shook his head. 'And the woman? I don't think I've ever seen anyone more terrified.' He shook his head. 'What use are you, Tuuran?'

'What use?' Tuuran spat. He ripped open his shirt and pointed to the scar on his chest. 'This! This is what use I am, Lord Grand Alchemist. You don't want me here and I don't want to be here, so just send me back where I came from if you can't send me home. Send me back to my ship. I was happy enough there.' He started to pace the alchemist's room, an animal in a cage.

'I don't know if I can. Li is hopping with fury. She wants you hanged.'

Tuuran stopped. A rough circle of dried skin covered in strange writing was on the alchemist's desk. It took him a moment to realise it must be the skin from the assassin the witch had destroyed. He picked it up and looked at it more closely, then grinned and bared his teeth. 'Well, how about I give you a reason?' He waved the skin in the alchemist's face. 'I've seen this writing before.'

The alchemist shook his head. 'In old books? On the walls deep inside the Pinnacles? I know. I just don't know what it means.'

Tuuran put the skin carefully down. 'Do I look like I read books? On a man, Lord Grand Master Alchemist. On a living man.' Crazy Mad. The great big birthmark – or whatever it was – on his leg that he always tried to hide.

34

The Layers of a Man

The Watcher was waiting for Tuuran in Vespinarr, shooing away the oar-slaves and the Vespinese soldiers who crowded around the gondola as it landed. Tuuran tensed and then made himself relax and look away. He knew well enough by now what the Watcher was for and how little point there was trying to stand against him.

'I'm not here to kill you,' said the Elemental Man, which made Tuuran laugh because no slave across all the worlds mattered *that* much, and if the witch wanted him dead she could have done it herself.

'So why are you here?'

'Because of the writing on the assassin's skin. I have seen it before. In two places, in fact. Where have *you* seen it?' He led Tuuran away from the open space full of gold and glass where the ships-that-flew brought their shining eggs, and towards a bridge of yellow stone over a wide blue rushing river.

'First time was in my homeland, deep in the bowels of an old palace, but that's not what interests you.' He frowned, struggling for breath. The air felt thin, as though he was high up in the peaks of the Purple Spur.

'The mountain air can be strenuous.' In the middle of the bridge the Elemental Man stopped. Tuuran looked around him at the city sprawled up the slopes on either side, at the Silver Mountain that overlooked everything else with its walls and palaces and old forts dotted across its slopes, at the massive towers of the Kabulingnor Palace on Mazanda's peak on the mountain's crown. The Watcher pointed down along the flow of the river. 'The Yalun Zarang flows that way for fifty miles to the edge of the plateau. It descends in a series of cataracts towards the coast, to the Lair of Samim and Tayuna. A mere handful of miles east of the city the Jokun river does much the same, but they never meet and through the Lair they wend their separate ways. The Jokun will lead you to Hanjaadi. It's the Jokun you see from the eyrie. Its cataracts are among the most beautiful things in all the world.'

Which was all very interesting if you were an alchemist, Tuuran thought, but not to a slave about to go to sea. He looked out over the frothing water rushing among its rugged boulders, filling his lungs with cold mountain air. 'Really.'

'To my eyes the City of Stone is unsurpassed. But they *are* beautiful. Tell me of this slave you know and the marks he wears.'

So Tuuran told the Watcher of Crazy Mad and his time on the slave galley as the Elemental Man led them away across the bridge and through the crowded city streets. 'He said it was a brand but I've seen lots of brands and it wasn't. I don't know what it was. Part of it was a scar, a great big one. Seen plenty of *those*. But not the signs around it. He was a strange one, Crazy Mad. Said all sorts of things but he kept the truth to himself. Very careful when he was awake. Not so much when he was asleep.' He told the Watcher how Crazy Mad had cried out at night, *Skyrie, Skyrie!* and of his grumblings of warlocks. 'Lots of hidden layers to him, that one.' He stopped.

'Warlocks?' The Watcher was listening with a sudden intensity, as though all of this meant something, which was more than it ever had to Tuuran.

'That's what he said. What do you want with him?'

'And this man was on your ship? And that's where you wish to go?'

'No, magician, I want to go home.' Tuuran shook his head and blew air between his teeth. 'But I'll take my old ship if that's what's on offer.'

'It is. You will stay close to him. You will be rewarded if you do.'

'I will, will I? And what's that reward going to look like? Going to slice off my head with that magic knife of yours when I'm no use to you any more like you did with that man who tried to kill my lord grand master?'

The Watcher shook his head. 'Serve your purpose to me and I'll have you sent back to your home. You'll be free.' A smile flickered at the corner of the Elemental Man's mouth. 'I let the second Regrettable Man go, didn't I?'

'Except his arm!' Tuuran looked the Elemental Man up and down and shrugged. 'All right. I agree. What do I do when I get to the ship? You want him brought back here somehow or do I just watch?'

The Elemental Man shook his head and walked in silence for a while, on through the streets and up the lower slopes of the Silver Mountain to an obelisk that stood in the middle of a great square in front of some great palace set at the foot of the mountain's roots. 'The Azahl Pillar,' he said as they drew near. 'Emperor Vespin brought it here from somewhere in the Konsidar. No one knows quite where. The inscriptions here are the oldest across the whole of Takei'Tarr. They were cut before the Splintering. They are the same as the ones on this slave, are they not?'

Tuuran rubbed his nose and squinted at the carvings in the white stone. 'Not *exactly*, but ...' He pointed at a few of the sigils. 'I remember that one. And that one.' He let out a long slow breath.

'But?'

He closed his eyes, trying to remember, trying to be sure. 'They're the same as the ones I saw back in the Pinnacles. Sigil for sigil. I think. Or maybe not *exactly* the same, I can't remember, but if not, then very nearly.' He grinned. 'Send me back and I'll find out for you.'

The Elemental Man ignored him. 'The Regrettable Man who came to Baros Tsen T'Varr's eyrie bore similar marks, though the one in Zinzarra did not. And they are like ... others I have seen.' They walked again, back through the city to the river and to a busy quay and barges packed full of slaves. The Watcher handed Tuuran a sliver of glass etched with words and symbols. 'With this you may call for aid from those who serve the sea lord of Xican. Show it when you reach Tayuna. Tell the harbour masters the name of the ship you wish to find. They will see to it.' He walked briskly down the steps to the riverfront and waved Tuuran aboard a waiting barge. Tuuran scowled over the frothing water. 'Watch the sail-slave with his marks. Watch for the grey dead men. Watch but do not intervene. I will find you when I can. If you do this for me then freedom is yours when it's done.'

'Watch him? For how long? How do I find you?' But the Watcher had already turned away and was quickly gone, lost in the riverside crowd. The barge master cast off his rope and ran to the front, yelling and shouting at the slaves there equipped with big thick poles. Tuuran made to stand up but the barge was moving now, getting faster, lurching and starting to spin in the surging river. 'Grey dead men?' he shouted back. 'Who are they? When *what's* done?' But he got no answer and was left to wonder whether he was alone now or whether the Elemental Man was still there, a part of the wind and the river; and then after that, as they bounced through the Yalun Zarang rapids and he was drenched in freezing spray, he was too busy clinging to the sides of the barge to wonder much of anything at all.

It took a week to reach the sea from Vespinarr, a week full of wild dashes down a river feisty with mountain snow-melt and of dangling in rickety cages lowered beside curtain-cascades of water, the Yalun Zarang cataracts. They crossed the river behind one of these on a ground-flat path of rock ten feet wide beneath a colossal black overhang with the river roaring down beside them, loud as the white witch's lightning and quivering the ground with its force. In Tayuna Tuuran found his way to the docks and showed his sliver of glass and said the name of the vessel he was looking for and was put on a ship that took him to another, and then to yet another; and whenever he showed the Watcher's glass the Taiytakei took him without question and set him to work, just another sail-slave, making his way around half the coast of Takei'Tarr and then a week across the open ocean to the horizon stain of the storm-dark. He counted through the stillness as they crossed it. Five hundred heartbeats before the ship lurched and shook and they were through to the other side and back amid the howling winds and the hurling waves and the churning violet-streaked sky.

That ship took him to another, with colours and signs on its sails that he'd seen before. He saw land again. They sailed towards it, beside it, to a cove in the middle of nowhere along an unfamiliar wild coast and lowered their sails and waited in the calm seas and turned to face the wind, and there at last was his corsair galley, his slave ship. He knew it at once and his heart smiled as he saw it. A strange feeling swept him through. A warmth. A relief and yet an anxiousness. He was as close as a man like him got to such a thing as home – as long as he could keep from memories of his *true* home.

The ship and the galley both lowered their boats, captured slaves leaving, barrels of water and biscuits and arrows coming the other way. Up in the ship's rigging the archer platforms were manned by sharp-eyed Taiytakei bowmen. Food and weapons and money for slaves, that was the way the corsair galleys worked. It wasn't the first time they'd met another ship in the middle of nowhere and exchanged goods like this but it was the first time Tuuran had been on the other side.

Oar-slaves rowed him over. Tuuran scrambled with ease up the heavy net lowered over the side of the galley, climbed aboard, put his hands firmly on his hips, took a deep breath and let it slowly out again, scanning the decks and smiling a toothy smile. A few new faces but most of them were familiar and he met their surprised eyes with his grin. *Tuuran is back. Old friends rejoice; enemies quiver and quail.* The sail-slaves watched him. Times like this they had little to do but the air was always thick with tension. Handing over the catch from the last few months always brought home what they were: slaves taken from their own lands and turned, now making more of the same for the very people they'd once sworn to hate. A few grinned back at him – old friends – but Tuuran passed them by. There'd be time for greetings and half-forgotten scores later. Some of the Taiytakei who remembered his face stared as well. A couple even grinned, maybe pleased to have him back, while others gaped. He passed them too. He was after Crazy Mad, and there he was, walking to the far edge of the deck, his back to the sailing ship as though he wasn't interested at all, looking down into the sea. Well, he wasn't going to get away with *that*.

Tuuran dropped a heavy hand on Crazy Mad's shoulder and clasped him tight. 'Hello slave. So now is your time to throw me in the water, I think.'

Crazy Mad jumped like he'd been stung. 'Tuuran! What are you doing back here?'

'What do you think? Back among my old friends. Missed all of our fun, missed stealing men and women from their homes to make into new slaves for our masters, of course.' And now he'd seen how those masters lived. Hadn't given it much thought before. 'You're not at your post, slave. Do you like rowing?'

In another world there might have been more between them

– an embrace, some acknowledgement of pleasure – but this was a slaving ship and everything that might be weakness was seized and devoured and destroyed, and so Tuuran said no more and left Crazy Mad where he was and set to shouting at all the other sail-slaves who'd been secretly glad when they'd thought he wasn't coming back. The old familiar world slipped easily over him like a favoured glove, close and comforting, and it was hardly a chore to keep half an eye on Crazy Mad and what he did, especially when what he did was exactly what every sail-slave did. Sailed, drank, brawled, gambled and told stories.

The sailing ship left and that was always a happy time for the sailors: a hold full of food and no angry captives. The galley continued in the routine Tuuran knew as well as he knew his own skin. A month passed and then another. They filled the slave pens with bronze-skinned men from a shoreline of arid rugged hills that the locals called the Kala, moving slowly north towards the southernmost coast of Aria. The sailing ship came again and emptied their cages and filled their larder and they moved on, edging up the coast; and it took even the Taiytakei by surprise when a second ship hunted them down only a few weeks later. It was a sleek warship, this one, far bigger than the one that had returned Tuuran and almost as big as the vessel that had taken him to the dragon lands. The usual platforms for archers hung amid the masts and spars but there were other things there too, and more on the deck, pointing over the side. Metal tubes filled with Taiytakei black-powder rockets, each with a glass bulb on the front filled with trapped fire. The ship stood off from the galley, weapons armed, nothing friendly about its manner at all, and lowered a boat. Just the one with a single Taiytakei aboard and some oar-slaves to row it, and three men in cowled grey robes who looked far too skinny and feeble to be working ships to Tuuran's eyes; and then a different thought jolted him: *Watch for the grey dead men.*

His eyes flicked to Crazy Mad. Took a long hard look. Crazy looked like he'd been struck by lightning, and whatever he did now, all of them would answer for it. Even before the grey-robes finished climbing aboard, Tuuran was alongside him, one arm wrapped tight around him, too tight, turning him away from the ship and towards the distant shore, away from these unwanted strangers. Whoever they were they weren't night-skins, so that made them slaves, and slaves had no place coming aboard a slaving galley unless it was to be put in chains and sold.

'I see that look and I know what it is because sometimes I have it too. One dissents, all are punished. You know this, Crazy Mad.'

'I have a *name*.'

'Yes. I keep hearing that. People ask about one slave or another, I tell them they're wasting their time. Slaves don't have names. But that's not really true. Turns out some slaves *do* have names after all. They keep them inside but they keep them nevertheless. They hold them tight and sometimes they let them out when they shouldn't. *I* have a name. *I* am Tuuran. And I'll hear yours too if you can make up your mind which one it is. But *not now*!' He let his arm loosen and risked a glance over his shoulder. The grey-robes were standing quietly on the deck behind the Taiytakei who'd brought them while he argued with the galley captain. 'So tell me, slave who has too many names and a mark on his leg, who are these men in grey and what do they want? Because it's you they're here for, isn't it?'

Crazy Mad struggled but Tuuran was by far the stronger and his grip was good and tight. 'One dissents, all are punished. Never quite got that through your thick head. What are these men in grey?'

Crazy hissed at him, 'Warlocks. Death-mages. Witch doctors. Necromancers! What other name do you need?'

'Where I come from there are alchemists and there are blood-mages. Alchemists are good. Blood-mages are evil and wicked and villainous. Or that's what I thought. I take it these are your blood-mages then?' Tuuran let him go.

Crazy Mad shoved him away. 'Stick it, Tuuran. You vanish for half a year; you come back; you bring them with you? I'll kill you! But not until I've done for them first!'

The grey-robes were filing into the cabins at the back of the galley. Somehow Crazy Mad had the knife out of Tuuran's belt. It was slickly done. Tuuran had to acknowledge that, even as he caught Crazy's arm, spun him around and slammed his elbow into the back of his head, dazing him enough to grab him and drag him away, kicking and swearing.

'This one's forgotten his manners,' he shouted at the Taiytakei guards on the deck. 'A couple of days in the bilges and a month back on the oars.' He took back his knife and hauled Crazy Mad to his feet. A couple of days in the bilges or as long as it took for the grey-robes to go away. But as he turned, there they were, the three of them with their hoods drawn back so Tuuran could see their shaven heads and their faces as pale as moonlight and the tattoos that started on their cheeks and ran down their necks and vanished under their robes. Symbols. Sigils. Meaningless to him, but as sure as he knew anything the same writing he'd seen on the pillar in Vespinarr, the same as on the dead slave from the eyrie, the same as on Crazy Mad's leg.

Soldiers stood beside them as well as the Taiytakei galley master in his coloured cloak, tattered and stained by so many months at sea. Tuuran saw the grey-robes and saw their smiles and then Crazy Mad thrashed his arms, wild-eyed, and Tuuran knew *that* look because it was the same look he'd had only just a few moments ago. *A knife! Give me a knife!* This time Tuuran was ready. As Crazy pulled the knife free again, Tuuran seized his wrist. They wrestled together, Crazy Mad screaming, Tuuran bawling in his face, 'We'll not all suffer just for you, you mad bastard!' And every shout drew more attention to them both and he needed to get this idiot out of sight, out of the way, because he knew they were here for Crazy, and Crazy Mad knew it too, only what he didn't know were all the things Tuuran had seen in his six months away. *Run at them with a knife, will you? Flame-addled idiot!* And it had to matter, didn't it, because this was what the Watcher had sent him to do, and if they took Crazy away to a place where he couldn't follow, he would never go home. Never!

The tallest of the three grey-robes swept towards them with contempt. His fingers curled around the hilt of his own knife, clutched with a religious reverence. Crazy Mad screamed. He and Tuuran lurched toward the side of the galley and whatever Crazy howled, Tuuran roared louder so no one would hear: 'Stupid slave! Take us all with you, will you?' The Taiytakei slavers had their wands drawn, tense and ready. 'One slave turns, all slaves die!' Crazy Mad's eyes did a frenzied dance around the galley, a wild animal looking for a way out, but Tuuran offered him none. 'And I ... am not dying ... for you!'

They hit the rail as the galley rolled and it was the easiest thing in the world to lower his hip and dump Crazy Mad over the side and watch him fall into the sea. He sank, and for a few seconds Tuuran stared after him but he didn't come back up again. When Tuuran turned, there was the grey-robe, the tall one, standing right in front of him with his knife. A strange blade, more of a cleaver than a dagger, with a golden hilt and patterns in the sharpened steel that swirled before Tuuran's eyes.

They stared each other down and then Tuuran pushed the grey-robe harshly aside. 'Piss off.' They were only slaves, after all.

He wondered what else he could have done. And whether Crazy Mad could swim.

35

The Day the Dragons Came

'Grand Master Alchemist. A private word, if you please?'

Nastria gave him a spherical glass bottle, stoppered and sealed with wax. It fitted nicely into the palm of his hand and it was filled with liquid silver. The knight-marshal had no idea, of course. There was nothing curious about what the bottle contained, but what was intriguing was how it had come to be in the knight-marshal's hands. It was a long journey home though and there would be plenty of time to ponder and plenty of comfortable inns and fine wine to help him think and dead Queen Aliphera would be there, watching over his shoulder, keeping him company.

He left the Veid Palace the next morning. He borrowed a carriage from the Viper and took a handful of soldiers for an escort while he was at it because last he'd heard there were snakes on the road to Farakkan, and so he'd need them. He tucked the knight-marshal's bottle under his seat, carefully packed in sand.

In the middle of nowhere the carriage stopped. A man made of rushing air tore open the door. He had a knife and blood glistened on its blade. There were bodies on the ground outside. Thousands of them, all blackened and burned. He opened his mouth to scream, but before he could, the knife flashed across his throat and his blood poured out of him and for some reason it wouldn't stop but just kept coming, more and more and more, and when he looked up the sky was filled with dragons. 'All but one are small. Freshly hatched from the egg, or so the alchemist says. There were three full grown beasts. The sorcerers took two, one for each of them. The third is ours.'

Bellepheros sat up gasping, panting, the cry of alarm still building in his throat. It was starlight-dark. There was no carriage, no knife, no masked men, but it still took him a moment to remember where he was.

Two long, slow, deep breaths. Dreaming again. The same nightmare that came back now and then. Once he'd caught his breath he chided himself for being surprised that it had come back tonight, after what the evening had brought.

In the far corner of the room a tiny candle burned on a stone slab. It was a slow-burner, something that would make a little flame all through the night. He stumbled out of bed and fumbled for his desk until he found the lamp he kept on it and lit it from the candle. There were no windows down here under the eyrie, but he knew from the glow of the white stone walls that outside the desert horizon would be a deep blue, not quite black. Dawn was an hour away.

He went to the desk and sat down. On another morning he might have tried to go back to sleep but not today. That bottle that Shezira's knight-marshal had given him was still there. He made a little mark on the underside of the desk. Another day. Two hundred and forty-five since the Taiytakei had taken him now, give or take a couple. He was an alchemist and nothing if not meticulous about such things.

A gentle knocking disturbed his despair and his door creaked open. 'Belli? Should I leave you alone?'

Yes. But that wouldn't do. 'No, no, come in. We have a great deal of work before us so we might as well get on with it.' Li. She was his watcher, his jailer, his assistant, but above and beyond all else she was his friend, and by the light of the Great Flame he needed her for that now. A few short hours and their whole world had been turned on its head. He rubbed his eyes and shook his head. 'Eggs. You were supposed to bring me eggs! Not this!'

'I have enumerated the dragon kin,' she said and pushed her glass lenses up her nose. 'There are fifty-seven hatchlings and the large one. Also I've made qaffeh.' She put a hot metal pot on the desk in front of him. The bitter smell made him smile. It was a Taiytakei drink and the likes of Prince Jehal and others who lived in the seaport of Furymouth spoke of it with awe. Bellepheros had never tried it until Li had all but forced it on him. She lived on the stuff. He couldn't think of a single time when she hadn't had a fresh hot pot of it to hand.

'Remember to keep away from the little ones,' he said absently.

The Taiytakei made a sticky sweet spongy bread which they dipped in their qaffeh and he'd acquired so much of a taste for it that even the thought was making his mouth water. 'They're easily young enough to still carry the Hatchling Disease.'

'They're dry. No residues of their birthing products remain.'

'So they may seem but they need to be washed, Li. By the Scales. Did they all feed?' No, wait, they did all of this yesterday didn't they? When the dragons suddenly popped out of the sky and filled the eyrie to its rim. Flame! There was nothing he could do for so many! Twenty-six Scales he'd prepared, far more than he'd thought would be necessary, and suddenly he needed five times that number. No. They'd started a feed and he'd run from one to the other, shouting and yelling at the Taiytakei and at all the slaves to keep away and stay underground and … and what? He pressed a hand to his forehead. He didn't remember coming back to his bed.

'They were all washed and they were all fed, Belli.'

'The adult? You're sure the adult fed? And drank?'

'Yes.' Liang bowed. 'I saw to every one.'

He could have held her hand and cried. She was better at this than him, she truly was, and if he'd had it in his power he would have turned her into a true alchemist so there could be two of them and the burden of the dragons wouldn't be his alone and never mind everything else. But of course he couldn't, because there was no essence of the Silver King for her to drink and weld into her own blood.

'Waiting for this?' With a flourish she presented a loaf of Bolo bread and tore it in half. 'Shall we break our night fast?'

He was shaking so much he didn't trust himself to answer but he took the bread and dipped it and let its sweetness melt over his tongue while he tried to push some order into his thoughts. If the dragons had eaten then they had his potions inside them. They'd be dulled for a while. It was the adult that mattered the most. If a hatchling woke they might still use the adult to hunt it down. If the adult woke and broke free then no force in the world would stop it.

'The moon sorcerers.' Li paused to wipe her lenses. 'I think I never quite believed that The Watcher and our sea lord had actually met them. I certainly didn't think they ever left their island.'

Lists in his head. Checking them off one by one. He'd made a lot of potion over the weeks and months since they'd brought him the dragon blood he needed. As much as his own blood would allow. Enough for today but enough for how long after? He didn't know. Not for ever, not as the dragons grew. There would have to be a cull. Better to do it sooner rather than later then. But how to explain? He could lay it out to Li step by logical step. Yes, and she'd see he was right. But Tsen? And the sorcerer-assassin who watched over them? *He* wouldn't.

'And you told me what a dragon would be and I had an idea in my mind, but ... by Xibaiya, Belli, it's as big as a glasship!'

Did he have poison? Yes of course. Enough? No. What else did he need then? He screwed up his face. Lists. He'd have to write it all down. What needed to be done. Each step, one after the other. *O Flame, don't make me have to do this in secret! I can't, I simply can't!*

'Belli?'

And soon. Sort out what needed to be done. All of it while Tsen was away. Before his sorcerer spy came back from wherever he was. However long he had. Let it all be done without their say, one way or the other, that was best. Argue about it after the fact. But so much, so much, and it all had to be done today! As soon as he could!

'Belli!'

Liang. If there was sense to it, she'd see it, she *would*. One thing they had in common, the way they thought. It bound them closer than their differences pushed them apart. *Help me, Li! You have to help me with this. Please!*

'Bellepheros!'

He jumped, his thoughts knocked sideways. She still called him that sometimes when he wasn't paying attention or when she was angry with him. 'What? What is it, Li?'

She pushed another chunk of bread his way and nodded earnestly. 'Qaffeh makes everything better.' He smiled as she put her hand on his. 'Chaos has come, Belli, but *we* shall make order. There's much to be done and some of it will be hard, but we shall prevail. You will show me what and why and I will stand beside those of your decisions that are right to my eye. You know this, Grand Master Alchemist Bellepheros, keeper of our sea lord's dragons. Tsen is in

Xican and will take days to get back here, if he comes here directly at all. The Watcher has gone to tell him that his dragons have come and even *he* can't travel such a way and back again in a day, and even when he does return, he'll not interfere. You'll do what you must, and I'll be beside you. So it's not so bad.'

Yes it is! Bellepheros took a deep breath. He let it out slowly and forced away the lists and the whirl of all the things that needed to be done. *Maybe* she was right. Maybe there was time if he was organised enough. And efficient. And didn't forget anything, and had everything he needed to hand ... A lot to do, though. A lot to do ...

'In fact, I don't think we'll be troubled much at all until the remnants of Sea Lord Quai'Shu's fleet make it back to Khalishtor harbour, charred and ragged by the sounds of things. And surely the worst of whatever they carried is here already. It *is* already here, Belli? There's not some other secret about dragons that I should know?'

Bellepheros laughed, slightly hysterical. 'Why? Isn't this enough for you?'

Li raised her cup and clinked it against his. She smiled. 'I know. You're terrified!'

Bellepheros giggled again. Couldn't help himself. 'Terrified? Yes! Of course I'm terrified. And if you're not then you don't understand them! One egg! I was ready to start from one egg and work my way up, not this. One slip, one thing forgotten ... and boom!' He threw up his hands. 'Woken dragons. Your world ends!'

She rolled her eyes. 'We're not helpless, Belli!'

'Really?'

'Really. The little ones don't bother me much.' Then she frowned. 'The big one? Yes, all right. Yes, that one ... troubles me. Is that what you wanted to hear?'

Bellepheros sipped at his qaffeh. Swilling its bitter taste around his mouth calmed him a little. 'Not really. But perhaps it helps to hear you say it.'

'You'd have to be mad not to feel it. It's so ...' She threw up her hands. 'Big. That's all there is to say, really. I could cage the little ones in glass and gold if I had to, or batter them with lightning. But the big one? No, I'm not sure I could make something to hold it.'

She reached across the desk and took his hand again and squeezed. 'But you, you scrawny old man, are the master alchemist. They shouldn't frighten *you*.'

He gazed at her face, so full of compassion and determination. 'Did you sleep at all, Li?'

'Don't be silly!' She laughed. 'How could I?'

'There are too many. They don't even fit in the eyrie!'

'Very true.'

'And I don't have enough Scales.'

'I can see that.'

'I don't even have enough potion! Not for so many. Not for long.'

'Well, admittedly I can't see *that*. But I believe you, Belli.' Her hand was still on his, still squeezing tight.

'We don't have enough food.'

'*That* I can help with.'

'No, no. There's not … there's not enough. Of anything!'

'I agree.'

He blinked. 'What?'

She let his hand go and took a sip of qaffeh. 'I agree. There are too many dragons. The eyrie isn't big enough. I'm sorry, Belli, but you'll have to get rid of some.'

'What did you say?' Was that a twinkle in her eye?

'I said you'll have to get rid of some. Quite a few, I'd imagine. I'm sorry if that upsets you but sometimes hard decisions must be made.' She watched him steadily and smiled. He probably imagined it but he could have sworn she winked too. She raised her cup. 'To us.'

He raised his own but his hand was shaking so much that he dropped it and spilt qaffeh all over his desk. 'Bloody bugger!'

'Belli! Language!'

He got up and found a cloth to wipe up the mess. His legs felt wobbly. 'Nigh on sixty dragons waiting outside means I can say bloody bugger if I want to! Bloody bugger, bugger bloody, *bloody bugger*!' For a moment the world spun and he had to hold on to the table so as not to fall, forcing himself to take long deep breaths, slow and steady. Li was on her feet in a flash, holding him, holding him tight, murmuring in his ear.

'You're a cranky old man but you're also brilliant and strangely likeable, and you can do this. You can.' She held on to him tightly until the shaking stopped.

'And you're a mad woman and a slave driver,' he said softly. She let him go and filled his cup again.

'You *are* my slave.' She gave him his cup. 'So tell me, truthfully, how many of them of them have to go? No, wait, let's have a wager. I'll wager I can guess. If I'm close, you make the qaffeh every day for a week.'

'And if you lose?'

'Well, it's not down to me to set you free and send you home, otherwise obviously I would, but since I can't let's just say that *I* make the qaffeh. I guess half.'

He told her how much more than half it would have to be. She simply nodded and didn't flinch at all and later, when she was bringing fresh qaffeh to his study each morning while the dragon yard was littered with hatchling corpses burning from the inside, he wondered whether that was when he'd fallen in love with her, or whether it had been much, much earlier.

36

In the Realm of the Dying Sun

In the stillness of the underworld the spirit of the dragon called Silence moved with wonder and deliberate purpose. It had come this way many times but on the previous occasions it had moved swiftly, eager for the call of a new skin, dulled dreamlike by the alchemical potions of the little ones. This time it was awake. This time it remembered. How? How did you make a poison that lingered even with the dead?

The dragon mused on that and then threw the thought away. It didn't move swiftly this time, but slowly. Carefully. Creeping among the ephemerals around it to the hole where the dead Earth Goddess and her slayer had held That Which Came Before at bay for so long. They were gone now and the hole was getting bigger and the Nothing was seeping through. The Nothing would kill more than dragons. The Nothing killed everything, annihilating all it touched. That was the nature of the Nothing. What it was called was what it was.

The dragon Silence lingered at the edge that crept ever further, staring, reaching in with its senses.

The Nothing. But its taste had a tang of the familiar nevertheless. The dragon dredged through ancient memories of its very first lifetime, hazy and dull from the centuries of alchemy it had suffered, until it found what it was looking for. When the Silver Kings had owned the world and the half-gods and the sorcerers had gone to war, it had scented this Nothing then. Just the once, right at the end.

Crazy Mad. Sinking into the sea, down and down, deep and dark and icy cold but at last he knew who he was. He was Berren, the orphan boy from Shipwrights' in the city of Deephaven, and the warlock Saffran Kuy was upon him. 'Dragons for one of you. Queens for both! An empress! The future, boy! See the Black Moon!' And the gold-handled knife jerked and the blade pushed into his skin and his own hands pressed it deeper and deeper towards his heart and he screamed but there wasn't any pain. Instead he saw himself as though looking in a mirror, but he wasn't seeing his skin, he was seeing what lay underneath, his soul, an endless tangle of threads like a spider's web wrapped within itself.

In the mirror there was something staring beside him.

Gelisya the Dark Queen, a child back then, standing in front of him and holding something out. A black stone pressed into Berren's hand. She closed his fingers around it. 'I suppose I have to give him to you now. I don't really want to because he's my friend. But I suppose you want him back.'

Facing him, no more than a few dozen yards away, he saw himself. He raised his javelin ready. His own face stared back at him, wild-eyed, spattered in blood.

'Well? Are you going to throw it or not?'

Silence remembered. It remembered fighting the gods themselves, burning the armies of their minions, crushing them, slaughtering their sorcerers. The splitting of the Quartarch. The scent of this Nothing belonged to the very end when the Black Moon had forged his greatest work of ice and the last of the silver ones had struck him down and the Earthspear ripped the world to splinters. The dragon had tasted the Nothing in that moment, a whiff of it, quickly clenched and crushed and buried away by the dead goddess and her slayer. Here. They'd trapped it here, all three of them locked together, the Nothing in its prison, the goddess the bars and the walls, her slayer the lock to its cage. In that moment the dragon called Silence had not understood. None of them had. No one except perhaps the silver ones and by then so very many of them were gone. Vanished away to wherever their abstention had taken them.

Crazy Mad. Holding fast to a weighted rope. Embraced by cold dark water but he knew who he was. Skyrie, bloodied and broken and crawling to his death in the swamps while the stars above winked out one by one. With a man standing over him in robes the colour of moonlight, his pale half-ruined face scarred ragged by disease or fire, one blind eye, milky white. Fingers that traced symbols over him. Air that split open like swollen flesh. Black shadow that oozed out of the gashes left behind.

'It fills the hole, you see.' Gelisya again. The Dark Queen as she would be, but back then she'd been only twelve. 'Like the Black Moon and the dead Earth Goddess fill the hole in the world. He showed me. You have to keep it closed. Otherwise something will come through. Not yet but one day. Before you both come back for the very last time. You have to keep it closed.' Even with her lips almost touching his ear, her whisper was so quiet he could barely hear. 'He's making us ready. To let it in when the Ice Witch sets it free.'

But he'd lost that black stone with the little piece of him inside. It hung around another neck and so now the hole was there.

He looked inside and saw he was not alone.

The dragon perched on the edge of the unravelling of everything and wondered to itself what might be done but it had no answers to that and so it wondered something else instead. A more dragon-like question, filled with an acceptance that all must inevitably end. *How long?*

Water came and water went. Air too, now and then. Gasped mouthfuls. Holding fast to a weighted rope with a hard wooden cliff over his head, always battering, pushing him under. So little left. Dragons and ice. Falling and falling, locked in an embrace of death with a goddess, and he *was the one who'd stopped their fall and* he *was the one who'd gripped her tight and* he *was the one who'd kept her from the final death, and it was* he *who had kept That Which Came Before from spilling into the world and unravelling the very weave of creation.* He had done all of that!

I.

The Bringer of Endings. The Black Moon who once killed a goddess.

The Nothing was come again, seeping through the hole, slow but relentless.

The hole that he'd made.

*

Hours after the warlocks and the ship that had brought them were gone, Tuuran went and stood where he'd thrown Crazy Mad into the sea. There was a sounding rope there, marked and weighted at the end. The sail-slaves used it for unfamiliar shallow waters to measure the depth beneath them. Out here in open water they didn't need it but it was still there. Tuuran pulled. It was heavier than it had any right to be so he gave it all his strength, and when he reached the end of it he pulled Crazy Mad back into the galley, soaked and freezing, half drowned and three quarters dead.

'Was the only way,' he said. The grey-robes had gone through every slave. They'd come looking for the mark on Crazy Mad's leg.

Crazy Mad sat in his own puddle of water. Shaking. Barely even there.

'They knew who you were.' And Crazy Mad laughed, in between coughing and vomiting up the sea, because most of the time that was more than *he* could have said.

The Watcher

37
Feeding Time

The Watcher approached. As he drew close he felt the air thicken as it always did around the eyrie, the tiny press of resistance, a drag trying to claw him down; but this time, instead of a tiny tug at the back of his thoughts, the thickening grew steadily worse. Instead of cutting though the wind like a sword through the air, the last mile felt like wading through an ever heavier sea. *Like walking in treacle* – that was what the Picker had said of the dragon lands, but that was there, not here. *Here* being the wind was no effort at all. *Here* he darted between Xican and the eyrie and half a dozen other cities like a bee between roses in his hunt for the elusive grey dead and it had hardly troubled him at all until the dragons had come. So it had to be them. Something to do with dragons.

For a few seconds after he materialised on the eyrie rim he couldn't do any more than catch his breath and look around the eyrie's outer edge, dotted with its cranes and shacks and crates and boxes. The gold-glass discs and spheres of two dozen fully built lightning cannon peppered the rocks among long tubes of Scythian steel pointing skywards – black-powder cannon to shatter any hostile glasship that strayed too close. Between them the litter of their building lay scattered higgledy-piggledy. The hands of the sea lord had moved quickly. Baros Tsen T'Varr had turned his eyrie into a fortress.

Once he'd recovered, the Watcher walked across the rim and up the steps shaped into the outer slope of the wall around Chay-Liang's dragon yard. His steps slowed as he reached the top. The monster, the big one, was wide awake and snarling, and even *he* couldn't help a shiver of awe. Its tail, thirty paces long, swished carelessly back and forth with enough restless energy to smash down towers. Its wings, when it stretched them out, were wider still. Its head was as large as a cart, big enough to swallow a horse whole, its teeth two neat rows of swords and knives. It towered over the dragon yard, dwarfed everything and made even the sun seem small. Its skin was a shining ruddy gold and every part was armoured with scales that shone and caught the light like plates of gold-glass. Its claws clenched and unclenched, its talons as big as a man and sharp enough to gouge stone. It was a thing to crush men simply by looking at them. Its eyes roamed, always hunting, never staying still.

Eyes. Those would be its weakness. He shook away the sense of awe. Every monster could be killed. He would just need a long enough spear. Yet even as he thought that, the dragon turned its head and looked straight at him as though it had read his mind and was already calculating how to kill him first. They sized each other up, monster and slayer. The smaller dragons stopped their restless pacings and snappings to stare at him as well, eyeing him as though he might be tasty. A dozen were awake, chained and tethered to the wall. The rest lay still, the forty or so more that the moon sorcerers had brought. Asleep, perhaps. The Watcher took them in, wondering how long it would take for them to grow. A year? Ten? A hundred? He didn't know.

The alchemist was there too, among the small ones and sur-rounded by his Scales, arguing with the enchantress Chay-Liang. Usually the Watcher would have merged with the wind and slipped through the air and appeared beside them, a constant reminder to them both of what he was and what he stood for, but not today. This close to the dragons he wasn't even sure that he *could* shift any more. Practice. The Picker said he'd grown used to it with practice. He'd have to try.

The alchemist turned and headed away across the dragon yard. The enchantress walked beside him. The Watcher followed them with his eyes and then looked back to the dragon. It was still staring at him, cold glacier-blue eyes never blinking. Then, as the alchemist entered the tunnels, the Watcher turned his back and walked down to the eyrie rim. With an effort he became the air again and forced his wind-self across the eyrie's heart and down into its tunnels. Passing the dragon was like walking into the teeth of a hurricane. He made himself do it though, then spiralled down to where the alchemist lived, passing the alchemist and the enchantress on his way. They were arguing, but as he blew between them the enchantress stopped and frowned and looked around her as though she sensed his presence. He kept on, and when he turned to flesh in the alchemist's room he was panting so hard that he could barely stand straight, and so perhaps it was for the best that he had another minute before they arrived. Thick as honey, those two, and better that neither of them saw his weakness before he left again and went back to his hunting.

He walked around the alchemist's study as he slowed his racing heart, one delicate pace after another, eyes flitting over the mayhem of open books and crumpled papers and bottles and vials and pots and jars which lay scattered across every surface without any hint of order. Elemental Men were, above and beyond all else, hunters of sorcerers and magicians and he knew in his belly that this alchemist was more than he seemed. There were books written by the enchanters. There were herbs and powders, and potions the alchemist had made. A dozen open glass beakers sat in a row on the alchemist's desk, all of them different shades of vivid green and each with a note beside it. The Watcher thought the notes were code at first – wondered even if they might be the same sigils and symbols he knew from the Azahl Pillar and elsewhere – but when he looked closely he eventually recognised a few of the words. Just bad handwriting. He shook his head. The alchemist made him uneasy. He'd brought almost nothing with him from the dragon lands but that didn't seem to have stopped him, had barely even slowed him down.

He caught himself. *Almost* nothing. On the desk, pushed aside in one corner but out in the open nevertheless, sat a small round bottle of silver liquid metal. The alchemist had brought *that*, of all things.

Outside he heard them coming, still bickering with each other, but they walked on past the alchemist's room and their voices faded. The Watcher followed on foot, keeping back, listening to their conversation.

'You need to stop, Belli. It won't take long. I've seen how you struggle. I've been meaning to do this for months. Yes, well, now you have no choice, because I'm *telling* you.'

In between, the alchemist was arguing and objecting that now wasn't the time although he never said for what. The Watcher dropped back a little further then stopped. He'd give them a moment to begin whatever it was the enchantress had in mind and then catch them in the middle of it.

He stood alone, his dark robes stark in the hostile white passages with their quiet inner light, and it felt strange to be loitering like this, flesh and bone, not turned into light or shadow. The eyrie had been floating out in the desert for as long as anyone could remember. Simply there, and no one had thought of what to do with it until Baros Tsen T'Varr had tethered glasships to its rim and moved it. It was a strange place, made before the world broke into pieces and then forgotten, and it resented the Elemental Men. Thoughtless and mute but it resisted their presence and it always had, even before the alchemist and his dragons. He gave them a few minutes, contemplating the eyrie's builders and who they might have been, then marched into Chay-Liang's workshop. The alchemist was sitting on a chair with a nest of metal wires over his head and a book in his hands, still complaining bitterly that he had other things to be doing. Chay-Liang was stooped in front of him, fiddling with the wires.

'Enchantress!'

The alchemist looked up sharply as he spoke which earned him a curse. Chay-Liang didn't even look round. 'Watcher!' She poked the alchemist. 'Be still, you! Where have you been, Watcher?'

'To the Grey Isle, lady.' He addressed himself to the alchemist: 'Slave! You will travel to Khalishtor at once to bow before our sea lord. You are to bring one of the monsters.' A hatchling could fit inside a gondola, if the gondola was a big one. The adult dragon, well, tails and wings outstretched it was probably the size of a whole glasship. He couldn't begin to see how they might move it. On a particularly large sled?

The alchemist blinked as though the Watcher was utterly mad. 'At once? Entirely out of the question.'

'Still!' Chay-Liang took two beads of glass and put them very carefully in among the wires right in front of the alchemist's eyes. She touched them and the glass began to flow. 'Close your left eye and look at the book and tell me when you can see the letters without squinting.'

The Watcher took a step closer. 'It is not a request.'

'No?' Chay-Liang still didn't look round. 'Then I shall call it what Belli is too polite to say: the absurd demand of the deeply ignorant! Completely unfeasible.'

The alchemist snorted then tensed. 'There! There! That! Great Flame, how did you do that? No! Back!'

'I'll do it more slowly this time.' Chay-Liang hunched closer.

The Watcher took another step. 'Enchantress, the dragons are your duty to manage. I am not interested in difficulties. I am only interested in your obedience to our sea lord's wishes.'

She waved a hand vaguely in his direction. 'Just wait a moment.'

'There!' The alchemist was beaming. 'There! That's perfect. Clear as anything!'

Chay-Liang sighed and straightened. 'I'm *so* glad I won't have to watch you squinting any more.' She shook her head and turned to face the Watcher at last. 'How long has he been here? And *how* long has he pretended that his eyes are perfectly fine, thank you very much?'

The Watcher hardened his voice. 'Lady! Our sea lord sends his commands! Your slave shall come with me to Khalishtor. At once.'

The smile fell off the alchemist's face like a stone off a cliff. 'Controlling the dragons is not something Li can do, Elemental Man. And *I* cannot *manage* them, as you so glibly put it, if I am not *here*!'

Li? Not *my mistress?* Not even *Lady Chay?* *Li?* The Watcher bared his teeth and drew out the bladeless knife. 'Slave! You will obey our sea lord! One way or the other.'

The alchemist met his glare, one eye strangely large through the glass lens Chay-Liang had made, the other hidden by unshaped glass and the nest of wire. He shook his head. 'This is the arrogance and ignorance of power without wisdom. It's stupid, dangerous and ridiculous. I refuse.' He looked pointedly at the bladeless knife. 'And how, exactly, do you think *that* will help?'

'Have you been waiting all this time, slave?' The Watcher smiled. 'Waiting for these monsters and now that they're here you disobey? Do not even think these thoughts, slave, for I will crush them right now before they grow roots. I do not wish to hurt you but I will if I must. Or others, if needs be.' He kept looking straight at the alchemist. Let him wonder who those others might be.

They stared each other down for a few seconds more and then suddenly Chay-Liang doubled over and hooted with laugher. 'Watcher! You didn't see what happened in the dragon yard when the Regrettable Man stabbed my alchemist in the neck but I assume you at least *heard*? And Belli, to be honest, right now you look slightly absurd. Watcher, our sea lord isn't here and doesn't understand. Two days ago fifty dragons came. You know that. You were here. We were expecting eggs and you know that too. It's nothing short of a miracle that my slave has kept these dragons docile. Give us some time. A week or two.'

The Watcher shook his head. 'You will do as you are commanded, Lady Chay. As will your slave.'

The alchemist snorted and then shrugged. 'Very well. If that's how it has to be. Do you see the big dragon with the harness? I'm going to poison it now. To *manage* it.'

He started to get up but Chay-Liang pushed him gently back. 'Belli! Sit down! You'll do no such thing and nor am I done with you here either. The sea lord—'

'Has no say!' snapped Bellepheros. This time he pushed past Chay-Liang and pulled the wires off his head. 'I built this eyrie for a dozen hatchlings raised one by one from their eggs, not fifty all at once! Poison it is. I'll do it right now. It was going to have to be this way anyway.' He marched out of the workshop into the passage, heading back for the dragon yard. Chay-Liang ran after him, shaking her head.

'Belli! I agreed to the poisoning of the others but destroying the adult would be against his wishes! *Do not do this!*'

The Watcher let them pass and listened to them go, arguing back and forth, then screwed up his strength and turned into the wind and blew past them and was waiting for them when they reached the dragon yard. The monstrous copper-gold dragon was where he'd left it, squatting on its haunches in the middle. It stared at him again. Even with his back to it he felt its eyes on him. As the alchemist came out of the tunnels, The Watcher drew his bladeless knife again and held it straight out, pointing at the alchemist's chest. 'Can you see the end, slave, where the air ends and the business of cutting begins? Keep walking as you are and you will find it.'

The alchemist stopped, then nodded and folded his arms. 'You couldn't simply walk, eh?' He glanced at Chay-Liang. 'I relish the chance to visit one of your cities, Watcher, I really do, but I don't wish to return to an eyrie filled with dead Scales and woken dragons! The adult needs to be fed and it needs to drink and if that cannot be done then it must go. I will not leave until either I see either a means in place to do this or the dragon is dead. Stab me, cut me, whatever you like, I simply will not.' He growled. 'I was ready for eggs, not for this!'

'I think you've made that clear enough, Belli.' Chay-Liang touched a hand to his shoulder but the alchemist shook her off. The Watcher felt the dragon's eyes fixed on them. He shrugged.

'There are plenty of beasts in the Lair of Samim.'

'But *they* are down *there*!' The alchemist threw back his head and rolled his eyes as though he was talking to an idiot. 'They are *not* up *here*! Or does one of you have a magic wand you've forgotten to mention – Flame knows you have enough between you – to summon the *entire herd that this monster and its little kin will devour each and every day as they grow*? No?' He clenched his fists and took several deep breaths. 'Watcher, the hatchlings I can manage where they are but an adult is always flown to its food, and we have no one here who can do this. Either you give me time to find an alternative or it dies. Almost certainly I'll have to kill it anyway.' He turned to Chay-Liang again. 'Choose. Between you. You know I'd prefer to be rid of it.'

'You did not prepare a …' The Watcher wasn't certain what word to use. Rider? Pilot? Navigator?

'*I expected eggs!*' The alchemist had to stop to take breath again. 'I have everything prepared for hatchlings but not for this! I have no one here who can ride this dragon.'

'It has a harness, does it not? Then I will fly it.'

'You?' The alchemist howled with laugher. 'Go ahead! I'll watch. You Taiytakei love to make your wagers – *I'll* make one with you. About how long you'll last.' He folded his arms and stood back. 'Go on! Riders are trained for years together with their first mount raised as a hatchling. They learn together. It requires a certain way of thinking and you certainly can't simply snap your fingers and *make* one. But *you* are an Elemental Man, and surely it cannot be too *difficult*, eh? It's only a *dragon* after all!'

'Belli!' Chay-Liang grabbed his arm. 'Enough! Mind your tongue!'

The alchemist rounded on her. 'Why should I?'

'Because he's an Elemental Man and you're a slave!'

Bellepheros snorted in disdain. 'Whoever and whatever, I'm correcting his ignorance! And yours, apparently.'

The Watcher left them to their snapping and slowly walked across the dragon yard to look at the monster more closely. He *probably* could – if he absolutely had to – merge with the air and appear on the creature's back. And there *was* a harness of sorts, from where it had been ridden before the moon sorcerers had taken it.

The dragon followed him with its unwavering stare.

He didn't even know how to ride a horse. What was the point when you were an Elemental Man?

'Thought better of it yet, magician?' called the alchemist with a scornful snort. 'I once told your master he'd have to bring me a rider. Someone who was trained. Someone who could train others. One of us *might* learn, but it'll take months that we don't have and I dare say a good few false starts. That dragon is hungry *now*. So, either bring me a herd of animals for it to eat or may I *please put it down*?'

The enchantress seized his arm and pulled him round. 'No, Belli!' She glared at the Watcher. 'But he *is* right: we have no way to feed this monster yet and so you can *not* take him away, not now.'

'Enchantress?' The Watcher slowly shook his head. 'It is not a matter for debate. It is your lord's *will*.' And so it was, and so he would see to it, and yet here they all were glowering at one another, doing nothing while the copper-gold dragon with its eyes like glaciers glared at them all. Hungry and getting hungrier. The Watcher stretched out his arms and tipped back his head and forced himself to merge with the air. He had to grit his teeth and summon all his strength and still he almost failed. The dragons were doing this to him ...

Understanding hit him like an arrow in the heart. It was there in the dragon's eyes as it looked at him – it *was* doing this to him and it *knew*. And he was afraid then because he'd never met anything like this before or even heard of it – something that could take away the very essence of what he was, and as he raced to the ground and felt the flow of the world ease around him until it was as effortless as ever, the relief was joyous. He reached the sand below the eyrie and kept on going, deep and far, revelling in the freedom before he circled back to find the inevitable camp of desert nomads that had grown up. It wasn't far from the eyrie, paid by Baros Tsen T'Varr for a steady stream of food and water and anything else that the alchemist required. Most of what the eyrie needed was ferried through the air by discs and sleds and glasships, but those were expensive and a t'varr was a t'varr, always trying to save his sea lord's silver.

There were a few dozen men and perhaps twice as many desert horses. The Watcher walked among them making the necessary arrangements. When it was done he blinked away again. Blissfully easy down on the ground, although even there he still felt the tissue-pull of resistance, yet harder and harder as he fought his way back. He lingered for a moment, watching the alchemist and the enchantress from high above. They *were* too close. She had him beguiled but she was blind to how much of a hold on her she'd given in return. The Hands of the Sea Lord would have to be told ...

The dragon tipped back its head and looked straight up and right at him. He was the wind, he was invisible and made of air, and yet it knew he was there. How? Maybe the alchemist would have an answer for that? He flew down and turned to breathless flesh again atop the walls, pausing to hide his weakness before he returned in footsteps across the open white stone of the dragon yard and bowed before Chay-Liang and her slave.

'The desert men will provide what you require. Lady Enchantress, you will please have the slaves build harnesses for their cranes to lift the Linxia you will need. Tell them how many you require and they will be provided. Have the glasships pull the eyrie as low as it will go to the ground. Right to the sand if you must.' He turned to the alchemist without waiting for Chay-Liang to reply. 'And you, slave! Draw up a list of all the men who work here. You will order the list by their value and you will entitle your list, "Menu in the Event of Dragon Food Shortage". You will give it to me when we are done. Am I exquisitely clear, *slave*? You will do this before we leave and we *will* leave today. Twenty Linxia each and every morning. They *will* be here. Do you wish them alive or slaughtered?'

The alchemist blinked. For a moment the Watcher thought he was going to rebel, and if that was how it was then he'd get carried from his eyrie over a soldier's shoulder like a naughty child. His lips pinched. But the alchemist closed his eyes and shuddered, shaking his head. 'Thirty animals, not twenty. And dragons can do their own slaughtering. They're very good at that. How long, Watcher, before I'll return?'

The Watcher's eyes bored into the alchemist. 'Are you tired, slave?'

'Of course he is!' snapped Chay-Liang. 'We all are! What did you expect?' She peered hard at him. 'Are *you* tired, Watcher? I didn't think that happened to Elemental Men.'

'It does not.'

Her look lingered but now the alchemist was busy talking of feeding schedules and the administration of the necessary potions, shaking his head sourly all the time as he did. *Wait for them to be hungry. Each hatchling must drink one flask every day. Tying the flasks around an animal's neck will suffice. Dragons are prone to eat their prey from the head down and in large pieces. Do not approach the hatchlings yourself. Remember they still carry Hatchling Disease. Keep the Scales segregated. They will have the disease in their blood by now.* So on and so forth. The Watcher listened. Chay-Liang was bored and barely paying attention as if she knew all of this already. So much the better if she did.

'The dead hatchlings are to be left. Don't touch them. We'll have a use for their residues but I'll deal with that when I come back. As for the adult?' The alchemist closed his eyes and shook his head. 'A war-dragon, and a large one. Empty the dragon yard and release the animals into it every day, each with a flask of potion strapped to its neck. Continue with more, one at a time, until the dragon is sated enough to allow the hatchlings to eat. While it feeds, don't allow anyone else into the yard for any reason. Beware the tail and the wing. In eyries far more die from those than from fire and tooth and claw. This dragon has at least been trained so it shouldn't devour our Scales, nor should it fly without a rider to guide it. If it does either of those things then poison it if you can and run far and fast if you can't. Pinned to the ground it will grow restless. Its hunger to fly will be voracious. We'll likely have a few weeks before it loses its last vestiges of self-restraint at which point, without a rider, I *will* poison it, whatever you say. You really might as well let me get on and do it now but perhaps it'll be a good lesson for you both to see what it's like, a dragon with no control. Perhaps then you'll listen with more open ears, eh?'

On and on. In days long past the Watcher had talked to Chay-Liang about her gold-glass arcana and how they worked, how she channelled the energy of the earth, but it was like talking with a different tongue. Listening to the alchemist was the same, how he could enter his blood and manipulate it to make his potions, how the essence of a half god buried and held at the brink of death under the mountains of his realm was also a part of him. Alien. And when the Watcher tried to speak of how it felt to become one with the elements of the world he found himself trying to describe colours to a blind man, sounds and timbres to someone who was deaf. The witch and the alchemist though; somehow for them it was different. They struggled but they'd found a common language, one he didn't understand.

The glasship to take the alchemist to Khalishtor came to rest high above the eyrie wall and the fragile golden egg it carried made its descent. The alchemist bowed to Chay-Liang as he readied himself to leave at last, already hours later than he should. 'Good fortune to you.' He sounded stiff and reluctant. 'A flask a day to each …'

'Of the hatchlings. And thirty to the monster. Yes, yes, I know. All will be well.'

'I know, I know. You only really need me for my blood, don't you?' He actually smiled as he said it, and the enchantress smiled back and the Watcher shook his head because this was not slave and mistress at all. 'The Scales, Chay-Liang. Watch the Scales. I've given them potions that will slow its progress but I fear the Statue Plague as much as I fear the dragons themselves. If I'm not back within a twelvenight and you have no certain word of me, poison them all without delay or hesitation.'

The enchantress wore the dour face of someone who'd heard the same admonishment far too often. She shooed him away. The alchemist gave an awkward bow and took a last look across the yard at the dragon and the hatchlings chained to the stone. The dragon *was* restless, even the Watcher could see that. It stretched out its wings and opened its mouth wide and bared its teeth. It was staring at the glasship now.

'Come, slave!' The Watcher ushered him to the waiting gondola.

'We all want to fly,' the alchemist said. 'I'll not have time to make a rider for this one. When I poison it on my return, by then you'll see why it has to be done, both of you.'

The Watcher sealed the gondola around them. When he'd done that, he bowed. 'There will be no need for that, slave. A rider waits for you in Khalishtor. Her name is Zafir. I hear she claims to be a queen.'

The look on the alchemist's face was delicious.

38

Khalishtor

Years ago, in the dragon realms in the court of her mother Queen Aliphera of the Silver City, ambassadors of the Taiytakei had come to pay their respects. Zafir had watched them carefully. Their colourful silks had made their faces seem even darker than they were. Their cloaks of bright feathers and gold and silver thread which they wrapped right around them swirled like wings when they threw out their arms to prostrate themselves before her mother's throne; and with the long braids of their hair scattered in an arc around their heads as they kowtowed, they reminded her of the ornamental birds of Bazim Crag. But what stuck most in her mind, what had lingered in the air of the Octagon long after they were gone, was the smell, the sweet musky smell that followed the Taiytakei everywhere. Xizic. The sailors chewed on lumps of it, the soldiers sprinkled it into their pipes. Even her slaves smelled of it. That morning when they killed Brightstar, she caught a whiff of it on the black-cloak's breath.

They forced her down to her knees and pressed her head hard into the floor. Beside her, the light hadn't gone from Brightstar's eyes. 'Like this!' snapped the black-cloak whose sword still dripped. As they pulled her up and dragged her away, her foot slipped in Brightstar's red blood, still warm. She almost fell and a trail of sticky red footprints followed her, quickly fading. Her head buzzed with what the Heart of the Sea Lord had done while his soldiers' hands held her arms hard enough to bruise. The urge crackled inside her to pull away and fight them, to kick them, steal their swords and stab them, but she pushed it away and walked between them straight and erect. She would *not* lose her control. She would not let them have that victory. A dragon-rider knew her passions. She revelled in them, embraced them and rode them like the hurricanes they were, but a dragon-rider was always, *always*, their mistress. If they couldn't ride their own, how could they ride the fury of a dragon?

The soldiers pushed and pulled her through the narrow companionways of the ship, up a tight flight of steps to the open air. Above the wooden masts and spars vast discs of glass and orbs of gold and silver hung in the sky, looming down and threatening to crush her. They were everywhere, spinning slowly and streaming bright shapes of sunlight across the deck in ever-shifting patterns. Others drifted languidly further out among the ships of the fleet and the smooth sculpted islands that surrounded them. They made her feel small.

No. She bit her tongue and made it bleed. Awe, rage, love, fear, they were all her children, not her masters. No, she would not gawk like some ignorant savage. She was the dragon-queen and nothing the Taiytakei could put in front of her could compare with the monsters that had been a part of her life from the very moment she'd been born. She let the cold breeze cutting through her silks fill her head, made herself look straight ahead and nowhere else, dismissed the bright sun-dazzled thing above her that was as large as a war-dragon with its wings outstretched. When they stood her in front of a gondola carved from solid gold, almost resting on the deck right in front of her, at first she refused to see that too.

But no, *that* wouldn't do either, and so she lifted her eyes and went to war. The gondola floated a few feet above the deck and seemed to move up and down but that was the ship rocking in the gentle swell. The egg hung motionless. It was the size of a small hall, large enough for perhaps a dozen men to stand upright before they felt pressed together. On the outside it was smooth-skinned, made of polished gold that shone brilliant in the sun, featureless except for windows of perfect clear glass in a single ring around its belly. At the tapered end of the egg in front of her a ramp hung open, yet more gold, ending in a few steps that hung by silver chains. The steps were clear. Glass. It all hung from chains of gleaming silver. Above her the gold-glass disc spun slowly, casting its fractured light over everything.

Zafir looked and took it in, every bit of it, and then held it up against her dragons, her Onyx and her Mistral and all the others, and made it small.

The soldiers pushed her forward. The ramp was laid with a deep red carpet. Under her bare feet it was thick and soft and warm. It caressed her skin. *Like a pool of warm fresh blood. Like Brightstar's blood.* The thought startled her. And then she was inside the egg and the black-cloaks had hold of her again and there was a man staring at her, fat and black-skinned with a jovial sort of face but also a sharpness to him. She forced herself to look at that face and nothing else: not at his brilliant blue silk robe with its streaming patterns of emerald and silver and crimson and gold, not at the cascading braids of his hair which spread across the floor around his throne of yet more gold still, with its arms carved in the shape of ships and its back sculpted to look like a sail, not at the white and silver and crimson feathered cloak that wrapped him nor the carved symbols that lined the golden walls, nor through the too-perfect glass of the windows nor the tiny door behind him that led to the front of the egg, hanging ajar. No, she looked at *him*. She met his eye and stood erect and let her mouth fall imperceptibly open. She cocked her head and imagined how it would be if he'd been her treacherous lover Jehal.

Not a flicker.

'I am Baros Tsen,' he said. And they talked, and as they did, she made sure to draw his gaze with her hands to her breasts, to her hips, to all the parts of her that every man she'd ever met stared at with their blunt hungry eyes. Yet not a flicker. It was strange. Confusing. Unexpectedly disarming.

'You don't desire me at all, do you?' She couldn't help herself.

'Not at all.' He waved her away; and when she went it was with a lightness to her step that she couldn't explain until the black-cloaked soldiers waiting outside seized her. *Their* eyes roamed freely, stealing devouring looks that perhaps they imagined she didn't see. She smiled at them. When she was a queen again, those were the eyes she would have gouged out first. They shoved and pulled her back down to her cabin. Brightstar's body was gone but her blood still stained the wooden floor. Myst and Onyx cowered and kowtowed as the black-cloaks chained her wrist once more and left, locking the door behind them. None of them spoke. Zafir put a hand on each of them and made a silent promise. *It will not happen again.*

Silent Onyx offered her a piece of Xizic. The taste was strong and made her gag at first but she chewed at it anyway, torn between disgust and curiosity while her slaves undressed her and bathed her and dressed her again, and as she did the world seemed to take on a new edge of colour. Sounds became crisper and a delicious warmth spread inside her. She almost forgot where she was. As they brushed her hair and oiled her skin she closed her eyes and couldn't help but see Jehal. The silks they put her in were tantalising against her skin. Jehal at his best with his fingers and his lips. With the olisbos he'd brought to her that last time they'd been alone. She could have lost herself in those thoughts but before they could grow into something more, the door of her cabin burst open once more and the black-cloaks were back, pulling her to the floor. They took the silver chain from her wrist and bound her with another, one that tied her hand to her ankle so she could barely walk, and when they were done they hauled her up and pushed and shoved her back to the deck. The golden egg was gone, a bronze one in its place; and this time she stopped and looked up at the glass disc in the sky, almost as long as the ship, and tried to make sense of it. It spun slowly around a lattice of silvery metal and more glass. Inside was another glass disc, spinning faster, perpendicular to the first, and then another and another and another, and then inside that a sphere and another disc, the last one turning so fast that its spokes were a blur. It reminded her of an object that her alchemist Vioros had once had, all concentric metal rings at strange angles to one another. An orrery, was that what he'd called it? Except his had been the size of a dinner plate while this dwarfed even a dragon.

But it doesn't breathe fire and it's made of glass. She tried to imagine what would happen if a dragon came upon something like this. It helped with the breathless wonder that threatened to overwhelm her. 'What is this thing?'

The soldiers hanging on her arms forced her forward. One of them said something like 'Glasship,' although through his accent she couldn't be sure. Then he said something else, guttural, and they both laughed. She didn't understand the words but she caught the meaning clearly enough: *ignorant savage.* She looked at the two of them, one and then the other so she could be sure to remember their faces. First their eyes and then their tongues, and then they would see how truly amusing a dragon-queen could be.

'I saw them fly,' she said with a smile. 'They are slow and clumsy.'

The soldiers spat their disgust at her feet and pushed her inside the egg, all bare metal and empty except for the men already waiting there and a single polished handrail of dark wood running around the interior below the line of the windows. The floor felt warm. She might have moved to the windows to look outside, to see how this flying thing felt beside the sensation of sitting on the back of a dragon with a hurricane howling through her hair, but her eyes wouldn't let go of one of the men already inside the egg. He was a slave like her, the only one in the ship who wasn't Taiytakei, and he was old but it still took a second for the rest of her to realise how she knew him.

'Alchemist?'

Grand Master Bellepheros. Older and thinner than she remembered, but it *was* him. He stepped away from the others and bowed. 'Your Highness.'

'I was crowned a queen, Bellepheros, to follow my mother, and then Hyram named me speaker. I've held the Adamantine Spear and it drank my blood.' She shivered at the memory then held out her hand so he could see the Speaker's Ring still on her finger. Through everything, no one had thought to take that away. He stared goggle-eyed in disbelief, and then his eyes glistened and his jaw dropped. He fell to his knees in front of her and pressed his face to the floor the way her slave maids had done before Shrin Chrias Kwen, and a bubble of joy burst inside her.

'Holiness,' he murmured, and for that she would have made him a king, right there and then, if she could.

'Rise, alchemist.'

The Taiytakei soldiers stared at them both in open amazement. Bellepheros struggled up, his old knees giving him trouble. As he rose, he stumbled and grabbed her arm. Zafir froze, flitting from crowning him to hanging him in a cage for the crows in an instant, but as he finished pulling himself up, his cheek brushed her ear. 'Do not bow to them, Holiness,' he breathed so quietly that no other would hear. 'They need us both.'

She smiled and took his hands in hers. *Not a king! For that I will crown you an emperor!* 'It's good to see you again, Grand Master. We thought you dead.' Bellepheros. Grand master alchemist. She'd barely known him. The last time she'd seen him had been in Furymouth at Jehal's wedding, spitting derision at him while her insides turned in knots, desperately afraid that he might peel back the riddle of her mother's death and unravel what she and Jehal had done. Before that she could barely remember him existing. Afterwards … After he'd gone she'd wished him back, but only because of spiteful vicious-minded Jeiros who'd taken his place. Yet here he was. An ally!

'The Taiytakei took me. As you see, Holiness.'

The smile stayed while she tried to look inside him to see what else was there. 'They took a great deal more,' she began, but then saw from his darting eyes that she should be wary. She looked past him at the other men. More black-cloaks in their gold-glass armour and one more who wore a plain sable robe woven with simple coloured strands along its hem from his collar to his feet.

The floor trembled as the glasship rose into the air. She almost stumbled.

'Perhaps you would care to share the view, Holiness?' Bellepheros gestured to the nearest window and grabbed for the rail beneath it. 'It is an interesting experience. Very different from dragon flight.'

'Slow,' she said. She moved beside him to watch as the ship fell away. The movement of the gondola was imperceptible at first; as it rose higher it began to sway a little, much like the ships down below rocking back and forth in the sea. Six more glass discs hung over the Taiytakei fleet. The closest, she saw, was being loaded with dragon eggs.

'Indeed. But comfortable,' said Bellepheros. 'How many do they have?'

It took her a moment to understand that he meant the eggs and not the glasships. 'Hundreds, I think. A good few hatched at sea. I don't know what became of them.'

'The Taiytakei have them. I beg to ask, Holiness, how could they have taken our speaker?'

Zafir smiled and put a hand on his, wondering what news he'd had of the dragon realms since he'd been taken. None? But she couldn't be sure. 'A long tale for another time, Grand Master. They took me when I tried to stop them stealing these eggs.' A tiny little truth. He could have that much. 'How many of these flying things do they have?'

'I don't know, Holiness. Many, but I'm rarely permitted to leave my eyrie.'

'You have an eyrie?'

He nodded. 'The Taiytakei have made one.'

She turned from the window and looked at him. There was something in his words that caught in his throat. Shame, was it? And she saw it in his face too. 'You helped them.' She couldn't keep the hardness out of her voice. He nodded. 'Are you not a slave then, alchemist?'

'I am, Holiness.'

'Yet you helped them? After what they've done?'

Bellepheros bowed his head. 'My duty is to keep the dragons in check, Holiness. Always and only that. I tried to dissuade the sea lord who took me. I failed.' He looked up again, now with a note of defiance. 'And it was right that I did. If I hadn't helped them to be ready when these dragons came ...' He shook his head. 'I have done my duty, Holiness, as I always have.'

'They could all burn, Master Alchemist, and I wouldn't shed a tear.' She leaned close, ready to whisper in his ear, *Let their dragons awake. Let them reap what they have sown. Let them burn, all of them.* But he was an alchemist. 'When we are alone, let me tell you what they have done to our home. See if you might reconsider where your duty truly lies.'

Abruptly Bellepheros turned around. He began pointing to the other men in the cabin. 'These two, as you may have already imagined, are our master's soldiers. Our master in practical ways is Baros Tsen T'Varr. Through these men he will hear every word we say. They are his ears. This one –' he pointed to the man in the middle, the one in drab black beside the rainbow colours of the soldiers '– this one is our sea lord's very own Elemental Man. Our master is the only sea lord to own such a magician outright. Do you know, your Holiness, what an Elemental Man is?'

Zafir pursed her lips. *Thank you, alchemist, for demanding that I show my ignorance.* 'I have heard many stories, Master Alchemist.

It would take a shrewd mind to discern the fact from the fiction.'

'Indeed it would, but our stories are largely true. They are killers of monsters, men who can become the wind, the water, fire or earth. I've come to know this one very well. I am sure you'll come to know him too.'

Ah. A spy then.

Bellepheros turned back to the window. The fleet was receding now, the city coming closer. 'Khalishtor, Holiness. The City of Gold and Glass. Imagine it as our City of Dragons. It is the centre of their realms yet a place where no one lord holds sway. The enchanters abide here, those who make such wonders as this glasship and other creations that will briefly amuse your eye. The navigators too, the ones who guide the sea lords' ships across the Endless Ocean and the Sea of Storms. At the Palace of Glass the sea lords hold their court.' Bellepheros glanced at the other men behind them. 'Our master intends to present us and one of his dragons. He wishes to show us off.' Zafir watched the old alchemist as he talked. He'd shown her already where his loyalties lay. Unleashing the dragons the Taiytakei had brought with them, letting them grow wild and untamed, letting them loose to do what dragons would do, in that he'd fight her tooth and claw; so for now she put the thought aside and stared out at the city as they drifted closer. It sprawled between two headlands. More ships cluttered the bay between them, closer to the land than Quai'Shu's fleet had come. Towers of glass or diamond rose in a circle from the far headland, glittering golden in the late afternoon sun. Between the headlands the buildings were packed in close and tight. A handful of the floating glass discs hovered in the air near the sea. Everything sparkled.

'That is where the Elemental Men are made.' Bellepheros pointed to the single mountain that rose behind the shore among gently sloping hills, its peak decked in a cloak of cloud, and then to the glass spires on the far headland. 'And there are the enchanters.' His voice dropped. 'There is little love between them.' A touch to the way he said it told her this was a thing for her to remember.

Smoke rose from a far point in the city near the sea. As Zafir watched, one of the hovering discs drifted towards it. Behind the press of buildings along the shore, strips of green and stands of trees sat among wide squat buildings. The glittering was golden glass, more of it in the more open parts of the city. A spire here, a tower there. Occasional black obelisks rose among them, several beneath flying glass discs. Tethers?

'Watch that one, Holiness.' Bellepheros pointed to the glassship close to the pall of smoke. Zafir did as he said. As the glassship reached the smoke, the air beneath it turned into a haze and then mist. 'Water,' said the alchemist with admiration. 'From the sea. They simply fill a gondola like this with it and then drop it from the sky! Their cities no longer suffer the peril of fire!'

'Slave!'

She didn't look up. At first she didn't realise the Elemental Man was speaking to her until Bellepheros gently nudged her. After that, ignoring the assassin was deliberate.

'Slave!' he barked again.

Bellepheros turned round, knelt and bowed his head. 'Master Watcher?' Zafir stayed exactly where she was, staring out of the window. They'd either kill her for disobedience or they'd tolerate it, and if they were going to kill her then they might as well get on with it. Better sooner than later.

When the Elemental Man spoke again, the edge had gone from his voice. 'Alchemist, if you have not seen the Crown of the Sea Lords, the view now approaches its best from the windows on this side.'

'Holiness!' Bellepheros was on his feet at once. 'It is their Adamantine Palace! A place of marvels.'

Zafir turned. She didn't meet the Elemental Man's eye – no need to gloat but now they both knew who had the power. Not him. Her life was in the hands of this Baros Tsen T'Varr, no other. She crossed to the windows on the other side, the Taiytakei soldiers moving away to give her room. She felt the Elemental Man's eyes burning her skin as she looked out. The alchemist was right. The Crown of the Sea Lords, if that's what this palace was called, was a jewel to make even her own Adamantine Palace seem drab and small. Scores of glassships floated over it but the palace made them all tiny. It covered the entire headland, a giant crown of gold and glass, a ring of thirteen glittering spires rising from a broad circle of white stone, each one taller than the Tower of Air. Spokes led from them to a central amphitheatre as big as her whole palace.

Between the spokes, patterns of trees ran in delicate lines and swirls among a swathe of gardens. Curves of water glimmered and sparkled between many-levelled lakes and ponds and manicured waterfalls. Flying glass buttresses rose over the amphitheatre to a gleaming silver sphere that sat directly over its centre. Flashes of colour caught Zafir's eye, puzzling things until she realised they were waterfalls running down the glass and fracturing into clouds of rainbow spray. Their own Diamond Cascade. As Zafir peered, she caught another glimmer of light like the sun off a spider's web, joining the silver sphere to one of the towers high above the ground. It flashed and then was gone and then she saw another to a different tower. Pathways. Bridges made of glass.

'Does it not take your breath away?' whispered the alchemist.

Zafir didn't speak. Yes, it was magnificent, and yes, it did. Sorcery beyond anything she'd ever imagined, beyond even the strange wonders left by the Silver King in the bowels of the palace where she had been born. Yet at the same time what she saw was a pall of smoke, the gleaming glass smashed to shards, the gold running in molten rivers while a hundred dragons circled overhead and the sky filled with flames.

Her dragons.

I am a dragon-queen. Nothing could touch her.

'Holiness?' Bellepheros was almost brushing against her again. Annoying habit. 'Holiness! Look up!'

High over the silver sphere hung a vast gold-glass star.

39

The Council of the Sea

The Watcher did what he did best: nothing at all. He stood in the corner of the bronze-panelled room, silent and still amid the noise and bright plumage of Quai'Shu's heirs, inconspicuous and half-hidden but overshadowing everything. As each man and woman came dressed in their dazzling silks and their shimmering oil-sheen feathered cloaks, fluffing and settling themselves for the battle to come around the dark rosewood table, they saw him and whispered and cursed under their breath. Prayers to gods in whom they should not believe, perhaps. Or maybe a simple *Why is he here?* Because his being here changed everything.

Sea Lord Quai'Shu sat at the head of his council of war and the Watcher stood close by. All others here were his servants. Quai'Shu wasn't the lord they remembered – he drooled and rolled his eyes now – but he *was* their lord still and the Watcher had come to be sure they all remembered it as they battled over the spoils. He looked at their faces and met their eyes one by one. Shrin Chrias Kwen, master of the black-cloaks and of Quai'Shu's network of spies and informants, whose men crewed and captained the sea lord's ships and ran the sea lord's empire. He'd be the first to turn. The kwen sat next to Elesxian, first lady of Xican, Quai'Shu's eldest grandchild and Zifan'Shu's named heir. Her claim to Quai'Shu's title was strong and the kwen was her secret lover. They'd see their ascension to power as rightful and inevitable, and perhaps it was.

Beside them sat Nimpo Jima Hsian. Quai'Shu might have dictated strategy but it was the hsian who advised him, the hsian who put the plans together, made the tactical decisions, whose schemes ran Quai'Shu's trading empire and his networks of spies and informants and never mind what Shrin Chrias Kwen might have thought on the matter. Beside him sat Baran Meido, Quai'Shu's second son, and Tetja Bronzehand, his third. Meido was bought and owned, body and soul, by the lords of Vespinarr. Bronzehand's own heir had been traded as a hostage to Dhar Thosis some years ago. They would both have their claims.

Last of all was Baros Tsen T'Varr, the glibly named supply master who ran Quai'Shu's treasury and was responsible for the providing of whatever was necessary to support absolutely anything at all. Who believed, whatever anyone else might say, that he quietly ran Quai'Shu's trading empire and probably his network of spies and informants too. Six tigers in a room. How Quai'Shu had stopped them from eating each other was a mystery, but he had. Now the Watcher was the only thing that made them pause from falling upon one another and devouring the first to show weakness, and that was why he was here.

He stepped forward from his shadows and reached for Quai'Shu's hand. The tigers were too proud to simply stop their conversing but they noticed, oh how they noticed. The Watcher opened Quai'Shu's fingers and placed a gavel in his hand and closed them again and made him bang the table three times, silencing their chatter. If he'd been like them, his wager would have been on the kwen to speak first. To stake his claim.

'There's no money left.' Tsen T'Varr beat Chrias Kwen by a heartbeat. The kwen's mouth was open but the words hadn't been quick enough. 'None. We're broke. No, I correct myself: we are sinking in debt and about to drown. Nothing more than the top of our mast remains above the water and even *that* is falling fast.'

'This venture has cost us a quarter of the fleet.' Jima Hsian sniffed. 'Thirty-six ships lost. Twelve more that will take months to repair. We must build. Our strategy is at risk.'

Tsen leaned back and clasped his hands behind his head. 'And to which shipyard shall we turn, Hsian? Who will build for us on credit with no promise of payment? You'll be lucky if I can pay Chrias's sailors to crew the ones you've still got.'

'The Vespinese shipyards in Hanjaadi will build if I ask.' Baran Meido smiled at them all through lidded eyes, as if they were all here for his amusement. '*If* I ask.' Chrias Kwen nodded. So, three of them already in it together.

'Your troubles to resolve, T'Varr. I cannot make money for you to spend without ships and crews to sail them,' said the hsian.

'Then I suggest you find some nice long voyages to places they might like to go.'

'Qeled,' said Bronzehand.

Elesxian rolled her eyes and clutched her head. 'Are you mad?'

'Give me ten ships and a good crew and this Elemental Man here, and I'll bring you something back from Qeled that will make our t'varr stop bleating once and for all!'

'*Another* reckless venture? Look at what this one has cost! You'll waste ten more ships and come back with nothing. *If* you come back at all.'

'Sounds to me like he should go,' purred Baran Meido.

Chrias laughed. 'Our lord has brought back dragons and our t'varr still squeals!'

'Likely as not you'd come back dead, little brother.'

Meido and Bronzehand stared each other down. Bronzehand's eyes shone. 'Is that a wager, brother?'

'Five ships.'

'Done!'

'Wait. Do you propose to let him have ten to waste in the first place?' Elesxian shook her head.

'He'll have none of mine.' Tsen T'Varr shrugged. 'Not unless our lord demands it.' He cocked his head. 'Don't think that's likely to happen by the looks of it. Wasted wager.'

Meido chuckled. 'Pay these penny-pinching prunes no mind. I'll have the Vespinese prepare ships for you, brother. For a half-and-half split of whatever you find between us and them.'

'Wait!' The Watcher coughed again but none of them seemed to notice until he banged the gavel. Then slowly they fell to silence until Bronzehand stood up.

'Gentlemen! Sister.' They all looked at him. He shrugged. 'Well, my father is incapable, isn't he? We must agree on someone to speak for him.' He looked hard at Quai'Shu. 'Unless, Father, you have something you wish to say on this?'

Chrias Kwen banged his fist on the table and glared at Tsen T'Varr. '*Why* have you not yet executed the slave who murdered Zifan'Shu?'

Tsen T'Varr met his eye. 'I will, Chrias. But not until I can afford it.'

'You'd get a good price if you sold her,' muttered Jima Hsian.

'She must pay!' snapped Elesxian.

Tsen smiled and offered out his hands. 'Exactly. She must pay. And she *will* pay for the murder of your father, first lady, when the debts that our sea lord has incurred are lessened. Until then she will pay in other ways. She is, after all, part of the fruits of his labour.' He stood up. 'Dear friends, tantalising a prospect as it is to dispatch a part of our rather ragged and meagre fleet on some expedition to Qeled, I suggest our discussions might be better centred on how we shall use the fruits of our *last* expedition to defray the expense of it. In other words, how shall these dragons pay their way?'

'The Sun King will pay you any price you ask,' said Jima Hsian. 'If you can find a way to take them to him.'

'Well, that's not why you brought them here, Jima Hsian, but why not start with it? Will one dragon suffice? A young one?'

'I think so.'

'Well, that's one thing settled. The navigators found a way to bring them here after all and we can certainly spare one of the little ones. *Hatchlings*, they call them.' He laughed a little as if they were all in on some joke. 'I will see that you get it, Jima, and then shall we talk of their other more ... challenging uses? And Chrias, find me someone to replace the dragon woman and I'll gladly put a hook through her tongue and hang her up for the jade ravens. Now how else—'

'*No!*' Quai'Shu snapped and the rest of them almost jumped out of their skins. Even the Watcher flinched. 'No,' he said again. They looked at him as though he was mad. 'You take my legacy and already you sell it to the Sun King. Do I have a say? Do you even bother to ask? Do I want to sell my monsters? You will not sell my dragons. You will not kill my rider. You will do none of those things.'

'Then perhaps I will sell your fleet,' snapped Tsen T'Varr, 'to pay for your indulgence!'

Chrias was on his feet in a flash. 'You will ...'

Quai'Shu waved a shaking finger across the table at Tsen T'Varr. He was quivering. 'Dragons. Nothing else. Let me see them. I want to be where they are. Take me there, T'Varr. You are master here. Tell them what we need. And take me back! I want my eyrie! I want my dragons.'

Quai'Shu fell quiet. Silence filled the room.

Meido stood up. 'I'll wager—'

'*Gentlemen!*' Tsen T'Varr had a good voice on him when he chose to use it and now he cut Baran Meido clean in two. 'I believe our lord has spoken.' He smiled at them all and turned to Quai'Shu. 'Sea Lord, we have so many dragons that I've already been forced to cull them. Please see reason. Let the Sun King fill our coffers. But!' He turned and shook a finger at the rest of them. 'I have only one alchemist and only one dragon-rider, and if we lose either then we really all might as well not have bothered. So we'll not sell anything to anyone – indeed, perhaps we *cannot* – until we have more. Chrias Kwen, I will ask you this: prepare a ship to return to the dragon lands. One will do. Tell me what you need. You may have the pick of anything you wish save for LaLa here. I think it may be best if you went yourself. It's too important and cannot be allowed to fail.'

'I will do no such thing!'

'He is needed here,' said Lady Elexsian coldly. 'In our time of weakness we do not send our kwen away!'

'*I* think our t'varr may be on to something,' drawled Bronzehand.

Tsen smiled at him again. 'If Vespinarr will loan you the ships, what is to be lost in going to Qeled save a wager?' He glanced at Baran Meido and his smile broadened. 'Although you too may not have LaLa. I'm afraid his place is firmly at our lord's side until the matter of a successor is settled. Jima Hsian will make us some money. Tell the Sun King he can have his dragon one day but make him pay! I'll keep the wolves away and give our lord's hsian and kwen what they need. I will beg,' he said, 'for that's where we find ourselves.'

Tsen bowed and sat down. The silence that followed was a long one.

'What if we were to offer a stake in the eyrie?' mused Jima Hsian. The Watcher shifted back into his shadows and smiled to himself. *There. That was how a sea lord did it. Tigers on the outside, kittens in the middle. As long as you promised them money.*

Chrias Kwen stood up. 'Ten per cent, Hsian,' he said. 'No more.

You may offer it as you see fit and get the best price you can. I'm sure that will be more than enough to spare Tsen T'Varr the ignominy of begging …'

He stopped as Quai'Shu suddenly rose. 'I need the water closet,' he said shrilly. Then he looked down at himself as the smell eked its way across the room. The Watcher took his hand before any of the others could do it. Before they fought over him as they'd fight over everything else.

'Our lord has spoken.' The Watcher said it so quietly that they had to stop and turn their ears towards him. *Who will strike at you first, old man? Would your kwen? No. Someone else then? Not Tsen T'Varr, that's for sure. You as good as made him your heir, old man. Did you mean to? Probably not.* He guided Sea Lord Quai'Shu gently towards the mahogany door. 'I will be attending the Great Sea Council,' he told them all. 'We both will.' He met their eyes one by one around the table. If there was murder then the Watcher would hunt the killer down. He let them see that, let them have no doubts at all, but even as he left Quai'Shu's sons were making a wager on how long Tsen T'Varr could keep him alive.

Baros Tsen T'Varr looked deep into the silver cup in his hand, into the pale heady apple wine. *When I look back, I suppose this will be the moment I started to wonder exactly who poured every cup I drink. My, my, won't that be fun. Did I really have to make the poison chalice so firmly mine?* But then hadn't it been so ever since Quai'Shu ordered him into the desert to built his dragon eyrie? Probably. He clasped his hands and found himself twiddling the many rings on his fingers. He wasn't the only one. Everyone here had rings, all of them much the same, all to counter the tiny slivers of gold-glass under the skin of each finger. The slivers had been Quai'Shu's way of binding them to each other but it had gone down like a lead glasship and they'd all found a way around it before long. About the one and only thing they'd all worked seamlessly together to achieve.

'A month at the outside.' Bronzehand smiled and opened his hands.

'You clearly haven't seen our t'varr's dragon fortress,' scoffed Meido. 'You won't get a Regrettable Man inside it and no one here can afford an Elemental, not any more. I say three months before our kwen or his lady find a way.'

'Someone already did,' said Tsen quietly, still gazing at his wine, but none of them seemed to hear. He glanced around the table but no one caught his eye. *Do I really think one of these sent a Regrettable Man to murder my alchemist? No. They're not that stupid, any of them.*

Chrias Kwen scowled. 'What are you saying?'

'Natural causes, I'm sure.' Meido shrugged.

'Three months, Baran Meido?' Tsen was suddenly on his feet, not quite sure why or what he was going to say but timing was everything. Fortune and timing, and this moment needed to be seized. Bewildered by what was happening around you or not, you didn't get to serve a sea lord for a decade without an instinct to grasp every opportunity as it drifted by and Quai'Shu had practically handed him his own boots. 'I'll take that wager. I'll make it six.' He offered his arm and grinned.

'Six. And I'll take your eyrie and your dragons if I win.' Meido smiled.

Of course you will. 'And I'll take everything you have in Vespinarr if you lose.'

'Wait!' Elesxian jumped up. She almost threw herself at the pair of them but the great table was in the way. *Too late. Oh dear, oh dear.* Tsen smiled at her and Chrias Kwen as he and Baran Meido clasped arms on their wager. *Have we just agreed that one of us will succeed Quai'Shu, one way or the other? No, we have a wager. Much more important!*

'The eyrie is not yours to give, T'Varr,' snarled Chrias.

'It is our lord's.' Tsen bowed to them all. 'I merely wager the onerous task of looking after it for him.'

'Against the heavy burden of our interests in Vespinarr.' Meido smiled too. *Good.* They had an agreement. *All I have to do is keep our lord alive through six months and a stream of assassins that will no doubt start very soon indeed. And now out.* Tsen left the council room in Quai'Shu's wake, hurrying through the glass cage that surrounded it and into the creamy open marble halls of Xican's tower within the Crown of the Sea Lords. The atrium was an indulgence of open space, half the height of the whole tower, the roof almost lost in the vastness overhead. Two sides of the tower were raw gold-glass, the one facing in towards the amphitheatre of the Proclamatory and the other facing out towards the sea. They let in the sun – when there was sunshine to be had instead of the usual Khalishtor rain – and so the tower was bright, even down at its feet. Men and women in peacock robes moved back and forth, some with cloaks and some without but all with feathers here and there, anything and everything from a single quill braided into their hair to a forest of plumage. Like every Taiytakei they wore their hair in braids, in different numbers and colours and lengths and Tsen could look at a man or a woman, look at the colours and the patterns, the feathers and their braids and know exactly their function, who they were, their family, to which sea lord they were tied, where they came from and where, most likely, they were going. *Each of us in his place and our place on display for all. Starting with the hair, and if your braids don't reach down to the backs of your thighs then you're simply not worth my time. Sorry but there it is.*

He waited outside Quai'Shu's private rooms until the sea lord emerged again, clothes changed, scented and sweet. Six black-cloaks and LaLa came with him. Not quite a guarantee against any assassin but certainly an open threat of the consequences that would follow.

'Well *you* don't look happy, killer. Does our plotting not amuse you?'

'It saddens me, Hands of the Sea Lord, that I have to wonder which of you will be first to try and poison my lord.'

'I can tell you it won't be me.' *And what other wagers were made after I left? Some, for sure. Alliances, bargains, some to be honoured, others to be betrayed. The usual goings-on of a sea lord's council.* He grinned to himself. *Pleasant though to hammer a wedge between Meido and his niece. Perhaps we should look and see if we can find another?* 'If I – if *we* – can see that he lasts six months, Baran Meido has thrown his support behind me. If not? Well, then the eyrie and the dragons will be his and I will be his servant. Lady Elesxian was most obviously unamused so I would say she and Chrias Kwen are my enemies for now, but it will be Meido who tries first, LaLa. I am sure enough of that to give you good odds on a wager of our own, if you like.'

They guided Quai'Shu towards the wall facing the Proclamatory, to the rising glass platform that would take them to the Paths of Words, the narrow glass bridges that reached from the towers of the Crown's outer ring to its silver heart and the Great Sea Council. Tsen sat Quai'Shu safely in the middle where he couldn't fall, then shielded him from darts and arrows with his black-cloaks. He tapped the glass with his black rod and then found his eyes darting from place to place, already looking for the first of Meido's killers. *Now there's a thought. Did he have that wager in mind before he even came? Wouldn't put it past him.*

No. Couldn't think like that or he'd go mad before even a day was out, and so he forced himself to be still and looked at the view. Even a sea lord never tired of this: the sun low behind him already setting the horizon aglow and firing the rippling sea. Orange light filled the void around him like a memory of a time when the world had burned and the pale stone walls were tinged pink as if with blood not quite washed away. In front of him the other twelve great towers gleamed and flickered, their shapes catching the sun and then losing it again as Tsen and his sea lord rose. The mighty coliseum of the Proclamatory was lost in an abyss of shadows. Above it the Paths of Words glittered while the evening sun turned the silver sphere of the Great Sea Council to a burnished copper. Much higher still, the vast glass Star of the Navigators shone like a jewel at the peak of a copper-gold crown. There lived the handful of men and women who held the knowledge to cross the storm-dark, the key to every sea lord's power.

It wasn't always this way. There was another world once, brighter than this one and whole. He glanced at LaLa. *However hard your sort try to make us forget. With no Endless Ocean and where the storm-dark didn't rage. Where every artifice of the enchanters would seem pale and shallow. A lost world. Useless to dream of such things and it might not even be true, but still ...* Tsen stared up at the Star. *Thing is though, if it is true, how did it fall? I'd like to know, because here in front of me is the font of every sea lord's power and I wonder how easily that too might fall.*

In the light of the setting sun the Star seemed to glow as though it was on fire and suddenly all Tsen could think of were dragons. He shuddered. *And now I'm just letting my imagination get melo-dramatic – clearly I need Kalaiya here to slap me to my senses.* He poked LaLa, because there was something about poking an Elemental Man that always brought him sharply back to the here and now. 'Bronzehand has bowed out and allowed himself to be sent to Qeled.' Along with half of what Baran Meido had promised in his wager, Tsen suddenly realised. *Cunning bastard. Gives away half his power to remove one rival and then negates his sacrifice by a wager of everything he has. Yes, too cunning by half.* 'Jima Hsian remains as enigmatic as ever. He's a hsian though. If he saw this coming then our lord would already be dead.' He could say things like that to LaLa. Not to anyone else. *Perhaps I should stop calling you that now? If I was you I really wouldn't like it. But there's that little devil that says I have to.*

The view blurred in front of him as the platform climbed the inside wall of the tower. There were men standing right in front of him on the other side of the great glass wall with short cropped hair, plain white tunics and brands instead of feathers. Slaves on a little platform sat atop a silver egg suspended by silver chains, cleaning the glass with rags and buckets of water. Tsen looked up. High above floated a glasship. Beyond that, clouds were sweeping in from the north. *Rain again? Ah, Khalishtor! But after so much time in the desert I suppose I shan't begrudge you a little of your favourite weather.* He glanced up at the glasship again. Extravagant to use one for such vanity. Maybe he should speak about that to the t'varr who looked after this tower. One of his own staff? Had to be, but he was buggered if he could think of a name. 'It would be best, first, to address our debts,' he said, largely to himself since LaLa surely didn't care and Quai'Shu had slipped into his daydreams again. And then the glass-cleaning slaves were far below and the glass beneath his feet slid in effortless silence to a stop.

There were no doors to the Paths of Words, only gold-glass that opened like a flower to the touch of Tsen's black rod. He tensed. *Never liked this bit.* Whenever he reached the top he always remembered the wind first, the howling gusts that blew across the Paths. There were no guard rails, nothing at all to stop a man from falling. It was a test, Quai'Shu had said many years ago when he'd first brought his promising young t'varr here. *Yes, and wasn't it just. Worst bloody weather in ten years. Howling great thunderstorm. Winds to snap anchor chains and pissing with rain. First thing that happened when you opened up the wall was lightning hit the Star of the Navigators and I almost fell off. Only those of courage may enter the Sea Council, you said. Only the ridiculously bloody stupid today, I thought, but I did it, even if you almost had to carry me. People still remember. We had the Great Sea Council to ourselves. Everyone else had far too much sense to be out in that weather.* Today was calm, but this was a different Quai'Shu now, old and broken. *Would it be such a bad thing if you fell? You wouldn't be the first. But if you do, then let it be because you've had enough, old man, not because of me, not even if LaLa wasn't here and the two of us were alone.* A witless sea lord was burden enough for any house, never mind one so crippled with debt, but Quai'Shu was Tsen's lord and master, had been his mentor once though there might not have been much love over the years, and even without Meido's wager he wouldn't simply stand by and do nothing. They walked side by side, arms wrapped around each other through the wind over glass as clear as water and then hundreds of feet of emptiness, and it seemed nothing more than two men who were well past their prime, both uncertain and a little fearful, holding on to one another to share what courage they had. *As you did for me in that storm. Although the glass is wider than it seems and there really isn't much danger of falling, not if your feet are sure, but it does things to a man's mind to look down, doesn't it? Straight through the air to the gardens and the trees and the contours of the water terraces so far below and you start to wonder, don't you, old man? What it would be like to fly, truly to fly.*

The glass platform sank back towards the ground. Others would follow bringing the alchemist and the dragon-rider and the little dragon. He laughed. *Yes. Little* dragon – the hatchling was as large as a horse and its tail made it more than twice as long. It would be interesting to see how *that* could be coaxed along the Paths of Words and he almost wished he could stay to watch. But Quai'Shu was his concern now; for the next six months, nothing else mattered. There were other people whose purpose was to see to such things as slaves and monsters.

From tower to Crown, the glass bridge was five hundred bold paces long, give or take a handful. Quai'Shu took far more than that and they were slow ones too, but Tsen tolerated it. When they reached the globe of gleaming silver that was the heart of the Crown, he tapped his rod against its bright skin and the silver shimmered and flowed like liquid, opening before him. The globe of the Great Sea Council was another relic, a thing from a different time like the floating castle that had become his eyrie. The enchanters had found it and resurrected it long ago. Did they understand it? He didn't know. Could they have made it themselves, this thing of liquid silver? He thought not, but he'd never know because neither the enchanters nor the navigators would ever speak of such things, not to one who wasn't their own.

He stepped through into an open comforting space that glowed with its own light – another thing that made him think of his flying eyrie. It was a simple structure inside, one quicksilver globe inside the other. The Great Sea Council sat in the inner globe and from there they ruled the six known worlds. A series of spacious halls had been built between the two layers where the entourages of the sea lords might mingle and wait for their summons to the council itself. And, on the council's more exciting days, occasionally stab one another.

The inner skin flowed and opened before the touch of Quai'Shu's rod. There were no guards here, no soldiers, no weapons. You either had a wand that would make the walls part for you or you didn't, and if you didn't then there simply wasn't a way in. Quai'Shu had one. So did Tsen, and Jima Hsian and Chrias Kwen. Probably not any of the others, not yet, but that would soon change. *Chrias Kwen will see to one for Lady Elesxian, so I should probably do something for Meido myself.*

Inside the inner sphere the black-cloaks gently manoeuvred Quai'Shu to his place among the thirteen thrones of the sea lords, arrayed in the shape of a horseshoe. Plain wooden benches were lined up behind each throne, simple and unadorned and desperately uncomfortable after not very long at all, but only sea lords sat in thrones. Four of them were already here, Quai'Shu the fifth, a sign of the importance of their twilight debate today. LaLa stood beside him – oh yes, and no pair of eyes missed *that* little statement, did they? – while the black-cloaks withdrew to the edge of the circle. Soft light shone from the walls, from the floor and from the roof, tinged with orange to reflect the setting sun outside. Tsen stretched his ears and listened to the whispering among the kwens and the t'varrs who served the other sea lords. Wagers, mostly, on who would attend and who would not. Across the horseshoe the throne for Lord Shonda of Vespinarr sat empty. Tsen touched a finger to his brow to salute the man who sat behind it, Vey Rin T'Varr. Rin smiled and returned a faint nod. More than half a lifetime ago he and Tsen had been friends together in the desert, chasing slaves. As far as it was possible for either of them, Tsen liked to think that old friendships still counted for something.

The walls parted and closed again as other t'varrs and kwens and hsians took their places, or now and then left and came back again minutes later, running petty errands for their restless masters. A hush rippled over them as three navigators entered, their braided hair almost touching the floor and as long as his own. Their cloaks of feathers were iridescent things, a deep blue but shimmering in every colour of the rainbow as they caught the light. Their robes were the same. The navigators had no thrones and stood in the centre, back to back and facing outward, meeting the eyes of the assembled lords, something that only a navigator was privileged to do. One of them held an hourglass. Tsen squinted at its sands. The speaking would begin when the sun fully sank into the sea.

More arrived, two more sea lords – seven of them in one place together, something almost unknown – and dozens of their kwens and their hsians. The murmuring grew. The sands trickled away, and as the last grain fell the navigator who held the hourglass spoke. Tsen smiled. Today wasn't about Quai'Shu's dragons, but one day it would be. *And how many of you will come then?*

'The Ice Witch of Aria.' There was a pause and then the navigator continued. Tsen sighed and tried to pay attention. Chrias Kwen would receive his own information. Jima Hsian probably knew everything he would hear today and far more besides. But Tsen listened anyway as the navigator went on. Aria was a realm that Tsen had never seen and in which he had no interest. He was a t'varr after all, charged with putting things in their correct places, and once they were there he had little interest in what they actually did. Given the choice he preferred his vineyards and his bathhouse. But the navigators' voices betrayed their alarm – they were anxious, all of them, even afraid. Sorcerers were growing in Aria like weeds, the strongest already a threat even to an Elemental Man, it seemed.

Their world was changing quickly – *too* quickly. They'd learned to forge near-perfect glass, might soon unravel the secrets of the enchanters, had taken Scythian steelsmiths and ...

A furore broke out at that. Not at steelsmiths being somewhere they weren't supposed to be – *that* was a mere annoyance and quickly solved by the swift cut of a bladeless knife – but for them to be there at all meant that someone had taken them across the storm-dark along with secrets the Taiytakei had chosen not to share. Now the sea lords smirked and twitched and looked among themselves to see if any face would reveal who'd made such a dangerous trade and what prize they might have won in return. The t'varrs and hsians and kwens behind them whispered to one another, exchanging wagers. Tsen heard Quai'Shu's name more than once. He closed his eyes for a moment. It would be easy to let go, to let others do whatever needed to be done. It would be like sinking back with a large happy sigh into warm scented waters, but that wasn't why he was here. Not why Quai'Shu and Jima Hsian – and even Tsen himself these last two days – had cashed in every favour they owned to have this debate here and now with a dragon in the wings outside.

The navigators waited, quietly letting the rest have their moment to build their little conspiracies, biding their time, and then the first navigator glared at the lords around him, fixing his eyes on them one after another. 'They were *taken*, my lords. Do not look within. A sorcerer from another realm has walked between the worlds.'

The silence unleashed was deep and long as the meaning sank in. *Someone other than a navigator has crossed the storm-dark. We have an equal.*

A competitor.

A threat.

And here it comes. My moment. In the silence Baros Tsen T'Varr coughed and had their attention at once. Ah, but this was going to be difficult and he wasn't even sure he wanted to do it. But he had eyes fixed on him. The lords and t'varrs and kwens and hsians of the thirteen cities. What he wanted was his bathhouse. His apple wine. His peace and quiet the way it had been a week ago but it was too late for that. He'd made this happen. This moment. *Inspired or mad?* He wasn't sure but now he stood up. 'I believe the lord of Xican may be able to offer a solution.' No going back now. 'A plague to ruin worlds.' That was what the alchemist had said when they'd taken him, wasn't it? Yes, and that, in the end, was why their lord had spent twenty-odd years of his life and broken his house's bank to steal these monsters. Because of Jima Hsian's warning: *Some day, in our lifetime, something will come. In the Dominion, in Aria, from out of the depths of Qeled, something will rise. Something that will threaten us all and we must be ready for it.*

Twenty-three years ago. Midsummer's night and every hsian in Takei'Tarr had said the same, but Quai'Shu was the only sea lord who'd listened.

'What plague?' The first navigator asked the question in all their eyes. Tsen let his smile grow wide. He had them where he wanted them. Every last one.

'I will show you,' he said. 'But there will be a price, my lords. And it will not be a small one.'

40

Dragon-rider

Zafir's breath caught in her throat. The Crown of the Sea Lords did that to her every time her eyes strayed to it. She told herself not to look, told herself that the Pinnacles, her old home, were larger and grander; and they *were*, three whole mountains carved and tunnelled and ... and *wrought* long ago by the will of the Silver King. But still she couldn't help the stolen glimpses and glances. So much glass, so much gold, so much light and so much sheer *size*! And the orb that floated far above it, all spines and spires of glitter. Each time it trapped her with its majesty she forced herself to see it shattered by dragons, its great golden shards falling like rain. Dragons. *They* were the true wonder. *She* was their mistress. She clung to that like a drowning man to driftwood.

The glasship drifted to a halt at the edge of the Crown beside one of the gold-glass towers. The black-cloaks pressed a stud in the wall and the bronze shell of the gondola split open. A ramp eased down. They led her out over a flat black circle of polished marble towards the looming tower. Brass gates as tall as a ship hung open. As she passed through them, she saw they were wrought from top to bottom with pictures beaten into the metal: a huge tower topped by a circle of cloud, ringed by lesser towers; a man standing on the prow of a ship facing a storm full of lightning; men bearing gifts, bowing in supplication. At the very top, etched right across the doors, were the twin lightning-bolts of Xican.

Beside her the alchemist was looking up at them too. 'Feyn Charin,' he whispered. 'The story of the first navigator.'

The black-cloaks led them on into the vast hollow tower, between walls of pale marble and gleaming glowing glass, across a floor of more black stone speckled with flecks of gold like the night sky. They took her to a glass disc that floated over the floor and pushed her onto it and stood in a circle around her. The alchemist, when he saw it, groaned and clutched his belly, and when he sat, got down by the edge, closed his eyes and gripped it tight with his hands. He looked old now, old and scared and she wondered why, until without any warning the glass rose and floated up through the inner space of the tower. Her heart jumped into her mouth at first but she quickly pushed it back where it belonged. The black-cloaks, if anything, looked bored. To them this was simply how things were, not to be given a second thought.

Dragons. She recalled sitting on Mistral, diving over the edge of the Pinnacles, the wind a storm in her face. They'd played a game, before her mother had forbidden it, with three great poles that jutted out of the cliffs, one at the top, one in the middle, one by the bottom, each with strips of coloured cloth tied to the end. One by one each dragon-rider took their dragon to the edge of the cliff and dived, the aim to snatch a coloured strip from each pole as they arrowed past, a test of skill and courage for rider and dragon alike. She'd been the fastest but it wasn't for playing the game that her mother had forbidden it. *That* had come when Zafir had insisted she be the one to climb out on the middle pole to tie on the strips so they could play again. It jutted fifty feet from the cliff, the ground half a mile below, no ropes, nothing to catch her, nothing to save her. She'd crawled along the top of the pole where the other riders hung underneath and the ground had stared up at her every inch of the way, and she'd stared right back while the wind that whipped around the cliffs had tugged at her clothes, and she'd felt so *alive*! She'd slipped twice, tying on the strips, nearly fallen each time but she'd caught herself, and when she finally came back, her heart was racing so fast and she was shaking so much she could barely stand. Now, as she looked at the black floor of the tower a mere few dozen yards below, she smiled. The Taiytakei thought they were so grand and so elegant, so full of arrogant poise and perhaps they were, but where was their fire?

The light of the setting sun streamed through the wall behind them. To Zafir it seemed as though everything was lit by distant flames. The disc rose high and then slid deftly sideways and stopped at a stone balcony overlooking the hall below. There was a circle of them up here and more above as the inner vault of the tower narrowed. From each balcony an entrance led to a cluster of glass-walled rooms. Zafir saw blurred shadows moving in some of them. People. Others had hangings blocking out the light, hiding whatever was inside. There was no other way up or down except by disc. No stairs.

Two of the black-cloaks led her onto the balcony and the glass disc drifted away, across the void to another. She watched as it stopped again and the other black-cloaks helped the alchemist to his feet and walked him away. When she turned back, Myst and Onyx were standing in front of her. They fell to their knees and pressed their heads to the floor. The black-cloaks didn't like that. One of them grabbed Myst by the hair and pulled her to her feet again. 'She's a slave like you. Get up!' They gave Zafir a shove as if to emphasise her servitude.

Her two broken birds took her to a room off the balcony. The soldiers didn't follow but she could see them still out there, slightly blurred through the gold-tinged glass, standing stiffly straight and staring back at her. She looked for a hanging or a curtain or something she could pull across the wall to hide from their gaze but there wasn't anything. The room was bare except for a silk rug that covered the floor, a chest of clothes, a bath full of warm milky water and a scattering of pots and bottles littered around it. Beneath the rug, she saw, the floor was the same glass as the walls.

Myst and Onyx fussed over her. They cut her hair short like their own and wrapped her in plain white silks. She didn't try to stop them even when they washed her and covered her in their sickly perfume. Instead she closed her eyes and imagined herself in the Adamantine Palace, imagined that these were her own maids dressing her to appear as the speaker of the nine realms once more. When they were done, they took her out to the balcony and waited until another glass disc rose to take them down to the cavernous heart of the tower once more. At the bottom, Bellepheros was already there. He had a hatchling beside him, fresh from its egg but still a monster. It squatted still and quiet, its eyes following every movement around it with a venomous hunger and a yearning hate. All the Taiytakei who passed by, who'd never seen such a creature, couldn't help but stop transfixed and tremble and then scurry away. Watching them made her smile. Made her sure in her heart that she was right about them, how they'd crumble when she squeezed. It gave her strength.

There were slaves beside the dragon, three of them. Scales with their hollow empty eyes. A part of her yearned to go to the dragon and touch it, to meet its eyes and stare into them and let it know that she was there, that one day, when it grew, she would be its mistress and its rider, but she kept away. The hatchling was too young and small to be properly clean and the slaves surely had the Hatchling Disease. It didn't show – the first patches of rough white skin on their knuckles wouldn't be visible for weeks – but they were Scales and so they had it, whether it showed or not. She sidled up to the alchemist instead, although he probably had it too. Most alchemists did.

'Remember who we are,' he whispered when they were close enough not to be overheard. 'Remember, Holiness. They need us both.'

She didn't reply. Bellepheros knew the secrets that would keep these stolen dragons in check but what use did they have for *her*? For a moment a quiver of doubt crept out. She took it in her hand and clenched her fist around it and put it back into the box where she kept all her others. *I am a dragon-queen. They cannot touch me.*

Shrin Chrias Kwen came strutting up, wrapped in his most brilliant feathers and surrounded by more black-cloaks, and she wondered briefly how easy it would be to get close enough to stab him in the neck and watch him bleed. But today she didn't have a knife and so she pretended not to see him, flicking lidded glances through her lashes now and then.

Another floating glass sled drifted across the floor, much bigger than the first. The black-cloaks poked and prodded her and Bellepheros and the Scales and the hatchling onto it. She sat at the edge beside Bellepheros, as far away from the hatchling and its disease as she could be, smiling at the black-cloaks who refused to stand anywhere close until Shrin Chrias Kwen planted himself in front of the hatchling's face with his lightning wand ready in his hand. *That* made her smile even more – the thought of the kwen's skin slowly turning hard as stone until he suffocated because he couldn't breathe. Delicious …

The sled rose, wafting through the space inside the tower to its centre and then rising towards its peak and another large open glass-walled space where the lords of this palace doubtless held their courts amid their gold-drenched glory. Zafir stared down past her dangling feet. Sitting over a void was strange, a very different thing from sitting on the back of a dragon. She dredged out another memory: standing on a cliff overlooking the top of the Diamond Cascade, watching as it washed over the edge of the Purple Spur and fell into mist above the City of Dragons. A few days before they'd made her speaker, with Sirion, old Hyram's cousin, beside her.

'Am I beautiful?'

'Of course.' He tried to step away, but as he did she caught his hand and pressed it against her breast.

'Am I desirable?'

'I am not to be had, harlot.' He'd pulled away but for an instant he'd hesitated. He'd felt her heart beating strong and fast. He'd been her enemy then, the most dangerous of them all, or so she'd thought, but for a moment she'd still seen the hunger in his eyes. A knife of last resort but always a weapon when she needed it, and she saw that hunger now in Shrin Chrias Kwen, even with her hair cut short and wrapped in these white silks, drab amid the colours of the Taiytakei. Not desire but a cruel lust to break her, fierce and brutal, to hurt her and crush her spirit utterly. A smile twitched at the corner of her lip. It made him weak.

Yet in T'Varr Baros Tsen, where she needed it most, there wasn't even a flicker.

High up, the sled stopped its ascent and drifted to the glass wall that faced the silver sphere at the heart of the Crown. Shrin Chrias Kwen touched a black rod to the gold-glass wall and it flowed away before him, opening into a portal leading onto a bridge of near-invisible glass. The black-cloaks pushed her onto it, wind howling in from the sea and the setting sun. The height made her head spin and her heart race. She strode out, head back, arms stretched wide to embrace the wind. This was more like it.

Behind her the Scales were coaxing the dragon out onto the bridge. It kept opening its wings, wanting to fly instead of walk. Its claws skittered on the hardness of the glass. Chrias Kwen walked with the Scales and the dragon as though it was nothing. Proving his fearlessness, perhaps? 'How young is it?' she whispered to Bellepheros. 'Does he not care about the Statue Plague?'

Bellepheros had turned the sickly yellow-white of old bone. He was gasping for breath, a black-cloak either side of him guiding him and holding him up. He barely managed to even look at her. 'He doesn't know, Holiness,' he gasped. 'I've held nothing back but not all men listen as they should. In some matters I feel little urge for repetition. Sometimes one must learn by seeing and doing and suffering a little from one's mistakes.'

He doesn't know? She smiled, a vicious little smile of imagining the kwen riddled by the dragon-disease, joints creaking, weeping sores forming over his hardening skin until he froze rigid and set like stone. 'Thank you for that thought, Master Alchemist. We must talk more.'

'Holiness, forgive me!' Bellepheros was too lost in his own misery to really listen. Maybe that was as well. 'I'm no dragon-rider and I do not take well to such heights. Caves and libraries are my home, not this.' He was shaking like a leaf in the wind and his face was now as white as her silks.

The black-cloaks urged them on, impatient. At the far end the kwen touched his black wand to the silver orb and its bright mirror skin flowed open to embrace them. Zafir's fingers brushed it as she passed through, trailing across its gleaming skin, ice-cold and glass-smooth and hard as diamond. 'There are places in the Fortress of Watchfulness where none of us go,' she murmured to Bellepheros as he stepped through behind her. 'Deep places. There are things left behind by the Silver King that are a little like this, though much smaller.' The alchemist didn't seem to hear her. He looked ready to collapse and the Taiytakei soldiers were as good as carrying him. Perhaps that too was for the best. The old blood-mages had never understood what the Silver King had made and the alchemists who followed had never been allowed close. Creations. They were mysteries that had never been unravelled.

Beyond the silver liquid skin warm wood walls welcomed them, exquisite but mundane. Across the floor some fifty strides away more silver faced her. A gently lit space arced overhead, following the curve of the egg's outer shell. Thick woollen rugs were scattered across the floor, full of colour, and after the glass bridge they felt lush and warm under her bare feet. She wriggled her toes in them and it felt oddly pleasant. She couldn't remember the last time she'd gone for so long without boots.

The kwen and his black-cloaks swirled around her towards a cluster of ornate bone-carved tables, chairs and crystal bottles of many-coloured liquids. Other Taiytakei circled warily in their rainbow clothes, with their cloaks and capes of bright feathers and their long braids. They watched but their eyes weren't on her; they were on the kwen and his hatchling. Zafir smiled to see them – yes, let *them* stare and gawk in wonder! The dragon was on edge. She could see from the way it twitched its tail. It sensed the fear and anxiety, the uncertainty all around it. Beneath the potions that dulled its mind lay old and powerful urges that even Bellepheros couldn't quell. These Taiytakei, what were they but prey? It made her smile. She caught the hatchling's eye and for a moment they regarded one another. *I understand.*

Bellepheros, gasping, moved beside her and sat down with relief. 'They need a rider, Holiness,' he said under his breath. 'The dragons and the Taiytakei both. They need someone who is trained. Some- one the dragons will understand. Someone who will not be afraid. They have one that is full grown and they have no one else to fly it.'

Zafir let that sink in. *That* was why they needed her? They hadn't thought to take someone else? Flame! There must have been a hundred riders across the realms who'd lost their dragons in the war! And *that* was the thread on which she hung?

The hatchling eyed her, almost as though it knew her. *Soon. When you're bigger and have the back for me to sit on and the sickness you carry is gone.* It would be months before the dragon could be ridden and even then it would really still be a hatchling. Yet it looked back at her hard as if to say, *Yes, but I will grow, and we will ride, and when the time comes my fire will be fierce ...*

One that is full grown. That meant they had one of the dragons she'd flown from Furymouth. The sort of monster she would need to bring this world crashing to its knees in flames and ash! Cloud Claw? Diamond Eye? 'But there were three, Bellepheros, not one. I saw them take three. If the Taiytakei have one, where are the other two?'

He didn't answer but she thought perhaps she knew. The silver men. Three of them. Three dragons. But then why did they let one go?

The kwen and his men helped themselves to the wine or whatever else the Taiytakei kept in their bottles. They hardly spared her and Bellepheros another glance. 'This is their heart,' she murmured. She could feel the power here. She saw it in the flash of all these colours, in the brilliance of the feather cloaks all around her, in the length of the braided hair. But she saw it in their eyes too, in the unflinching stares, the pinched mouths. Used to obedience, all of them.

'As I have said, Holiness, this is their City of Dragons,' said Bellepheros. 'Their Adamantine Palace.'

'Is it true they have no speaker?'

'Kings and queens they call sea lords. Their enchanters and the navigators who dwell above us are perhaps their alchemists but they have none to speak for them as one.'

'Then they may be turned against one another.'

'Perhaps.'

Perhaps? Kings and queens *always* turned against one another. She flinched away as the hatchling moved restlessly closer then realised that Chrias Kwen was watching her. He laughed at her. 'Afraid of your own monster, slave?'

So much disgust. So much hate. Anger? Yes, anger. *Envy?* Is *that* what she saw there amid all that hungry desire to hurt her? She threw back her head and laughed right back in his face. 'Fear?' Angry men were easily made into fools, and lustful men too, and this kwen was both. She shivered. 'Fear?' she said again. 'Of that? What you misread, Shrin Chrias Kwen, is disdain. *That* is a toy. A pretty thing for your master to show to his friends but *that* is not a dragon, not yet.'

They glared at one another until the inner wall flowed open and there was Baros Tsen T'Varr himself. 'Chrias Kwen.' The t'varr smiled, showing his usual jovial mask. Zafir watched the looks that passed between them. No love, not a bit of it. In a dark street with knives at their sides and no eyes to bear witness, only one of them would ever walk away. 'Bring the dragon and the slaves. Our lords wish to see them.'

She followed the kwen and the t'varr as she was bidden into a wide circle of a room whose walls were silver, whose floor was solid gold, where a soft light fell from above and marvellous thrones surrounded her. They stood her in the middle with the alchemist to one side of her and the hatchling kept carefully away from all the Taiytakei in their magnificent clothes. The black-cloaked soldiers pressed close as if fearful that Zafir would launch herself in another murderous fury. *And one day I will. But when I come again it will be with dragons, and nothing in the skies will save you.*

Tsen started talking, preaching about how he and his dragons would pour fire over a place whose name she'd never heard and turn it into ash. She watched the other Taiytakei as they listened. They were curious at first. Fascinated, but they weren't afraid. If anything she felt scorn from them. What could such a tiny monster achieve against a nation mighty with sorcerers?

Tsen talked of an army of dragons but he spoke in terms that were absurd and Zafir could only shake her head. A year? A hundred dragons? But it would take ten before they were grown to their full size. Did he mean to go to war with a hundred yearlings? Even her Adamantine Men would have destroyed them, no need for any blood-mages.

A Taiytakei in a cloak so cleverly made that he seemed to be garbed in flames rose and asked Tsen how much all of this would cost. The answer came in words that Zafir didn't understand but the meaning was clear enough. Something preposterous. Around their circle the Taiytakei fell to laughter and derision and discord as the soldiers bustled her and the alchemist and his hatchling away again. And that was that, and Zafir laughed as she left because for all their gleam and colour and glamour they were so much like her own Council of Kings and Queens. So deliciously, delightfully familiar and so utterly pointless. With no speaker, how did they ever do more than bicker?

It was as she walked away that she touched a finger to the soft skin inside her elbow and noticed a roughness there. She stopped and stared in horror at the first little whiteness on her own skin. She knew it for what it was at once – she'd seen it enough times after all – but it was too soon by far to have come from the hatchling Tsen and Bellepheros had brought today so maybe she was wrong ... And then she understood. The hatchling dragon on the ship. The woken one that had so very carefully cut her with its claw and then let her live. It had done this to her. It had given her the dragon-disease.

41

Unnatural Selection

High in the gold-glass tower, back across the Paths of Words, Baros Tsen sank deeper into the water, deeper and deeper until his nose and his eyes were all that broke the surface. *Like a crocodile*, back when he had space for such frivolous thoughts. *A big fat happy crocodile. But not so happy now.*

He surfaced. The bathhouse here was nothing like the one buried in the bowels of the Palace of Leaves in Xican. *Here* was far above the ground with a gold-glass roof and walls. Anyone who happened to pass over the top of the tower on a sled or a disc could look right down and see him in all his glory if they were curious enough. And the bath was far too small, and they never got the water quite right, and the Xizic oil wasn't the oil he liked, and the steam just made the glass absurdly slippery and, really, it was a surprise no one had yet broken their neck in here …

At least it was dark outside now and, since he hadn't brought any lamps, no one would know he was here. Dark was good. Dark with a bit of moonlight in between the gathering rainclouds. He sat very still and when the water was smooth enough for him to see his own dim reflection, he wagged his finger at it. 'You know what? That could have gone a little better. Just a bit. Maybe, perhaps, without the part where they all started laughing.'

His reflection stared back at him. At least the bath wasn't glass too. Someone had kindly lined it with the same black marble they'd used for the tower, with the gold flecks. In the dark they glowed. It gave him the odd sense of seeing his own face loom over him out of the night sky.

'Go on. Say something. And it had better be something useful.' A plague of dragons to scourge away the curse of the Ice Witch and her sorcerers across the storm-dark in Aria. And it wouldn't come for a year or two because that was how long it would take for everyone to be ready, and the dragons would be bigger then, big enough for men to ride on their backs.

If Quai'Shu had been able to speak it would have been different. *He was the master of that, not me. I read them; he's the one who would take their minds and transform them. And I thought my dragons would be bigger.*

It had been an odd failure though. Too thorough and complete to quite make sense, as if someone had been ready for his play and carefully laid the ground against him in advance. He should have brought the grown one. Maybe that would have made a difference, if they'd all had to traipse outside to even see it. But then again maybe they just wouldn't have bothered.

'Did it come from within?' He looked at his reflection and his reflection shook its head. No. Just like the assassins trying to kill the alchemist, no one from Xican wanted to see the eyrie fail. They wanted to see *him* fail but not the rest, because if they destroyed the rest then what was there to inherit save an insurmountable debt? 'Well then, if not from within, who wants to see a sea lord fail?'

His reflection laughed. *Who wants to see a sea lord fail? Why, everyone ...*

He stopped, suddenly aware he wasn't alone. He stayed very still, listening, until he was sure that he knew who it was and then turned. 'LaLa, a bath is a man's private personal place. I come here to be alone, not to be bothered, even by you.' *Even when I come with Kalaiya, it's not what all the rest of you all think it is. Not that I care a whit.* 'You'd better be here to tell me that Quai'Shu's dead or something equally grave.' *I could put metal doors on my eyrie bath-house and line the walls and floors with brass to keep you out. My petty little thumb up my petty little nose to you. Shall I do that?*

The Watcher lit a lamp. He bowed. 'Sea Lord-in-Waiting, I do not come with news.'

'That's a relief. It's been a long enough day as it is. And why do you keep calling me that when I'm not? Quai'Shu is our sea lord. I'm merely his t'varr, LaLa, and we've seen there are plenty of others equally keen to step into his shoes. One or two of them might even be better at it.' *And even if they're not, they'll certainly think it now. Well done, Tsen, well done. But who was it who set the trap?* 'They're all preening themselves, but do you know what outcome *I* would most like? *I* would most like my sea lord to recover his wits and lord it over us all for another ten years more, that's what *I* would like. And if he doesn't, I might still change my mind and content myself with what I have, you know. Wisdom and the desire for a long life both recommend it and I can hardly complain about the conditions of my current position. Certainly far less than I'd complain about losing it. Besides, after today I'm inclined to wonder if almost *any* of the others might make a better job of it. What happened in there, LaLa? We were ambushed, that's what, and I had no idea it was coming. Would you care for some apple wine?'

The Elemental Man shook his head as Tsen knew he must. *Only water fresh from river or sky, untouched by the hand of any man.* 'Our master Quai'Shu chose you, Hands of the Sea Lord. Do you not wish to be master of Xican?'

Now there's a question. 'Which one, do you suppose, will try to kill me first? Would you care for a wager?'

'I do not wager, Hands of the Sea Lord.'

'No.' Tsen sighed. 'You're really no fun at all, LaLa. And, in a way, that's why I'm not screaming for the guards outside. Fat lot of use they'd do me anyway. But which one. Pick one.'

'None of them. I am your protector.'

'What? And you think because of that they won't dare? How very pleasantly optimistic – but you're not *my* protector, LaLa. You belong to Quai'Shu.'

'They will not see the difference now.'

'Well I suppose I hope you're right but I can't say I don't have my doubts.' Tsen sat upright and poured a glass for himself. He savoured the fire and the apple in his mouth and let out a heavy sigh. 'I should have stayed where I was happy. With my orchards.'

'Is that what you wish?'

'Why do you keep asking me? What did you come here for anyway, LaLa? I certainly didn't invite you.'

The Watcher came closer in slow careful steps. At least inside the bathhouse he had the decency to get about like a normal man instead of simply vanishing from one place and appearing at another. Tsen gazed out into the steam-hazed gloom. They were alone. If the Elemental Man decided he was to die then that was what would happen. Nothing could stop it, yet mostly he felt annoyed at the intrusion and despondent about the day as a whole. Fear? No, no space for that any more.

'It is important that I know.' The Watcher stared at him, all pretence of servitude momentarily gone.

'Why, LaLa? Why? Why is it your business at all?'

'I am owned. I am Quai'Shu's slave, Sea Lord-in-Waiting.'

'Ha!' Tsen laughed. 'An exquisitely expensive one. Are you free when he dies?'

'I will serve whichever sea lord follows him.'

'Yes, well, I suppose I can see how there would be flaws in Quai'Shu's scheme otherwise, eh? An unstoppable assassin bound as a slave but free upon his master's death? Yes, I do believe I see a weakness or two in *that*. Other sea lords hate us and fear us, LaLa. You make us unique and some would see us fail simply because we have you. And now the dragons. It's as though Quai'Shu has set about acquiring a menagerie of monsters. Unfortunately, the other thing that makes us unique among our peers is our debt. I could sell you, I suppose. That might steady the ship.'

'Will you do that, Baros Tsen T'Varr?'

'No.' No, he knew that already. 'You'll be the last thing I let go. Right after I let some other grasping lord have Quai'Shu's dragons.' He drained his glass, poured another and looked the Elemental Man hard in the eye. 'I asked Quai'Shu several times how he managed to buy you and he wouldn't give me an answer. If I'm going to own you, LaLa, I want to know: why did your masters give you to our lord? It can't just be money otherwise the Vespinese would have gone and bought a dozen of you just because they could. Your masters wanted something in return, something only Quai'Shu could offer, and they wanted it enough to do a thing they've never done before or since, something that upsets the balance they strive so earnestly to keep. What was it, LaLa? Do you even know?'

'Our lord bought a service from one of my kind. This one failed.'

'No, no, LaLa. You can do better than that. Elemental Men don't fail, and if they do then another one comes to do the same work, and if needs be then another and another until it's done. And then they go away again. What did your masters want from

Quai'Shu? More to the point, what are they going to want from whoever follows him?'

'Our sea lord has a vision.' The Watcher spoke softly. 'We are a part of that. Where it goes, I follow.'

Tsen laughed. 'Bringing dragons to Takei'Tarr? *That's* what your masters wanted?'

The Watcher bowed his head. 'I cannot say, Hands of the Sea Lord, for I do not know.'

'Really?' *But that's why you stand beside whoever keeps that vision and nurtures it, isn't it? And that, of course, is why I do too.* 'If that's the case then your work is largely done and so is mine. I won't sell you, LaLa, but we need the money. Can I hire you out? Is that allowed?'

'The Elemental Masters would likely be displeased.'

'Why? Because it would be stepping on their toes? Breaking their monopoly?' *But Quai'Shu must surely have had the same idea. He'd never done it so there was surely a good reason. Would they have had him killed? Ach, there is so much more to this than money!*

Ah, but that's what makes it so spicy and unusual and interesting and why you're going to play along, even against your better judgement, isn't it?

Quiet, you. Although … 'I *am* left to wonder, LaLa, how many of us are puppets and who pulls our strings. Thoughts?' *You were a suspicious-minded old man, Quai'Shu. Did you ever wonder who was the tool and who was the craftsman here? Of course you did but you let it happen anyway. So you must have known what it was. Pity you went mad before you chose to share your thoughts.*

The Watcher bowed. 'I am but a servant.'

'Of course you are.' *And exactly how do I go about spying on a man who can turn into the wind and the rivers and the earth again? Oh, of course! I hire another one, and from the same masters! Surely that can't possibly go wrong at all, can it?* His lips settled into a wry pucker. 'I see there'll be no answers for me today. But, LaLa, whoever takes Quai'Shu's cape, they *will* need to know. Is that why you came? To see if it would be me? Well I don't know if I want it.' *Of course I do.* 'And even if I did, whether I can get it.' *Yes, a bit more to the point that.*

Tsen sank back into the bath. He turned and slid across to the other side so the Watcher was behind him. 'Since you're here, you can make yourself useful. Usually I talk to Kalaiya when I have days like today, but as she's not here I shall use you instead. Since you're nothing like her, I suggest you keep back in the shadows, and if you absolutely *have* to say anything, do it in a nice falsetto, and for the love of the sea please don't actually express an opinion on something I say or you'll ruin it completely. I shall call you Not Kalaiya until I'm done. Are you still there, LaLa?'

'I am, Hands of the Sea Lord.'

'I asked for falsetto! You didn't even try!' He laughed. 'Oh, then just don't speak at all, Not Kalaiya. Listen though. Whoever is sea lord must decide quickly what these dragons are worth. I want to keep them but they must be put to good use. They're tools of war, Not Kalaiya, useless without one. They must show their worth, but where is the war? My lords mocked our little hatchling today. They were turned against our scheme to use the dragons against the Ice Witch. Whoever did that turning I think must have another war in mind, perhaps a very different one and one that none of us yet see. Find out who did it for me, Not Kalaiya. Ask Jima Hsian. Find out why and what it is they want from us, for little monsters must grow into big monsters, and the bigger they are the more terrible they will become. And there is another matter: Quai'Shu, the alchemist, his dragons, that blasted slave who can ride them, even Chay-Liang. You must watch over all of them and keep us alive.' Had he just told the Watcher that yes, he did have the will to become the next sea lord even if it meant he went to war with Chrias Kwen? But he already knew the answer to that. The little hatchling had bewitched him. His dragons would change the world, and for all he was a t'varr, fat and happy and sleepy in his bath and with his wine, he *was* still a crocodile. He put down his glass, sighed and stood up. There were no slaves here, no one to robe him. He preferred the solitude.

'We have no money, Not Kalaiya. We drown in debt to half the other lords of the Great Sea Council and they all know it. They'll strangle us and starve us and bleed us until we fail; and then while we're dying but before our heart quite stops beating, they'll fall on us and carve up our corpse. *That* is how they will try to take my dragons. If we fight among ourselves for our sea lord's power, we only make it easier for them. That's the truth of where we are.'

The Elemental Man came closer and offered Tsen a towel. *Of course it is. But we'll still fight.*

'The others won't see the debt. They'll be blind to it – a t'varr's problem for when the dust clears. Every one of them would trade our dragons to have Quai'Shu's cape. All of them except me because the dragons are all I have.' Tsen wrapped the towel around himself. It was like putting on a fur. 'So somehow we make them show their worth and start the bargaining. We must begin by putting Shrin Chrias Kwen in his place. Firmly so.'

The Watcher nodded.

'The eyrie will be our fortress, Not Kalaiya. We'll keep the dragons close where they cannot be touched. We'll need glasships to and from the eyrie every day and *that* will be expensive, and that will also be how they try to get their assassins in.' He sat on the edge of the bath and took a few great lungfuls of steam. Sweat beaded on his skin. *Is this how it will be now? For the rest of my days, living in a cage of my own design?* Tsen laughed. 'How do I truly keep us safe, Not Kalaiya? How do I keep *you* safe, above all? Perhaps I shouldn't do this. I'd need a lot of metal to encase my whole eyrie, and Liang has far too much to do already and where will I find another enchanter who will build such a thing and know they will not – *can* not – be paid? But I can't say it isn't tempting. Other lords might easily afford an Elemental Man, if only for the day it would take to open my throat and see me bleed dry.'

The Watcher shrugged. Tsen shook himself. Even this stupid pretending game was making him miss Kalaiya far more than made any sense. She helped him *think*, that was it. He turned and poked the Watcher in the chest. 'Very well. Yes, Elemental Man, I'll preserve Quai'Shu's dreams. We shall have dragons, and we alone. Does that appease you?' He thought he saw LaLa smile but it must have been a trick of his eyes in the gloomy haze since Elemental Men never smiled, and it *was* very dark. They never got angry either. All they ever got were whatever tasks they were set done, ruthlessly and completely. Tsen had to laugh again. Couldn't help himself. 'Oh, they'll all try to kill me sooner or later, won't they? Dissuade them as best you can, LaLa, if you would? Now go. Oh, and have someone make the slave woman ready to receive me. My dragon-rider.' He let his distaste bleed out into his words. Then he stopped and shook his head. 'And why *did* you come and bother me in my bath again? You never gave me an answer to that.'

'To ask you a question, Sea Lord-in-Waiting.'

'Have I answered it?'

'Yes.'

'Good. At some point you can tell me what the question was. Just so we can both know when it turns out I was joking or otherwise didn't quite mean it.' He took a deep breath and sighed. 'Go on then. Run along.'

The Watcher paused. 'Sea Lord-in-Waiting, I cannot pass the white stone walls of the eyrie. It is like metal to me. This is not known to others. You will not need your enchanter.'

They regarded one another long enough to be sure they both understood. Then the Watcher knelt and pressed his head to the floor, a thing that an Elemental Man was rarely called to do, and vanished into the warm stone floor. Tsen poured himself another glass of wine. Beautiful stuff. Far too delicate to be wasted on an Elemental Man. You had to work for years to forge a palate capable of appreciating the delicate nuances within its richness. For some reason the bathhouse steam, with its touch of Xizic, brought out the best of its flavours. Enhanced it. And that was what a sea lord did, wasn't it? Brought out the best in everything around him?

The Elemental Man had touched his head to the floor as if bowing to a master, not to an heir or a regent. *Am I starting to do something right?*

Outside he wrote a note to be sent by jade raven to Chay-Liang at the eyrie: *'Doors on all the ways in from the dragon yard. On anywhere that must be safe. Not glass or wood. Sealed in iron. LaLa cannot pass through the stone.'* And she would understand, perfectly, what he meant and why.

As an afterthought, he added, *'On my bathhouse too.'*

42

A Dragon's Touch

Baros Tsen called for Zafir again that same night after she discovered she was slowly dying and there was nothing that anyone but Bellepheros could do about it. It was late, long after dark and she was already asleep, curled up on her thick rug when the black-cloaks came. Myst and Onyx did their best to dress her in the few minutes the soldiers allowed. When she walked to the balcony and stepped onto the waiting sled, she looked back at them. They were staring out through the wall, watching her. Then the sled slipped away into the starlit gloom inside the tower and rose into the darkness until it emerged into the upper space and settled on a glass roof. Tsen was already waiting, and he waved the black-cloaks away. When they were well out of earshot, his words were blunt and straightforward.

'How long will it take for these hatchlings to grow?' Her answer didn't please him, but he surely knew it already from Bellepheros. 'I have one fully grown dragon,' he'd said at last. 'I wish to show my rivals what it can do. For that I am told I require a rider. Can you do that?'

Yes. He asked her what she needed and she told him that too: Bellepheros the alchemist. A harness. Armour. The simple truths of the matter. If she'd had her wits about her she might have asked for so much more – lied and lied and who was *he* to be any the wiser? But tonight all she could think of was the disease, the horrid mark on her skin that would never go away, whose spreading, above anything else, must be stopped. Right there and right then she would have given him anything if he could have promised her that.

'Where is the alchemist?' she asked, the only question in her head, burning away all other thought.

'I sent him back with his monster.' The t'varr gave her a look then. A kindly look almost like a father, although she'd only known those as monsters too. She had to bite her lip not to beg him to let her go to be there with the dragons and the alchemist whose potions she needed more than water. But she did not beg, *would* not. Not ever. Not to anyone, not for anything.

'You killed my sea lord's first-born son and heir,' Tsen said, and his face never changed. 'You have enemies – Shrin Chrias, my lord's kwen. I don't know what you did to *him*.' He shrugged. 'Others. I'll give you someone to watch over you. He'll keep you safe and he'll keep you to your promises, but for now he has other matters to address and I can't spare him. So you'll remain here, a slave and nothing more, until I'm ready. You will not be seen to matter. Have no fear though.' He smiled a sad little smile. 'My desires are not theirs. Not what a sea lord should crave. Serve me well in this and for as long as you do I'll not turn you over to them. Cross me even once, slave, and you're dead to me. I do hope you understand.'

'I wish to be with my dragons,' Zafir said, as close as she could bring herself to ask for what she truly wanted.

'But for now I wish you to be here, slave.' He sent her away and waved for the black-cloaks to take her back.

For the next few days they kept her in the brightest of cages, gleaming and gilded with bars that she never saw but sensed nonetheless. Tsen sent her more slaves, maidens to wash and clean and feed and clothe her, and Zafir sent them back. The first two, Onyx and Myst, they were enough. They'd seen her face down a dragon. They'd seen her face down Shrin Chrias Kwen who'd murdered Brightstar. She owned their souls now while the others, however skilled, were surely spies.

One day Myst and Onyx covered her with perfume and Tsen himself took her on a glasship. They drifted above the glittering spires of Khalishtor and he pointed to all its wonders. None of it mattered but she forced herself to go through the motions he wanted of her. She saw the magnificence of his world, the opulence, the richness, the sheer delights to be had at every turn for those who were close to a sea lord. This man she needed somehow to own, and yet all she ever saw when she closed her eyes was that little patch of skin, Hatchling Disease, the dragon on the ship that had given it to her and the vengeful look in its eye. She tried to rub the roughness away, rubbed it red and raw until all the flakes were gone but they were back again two days later, and there were other parts of her too now that she thought to look. Other places where she was not quite as soft as she'd once been. Little calluses, so small and slight she wouldn't even have noticed if she hadn't been looking for them.

Six days after she'd stood in the Great Sea Council and smiled a coy smile and tried to hide her laughter, the black-cloaks led her onto a disc and down to the black floor of the tower. This time Myst and Onyx came with her. Rain hammered from the sky and the great open emptiness of the tower thrummed with a deep rumble. More soldiers waited, not black-cloaks but men with cloaks whose feathers made a shimmering pattern of burning orange flames with a rampant red dragon in their midst. Tsen's own soldiers. Dragon-cloaks. They led her through the open brass doors and outside over the black marble where the glasships came, slick with water. The rain drenched them all, cold and angry, clinging her silks to her skin. The wind tugged her sleeves. Myst and Onyx shivered and huddled and screwed up their faces, but they were palace slaves, not dragon-riders. In the space outside the Crown, where the glasship pods hovered a hair's breadth above the ground, Zafir lifted her head and stretched up her arms as if she was worshipping the sky and let the glory of the rain and the wind remind her that, despite all she had endured, she was alive. Above her the glasships barely moved despite the wind. The ships-that-flew might be slow but she'd seen they could be precise, for what good it did them. She closed her eyes as the rain battered her face and imagined how it would feel to smash one to splinters with a dragon. A pleasure enough to dull the terror of the Hatchling Disease for a moment.

In the middle of the circle of black marble a golden egg opened for her. Myst and Onyx fell to their knees, faces pressed to the wet stone. Tsen sat inside the gondola with a trio of brightly coloured dragon-cloaks standing to attention around him. As they left, he beckoned Zafir to take their place beside him. The ramp closed behind her and they were alone. A t'varr and a dragon-queen. She could kill him, she thought. It would be so easy. No obvious weapons but he was a fat old man, while beneath her hardening skin was a warrior's heart, fierce and furious when she wanted it to be. The glasship rose, a faint sensation she might never have noticed if she hadn't been tense and waiting for it. Tsen pored over a map, ignoring her. There was one other chair. She sat without waiting for his invitation and lounged and yawned until Tsen rolled the map away and smiled his ever-amiable smile. He leaned back in his chair and folded his hands behind his head. 'Dragon-Queen.'

'T'Varr.' The half-smile, the slight opening of the mouth, the tilt of the head, the lick of the lips, they were all instinct now and rarely wasted; and though her silks were thick they were soaked through and clung to every curve. But from Tsen? Nothing. She found it hard not to admire him.

'I'm having trouble with my eyrie,' he said. 'My enchanters have yet to discover how to make it move on its own and so we must tow it from place to place with glasships. It's an expensive business.' He frowned. 'Also I have been making a list of my enemies. It has become very long. I was wondering whether I should put you on it but I seem to have run out of space.'

He was looking at her hard. Reading her. She met his eyes. 'Your enemies will desire what you have. They will desire your dragons and they will desire me.' She tipped her head and turned her shoulder and dipped her eyes at him. 'Perhaps they will make offers.'

'Oh, I'm quite sure they will, but if they do, *you* will not hear of them. You will remain in the eyrie now.' He frowned. 'Let us not pretend: you're no ordinary slave but you're not *that* special. You have something I want but you know that with time and effort I can get it elsewhere. I'm not going to let you go, but if you're trouble to me, I *will* get rid of you. I want you to consider this for a moment: do you wish to be a little piece on the board of a big game, moved from one square to another, bartered and traded and in the end sacrificed as all little pieces are?' His brow furrowed. 'You were a ruler in your own land. It must have crossed your mind that my ships are already on their way back to bring me more dragon-riders. And they won't just be *my* ships either. When they come back, you will become ...' He turned up his palms and snapped his fingers and blew a little puff of air across the table at her. 'Nothing.' He shrugged. 'Or I could let you be what you are, within reason.

You may be mistress of my dragons for as long as they follow my wishes, however many riders I may one day acquire.'

Zafir found she believed him. Not that it would stop her in the end. 'Let us say I'm yours for now.' Another flutter of her eyelashes, completely wasted, and now the wet silks were simply irritating and making her skin itch. She tugged them back into shape.

'So.' Tsen rubbed his hands. 'Tell me: what does a dragon-queen do when she's surrounded by enemies on all sides?'

Burn them. Burn them like she'd burned them at Evenspire. At the Pinnacles. At Furymouth. Yet as she opened her mouth she thought of Jehal, stopped and met Tsen's eye. 'I would look very hard, Baros Tsen T'Varr, for the enemy I had not yet seen hiding among such a crowd. The one who stands beside me and calls himself a friend.'

Tsen laughed. 'You have the makings of a kwen!'

'And then I would burn them. All of them.' Her jaw clenched. She hadn't meant it to show but the anger inside was too much. Jehal. Tsen. Chrias. All of them. Every Taiytakei in every realm and every dragon-lord who'd ever flown against her.

A half-smile wrinkled the t'varr's face again. He raised his eyebrows at her. 'But does not war destroy us all? Perhaps subtlety and dragons do not mix. They don't seem very subtle creatures. I've heard a great deal from the alchemist about what must be done to raise and train one of your monsters and also what they can do, but not what they are *for*.' He leaned forward and rested his elbows on the table, head on his hands, his eyes on hers. 'Let us begin. You are the rider, so answer me – how far do they fly before they tire?'

Zafir shrugged.

'You don't *know*?'

'No one does.' She gifted him a slight smile. *Deluded fool.* 'They fly on and on.'

'Then how far do they fly before *you* tire?'

'Far enough.' She took his map and unfurled it, noting the slight flicker of irritation that caused, but there was no indication of the distances between the islands and the cities it showed her. 'From one realm to the next in a day. If the need was strong enough, one might fly days and nights one after another without end. One must make certain arrangements for such journeys. One must be properly equipped. But it can be done.'

'And the dragon itself doesn't tire?'

'I'm told not. But you must know this from Bellepheros already. Why ask me?'

He brushed the question aside. 'The fire. How much fire may it breathe?'

Zafir laughed at him. 'Dragons don't *breathe*. Have you not seen?'

No, he hadn't, he'd barely even seen his own monsters! And no one had told him either. But then why would they? 'All creatures breathe,' muttered the t'varr.

'Not dragons.' Zafir took a deep breath. 'Baros Tsen T'Varr, they do not tire. Ever. They will gout fire without end if you demand it of them. It will simply make them hungry. Starve them of sustenance for long enough and they will wither and burn from the inside and die, but they don't tire. How long that takes depends on their size. A week for the newly hatched, perhaps longer. A month or more for an adult but Bellepheros will know far better than I. Drive them hard for long enough and again they will grow hot and burn from the inside if they're not allowed to cool. They last better amid glaciers and mountains than deserts but I doubt you'll much appreciate the difference.'

'Are they damaged by their own fire?' Tsen looked incredulous.

'It washes over them like water.'

'Then by what?'

Another shrug. Zafir chuckled. 'Poison.'

'Poison?'

'There's no other way to stop a dragon, Baros Tsen T'Varr. Not that's known to me, save to take its will for the fight. The rider. The rider is always a dragon's weakness.'

'You.'

'You're right to look for others. You'll need them. I'll do that for you. I'll train them.' *If you have a blood-mage who can make a potion to force me against every grain of my will!*

'And how long will that take?'

As if he hadn't asked the alchemist already! 'For ever.' She stretched, letting him see her curves. Still wasted. 'The longer a rider is with his dragon, the better they're paired. A few months, perhaps, before they can do something useful. You should begin now. Choose the men who will ride your hatchlings once they're grown in years to come.' A little light emphasis on the *years*. Time was *her* friend, not his, and they both knew it. 'Take all the riders you like from my realm. It will be quicker but they must still bond with the dragon they'll fly.' There was even a grain of truth to that. She'd leave it to him to imagine how long that bonding would take, that it might be months or years and not merely a few scant hours or sometimes even minutes.

Tsen frowned. 'Look outside.'

They were up in the clouds. The sky was a dense white, just beginning to break up as the glasship rose through to the clear sky above. She caught glimpses of what looked like line after line of great white waves, frozen still. As they rose higher she stood by the window as the waves became a rolling white sea. To be high in the sky like this, yes, she missed that, but with the howling wind in her face too. More than anything, *that* was what she missed.

'How high can a dragon fly?'

There was a mountain, the same mountain that rose behind the city and vanished into the cloud except now it rose from the white sea and she could see its peak, still verdant green. 'Higher than this.' She had no idea, really. At Evenspire they'd come from above the cloud so as not to be seen from below, and Hyrkallan had done the same but from higher still. There'd been times she'd flown so high that she couldn't breathe, high enough for the sky to turn a deep deep blue, for the world below to become a formless haze, for the far horizon to be a blur and, if you looked hard, to seem not quite straight any more.

'But how high?' asked Tsen politely. 'Would they cross the mountain of the Elemental Masters?' He flicked his eyes at the peak outside the window.

'With ease.' High enough to feel sick and for her head to ache and spin, for the air to be as cold as ice so it hurt her lungs to breathe it, but the dragon hadn't been troubled at all. 'As high as the stars perhaps. I don't know how high a dragon might fly alone.' She stared at the mountain peak. The glasship was flying away from it now. They were leaving the city at last.

'I've been told what dragons did to my fleet. What would a dragon do to my glasships?'

Zafir smiled over her shoulder and tugged at her damp silks again. 'Do they burn?'

'They are glass and gold.'

'If *I* were to ride a dragon against one of these, I would seize the egg where people are carried and rip it away. I would snap the tethers that hold it and hurl it through the air. Or, if I was playing, maybe fire would amuse me. Gold will melt in dragon fire, and silver too, but only long after all those inside would be dead, black and charred and brittle. Or perhaps seize the ship itself and smash it into the ground. Are they fragile? If they are I might shatter one with the lash of a tail.' She tore herself from the window. 'We're leaving your city and you ask me questions of dragons that are filled with war, Baros Tsen T'Varr.' She glanced at the map, once more rolled up in front of him. 'Is there something else you wish to share?'

He shook his head and put the map away, and for a time they talked of other things, of her life in the realms, of the eyries she knew, of dragons and how they were raised, of the wars the realms had seen, old and new, and how dragons fought. They talked for hours and grew slowly tipsy together on wine that Tsen had brought that tasted like apples and honey and fire on Zafir's tongue. She flirted with him constantly. Couldn't help herself. Instinct, but she never reached him and never got anything back from him, not once.

'Do you prefer men?' she asked him when the wine made her careless. She thought he might blanch or frown but he only shook his head. 'Are you a eunuch then?' He just laughed. 'Then what are you?'

'A t'varr,' was all he said, but she could see she'd touched something. He hid it well but not well enough. A sadness, perhaps, and a flicker of resentment. And then they went back to dragons and ships and how large a sea lord's fleet might be as they slowly finished getting drunk. Whatever she asked, Tsen smiled as he answered her. Did he always smile? He seemed to, and nothing she asked bothered him. Even glow-cheeked on his apple wine he gave nothing away. She'd never met anyone quite like him, one who could keep his passions so contained.

Night came and went. They slept in beds divided only by a thin curtain of silk, yet Zafir slept with an ease she couldn't remember, not since Jehal. The second day passed as the first, filled with talk and more apple wine. She took his hand on the second night when they were drunk again and looked at the lines there and told him his fortune in some preposterous way that made him laugh, and then he took hers and did the same. He didn't flinch from her touch, merely chose not to seek it. He was ever kind and gentle and yet somehow oblivious. She came at him from every way – coy, sly, eager, angry, bitter – and none of it made the slightest difference. If there were gaps in his armour, ways to reach through to the soft heart inside and fix her talons around it, she didn't find them. It was a failure that vexed and intrigued her. Maybe he simply didn't have one?

'People assume a great deal,' he said as they slipped under their separate sheets on their second night in the sky. 'Do not let it concern you.' And she realised that yes, people *did* assume so very much, and that she'd come to count on it.

'What are you trying to show me with this?' she asked. 'Do you have some guard here I cannot see who keeps you safe from me? Alone, so very much could come to pass. It still might.'

'And little of it good –' he yawned '– and yet here we are and you haven't murdered me even once.'

'It's always there, that thought.'

'I suppose it is, and I'm quite sure you could have done so if you wished. I am just a fat old man, after all. And no, there is no guard.' He laughed. 'Although of course I might be lying.' He smiled again. 'I knew another slave once. Like you in some ways, very different in others. You wouldn't kill me even if you were certain there was no hidden guard to stop you. If you wanted to die, you'd be dead. And we will never quite trust one another, and one day, if I'm foolish enough or you're clever enough, you'll find a way to be free. But I don't think I can have what I want from you any other way.' Another chuckle. 'Yes, Dragon-Queen, you're being tested just as you have been testing me. We both know this. I think we've both done quite well too. Perhaps even surprised one another.'

Tested? But in more ways than the obvious, surely. She felt the answers there as she fell asleep, flitting and fluttering at the edges of her reason yet always dancing between her fingertips as she reached for them. It dawned on her as she dreamed that this t'varr might be a lot more dangerously clever than he seemed.

On the morning of the fourth day the clouds thinned and faded away. They flew over dry brown land wrinkled and scarred by rivers, crossed a line of hills and drifted towards a scorched and yellow desert. The glasship sank. Tsen went to stand by one of the windows at the front above the little door leading to the place where the pilot golem was. In the warmth Zafir shivered when he showed her. The closest a Taiytakei could come to being a dragon-rider and they replaced their pilots with automata. Then he beckoned her to stand beside him and pointed. To share his window they had to stand close, so close that now and then they touched.

Sitting on the desert ahead was a huge rock. 'My eyrie,' he said.

No. Not *sitting on* the desert but *floating over* it, and on its back was a round fortress of thick sloping walls and low squat towers and … other things whose nature she couldn't make out from so far away. It reminded her a little of Evenspire with its sloping walls meant to stand up to dragons. She saw it and laughed. *It floats in the air so has no tunnels deep under the ground and so there's nowhere to hide when the dragons come.* 'Whoever is master of that eyrie had better make victory a habit,' she murmured.

Maybe Tsen misunderstood her. He pulled away, faced her, reached out a hand and touched her brow with two warm fingers. 'Yes,' he said. He went back to his chair but Zafir stayed, watching until the floating eyrie was beneath them and she couldn't see it any more. She'd seen the one thing that mattered by now. The golden war-dragon perched on one wall. A monster. *Her* monster. Her heart skipped a beat. She knew him at once. Diamond Eye, for the deathly pale blue of his eyes like glacier ice.

The glasship slid slower and lower through the air and finally came to a halt on the sloping wall. Through the windows Zafir took in Tsen's eyrie. The space was huge, bigger than any walled circus she'd ever seen, bigger than the Speaker's Yard in the Adamantine Palace. Bigger even than the spaces inside the vast walls of Evenspire and yet almost empty. A few huts in the middle, a lot of crude tents around them, lines of sails strung up on ropes, partitioning the yard like low walls, flapping in the wind. In one area she saw hatchlings chained to the stone. She tried to count them. A dozen perhaps, give or take.

The back of the gondola split apart and the ramp of gold and glass lowered. Tsen made a little gesture and Zafir stepped outside, but the t'varr made no move to follow her. On top of the walls were squat towers, little more than a few stone pillars with a roof on top; along and below the walls were dozens of long blunt-ended tubes made of thick iron. Each was mounted on a mesh of metal wheels built to turn quickly. They were nothing like the scorpions defending the Adamantine Palace: the tubes pointed up rather than out and there was no dragon-scale shield to protect the firer. Strange.

At last she let herself look at the dragon, like a treat saved for the end, and all else was forgotten. Diamond Eye. A war-dragon from her own eyrie, massive, mature but still in his prime. A real monster, almost eighty strides across the wing and thirty tall when he lifted his head, scales of gold and gleaming crimson but also silver and greens and blues across his belly, a tail that could bring down castle walls with a single swipe and the strength and the power to lift a Taiytakei ship clean out of the water and crush it to firewood. *That* was a dragon, and *this* was what it meant to be a dragon-queen.

A tightness crossed her face. A flash of sadness, quickly twisted to an anger she couldn't hide. *Her* dragon, ridden by riders she'd trusted with her life, and the Great Flame knew there'd been few enough of those by the end. Dead now and gone for ever. She stared at Diamond Eye and the sadness flared again. They'd served her to the end. Even in their dying, they'd served. No other riders left but her and so Shrin Chrias Kwen was denied his hanging and she was alive and here and given, once more, a dragon to fly. *And we will, my beautiful deathbringer. We will. We'll show this world what we can be, both of us.* The anger shifted to a fierce glee. The hunger she'd felt before Evenspire. *There will be a reckoning. One day we will burn them all.* And as she thought it, the dragon lifted its head and turned towards her, and she could almost feel it noticing her and seeing her for the first time and knowing who she truly was.

As it should be. For I sat astride you many times, my deathbringer. I felt your wings beat at my command and you heard my thoughts and my will. You're mine and we will be one again.

As if he heard her, Diamond Eye spread his wings and lifted his head and snorted a column of fire into the sky. The soldiers around her flinched and she laughed. *You know nothing. You all call me slave but you know nothing.*

Tsen came out of the egg at last, the Elemental Man beside him, and she smiled some more and nodded to herself. He'd been there all the time then, as the alchemist had warned he might be. Loitering, so there *had* been a guard, and Tsen hadn't been quite as much at her mercy as he'd wanted her to think. He'd tricked and lured her and lulled her and she had the vague sense that a game had been played between them these last few days, one she didn't quite understand and had comprehensively lost. But the dragon filled her head now. Tsen could wait.

He looked serene, untroubled as he stared at the monster on the walls. 'Well, yes,' he said after a bit to the Elemental Man beside him. 'You said it was big but I suppose it's one of those things you need to see for yourself to really understand what *big* actually means. My, my. What a difference it would have made had we brought *this* one to Khalishtor.' He looked at Zafir. 'And you will fly this creature for me.' And she wasn't sure whether it was a question or simply a statement of what would be.

Parts of a harness still hung around Diamond Eye's back. 'Yes,' she breathed and had to fight back the urge to go to the dragon right now, to look for the mounting ladder and climb straight up onto its back, even in this useless slave-silk tunic they made her wear. Seeing the dragon now, the longing was a physical pain. 'And so will you,' she said.

Tsen laughed and his belly shook under his peacock robes. 'No, slave, I will not.'

'Oh, you will.' She smiled at him. 'How could you resist?'

He was still laughing. 'It will be very easy.' He walked away along the top of the walls and then down steep steps into the dragon yard. Zafir watched him go until he vanished through a hole in the base of the walls. She was for a moment alone. For the first time in days.

The dragon. Still looking at her. Calling her. *Come, rider, for I yearn to soar and do you not feel the same?* And she did, but the thoughts must have been her own because dragons didn't talk, not when they were dulled, and if the alchemist's potions had somehow failed wouldn't the eyrie be a smoking ruin?

But still ... *Yes, Diamond Eye. We'll fly soon.* A promise to herself. She started along the wall and down the steps, looking for Bellepheros and his potions.

43

The Sea Lord's Granddaughter

Shrin Chrias Kwen sent the fleet on its way home from Khalishtor, gathering as many soldiers as he could before it left. They were poor troops – slaves mostly, ill trained with little armour and old weapons that would break as likely as damage anything else – but they were the best he could get in a few days. In Xican he might find more.

Once the fleet's orders had been given, he took his own glasship and followed, taking the direct route over the land. He crossed the gleaming aqueduct of Shevana-Daro which ran like an arrow of light from the city to the edge of the mountains. Then over the sea past the Zinzarran island of Bal Ithara with its sheep and its rain and its bloody-minded farmers who eked what living they could from a land that hated them, and from there on to the Grey Isle and the City of Stone. Home.

Go and find more riders. Quai'Shu had already lost them some thirty ships, burned by dragons while anchored in the bay outside Furymouth, and that had been *before* he'd helped King Valmeyan steal all of the Prince Jehal's dragon eggs. Perhaps the Mountain King had won his war but Chrias Kwen had met both and thought he probably hadn't. If the prince was back on his throne in Furymouth then the best that any Taiytakei could expect was to have their ships burned to ash around them. The fat fool of a t'varr was right, though. One alchemist and one dragon-rider was too few of either.

He looked down over the desolate rain-swept stone of the Grey Isle. Here was as good a place as any for monsters, wasn't it? Elesxian could start building, have the Stoneguard dig tunnels and caves ready for the slaves and the dragons when he found a way to wrest them from Tsen's grip. They'd need their own alchemist though, ready and waiting, and as for a rider ...

He closed his eyes. An expedition to the dragon lands meant paying for a navigator to take them across the storm-dark. It meant half a dozen ships at the very least. He'd have to land his men far away from either city or eyrie so the ships wouldn't be burned by wandering dragons with their riders. He'd have to find the sort of men who could stay hidden in a hostile land for weeks, perhaps months, who could slip into an eyrie full of dragons and slip away again with captives who'd be far from happy about being taken. One of the lesser shifters, one of the failed Elemental Men, a windwalker or an earthshifter perhaps, but again they cost a small fortune and Quai'Shu had already almost ruined them.

Almost ruined? Such things were a t'varr's domain and t'varrs were always prone to exaggerate, but Chrias had his own spies. As far as he could see, Tsen was right. Xican was so deep in debt that they'd all be slaves before another year was out and for what? Eggs and babies! Vespinarr would own them all before much longer! If they had their way, they'd take Tsen's eyrie and everything in it for a fraction of what it was worth and put Meido on his father's throne, no better than the Vespinese puppet lord of Tayuna; and yes, Tsen had no love for the Vespinese either and he might fight them tooth and nail, but how, when success depended on a slave who brewed potions from his own blood and would doubtless soon be murdered and that ... that murderous whore-slave who ought to be hanging from nails through her feet for what she'd done to Zifan'Shu ... Yes. Alchemists and riders, another few of each and soon, but not given to Baros Tsen and his eyrie. They'd be held safe and in secret in Xican, out of harm's way.

He sighed. Tsen was actually damn good as a t'varr. Why couldn't he be content? What did he want that he didn't already have? But there was no point dwelling on that – Tsen clearly *wasn't* content and so he'd have to be brought to heel and that meant taking his power away. Chrias turned from the window and paced tiny circles inside the gondola. He couldn't send his black-cloaks to the dragon lands – they were Taiytakei and could never pass as anything else. It would have to be slaves. Slaves from the dragon lands themselves. The Taiytakei had plenty, and mostly they hated the dragon-riders and the alchemists. If times had been different he'd go among the sword-slaves who'd come from there and pick them himself and yes, he'd probably lead the expedition with a handful of his own best men but not now, not with Quai'Shu as he was. He'd need someone else. Someone he could trust with six ships and two hundred men and possibly the future of the Grey Isle itself.

He stopped his pacing and smiled. Someone to be the next kwen when *he* wore Quai'Shu's cape. Now there was a prize worth having.

The glassship wafted through the stone spires of the city and drew to a silent halt over the Palace of Leaves. It nudged itself up against the spike of a black stone monolith; its rim touched the very top of the stone and the arcane energy of the earth trickled through, charging the glassship for its next journey. As it did, the golden gondola eased down on its chains. It came to rest a finger above the earth, and through the windows Chrias saw that Elesxian was waiting for him. Elesxian of the Grey Isle. She was Quai'Shu's eldest grandchild, heir of his heir, the treasured daughter who ruled the city in Zifan'Shu's name while Zifan'Shu sailed at his own father's side, and of all Quai'Shu's bloodline by far the best choice for the city's next sea lord. Chrias took a moment to compose himself. Every gesture between them carried meaning. Some to those who watched, some only to himself and Elesxian. She'd left Khalishtor too soon. He needed her to see that matters had changed between them and he needed her to see that at once; but at the same time there would be other eyes on them, and those eyes would have to be blind – all they must see was a kwen come to his sea lord's vassal to call upon her resources.

He opened the egg and stepped outside and bowed. Not the kowtow a sea lord would demand but a bow of almost-equals. He let himself dip perhaps an inch lower than usual. She would see that – and yes, a moment of hesitation before she began the ritual of greeting, old words known by rote, offering her home and her fire and her water. He replied with the formal words every Taiytakei knew by heart. Rituals like these were useful. They broke silences, calmed and settled angry thoughts, and today they filled the awkward handful of seconds it took to walk from his own glassship to hers, brought down to take him to the airy rooftops of her palace. As they entered her own egg – silver this one, streaked with gold, but a true golden egg was for the sea lord and his first servants only – he saw she'd come alone. As had he; and as the glasship rose and there could at last be no eyes watching through the windows, Chrias offered her his arms.

'I'm sorry for the loss of your father,' he said, the first time he'd truly been able to offer her any comfort. In Khalishtor everything had orbited Quai'Shu and his broken mind. Everyone else had largely forgotten his murdered son but Chrias. Zifan'Shu would have been a fine lord. The succession would have been clear and no one would have questioned it.

Elesxian looked away. Instead of coming to him she sat among the gold-embroidered cushions heaped around the floor. 'I would have followed him.'

'Yes.'

Chrias sat down beside her. He came close but she leaned away and held up a hand. 'Stop. That's not what I want now. My father's dead and our sea lord has lost his mind, and all for marvellous treasures that turn out to be monsters. And where are they? Out of our hands. Uncle Meido has turned on us and now he and our lord's t'varr seem to think they can exclude us. They forget who is the lady of this city. Will you be here for long?'

'Not long.' In Khalishtor she'd worn her masks well. He hadn't realised how bitter she must have felt. 'The fleet is on its way. I'll make arrangements for its replenishment and another foray to the dragon lands to acquire an alchemist of our ow—'

'Another? To what end, Chrias? To burn more ships?'

'What Baros Tsen T'Varr has is far too fragile. I'll be careful.' He snorted. 'And yes, I'll be cheap. But that will likely take months before it's done. Until then I'll move between here and Khalishtor. We both must. Tsen can't be left to act freely there or he'll become Quai'Shu's voice while he keeps our lord alive and stifled in his eyrie.' Supplying the fleet was a t'varr's job too, and so he could easily have sent one of his own t'varrs here to arrange the expedition instead of coming himself. People would wonder why he hadn't. He'd have to choose. Let them see the squadron forming to cross the storm-dark or let them see his real reason. He looked at her. Elesxian. Grief was making her older than her years but she was beautiful. Skin black as the dead of night, hair braided down to her feet like a cloak, soft rounded belly …

'Tsen!' Elesxian suddenly threw back her head and snarled. 'That impotent! What fool dragged him out of his bath and told him he could have a say in this?'

'He's not stupid, Elesxian.'

'Our sea lord named my father to follow him, not that fat fool. Gods! You came here to replenish our fleet? With what? Do you have money? My coffers are beyond empty and frankly I have no idea who will lend to me. I've already sold more than you'd care to hear and I have little left but my city. Shall I auction it off piece by piece? And our t'varr who made this calamity will now be the one to save us from utter catastrophe? I doubt even the great Shan Su could have pulled us from this mire, but Tsen? *Tsen?*' She made a strangled noise and shook her head. 'Open the ramp! I may as well hurl myself into the abyss right away and save myself the pain of waiting. And by whose command? Who chooses that it will be Tsen?'

'The Great Sea Council will choose if there is choosing to be done. But our lord is not yet gone and so much may happen.'

Elesxian hissed, 'It should be me! *I* am my father's heir!'

'And that, my lover, is why I am here.' The kwen smiled.

Elesxian didn't. 'But you came too late. I already have a guest. A snake but I can hardly be rid of him since he holds most of my debts.'

Shrin Chrias Kwen looked through the window; there, high up amid the floating glass discs that held the Palace of Leaves in the sky, was a glasship with a pure silver gondola. Silver for Vespinarr. 'They send their minions? Send them back.'

'Minion?' Elesxian barked a laugh. 'This is no *minion*! This is Shonda's own brother. Straight from Khalishtor. He didn't even bother going home first.' She spat. 'Though he's been free enough with my jade ravens since he came and shows no sign of going away.'

Chrias nodded. He would have held her if she'd wanted it, but mostly his thoughts were veering to the murderous again. Vey Rin T'Varr. Another one.

44

Hatchling Blood

You wanted something done, you did it yourself. Not something Bellepheros was used to but he was finding out the hard way. In the realms when he wanted something done he had dozens of alchemists at his beck and call and hundreds of Scales. Thousands of people across the nine kingdoms. Strictly speaking the eyrie masters of the realms were his too, and that meant he could call on their dragons. *Strictly* speaking, even kings and queens were his to command and so were all *their* dragons too, not that he or any other grand master had ever actually tried it because they all knew *exactly* how that would end but, *strictly* speaking, he answered to no one.

Now what he had were a handful of dull-minded Scales and nothing else, which was why he was standing right in the middle of the white stone of the dragon yard, as far from anywhere else as he could be, dressed in leather coveralls spattered in blood, gasping for air and holding a big axe that was too heavy for him. He wore leather gauntlets that reached up to his shoulders and a leather mask with large round glass eyepieces covered his face. Everything was tightly buttoned together. Behind him a newborn hatchling hung from a wooden frame as tall as a house. It had been winched up by its back claws and it was quite dead. A large barrel full of its blood sat beside its half-severed neck. Bellepheros leaned on the axe and tried to catch his breath. *Too old for this. Much too old.*

The mask was probably why he hadn't noticed the arrival of the glasship that now hung over the edge of the eyrie, its golden gondola sitting on the wall opposite the monstrous copper dragon. The dragon wasn't looking at the glasship though; it was looking at Bellepheros. It hadn't taken its eyes off him from the moment he'd strung the hatchling up. In fact it had hardly moved at all.

Bellepheros sighed. The gondola was Baros Tsen T'Varr's

personal egg. The t'varr was back and doubtless that would mean all manner of trouble over how many hatchlings Bellepheros had killed. But he'd done what needed to be done. He could manage what they had now. He could make enough potion and had enough Scales and they'd survived the first few weeks and no dragon had woken or escaped. And that, he told anyone who'd listen, was a minor miracle.

There was a woman crossing the yard towards him. Dressed as a slave and with her hair cut short, it took Bellepheros a moment longer than it should have to recognise her.

'Holiness!' He stiffened. Zafir stopped fifty yards away. The adult dragon shifted, very slightly. Now it was looking at her too. The hatchlings were away on the far side of the yard, hidden from view behind the huts and tents of the Scales built around them. There were Taiytakei watching him too, but at a distance. He'd told them to keep away, as far as they could, and they had. They didn't know what to make of him, any of them.

Zafir was alone. 'Stay back!' His words were muffled by his mask and she probably couldn't hear him but he didn't dare get too close. 'The hatchling was fresh from the egg.' Hatchling Disease was simply something that happened, whatever you did to avoid it. The Scales, the ones who worked with the dragons all the time – even with the best potions he could make – still died. Those back in the realms sometimes lasted ten years or more but it got them all in the end. They simply stopped being able to move. Eventually they suffocated because they couldn't breathe, or starved because they couldn't eat, but usually the alchemists dealt with them quietly long before it went that far. Most Scales were eaten by their own dragons in the end, out of sight where no one else would see, and by the time the disease was that far gone almost every one of them was happy to die. A Scales that far gone was long past caring about anything except the handful of dragons they loved.

For some reason the disease was working faster on the Scales he'd made here, that or his potions were missing something. He gave them a year at most and probably a lot less. Alchemists? Some of them only lasted weeks before they showed the first symptoms, some of them years, some even longer but they all eventually caught it one way or another. It wasn't so bad if you took your potions every day and weren't exposed too often. If the disease found a way through his leathers and his mask today then it would get a little worse; but he'd take his potions and it would slow to its usual imperceptible crawl again and he'd lose his sleep each night to far more pressing troubles. Speakers, though? Dragon-kings and dragon-queens? They were kept away. The disease stayed within the order. Within those who'd been conditioned and trained and bred and fed potions since they were babies to control it. Kept to those who understood how dangerous it could be.

Zafir kept on coming. Bellepheros shook his head. Was she mad? He walked towards her quickly to keep her away from the dead hatchling. This was when they were at their absolute worst and surely she knew that!

'Holiness!' he gasped. He had to stand right in front of her to stop her.

'Master Alchemist.' She was smiling, peering at him, through him even, eyes as full of hunger as they always were and with a touch of madness too. Looking past him to the monstrous dragon perched up on the wall, quivering with want.

'Holiness! Stay back! The hatchling is …' Zafir held out her arm and pulled back her sleeve and showed him her skin. In the crook of her elbow a tiny patch was rough where it should be smooth. No bigger than a fingernail but there was no mistaking what it was. Bellepheros looked at her agape.

'Yes, Master Alchemist. I have the disease already. So your dead hatchling hardly matters to me. Now tell me—'

'How?' he blurted. She hadn't been near the eyrie. She hadn't been near the hatchling he'd brought with him to the Taiytakei city; and that one had been made clean, washed and washed and washed again until all residue of the egg must surely have been gone, and yet she had it, and if *she* had it then who else might have it too?

'When the dragons hatched out at sea, Bellepheros. It was a hatchling minutes fresh from the egg and it was awake. It remembered. It …' She ran a finger over the red mark that ran down the length of her neck and looked at him for a long time. 'Tell me you can stop it. Tell me you can make it go away.'

'I … I have potions, Holiness.' Not ones to cure, though. Potions to arrest the disease, to slow it, to almost but not quite stop it. But to get rid of it? No. 'There are ...' He shook his head. Did she need to know? Perhaps she did. 'There are ... there are consequences of the disease that I cannot treat, Holiness.'

Her face grew brittle. No, she didn't like *that* at all. 'You'd best enlighten me.'

Not here. He looked around. The Taiytakei watchers were keeping their wary distance but he never knew for sure where the Elemental Man was hiding. He hadn't seen much of the Watcher in the last few days, but for all Bellepheros knew he was lurking in the stones right under their feet. He cast his eyes about, floundering for a place and a way to be sure they weren't overheard. He nodded to the dragon as he did. 'Will you fly it, Holiness? They're all restless and agitated. Something here vexes them and they won't settle. It would be ...' *It would be a blessing to have someone fly that monster, just to burn some of its energy.*

Zafir glared at him. 'Of course I'll fly him! Tell me what I need to know!'

The glasship from Khalishtor! It was still hovering over the eyrie, its golden gondola resting up on the walls, open and empty. He nodded towards it. 'Come, Holiness!'

Bellepheros hurried towards the wall. They wouldn't have much time. Zafir called after him, 'Alchemist! Stop! I have asked you a question.' Anger streaked her words. Bellepheros tore off his apron and his mask, left them on the ground and began to climb the steps carved into the inner face of the wall. They were steep and tall and went hard on his knees. He glanced back and at last Zafir turned and strode after him. At the top he walked straight for the gondola, praying to the Great Flame that she'd follow him in. He didn't dare run lest the Taiytakei start wondering what he was doing, and he couldn't bring himself to grab her and pull her with him either – she might be a slave but she was still the speaker of the nine realms and he was still her servant, still her master alchemist. But she did follow him, anger sharp as a knife written into every movement. As soon as he was inside the glasship's golden egg he touched a spot in the wall and the ramp closed behind them, sealing them in.

'Alchemist!' She was furious now.

Bellepheros whipped around to face her. 'We don't have much time, Holiness, before they come for us, so I ask you to please listen! The Watcher. The Elemental Man. He cannot enter here when the door is closed. Gold and silver and their golden glass – the Elemental Men cannot pass through them but if you are not encased in any of those then you must assume he's there, somewhere, in the walls or in the air, listening. We can speak freely here, Holiness. Here and now but nowhere else.'

'Alchemist …' Dark clouds filled her eyes. But he needed this, *needed* to tell her these things and there might never be another chance.

'Yes, yes. The Statue Plague.' He bowed his head. 'The disease is voracious among these Taiytakei. Worse than I've ever seen. They have no resistance to it. Or perhaps there's something to the nature of their world that encourages it to thrive. Or perhaps … perhaps my potions are not as strong as they were.'

Zafir's eyes were savage. 'You *will* keep it contained, alchemist. You *will*.'

'Of course, Holiness.' He bowed again. 'There are other—'

'Other *what*?'

'Listen! Holiness! Please! I will treat your disease as best I can. It can be slowed – stopped, even, if you keep away from eggs and the youngest hatchlings – but it cannot be removed. Drink my potions and do as I say and it will not spread further. Do not share your blood or your bed with any other or the disease will pass to them.' His shoulders drooped and he shook his head. 'You cannot bear heirs. They will die. I'm so very sorry.'

Zafir looked aghast. 'Heirs? *That's* the first thing you think I need to hear?'

Bellepheros was still shaking his head. 'I'll warn Baros Tsen T'Varr if you wish. Perhaps that's for the best. But listen! Listen! I'll tell you more later, everything you want to know, you have my word. What matters now is this: the Elemental Man, *he's* the danger, to you most of all. I'll help you to fly, I'll help them to make whatever is needed – harnesses, armour, everything – but you'll have that man at your shoulder every moment of your life now and you must know that he's there. He'll hear every word and see every deed. Whenever the time comes and you turn on these men who have enslaved you, I will not stop you nor will I speak of it, but my duty above all, above either my freedom or yours, is here among these dragons now. I must keep them from waking. There is no one else who can. Do you understand what a woken dragon means, Holiness?'

'I …' He could see straight away that she didn't. Someone had shown her the dragon they kept under the Purple Spur, the woken monster weighted down in chains. Every speaker was shown the same. A dragon, true and undimmed, and yet they rarely understood because the dragon was chained and held in a cavern too small for it to ever escape. It was a rare speaker who had the vision to see what it would become, free and in the sky and with its chains shattered.

'No. It doesn't matter. The Elemental Man. Whatever you do, you must think his eyes are there. One slip and he will know. Enchanter's glass, gold, silver – he cannot penetrate those things and that's why they build with them. There may be others, but if there are I don't know of them.' He glanced out of the windows. Taiytakei soldiers were hurrying towards the egg. They didn't have much time. 'There's something else. The dragons. They're …' How to make her understand? 'There's a reason why there are no Elemental Men in the realms, no enchanters, no artificers, no navigators, no sorcerers, no warlocks, no arcane priests, mages or whatever else they like to call themselves. The dragons … they *eat* their power. They drain it from the world. I've seen it already. The Elemental Man – when he comes here, the dragons make it hard for him. It might be a way to stop him. But it's making the dragons restless too. They have a vigour and an energy to them, more than I've ever seen. You must know this. Be wary when you ride them …' The soldiers had reached the egg. Bellepheros closed his eyes. There would be punishment for this. They wouldn't know what he'd said but they'd know he'd come here to deal in secrets and somehow defy them.

Zafir tore at her silk tunic and raked her hands through her hair. One hand snaked around his neck. For a moment her fingers dug into his throat and he felt how strong she was. She was quivering with anger. She hissed at him, 'Never forget who I am, alchemist.' Then she took his other hand and pulled it to her. As the egg split open once more, she pressed him to a wall, her face to his. She was hard and soft under his fingers. She held him exactly for the moment the ramp opened and the soldiers outside stared at them, then let out a little groan and breathed in his ear, 'Let them think this is why. But do not forget this, alchemist. Any of it.' She stepped away, shameless, licking her lips, all curves and shadows beneath the disarray of her silk, then stopped and looked at him again, puzzled. 'What were you doing, alchemist, out there with that dead hatchling?'

'More eggs are hatching, Holiness. I need their blood for my potions.'

'Every dragon, alchemist.' She shook her head as though they were back in the realms. 'Every egg that hatches is a dragon and every dragon is precious. If you were my eyrie master and this was my eyrie, I'd have you hung to die in a cage for that.' She smiled at him, smiled at the Taiytakei soldiers, straightened her tunic and strode out of the egg, swinging her hips. The soldiers' eyes followed her along the wall.

'But you are not my eyrie master, Holiness,' he whispered. Did she know how many hatchlings were lost every week and every month in every eyrie across the realms? Did she know about the dragons who hatched and snapped and hissed and wouldn't eat because they'd already woken in some previous life and knew exactly what awaited them? Who starved themselves rather than take his alchemists' potions, who wilfully withered and died and were reborn again, over and over and over? One egg in four failed but they were the same handful of dragons, again and again. Did she know?

Beside Bellepheros the air popped and there he was, as expected. 'I had understood that alchemists were celibate.' The Elemental Man's voice was flat and empty of either feeling or judgement. His face was flushed and he was out of breath.

'You understood very wrong then.' Bellepheros blinked. 'We prefer our own kind, that's all.' *Because we carry the disease and so we keep to ourselves, because we know what it would mean to spread the plague.* But he couldn't say that because then they'd know it wasn't just the Scales who would catch it. Sooner or later it would spread. The Elemental Man would be busy that day. He shrugged.

'We have the same needs and urges as everyone else.' Apparently more than he'd thought. The feel of Zafir's skin against his fingers wouldn't leave him alone. He was a man after all. Old, perhaps, but it had been a very long time since he'd felt a woman's touch.

'Do not come here again, alchemist,' said the Watcher.

Bellepheros laughed suddenly. 'Actually I came here to summon you, assassin. I have need of something.'

'Then ask a t'varr.'

'This is not a t'varr's work.' He stared hard at the Elemental Man. Ridiculous really, but he always hoped that he might see, somehow and simply by looking, what made such a creature work. A man on the outside, but under the skin? What was he in there? Something else. Something more. Something … *other*? He was almost sure, but all the books that might have told him, all the ancient scrolls that might have held the clues to put together, they were lost to him now, far away in the dragon realms, deep in the archives under the Purple Spur and the monastery of Sand. 'What I need is knowledge.'

'Then you need a hsian.'

'I need to know what your moon sorcerers know about dragons.'

The Elemental Man shook his head. There might have been the start of a smile as he looked away. 'You will get no answers, old slave, not from them. No one ever does.' He looked Bellepheros up and down. 'Should I send a woman to your study tonight? I do not think the Hands of the Sea Lord will allow you to have his dragon-rider.'

Bellepheros snorted. *Idiot.* 'Who are they, assassin, these Moon Sorcerers?' Men of silver, when every man, woman and child who lived in the nine realms knew the name of the silver half-god who'd tamed the dragons. Isul Aieha. The Silver King.

The Watcher walked away and Bellepheros was left to stare at the three Taiytakei guards who'd opened the egg. He was about to follow but something made him pause. Some thought that for a moment he couldn't pin to the floor of his mind to dissect. But only for a moment.

Walked. The Watcher had *walked*.

45

The Hsian

A HSIAN IS NOT BORN AND A HSIAN IS NOT MADE. A HSIAN IS BOTH. The words written across the entrance to the Palace of Forever where every hsian who ever served a sea lord was trained. It was called the Palace of Forever because, while a t'varr concerned himself with matter and the moving of it to be at the right place at the right time and a kwen concerned himself with the minds of men, with spirit and courage, a hsian concerned himself with time itself. *All you have to do is think further ahead than any other and you will be the greatest among us.* It was a simple and yet impossible creed.

The thinking that had brought him to this day had started twenty three-years ago when a new star lit up the sky above the Godspike. It first bloomed like a new moon on the night of midsummer, the last night of the year. It had lasted for a week, and every hsian across Takei'Tarr had seen it.

What does it mean?

There were old gods. Forbidden gods now, and not to be spoken of, but a hsian knew of these things because a hsian was nothing without knowledge. Probably every single one of the great savants of the thirteen cities had their own secret copy of the *Rava*, carefully hidden and always denied lest the Elemental Men kill them for simply knowing the old gods' names. They'd met in secret in their Palace of Forever to wonder what this new star, born so bright and yet already dead, could mean. An omen, they agreed. Something was coming. Something to do with the ancient mistress of the night sky, most forgotten and least understood of the old gods. And then they'd looked at one another askance and each had gone their own separate way.

Jima Hsian had thought long and hard and deep, and all that thinking had brought dragons to Takei'Tarr, and now it was taking him to the far corner of the sea lords' empire, to Dhar Thosis and the Sea Lord Senxian, Quai'Shu's greatest rival. Not an easy journey, even for a hsian with a glasship. He'd be missed, no doubt about it. A week away from Khalishtor could never pass without comment even at the quietest of times, and Quai'Shu's monsters were anything but quiet. For most of the journey there weren't even any places to stop. From Khalishtor he flew beneath the perpetual clouds around Mount Solence, mountain of the Elemental Masters, then over the rolling plains and hills to the high peaks of the Konsidar where the Righteous Ones still dwelt in their endless tunnels and caves, guarded from intrusion by the wrath and fear of the Elemental Men. He made a stop there, high among the Konsidar, too high for the Righteous Ones to mind or even notice he was there. The enchanters had built a mountaintop retreat, a quiet and comfortable place for sea lords and hsians and kwens and t'varrs who desired a few days of peaceful rest and tranquil meditation. It was spartan in its luxuries but kinder than the cramped living aboard an egg beneath a glasship. They shouldn't have built it, not really, not in the Konsidar, but the Elemental Men had turned a blind eye for once. Perhaps Senxian and his predecessors had found a way to twist their arms, for it was a long hard flight across the deserts to the Kraitu's Bones.

The place was rife with spies, of course, and everyone would know he was there. He put it about that he was doing exactly what he really was doing – crossing the deserts to the far coast and Dhar Thosis. No one would believe that he'd simply told the truth for long enough for it not to matter any more.

Past the enchanters' retreat he flew alone again, trapped in a golden cage for eight days and a thousand miles. The Konsidar became bleak and dry. A little ice capped some of the mountains but the sky was blue and there were no clouds in sight and the sun was remorseless. The Righteous Ones lived far below, in tunnels so deep that they didn't care about rain or sun, night and day. Throwbacks. An Elemental Man had called them that once, but throwbacks to *what* Jima had never been sure. What he did know was that something had happened to make them restless. It had happened about six years ago but he had no idea what it was; nor, to the best of his knowledge, did anyone else.

After a day the peaks sank away beneath the glasship, although

Jima Hsian kept it high, so far above the ground now that any prying eyes down in the desert would never see him, not that anyone could live in the waterless inferno below. A lot of it was bare rock, so hot it burned the skin. Gravel flats rose gently away from the mountains and then fell sharply in their turn into the broken cliffs and cracked valleys of the Tzwayg. Another day took him deep into the boundless expanse of the Empty Sands, dunes ruddy and immense, a thousand feet tall, on and on until they too sank into a shapeless flatness, stained by dark scars that might once have been lakes before the Splintering had cracked the world a millennium ago. The deserts were one huge space filled with heat and dead stone and nothing else.

No, not *nothing* else. There were *things* in the desert. Relics. The bones of ancient monsters as large as cities. The hsian had seen a few and knew there must be more yet to be found if anyone could be bothered with the effort of looking. A thousand miles by a thousand miles of nothing, though ... Too much trouble. Easier to trade with Aria, with the Dominion, with ... other places. But Quai'Shu's eyrie had come from here, sitting abandoned for however many hundreds of years before someone found it, and even then for another fifty, doing nothing except floating impossibly above the ground on its cushion of violet light and its cracks of lightning that meant you couldn't help but think of the storm-dark. Enchanters had been and gone and none had been able to fathom its secrets, and no one had much use for a large floating rock when they had sleds and discs and gondolas and palaces of gold and glass, all so much brighter and prettier and less ... less frighteningly *old*; and so in the desert it had stayed until Quai'Shu had sent every glasship he possessed to drag it hundreds of miles and turn it into a nest for his dragons.

Yes. There were things in the desert that had been found and taken, and others that had been left and never understood, and doubtless many more that had never been found at all. Mysteries and mysteries, but they all lived in the shadow of the greatest. Another day into the desert and he began to see it. The Godspike.

No, what he saw first was the strange darkened air around it. A thick roiling darkness. Not clouds like a storm but something else, stricken with lightning that lit up the night-time desert for a hundred miles – a snip of the storm-dark itself. It began at the Ring of Fifty Needles, fifty white stone monoliths perfectly smooth and never mind their age, each a mile high and sharp as a sword point. They were like the black monoliths the enchanters made to draw power up from the earth for their glasships, but ten, twenty, fifty times their size and white. They made a circle around the Godspike a dozen miles across. Outside the circle the air was the same air as in every other realm and the desert was the same desert that stretched for a hundred miles in every direction. Inside … inside was different. Electric. The storm-dark churned above, reaching down to touch the needle points but never straying below, cooling the air while perpetual violet lightning flashed through it. Every hsian went there – in glasships careful never to fly too close – just as every hsian went to sea to stare at the storm-dark with its own black roiling clouds and their lightning. To any who saw both they were clearly the same, yet the curtains of the storm-dark at sea went on for ever, up and down and from side to side, impenetrable and infinite and no one but a navigator could cross them. The Godspike was different. Feyn Charin, the first navigator, had entered the storm-dark here and crossed to another place and returned again, a feat no other navigator had since managed to repeat. They all simply vanished. Nothing that went in came out.

From the air it was the storm-dark and the lightning that caught the eye, as it always did for any who came this way, but on the ground the storm-dark was high above. Its shade became a relief from the desert sun and heat, flickering a little but otherwise a welcome shadow and not much more. On the ground what pinned a man to the spot and never let him go, not ever, not even when he'd put years and thousands of miles between them, was the Godspike itself. Pure white like the other monoliths but vastly greater – and *they* were large enough. It was perfectly round and perfectly smooth and a thousand paces across, give or take. It glowed a little and it was so high that no one had ever seen the top of it. It rose into the storm-dark, pierced it and came out the other side, and since no one could see through the storm-dark from below, and since no one dared fly through it and few had the courage to go over it, what lay at the top of the Godspike remained a mystery. As far as the hsian knew, the Godspike simply rose from the top of the storm-dark and went on, fading into the sun-haze of the sky. Maybe an Elemental Man had once merged with the air, or even with the stone itself, and sought the summit, but if he had then he had never spoken of it to any but his own. Jima Hsian liked to think it was a mystery even to them.

He'd touched it, the one time he'd been made to see it from the ground, when he and the other hsians of his class had been brought here to be awed by it. He'd been the only one who'd dared and it had changed him. It was so immeasurably old, so massively big, so beyond everything he knew, that it had changed how he thought about time. Everything that seemed large became small. And that, he supposed, was why he had become the hsian that he was.

He steered his glasship around the Godspike, staying well clear because if there was one place in the western desert where eyes might be, it was here. He tried not to look but it was impossible. The Godspike drew him in as it drew everyone. He stared and stared for hours on end as the glasship made its slow circum-navigation of the outer needle ring. It dwarfed him in every way. Him and everything about him, every deed and every hope, every aspiration and every scheme, it made them into nothing. *Sea lords should be made to come here*, he thought. *All of them, to see what trivia they really are.*

On the far side, away from the Konsidar, he should have turned to cross the second great desert, the Desert of Thieves, to finish his journey, but now that he was here he couldn't resist. In the years since he'd last come the storm-dark over the Godspike had changed, the first record of such a thing since there had been records at all. He pulled out a farscope and studied it as best he could and still wasn't sure, so he turned his glasship toward it and spying eyes be hanged. When he got close, he could see that one end of the storm-dark was hanging a little low, covering the tip of one of the outer needles.

He moved closer still, as close as he dared. He was lost to this now. There were men a mile below him on the ground, clustered around the base of this needle. Tribesmen probably, although he couldn't be sure there weren't others among them. All could be spies, and they'd have seen his ship because they were looking up at the needle.

The needle was cracked. It wasn't a big crack and it didn't go far, but it was there, a jagged dark line running from the top where the storm-dark had come down. The flaw in the white stone ran for a hundred yards until it faded to nothing. The hsian thought about this for a while. Then he thought about whether he should bring his ship down low to silence the tribesmen and blind their eyes with his lightning cannon. But perhaps that carried more risk than it removed and so he simply flew on, out across the Desert of Thieves.

Six years. Six years since the storm-dark had begun to change, slowly creeping lower and lower at that one point in the circle of needles. *Six years.* The thought horrified him. *I haven't been this way for that long? Gods! I'm old!* Six years. At the same time as the Righteous Ones had begun to stir. A hsian noticed such things, but Jima had no idea at all what they meant.

Away from the Godspike the desert changed again, morphing to a maze of mesas and broken cliffs and canyons, some of them so deep and dark he couldn't see to the bottom of them even when the glasship was directly overhead. He veered off course to the biggest and deepest canyon of all, the Queverra. There were some who liked to suggest that the Queverra was somehow the antithesis of the Godspike but Jima was sure this wasn't true. Very deep and very sharp and very dark, rather like some unfeasibly large god had slit the desert open with a knife. It had a bottom, though, and people had been there. The upper terraces were home to desert tribesmen, kept cool and shaded by the canyon walls for much of the day and there was even a little water to be had and places where plants would grow and animals could be fed. Further down in the darkness where the sun almost never reached, *things* were said to live. Jima had never quite grasped what these *things* were, exactly, and suspected they were ghosts, shadows and other products of the imagination rather than anything real; but since he'd never been down there himself and never would, he was cautious about where he poured his scorn. Glasships that flew over the centre of the Queverra sometimes mysteriously lost their buoyancy and plunged into the darkness, never to be seen again, and there were plenty of myths and legends of monsters. The caverns that opened into the walls of the Queverra were supposed to run right across the Desert of Thieves, for hundreds of miles under the Empty Sands to the ruins of Uban and into the Konsidar. They were *supposed* to reach down into Xibaiya itself.

Stories. Everywhere had its stories.

It took another full day from the Queverra to reach Dhar Thosis. He came to it early in the morning, and the first things he saw were the two great pieces of stone that rose out of the sea around its harbour, the larger Eye of the Sea Goddess, which from this angle, coming straight from the desert, looked more like a nose, and the pinnacle of the Dul Matha, the Kraitu's Bones. He could even see the arrow-straight line of the Bridge of Eternity, the span made of enchanters' glass and gold that crossed the sea between the two, hanging a thousand feet above the waves. The stories of the desert men had it that the Kraitu had come from the Queverra, sent by the desert gods to battle the sea. The great serpent of the ocean, the Red Banatch, had fought it in the shallows here and the Kraitu had been crushed in the serpent's coils; the Kraitu's body had become the monolith of the Dul Matha, and the marks of the battle were still there to be seen if you believed in such things, the long dark gouges down the side of the sheer stone stack. The Red Banatch had returned to her depths, but not before she stole the Kraitu's essence and laid a thousand eggs along the shore, the offspring of earth and sea. Half had hatched into the sea titans, little images of the mighty Kraitu itself, and the other half into dragons.

Odd, the hsian mused, to be coming to one of the few places in Takei'Tarr that had a story about dragons in its past when he was driven by the ones that Quai'Shu had brought to the present. The dragons of Dhar Thosis were myths, and even if they'd once been real were long gone, but not so the titans. The old story went that the titans had savaged both land and sea with storms and floods after they hatched from the serpent's eggs. The dragons had plucked them from the water one by one and dropped them from the top of the Dul Matha – the shards and lumps of broken stone around the base of the cliffs were said to be their bones – until the last few swore an eternal oath to become guardians of the coast here for ever. In the cataclysm of the Splintering the dragons had vanished as the world fell to chaos and darkness but the titans were still there, lurking under the water, ready to come if the sea lord master of the Kraitu's Bones called to them. No one, as far as Jima knew, was quite sure any more whether the titans were real or merely an elaborate and exquisitely crafted story to instil caution into the city's enemies.

Time. Such scales of time and space and change beggared lesser minds. But not a hsian. *Why would there be dragons here?* He could see, as the glasship flew over the city and across a narrow stretch of sheltered sea full of ships at anchor, how it would be a fine place for dragons. The only ways to the top of the Dul Matha were to fly or else to cross the water to the Eye of the Sea Goddess and climb her winding roads to the Bridge of Eternity, both of which would be next to impossible for any unwelcome invader. Perhaps not quite as safe as Baros Tsen's flying fortress, but Jima Hsian was about to bet his life that the Palace of Roses on top of Dul Matha was a great deal more impenetrable to what was by far the most dangerous threat to any lord – an Elemental Man.

The glasship nudged up against a black enchanters' monolith. They would need to stop here for a full day to recover enough energy to cross back over the deserts. Seneschals cloaked in feathers of emerald and blue, the colours of the city, greeted him with kindness and courtesy, exactly as the protocols of a good host demanded, and never mind the enmity that existed between their lords. They led him across the open yards between the three great glass and gold towers at the heart of the Palace of Roses. They opened the tower walls for him with their black rods and took him to a beautiful hall filled with scents and pleasures where they entertained him while their lord decided what was to be done. An hour passed and then another, and then the inevitable black-cloaks came. Polite to a fault, they blindfolded him and led him through a maze. *Down*, he thought. *We went down, not up. Down into the Kraitu's Bones.*

When they took the blindfold away, he was at the end of a passage filled with fine silver chains hanging from the ceiling, so thick with them that every step was like walking through thick mud.

'They say the Elemental Men cannot pass such a passage in any form other than flesh and blood,' said Sea Lord Senxian on the other side.

'And are they right?' Jima finished pushing his way through.

'We will probably never know.' As he emerged from among the

chains, Senxian led him on into a small room lined with gold and lit with candles in such a way that no shadows could exist. They exchanged the necessary words, spoke of their families, their business interests, all the things that needed to be said before the reason for the hsian's coming could be reached.

'I have considered my sea lord's position carefully,' said Jima Hsian at last. 'It is no secret that the acquisition of dragons from the western realm has placed a huge burden upon him. There are some who question whether he can survive. My sea lord will require considerable additional loans before his debts can be stabilised and brought under control. I have made my assessment of those who will be sympathetic and those who will not, of what assets will be traded fairly away and what cannot be lost. I have assessed those among the sea lords who see an ally in need, those that see an opportunity for partnership and advantage, and those who see a giant about to fall. Sadly, the state of Quai'Shu's health and the fragility of his mind will have a significant and substantial adverse affect on the confidence of our friends and allies. In short, he does not have the trust and faith that he once commanded. Had that been otherwise I believe the fleet of Xican would weather this storm. As it is, I have concluded that it will be you, Sea Lord Senxian, who will hold the balance. The fate of Quai'Shu's fleet will rest in your hands. You will decide whether Xican remains proud and free or whether it becomes a second vassal to the bottomless wealth of the Vespinese.' *Quai'Shu*. Not *My sea lord*. There was a hint in that if Senxian cared to see it.

'My hsian concludes the same,' Senxian said.

'Feyn'Channa. A great and dear friend and colleague.' *If you could say that about a man who was a venomous snake.* 'We studied together for a time.'

'Yes. Be clear to me now, Quai'Shu's hsian. Have you come to beg? If so, what does your master offer?'

'My master hasn't sent me,' said Jima Hsian. 'My conclusion is that you would see him fall and we will become vassals to Vespinarr.'

'Do you seek new employment then, Hsian? How curious. What would you offer?'

'You know there's only one thing worth either of our considerations.'

'The dragons, Hsian? Why would I want them?'

'Not the dragons. The alchemist, Sea Lord. Whoever controls the alchemist controls the dragons. Feyn'Channa, I'm entirely sure, has already told you this.'

'Yes. So I have … heard.' Senxian didn't believe him! Which meant Jima had missed something and all his calculations were wrong or …

He started to get up, then stopped as Senxian stood up too, shook his head and rang a little bell. 'Why not meet the man who believes otherwise, Hsian, since you've come such a way.'

A cleverly concealed door opened behind Senxian, one that Jima Hsian hadn't seen. Beyond it stood a slave, a very tall man with skin so pale it looked like moonlight, dressed in grey robes and with tattoos that ran from his cheeks down his neck and vanished into their folds. A slave. Worse – one from a distant realm. The hsian wrinkled his nose.

'This was once the home of your dragons, Hsian.' Senxian smiled. 'They belong to this stone. Perhaps this slave can explain more clearly than I can.'

The slave pulled a weapon from his robe, a cleaver with a gold handle covered in stars. He held it up and bowed. Jima Hsian started to rise from his chair again, quickly this time, pricked with fear. *A trick! Betrayed!* But the slave was already on his feet and quicker, and the knife came down fast and sharp.

Three little cuts. You. Obey. Me.

But that *wasn't* what happened, at least not how Jima Hsian remembered it later, and when the slave had explained and made everything perfectly clear, the hsian scoffed at his own childish fright. For Sea Lord Senxian had shown him something he hadn't known before, something that changed a great deal, and he knew now that he'd made the right choice to come here, that he would stay and serve Senxian as he'd once served Quai'Shu. That he'd give him every possible help and, for him at least, everything would end exactly as he desired. At night, as he lay in his new bed with his new life around him, the strangest thought came to him: the white stone walls that glowed, the ones inside the eyrie he now meant to help Senxian to steal, they'd felt under his hands exactly like the stone surface of the Godspike.

46

Slaves and Executioners

Tuuran jumped over the side into the churning surf. The water was cold. A wave lifted the boat beside him, bumping him, almost knocking him off his feet. Crazy Mad was beside him. There were a lot of things wrong with Crazy, but how he handled himself in a fight wasn't one of them. Life felt good. It was one of those days for revelling in being alive.

'I've been here before.' Crazy Mad's eyes gleamed. They fought through the surf. 'Not *here* here. Probably not even this world. But somewhere, leaping out of a boat like this, crashing through the water up onto a sandy beach towards waiting lines of trees. Oh yes. You were there too. You were called Tarn.'

'Tuuran, slave. Always Tuuran. One name's good enough.'

Crazy Mad ignored him. 'That was the day the Bloody Judge was born.'

Six months back at sea. Six months away from the choking desert and the mad devices of the Taiytakei and their slaves and the alchemist and his shameful submission. Three months since the grey-robes had come and no one had known why or what they wanted; and no one else had been on the deck after they'd gone and Tuuran had hauled Crazy Mad back up out of the sea, and so no one else had seen him sit bolt upright and stare at Tuuran with eyes that blazed with silver-white fire like the full moon on a cloudless night.

'I am the Bringer of Endings.'

Three months. The grey dead hadn't been happy not to find what they were looking for but they hadn't come back. Three months and Crazy Mad's eyes had stayed crazy and mad but they hadn't burst into moonlight flames again. Tuuran had quietly decided he must have imagined it. Easier to bury that way.

'Run, you dogs!' he roared. 'Run! Out of the water!' The sand felt sure beneath his feet. He raced to the beach and stood, naked steel, teeth bared, a roar poised on his tongue. The other sword-slaves were still struggling out of the water. *This is what I am. This is what I was made to be.* 'To the trees!' He ran and Crazy Mad ran beside him, long loping strides. Crazy Mad, still alive. No one had thrown him into the sea or sold him to another ship and now he was a sword, a soldier, and Tuuran was proud of him. Whoever he thought he was, he'd grown into his madness now. He'd made it his.

'The last time I did this there were soldiers waiting in the trees.' Crazy grinned. Sometimes he was frightening. His hunger for a fight put even some Adamantine Men to shame.

The second and the third boats were nosing into the shore now. The rest of their little company of sword-slaves and Taiytakei with their bows and their wands and their spiked clubs to keep them all in line. When they'd given Crazy Mad his first sword, Tuuran had seen the wondering in his eyes: how easy might it be to take them down, to cut them apart and seize their ship and be free? But that was what every sword-slave thought when they were given their spear or their blade or whatever weapon they chose.

'And it happened too – once,' Tuuran told him, as he'd been told in turn. 'A whole ship threw off its chains. And the Taiytakei hunted down that ship and every slave who sailed her. They sent a sorcerer who could become the wind and the sea and every one of them died a horrible grisly death, and you may scoff as I once scoffed but I've seen those sorcerous killers with my own eyes now and I've seen what they do. So think it, slave, and then think that you'll have to cross your sword with mine and every other here. Better to take what is freely given.'

And Crazy Mad *had* thought it, and Tuuran had wondered for the first time in a very long while whether this was a man with whom he might cross swords and lose. But it hadn't come to that, not yet.

He waited for the other sword-slaves and lined them up, pairing them off.

'Where are we?' they asked, and Tuuran shrugged. The slave ship sailed where the slave ship sailed. None of them, save perhaps a few of the Taiytakei, knew where they went.

'None of your concern, slave.' He shoved a man at Crazy Mad. 'This is Jris. He's yours.' He took a step back and looked along the two lines of men. 'You're slaves. *Proud* slaves. Slaves with names. You look after each other. What happens to one of you, it happens to the other. If one of you runs, we are all punished. If one of you brings back a new slave, we are all rewarded. We are as one.' He pointed down the beach. 'A mile that way, some people are stupid enough to be living. Bad for them, good for us. We want more slaves. Men to work so you don't have to. Women for pleasure, because we get little enough. Or boys, if you prefer, or more men, or girls, or donkeys if you're Amrir here. I don't care. The sick and the old have no place in our ranks. If they fight then take them. We like a fighter. If they fight too hard then put them down. Don't break them unless you have to, but if you do, make sure whatever you break stays broken. Burn, loot, plunder, take whatever you like but you won't get to keep it. What's yours is mine and what's mine is theirs.' He pointed to the Taiytakei. 'You fall, you get up. You get hurt, you make like it's nothing, because there's no place here for the wounded and there's two ways back to the sea – on your feet or rolling in the surf to feed the fish. Now run! Run with me, you dogs!'

He loped down the beach with a long pace that drove them hard. The sword-slaves followed in their two lines, the Taiytakei a little way to the rear. No one said a word because no word was needed. They were slavers today, tearing men and women from their homes. They'd strike a village and rip it to pieces, take what they could, and by the time they were done the galley would be close to the shore, the boats beached, and they'd run and be gone before any warning could be given. He'd done it a dozen times and seen it more often than he could remember. Every few days in a different place until they had a hold full of slaves, then away to one of the deep-hulled Taiytakei sailing ships in some hidden cove, and then back somewhere else, somewhere far removed. Sometimes they stayed with their sailing ship and crossed through the storm-dark to a different world. Tuuran understood that much better now although the Taiytakei never spoke of it. They'd move again soon. In the last few days they'd struck three villages along this coast already. The galley hold bulged with screams and tears.

A flash of light across the water caught his eyes. He glanced out past the breaking surf. The galley was there waiting for its boats but something else was there too. A bright orange spark in the sky, racing above the sea faster than any bird could fly, skimming the whitecaps, coming from further down the beach. The way he was taking them.

The spark reached the galley. Behind him the slaves had slowed to look; and then from the deck of the galley a pillar of fire erupted into the sky. Whips of it cracked out across the sea. There were no screams, no shouts, nothing that rode over the gentle hiss of the breaking surf. Tuuran faltered and then stopped to stare. Even the Taiytakei had stopped running.

A black dot arced up off the galley towards the beach. It came right at them, sailed a dozen feet over Tuuran's head and slammed into the sand so hard it made the ground shake. It broke into pieces, brittle and charred right through but it had been a man once. There were fingers, a hand, an arm … a stump that had been a head and a face. Tuuran stared at it like they all did, but unlike the others he'd seen this before. This was what happened when a dragon unleashed its fire, although the spark they'd seen streaking across the waves had been too fast and too small. Still, maybe that was why he was the first to look up, that age-old instinct to look to the sky. A dozen more specks were hurtling from the galley as if thrown by trebuchets.

'Run!'

There was no way to dodge the bodies but that didn't stop some of them from trying. Tuuran bolted up the beach for the trees. A dead man hit the sand in front of him and shattered into blackened pieces. Burned fragments of skin and bone flew up into his face. For a moment the world stank of charred flesh. He glanced back. Most of the sword-slaves were standing there staring up at the sky in horror, or running back and forth, trying to get out of the way of the raining dead. Only Crazy Mad had followed him for the trees. But Tuuran saw something more. The spark had left the galley. It was coming for the beach.

He reached the trees. On the beach the sword-slaves screamed and scattered as the spark shot across the sand and then stopped and became a woman wreathed in flames. Bolts of fire arced from her hands, three or four at once, cutting men down, so hot and fierce the fire went straight through them, burning them apart and searing their legs from their bodies and leaving holes as big as a man's fist. It was done in seconds. Every single soldier on the beach. Every single sword-slave except for him and Crazy Mad, hiding in the trees.

The woman became a spark again and flashed after the Taiytakei. He heard booms of lightning and saw flashes through the trees. A moment later and the screams started again. Wands, armour, it made no different. The Taiytakei fared no better than their slaves.

'What in the name of the gods that are no more is that?' Even Crazy Mad had no answer. They were paralysed. Waiting for it to go away, or to find them and end them. For the first time Tuuran could remember, Crazy even looked scared.

The screams stopped. For a brief moment there was silence. Tuuran stared at the beach, dumbstruck.

'You.'

His head snapped round and there she was: the woman wreathed in flames, a dozen yards further in among the trees and pointing a finger straight at him.

'Run,' he hissed to Crazy Mad but Crazy didn't need telling and had already vanished into the undergrowth so quick and so quiet that Tuuran hadn't even noticed him go. Tuuran raised his hands. 'I'm just a slave.'

'The beach!' If she was going to kill him, she'd have done it. There had been no mercy for the rest. No pause and no hesitation. So he stepped back onto the beach, cautious but not fearful. She wanted him for something.

'Slavers,' she hissed and pointed across the sand to where the Taiytakei had been. They were there still, only now they were one great black and gently smoking heap. 'Slavers,' she hissed again.

Tuuran shook his head. 'I—'

Fire from her finger seared his cheek. He screamed, clutching his hands to where it had touched him and then tearing them away. She'd burned off his ear, nothing left but rags of crispy skin.

'Your black-skin ships will leave this land. Any who return, this is what will happen to them. Take that message to your masters, slave. Tell them what you have seen.'

She vanished into flame and was gone, straight up into the sky. Out to sea, the galley was floundering in the waves. Tuuran glowered at the vanishing spark and raised his fist. 'And how? Just me? How do I find them to tell them when I am all alone in this land? Stupid sorceress!' The whole side of his face was a blazing mass of pain.

Crazy Mad crept out from among the trees, dazed-looking but with that mad gleam in his eye again. He kicked at the charred remains of a head. No way to tell who it might have been.

'I've seen dragons do that to a man,' Tuuran said.

Crazy Mad giggled. 'Is that Fire Witch a dragon then?'

'Dragons look like dragons, not like that.' Tuuran frowned. 'Who would have thought it, eh? Been hearing a lot of whispers about this place.' Damn but his face hurt. The whole side of his head.

Crazy Mad wandered across the sand and stood beside him. He peered at Tuuran's ear. 'Nasty. What place is that then?'

'Aria,' whispered Tuuran after a time, long after the woman was gone. Boats were on their way from the galley now, closing in on the shore. Oar-slaves. The witch hadn't burned them; she'd set them free. 'We're in Aria.'

'Aria.' There was a smile in Crazy Mad's voice and Tuuran understood it, as he understood now what the witch wanted him to do.

Home.

47

The Walking Man

You will get no answers, old slave. Not from them. No one ever does. The voices of the moon sorcerers were always there, soft like a spider's web across the Watcher's thoughts. Around the eyrie, becoming the wind or the stone was getting harder every day, not easier. It had to be the dragons. Something about them. In Khalishtor, in Dhar Thosis, in Vespinarr, in any other place he went he felt the world bend to his will as it should. Just not here where he needed it most.

When he was done with the alchemist, the Watcher took himself to the edge of the eyrie where no one would see the lines of pain on his face and his clenched fists as he turned himself into air and vanished away. The world rushed by. As the wind he had no eyes but there was a sense of the shape of things, the rise and fall of the land, the taste of running water, the tiny bright pinpricks that were hard barriers of silver and gold and gold-glass.

He turned away from his course …

… and appeared from the air atop a mountain deep inside the Konsidar, far from any city, in a place that no one but an Elemental Man would ever go, a hundred miles from the nearest Taiytakei or slave. From the peak he could see right down the mountain on every side, but on one particular side the descent never stopped. The mountain slopes reached down, but where they should have joined the lower slopes of another and made a pretty tree-filled valley with a stream rushing and bubbling through it, instead there was a colossal rift. It always looked to the Watcher as though some god had reached down and pulled the mountains apart, splitting the skin of the earth between them. It reminded him of the Queverra. The rift ran for miles though the Konsidar, a sheer-walled and depthless chasm between the mountains. Somewhere down there lived the Righteous Ones. Instinct had brought him here. It wasn't even on his way to where he was going but he'd come nevertheless, and as he looked down on the rift he knew why. Something was happening. The Righteous Ones had been caught creeping out of their caves of late. Something had changed down there, some years back, and at the same time out in the desert by the Godspike one of the ring of needles had cracked and the storm-dark had started to shift. Further back still and the Elemental Masters had allowed Quai'Shu to buy him and to buy the Picker too, as though they needed Quai'Shu's hunger for dragons to be fulfilled. As much as anyone, his makers had brought the dragons here. They hadn't merely allowed it to happen; they'd been its architects every bit as much as Quai'Shu. And the moon sorcerers too, who never came out of their towers, who were myth and legend until that day on the beach, *they* had made this happen. Whatever it was they'd seemed to want in return – his hunt for the grey dead ones or the Adamantine Spear of the dragon lands – what they *really* wanted was for dragons to cross the storm-dark. He could see that now. Perhaps that was the one thing they couldn't do, cross it themselves, and so they'd needed Quai'Shu and some navigator to make it so. Dragons in Takei'Tarr. That's what they wanted all along. In hindsight it seemed so obvious. They knew something, and the Righteous Ones, in their gloom, they knew something too.

The voices had stayed with him since that day on the shore of the Diamond Isles. He could never quite hear them, never quite understand what they were trying to say. He'd been a gift. Quai'Shu had given him to the sorcerers with their diamond towers. The Watcher had never forgotten that and nor had they. *Become as one.* He was their servant now. But servant in what? To what end?

He sat on the mountaintop in the biting cold air which cut like little knives and held his head in his hands until the voices found a calm. Passions clouded the mind and a clouded mind could not become the wind, the earth, the ice, the light, the water, the fire or the dark. Among his own kind a few whispered that the secret of the last element, of metal, was to be bursting with joy or love or hate or fury, but no Elemental Man had ever mastered metal and so whispers was all they ever were.

The voice of the moon sorcerers never stopped. The Watcher changed it in his head to make it a more soothing thing. His other master was Quai'Shu, whom the dragons had made mad. Men were plotting to kill him and the Watcher would stop them. *That*, at least, was a simple enough thing to see.

Become as one. He had no idea what that was supposed to mean. *What* become as one? Was he supposed to stop it or make it happen? They'd told him just enough to pull at the loose threads of the tapestry of something when they could simply have shown him the tapestry in its whole, the picture it made, and told him what to do. So why hadn't they done that?

He drew out his knives one by one, the blades of each so thin that light passed through them, leaving them all but invisible. Bladeless knives. Enchanter-made, sharp as broken glass and hard as diamonds. He cleaned them, cleaned away every speck of dust until he could barely see they were there, and as he did, a stillness settled over him like a weighted net. They'd given him a purpose and a mission, and in that purpose they'd given him a reason for what they'd done. And now he saw why: it was to stop him from looking for another one, purely and simply that. Dragons on Takei'Tarr. Their intervention after the crossing – leading away the hatching dragons and dumping them in Baros Tsen T'Varr's eyrie – was almost unseemly in its blatant purpose. Tsen and the other Taiytakei were too busy with their own problems to notice but a hsian would see at once. Quai'Shu's hsian. He could start there. The hsian was due a reminder of whom he served but perhaps he could serve just a little more. It would be ... interesting. For both of them. The Watcher would start with why he, alone among the hsians, had decided to bring dragons to Takei'Tarr because of the Midsummer Star and how, exactly, he had made that choice.

He wrapped his knives in their silks and stood up, breathing in the mountain air. Before that he had one other thing to attend to. The kwen. The kwen was in Xican, and that was as good a place as any to do what Tsen and Quai'Shu had asked. The city of the sea lord's first grandchild, wilful raven-haired Elesxian. Baros Tsen T'Varr should probably marry her. It would give both of them what they wanted but the simple fact was that Tsen wasn't ever going to marry anyone. No one would ever marry him. It would be a waste of everyone's time.

He blinked, changed to a breath of wind, and the mountaintop became still. A moment later it was a distant shape on the horizon.

Another moment and it was gone and he was gusting across mountains and forests and islands and seas to Xican, to the city of stone carved out of the iron-grey and obsidian-black of the Grey Isle where nothing grew. Not a single thing lived there if it didn't live in the city; in fact most of the island wasn't even an island but more a collection of boulders, large and small, smashed together, which still rolled and shifted from day to day. The enchanters had done something to the city itself to keep the stones around it still, the ones from which it was carved. Except for the plateau at the centre, the rest of the island changed constantly. Slowly, yes, but never the same. For a long time it hadn't been much more than a staging post, a first and last place for the great Taiytakei fleets of the sea lords to stop and rest before they crossed the storm-dark to the other realms. That was how it had started.

The Watcher appeared on a pinnacle overlooking the hollowed stone spires of the city. The weather out here on the far edge of the island was always the same, always bright and sunny and clear and never a drop of rain, even when a deluge of storms hammered at the plateau only a dozen miles to the east. On the horizon, twenty miles away more or less, sat the grey veil edge of the storm-dark. When it was as close as it was today, the Watcher liked to sit and look at it because Xican was the only place in the whole of Takei'Tarr where the storm-dark now and then came close enough to the shore to be seen from land. Through that veil lay other worlds, the dragon realms, the Diamond Isles, Qeled, Aria, all the rest, and it was a veil that even an Elemental Man couldn't pierce. Not like a wall of silver or glass or gold, which became like a solid thing, hard and impenetrable; no, the veil of the storm-dark was soft like a curtain, always pushing him aside so that no matter how carefully he trod, he always found himself back where he began. It moved too. It drifted back and forth. Some days it was within sight of the Grey Isle, but on others it was far out to sea, hundreds of miles into the ocean perhaps, days of sailing. Most often it was out of sight, but there were some who said that the clouds of the storm-dark had once come closer still, that they'd touched the Grey Isle itself, and that was why it was as it was. To the Watcher the storm-dark was a marvel, a miracle and a wonder left over from the Splintering. For ships and more mundane men it was simply a place of horror and death from which nothing returned. For the Taiytakei that was a much easier thing to understand.

The Watcher looked down. After Khalishtor and Vespinarr, Xican wasn't much of a city, not much more than a swathe of rocky spires all jammed together around the water's edge and hollowed out. A few ships sat in the sheltered bay, pieces of Tsen's broken-up fleet. The kwen might be there or he might be in among the spires, still searching out the men he'd need to creep back into the waters of the dragon realms and steal another rider.

Or he might be somewhere else.

The Watcher turned his eyes to the Palace of Leaves floating in the air above him, a glasship of absurd proportions, a dozen and a half gold-glass discs with scores of silver and golden eggs hanging beneath them, hovering over a cluster of gold-glass towers that reached up like fingers and cold black obsidian columns from where the enchanters drew the energies that kept the palace aloft. Yes, the kwen could be on his ship or in the city minding his business, or he could be up there.

The Watcher blinked. Vanished and appeared on the surface of the highest part of the palace. Blinked again, working his way down, peering through roofs and windows. He moved from place to place, watching and searching, and although it took days, he kept on until he found what he was looking for and knew that he was right. Which only left the far more straightforward matter of getting inside to put an end to it.

He blinked again, back down to the surface and to the gates of the first glass tower. Glass and silver and gold. They all thought it was so easy to keep his kind away. The gates were closed of course, or what would be the point? The Watcher appeared out of the air before them and made a show of inspecting them. There were gaps, always gaps, but they were too small and too narrow. Beside the gates a face stared at him through a window of clear fine glass. The Watcher made a gesture to the door as if asking for it to be opened. The face frowned. The Watcher blinked and reappeared a foot to the left so the face could have no doubt what he was. The eyes within the face grew wide and the face turned away. The Watcher's fingers began to quiver. He raised a hand to touch the glass, placed his palm against it and the window shattered. One decent-sized hole. That was all it ever took. He blinked through, knives out now. The face from the window was running but he hadn't gone very far. Pale skin. A sword-slave.

Blink. The Watcher appeared in front of the running man and held out a bladeless knife, then blinked again as the man stopped. Appeared behind him and ran him through. The slave shouted an alarm as he died. Blood sprayed across the floor over cold white marble. There were other soldiers here in the open space behind the gates, the great open hollow inside the glass spire. He let them see him holding his knife towards them. They could see its blade now, a crimson edge made from the blood of the dead, but they weren't afraid of him, not yet, not when he was only one and they were fifteen and they hadn't understood what it was that had come for them. More sword-slaves. Skins of all colours.

He shifted. He was behind them as they skittered to a stop. He slit a throat. Broke a neck, twisted a head clean round so its eyes stared backwards at him as the light inside died. Ran another through as he turned.

Blink. Back the other way. Knives in clenched fists now, wading into the middle of them, striding between two with their backs turned, a blade to the heart of each as he passed them. They wore coats of metal plates layered under leather but their armour was worthless against a bladeless knife. A soldier in front of him began to turn. The Watcher opened his throat in a flash of light. Blood sprayed. Another knife rammed hard up under a sword-slave's chin. These men had done nothing wrong but there was a point to be made and they were only slaves.

Blink. They were quicker this time. Credit them for that. Blade into the kidneys of another and then the Watcher even had to duck. Shifted away a while now. Up high where they wouldn't think to look. Listening to their screams, the shouts, the terror and the panic. They needed to feel it. The whole palace needed to feel it from the top of its floating glass to deep within its rocky roots. It needed to feel the dread of an Elemental Man. The kwen, *he* needed to feel it.

Nine dead in as many seconds. They didn't know what to do. One of them ran ...

Blink.

... onto the point of an outstretched knife he couldn't even see.

The Watcher let him fall to the ground. Let the last few savour it. They stood in a circle now, backs together, swords out, pleading for help and mercy, doing the best they could do not to die, not that it would save them. Around the edges of the tower in their little rooms aghast faces peered out. Slaves and servants. Little kwens and t'varrs and maybe even a hsian or two, but mostly they would be t'varrs. Someone was already riding a disc up the glass side of the tower towards the tip of the spire and the hanging palace of orbs above.

Blink. Up beside the last of the soldiers close enough to smell their breath, to taste their fear and see the quiver of their skin. Right inside their guard. One knife up under the chin, the other down into the soft hollow of a collarbone.

Blink. As they fell. Down low at a crouch. Knives deep into feet. One each.

Blink. So fast the first bodies were still falling. Behind the man with the bleeding feet as he dropped his sword and opened his mouth to scream. Opened his throat instead. Snapped into air and back again, falling this time, straight down, head first, face upside down before the last two. They had a moment, a flashing instant to see what would come before the bladeless knives found their open mouths and they saw him vanish before their eyes. He appeared between them as they were still falling. Made sure that the faces peering from above had plenty of time to see him, to see who he was and what, standing in the middle of a circle of bloody death. His eyes settled on the disc rising up the wall. A face stared back at him. Screams echoed through the huge space inside the tower. Shouts, the terror spreading among the slaves and the servants who worked down here, the ordinary palace folk faced by a horror beyond their understanding save that they knew him as death. An Elemental Man. A bringer of endings.

He let them see and then vanished and appeared on the disc. The man there was a Taiytakei, not a slave – a t'varr by the feathers he wore – but the fear in his face was the same, a tangible thing. The Watcher took a step and the t'varr backed away. Another step forward and another step away, and then there was no glass beneath the t'varr's feet, only air, and he fell and smashed on the white marble floor far below.

Fear. The all-consuming power of the Elemental Men.

48

The Lord of Silver

Chay-Liang stood next to Baros Tsen, watching the Vespinese glasships drift in towards the eyrie. As the ships drew closer she could see that some were different colours, not the plain gold-glass of Xican and most of the other sea lords. Emerald-green, ruby-red, sapphire-blue and one that was almost midnight-black, surrounded by a dozen of the plain glass and gold she was more used to seeing. Huge streamers hung beneath, trailing from their gleaming silver gondolas. The wastefulness of it irritated her, but then she was already irritated with having to fit iron-clad doors into the white stone passages of the eyrie – stone, she noted sourly, that would not be scratched or pierced by any tool she could find – and she'd barely even finished when Tsen had told her to take them all out again.

For a moment the annoyance of it all got the better of her. 'Why do I have to take all the doors off for them? Do they not have doors in Vespinarr? Does it offend them?'

Baros Tsen smiled beside her, the same affable smile he always had. 'You don't need me to answer that, Chay-Liang. Think about what they're for. And of course you'll be putting them back again as soon as our guests are gone.'

'What a delight.' She gave him an acid glare. 'I can barely contain myself.' But yes, she understood. The doors were for stopping an Elemental Man, and the first thing anyone who saw them would wonder would be what use they were when an Elemental Man could simply merge with the stone instead and simply pass round them. And the second thing that a man like Shonda would then realise would be that the doors must mean that they *couldn't* pass through the stone. And Tsen didn't want them to know that.

The t'varr shook his head. 'They always have to show off, don't they?'

'The Lord of Silver flaunts his wealth? When will *that* ever change?' Chay-Liang sniffed. There was more to life than silver. Other kinds of wealth worth more than money.

'Oh, I hope never.' Tsen turned and flashed her his perfect white teeth and she had to crush the urge to slap his smile off him. 'And the question you really wanted to ask is *Why are they here?* Well think about that one too, mistress of our lord's eyrie.'

Chay-Liang jumped as if she'd been stung. 'What? *Me?*'

'Not really, of course, but that's what they think. They're here to see our dragons … *your* dragons. Their, ah … *investment*. And to see our sea lord since he's so close by. And of course they're *really* here to see whether Quai'Shu is as ill as they think he is and how much of a stake in our little enterprise they can wheedle out of us in exchange for the debt our lord has amassed.'

'You mean *you* have amassed.'

Tsen's smile didn't waver. 'I suppose I do. I suppose what I really mean is *we* have amassed.' He patted Liang on the shoulder. From almost anyone else she might have taken offence, but Tsen was wearing his harmless amiable fat-man persona and he slipped into it so well that it worked even on her, even now, even when she'd known him for so long that she knew it for exactly the façade it was. 'Go on, go and get your alchemist and your dragon ready. I'm sure that's what they really want to see. Your dragon-rider too if you can be sure she won't suddenly set about them.' He laughed. 'Not that I'd particularly mind in some cases. Oh, and LaLa is about some other business and not here to keep an eye on things. There's no way they should know that of course, but you can never be too cautious with our dear friends from the mountains. Keep your alchemist safe.'

'Not here?' Chay-Liang raised an eyebrow. 'Exactly when we need him! Their arrival shows interesting timing.'

For a moment Tsen's mask slipped and his eyes glinted like a pair of daggers. 'Doesn't it just?' He shook himself and turned away. 'There's going to be a big formal meal and all the usual hoo-ha. Meido and Bronzehand are both with the Vespinese but don't you worry about that. My problems. Just make sure your dragon doesn't eat anyone. Or your rider either.'

'They are not *mine*, T'Varr!'

'Today they are, Liang, today they are.'

Tsen strolled away down the battlements towards the steps that led to the dragon yard. Chay-Liang watched him go. He passed a cluster of air cannon, the black-powder guns that pointed into the sky to shatter any glasships that strayed overhead. They were inferior in almost every way to lightning cannon except for the one crucial flaw: a lightning cannon wouldn't trouble anything made of gold-glass.

Would they trouble a dragon? She looked past Tsen across the dragon yard to where the monster was perched on the far wall. It was staring at the approaching glasships with the fixed intensity of a predator. Even from here she could feel its restless tension. She could feel its hunger. *It wants to fly*, Belli said. He was on the wall too now but on the far side, close to the dragon and with the rider beside him. Liang bristled as she saw them. It had been a bad day from the start and now she had to get this slave – Zafir, was it? – to cooperate when neither of them liked each other even one little bit. A slave who owned slaves of her own? Tsen should never have allowed that; and the woman might have been a queen in her own land but here she certainly wasn't. She was a slave, that was all. An unbranded slave, which made her a nothing, yet she strutted as though she was mistress of everyone.

Mentally Liang slapped herself. The alchemist was an unbranded slave too, and *they* got on just fine. Or they had until the rider had shown up with Tsen. The whole eyrie had heard about what had happened next. It had run through the slaves like wildfire. And in Tsen's own gondola too, and barely a few minutes after she'd arrived! Disgusting.

Jealous, Liang?

Yes, she was, and deathly disappointed that Belli would do something like that, and damn the stupid alchemist because he seemed to worship the ground on which this woman trod when he should really have known better. *She* treated him like a slave and he took it! He took it as though it was perfectly normal, when *he* was the one who made this eyrie work, *he* was the one who made the potions and tamed the monsters. What did *she* do? Nothing! She could fly their monster, could she? But so far all she'd done was flaunt herself and strut and look down her nose at everyone.

Everyone! She barely deigned to show any respect even for Tsen.

Liang huffed and turned her back on the Vespinese glasships. Stupid to let a slave get under her skin like that. She walked to the dragon yard. Bellepheros had come down from the wall to be with the Scales now, herding the hatchlings towards the wall to make space for the gondolas to land. She laughed a little as she walked over to him. Wouldn't do for Tsen's visitors to catch the dragon disease now would it? It had already crept out once and now Belli had all sorts of quarantine rules in place. *No one is to have intimate relations with anyone else for two months.* He'd actually said that, and when she'd blinked and looked at him and he'd smiled at her and said, *I mean no sex – that's how it usually spreads*, she'd turned bright red. And yes, it *had* been funny, because yes, she *was* a bit of a prude, even among the Taiytakei, but at least she wasn't too full of her own importance to admit it. The alchemist, as always, was shockingly direct. All he could ever find to do with her squeamishness was laugh at it. Usually she ended up laughing too; and obviously she *had* known what he was talking about in the first place.

Today her laughter died. *No intimate relations? Tell that to your rider. Tell that to yourself every time she's around.* Maybe the slave could catch the disease. Liang smiled again at that. She'd seen what it was already doing to the Scales. *Wouldn't that be a shame?*

She waved at Belli in the dragon yard and he waved back, warning her not to get too close, and then he left the hatchlings with their Scales and came to greet her. He always used to smile when he saw her but not any more, not since Zafir had come.

'We have visitors,' she told him. 'They'll want to see you. They'll want to see the dragon too.'

'They can probably see Diamond Eye already.' Yes, and there was another thing. He'd taken to calling the dragon by that name the moment *she* had told him to. Liang looked up at the battlements. Zafir sat beside the monster, looking at it while the dragon lowered its head and looked back. Their faces were a few feet apart and the dragon made her seem so incredibly small. It would have made anyone seem small, but Zafir was the only one who would sit so close to it. The only one who wasn't at least just a little bit afraid, damn her.

'I don't trust her at all,' she muttered. 'Look at them. It's almost as though they're talking about us.'

A month ago Bellepheros might have laughed at something like that. Now he just turned away. 'Dragons don't talk, Liang. They have nothing to say for as long as they take my potion.'

'But *she* does.'

'Her Holiness?' Bellepheros turned back and looked her in the eye again. 'Of course. You've made her a slave. Just as you did to me and I have done to Diamond Eye.'

Damn you, woman! Bellepheros had almost forgotten that he was a slave here. For months and months, ever since the bodyguard from his own land had been sent away, he'd never even spoken of it. Before, even. And now this rider came and suddenly it was always there and held against her again.

Is it my fault? No! She caught his shoulder. 'Remember, Belli. It's not about right here and now. You told me yourself: what matters is the future, the faraway years no one else thinks to imagine. Remember what we talked about, of the way it could be between our two realms when we're both old. Now that she's here to show what our dragons can truly do, are we not a step closer? You should be happy!' She looked up at the rider again, Zafir, once the speaker of the dragon realms, and suddenly she wasn't so sure that her future would work. Was that what was bothering him? Did he see the same?

He turned away from her and looked at the smaller dragons being tended by their Scales. 'Whoever these people are, the older hatchlings are safe now. They shouldn't go near the new one. If they wish to approach Diamond Eye then her Holiness must accompany them.'

Holiness? As though she's some sort of goddess! It made her want to retch. She swore she saw the Watcher grind his teeth every time he heard it as well. 'When is she actually going to fly it?' she snapped, irritation getting the better of her for a moment.

'When *you* have finished making what I asked of you.'

Liang threw up her hands. 'Which I would have done by now if Tsen hadn't demanded doors and doors and more doors and then no doors at all! Is it necessary? All of it?'

'The harnesses are already done. We're just waiting for you.'

He walked back to his hatchlings. Liang turned away as well and stalked towards the middle of the dragon yard. The glasships were overhead now, the silver gondolas of the Vespinese easing down to touch the stone. Dragon armour! He wanted her to make armour for their rider. Armour to resist the tear of the wind and the burn of the flames, and while she was at it anything else that might be thrown at the rider which, as far as Chay-Liang knew, meant that it had to turn lightning, as that was the first thing any sea lord would turn on such a monster. Even if the dragon survived, what was the use if the rider was dead? Armour of glass and gold and of dragon-scale. Tricky. Challenging. Interesting though, and for anyone else she might have relished the novelty of it, but not for this one, not for *her*. She'd had to deal with the slave-rider, take her measurements to get the armour right, and Zafir had left her feeling like a common tailor. *Bitch.*

Oh by all the elements get a grip, woman. How old are you? She could be your daughter and she's a slave and of course the alchemist finds her pretty. Maybe he only likes his women pale-skinned. She closed her eyes and touched her temples. *Did I just think that? I did. O Charin preserve me!*

'Are you unwell, Enchantress?' Tsen sidled up beside her as two of the three silver gondolas opened their doors. A handful of Taiytakei soldiers in cloaks of pure white feathers and armour of jade and silver-glass lined up, and Baran Meido and Bronzehand too, but Chay-Liang barely noticed as the third silver egg split open. Two men stepped out of it. They were both wrapped in flowing silk, pure snow-white like a slave's tunic but each had three emerald and sapphire dragons entwined on their garments, and as the gentle breeze tugged the folds of their robes the dragons seemed to writhe and chase each other. Their cloaks were the same, a million tiny white feathers with three shifting green and blue dragons wrapped around one another. Even when the air fell quiet, the dragons still seemed to move. Both men wore the braids of their hair down to the ground, so long they touched the white stone of the dragon yard and dragged across it. Liang always told herself not to be impressed by cloaks and silks and feathers and braids because they were all nothing more than money, not a measure of a person's worth at all, but today she stared. Couldn't help herself, for the two men who'd stepped out of the silver egg were possibly the two most powerful men in all the worlds. Sea Lord Shonda of Vespinarr was certainly the richest and his t'varr, who also happened to be his brother, Vey Rin, decided on what those riches should be spent.

As her eyes flickered from one to the other, she realised she couldn't tell which was which. A t'varr and a sea lord standing together. Even their braids were the same length.

'You've never seen them before, have you?' hissed Tsen from the corner of his mouth. 'Left or right? A salver of jade says you get it wrong.'

Liang ignored him. On the other side of the t'varr their own sea lord sat on a chair on a gold-glass disc that Liang had made for him, and she knew that Tsen had pushed Quai'Shu up into the dragon yard himself. Quai'Shu had deteriorated steadily since Khalishtor. Moments of clarity were few and far between. Mostly he asked to be taken to see his dragon, to sit with it, which meant sitting with *her*, the woman who'd murdered his first son. He seemed not to notice, or else he didn't remember, but to Liang's surprise seeing the two of them together troubled Tsen more than anything. Liang had no idea why.

Shonda and his t'varr stopped in front of Quai'Shu's makeshift throne. Tsen fell to his knees and pressed his forehead to the hard white stone of the dragon yard. Liang did the same. All of them did except for Quai'Shu, who simply stayed where he was and stared blankly into the air. Sea Lord Shonda of Vespinarr took one look and wrinkled his nose. He pointed up to the dragon on the battlements. 'Is it ready?'

Tsen rose again, a cue to the rest of them. 'No, Sea Lord, it is not yet ready to be flown. If you had waited a few more days—'

'I came when it suited me.' Shonda beckoned his white-cloaks and walked past Tsen and Quai'Shu towards the dragon. 'When it's ready to fly you can tell Mai'Choiro Kwen. He will come and you will show him.' He swept past with Vey Rin T'Varr at his side. His white-cloaks followed and then Baran Meido and Bronzehand.

'My father doesn't look at all well. At least he's still alive, eh?' Meido winked at Tsen as he walked past. 'Doesn't look like he's going to last much longer though.' As Tsen fell in beside him, he leaned closer. 'Bronzehand leaves for Qeled in a week. By the look of things I might win both my wagers without even having to do anything.'

Liang followed a few steps behind. Tsen let out a great sigh and held up his palms. 'I keep him as well as I can. Dragons are very dangerous creatures.'

Shonda of Vespinarr climbed the battlement steps and stopped on the top of the wall a respectful distance from the dragon. It had noticed them now and had torn its eyes off the glasships to watch them, jaws ajar, lazily flicking its forked tongue over its sword-like teeth. The rider had noticed them too. She was standing up, preening and flaunting herself again. Liang gritted her teeth.

'Impressive creature,' said Shonda with a mildness that sounded a little forced. He turned his eyes past Tsen to Chay-Liang. 'Will it survive your arsenal, Enchantress?'

Liang felt herself quivering. She dug her nails into her thumb. *Stop it!* 'We have yet to try, Sea Lord.' She bowed.

'It would be unwise to—' Tsen began, but Shonda shut him up with a wave. He whispered in the ear of one of his white-cloaks. The man bowed deeply, hesitated a moment, then turned and walked towards the dragon. He stopped halfway between them and stood there. Hairs prickled on the back of Liang's neck.

Her mouth fell open. 'Sea Lord, may I ask what ...'

The white-cloak pulled his golden wand from his belt.

'No! Sea Lord! Please! Do not!' She saw Zafir between the white-cloak and the dragon. The slave was shaking her head but she was smiling, the bitch was *smiling*. Even as the white-cloak raised his wand and pointed it at the dragon, Zafir dropped to one knee, ducked and pressed her hands over her ears. Liang looked away. The noise shook the eyrie, lightning as strong as a wand could make, a crack of thunder so loud that even the hatchlings at the far end of the dragon yard stopped snapping at one another and turned to look. The lightning hit the dragon square on the nose. Tsen and Bronzehand and a few of the white-cloaks who hadn't had the wit to see what was coming and look away reeled and staggered, stunned by the noise and the light. Liang looked back, horrified. The dragon bared its teeth. Its eyes narrowed and its wings flared, sending a wind along the battlements that almost knocked her off her feet, but that was just the dragon keeping its balance as its tail whipped around from behind its legs. The dragon-slave threw herself flat as though she knew exactly what was coming but the white-cloak didn't see it at all. The end of the tail took him from the side like a mountain falling from the sky. It hit him with such a force that his armour exploded, pieces flying off it in all directions. It probably shattered every bone in his body as it hurled him hundreds of feet into the air, away over the edge of the battlements. Liang watched him fall to the desert far below. He didn't scream.

Everyone moved at once. The white-cloaks all went for their wands. Zafir was on her feet, running straight at them, but the dragon was quickest of all. Its head shot forward. Frighteningly fast, faster than Liang had ever seen it. Its eyes were locked on Sea Lord Shonda and Liang's blood ran cold. It knew! It had seen the sea lord give the order and it knew! Its mouth opened and Liang could feel the heat of it.

'No! Stop! All of you stop!' Zafir was between the dragon and the white-cloaks, one hand thrust out each way, palm up. 'Do not, do not, do not!' Her voice cut the air. The white-cloaks had surrounded Shonda, wands all raised. Shonda somehow managed to stay still. Zafir turned her head slowly to the dragon, hands still up. 'No!' she commanded it again. 'You may *not*.' They stared each other down, dragon and rider, for ten long heartbeats, and then Zafir's head snapped back to the white-cloaks. 'That was foolish. Now withdraw or it will *eat* you.' She pointed a finger straight at Sea Lord Shonda. 'It will eat *him*. It's not stupid.'

'Sea Lord …' Tsen had misplaced his voice for a few seconds, but now he found it again. Another handful of heartbeats passed and no one moved. Then Shonda turned his back on the dragon and walked with deliberate slowness away.

'We have seen enough,' he said, and Liang had to admire his control. He *was* shaking, but only enough to see if you really looked.

49

Men of Stone

Blink. Two soldiers stood in front of the Watcher, backing quickly away. The next moment he was behind them. They fell as blades thin as a hair slit them open.

The glass palace of Elesxian was small as palaces went. Xican was a nothing place, dull and lifeless except for the docks and the sailors who came and went with the sea lords' fleets. A fine place for listening to the wind though, and for learning what moves were afoot among the lords who sent their fleets this way. The quickest paths to both the Dominion and the dragon realms lay through the storms that danced across the seas off Xican.

Blink. A half-shut door, two men on the far side desperately trying to close it. Glass, not that glass would keep him at bay for long. They were too slow and there was a gap and it was enough, and he was through and behind them. The bladeless knives flashed and blood sprayed across their glitter. Wasteful to kill so many. Shameful for one who'd learned to move like a ghost in shadows but he wasn't here to kill, not really.

Blink. A screaming servant saw him and ran. A Taiytakei. A little kwen or a t'varr, lowest of their rank, quivering in a corner, perhaps hoping he wouldn't notice him. He walked on past, blood dripping from the blades that could not be seen. He wasn't here to kill. He was here to teach.

They'd sealed the glass palace itself. Hardly a surprise since he'd let them know he was coming so that they could do precisely that. Now he would enter it anyway and show them how futile it was to even try. *That*, after all, was the point. That was the lesson.

Blink. A glass door. Sealed. The last and only entrance to the inner palace, to Elesxian's inner heart. He tapped and listened to the music that the glass played for him and then reached out a hand and set it quivering to the same song. The door shattered.

The enchanters were always finding ways to mix metal and glass together to try and defeat an Elemental Man and the Elemental Men were constantly proving that it could not be done.

Blink. Another door. Gold. Gold or silver that wouldn't shatter, that was far better but even then not perfect. A gold door? It was new. Elesxian's palace had changed since last he'd been here. No matter.

There were more soldiers coming from behind him. Ones that didn't turn and run. He blinked behind them and slashed but for once the bladeless knives didn't bite.

Stoneguard. Xican's little secret, although not as secret as Elesxian liked to think. Golem soldiers made of stone, enchanted to life and merged in some way the Watcher didn't understand with sword-slaves. Creatures made of stone who moved as men. Enchanters' work, a darker side of the golems they made for digging and tunnelling the ever-growing City of Stone.

They lunged at him but he wasn't there.

Creatures made of stone.

Perfect.

He was inside them.

50

Damage

Ah, the joys of hosting one's betters! How can one ever get enough of it? They went through the motions. Tsen was good at that and always had been. A part of his mind listened to Lord Shonda and his questions, and to his own answers as he guided the Vespinese lords around his eyrie. He showed them the hatchlings and the alchemist, the Scales and the dragon-scale skins they were drying. All the while another part of him thought of his bathhouse deep in the eyrie's heart and of Kalaiya. He'd need her tonight, her soothing words, her presence and her scent. *I nearly died today* he could tell her, and she'd laugh at him, but it was true. He was quite sure the dragon would have eaten them all if its rider hadn't stopped it. A part of him wondered why she'd bothered, and yet another part of him wouldn't have blamed her at all if she'd just let it rip them all to pieces. *What sort of idiot walks up to a monster like that and hits it with a lightning bolt?* He supposed he should admire the loyalty of Shonda's white-cloak for doing it at all. *Makes you wonder how loyal the rest of them will be when the next time comes.*

'A good test of your control of the beast,' Vey Rin T'Varr said while Shonda was talking to the enchantress and the alchemist. They were the only words to come from his old friend from long ago, and the cynic in Tsen decided that Rin was only saying them to distract him from listening in on whatever Shonda was talking about. Not that he needed to. Shonda's agenda was obvious. He was a sea lord and his thoughts were sea lord thoughts: *How can this be mine?* Rin himself didn't seem interested in the hatchlings or the alchemist or indeed anything. *Because you're only here to talk about all that money I owe you? Ah well, considerate of you not to pretend otherwise.*

Nasty little thoughts.

Tsen had planned to show them around the inside of the eyrie too, including the alchemist's laboratory and the quarters where the Scales lived – wearing the alchemist's leathers and mask and with dire warnings, of course, which would only have made them all the more keen. He might have taken them to his own study. He had a sumptuous feast prepared but it was all wasted. Shonda stayed for scarcely more than an hour and never left the dragon yard after he'd almost got himself eaten – was that what a dragon did? Or would it have burned them? He hadn't seen the dragon's fire yet, but that's what they did, wasn't it? Burned you and then ate the charred mess that was left? He realised he didn't know. He'd have to ask.

He bowed and kowtowed and did all the things he was supposed to and pushed Quai'Shu's disc up to the gondolas to make the pretence of a formal farewell. Quai'Shu was muttering under his breath, something he'd been doing more and more and none of it made any sense. They watched Shonda leave. Meido and Bronzehand followed him, little ducklings paddling furiously to stay close to their mother leaving Tsen alone with Vey Rin T'Varr and the business that really mattered. The two stood side by side, watching the Vespinese glasships recede into the sky with the sea lord and Quai'Shu's sons safe in their thin silver shells.

'I don't think,' said Vey Rin, stroking his chin, 'that I will ever see a glasship in quite the same way again.'

Tsen said nothing. They'd been t'varrs together for years. Long before that they'd actually been friends – real friends – two wild young things who thought the world existed for their amusement and pleasure without much of a care in the world or thought for the consequences of what they did. Nowadays they were sometimes friends, sometimes adversaries, always too much of one to fully be the other, but they still had an understanding. They'd come to know each other well enough to know each other's silences.

'I've always rather taken them for granted,' said Rin after a while. 'It never had occurred to me how fragile they really are. Now it does.'

My monster could rip a gondola from its chains as easily as you or I might pluck a flower. It could throw it through the sky as you or I might throw a ball for fun. That about right? Frightening, is it? I suppose it must be. 'Glasships have their lightning cannon,' said Tsen mildly. *And whatever else your enchanters have secretly done to them.*

'And you really haven't seen what happens when you fire one at that thing?' They were still staring at the gondolas, watching them fade into the desert haze, little gleaming pricks of light in the sky.

'I really haven't.' *And now you can have some fun trying to decide whether to believe that or not, and I can have some fun too trying to guess which way that goes. We already both know what worries you: that I have tried it and that the dragon survived. What then, eh?* 'I was thinking,' he added, 'of not finding out at all. If the cannon kills my dragon then I will have to wait for the little ones to grow. If the dragon kills the cannon then I can imagine a few sea lords might find that a touch upsetting.' *Which is like saying the dragon is a touch big, even if we all know that the Elemental Men would never allow me to turn my monster against my dear friends in the Great Sea Council.*

'Uncertainty can be your ally only for a while, my friend.'

'True, but there are no lightning cannon in Aria.'

'Point.' Vey Rin turned away from the drifting points of colour in the sky. For a while he stared at the dragon. The monster was watching the gondolas too and you had to wonder what it was thinking. Nothing, if you believed the alchemist, but Tsen wasn't sure that he did. The creature watched the world around it with far too much purpose in its gaze.

Rin shivered and pulled his eyes back to Tsen. 'And that is something I should like to discuss. Along with one or two other more tedious matters.'

Money. Tsen smiled. 'Of course, old friend. The usual?'

'Yes, I would like that.' Vey Rin smiled back and for once he really meant it. They walked together across the yard, past the dragon on the battlements. Zafir was sitting beside it again, head tipped back, sprawled under the desert sun. Rin pursed his lip. 'Interesting slave you have there.'

'Oh, I have several.'

'I think you'll particularly want to watch that one.'

Really? Why, I don't think that would ever have occurred to me without you mentioning it. Thank you so much, you patronising sod. 'I think we have an understanding.' *We have a something, anyway.*

'You have other slaves who can ride the dragon?'

Tsen laughed. No point in even *trying* to lie about *that*. 'You think I'd use her if I did? It is being arranged, Rin, as with many other things. Our lord had planned for hatchlings and eggs. The adult is an unexpected bonus to which we are adjusting as best we can.'

'I'd adjust quickly if I were you.' They walked into the cool shade of the spiralling tunnels. 'We might talk about how Vespinarr can help you with that.'

'I'm sure that will be most pleasant.' *You mean we might talk about how much more debt I can accrue and what you'd want for it, and how difficult my life might become if I don't do things as you want them done? Yes. A delight indeed.*

He led Vey Rin down into the depths of the eyrie and the bathhouse. As they walked thorough the curling white stone passages with their quiet light, they gossiped and idly speculated on the nature of the eyrie itself. As much a wonder as the dragon in its way, but it had sat abandoned in the desert for decade after decade, floating above the sands because no one had found a use for it. An inexplicable oddity, too dour and drab to be a palace, a thing of almost no value at all and yet still a mystery and a miracle. *Just because it has slept and done nothing for all these years, don't imagine there is no danger dormant within it. Thank you, Jima Hsian, for those last words to keep me up at night.*

The baths were ready for him as they always were. He let Rin have a good look at them, though there wasn't much to see. The chamber at the eyrie's heart was a hemisphere of white stone that glowed too brightly in the daytime, just right at twilight and was a little too dim at night. Tsen had tried to think of ways to change it but the stone did what the stone did and it turned out there wasn't much to be done about it. Ten white stone archways ringed the centre of the room. They weren't much to look at, not ornamented in any way, just arches. Somewhere in the middle, when they'd first found this room, had been a plinth of yet more white stone. Tsen supposed it was still there but now his bath filled the space inside the arches. Black marble flecked with gold, the same as he had in Khalishtor. Shallow steps between each arch led up to the bath. He'd thought at the time it was a shame they hadn't been able dig through the white stone and set the bath into the floor as it should have been; now he knew a little more about what this white stone did, he didn't mind so much, even if it *was* all a bit of an ugly hodge-podge.

Vey Rin walked around the outside of the cavern and then up the steps to the bath and dipped his hand into the water. He didn't say a word, but when he came back to Tsen he nodded. They left the last of Shonda's white-cloaks and Quai'Shu's black-cloaks outside, disrobed, then let the eyrie slaves take their clothes and close the iron doors to the bathhouse behind them. The only doors Tsen had told Chay-Liang to leave as they were.

'My quiet place.' Tsen smiled once they were alone. He walked up the steps and eased himself into the water. The slaves had got the temperature just right for once and his old favourite Xizic oil too. His, not Rin's. Rin preferred the subtler Xizic of Shinpai. 'A shadow of my bathhouse in Xican and a mere speck of dirt beside your own in the Kabulingnor, but one makes do as one can.'

'Apparently one does.' Rin slipped into the water beside him, clearly unimpressed. Tsen gestured to the white stone of the cavern, glowing as it always did.

'Even my enchanters cannot mark this stone. It is impenetrable to them in some way.' He shrugged apologetically. 'It has forced many compromises into my design.' *Ha! And there's a thing you probably didn't know when you came here and I probably shouldn't have told you at all, but there you go and now I have. Startling enough to merit a word with your lord and a small panic at Hingwal Taktse, I should have thought. I'll tell Chay Liang to expect some guests shortly, shall I?* Little moments like this came between them rarely. He made sure to savour it. He could see Rin thinking, trying to decide whether he was lying. *I wonder how you would take it if I told you how impenetrable my stone is to certain others too, eh? Elemental others, but I think I'll continue to keep that little jewel to myself.*

'Will your usual slave not join us?'

Yes, and thank you for that little needle-nod to my weakness. 'Kalaiya? Do you think she should?' *Of course not, not when we're here to discuss the future of both our lords, or do you already know that I'll tell her everything anyway?*

'Perhaps not.'

Tsen nodded. 'It is a place, after all, to be alone. For words to be spoken that will not spread.'

More slaves brought food from the abandoned feast. He told them to take the rest and to share what was left among everyone, slaves too. No reason not to be generous sometimes. The two of them ate and talked of old times. They chewed over how things were when they'd been younger men, of how things had changed over the years. Vey Rin talked for a while about his family and his many sons and daughters. Tsen stayed quiet for that, listening with little to say of his own. *I envy you, in a way. All that love if only you can find the time for it and choose not to waste it. All that life. Just never what I wanted.* At least Rin knew him well enough not to pry. They both knew he had his Kalaiya, that he loved her more than he loved his own lord and that he'd never taken her to his bed, not once. A mystery to everyone, even to Tsen himself.

They ate and talked until the apple wine came and the doors closed and they were alone again. Rin smiled into his glass. 'How are you managing, Tsen? Well, I hope?' Which could have meant almost anything, but there was the slightest change in his posture which said, *Business now*, and so Tsen knew exactly what he was talking about: Quai'Shu's fleets and the money to keep them going.

'Adequately, under the circumstances.' *Of which you are probably even more aware than I.*

'Good.' *Liar.* 'If there is any help you wish from your friends in Vespinarr, you have but to ask.' Rin eased back into the bath, letting the water lap at his chin.

In exchange for a piece of my dragon? Tsen smiled. 'I am ever grateful. I'm sure there is something.' *Yes, we both know there's no avoiding this, given how much I owe you. Yes, you can have a piece, and no, not as much as you want.* He leaned forward. 'The Great Sea Council's concerns regarding Aria interest me greatly. The dragon is a powerful weapon. It can be taken across the storm-dark, that much we already know.' *And push me hard enough and I might just try and go on without you, and we can both imagine how painful that would be for everyone.*

'Perhaps we should consider a cooperative proposal?' *No, I won't push you that hard. Too risky. Too uncertain.*

'Perhaps we should.'

'The council will need to understand what else will be required.'

I want to see what your dragon can really do so we both know how much it might be worth.

'Yes.' *Well, it's not like I didn't see that coming.* 'I was thinking of a demonstration. Bom Tark.' *And that look of shock you should be wearing on your face right now* ... Except there was no such look. If anything Rin looked disappointed.

'Bom Tark? Why?'

Tsen frowned. Rin didn't like this idea at all. Tsen had expected surprise, perhaps a little admiration for such audacity but not this, not disapproval. Was he *frightened*? But that wasn't the Rin who'd gone slave hunting across the dunes thirty years ago, and it left Tsen thinking he'd missed something. *Enough sparring then.* 'Where else, Rin? The dragon is a monster. A weapon. Bom Tark is a city of slaves, of outlaws and renegades ruled by no one, commanded by none and outside our law. It's been a thorn in the Great Sea Council's side for a century. How many times have we contemplated getting rid of them? But each time it's just not important enough for anyone to take the risk that they'll lose more than they gain. I have nothing to lose and a great deal to gain. Bom Tark. One dragon. Even Shonda would have to pay attention.'

'He would.' Rin nodded. 'But Bom Tark is ... useful. Sometimes.'

'And now it can be useful to me. By burning. If the dragon can do it there then it can do it in Aria. One terrible beast. Let it ravage half their empire and let them wonder where it came from. We won't destroy them completely. Just enough to cripple them for another generation and pull the Ice Witch out to where the Elemental Men can finish her.' The look on Vey Rin's face was still all wrong though. This wasn't him being appalled that Bom Tark was a city of ten thousand slaves and refugees and Tsen was talking about burning it. It wasn't about all the little uses the sea lords found for them either, the things that had kept them from being scorched off the map of Takei'Tarr in swathes of lightning long ago. For a moment Tsen was lost. *What are you thinking, old friend?*

'Bom Tark would serve as a demonstration for the council, I suppose. But ...' *But? Something ... bigger? I thought to take you aback with the scope of my ambition and now you tell me that yes, you're taken aback, but by the lack of it?*

Tsen raised his hands in defeat. 'You'll have to be a little more clear, Rin. You have something on your mind but I don't see it.'

Rin leaned forward and bared his teeth. 'There is *one* thing. Something that would wipe our slate clean. No debt, and Vespinarr will claim no part of your dragon or your eyrie or anything else. Your debts to others are another matter but I'm sure they're quite manageable.'

Yes. As you well know, since you've quietly bought most of them. Tsen could barely think. The enormity of what Rin was offering was staggering. *All our debts? No part of my dragons? So it cannot be anything but a trap.* 'I struggle to imagine, my friend, what could be worth so much.' He tried to laugh. 'You've beaten me. Enough. What share of this eyrie and these monsters do you want? Let us haggle and be done with it.'

Rin shuffled around the bath until they were sitting beside one another. 'Do Bom Tark for the council if you like, but I'm not interested. You know what I want to see scorched? Think about it.' His fingers drew a shape in the air. An unmistakable outline of two islands. With a flourish he put a little bridge between them and shuffled away back to his side, smiled and raised his glass. Tsen was too stunned to move. 'Where is your other little pet anyway? What do you call him? LaLa? You must like to live with danger, my friend. I wonder: why is your lord so driven to collect such weapons?'

'Quai'Shu keeps his own counsel there.' *Although I suppose we could ask him if he wasn't demented.* His head was full. *You want me to burn where?*

Vey Rin clambered out of the bath. 'You might want to have him check up on your friend Jima Hsian. Strange friends he has recently. *Unlikely* ones, all things considered, and you might find it clears your mind to my proposal.' He stretched. 'I think we're finished. You've done some nice design here, given what you had to work with. You always did have a taste for how a bathhouse should feel. If this all turns bad for you, Tsen, I have a place for you in Vespinarr. You'd do a much better job of this than I ever did. We could go to the tiger pits together like we used to.' Rin chuckled and shook his head. 'An evening with you and we haven't made a single wager? You must be working too hard.'

Tsen followed him out, even though all he wanted was to stay exactly where he was and have Kalaiya come and join him to tell her about the madness that Vey Rin T'Varr had just put in his head. But he didn't. Partly because what kind of a host would he be to let Vey Rin see himself out, and partly because of that last little needle there. *I could live in Vespinarr? I could be a part of your family? I could be your bathhouse designer? One tiny step above a sword-slave? I don't think so, Vey Rin T'Varr.*

It took Kalaiya, much later when Rin was gone, to point out that his offer hadn't been an offer at all. It had been a threat.

51

Lessons in Diplomacy

Patience was the prime virtue of an Elemental Man. The golems of stone stood unblinking, unmoving, sealed between doors of gold and broken glass, but patience, beyond all the Watcher's other talents, was always his greatest weapon. Sooner or later the kwen and the Lady Elesxian would decide that he was gone.

The light outside began to fade. Sooner or later they'd grow hungry.

And so they did. He admired them for their care, placing a screen of beaten golden plates where the last glass door had been, passing through curtain upon curtain of thick silver chains, keeping him out from where the Stoneguard stood if he hadn't already been inside one of them. But the golems were stone and not flesh, and so inside he was and they took him to exactly where he had wanted to be. To Quai'Shu's kwen and to Elesxian, his eldest granddaughter, whom Xican had made crude and brash. Elesxian, when the Watcher closed his eyes, sounded a lot like her father. They were talking about him, about who had sent him. Shrin Chrias Kwen had her hand in his own and knelt before her. It was all very touching.

The Watcher almost wept for them. Were they so stupid? *I serve my lord and only my lord.*

Blink. The sea lord had been explicit about the Lady Elesxian. Less so about his kwen and so he chose the kwen. He burst into the air behind him, knife at the ready. Chrias was quick. He dropped and rolled away before the Watcher could get his knife around the kwen's neck and sprang back into a defensive stance, blades drawn and swinging around him. Not that it would have saved him on another day, for the Watcher would simply appear above him, knife point down, or else burst from the ground beneath. But the kwen and his kind liked to think there was no attack that could not be blocked and the Watcher saw no reason to disabuse of him of such a ridiculous idea, not today. So he stayed where he was and sheathed the bladeless knife and held up his open hands.

'Your sea lord sends his salutations to the divine and beautiful daughter of his blood and to his faithful and ferocious kwen.' The Watcher's words were bland, the greeting carefully neutral. Elesxian spat at his feet. She was shaking. Not so stupid that she didn't realise she had no escape. Shrin Chrias Kwen shook his head, blades still a-whirr.

Blink. Inverted over the kwen's head. Finger outstretched to touch the tip of his ear, a brush of skin on skin, no more. Then back exactly where he'd been an instant before. 'You may cease your sword dance. It cannot do what you ask of it.' A pity. Now this kwen would tell others.

Shrin Chrias stopped. For a second he stood frozen. Then he sheathed his swords and one hand touched his ear.

'Baros Tsen is no sea lord!' hissed Elesxian. 'Our sea lord is Quai'Shu and he chose my father to follow him. And my father—'

'Chose no one,' said the kwen softly.

'It would have been me!'

The Watcher tried again, a little more slowly this time. 'Sea Lord Quai'Shu sends his salutations to the divine and beautiful daughter of his blood and to his faithful and ferocious kwen.' He gave the words a little time to sink in and then, while they were still staring at him and wondering what he would do next, he walked calmly to the improvised door of beaten plates of gold, pulled it open and vanished into the air.

A warning. That was all. They would understand. Shrin Chrias Kwen would not be a problem again.

52

The Touch of the Wind

After the foolishness with the alchemist Baros Tsen sent her the pick of his men. They were fine enough, sturdy specimens, well built and well hung and they claimed to be skilful. But they were slaves. Zafir scorned them and sent them back.

'*Real* men.' She smiled at Tsen when he called her to him. 'I like to hunt and stalk my prey, not pick up the leavings of others, however pretty they may be.'

'A tigress,' he said.

Her smile faded and she shook her head. 'A dragon-queen, Baros Tsen.' Maybe he meant it kindly. She could almost believe it. But if she'd had a knife with her right then she might have stabbed him for that, and patience and waiting and consequences be hanged.

When the lord of Vespinarr in his dragon robes had his moment of madness, she'd stopped Diamond Eye from killing them all. Tsen owed her for that. Another second and the dragon would have burned all the Taiytakei to ash where they stood, and Tsen too. And she could have let it. All she'd had to do was nothing at all and they'd have been dead and Diamond Eye would have feasted on their bones. She could have climbed onto his back and flown away. But she'd done what she'd done and held Diamond Eye back, and afterwards she wondered why. Because she could? To show them that she was the mistress of their dragon? Both reason enough, perhaps?

In the days that followed she thought about what might have been. Climbing onto Diamond Eye's back. Jumping off the edge of the eyrie. Vanishing out into the desert. What if she'd done that and their lightning hadn't brought her down before she got away? What then? The Elemental Man would have come for her, that's what Bellepheros always said. She'd get a mile or two before he caught her and cut her head off her shoulders and there wouldn't be a thing she could do to stop him. But when she looked, it wasn't that that had stopped her.

What if he hadn't caught her? What then? Alone in the desert. They'd hunt her. Fine – she had a dragon – she'd hunt them back. Whatever came for her she'd fight it, and sooner or later she'd die because she had nothing to protect her from the lightning or from Diamond Eye's fire.

But it wasn't that either. Maybe it was because whatever she did, whatever battles she won, she could never go home. Her old life was a world away, a crossing of the storm-dark, but it wasn't *that*. Even if she smashed and burned their world piece by piece until she forced them to take her home, even if she found a way to do that without them slitting her throat, what then? What was there? What would it look like? One rider and one dragon against whoever had taken her throne?

Closer to the mark now.

She was waiting. She hadn't realised it until now but that was the truth of it. She was waiting for something to happen. She didn't know why or what but it felt right. And she *would* return to take her throne one day, but when she did it would be with an army at her back. And she didn't know how or when, but that was how it would be, because she was who she was.

And all the time Tsen orbited those thoughts, every single one, and she had to wonder why that was. Did she like him? *Flame, I hope not*. But no, not particularly. He'd made her a slave and one day she'd kill him for that, and the thought didn't particularly trouble her. And yet while she was waiting and had nothing else to do, he fascinated her. It was his simple lack of interest. She didn't know what to do with that. However hard she tried, it wouldn't leave her alone.

The days passed. The eyrie took to moving slowly over the desert again. Three glasships floated above, pulling it along by their tethers, inching it above the dunes, hour after hour, day after day. The salt marshes and the distant rivers of the Lair of Samim vanished in the night, replaced by a sea of sand. On the far horizon a range of mountains was a constant outline in the haze. Other glasships came and went, sometimes more than one each day, and every morning great floating glass sleds drifted up carrying soldiers and desert men and barrels and crates and pens full of Linxia for the dragons to eat. They came early in the morning and spent half the day shadowing the eyrie while the rim cranes lifted animals and men and supplies for slaves to take over the wall into the dragon yard. Usually they were done by midday, sometimes not until the middle of the afternoon, and then the sleds would go south again, only to return the next morning as the eyrie made its relentless way north. With little else to do, Zafir spent her days watching the other slaves at work or dozing beside Diamond Eye, sprawled in the hot desert sun, thinking the same lazy thoughts in the same lazy circles.

Waiting. But for what?

Sometimes she picked and bit at the little hard places of the Hatchling Disease. She wore a gourd around her neck now, wore it constantly since the alchemist had given it to her. *Drink it slowly through the day, every day. Take more before you sleep. It will stop the disease from getting worse. I can do no more.* It tasted foul but she drank it anyway, and whatever was in it, the disease hadn't grown. She'd seen alchemists with these gourds before, plenty of them. When she'd been speaker she'd never known what they were for and had never thought to ask.

Tsen had seen her wearing it too but she'd heard the alchemist explain: *All riders drink this. It helps with the control of the dragon.* Her words in his mouth, because if he'd told Tsen the truth she would have ripped him apart. No one else could know. No one.

She watched the glasships as they came and went. Sometimes with Taiytakei in bright-coloured cloaks and robes and long braided hair, sometimes filled with slaves and crates and boxes quickly scurried away underground. She had no idea who or what or why. Everything she heard came from Bellepheros, and most of what *he* heard came from the enchantress, and the enchantress had become tight-lipped of late. Strange things were happening among the Taiytakei. She could sense it. Lots of to-ing and fro-ing. Something was coming, and all since that day with the mad lord from the mountains. Whatever Bellepheros knew, that was only the tip of it.

'Shrin Chrias Kwen came in the night,' Bellepheros told her, and then stopped and frowned as sparks lit up her eyes. When she asked him to go on he told her how the kwen had gone straight down the tunnels and spent the small hours of the night shouting and raving at mad old Quai'Shu. She listened, but as she did she saw the memory of Brightstar's blood spreading across polished wood. When he was done, she walked to his workbench and picked up the first knife she saw. He raised a hand, opened his mouth, then closed it again. She smiled and nodded as she left.

'A wise man knows when not to speak.' She hid the knife in her room.

When she went outside next, another glasship was over the eyrie, a silver gondola coming slowly down on its chains. Another Taiytakei lord come to see Diamond Eye. A kwen from the mountains this time, but he wasn't the kwen she was looking for.

Shrin Chrias Kwen. There was no knowing how long he'd stay. She might not have much time.

'Slave!'

She jumped. The black-cloaks had come up behind her and she'd been so deep in ways to kill their kwen that she hadn't even noticed. They led her away to one of the squat towers that dotted the flying castle's walls. Tsen was there, staring out at the sand. The t'varr didn't turn to look at her, just waved the black-cloaks away. Something had changed in him the day Diamond Eye nearly burned them all. She'd wondered at first if the dragon fear had got to him, but it wasn't that. His mind was somewhere else. Some heavy new burden he carried. One heavy enough to show.

'I found this eyrie three hundred miles from here,' he said without turning. 'It took me a month to move it. Quai'Shu thought it would serve well for the dragons. It would appear he was right.'

Zafir looked out across the desert. Far off to one side the dunes gave way to stone crags, lifeless and bare, before rising on to the distant mountains. Ahead was a sea of sand, rolling as far as she could see. This was how the northern dragon realms had been, though she'd never seen them with her own eyes. Hyram, Shezira, Lystra, they'd all come from a land like this.

Lystra. For a moment her fists clenched. Sometimes her ankle still ached, even now.

'You disagree?' Tsen misread her.

'Safe enough from assassins and thieves and poisoners.' She shrugged and took a sip from her gourd.

'More so as we fly further into the Empty Sands but there will soon be no herds of animals for our dragons to eat. The alchemist says this is necessary. Is it?'

Zafir shrugged. 'In Bloodsalt riders used to fly their beasts from the eyrie to far-off feeding grounds.' Bloodsalt. Another place she'd never been, but Hyram had come from Bloodsalt. He'd talked about it sometimes after he'd spent himself inside her, while she was trying to keep herself from being sick. 'Perhaps it makes matters hard for the alchemists with their potions – I wouldn't know – but otherwise I see no reason it couldn't be done here once Diamond Eye can be flown. Why would you move, though. Nowhere is safe from your Elemental Men, is that not so?' Nowhere that wasn't surrounded by gold or silver or iron, if she had it right. Was that why the eyrie had grown so many iron doors of late? Curious how they'd arrived and then gone and then come back again, either side of the mad mountain lord coming to visit.

Tsen beckoned her out onto the walls. Diamond Eye was perched across the yard, his claws and his jaws clenched tight, tail lashing back and forth with a tense energy. Now and then he opened his wings and stretched. He'd been like this for days now, pausing only when he was fed as though he sensed what was coming. 'The alchemist says you do not need your dragon-rider clothes, that thick furs will do.'

Look at you, Diamond Eye. How eager you are. You yearn to fly, don't you? How long have they kept you tethered? Well so do I, and so we shall! Zafir looked to the part of the yard where Bellepheros had hung the skins of the hatchlings he'd butchered for their blood. An adult dragon would take a month to burn from the inside and be cool to the touch again. For some reason hatchlings took even longer. Their skins were hanging now, the Scales treating them with vinegar and scraping them with salt. 'Yes,' she said. 'If they're thick enough to turn the wind and the cold. But I will need a helm. The wind is blinding and a blind rider is of little use.' Another few days and the skin would be ready to cut. Hatchling skins weren't as thick as dragon-scale from an adult but they made more flexible armour, and either would turn fire and that was mostly what mattered.

'The harness is sufficient?' Tsen was looking down too, but

not at the hatchlings. He was looking at the silver gondola from Vespinarr, and Zafir wondered why he wasn't down there welcoming today's guest. It wasn't like him.

'It is.' She'd seen to *that* at least. Diamond Eye must have worn the same harness for almost a month by now without it being changed once. Bellepheros apparently didn't know how. They'd have to do something about that.

Tsen still didn't look at her. 'Chay-Liang says your helm is ready. Today you'll fly for me and show me what a dragon does.'

Zafir almost purred. 'And once I'm in the air, how will you stop me from turning my dragon against you, from burning every creature here to ash and smashing your castle to rubble?' Down on the wall Diamond Eye turned his head and looked straight at her almost as though he'd heard her thoughts.

Tsen barked out a laugh. 'In time Chay-Liang will make a collar for you so you cannot turn your dragon against me, slave. For now you will have a guardian. The Watcher. You will do as you are told today or he will kill you instantly and never mind that I have no other rider. Do you understand me?'

Zafir raised an eyebrow at his back. 'I understand, Baros Tsen T'Varr. Are there enemies out in the desert? A city you wish me to destroy? For *that* is what dragons do.'

'Not yet.' At last Tsen turned to look at her. He held up his hands and then bared his teeth. 'I would apologise for my terrible manners, slave. But since you *are* a slave, I shall not.' He had a coldness to him, something she hadn't seen when they'd flown across the world in his glasship together. It had come over him in the last few days. He seemed somehow disappointed in her and it made her want to please him, and that in turn made her unreasonably angry. *Please him? Who is he to call a dragon-queen his slave? Burn him, that's what you should want!*

And I do, she told herself. *And I will. But it's more complicated than that.*

Complicated? When was the last time it had mattered to her to please anyone at all? She'd wrenched that out of herself years ago, hadn't she? But as she wondered, she found herself staring into a wall of doubts and fears that she didn't dare to touch.

I want to break him.

You'd better.

'Have I upset you?' she asked.

'*Upset* me?' Tsen closed his eyes and shook his head and looked away at the dragon. 'You are a slave, dragon-queen. An important one, I will allow, but that is still what you are. Show me what this dragon can do today. Show me that my sea lord's madness and his ruin of our fleets has not been in vain.'

He beckoned her away from the tower and they walked together past the first of the long tubes pointed up into the sky, mounted on the familiar pivots she knew from the scorpions in the Pinnacles and the Adamantine Palace. The tubes were set at a high angle, several of them to each mount and all slightly different. She looked at them. Bellepheros had said they were weapons, but if they were she had no idea how they worked. 'These. They are like scorpions?'

'Cannon,' said Tsen, his thoughts somewhere else.

'That's a name for which I have no meaning.'

He paused for a moment, gave her a puzzled look, then stepped towards the nearest. As he did, soldiers came hurrying along the wall towards it, anticipating his desire. They were Taiytakei, these soldiers, not slaves. Tsen turned back to Zafir and for a moment his coldness was gone. 'In our world our power lies with our fleet. Our ships are our heart, our wealth, our treasure. You understand that, I think. They are that which makes us what we are and so they are perhaps a little like your dragons. It's been a very long time since one sea lord last waged war against another.' His eyes wandered just for a moment and there was a flicker of a hesitation in his voice. He caught it quickly, so fast she almost didn't hear it. Almost. Then he was smiling, his mask intact again. 'The Elemental Men respond quite, ah … *finally* to such things, you see. But there are others who ply the seas.' He looked up to the glassships towing the eyrie deeper into the desert. 'And also the skies.' One of the Taiytakei soldiers had hopped onto a small sled and had flown to the top of the tubes now. Zafir watched. The soldier dropped a cloth bag as large and heavy as a sack of flour into the top of one of them. Then a bundle of straw rammed in hard with a long pole. Finally he tipped in a basket of black iron balls each as big as a clenched fist. Tsen beckoned her on, away. 'At sea a ship may outrun a glassship but a fleet at anchor or a city or this castle cannot. You have seen a glassship float above Khalishtor and pour water upon fire; imagine if you will that it might pour fire instead.' He turned back to the soldiers around the cannon. 'Put your hands over your ears, slave, and watch carefully the mouth of the barrel.'

Zafir put her hands over her ears. Tsen made a gesture. The soldiers retreated, all except one who struck the base of the tube with a heavy hammer. A flash of flame burst from the mouth of the cannon. The entire castle shook beneath Zafir's feet and then came a smell that reminded her of sickening dragon. The noise, though, *that* was a terror, worse than the lightning-throwers the Taiytakei soldiers carried on their belts. Even with her hands pressed to her ears it reached inside and filled her, and as it left it shook her bones so hard she thought she might never hear again.

'The balls of iron fly into the air.' Tsen's voice sounded strange until Zafir realised he was shouting at her and it was the ringing in her own ears that made him sound so odd. 'Hard enough to shatter the glass of a glassship. Did you see them?'

Numb, Zafir shook her head. No, all she'd seen was the flame, and then the noise had devoured everything. And Diamond Eye, jerking on his wall across the eyrie, snapping round to stare, wings flared, fangs bare.

'No. They travel very fast. These cannon, as you see, are tiresomely slow to prepare and desperately unwieldy. It is a delicate dance between sky and ground, slow and fatal. Sadly, unlike a lightning cannon, a weapon such as this cannot be placed on any ship. I wonder, though, how useful it might be against a dragon.' He cocked his head but Zafir couldn't even think yet. She closed her eyes and shook her head and staggered away and Tsen had to get one of his soldiers to help her. It took minutes before the ringing cleared enough for her to take a deep breath and turn and look back at the cannon. A slight haze of ugly brown smoke still hung around the end of its barrel.

'No use at all, I would say,' she said at last, as her mind found its sharpness again.

'None?' He laughed at her.

'I've seen dragons carry stones and casks of fire and drop them from on high but that is not a rider's way. Fire and tooth and tail and claw. I will come at you low and fast.' She laughed at him.

'Take me to my Diamond Eye, Baros Tsen T'Varr, and you will see.' Her ears were still singing to the sound of the cannon but she could barely hold herself in now. The anticipation. The thrill. *To ride a dragon again* ...

The Scales were waiting for them, and Bellepheros and the usual Taiytakei black-cloaks with their spiked ashgars. The alchemist held up a thick and formless coat as Zafir came near. Like a rider's dragon-scale riding coat except there was no dragon-scale and the coat was made of thick furs and looked as big as a tent. Two Scales stepped out in front of the alchemist and placed a pair of boots in front of Zafir's feet. They were enormous, heavy leather and lined with more fur. She felt immediately clumsy with her feet inside them. 'I look ridiculous.'

'It is the best I can do with what is here.' Bellepheros hung his head. 'The dragon-scale will be another week before it's ready. These will keep you safe from your own fire, though. The coat is clumsy too.' Then he shook his head and looked even more ashamed. 'The gauntlets are worse, I'm afraid.'

He held them out to her after she'd wrapped the coat around her like a robe and the Scales had tied a steel chain around her waist. Mittens! She looked at the alchemist, horrified, but it was that or nothing, and on a dragon's back the wind could flay the skin from your fingers and freeze your hands to your harness, while the wash of your own dragon's fire could burn them to the bone. Still ... Zafir shook her head. 'This one time, Master Alchemist. I will not fly like this again.'

The alchemist lifted his eyes to hers for a moment. 'Holiness, I beg this may be a small compensation. The first part of your true rider's armour.' A Scales lifted some shapeless thing off the ground; Bellepheros pulled away the cloth that covered it, and underneath was the most perfect dragon helm that Zafir had ever seen. There was no wind visor, no fire visor, only a perfect curve of gold-glass. The cheeks were golden, puffed out and with a series of wide slits below the ear like the gills of a fish for breathing in the wind, and the crown and the sides and the back were yet more gold, ornate and carved with rampant dragons, yet swept back so as not to drag in the wind. The nosepiece was pointed like the beak of a bird, gold again, and the parts that covered the mouth and jaw pivoted open beneath the ear and were lined with more air slits. Fighting dragons entwined around one another, etched into the metal. She'd never seen anything like it, and when she put it on it felt so light on her head that she might almost have been wearing nothing at all. She closed the jaw piece. Breathing was effortless. And she could *see*. She could see as though she had nothing on at all. In all the dragon realms there had never been a helm so magnificent. A shiver ran through her. *To see, finally to be able to see as Diamond Eye breathes his fire. No blurry-eyed wind visor, no blindness as the fire shield comes down! To see it all, all the terrible beauty ...* A shiver ran through her.

'Liang made it to my design.' Bellepheros looked pleased with himself and for once Zafir didn't think to slap him down. For this even she would let him puff his chest. 'Dragon-scale would be better than gold, but the glass will not melt until long after you no longer care and the gold is mostly decoration.'

A helm of glass and gold. 'It's exquisite.' A dragon-rider's dream. Any one of them would sell their ancestors for a helm such as this. She bowed to him, something a speaker had never done to a grand master of the Order of the Scales since Narammed, but he deserved it for such a gift in this strange place. She smiled as he blanched and almost staggered in gratitude. 'It's a pity I can't honour you for this as you deserve, Grand Master.' She wiggled the jaw piece, locking it into place and then opening it again. It was perfect and it made her look once more at the glasships dragging them through the air. *Do they make everything like this? No wonder we seem to them like barbarians.*

Barbarians with dragons, she reminded herself. She let out a deep sigh of pleasure and smiled, then turned to Tsen with the helm still on and was pleased to see him at least blink. *What a sight I must be. You should see me with the dragon-scale armour I wear for war. A true dragon-queen to make you wet your precious silk pants. Pity it all went to the bottom of the Sea of Storms.* 'Shall I mount?'

Tsen clicked his fingers. 'Watcher!'

'You don't need him today. Today I'll fly for you because I desire it, and for no other reason. And because you've both given me such a pretty helm, I'll show off as best I can what my dragon might do for you.' She cocked her head at Tsen. 'Thank you, Sea Lord.' He wasn't that, of course, but she knew it both needled and flattered him.

'The Watcher will be there, nonetheless.'

She let her smile linger over his disdain. 'When you ask me to fly to war, and you will, I would like a sword. Not much use for a dragon-rider, I know, but still it is a tradition. I think your enchanters must make quite exquisite blades.'

Tsen snorted. 'Mount, slave.' He meant it as a slight, a retort to her refusal to address him as anything more than an equal and to the mocking she let slip into her voice. But that was good. Every little reminder of her fragile place in his order of the world added to the flames in her belly. *I will have you. One way or the other I will get my fingers under your skin and you'll be mine. Jehal, Hyram, Tichane, they all fell one way or the other. I'll find your weakness, Baros Tsen, and then I will own you.*

She turned and walked to the dragon, waving it down, head cocked, arms outstretched, clucking her tongue, gestures any trained dragon should understand. It responded, lowering its shoulders and its neck, bending its head down to the ground.

'I remember you, Diamond Eye,' she said, quietly and to no one but the dragon. 'I watched you grow. I picked you out to be one of my own. You were never as huge as Onyx or as fast as Glory but I never forgot you. You must be getting old now.' Of course the dragon couldn't hear her, couldn't understand her, not if Bellepheros was feeding it his potions. But it was watching her. It had its head turned towards her and its eyes followed her steps. *Potions or no, you do understand at least a little, don't you?*

Diamond Eye bared his teeth. He flared his wings, sending a wind across the yard.

'Frisky today!' She smiled. *Good. We both need this. We both want the same thing.*

Behind her she felt the air pop.

'Do not forget I am watching,' said a voice, and when she turned he was there, the Watcher standing rigid behind her, stony-faced and teeth gritted, taut with tension and breathing hard. He nodded to her and there was another pop of air as he went rigid and vanished again.

'Oh, but I will,' she whispered. 'For a little while I will forget everything.'

The mounting ropes were in a terrible state but at least they were there. She climbed up onto Diamond Eye's back and began looking for the buckles. The last time the dragon had flown, it had flown to war. The harness was meant for battle where it would become a part of the rider's armour from the waist down. Which was a blessed relief, because it meant she could throw away at least the boots. She struggled to fit inside with Bellepheros's bulky coat around her, had to lift it up and balloon it around the saddle. But she did, and if she'd had to she would have thrown away the coat and ridden in silks to be on a dragon's back once more. With the last strap done she sighed into the harness and smiled at the sky and closed her eyes.

'Everything,' she whispered. 'Now fly, my winged half-god, my deathbringer. Fly and show them who you are.'

Diamond Eye leaped into the air. He was flying in a single bound and one mighty pull of his wings and with such strength that Zafir pitched backwards and would have fallen off if it hadn't been for the harness. He drove into the air, strong and urgent and powerful, exultant in his freedom from the earth. On other days Zafir might have felt a twinge of caution, for the Diamond Eye she'd known had never been so strong, nor had any dragon she'd ever flown, but the dragon's joy of simply being aloft once more flooded through her, merged with her own and drove all other thoughts away. *To fly! To be free!* Up and up and up until the castle below was a dark speck in a sea of orange waves. The wind was a hurricane over her. It tore at her face and at her furs, but the helm held and she could see as she'd never seen before. If there had been clouds then she would have gone on higher still, up above them and into the deep and endless blue above, to the holy sky where only a dragon-rider could fly and sometimes the ancestors and even the gods themselves would send their visions. But there were no clouds in the desert and so she turned Diamond Eye and dived towards the ground once more, wings tucked in, legs pressed back, her own head squeezed into the dragon's shoulders as the hurricane became something more and the roar of it was as loud as Tsen's cannon in her ear.

The ground hurtled back at them. Diamond Eye spread his wings. A monstrous hand crushed Zafir into his back, pressing so hard she thought she must snap into pieces. The world went grey and narrowed to a single spot of brightness and then she must have passed out for a few seconds, for the next thing she knew they were hurtling straight at the eyrie, sideways on, faster than she'd ever flown before, and the perfect helm was such a weight that she thought her neck might snap rather then keep her head pressed down into Diamond Eye's scales.

Straight at the eyrie wall. At the last second Diamond Eye dropped his nose and rolled. He shot beneath it. Purple light filled the air and a bright flash of violet. Zafir had a moment to see the lightning and then Diamond Eye twisted and stretched out his wings and flipped onto his back between the castle and the sand. He shot upside down between them with the sand howling past a few spans beneath Zafir's head and a part of her wanted to scream at the pain as her muscles wrenched her down against the wind, to cry out in alarm, for a dragon had never flown on its back for her before and she couldn't remember the last time she'd had so little control; and at the same time she was whooping with joy at the madness, the power, the freedom, the unfettered joy. Out from under the castle Diamond Eye rolled again. 'Up, up!' she cried, and so he climbed and they spiralled high once more until he found what she was looking for. A dozen miles away, deep in the sands on the edge of a black tar lake, far out of her own meagre sight. A tented town of nomads, of dark-skinned Taiytakei, of their horses and their Linxia, and the hunger was like a sharp spike through her belly and she wanted to feed, to hunt, to *burn*! *NOW!*

'No!' She brought Diamond Eye back down, his resentment squirming through her like a knot of angry snakes, and flew him across the sands in front of the eyrie instead. She let loose his fire there, down in the open where the watchers from the eyrie would clearly see. The dragon ravaged the dunes, burned and burned and burned them in an endless stream of fire until the sand became glass and she could smell the smouldering of her furs amid the heat around her. As they passed the eyrie again, Diamond Eye lashed the empty wall with his tail, slashing out a great chunk of the white stone that even the enchantress couldn't mark. *See! See what I can do! See what* we *can do! Find us with your cannon if you can, Baros Tsen!*

She let Diamond Eye have his way now and flew to the nomads and their tents. She let the dragon burn them black and eat his fill from the savaged remains and she couldn't have said which one of them it satisfied more. They were Taiytakei, and she was a slave.

And when they were both done, when they'd gorged themselves and were finally sated and bloated with the exhilaration, when Diamond Eye came to rest and paced the ground, she climbed down and threw away Bellepheros's stupid furs and his stupid mittens and felt the sand under her feet, the first true earth since she'd flown to war above her beloved Silver City. She felt the wind on her skin and the eyrie was small and distant, a dozen miles away across the sand.

Free.

Behind her the air popped. She wondered, briefly, if the Elemental Man had come to kill her for what they'd done, and found that she simply didn't care. She'd laugh in his face as she died, and then Diamond Eye would eat him.

'It would be best for you to return,' he said. 'They are becoming anxious.'

Zafir laughed. When she climbed up into the harness, the Elemental Man came up and sat behind her. Diamond Eye launched himself into the air once more, fat and slow and languorous this time. 'Are you impressed?' she called as they rose into the sky, but he didn't answer and when she looked round the Elemental Man was gone again.

A little frisky she would answer later, when Bellepheros asked how Diamond Eye had flown. The glorious truth was something that would for ever be hers alone. No dragon had ever flown like that for her before. Nor for anyone.

53

Stiff Around the Edges

Bellepheros watched the dragon fly away, squinting into the brightness of the desert sky and the glare of the sands. He watched the faces of the soldiers and of Baros Tsen and of the Taiytakei from the silver gondola, the kwen from this other place of Vespinarr. If he believed Li, the whole day was staged for this man. The Taiytakei kept their awe well hidden, but now and then a twitch gave each of them away. A touch of amazement at the speed of the dragon's ascent – even Bellepheros was surprised by *that*. A twinge of fear as it flew so high that it vanished from sight and they stood with their heads tipped back, faces screwed up against the sun and vast blue sky – always the chance that Tsen had somehow misjudged, that Zafir would choose to flee, that the dragon would escape even from an Elemental Man. Staring up alongside them, hands doing their best to shield his eyes from the sun, a part of Bellepheros hoped that Zafir did exactly that. Another part of him hoped she didn't, but with Zafir he simply couldn't be sure. Quietly, in the inner thoughts he never shared with anyone, it beggared belief that anyone had thought she'd make a good speaker.

For a minute or two he really thought she'd gone, rocketed off across the desert never to return, but then she came back and boiled the sand into glowing glass, and not even the Taiytakei could hide their shock at that; and when the dragon lashed the wall with its tail and sliced a chunk away and the whole castle shook beneath their feet and pieces of stone as big as a man's head fizzed right across the dragon yard and soldiers and slaves and Scales ran screaming, the Taiytakei watching from the wall cried out too, a sharp dagger of fear through them all, their masks for a moment broken. In their part of the yard the hatchlings shrieked and flapped their wings and strained at their chains at the frightened Scales around them.

Bellepheros hurried off the wall to restore some calm. She should have come back right then, he thought. Swerved in the air and crashed into the wall right in front of them before they assembled their faces again. She could have seen them as they truly were; but instead Zafir flew Diamond Eye away and for a long time there was nothing save a pall of smoke on the horizon. Even after he'd settled his Scales and the hatchlings, she still hadn't returned, and by then the Taiytakei had begun to lose interest.

Later he watched as the Elemental Man came and went. The killer had something wrong with him and it was never more obvious than today. By then most of the Taiytakei had gone and weren't there to notice, but the Watcher was almost dead on his feet. He was struggling to shift, exhausted every time he did it, gasping for breath and wet with sweat. Even under the desert sun Bellepheros had never once seen the Elemental Man sweat until the dragons had come.

When Zafir returned, the Taiytakei came back up to the walls to watch the dragon land. The dragon came slowly, with long leisurely beats of its wings. It pitched up and landed gently, towering over the white stone wall, the sun behind it so that when it reared up and stretched its wings it cast the whole of the yard into shadow. The air filled with a sweeping satisfaction. It oozed from the dragon like honey, a cloud of feeling spreading out across the eyrie to touch them all. Bellepheros had been around dragons for long enough to know it for what it was and brush it aside but its force unsettled him. Diamond Eye had an energy, a hunger, a *need*. Dragons always did, all of them, even back in the dragon realms, but not like this. Here all those things were somehow magnified. It wasn't only Diamond Eye either – the hatchlings were the same. He had no idea why this world should be different but it was, and it left him with a deep and lingering unease that he could never quite shake. Dragons took the thoughts and emotions of their riders and mingled them with their own, even Zafir knew that, but they sensed other things too. Was it the eyrie? They could feel things that were beyond the senses of any rider or alchemist. Old things. Deep things. For all the discipline of the Order of the Scales, their potions, their lore, there was so much they didn't know. So much lost when the Silver King was struck down.

He watched Zafir slide down from the saddle and walk away

from Diamond Eye, sashaying along the wall. Alchemists learned to wall away the hungers and desires that came from the dragons around them; riders did the opposite. They rode those desires, mingling them with their own, guiding and steering if they could, if they were strong enough, succumbing to them if they weren't. Zafir, he could see, was on the edge. She was a like a lizard basking in the sun, a sleepy lioness sprawled with a full belly beside a fresh kill. She walked barefoot towards the watching Taiytakei, furs left Flame-knew-where, helm under her arm and swaying as she walked, swinging her hips in the afterglow of the dragon's flight. As for the Taiytakei? He had no idea how the dragon's desires would touch them or how deep they might reach.

'And now you know,' Zafir smiled at Tsen as she reached them and touched her finger to the tip of his nose, 'what a dragon can be. I trust you are now pleased?'

Bellepheros had seen the Taiytakei after she'd lashed the castle wall, the naked awe raw and impossible to hide, but that had been hours ago. Tsen had found his calm again. 'You damaged my eyrie, slave,' he said.

'Because you wanted to see, Sea Lord Tsen.' Her eyes glittered. 'They are for war, these glorious creatures. Nothing else.'

She was too wrapped up in her own satisfaction to see the tension in the t'varr. They each turned away from the other, Tsen back to his guests and soldiers, Zafir to Bellepheros. She lifted an arm towards him and for a moment he thought she meant to put it round his shoulder. She caught herself, frowned and then smiled.

'Were our lords pleased?' This close he could see her eyes were as wide as a dust-eater's, drunk on the dragon's joy. Dangerous. She was bright, flushed, face agleam with sweat, her hair matted and wet, damp patches where her silks clung to her skin.

Bellepheros bowed, cautious. He took her by the arm and led her gently away, and for once she didn't resist, didn't slap him with her eyes for his audacity. She needed to be away from the dragon, he thought, as far away as he could take her. 'They were, Holiness. And fearful, though they do not show it now.' Perhaps if they were quick, there would be time to talk alone now. Distant eyes always kept watch on him, but Tsen liked to give his slaves the illusion that they were free, that they were his guests. It was a dangerous freedom and yet a cunning one. *They make us a part of their own but the words we think we speak in secret are always overheard.* Tuuran might have said that all those months ago, but perhaps while the Tsen and his generals and his Elemental Man were all together, engrossed ...

He stole a glance at the dragon purring on the wall. *Is an alchemist ever free? No. We enslave one another, monster and man.*

They crossed the dragon yard, past the hatchlings still chained to the walls. The hatchlings were furious – he could feel the rage as he passed them. Maybe Zafir could work with them soon. Maybe the bigger ones were ready. Perhaps it was time to start making harnesses for them.

'They want to fly,' Zafir said.

'They do.'

'They're envious of me.' She laughed. 'And who wouldn't be?' She stopped him out there in the yard, right out in the open beside the snapping hatchlings, and pressed a hand to his chest. 'There's something about this place, Bellepheros. I've never known a dragon fly the way Diamond Eye flew for me today. Never such ... *passion*!' She dropped her hand and looked away. 'You said it might be this way and you were right. Why, Master Alchemist? Why do they have such a hunger here? My skin tingles with it, my blood is hot. They have so much desire! I haven't felt like this after flying for years!'

Bellepheros shook his head and took a step away. 'A mystery, Holiness. I cannot tell you why it is so, but yes, I have seen it.' He tried to move her away from the hatchlings, further away from Diamond Eye. Get her down under the ground where at least they couldn't see each other. 'You shouldn't stand here, Holiness. The Hatchling Disease ...'

'Yes.' She smiled at him again but now her eyes had changed. The wonder was gone. She was a predator. As he guided her towards their passageway beneath the eyrie, her feet dragged. On the steps into the cold white glow of the tunnels, she stopped again. Her gaze lingered on Diamond Eye and the dragon stared back, a look of shared secrets.

'I have something for you,' Bellepheros said, reaching for anything he could think of.

Zafir's eyes snapped to his, curious and eager. 'What?'

'Come, Holiness.'

He took her down the spiralling tunnels. Zafir kept walking ahead, long strides, then turning, waving at him to hurry up until he was almost running at her heels. When they reached his study, Zafir closed his new iron-cased door behind them. Bellepheros never bothered. There was a lock too and he never used that either, because locks in this place were an illusion. Perhaps the Elemental Man could move through the white stone or perhaps he couldn't but he could certainly move through the air. His ear might be anywhere, always.

'What? What is it?'

'Here.' He gave her a fresh gourd. Zafir tossed half of it down with a careless lack of interest.

'This?' She snorted and hung the gourd around her neck. 'You brought me down here for *this*?'

'Not just that, Holiness.' He turned and started to rummage through the papers and books and glass beakers on his workbench. He could have given her poison just then and how would she have known? But then dragon-kings and dragon-queens had always trusted their alchemists to do as they were told for the greater good of the realms. It was just that it was a little more complicated now. *Whose* greater good and *which* realms had never been problems for any master alchemist before.

'Well?' He could feel her impatient energy, even with his back to her. He just needed to keep her here a while, that was all.

'I'm afraid that potion's not as good as I could make were I in the Palace of Alchemy.' He wondered how much to say, but in the end she was still his queen and more his mistress than Tsen or any of the Taiytakei. Trust. It all came to trust. Zafir trusted his potions and that he would keep the dragons calm so he must trust her to speak for the realm that had once been their home. 'The dragons *are* restless here,' he said, slow and unsure of how far to go. *Do you even care?* At last he found what he was looking for and mixed a little of the powder with a drop of his own blood, carefully so she wouldn't see, and a cup of water. He offered it to her.

'I could hardly not have noticed, Master Alchemist.' She gave him a hungry smile. 'Was that why you brought me down here, out of the sun and the light? To tell me that?'

'Holiness …' Were the Taiytakei somehow different too? Because they *were* different, from the colour of their skin onwards. Was that it? He put the cup on his workbench and pushed it towards her. 'Please … This will help with the … to regain your composure, Holiness.'

'What do you mean, alchemist?' Her eyes narrowed and bored into him as though she already knew. *Trust trust trust. And how much, really, should I trust you? For when I was taken from the realms you were barely a queen and Aliphera's death was far too strange to ignore, and yet in a few short months you became ruler of us all. And so young! How, Dragon-Queen Zafir? May I ask how?*

'There is no shame, but …' He stopped. She was nodding. He winced, half expecting her to strike him down where he stood. A slap, certainly … but no. She just looked at him, that hungry predator look she'd worn ever since she'd come down from the back of the dragon. Full of scorn and desire.

And then burst out laughing. She took his cup and threw it away. 'Alchemist! I am not some squealing virgin back from her first dragon. This hunger?' She clasped a hand to her breast. 'Do you think I don't know it for what it is?' She leaned over him, her face close to his, and he sank back into his chair. 'I am a dragon-queen, alchemist, and I am mistress of both of us, and this … *thing* that you think you see? I am still its mistress even if I revel in riding it.' She bared her teeth. 'It *is* strong, though.'

Like a dragon. Bellepheros swallowed hard. 'The Taiytakei will listen to you,' he said, 'for a time. You have their minds. They have seen the possibilities and they will want to know more. Everything. Give them what it pleases you to give, Holiness. Tease them.' He could feel the heat of her as she stared down at him, burning through her shifting silks. 'Tsen had the Vespinarr man beside him to watch you but there were others. Many others. I couldn't see them where they stood so I cannot speak for the faces they wore, but for any who saw you fly today, their world has changed.'

'Shrin Chrias Kwen? Did *he* see?' Her face lit up. He watched her hunger turn murderous. *Prey.*

'I do not know, Holiness.'

'No matter. I can't imagine he missed it.' She licked her lips and ran a finger along the skin of her neck, over the scar from the hatchling on Quai'Shu's ship. Then held out the dragon helm Li had made. 'A fine gift, Master Alchemist. You must tell me one day how I may reward you. Make the rest as you made this and I will be pleased.'

He bowed. 'Holiness.'

Zafir tossed her head, turned for the door and then paused. 'Bellepheros, the potions you make for your Scales, the ones to keep the Hatchling Disease at bay, have you told your mistress Chay-Liang the secrets of their preparation?'

'Some but not all. I have been careful, Holiness. Besides, only those with the Silver King in their blood can make such potions.' He bit his lip.

'Keep that secret safe, Master Alchemist. Keep it very safe.' Half a smile twitched at the corner of her mouth. Perhaps he imagined it but there seemed a terrible purpose to her eyes. He bowed as she walked away.

'Holiness ...'

She didn't turn back. 'Bellepheros?'

Did you do it? Were you the one? Did you throw your mother from her dragon's back? What did I see back there in Furymouth between you and Jehal? How did you come to be speaker when it should have been Shezira? What happened in the realms after I was gone? Subtle clues for the subtle mind here and there. And the not so subtle, for here was a dragon-queen, the speaker of the nine realms no less, taken as a slave; but the dragons had taken all his time and all his thoughts until now. *What did you do, Speaker of the Nine Realms? What did you do?*

The words froze in his mouth, unsaid. They were here now and surrounded by enemies and so perhaps it shouldn't matter any more. He bowed his head. 'I serve you, Holiness. You above all.'

Zafir laughed, a little singing sound. 'Well that's as you should, Master Alchemist, and very good to hear.' And she was gone, and all he could do was wonder, *Am I doing the right thing? I whose duty is to enslave monsters?*

54

The Devourers

The dragon was doing it. The Watcher blinked deep in the night under the desert stars, closer and closer to the monster's side to be sure, but it *was* the dragon, its very presence. The closer he came, the harder it was, and that was the simple truth of it. In the dragon realms a windwalker had been killed by a man with a crossbow not long before Quai'Shu stole the dragons. Beneath his scorn the Watcher had been shaken by that. A man who could become the wind should never fall to a mere crossbow. The Picker used to swear the hardness of shifting his form in the dragon-realm came from the dragons themselves; now the Watcher knew he was right.

He flew with the air to Khalishtor, where Nimpo Jima Hsian was supposed to be taking their sea lord's place at the Great Sea Council, as a hsian often did, but of course he wasn't there and had passed on the duty to his own t'varr. Another thing a hsian often did.

From one place to the next, then, one man and then another, holding the bladeless knife at their throats and asking where Quai'Shu's hsian might be found. A tedium made bearable by the relief of shifting effortlessly from place to place within the City of Gold and Glass. It didn't take long to find the answer. The hsian was in Dhar Thosis. The Watcher tried to see the reason behind such a defection, for there could be little doubt that was what it was. The lord of Vespinarr had already known and told the Hands of the Sea Lord where to look, in his own subtle way.

Before he left for the long crossing of the desert, he stood at the edge of the sea and faced the city where no one ruled, shadowed by the mountain of the Septtych of the Elemental Masters. He bowed to both and stepped back over the edge of the harbour wall and fell in among the waves, and as he touched them he became the water. Currents. Temperatures. All too subtle for a man to see but the Watcher felt them. They were his guide, his map and compass. They took him a little way up the coast to the old Tomb of Ten Tazei where he walked past the shrine and into the cave and passed effortlessly through the wall of stones that barred its end and on to Ten Tazei's path to Xibaiya and the land of the dead. Secrets lay here. Old ones best forgotten, and the Elemental Men were their guardians.

'These dragons make me weak.'

The sand and the stone took his words and ate them with silence. The Watcher closed his eyes and tasted the air, filled with salt and the sea. The distant hiss of waves on the sand kissed his ear. The cave was still. Time could stop in a place like this. He'd come here sometimes with the Picker. Now he came here alone, but it was still their place to speak together. He felt the Picker's memories most closely here.

The men here have their navigators and their enchanters. In Aria they have sorcerers of the old ways once more. Pale nothings beside the silver half-gods of the moon but they are learning at last. The priests of the Dominion call power from the old gods themselves. But in the realms of the dragons? Nothing. Alchemy. A dance with potions and a dabble with blood. There's nothing there for the likes of us to hunt.

Blood. The alchemist got his power from his own blood. The last refuge for a sorcerer's power. The most potent place.

Why? Why did the dragon realms alone have no true sorcerers? The answer had been staring at him. There were no sorcerers in the dragon realms because the dragons had devoured the nameless boundless flow of life from which all mages drew, even the Elemental Men.

'How?'

No answer.

'Can they not be destroyed?'

The cave and the endless tunnel downward mocked him with their stillness.

55
Need

Zafir walked back out across the dragon yard, smiling at Diamond Eye and at the sun, Myst and Onyx trailing in her wake. She felt drunk. Tipsy with joy. Her skin tingled, hot in the desert heat. Her head still buzzed from the sheer ecstasy of the dragon. Maybe once, maybe the first time she'd ridden on a monster's back with her mother in front of her to guide the beast, maybe then she'd felt this before. Or the first time she'd taken old Azure into the sky alone with no one to sit beside her and watch over her and tell her what to do, just weeks before Hyram had taken the throne she stole from him ten years later. The sheer unadulterated freedom. Azure, slow and small and old. He'd burned to ash from the inside not many years later but she remembered him as well as she remembered any of them. Pale blue scales that flashed in the sun, and if he was old and slow then he hadn't seemed that way when she'd ridden him up above the three mountaintops of the Pinnacles, higher and higher until everything below was specks and streaks and had lost its colour, where the air was so thin she could barely breathe; and then they'd dived, three miles straight down, and her head had roared and swum and she'd known that nothing, *nothing* in the world, could possibly be like this, and for all the horror that awaited her, whatever they did to her when she came back to earth, none of that would matter any more, and the pain and rage and the fear of even being alive, they all became small things, a suffering that no longer had substance. They'd flown for hours, far longer than they were supposed to, and she'd been punished for that, but it had been worth it. She sometimes thought it was the greatest lesson her mother and her many lovers had taught her. They'd surely never meant to, they'd certainly very quickly regretted it, but she'd never, ever, forgotten. That sometimes there came a point where punishment didn't matter any more.

In the middle of the yard she paused, looked up to the sky, closed her eyes and soaked in the sun and the warmth and the dragon's wild hunger. In the years after that day with Azure she'd flown more and more. She'd become a rider, a dragon-princess. The joy had faded, too familiar perhaps, but she never quite forgot, and every time she climbed onto a dragon's back she closed her eyes and thought of that day and of what had come after. She'd looked for it everywhere. With dragons at first. With men, when she'd come to understand what they could do for her. She'd found it for fleeting moments with Jehal, who would die a thousand deaths if she ever found him again. She'd come close over Evenspire in the wild mad fury of that fight; lost herself here and there for little moments until the battle had turned sour. Afterwards, when she was sure she was alone, she'd wept, wept as the little girl who'd found the door to heaven and lost it again.

And here, of all places, she'd found it once more. *Joy.*

'Mistress is pleased.' Myst had found her voice these days.

'Mistress is,' murmured Zafir, still with her eyes closed. She held out her arms and stretched.

'They're looking at you.' Myst meant the Taiytakei. Zafir opened her eyes and saw that they were, all of them. Watching her, some of them openly, some of them furtively from the towers. Tsen T'Varr and Chrias Kwen and the lord from the mountain city and a dozen others in clothes and feathers that would put rainbows and peacocks to shame were gathered together up on the wall. They were well away from Diamond Eye, but the dragon loomed over everything. And Diamond Eye was looking at her, and so now the Taiytakei were looking at her too. She wondered what it was that drew them in – the power? The hunger? *But today they want me. All of them. One way or another they want me for what I have. Even Tsen.*

Taiytakei black-cloaks followed as she walked to the castle walls and mounted the steps. She lounged against the stone parapets, dressed in white silk and barefoot. The desert sun beat down and made her skin hot. Her face tingled. She stretched her arms and arched her back, soaking in the heat while Myst and Onyx stood beside her, heads bowed, still as statues. With her long tunic loose around her shoulders and her waist, her arms and ankles bare, the desert was bearable. The soldiers around her with their metal plates stitched into cloth, in their glass and gold and their long florid cloaks, she didn't know how they could bear it. They must be sweating rivers. She looked at them, wondering, and they looked back, desire and envy and disgust mixed together in their gleaming faces while their hands gripped their ashgars and their lightning wands. They couldn't help themselves. *They think I'm a whore.* She laughed at them and smiled and shook her head. They wouldn't be the first, and whatever they thought it didn't matter. Taiytakei women kept themselves covered from chin to ankle. So what? She wasn't Taiytakei and none of them would ever have her unless she chose it. Another rule of steel forged on Azure's back that day. Never again a slave to any lusts but her own.

The Taiytakei gathered on the wall began to disperse. Tsen paused. He saw her flaunting herself in his path and turned and went a different way. *What's wrong with you? What are you afraid of?* But it wasn't Tsen she wanted anyway, and the arcane rules they lived by said that none of the others could follow in his wake save the lord who was his guest. Shrin Chrias Kwen – *he* was the one she wanted. She set her eyes on him and ignored the others. *Later. This one first.*

Chrias Kwen met her gaze as he approached, and with a venom that made her heart beat a little faster. She let the dragon hunger wash over her, let him feel it burn his skin. As he passed, she kept her eyes on his and brushed a hand across her neck as if to wipe the sweat away. 'Do murder some more slaves, Kwen, if it troubles you that I'm still here.'

Myst and Onyx flinched. The muscles in the kwen's neck tensed. He'd heard her. She laughed, a tinkling mocking laugh in case her words hadn't been enough. He walked on. The others passed her and she pointedly watched each one as they did. A few turned to look back and then quickly looked away again, embarrassed to be seen to stare at a slave, even one who was a dragon-queen. When they were all gone, Zafir turned and leaned over the parapet into the gentle touch of the breeze. She stretched out her arms and tipped back her head, closed her eyes and flew once more on the dragon's wings.

'Mistress, why?' Myst again. Zafir still didn't know her real name and didn't care to, either. Myst was good enough.

'I'm thirsty.' They followed her down into the white circle of the dragon yard and into the soft light of the tunnels beneath. Tsen had quartered her among the eyrie slaves at first to remind her of what she was, but he'd moved her before long, away from the others and put her in among the Scales. To keep her safe, he'd told her, but she saw the lie. He'd moved her to shut her defiance away.

She let Myst and Onyx wash and perfume her. They made jasmine tea and chewed Xizic together and Zafir looked at them. They'd been with her for months now, ever since the ship. They were hers, body and soul, and she'd come to take them for granted because they were slaves, *her* slaves, which made them much the same as the servants she'd once had. But now, today, there was a chance they were about to die and so she saw them afresh. Not as slaves who dutifully loved and groomed and fed her but as people who had once had hopes and hungers of their own, just as she did. She took Myst by the hand. Her skin was so dark it was like staring into the moonless night.

'Were you born a slave?'

Myst shook her head but Onyx was the one who answered. 'None of us were, mistress.'

'I was born in the desert,' said Myst.

'We both were. The sword-slaves came out into the Empty Sands and the Desert of Thieves. They bought us from our people and took us back to the slave markets of Cashax and sold us to our first master.'

Zafir listened to them talk as they told her how they'd been taken, each of them, to some Taiytakei lord who made slaves from the desert into bed-slaves fit for a sea lord. How they'd been taught about men and how to pleasure them, how to groom themselves, how to make themselves as perfect and as desirable as possible. They talked of friends made and lost as those who failed to become someone's favourite were thrown aside. The men who were their masters, the kind ones and the cruel, and the women who taught them, who were often far crueller. Zafir half heard their stories and half listened for the crack of the iron-shod boots she knew would come on the stone outside their door, yet while she waited an unexpected sadness crept into her. A kinship for these slaves who should have meant nothing to her – who would have meant nothing to her back in her days as a dragon-queen. Not for their slavery, but for what had come with it. And a sadness, because she ought to send them away now to make them safe but she couldn't quite bring herself to be alone, not in the face of what was coming. She could already feel her resolve weakening.

Which wouldn't do. There was no space in the world for pity, not for her, not for anyone. She'd learned that long ago. Even the idea of it, here of all places, made her furious. She jumped up and stepped away from them. Myst almost whimpered. 'Mistress? Have we said something wrong?' They looked at her like whipped dogs.

No, and anger wouldn't do either. That wasn't what she needed, not with what was about to happen. The dragon. She needed the dragon. She sat down beside them again and pulled them close. 'No. You haven't.' Sitting on the back of Diamond Eye. The feeling of him. The warmth, the speed, the hunger, the desire, the freedom and the joy. She took herself back and lived it again. 'Tell me something else. Something precious. The memory you hold on to on dark days. Something that brings you joy.'

Onyx looked sad, but Myst's eyes were suddenly bright. 'I remember a night in the desert,' she said. 'The air was cool, the sky clear like every other desert night. I am hidden, stolen away from my family and my people, not far, but out of sight and out of sound. We are on a journey across the sands. The shaman has decided it's the way we should go. There are whispers of black ooze rising from the dunes and harvesting the ooze for the city lords brings us riches and fat bellies. But we are still on our way. We have reached the old place the city men call Uban. Much is buried under the sand but some pieces still rise above it. I have never seen a city before, even an old and ruined one that is almost buried. It seems a magical place outside the world I know. I am waiting behind a stone that rises out of the sand, tall as the sky, for the boy that I want. And he comes to me and I see him, and his eyes are like stars.'

She looked so far away. Zafir, riding on the back of her dragon, understood. She'd never found that anywhere but in the sky. No man or woman had given her that happiness, not even Jehal on the best of his days. 'I am the dragon,' she murmured, and she might have said more but that was when the footsteps came at last from the passage outside. She hugged her two broken birds close. 'I am sorry for this. Truly I am.' And she meant it, and for a just a moment the fear began to escape from its cage inside her and almost overwhelmed her. Almost, but not quite, as she turned it to cold fury.

The soldiers didn't bother to knock, just smashed in the make-shift door. The kwen and a half-dozen of his black-cloaks. They grabbed her arms, pulled her away from Myst and Onyx and al-most hurled her to the ground. The kwen just stared. Zafir waited, silent and with the dragon wrapped tight around her. It had always been a dangerous game to play with this one.

'Bow, slave!' One of the black-cloaks slapped her. She tasted blood.

'Kwen.' She ignored the black-cloak, cocked her head and ran her tongue across her teeth. 'Do you have something for me?' *Bow? I'll die first, and then who's going to fly your precious dragon?*

Shrin Chrias Kwen faced her, his six men around him. 'I do, slave. I hear Tsen sends you men and you turn them away. So I have some *real* men for you.' He spat his words at her and turned to his soldiers. 'Hurt her if it amuses you but don't break her. Do what you like with her slaves.'

Zafir threw back her head and laughed at him. 'These? *These* are your real men? You disappoint me, Kwen. I thought you'd be one to fight your own battles. Sword not sharp enough?' She stood straight and tall. 'Well I am here, little man. *You* can do nothing to me.'

'She's all yours, boys.' Chrias turned and walked away. Zafir lunged after him. *Oh no. No you don't. You don't get away from me, you limp-dicked shit, not this time.* As the first black-cloak snatched for her she danced aside, pulled his dagger out of his belt and rammed it under his chin. She let go as a river of blood ran down his throat and his shirt and flicked the few drops from her finger-tips onto the ground. The rest of the soldiers paused, suddenly uncertain. Hands fell to hilts and to wands. Zafir bared her teeth. 'Yes, cut me down, Shrin Chrias Kwen. Murder me if you can. Touch me if you dare, but if you do *not* dare then take your flock of sheep away with you and go and baa at some grass. *My* soldiers were Adamantine, untouchable, unbreakable, their captain a titan to wrestle with dragons, yet he still was my toy to tinker with as I chose and so are you.' He'd stopped. Hadn't turned, but he'd stopped and that was enough. She bent down and tore the dagger out of the dead soldier's neck, then held it to her own throat as she walked towards him. The black-cloaks moved apart, backing away from her as she came on with the knife still at her throat. Rage and confusion simmered in their faces. 'I have killed the first man who tried to touch me. Do you not remember the ship, Kwen? You were not there but you've heard every last part, I'm sure.' The kwen turned at last and she wasn't sure whether it was hate or lust or perhaps even fear that she saw in his face. Perhaps all three. She stood before him.

'Kill yourself then,' he spat.

'Why would I do that?' She let the knife move a fraction away. Not far, but far enough so that when he lunged at her, quick as a striking snake, he had her hand gripped in his own before she could cut herself. She didn't move, didn't struggle, didn't even try to resist as he twisted her arm and the knife fell to the ground. He was holding her tight. She'd have bruises in the morning but the bruises so far were only the start of what she'd have from this. A small price. She'd known that the moment she'd left Bellepheros.

I am the dragon. She could feel the heat rising through her. They were inches apart. 'Tsen sends me slaves? You send me soldiers? I am a dragon-queen, Chrias Kwen, and I deserve *better*.' She snatched at the knife on the kwen's own belt but he was quicker, jerking it out of its sheath and tossing it to the ground behind him. Not quick enough to stop her sinking her fingers into his throat though.

'Now what, Kwen?' She felt the dragon inside her watching them both from up on the eyrie wall. The two of them pressed together. The hunger, the desire, the need for *something*, the clenching urge to take, take, *take*! When he didn't move, she hit him square in the face with an open palm, hard enough to make him stagger. 'Better,' she hissed, 'I want *better*!'

As he blinked from the punch, she slashed him with her nails and finally he broke. He twisted her arm behind her back and hurled her into the room. 'Out!' he roared. 'All of you! Out!' The black-cloaks scurried away as he pushed through them and grabbed Zafir by the throat. She made no effort to stop him. Maybe, if he'd still had it, she could have taken his knife this time and stabbed him after all, but that wasn't why she'd drawn him here. She had a much nastier death in mind for this one.

I am the dragon. I am the dragon.

He pushed her down to the ground and ripped her tunic. Her fingers curled into claws. She tore at his face. He pinned her down, all his weight on top of her.

I am the dragon.

He wrenched her over onto her belly and pulled her legs apart. She bucked underneath him as he took her there with her slaves watching, and for a short time she couldn't have said whether she meant to throw him off and murder him or whether she meant to pull him deeper and deeper until every part of him was inside her skin.

I am the dragon.

A wall of fire burst inside her. It burned her sweat to steam and scorched her skin to ash. She was high, high as the stars and falling into the hurricane, wings tucked back, shattering the sky and the fire filled her, tooth and claw and tail, with a strength to smash the world itself to pieces.

I am the dragon.

The feeling faded as it always did. She remembered where she was again. She felt the kwen stabbing away inside her, listened to his grunts and quietly remembered another time and place and said nothing. When he was done and drawing away from her, she rolled onto her back. Her eyes glittered. Her lips curled for him, a smileful of hate. Still in his armour except for one shrivelling piece. *Men. Wherever they are they make their armour the same so that can be the first part of them to come out of it. What does that say about what you are?*

'I remember you,' she breathed. 'So full of what you are and so empty of any meaning.'

The kwen shouted at his soldiers and stormed away, and what-ever he said was so harsh and sharp that she couldn't understand; and it was only when the soldiers came down on her, one after the other, that she knew. She fought these ones – couldn't not – but they'd left their knives outside and there were six of them and only one of her. She remembered the faces, though, of the ones who took her with gleeful lust, the ones who twisted their lips in disgust, and the one whose eyes showed pity. The one who didn't touch her at all would be the one who would live. The rest had sealed their fates right there. Each one would die, and she wouldn't even have to lift a finger.

They left her on the floor when they were done. Myst and Onyx stared, untouched. The dragon inside looked down as if to ask why and what she meant by this. She met its eye. *No regret or sorrow. I sought this out. The pain will go and the vengeance, when it comes, will be a long and lingering joy and I will feel not one iota of remorse. No one can touch either of us. Not while we can fly.*

She struggled to her feet. Painfully. All three of them were still alive. That was something. Better than she'd feared. For a time they huddled together, and for a little while Zafir wasn't the dragon-queen any more, she was just Zafir, and the locked dark room was a thing that hadn't happened yet. She whispered softly in the ears of her broken birds, 'They came because I made them come.'

'Mistress?'

'And I was afraid for you. I was afraid of what they'd do to you. And I should have sent you away, but I couldn't bear to be alone.'

Later, when Myst and Onyx had bathed her and clothed her and oiled her bruises, she went back to Bellepheros. She couldn't quite hide the awkwardness of her gait. She waved the gourd around her neck.

'More.'

'You don't need more, Holiness. It will not help.'

'All of it. I want all that you have. Every single last drop.'

He frowned and looked her up and down and then frowned some more. 'Has there been a change, Holiness? Are you hurt?'

Zafir smiled, sour and tired. 'I have ridden long and hard today and it has been a while. I am stiff and sore from the saddle, Master Alchemist, nothing more. Why? Do I concern you?'

'My duty is to keep these dragons dull, Holiness. You will understand that, I know, for you were speaker once. But beyond that my duty and my love are yours.' He began to gather the potion.

Zafir watched where he went. One bottle from his desk, two from a chest beside his bed. 'I do need them, Holiness. The Scales will die far more quickly without the potion.'

'Then they will die but you may give them something to think they are still loved. Is that all you have? Give them to me. All of it.'

He did, and he looked infinitely sad as she tipped them out onto the floor, one by one. When she was done, he held up another bottle. 'And I, Holiness? May *I* keep the Hatchling Disease at bay?'

She smiled at him. He was an old alchemist and so of course he carried it. 'Yes. But keep it safe and keep it close.' She tapped the gourd around her neck. 'There will be others, you see. Taiytakei. And when they come to you with the Hatchling Disease, the potions you give them will do nothing at all; and when *that* comes to pass they will take whatever you have, for that is what desperate men do. Be ready for that day, Master Alchemist. I'm sure you'll make more. I won't forbid it, but hide it well.' She turned to go and then turned back. 'I almost forgot. I require another gift from you. A small thing, one that's so far beneath you I hesitate to ask but I must. Dawn Torpor.'

Dawn Torpor so I will not grow fat from you or your men, Shrin Chrias Kwen. She watched the alchemist's face, watched his eyes go wide and his mouth hang open, his face blanch.

'*Holiness!* What—'

She cut him off with a fierce clenched fist. 'They took what they wanted, Master Alchemist, as they took us from our homes and made us slaves. They did not ask, they were not kind, they are not dragons and you owe them nothing. When the Hatchling Disease begins to take them, they will come to you. You will do nothing to help them. They will all slowly die in lingering fear and agony and I will watch and spit in their faces. Do you understand, Grand Master Alchemist?'

When she left, she was on Diamond Eye again, tearing the air, clouds of sand billowing in their wake as they burned the desert to glass. She was almost singing.

56

Dhar Thosis

The Watcher appeared on the Divine Bridge a thousand feet above the sea. To his left, rising still higher, stood the Dul Matha, the Kraitu's Bones, which rose half as high again from the sea below in rings of walls and steps with the gatehouses that guarded the Palace of Roses at its peak, the home and dwelling of the ninth sea lord Senxian. It had been a shrine once, in the very distant past before the enchanters had made the first glasships. Pilgrims had come thousands of miles from every city, from every fledging realm, to bring their offerings of hope to the Goddess of Fickle Fortune.

Dhar Thosis. The City of Golems, they called it, although there were hardly any here and the name belonged better to Xican with its Stoneguard.

The Watcher looked past Dul Matha to the larger but much lower island a little way beyond it, Vul Tara, known as the Pilgrims' Island because visitors to the shrine always came that way if they arrived by ship. It was a fortress now, armed with bolt throwers and black-powder and lightning cannon, but the shelters remained, the refuges and the hostels. Unclean godliness remained scattered across Vul Tara, despite its weapons. He couldn't see the seaward side from the top of the Divine Bridge, but that was where sheer-walled monasteries rested on the tops of low black cliffs, and on the lower parts of the island poor pilgrims still came to pray to the relics from the shrine that Ten Tazei once built on the top of the Kraitu's Bones.

The pilgrims' ships would have anchored where ships still anchored now, in the sheltered open water between the shore, Dul Matha, Vul Tara, and the third and largest island, the Eye of the Sea Goddess where the sea titans slept and where Senxian's administrators and sea captains now lived, each in their own palace with their own kwens and t'varrs and hsians, servants and soldiers and slaves. A whole island of palaces now, each striving to surpass its neighbours, but it had not been so back in the time of the shrine. They called the island the Eye of the Sea Goddess but they should have made it her nose because that was the shape of it from far away, rising gently from the sea beside the shore, curving up ever sharper to a rounded summit that fell away to a sudden sheer nothing from a thousand feet in the air. Sprawling stone villas loosely jostled one another down by the sea, while at the top rose a forest of gold-glass towers, packed together like slaves in a gondola. The towers were the richer palaces. Few could afford a home built by enchanters.

Two hundred paces across the sea from the peak of the Eye of the Sea Goddess, the Dul Matha rose. The Divine Bridge crossed that space now, floating on enchanted gold-glass, but the Watcher wondered how it might have looked to those ancient pilgrims as they climbed down from their ships squeezed between the towering islands; as they rowed to the Vul Tara and their first night ashore, heads craned back to stare at the sky and the Divine Bridge high above them, searching for a first glimpse of the most famous shrine in the world – or so it had once been. They would have looked again as they rowed back the other way, across to the mainland and to what had once been a swamp, the salt marsh grown over time into the working rump of the city of Dhar Thosis. The swamps and the channels of brackish water were still there, some of them built over, others built around, others still slithering their way between the packed-stone streets of the shore city. There might have been jetties where the shore-side docks now stood, with a few little wooden huts perhaps sheltering sellers of slivers of wood or bone claimed to have come from the shrine. After that the pilgrims would have walked the swamp trails, now city streets with names like Pilgrim's Path and Quicksand Alley. They would have turned their backs on Dul Matha at first, following the curve of the shore until the Kraitu's Bones vanished behind the Eye of the Sea Goddess where they would have crossed the causeway, a treacherous tidal path now supplanted by the gleaming glass and gold spans of the Bridge of Eternity. They'd have climbed the winding paths up the Eye towards its peak, past temples and other shrines long since flattened to make way for palaces. All the way to the top of the Eye and they'd have come here, to where the Watcher stood now, to the start of the Divine Bridge.

Like the Bridge of Eternity, the Divine Bridge was now a thing of gold and glass, one great magnificent span crossing the sea far below, but back when pilgrims had come to the shrine atop the Kraitu's Bones the Crimson Sunburst had yet to be born and Hingwal Taktse and the Dralamut were just two warlord castles among many. There were no golems, no gold-glass, no enchanters, no navigators, no sea lords with their palaces and the Divine Bridge had been nothing more than two great ropes strung across the void. A place to be at one with the air, with the sea below and the unforgiving cliffs to either side. Bones still littered the rocks where the Goddess of Fickle Fortune had chosen not to cast her favour on her pilgrims. They said the ropes of the very first bridge were made from the hair of Ten Tazei, the first man to stand on Dul Matha's peak; but then they also said that he'd been carried there by an eagle, that he'd lived for three years on top of the rock eating birds and eggs and fish brought to him by the gulls – who for some reason didn't much like the eagles – until he'd grown his hair long enough to make the rope that would become the first bridge.

They said a lot of things in Dhar Thosis, but the rope bridge was long gone and nothing of it now remained. The enchanters had come with their glass and gold and a sea lord had followed. Parts of the shrine were still there, walled within Senxian's palace where only the greatest of men were allowed to see them. The Elemental Men had seen to the rest. The shrine was a curiosity from another time, a relic of ideas now forbidden.

The Watcher, by his nature, had no time for gods. The Elemental Men had wiped out their religions long ago, casting out all but their most distant echoes. It seemed a shame, though, that the enchanters had built this bridge. The Watcher tried to picture it as it had been in the stories, two great strands of rope, a coming together of air and stone and sea when Dul Matha was untouched.

The stories belonged to another time. The Palace of Roses had stood here for hundreds of years now and the sea lords had thrived as all sea lords did. Evidence perhaps that the Goddess of Fickle Fortune was nothing but a superstition, for surely to wall away her shrine was nothing if not insulting and yet she had rained no great misfortunes upon the lords of Dhar Thosis to punish them for their hubris – at least not until now.

Or perhaps that was simply why she was called fickle? The Watcher smiled to himself. He became the air and vanished and appeared again atop the highest of the gold-glass towers of the palace, looking down on the city so far below that even the ships were little more than specks in the grey rippled sea. There were no doors here of course, none that could be opened from the outside, no point of entry for an Elemental Man. The palace wore a shield of gold, armour against such killers. The Elemental Masters would never permit one sea lord to strike against another and so such armour should never be needed, but the sea lords dressed their palaces in it nonetheless, never quite trusting the Elemental Men as they never quite trusted their peers, their kin, their kwens and hsians and t'varrs. They built their world of opposing forces kept in carefully weighted balance to prevent any one from overwhelming the rest. An illusion, all of it, a fallacy. The Watcher knew this and the sea lords perhaps knew it too at their core, but for as long as the Elemental Men obeyed their masters and as long as the masters kept themselves to themselves, this tension of oppositions worked.

And that, he knew, was why the sea lords of Vespinarr and Cashax and Dhar Thosis and all the other great cities feared Quai'Shu and his dragons. Quai'Shu had ruined his house to get them. None of the others knew quite what for, but the not knowing made them afraid, and through the visor of their fear all they saw was a crippled house ripe to be brought down and a corpse to be picked over. None of them even knew what these dragons would do to them, not even Baros Tsen T'Varr, to whom the beasts answered, but they were right to be afraid.

They had to go. Back where they came from. All of them. The balance must be preserved. These were his own thoughts, unshared as yet, and there would be a time to bring them to the minds of others, but not today. Today the Watcher waited. A sea lord had not fallen for nearly two hundred years. An Elemental Man had not struck in a gold-glass palace for even longer. They had forgotten the fire with which they played.

A glasship rose from the city below, drifting in its leisurely way across the water and up towards the palace. It floated higher and higher, beyond the Divine Bridge, and then arced closer. The golden egg of the gondola beneath gleamed in the sun, catching the light like fire. The ship came over the palace. It nestled itself into the needle of black stone that the enchanters had raised here to feed it. As it stopped, its gondola sank gently on silver chains until it came to rest deep among the roots of the towers. It opened and waiting men came to take whatever it carried inside – food, water, simple things that any palace would need.

The Watcher looked down on the slaves as they worked. Glasships were a marvel, the pinnacle of the enchanters' arts, but often they were treated no better than a wagon and a few mules. Such was the way of a sea lord. He shifted from his perch. There was always a way through any shield of gold that the sea lords made. Men were men. They had to eat and they had to drink. He admired Baros Tsen T'Varr sometimes for not hiding himself away like the others, for seeing the futility of even trying, but then Tsen T'Varr had an Elemental Man of his own and Quai'Shu had always been different.

He chose a barrel filled with wine and a moment later was inside it. The men who carried it never knew he was there. They brushed through doors of beaten gold and the sea lord's shield was punctured. It was that easy.

Once inside, the Watcher shifted again, into the floor now, into the stone of Dul Matha itself. He felt his way towards the palace centre. There were more layers, more walls of gold and silver, animated sentinels of glass and jade like the Stoneguard of Xican. He passed through them one by one, always patient, always waiting until the moment came to move unseen.

In this slow methodical way he finally found the hsian. It would have been easy to strike in that first moment, to appear and open Nimpo Jima's throat and vanish again to leave his death a mystery, but there was a greater purpose to his being here and so he waited and watched for another day until Quai'Shu's traitor of a hsian was called and walked alone into the inner sanctum of Sea Lord Senxian himself. The Watcher followed. He would kill the hsian in front of the sea lord. He would kill him so that the hsian's blood stained the sea lord's shoes. The message would be as clear as it could possibly be. *It could have been you. But sea lords do not strike at one another.* And Senxian would understand, and the plans that he and the hsian were laying against Baros Tsen T'Varr and Sea Lord Quai'Shu would fall quietly to nothing, and there would be no more to be done.

He merged with the air, following the hsian. Nimpo Jima sat down on the floor beside a low table. On the other side knelt Senxian in a robe of shimmering rainbows, large and strong but fat with age. On the walls hung cloaks of dazzling emerald feathers. Cups of crushed leaves sat on the table beside a coppery bowl of steaming water.

'Hsian.' The Watcher waited, one with the air until the moment when they were close enough for the hsian's blood to touch the sea lord himself. The song ran strong in his head here, the voices of the moon sorcerers. *Mooncrown. Earthspear. Suncloak. Starknife.*

Somehow – he would never understand how – he didn't see the tall pale-skinned slave who had no place at all being in the same room as a sea lord. Didn't see him until the man stepped behind the air that he had become and drove a gold-handled knife into the place where he was. The slave was dressed in grey with a tattooed face and the knife hilt was engraved with stars, and suddenly the Watcher was flesh and bone and the gold-hilted knife was inside him. He shuddered. *How?*

Grey robes. The grey dead men and making something ...
How didn't I see him?

The knife held him fast, paralysed. It didn't move but he felt three little cuts, three little pieces of his essence sucked away, and then a voice like thunder in his head, crushing and destroying, like the moon sorcerers had been but stronger by far. The knife withdrew and he fell to his knees. Terror welled up inside him and he had no idea what to do with it because Elemental Men had nothing to fear and so were never afraid, because nothing in any of the worlds of the Taiytakei could ever touch them.

The Picker, he reminded himself. *The Picker died too. And the one before.*

He couldn't move. Not a muscle.

'You're not going to die,' said the grey dead man. 'None of this has happened. I was never here and no one ever touched you. You will never see me, as these men never see me, even when I am right in front of you, for your eyes will simply look elsewhere, but now and then you will hear my voice. Do what you came to do and return with the knowledge that Sea Lord Senxian will make war on Sea Lord Quai'Shu for his dragons no matter what warning is sent. When that war comes, you will find a way to steal one of your master's dragon eggs and you will take it to those who dwell beneath the Konsidar. When that is done, you will go to some place so remote that you will never be found and you will cut out your own heart.'

The knife vanished and with it every memory of what had happened, and all the Watcher knew was that he was no longer the air but flesh and bone and the two men in the room in front of him had turned to stare, horror covering their faces.

He blinked. Shifted. The bladeless knife flashed and the hsian's blood sprayed across the plates and the steaming water and spattered Senxian's arm. The Watcher stood for a moment, let the sea lord drink him in, let him understand, and then was gone, slipping slowly and steadily back through the layers of Senxian's palace with the same care with which he had come.

57

Shades of Entanglement

The shade of the dragon called Silence slipped among the ghosts and fleeting spirits of men. It closed its thoughts to the siren calls of waiting eggs and opened wary eyes to the slowly awakening things that now moved among the ruins of what the little ones called Xibaiya. It moved with careful speed and purpose back to the edges of the hole and the oozing spread of That Which Came Before. The door of its prison was gone, the door that had once been the Earth Goddess frozen at the moment of her death, mingled with the essence of the half-god who'd slain her. The dragon had known this already but now it sat and watched, pondering the open hole and the Nothing beyond. There was no hurry to the void and the chaos. It crept hither and yon around the rip in creation that the Earthspear had made, devouring what it touched but touching with no purpose. It was easy to stay away from those wandering tendrils of nothingness, slow and blind as they were. It would be less easy later, when everything was unravelled and only those tendrils remained.

How long will it take?

It tried to catch a passing little one but the shade fluttered away. They were such ephemeral things, these children of the sun. It would be interesting, the dragon thought, to feed one of their souls to the Nothing and watch it be consumed. Perhaps there was an insight to be gained into the nature of things. Or perhaps not, but either way it couldn't catch them. They winked into the under-world and quickly sped away, and when the dragon chased them it was slow and they were quickly beyond its senses.

Silence.

The little ones had given it that name. It had snarled against such a crude word when it had first woken, but other dragons had kept their human names and its own thoughts had subtly changed.

Silence was a blissful thing. Death was silent. Here was silent. In the living realms with the little ones all around, their thoughts gibbered and jabbered constantly. Silence was beautiful.

I will keep it. I will become it. I will bring it and I will surround myself with it.

After a time it tired of watching the mindless Nothing grow, inch by tiny inch, the cancer of creation. *How long will it take?* Lifetimes, and the dragon was too impatient for such things. It felt the call of eggs, here and there and everywhere, scattered in places unfamiliar as well as those well known. The little ones with the ships, *they* had taken eggs. Perhaps it would be amusing to bring some silence to them?

It moved, but not yet towards the eggs. There was another thing, close to the bleeding wound of the underworld. Something else that lingered. A familiar taste.

Sister? Brother?

But it wasn't a dragon. Something like a dragon, but not. Something more. A silver half-god, nothing less, and the dragon wondered how one of the makers was here. The half-gods didn't pass through Xibaiya and never had. They'd had their own ways, even before they were banished by the earth.

Curious then that one of them should be here, and more curious too that it was close to That Which Came Before. *Did you come to see, old one? But this is not your domain and you should know better than to be here.*

As it came so close that they might have touched, it tasted a second shade, a little one, and now it understood. The two were locked together, each held fast by the other so that neither could move, a tiny mirror of the Earth Goddess and her slayer wrapped in their prison.

Old one?

The shades writhed and screamed together. The dragon turned away, sorrow and disgust all at once. Yes, an old one, one of the silver half-gods, a maker, but diminished to almost nothing, a barely flickering ember of the bright light it had once been long, long ago.

Old one?

The little one had trapped it and almost unravelled it so that only the barest essence remained. The dragon wondered how a little one could do such a thing but it had no answer to that. The half-god was all but gone, not enough left for it to know what was happening to it, much less talk. The dragon took the two shades in its claws and picked them patiently apart until they were separate things, each straining to be released. One for the sun, one for the moon.

Old one? It tried one last time but the half-god was too damaged to understand. Perhaps the night lord would make it whole again, perhaps not. There was a sense of recognition though. This was one of the half-gods who'd turned with old wise Seturakah for whom the dragons had first flown. One of the few who'd stayed and fought, who had turned against the old gods and failed and lost and been broken.

Were you too close when the end came? Is that what happened to you? It looked at the mangled shrivelled shade. *So few, and yet you were so great and so close.* It let the old one go. *Be with your creator. Make your penance and your peace. Is he merciful in his victory, the night lord?* The dragon had little idea what such things meant. Mercy, revenge, forgiveness, spite? Those were not dragon thoughts – for dragons there was only what was food and what was not. It had learned these other words from the little ones. They seemed to think them somehow important. The dragon couldn't see why they should matter. Mostly what it understood was the rage, the wild impatient fury that always undid them. *Why are we this way? Why are we made to be so quick of thought and claw and yet so fleeting?* It mused on this for a minute or two, and when it saw that there was no answer to be had to that either, its thoughts moved on. It did not understand resentment either.

It still held the little one. The little one wasn't damaged at all.

Who are you? It began to move back to the broken prison. The little one squirmed and tried to get away but the dragon held it fast. Nor did it answer; but little ones, as the dragon had often observed, could rarely control their thinking. All the dragon had to do was to listen.

You were a lord among your kind? The little one had a name, but the dragon had no interest. *I have never heard of your home. If I find it I will burn it. No, I will not let you go. I mean to feed you to the Nothing to see what will happen.*

The little one struggled but it had no hope of escape. The dragon reached out as close as it dared to the hole and its questing devouring tongues. It dropped the little one inside.

How? How did this come to pass? How was the old seal broken? Where did the dead goddess and her slayer go? Did they flee or has the Nothing consumed them? Not that, it thought, for the two of them had held the Nothing at bay for an age and more. No, they had gone somewhere.

A weight of understanding closed over Silence then. If they truly had *gone* somewhere then they could be found and they could be returned, and That Which Came Before could be locked away once more.

I do not want the burden of this knowledge.

The little one flickered as the Nothing closed around it and then it darted through a tiny space the dragon hadn't seen and flashed away, gone towards its creator, the Lord of Light and Warmth. The dragon lunged, annoyed, but it was slow and the little one had already vanished. As it went, the dragon caught a fractured fragment of a thought.

I was there. I saw it happen.

And with that a flicker of something else. Of pride and a place and a face.

The dragon snarled. If the little one had seen it then so had the old one; and if the little one was gone to the sun, so the old one was gone to the moon and the night lord. And the night lord was known to dragons.

So, Gods, I have sent these souls with their knowledge and their memories back to you. What will you do?

What gods always did. Nothing.

The Bloody Judge

58

Never Forgotten

By the time the boats from the galley came ashore, the pain ran right from the top of Tuuran's head down his neck. His face felt like it was still on fire and it wasn't going to get any better in a hurry either. Adamantine Men knew all about fire. When old Hyram had taken the Speaker's Ring, he'd put on a tournament and games for the dragon-riders who came from across the nine realms to kiss it. They'd fought mock battles, strafing legions of the Adamantine Men with dragon fire while the soldiers hid behind their dragon-scale armour and walls of dragon-scale shields. It was supposed to show how fearless the speaker's army was, how they could stand up to anything. And it had, but they'd still lost fifty men over the space of the five days and a hundred more carried their burns proudly, scars to prove who they were. Tuuran reckoned the good soldiers were the ones who'd managed to get themselves and their brothers beside them properly behind their shields, but anyone who got burned got treated well enough. Burns *hurt*.

He growled and waved his sword at the slaves from the galley and turned them right around. 'That's a ship, that is,' he bellowed at the oar-slaves and the sail-slaves as they struggled in through the surf. 'That's a ship, and we know how to sail it and that makes it our life. What are you going to do? Run into the woods barefoot? Do you even know where you are?' The men from the cages in the hold came from up and down the coast here but the galley slaves came from everywhere, mostly the little kingdoms like the one Crazy Mad said he was from, all around the fringes of the Dominion. They'd be lost here, as lost as he would, so he rounded them up, sail-slaves, oar-slaves, the men from the cages, and made them have a good long look at what had happened on the beach. All those dead Taiytakei, that was the sort of sight a slave ought to see now and then. The sort to remember. No one questioned that

he should be the one giving the orders now.

'Any of our slave masters left on the galley?' he asked. The pain across his face turned everything he said into an angry snarl. But no, the Fire Witch – or whatever she was – had burned every Taiytakei to ash. So he looked at all the slaves, standing there on the beach, shitting and pissing themselves and gawping at the mangled remains of their masters, and left them to wonder for a bit while he picked up one of the lightning wands and waved it about in case he could make it work. Everyone knew the wands only worked for the dark-skins but it seemed worth a go. Turned out everyone was right, but it didn't stop them from flinching when he pointed it at them. He'd keep it, he thought, and turned and waved it at the slaves and asked them, 'You really want to stay here? Stay. The rest of you, we go back to the galley because it just became ours.'

About half stayed, mostly the ones from homes up and down the coast. Back on the galley, once the rest of them had scrambled aboard, it turned out that not all the dark-skins were dead after all. The galley slave masters might all be burned to crispy ash and yes, the deck smelt like an eyrie from back home, but down among the oars they found a pair of Taiytakei oar-slaves cowering under the rowing benches. Tuuran had no idea what they were doing there – putting Taiytakei slaves in among the oars was just another way of killing them, everyone knew that – but there they were anyway, terrified. Tuuran dragged them out and gave the others a choice: kill the dark-skins or keep them and they voted almost to a man for keeping. It didn't surprise him. Slave or not-slave always counted more than the colour of a man's skin.

Flame but his face hurt! Cursed Fire Witch or whatever she was. And he still kept wanting to touch it and still kept having to stop himself. Burns. You had to keep them clean – every Adamantine Man knew that – and so you didn't touch them, didn't wrap them, just let the air do its work and maybe a little cold clear water for relief now and then. Damn but he'd have killed to get his hands on a decent alchemist now, or at least a bit of Dreamleaf.

It slowly dawned on them all that they were free. They broke into the hold and hauled out the Taiytakei food and the little barrels of wine and spirits and drank themselves stupid. Tuuran drank until he couldn't stand up any more. It took the edge off the pain. He passed out as the sun set, same as half the rest of them. He thought maybe he saw Crazy Mad's eyes burn silver again right as the sun turned the sea into a lake of orange fire, but afterwards he couldn't be sure and he'd been drunk enough to see faeries and dragons dancing on the moon too. In the morning, face still burning, head pounding, guts churning, he tried cleaning up the messes that the Fire Witch had left behind. Not that he particularly minded them, but it was something to do. Didn't get far though. The Taiytakei slavers – what was left of them – were little more than ash and charcoal burned into the galley's wooden hull. He tried to scrape them off but they were welded in as though wood and flesh had melted and then set again, merged together.

He went off to puke into the sea in case that would make him feel any better. It didn't, but then Crazy Mad showed up with a pot of something he'd looted from the galley captain's trunk, and when he smeared it on the side of Tuuran's face where his ear used to be his skin went numb and the pain just wafted away. Crazy had found some Xizic too, and after a while chewing on that, the world was suddenly a whole lot better and Tuuran took to doing what he did best: strutting the deck and yelling at people, and it never once struck him as strange how easy it was to send the oar-slaves back to their oars and the sail-slaves back to their sails. How easily he became their captain and Crazy Mad his mate.

'Aria,' he muttered to Crazy once the galley was moving again. 'You reckon that was that Ice Witch the night-skins keep whispering about?'

Crazy Mad looked all deep for a moment and smiled one of those smiles of his, the one where it looked like he knew all the dirty little secrets of the gods and was wondering what to do with them. 'No. Not her.' Then the smile hit his eyes and the chill was gone as he laughed and shrugged his shoulders. 'Well, not exactly ice, was it?'

Tuuran scuffed at some charred remains on the deck beside him. 'Seen dragons do that to a man once. Just burned and burned him until there was nothing left but a handful of charcoal.' He stood up and looked out at the sea and the sky and the land. 'I don't know where we are, Crazy. Not the first idea. Even if I did, I wouldn't have a clue how that would help me work out which way to go.'

'I want to go to Tethis. I want the man who took my life.'

Tuuran shook his head and wrinkled his nose. 'It's the Judge in there today, is it? Well, Judge, I never heard of Tethis save what you've told me and most of that I don't believe. But even if I did, there's no going back home for either of us, not yet. A galley can't cross the ocean and none of us can navigate the storm-dark and your Tethis lies on the edges of the Dominion, does it not? We're in the wrong world for either of us. Shall we say Deephaven? To be blunt, in this world I don't even know the name of anywhere else.'

Crazy Mad spat. 'Deephaven then.'

'At least I know it exists beyond your say-so, eh?' He grinned. 'And it sounds a good enough place for a shipload of sailors to make their home. I've heard there are Taiytakei anchored there often enough too. Traders, not slavers. Maybe you could persuade them with that sharp-edged charm of yours to take you home. Maybe I could too!' He laughed.

Crazy Mad shrugged and turned away. 'Bad memories. Bad things happened in Deephaven. Someone died. But that was a long time ago. There's others who might know it better by now.' Crazy didn't like Deephaven today by the look of things. And on his bad days Crazy Mad could be, well, crazy. And mad.

Tuuran gestured vaguely at the sea. 'Look, I don't care where we go. You know another place? Choose it.'

'No, you're right – there always used to be Taiytakei ships in Deephaven. I remember them. Sharp-edged charm or not, they can take us both home. If we can think of something they want bad enough to do it.'

Tuuran snorted. 'Or they can make us slaves again.' But Crazy Mad didn't say anything more and Tuuran still had the glass shard given to him by the Watcher, the one that would make the Taiytakei give him aid, and so maybe they *could* get home, one way or another. He jabbed a finger at the coast. 'Pick a direction. Left or right?'

Turned out neither of them had any idea where Deephaven was, and so they sailed with the wind because at least they'd cover more ground that way, and it was only later that day that Tuuran heard the oar-slaves talking among themselves about the Fire

Witch who'd freed them and stopped to listen, and of course as soon as he did, the oar-slaves all stopped talking and made a point of some vigorous rowing and he had to remind them that they weren't wearing chains any more, that they weren't slaves and that he wasn't some Taiytakei with a whip; and when he'd done yelling that at them, he set them to rowing again. Much later, as the galley drifted through the night and they sat around their braziers on the deck, doing what they'd always done and telling each other stories, he found those oarsmen again and told them to tell everyone else what they'd heard.

'Everyone knows the Fire Witch. She came to Deephaven after the day the knives fell from the sky. That was the day the silver sorcerers came and raised the dead to walk and lifted an army from the earth. The Ice Queen drove them all away. And then the Fire Witch came.' Which was about the most ridiculous story Tuuran had ever heard until he thought about the tales he might tell of dragons and a stolen alchemist and an ancient flying castle drifting over a desert.

'They say the Fire Witch burned the risen dead and put them to rest.' Several of the oar-slaves made a little sign, a strange gesture of reverence and protection and fear mixed together. They'd been on the galley when she'd freed them. 'She cleansed the city and let the living come back. It's hers now. She rules it for the Ice Queen.' Again they made the same gesture. 'The risen dead are everywhere. They covered the streets to keep the sun at bay. Half the city is theirs.' The slaves from Aria made another sign, the sign of the sun this time, a ward against evil.

Tuuran scratched his chin, not much liking the sound of any story with so many witches in it. 'Maybe we shouldn't go that way after all.' Not that he thought much of stories in which wizards who could really only be the Silver Kings themselves suddenly showed up and raised armies of the dead, seeing as how the Silver Kings had been gone for a thousand years and probably then some. But none of them knew anything better and he couldn't quite shake that memory of Crazy Mad and the way his eyes had flared after the grey dead men had come with their golden knife. And the Ice Witch was real enough, or so the Taiytakei had said before they'd burned. He looked around at the faces lit up by the glowing coals of the braziers, all equal men for the first time since they'd been ripped from their homes. *Home*. That was what they all wanted, but home was scattered across four worlds and a dozen different kingdoms and Deephaven was the only place where they might find ships to take them across the storm-dark.

They argued some more. No one much cared for a city of the dead ruled over by a witch who could burn men to ash with a blink, that much was obvious. Even Crazy Mad didn't like it. Deephaven might have been where he'd been born on the days he called himself Berren but he'd severed his ties with that past long ago. In his moments alone Tuuran quietly reckoned that Crazy had severed his ties with rather too many things. But in the end, since none of them knew which way it was to Deephaven anyway, they stuck with the wind and kept the coast on their port side and hoped for the best. The other slaves prayed, but not Tuuran and Crazy Mad. Tuuran's only god was the fire that burned everything at the end of the world and Crazy didn't have any gods at all any more.

The coast grew wilder and soon all they found were coves filled with reefs, treacherous shores, few chances to take on water, little food and no sign of habitation. They had supplies for months though and so it was the restless boredom that bothered them the most; and after another week the shores grew tamer again and they started to see huts and farms and here and there a boat and then villages and fishermen, and someone even made a joke about how they should go ashore and do what they'd always done: take some slaves and look for a place to sell them. When Tuuran heard and found out who'd said it, he threw him into the sea. *He* could go ashore, right enough.

His face still hurt.

A few days later they rounded a headland to a bay outside a city that none of them had ever seen but whose name Crazy Mad reckoned he could guess – Helhex, whose whitewashed walls and temples and houses gleamed in the summer sun with such a fearsome light that Tuuran had to screw his eyes up to look at them. The White City, most people called it, home of the witch breakers of Aria. They anchored in the bay and Tuuran tried to keep the galley slaves together as he and Crazy Mad went with a boat to the shore, but none of them knew where to even start when it came to selling something like a Taiytakei slaving galley. By the time he got back they'd already fallen to fighting and looting, the other boats were all gone and the slaves too and the galley was empty, ransacked. Tuuran looked about him, hands on hips, trying not to laugh and trying not to rage. Crazy Mad stood beside him, blank like he simply didn't care. They ripped out whatever was left that they could carry and Tuuran thought he could sell. Then he split open the casks of oil in the galley that were too heavy to move, lit a torch and set fire to it, because it *was* a slaver and maybe it was better if no one had it at all. It felt good, cleansing himself of the Taiytakei. Crazy didn't lift a finger to stop him, just laughed and laughed as they watched it burn together, rowing for the shore for the last time. It was a strange feeling, an uncertain future in collision with an unkind past. Hope and loss and victory and fear mingled together.

The slaves from the galley dwindled away over the days and weeks, drifting off to other places, falling into trouble, finding ships and setting sail, but Tuuran and Crazy Mad stuck together. They sold what they could but they hadn't come with much. The taverns they stayed in became steadily cheaper and seedier, the wine more sour with each day, and before very long all Tuuran had left was Crazy Mad and the clothes on his back and a last few pennies and a handful of Taiytakei treasures that he had no idea what to do with. And that, he mused, was still a lot more than he'd had for a very long time.

'Here's to us.' He raised his cup. They were drinking the cheapest wine he could find. Too much most nights, if he was honest, but that had always been the vice among the Adamantine Men. Mostly Crazy Mad just sat and watched.

'Here's to sleeping on the streets.' Crazy touched his cup to Tuuran's. 'At least the nights are warm here.'

'It could be worse. We have what we hold, nothing more and nothing less. We have our strength and we have our swords, and what more could a man ask than that?'

'Comfortable bed and a clean woman would be nice.'

'We are Adamantine!' Tuuran was drunk and he knew it. He banged the table. 'We take what we want! What we need!'

'Not here we don't!' Crazy Mad laughed, which earned him a

growl. He wagged a finger in Tuuran's face. He'd taken to doing that a lot since they'd come ashore and Tuuran always wanted to grab it and snap it off. 'You start up with the *I am an Adamantine Man* thing again here, you're going to get us in a fight.'

'Good!'

'Which—'

'Which we'd win!'

Crazy Mad looked all set to start going on about militias and witch breakers and the hundred and one different kinds of trouble that Tuuran might bring down on them but then he stopped abruptly. His whole face changed from bloody warrior to that of a boy, almost forlorn and a little lost. He blinked a few times. 'I saw three sword-monks this afternoon,' he said after a bit. 'Walking the street in the middle of the day. Yellow robes with those twin curved swords they have crossed over their backs and the sunburst tattoo scrawled over their faces. You'd know them if you saw them. One of them, they'd rip us to pieces, either of us.'

Tuuran shrugged and looked into his cup. When Crazy Mad went rambling off into one of his stories, some bits might have some truth to them but you could never tell which. He swilled his wine. Enough for one story. Maybe not for two.

'Twenty years and I've never seen a sword-monk since, and there they were, right in front of me. Sun and moon, can you believe I'd forgotten her?'

'Forgotten who?'

'The teacher I fell in love with. Tasahre. Back like a punch between the eyes, she was. Gods and soldiers! I haven't thought of her for years.'

'Two decades?' Tuuran took a large gulp of wine and raised his eyebrows. 'And how old were you at that particular time?' Because if Crazy Mad had been doing much more than crawling twenty-odd years ago then Tuuran was a dragon in disguise; but then they'd been round this particular island so many times that they both knew every spit and cove. 'Oh, right. That was before those nasty warlocks changed your body for you, eh?' He rolled his eyes.

Crazy Mad ignored him. 'I saw the blood. I held her hand and I felt her heart stop. But I never saw her burn. The last thing I remember was another one of them leaping towards her. And today all I could think of was to chase after those monks and ask them whether there was a monk called Tasahre, whether there'd been some miracle and she somehow hadn't died after all. I *knew* what the seal of the sun could do ...'

'The what?' Tuuran's cup was almost empty. He waved for another.

'There was always a chance, just a tiny, tiny chance ...'

'We're out of money.' Tuuran drained the dregs from his cup and poked forlornly at the last pennies on the table. Crazy had more stories than Tuuran had seen dragons, and this was sounding very much like one of the dull ones. 'So here were are, two soldiers with no war to fight and good for nothing else. Where do we start one?'

Crazy Mad suddenly had a bit of a look like maybe he might be about to punch Tuuran in the face and possibly tear down half the tavern for seconds. But it only lasted a moment and then he let out a bellow of laughter. 'You want to start a war?'

'I've been forged for it from the day I could walk, sword-slave.'

'You can call me by my name now.'

'Ah, but aren't we both slaves to our swords, even as we think we're free? What name would you like, Crazy Mad?' He had too much drink in him. The curse of men forged to fight a war that would never come, penned in by their code and their loyalty and their honour. Wine had been his lover once. Where else was there to go?

Crazy Mad was still laughing. 'For as long as I can remember I wanted to know how to fight. In Deephaven back then you learned to run, always to run. I hated it. Hated how there was always someone bigger, someone stronger, someone who'd simply take whatever they wanted. And so I learned the sword; and then I went to war, more by accident than anything else really, and I found it was no place for flashing blades at all, Tuuran. Scrums of men grunting and heaving at one another, poking at eyes and feet with spikes of metal until one side broke. The slaughter of a sky darkened by arrows. Whole companies of men crushed into the mud by waves of armoured horse, or else it was a sea of fire, or lightning called from the sky, soldiers skewered by spear throwers that could drive a shaft through a stone wall, flesh smeared into the earth by boulders the size of a man's head, hurled across a river. Nothing flashing, nothing dashing, no heroes, only screams and blood and shattered bone. But by then it was too late. It was my trade. My art. I'd sold my soul to it.' He stopped and stared at Tuuran as though he'd seen a ghost and then bared his teeth as his eyes went wide. 'Or someone took it. And I knew nothing else, and for all its horror it became my love. I had enemies, you see. I was the Bloody Judge of Tethis, the king's assassin, the Crowntaker, for ever until the end. Or so I thought until I woke in the skin of a stranger.' He laughed and spat. 'Maybe those warlocks did me a favour.'

Tuuran let out a ferocious fart. *Here we go again. Crazy Mad with his stories. All these things he can't possibly have done.* 'They raised me to fight dragons. Fight and die. Simpler really. Dragon comes, dragon burns. None of the rest of all that stuff you were on about. Get eaten, that's all an Adamantine Man needs to do. And what about this Skyrie of yours? What's his story? How did *he* get to be a slave to the sword?'

Crazy Mad hardly seemed to hear. 'Skyrie? He's mostly gone now.' He was lost. Off again. 'I had a son once. By a bondswoman, which was just another fancy way of saying a slave. She belonged to the queen of Tethis. I stole her and I stole my son. It took three years of my life to do it and I gave no thought to anything else. I went to war. I killed men and I stripped the dead. It was the only thing that mattered and not one second of one day went by when I didn't think of her and of the son I had waiting for me. The other soldiers drank and bought women while I counted my silver until I had enough to buy her. And then in the end when I finally took her and she saw what I'd become ... well, she didn't see it right away and there were some good times. The best times ...' Crazy Mad looked away. Tuuran stared, wine forgotten. The mad bugger looked all but ready to burst into tears. But then Crazy took a deep breath and pulled himself together and emptied his own cup and now he just looked lost again. 'It didn't last. She saw who I was, saw the blood on my hands and wanted nothing to do with me any more. So I let her go and I never saw her again, nor my son, because I knew she was right, and nothing good could come to anyone who lived their life around me. I gave her everything I had and I sent her away and I went back to war but I kept my eyes and ears open. Was going to look after them the best I could. See they didn't want for much. Send them money, that sort of thing. And I did too, for bit. And then the pox came and that was that. Gone. My boy. The one I swore wouldn't grow up like me. I want my life back,' hissed Crazy Mad. 'The one they took from me in Tethis. The first one they took from me when I did what they wanted and they threw me in the pit for it. Never mind the rest.'

'You can never go back, Crazy.' Tuuran belched. 'Besides, doesn't sound like it'd be much use to you now.'

'The warlocks who came to our galley. You remember them?'

The last pennies were gone now, the last cup of wine in front of Tuuran and they were flat broke with nothing to their names except what they carried on their backs and at their hips. And Crazy Mad was so full of shit. Too young to have done all the things he claimed – as long as Tuuran didn't look at that memory he had, carefully locked away, of Crazy Mad with his eyes like burning liquid silver. Maybe not too young to have fathered a child. He'd looked forlorn enough about that. Maybe *that* bit was true. Maybe. And *maybe* he just didn't care, because what did it matter? Tethis? He had no idea where that even was except that it was near the Dominion and across the storm-dark and so might as well have been on the moon. He started eyeing the loose pennies on the tables around them. He wanted more wine. 'Yes, yes. How could I forget throwing you into the sea? One of my fondest memories. Is this going to take long?'

'Where are they?'

'Bugger me if I have the first—'

In a flash Crazy Mad was across the table, a fist clenched around Tuuran's collar. 'Tell me! Tell me what you know about them!'

Tuuran looked at the hand at his neck. With delicate care he wrapped his fingers around Crazy's wrist and squeezed, harder and harder, until he let go. 'I could crush your bones, sword-slave.' Then he laughed. The men on the next table were looking carefully away, very pointedly not seeing anything. While they weren't looking, Tuuran reached out and helped himself to some of the money on their table. Not all of it, just a couple of pennies for another cup. He waved for a refill. 'They weren't Taiytakei, even you could see that much. And that really is about as much as I know. They didn't stay for long. They were looking for you; they were sure you were there and they were mighty upset when they didn't find you. When they left I don't know what they were thinking but they were certainly wondering who it was I threw into the sea. They peered into the water a lot until everyone decided you'd drowned; or maybe they thought you couldn't have been who they were looking for.' Tuuran rubbed his nose. 'Mind, something was off with them. I'd keep my guard about me if I were you, if you see them again.'

Crazy Mad bared his teeth and hissed, 'If I see them again, I'll rip them to bloody shreds! You told me, after you came back from your flying castle over the desert, that you'd found out who all the Taiytakei lords were and what their cities were called and the flags and insignia and all that.'

'That's true. Although fat lot of use it is to a slave.'

'You saw the ship that brought the warlocks and took them away again, Tuuran. Where did it come from?'

Tuuran picked up his pennies and stood up, swaying slightly. 'I like you, Berren Skyrie Bloody Judge Crowntaker Crazy Mad, whoever you are. But I was a slave and no one tells slaves where things are to be found. You want your grey dead men, you'll have to ask one of *them*.' He waved and bellowed something across the tavern floor and sat down again. 'The night-skins. Our masters. Black on the outside but they bleed like the rest of us. Go ask one of them. You know where to find some? Deephaven, I'd say.' He smiled and sighed as a tavern boy filled up his cup. 'The flags said the ship came from one of their cities. Dhar Thosis. For what it's worth, I happen to know that. But don't ask me where it is because I haven't the first idea.'

59

All Debts Paid

An emerald glasship hung beside Baros Tsen's eyrie, carefully out of the way of the long snouts of the black-powder cannons. There wasn't much it could do about the dragon though. Tsen supposed Vey Rin simply trusted him, which was comforting in a way: at the very least it proved that Rin couldn't read his thoughts.

They stood side by side on the battlements watching the dragon fly. The rider took it into the air every day now. It was a little miracle, he thought, that she hadn't turned on the eyrie and destroyed them all. She was a terrible slave, utterly the worst sort, wild and with a dark vein of self-destruction inside that fed her and made her impossible to control or even to contain. Slaves like that were almost always put down, yet so far Tsen hadn't done that and she hadn't burned them all either. Perhaps he had that same vein hidden in him somewhere. Maybe that was why he didn't just go back to his orchards and make wine and build bathhouses for people like Rin. It seemed that he and this unruly slave somehow got along, in their strange way.

Tsen glanced at Rin and for a moment struggled to remember what exactly it was that had brought them together all those years ago in Cashax. Half his memories of those days were lost in a haze of wine and Xizic and Devilsmoke dens. Tsen had been the leader of the pack back then. Maybe a dozen of them at times – rich, young, soulless and cynical, Taiytakei destined for power and greatness, all of them. He struggled to even remember most of the names now. They'd done whatever they could to make each day wilder than the last. Things that were best forgotten sometimes but Tsen remembered them clearly. For a while he'd been the worst of them all. And then things had happened and people had died, badly, and the others had drifted away and suddenly he and Rin were the only ones left, and Rin had dragged him out into the desert to go hunting desert men with a slaving gang who'd been only too happy to have a couple of rich boys with their sleds slumming it out in the sands. His heart hadn't been in it any more by then. In fact most of the time out among the dunes he wasn't sure whether he even had a heart at all.

Thirty years later he knew that he did. It had taken quite a while but he'd found a certain peace again. *And so would it be so bad to give in to wisdom and let it all go and live a long quiet life somewhere doing the things I love?* But the more he looked at Rin, the more all those old memories kept coming back and the more he knew that yes, it would. *Ah, the follies of pride.*

'I've explained matters as succinctly as I can to Sea Lord Quai'Shu,' said Vey Rin. 'He doesn't seem to be terribly … coherent.' Overhead the dragon twisted in somersaults, jinking and rolling into a series of tight turns far too fast for a lightning cannon to follow. Rin wasn't really looking – didn't seem to care at all – but Tsen often came out to watch the dragon when it flew now. Not that he wanted to actually get onto the back of the thing – the thought made him shudder every time – but he *did* find himself wondering what it felt like up there. He'd sailed sleds over the desert after all, him and Rin and the rest of them. From what he remembered, it had been a lot of fun.

'Quai'Shu has lost his mind, Rin. He and coherence parted long ago and you knew that before you came.' *Charades and masquerades. Is that all we are?*

'At least he's still alive. How much longer before your wager with your friend Meido is done?'

'A little under two months.' *Your friend Meido? What have you promised him?* He wondered at his own irritation. *Would Meido be so bad? Of all the rest, would he really be so bad? No, he wouldn't. So why not just let him have it?* But he couldn't. *Why? Because I can do better, damn you all, that's why. And because Meido would give Shonda what he wants, and for some reason I simply can't bear to let you have these monsters, Rin. Because you and Shonda never really changed.*

Rin shook his head. 'My brother is growing impatient. He doesn't wish to wait for two months. He wonders with whom he should speak regarding matters that affect the future of our business together.'

Tsen watched the dragon, a distant speck in the sky now. *With her. With that.* He wondered, as always, if today would be the day she simply didn't come back. 'I suggest the Great Sea Council, my friend. Or for matters less public, perhaps my Lord Quai'Shu.' Tsen smiled, though Rin knew him far too well for that to work.

'I didn't come here to be mocked, Tsen.'

'And I won't be the one to set that monster on Dhar Thosis. I see no profit in it.'

Rin shrugged. 'All debts paid and you see no profit?'

'Oh, if my dragon is destroyed by Senxian and his stone titans and his lightning cannon then you'll find some other way to keep me in your pocket; and if by some miracle my dragon destroys his city, the Elemental Men will rip *both* of our houses to pieces and I shall be too dead to even wag my finger at you and say *told you so*. Perhaps I might ask them to take my corpse to yours and re-enact the scene. How many thousands dwell in Dhar Thosis?'

'Many. How many thousands dwell in Bom Tark, Tsen?'

A scream rang out from one of the towers. A welcome distraction from an uncomfortable thought. Rin had put a slave in a cage up there and lined it with silver to draw the eyes of his jade ravens, his messengers to and from Vespinarr while he was here. One was perched on top of the cage now, the size of a hawk but with feathers of a deep iridescent green and an emerald beak like the emerald of Rin's glasship. Rin kept his eyes on the dragon while Tsen watched the bird. The jade ravens made his skin crawl; he'd been glad to be rid of them after Quai'Shu lost his mind and now Rin had brought them back again. They came from Qeled and they were, as far as Tsen could tell, fitting ambassadors of their realm. The silver drew the raven to the cage, but it was the slave it was after. The bird hopped down and squeezed through the bars. The slave kicked out but the raven was too quick. It flapped and jumped and dodged and pecked the man on the foot. It couldn't have been more than a tiny puncture but the slave only had time for one pitiful scream as he turned green and then shattered, transformed by the bird's poison. The jade raven poked at the debris and began to devour the fragments, the broken chunks of what had once been flesh, pecking at them then hopping from one to the next like a crow. From a distance it seemed as though the birds turned men into glass, but that wasn't true. Hard and brittle but more of a resin, like amber or Xizic. Tsen shuddered. *More monsters. As if we don't have enough of them.* He had a dim idea that someone at the Great Sea Council had said something about letting them loose to trouble the Ice Witch. A thing already done? He wasn't sure. *But if we do then I'm quite sure it won't be the Ice Witch they devour.*

Rin was watching the dragon come in to land. It came down hard. Tsen didn't know whether it was the dragon or the rider that liked to do that but they did it every day, and so every day the castle shook to its core. Wherever you were, the stone trembled under your feet to tell you that the monster was back. Zafir threw off her riding leathers and swaggered past them, hips swinging. Rin stared after her. 'That's some slave you have there.'

'Yes. I suppose so.' Every flight was the same; and after every landing, after the dragon announced its return, she sauntered across the eyrie in front of everyone with such a fierce magnetism that every slave and Taiytakei alike stopped to stare. *Look at them. All except me and the alchemist. It's the dragon, you cock-brains, not her!*

'But she *is* a slave. Send her to me.' Even Rin. Tsen shook his head. He wasn't sure whether to laugh or cry.

'I'd keep my distance if I were you,' he said quickly, before Rin let out something stupid that he'd have to make up for later by driving Tsen even harder into his corner. 'She kills. Even when Chrias Kwen wouldn't take no for an answer it cost him one of his black-cloaks.' Now there was a thing he still hadn't made into any sense. They had loathed each other before and now they loathed each other even more. He struggled to imagine what Chrias had been thinking, making such a fool of himself. Did he see it as some unkind little victory? If he did, Tsen thought he was wrong. *Her eyes say otherwise, Chrias my dear sweet enemy. Her eyes say it was hers. Not that I much care, but I do wonder how that can be. What has she done to you? Something bitter, I hope. You brought it on yourself and so you deserve it. I'd ask but – wait – I can't, because you're not here, because you're off assembling a fleet and an army for our dear friend Rin while he helps you into Quai'Shu's cape. Not that I'm supposed to know anything about that ...* He tried to hide his unease behind a laugh. Rin didn't much like it but as far as Tsen was concerned he could choke on it. 'I wouldn't wish to explain to Lord Shonda why he's suddenly missing both his brother and his t'varr. I imagine he'd be irked.'

The jade raven was fat and bloated now, dopey and slow but it came when Rin called in clicks and whistles, hopping out of the cage and the ruins of the slave who'd once stood there. It flapped lazily onto Rin's arm. Tsen couldn't help but recoil a few steps, but the bird didn't seem interested in him. It preened a few of its feathers and then settled. Rin gently tugged the silver ring from its leg. He stood calm as he squinted at it with the bird on his arm, a lethal enigma of a creature made by sorcerers long dead and that no one understood, and Tsen wondered at the absurdity of Rin's blind belief in his own invulnerability; but then the dragon shifted on its wall across the eyrie and he felt the castle tremble under his feet again and laughed at his own absurdity instead.

Rin peered at the message ring, struggling with the tiny words, then threw it high into the air over the rim of the eyrie. It glittered once as it caught the sun and then vanished towards the sands below. He clapped a hand on Tsen's shoulder. Tsen flinched – Rin still had that damned bird perched on his other arm. 'Well, there's a thing. The Great Sea Council *has* agreed to turn your dragon on the renegades and outlaws of Bom Tark.' He smiled. 'It seems that not one lord raised an objection. I dare say there will be quite a turnout to come and watch.'

Tsen winced. He only had himself to blame. Bom Tark. A few thousand runaway slaves. He'd made the suggestion before he'd seen the dragon fly. A few houses burned and a few hundred slaves killed, he'd thought, and then it would be done, but he knew better now. It wouldn't be that way at all, not with that monster and not with her. A chill ran over him and prickled his skin, even under the blaze of the sun. *And a dozen glasships hovering overhead filled with fat old men like me. Hsians and kwens and t'varrs and maybe even sea lords peering out from their nice safe gold-glass windows. Scratching their chins and complaining about the wine as thousands die, clucking their tongues and furrowing their brows and making notes, complaining about the smoke spoiling their view and and feverishly wondering who might burn next. And my dragon-rider ...* He shook his head.

She'd leave no room for doubt. She'd be perfect. Meticulous and ruthless and utterly thorough. She'd leave Bom Tark a black scar on the jungle coast. Every ship and building burned, every single man, woman and child dead. Worst of all, she'd delight in it.

'Are you cold?' Vey Rin raised an eyebrow.

'I am disheartened.'

'You are also, to remind you in your own words, drowning in debt. The dragon is all you have. You have to use it or sell it, Tsen, and you know that perfectly well. Lord Shonda would buy you in a flash. Live your life with us in every bit as much luxury as you live it now. Full of comfort but empty of any danger. Grow your apples and make your wine and spend your days in your bath with your slave. Why not, Tsen? Really, why not?'

'While you burn whatever amuses you?'

Rin's face went cold. That was the end of their friendship, such as it was now, right there, which only went to show how little it had been worth. 'Aria, T'Varr. I speak to you as one of our discipline to another but you're not the only one who might one day be lord of Xican. Don't imagine that Lord Shonda doesn't speak to the others.' He frowned. 'What's happened to you, Tsen? You saw everything so clearly not all that long ago.'

Tsen laughed in his face. 'Your lord can speak to whoever he wishes. The dragons are here and they're mine. They will go where I say.'

Rin shook his head. 'Your thinking has grown muddy, old friend.' He didn't wait for an answer but instead walked towards the dragon. A Scales sat beside it, but neither the alchemist nor the rider was nearby. *Safer to be close to them when they've flown than when they haven't, but safest of all to simply stay far away. They can be careless even when they are not malicious.* The alchemist had told him that weeks ago and Tsen had been perfectly glad to heed his warning.

'Rin!' Tsen stopped fifty paces short, safely further than the length of the dragon's tail. Rin didn't. 'What are you doing?' In a flash of madness he found himself almost hoping that Rin *did* get too close, that some accident *did* happen. *And then I should just get on with it and burn the Kabulingnor while I'm at it? Idiot! Shonda would murder us all!*

Rin turned and Tsen could see the strain on his face, the fear. 'I want to touch it,' he called. 'Before I go.'

'Are you mad? You sound like Chrias. He did the same, but he's a kwen and you expect that sort of foolishness from kwens! Rin, please!'

Rin walked right up to the dragon. The Scales was waving him back but the Scales was a slave and Rin was a t'varr, the Hands of the Sea Lord Shonda. He reached out and touched the dragon's foot. The dragon didn't seem to notice. Rin backed away, turned and walked as fast as his dignity would allow and it was over and no one had died. Tsen found he was sweating and panting and he hadn't even moved. Rin was shaking when he came back. He still had that bloody bird on his arm too.

'Are you happy now, Rin? Or would you like to dive off the rim of my eyrie and see if my dragon can catch you? Would *that* be enough excitement for you?'

Rin's eyes were wide. He grinned, and for an instant he wasn't a t'varr but just a man, one that Tsen had once rather liked. 'I remember a Baros Tsen who would have raced me to be there first.' He stared at the dragon. 'It's so ...'

'Big?' That was a word for the dragon. Big.

'Yes, but not just its size.' He was gasping for breath. 'We're safe here? Yes? Out of its reach?' There was a quiver in his voice. Fear. Not surprising after what he'd just done but there was more, something ...

Rin clucked and clicked his tongue and lifted his arm. The jade raven launched itself into the air and flew straight at the dragon. Tsen stared in disbelief. 'Rin!' His mouth stopped working and simply hung open. No words. He had no words for this.

'I'm sorry, my friend,' and for once Tsen truly believed him, 'but Lord Shonda commands it.'

'*Why?*'

'There are sorcerers in Aria.'

The bird landed on the dragon's back. The dragon ignored it. 'Couldn't you have at least tried it on one of the small ones?' Tsen wanted to punch someone. *No. Because if it works then everything changes and I have almost nothing and Shonda has the power again. And to think I called you a friend once. You bastard!*

The dragon's head snapped round. The jade raven jumped into the air. The dragon shot fire, missing it but spraying flames across half the dragon yard as the bird flew between its legs. The dragon stamped, the shock shuddering through the whole castle. Tsen staggered into Rin. 'You stupid t'varr! What have you done?'

The bird flew out into the open space outside the eyrie. The dragon's tail flicked out, precision perfect. The jade raven plunged at the last moment, but the dragon seemed to anticipate the dive. The very end of the dragon's tail caught the raven like a whip and the bird exploded in a cloud of gleaming green feathers that hung for a moment in the sky before they floated slowly away. What was left of the bird fell towards the desert and out of sight, as broken as the slave it had just eaten.

'It didn't work.' Rin's eyes gleamed. 'It didn't work, but it felt it!'

Tsen gaped. 'And are you pleased or disappointed? I have a mind to put your name to my Elemental Man for that.' And he might have said more, or simply pushed Rin off the edge of the eyrie himself, but now the dragon had turned. Its eyes fixed on Tsen and Vey Rin and it stared, exact and calculating, hungry and malevolent. Tsen cringed. The alchemist had said fifty paces but even a thousand would have felt futile now. He couldn't move and the monster was towering over them both and it seemed almost as though it was inside his head, pinning him to the stone beneath his feet. When it came it came fast, crushing the Scales beneath its feet as though it had forgotten he was there, intent focused entirely on Tsen. He felt himself falling apart on the inside and *still* he couldn't move. Was this what happened to Quai'Shu?

The dragon lowered its head right down, as big as a cart, with eyes like glistening boulders of glacier ice and teeth like swords.

'Rin,' whispered Tsen in such a broken voice that he wasn't sure he'd even spoken at all. 'It was Rin.'

The dragon's eyes shifted very slightly, and then it reached out one massive claw and picked up the t'varr from Vespinarr. For an age everyone was frozen where they were, Tsen still rigid with dread, Rin held in the dragon's claw high up in the air, eyeball to eyeball with the monster. A strange noise echoed over the eyrie, and it took a moment for Tsen to realise what it was. Rin. Screaming.

'Put him down! Put him down!' Dimly Tsen registered that the alchemist was shouting too, but the dragon didn't move and the alchemist was left to wave his stick in futile anger until at last the rider came out and told the dragon to leave Vey Rin T'Varr alone. Much to Tsen's surprise, Rin was still alive.

Later they had to help him to get into his gondola. He didn't say much. Tsen didn't think he'd be saying much for a long time, but at least Shonda still had his brother. He might need a new t'varr now, but no one had died and so they weren't going to war, and maybe there would be an Elemental Man coming for him or maybe not, but with a bit of luck not as long as he gave Shonda exactly what he wanted and sent the dragon to burn Dhar Thosis.

The thought made him smile and weep both at once. Shonda had something else now too, something unexpected. He had someone who understood exactly what had happened to Quai'Shu.

For what that was worth.

Goodbye, Rin, old friend.

60

An Orphan Boy from Shipwrights'

He lay in bed at night, wide awake, shaking and sweating and shivering. Trembling at the memory of a dream he could barely hold but to which he clung with every finger of memory hooked into it like talons. All his people were dead. His family. But he knew who he was and he knew his purpose.

In his dream he'd been someone else. More than someone else. The hooded man with the half-ruined face and the one blind eye had been there.

He'd been begging, pleading on his knees. There was someone inside him. Another name. He scratched and scrabbled at the dream, clawing at it to drag the memory back but it wouldn't come. All he remembered was the name.

Skyrie.

Berren Crowntaker, the Bloody Judge of Tethis, sat up, fists clenched and eyes wide. He was surrounded by straw and everywhere was dark, so dark he couldn't see even a glimmer around him. He didn't know where he was. *Tethis? The Pit?*

The shades from his dreams lingered. There was another pit, one they remembered but that he'd never seen. In another dark place lit by a column of golden light and the broken goddess of the dead earth was there and the Black Moon, and he'd come so close. So close to …

So close to what? It made no sense.

He stared around him. The dream was fading but in the darkness he could still see it. He saw a woman bent over a man, and the man had an arrow in him and he was going to die; and the woman was trying to save him, but that didn't matter because the woman needed to die too because she was the last lock on the gate he'd so very nearly opened, and there was something about her, something inside her that made her like him, more than one person at once, but there was another voice far away calling him and his hands wouldn't move, wouldn't make that last tiny little gesture to make him free, and the rage and the frustration and the despair were like tidal waves crashing through him one after the other.

He roared and jumped up off the floor and lunged for the door he couldn't see. 'Leave me alone!' *Not my memories. Not my memories.* It was there somewhere. He knew it. He still couldn't remember where he was but he knew this place. He fumbled for the wall.

A hand landed on his shoulder. 'Great Flame. Again?'

He jerked. Tuuran. And with his name the memories that didn't belong shattered to glittering shards and faded like smoke in the wind and yes, he knew where he was: he was in Deephaven. The place he'd once called home. Deephaven, looking for Taiytakei and their ships to take him to Vallas Kuy.

'Come on. Out, out!' Tuuran was pushing him through the door into a passage every bit as dark as the room where they'd been sleeping. He thrust Berren ahead of him up a steep flight of stairs. There was light here now. Gleams and slivers of something bright at the top. A trapdoor onto a rooftop.

Deephaven. His head was clearing. He remembered now. They'd found a ship and worked their passage up the coast and he'd let himself sink away again and for a time he'd become ... the other one. *Skyrie*. Still in there. Lurking. Hiding. But now he was where he'd been born and Skyrie was the weak one, and he wanted this, this place with its memories.

Tuuran pushed the trapdoor up and Berren almost fell back down the steps as he reeled from the brightness outside. It was the middle of the day. He climbed up and looked, and all his strength was suddenly gone because he was *here* again and seeing it was like a punch to the gut. Twenty years since he'd trained with the sword-monks of Torpreah when they'd come to Deephaven for a summer. The start of a civil war, his master had said, but it had come to nothing. Twenty years and yet he could see Tasahre as though it was yesterday, dying at his feet as he knelt beside her. He blinked and shook his head, trying to tear himself away from the past and the deck of that ship, from the Emperor's Docks and the Deephaven he'd known half a lifetime ago, but he couldn't. It had gripped him from the moment they'd sailed round the Blue Cliffs and the needle-like spikes of Deephaven Point. When the ship had brought them into the bay, it had all come crashing back. He'd seen the city from the sea before, but only the once, from the ship that had taken him away all those years ago. The docks were still there, the castle-like House of Records at one end where the harbour masters lived, the great warehouses, the Old Harbour Watchtower at the other leaning like a drunkard over the Kingsway but still not fallen down. He stared at it all, fifteen years old again, the Bloody Judge and the Crowntaker both names that hadn't yet found him. Just Berren, the thief-taker's boy, the day after his life was shattered. He felt as though he'd stepped back in time, as though he'd gone back to those days to walk through them again, only this time he was walking backwards ever further into the past. He'd watched the city come closer and he'd wept, because if he was walking backwards through his life he knew exactly what happened next; and also because he knew that he wasn't, that the sensations weren't real, and that however hard he wished, he wouldn't be seeing his Tasahre again.

From a distance the city had seemed much the same. The changes were small and subtle and it took being up close to see how deep they ran. And not so much *see* as *feel*. As he stepped off the boat and onto the docks, a tension had embraced him like a poisoned shroud. He'd walked up the Avenue of Emperors, drinking it in, the rich taverns on one side and the hostels for sailors who could afford decent lodgings. The Assayers' quarter, as he remembered it. On the other side should have been the first fringes of the Maze, and *that* was where the city had changed. But not just changed. Every single street and alley had vanished, simply not there any more as though all the taverns and bawdy houses and the jewellers and the goldsmiths and the Moongrass dens and the sailors' flophouses had all shuffled up while he was gone and quietly closed them off. Further on it was suddenly familiar again. The two great curved swords still reared over the top of the Avenue, the Swords of the Sun proclaiming the virtue of truth and a terrible fate for thieves and liars. The old statues he remembered were still there: the first emperor and the last, except the statue of Ashahn the Wise had now gone and there was another in its place, a young woman. She might have been beautiful and regal once but her face had been scratched and scarred and daubed with paint.

Hang the witch.

They'd found a place to stay. He hadn't been paying much attention. Memories came at him from everywhere. He must have fallen asleep, and then the dreams, and now he sat beside Tuuran on a rooftop in the sun.

'You never believe me when I tell you who I am.' He said it without any bitterness but with a sadness that came of simply being here. From the rooftop they were looking over what had been the Maze, back when he'd been an orphan boy from Shipwrights'. He should have been able to see other places he'd known once: the Sheaf of Arrows where he'd hidden with Lilissa, the Barrow of Beer where old Kasmin had lived. He should have been able to point them out to Tuuran but he couldn't. The Maze he remembered was all gone and a new Maze had risen in its place. The House of Embalmers and Morticians stood on one corner, a place that hadn't existed in Berren's day because burying the dead had been a terrible sin and still was. The streets of the Maze were covered over now, *everything* was covered over, windows boarded and curtained or bricked up and it didn't take much to understand the why of it. The Maze had become the Necropolis, a city within the city, a city of the dead just as the oar-slaves in the galley had said. Every street he knew had been barricaded from within and then blocked by the living except for one – Taphouse Way once, but now they called it Dead Man's Walk.

'I know you think I'm mad.' He didn't look at Tuuran's face but pointed out over the city. 'There. Those towers up there. The Peak. The tower capped in gold is the Temple of the Sun. The one that seems to have wings is the Overlord's tower. They're the same height so neither overlooks the other.' He peered at them. They were still exactly as he remembered them. His arm moved round. 'That tower poking up over the rooftops is the Temple of the Moon.' Old Garrent who had always put a smile on his face. 'Beyond lies the Godsway, which runs from Arr estuary and the River Gate to the Square of the Four Winds.' Right past the House of Cats and Gulls where Saffran Kuy once lived. His arm moved again. 'Down there runs the Avenue of Emperors. All the way to the sea. The one we walked up yesterday from the docks. Next road along is the Kingsway.' His arm swept further round. 'Pelean's Gate and the Sea Gate are over there. Then somewhere are the old city walls. On the other side there used to be a canal. It was supposed to go from the river to the sea and make Deephaven into an island but they never finished it. It's mostly covered over now, but the canal's still there underneath the slums. You go and see, Tuuran, and then come and tell me how I know all this.'

'Never said you hadn't ever met someone who'd been here.' Tuuran snorted. 'Just said you were too young to be the Bloody Judge, that's all. Thought you were a bit pale to be from here too but I see they have all sorts.'

Berren rocked on his haunches. 'Bit of everything in Deephaven. Anything you want, you can find it.' *Almost* anything. The boat from Helhex had brought them round the mouth of the river. He'd seen the Emperor's Docks where his thief-taker master had killed his first love. The memory felt as fresh as dripping blood. He knew he'd never find someone like her again.

'We could stay here. In Aria. In Deephaven,' said Tuuran.

'No.'

'There's work for a good sword here.'

Snuffers. He meant they could be snuffers. He was right too. The snuffers the young Berren inside him remembered, the old soldiers from the civil war, they were all gone now, dead or hung up their swords. The city hungered for more.

'There's a war coming.' Tuuran said it almost like he was saying a prayer. A war, except there were no dragons here for him to slay.

On the rooftop, sitting in the sun, staring out over the Necropolis, Berren Crowntaker turned. 'No,' he said. 'We're not staying.'

Tuuran sniffed. 'I've been listening out,' he said. 'Keeping my ears alive while you've been sleeping the day away. That Ice Witch rules here now, and these risen dead, their presence, the tolerance she gives them, the fact that she doesn't have them all burned, that's proof enough of what she is.' Tuuran made a gesture of the sun, a warding away of evil. 'You should look for your warlocks and your blood-mages here, not somewhere across the sea.' He drew his knife and tested its edge with a finger. 'They say she rules as regent for her younger brother but that when he comes of age he's going to move against her. There's going to be a war. They say she's built a vast fortress up the coast from here, a huge thing as big as the Palace of Paths. All black stone risen out of the earth and welded into shape by her magic.' He shivered.

'Stay if you want; I won't.' Berren got up, leaving Tuuran out in the sun, and clambered across the rooftops looking for a way down. On the whole he'd seen enough of war, and now he'd seen enough of Deephaven too, but he had to have a look at what had once been the Maze, just the once before he left. Had to, because what was now the Necropolis had almost been his home.

'They don't like the light.'

Berren was following a man and a woman down Dead Man's Walk, loitering behind them because the woman seemed to know what she was talking about. The man was obviously new to the city – it was all over him in the nervous way he walked and how his eyes darted from side to side, in the unease that clouded his face; and who could blame him, heading into the gloom to where dead men walked and spoke and haggled over pieces of bone. The windows overlooking Dead Man's Walk were boarded up, the side alleys and streets blocked with rubble or walled shut. A patchwork of boards and blankets and sails hung between the rooftops overhead. The street became a tunnel. In places the stone was blackened and charred. There had been fires here.

The man looked around him and gawped and Berren stared too. *Fire destroys the walking dead.* He wished he knew how he knew that.

As they walked deeper in, only a few dim rays of sunlight filtered down to the ground. His eyes began to adjust to the strange twilight. He could see where daylight burst in again at the far end of the street, where the Necropolis ended once more. Between there and where he stood lay a small square, the Speaking Square in his day although it doubtless had another name now. A dozen or so figures stood within it, clustered in twos and threes.

'This is where they do their business with the outside world.' The woman was talking again. Berren stopped close enough to listen. She pointed down another street, a black hole leading away from the square. 'There lies the heart of the Necropolis.'

One of the figures in the square turned to look at him. It was the face of a doll, beautiful and perfect and cold and lifeless; and as Berren looked around he saw they were all like this, and they were *all* turning and looking at him. They started towards him, all of them at once. Though they moved as though they could see as well as anyone, each had their eyes sewn firmly shut. The woman fell silent. Sudden fire flickered from the tips of her fingers.

Berren turned and fled. Bolted like a frightened little boy until he was back in the summer sunlight once more, holding his side and gasping for breath. People passed him on the street with wry smiles. Someone running out of Dead Man's Walk like his arse was on fire? They probably saw the same thing every day. He waited until he caught his breath but no dead men came shambling after him. Out here the rest of Deephaven, the rest of the empire and beyond, everything was exactly as it was when he'd entered. Perhaps ten minutes had passed, and yet as he emerged into the light he came into a different world. Nothing would be quite the same. His home was gone for ever. He'd leave on the first ship he could find now and Tuuran could do whatever he liked. He didn't think he'd ever be back.

He walked to the Temple of the Moon. The priest Garrent had been a friend once. Perhaps a priest might understand what the warlocks of Tethis had done to him, but when he went in and asked he found Garrent was dead five years, and when the priests of the moon looked at him closely a horror spread across their faces and moonlight began to shimmer around them and their fingers pointed at Berren's heart and he backed away while they flung words like stones at him: *Monster! Abomination! Anathema!* The words Tasahre had hurled long ago at the warlock Saffran Kuy. He ran, scared again, and it was only when he was halfway down the Godsway to the river docks that he realised the moon priests had been scared too. They'd been terrified. Of him, and he had no idea why.

Even as he thought that, he saw the one-eyed man in grey in the night with the stars winking out around him. Skyrie's memories, haunting him.

At the bottom of the Godsway he went looking for the old house of Cats and Gulls to see if it was still there, for the relics of his old enemy Saffran Kuy, but the rickety wooden riverfront warehouse was gone. It had been torn down and a stone one built in its place, and the cats and the gulls and the stink of fish were gone too. He stopped there for a long time, looking, but Saffran Kuy was dead. Berren Crowntaker had killed him on a ship in Tethis long ago. The warlock of Deephaven was gone. And yes, there had been others, but they were somewhere else now.

He found Tuuran exactly where he'd left him, hours later, and it looked like he hadn't even moved. The big man didn't look up. Just grunted. 'Well?'

'First chance I get, I go.'

Tuuran muttered something under his breath. He nodded. 'War's a year or two away yet. It'll keep. I can always come back for it later, right?' He grimaced and pointed towards the docks and the sea. 'There's your ship.'

Berren peered down the slope across the maze and the docks to the sea and smiled. How many times had he done this? He remembered looking out over the bay almost every day, counting ships, seeing which ones were new and where they were moored so he could go and check the flags they flew in case the one that Master Sy was waiting for was there.

The smile faltered and turned into a lump in his throat. Tuuran groaned and got up. 'I hear they don't come here as much as they used to. Don't get on with this Ice Witch. Well we've seen how that goes, I suppose. But they still have their little palace up among the rich folk.' He gestured over his shoulder towards the towers and spires of the Peak.

'Deephaven Square,' said Berren.

They walked down the darkness of the stairs and along the passage with its closed doors and boarded-up windows to keep the dead at bay. An invisible wall divided one Deephaven from the other. The Barrow of Beer, old Kasmin's haunt, was only a few streets away on the other side of it but it might as well have been across the sea. Berren led Tuuran away, through the market and up into Weavers' Row, past the little street to the Upside-Down Temple and then down the other side, through the heaving crowds until Weavers' Row became Moon Street and Berren could see the corner of Godsway again and the Temple of the Moon with its tower which looked out over half the city. He kept away this time and cut through the side streets to Four Winds Square, right past the yard and the little house where he'd once lived, a thief-taker's apprentice who'd only cared about learning swords. They crossed the endless parade of carts and wagons that rolled between the river and the sea and then they climbed the Avenue of the Sun to the beating heart of the city, to Deephaven Square. It was all as he remembered it. The guild house. The Golden Cup beside it. The Overlord's palace at the far end and beside that the Temple of the Sun. For a moment Berren felt again as though someone had ripped his heart in half right there. Memories burst in another downpour, enough to drown. Swords. Priests. Monks. Tasahre. Master Sy. All torn away. The pain made his eyes water and the square started to swim. This was where his life had been cut clean apart by Kuy and his kind.

Why me? Why me? But that didn't matter. Him because he was there, because he'd been in the way, because he'd fallen in with the thief-taker and no other reason than that. Sometimes the why didn't matter any more, sometimes the what and the how and everything they'd done to him, sometimes even *that* didn't matter. What mattered was that he would find them, all of them, one by one, one after the other, and when he did they'd pay in blood and pain and suffering, because *they* had done this to him.

I am the Bringer of Endings? So be it.

Tuuran nudged him. 'You still here?' He was pointing too. 'See? There's the night-skins' palace. Now as to getting them to take us where you want to go, you leave that to me.'

He cracked his knuckles and strode towards it.

61

The Point of Balance

Bellepheros understood the prickling in the air for what it was. The Adamantine Palace had felt this way after Queen Aliphera had died, when Speaker Hyram had set himself against Prince Jehal. He barely understood what had passed in the dragon realms since the Taiytakei had made him their slave; what little Zafir let slip spoke of a war, and that she had been on the losing end of it, and beyond that he couldn't see past the half-truths and lies. Maybe Zafir was mad. They'd said that about her in the Palace of Alchemy, quietly where no one would hear. All the queens of the Silver City, hidden away in their fortress of treasures, surrounded by the relics of the Silver King which they could never understand. One by one they all lost their minds.

Yes, he remembered how the palace had felt before he'd left that last time, and Baros Tsen's eyrie felt the same now, full of unheard whispers of war. The Taiytakei told him nothing, of course, but there were no new riders, no new alchemists, not a word. When he asked Li, it was obvious she felt the same, and obvious too that she knew little more than he did. She tried to hide it, but he could see how much it bothered her.

'I've done it. It's made.' She stood in the door of his study now. 'Would you like to see?' He turned and saw the twitch of a self-satisfied smile on her face and couldn't help smiling back. The dragon-rider armour. She'd been working on it for weeks. It had sucked her into its novelty and complexity, however much she despised Zafir. Tsen had been nagging her to finish. Another little sign of war.

'Will I be impressed?'

'She liked the helm, didn't she?'

She. Hissed out with sour distaste as if someone had force-fed her lemons all morning. 'You don't fool me, Li. You're pleased with yourself. Smug, and I like you smug.'

The smile came back. 'Yes, perhaps I am. I've surpassed myself for the rest, even if I say so myself.' She gave a little bow and Bellepheros's own smile widened. He couldn't help but admire her. Dedicated, devoted, talented. *You should be running this eyrie.* But then he'd been thinking that for months. *We* should be running this eyrie.

'You, who could build a glasship. But I like that look on your face. Show me then.' He put down the book he'd been reading on the flora of the Konsidar and let her lead him. He walked behind her, not at her side. He was supposed to be a slave and she was supposed to be his mistress after all, even if no one else in the eyrie gave any weight to that now. Outside her workshop he waited for her to call him in. There was always a sense of anticipation and he liked to draw it out, wondering what marvel she might have for him. The enchanters' works filled every corner of the Taiytakei system of the world. They made it tick. Their constructs were everywhere; their engines drove and powered almost everything more complex than a horse or a mule and yet it seemed to Bellepheros that the enchanters themselves were treated little better than slaves, poor relatives to the revered navigators and the terrible Elemental Men. *Always the fate of those who are builders.* They were like alchemists, perhaps, servants to the dragon-lords of the nine realms, but every alchemist knew that that wasn't really true. Alchemists were slaves to their dragons, not to men.

He shook his head. The kings and queens he remembered had been the same as these sea lords. Mad, all of them, and if Baros Tsen were forced to choose between Zafir and Li, Bellepheros was quite sure the t'varr would choose his slave and let his enchantress go. Zafir, who rode dragons. He could always buy another Liang.

'You can come in now,' she called.

And by the oaths I once took I should choose the same, but I'm not so sure that I would. The greater good of the realms seemed as insubstantial as a vapour now. He shook himself and walked into the workshop. 'They treat you as they treat me,' he said as his eyes darted around, looking for what was new or different since the last time. 'Doesn't it trouble you that you build their world yet receive so little of its glory?'

Li looked at him and smiled and shook her head, and maybe there was a trace of something sad in her eyes. 'Oh, we enchantresses talk sometimes among ourselves of what they'd do without us.' It was an old conversation, he saw that straight away. 'Back in the Hingwal Taktse. We all think it at some time or another. We could stop making their glasships and the black needles that give them their power. We could take away the glass and the gold. They'd manage perfectly well without us for a while. The consensus when I was there was three years before enough things broke down to trouble them, five and they'd be on their knees. That's a long time, Belli. Plenty of time to destroy us or enslave us or persuade us. But what's far more likely is that we'd all grow so bored with nothing to do that we'd give in and give them back what they wanted. Just for our own pleasure of building it.' She smiled. 'There's no running from an Elemental Man, Belli, and we all take far too much pleasure in what we do to stop. We're like you. When all is said and done we love our creations, and that's enough for us to be happy with what we have.'

'Like me?' He couldn't argue with that. 'Ah, what we could do, you and I, with the knowledge we each have. Imagine if we could take it away and share it all with no secrets between us! Give us a year and we could turn both our worlds on their heads but we'll never get the chance. Baros Tsen T'Varr will keep us apart because he doesn't understand what we might do if we truly worked together; and if ever he did, he'd still keep us apart for fear of it.' He laughed. He'd had that thought for months too, but until now that was all it had been: a thought.

Li stared deep inside him, eyes a-sparkle and a smile flickering around her lips, and he saw she knew it too. 'But Belli, why would I want to turn my world on its head? Or yours, for that matter? For the most part I like it. It's comfortable. I get to do what gives me pleasure. What should I change?'

'Your people's hunger for slaves.' The words jumped out as though afraid he'd bite them back if they gave him any time to think about them. Probably would have too. The two of them stared at each other, struck silent for a moment. 'Could you not build a dragon of your own?' he asked her. 'One of glass and gold?'

'I built two. Little ones. Gold with jewelled eyes and little dim minds of their own.' She led him across her workshop. It was far larger than his own study but so crowded with bits and pieces she was working on that it always felt cramped. He'd come to know it well. Sometimes when she was moulding glass he came in just to watch. Of everything he'd seen, the Taiytakei glass still struck him the most. So clear, like water, and he'd watched her do it a dozen times and he still didn't understand how she made it like that.

Different sand she always said when he asked why her glass was so perfect while everything he remembered from the realms had been dull and warped. *Different sand and hotter fire. Did you see what your dragon does to the desert sand? Your glass makers should take their work to your eyries. Then you'd have much better glass.* And he'd thought about that afterwards and saw that maybe she was right, and that he'd never have thought of that on his own. Not a chance.

'Do you like it?' The armour was strewn across the benches in pieces. Bellepheros tried to imagine how it would look when it was put together, all overlapping plates of silver and gold and enchanted glass. 'I started with your dragon-scale ,' she said. 'I put a very thin soft leather underneath it. I don't think you have one quite like it where you're from.' She tossed him a strip of brown cloth. 'Here. Feel.'

'Rabbit skin?' It was soft enough and light enough but there was no fur. *Almost* no fur.

'Ratusk. They're bigger. But it serves the same purpose. The strength lies in the dragon-scale.' She pouted at him. 'You never told me how hard it is to work that!'

'I certainly did!' They'd been arguing about that ever since she'd started.

'You told me it was hard; you didn't tell me it was next to impossible! So the dragon-scale holds it together. There's padding on the inside where you said it should be. I would have fitted it to her in person but she is ... hard to borrow.'

'Hard to borrow?' Bellepheros snorted. 'When she's not riding the dragon she sits around all day doing nothing! You mean you don't like her.'

Li's nose twitched. 'No, I don't, and I won't have her here. She's broken and she's dangerous and she troubles me; and what troubles me more, Belli, is that you don't see it.'

'Li, do you think I'm so blind? But she's my queen, my speaker. I have a duty to her. I swore an oath.'

'She is a slave now, Belli.'

'And so am I.' And for that he closed his eyes to Zafir's madness. Deliberately, wilfully, and he knew it, and it made him angry, angry with himself for being an old fool. 'In my world she would have been my mistress. She was a sea lord and more.'

'I think she seeks to supplant our kwen.' Li laughed aloud, but Bellepheros didn't.

'I've been asked to prepare the dragon for war. Does our lord mean to burn somewhere? Because if he does then I think you might ponder long and hard before you reserve *all* of your disdain for our dragon-queen.'

'O Belli!' She frowned and poked him. 'Yes, they're speaking among themselves of a war with Senxian, even if they don't admit it to the rest of us, but it won't come to that. Senxian is a sea lord and the Elemental Men will not allow it. The consequences would be fatal and far-reaching and Tsen knows it and he's not stupid. And I promise you, Tsen T'Varr is not a man to burn cities either, not really. He's too ... well, content, I suppose. It's all posturing and noise and flapping of wings, nothing more. They'll not fly your dragon to anything that matters. Tsen simply wouldn't do that.' Which wasn't what Bellepheros had been hearing in what little time he had with Zafir these days, nor what his own eyes were seeing around him, but then he and Zafir were merely slaves and sometimes wars truly were phoney ones, fought without swords and blood and dragons but with merely the idea of them. Sometimes.

'I hope you're right. The dragon is made and bred and ready for such things and her Holiness is quite beyond my influence or control. I don't think Tsen or any of the rest of you quite understand what you'd unleash.' Li gave him an odd look, as if trying to peer inside his head. A dark anger came over Bellepheros and he snapped at her, 'Come and learn our ways instead of taking us as slaves and then you'd know!'

The venom stung even him. Li touched his arm. 'I will, Belli. One day, I promise. We have to show Tsen T'Varr our need for one another. He'll be our next sea lord, I think, and when that's decided we can talk to him. Properly. About all the things we've talked about among ourselves. Alchemists to come to our world, enchanters to go to yours.' She squeezed his hand. 'I promise. We *will* do this.' Then she let go and made a face and shook her head. 'Mind you, your *Holiness* is not helpful in that regard. She is ... inappropriate. She has slaves to wait on her, the best, trained to serve a sea lord's son. They could expertly guide her in proper dress and demeanour and yet she behaves as ...' Li paused as if looking for the right word and not finding it, then huffed in exasperation. 'She's *indecent*, Master Alchemist. Are all your women this way?'

Bellepheros laughed, thinking of Zafir in the golden egg beneath the glasship, the first moment they'd had alone to share their secrets. She'd been protecting him, making it seem as though she was the one at fault, but surely there could have been other ways. She could have put a knife to him for a start – wouldn't that have worked just as well? 'All of them? No. Those born to ride on the backs of dragons, though? Yes, perhaps they are, men and women both. Indecent and arrogant.' He shrugged. 'They don't care what you think of them, Li. Why would they when they're dragon-riders?' He sighed and looked at the floor. 'And are all Taiytakei so ... so ...'

'Squeamish?' Li cocked her head. 'You can say it. I don't mind. And no, not all of us. In the lesser quarters of Xican and one or two other places your dragon-queen might fit in perfectly well. But *most* of us were brought up properly, thank you!' She stared at him, eyes strong and defiant and daring him to mock her for it. Bellepheros took her hands.

'And you're all the better for it, Li. But see the world for a moment from other eyes. For me, and in my shoes I think you would be the same, this slavery isn't so bad. I continue to do as I've always done. The place is different, the time, the circumstances, the materials around me, the people, the words, but the task is the same. The nature of my bondage hasn't changed, merely the clothes that it wears. I'm a slave to my dragons and always have been, far more than I will ever be a slave to you or to Baros Tsen.

And you, Li, you enchanters, all of you would understand this. You would forge your magics of silver and glass and gold for Zafir and make little complaint of it in time, I fancy. But for her ... she's a dragon-queen and she cannot serve any will but her own. Look at the dragons. Look at Diamond Eye! *That* is what would be her master before any of us, and she cannot allow it, nor could any rider, and so they learn never to bend, never to flex. In their own minds they *must* be free. They *must* be their own mistress or master, for how else can they be mistress or master to their monsters? Sometimes they snap and break – I've seen a good few – but Zafir will not bow to anyone, ever, and she must show that in every deed and every thought, and if Tsen finds another rider then I'm afraid you'll find that one to be much the same, for the dragons have a different name for any who are otherwise. They call them prey. Do you see? Zafir doesn't wilfully set herself against your traditions or your people. She sets herself against the will of a dragon. She's been raised from childhood to do this. For her every breath is an act of defiance and she has no more choice in that than you or I. It's the way the best dragon-riders are made.' He gazed at the armour lying on Chay-Liang's benches. 'How does it work, armour made of glass? Doesn't it shatter?'

'If struck hard enough, which is why the soldiers you see carry ashgars, those spiked clubs you keep staring at. But this is to be worn on the back of a dragon and so I haven't designed it for swords and arrows but for fire and lightning. For a black-powder cannon there's little I can do.' She stopped abruptly. 'I've heard that she's been taking men to her bed of late. Taiytakei men, not slaves. Is that true?'

Bellepheros closed his eyes and took a long breath. 'No, Li, and why would you ask?'

Li gave a helpless shrug. 'Prurient fascination, I suppose. So the rumours are not true? How can you be sure?'

'There are reasons why I would know if she had, and she has not.' Another deep breath. 'There was ...' But no, say it as it was, and if Li didn't like it, it was hardly *his* fault. 'Some soldiers forced themselves on her. Black-cloaks. It was a while back. Afterwards she came to me to make sure there wouldn't be a child. So I would know, Li. I would know. She's not what you think.' He looked away, aware of a nagging inside him. *Think, alchemist! Think! What did you just tell Li about the nature of dragon-riders, how willing they are or are not to bend ...?*

But I saw how hurt Zafir was! Bruised and battered. How can I even think she had a choice? He turned away from Li, ashamed of himself. 'They said the same about the queens of my home too, Shezira and Aliphera when they grew powerful and ruled with no king beside them. Perhaps a dragon-queen is easier to accept if you call her a whore? Perhaps an enchantress too, if she grew too strong and wilful and called herself better that you? No, Li. That's simply the unkind lies of jealous men.' *So I trust her then, do I?*

She has the Hatchling Disease. Who would touch her?

But they don't know that and they don't know the signs.

'Belli? You look ill. Have you been forgetting to sleep again?'

Bellepheros forced a smile. 'A touch of indigestion. Sometimes I still have to convince my ageing stomach of the merits of your food, fine as it tastes to my tongue.' He grasped for anything else. 'You said fire and lightning. Fire I understand. Lightning?' *There can't be more. She'd come to me for Dawn Torpor. She would. And so I would know!*

For a long time Li stayed silent, watching him. Then she turned and stroked the dragon armour. 'Would you like to wear it? I made it for the dragon slave so it won't be a good fit but you'll have some sense of its design at least.'

'You're more her size.'

'I am *not*!' But when he cocked his eyes and glared at her, she shook her head and snorted and wrinkled her nose at him. 'Well turn your back for a moment while I take off my robe then.' Bellepheros dutifully turned his back as Li began to put the armour on. Because she wanted to, really, and they both knew it.

'Lightning, Li? Why lightning if not for war?'

'It's just the way we do things.' He heard a rustle of clothes and some muttering as Li put on the dragon-scale leg wrappings first, then the soft leather undercoat. 'You can turn round now.' When Bellepheros looked back, Li was struggling into a pair of boots, elegant and thin, dragon-scale covered in gold. Zafir would like them. On top of the leggings, overlapping the boots, came moulded glass plates covered in woven patterns of silver and gold to cover the shins and thighs, turned to face out from the dragon. Overlapping at the knee. Strange-looking, like the segmented armour of an insect.

'But why protect her from lightning when that's how you defend yourselves? What if you need to stop her? Your wands and your cannon wouldn't ...' *Oh yes.* He began to see.

'Belli!' Li wagged a finger at him. 'Yes, she is being dressed for war but I *told* you: it will come to nothing. Tsen won't allow it, and even if he did, the Watcher would stop him.'

Bellepheros shrugged 'Then I'll imagine that lightning storms are more common in these parts than they are in my home realm.' He couldn't see her face now. The next part of the armour was a long coat of dragon-scale. Hatchling skin was soft, the best for making armour and also the rarest, for the duty of every eyrie master was to see that as many hatchlings as possible survived. It always made him laugh when some king or queen started banging that old drum again. Survive? As if they needed any help with that! The ones that died were the ones that *chose* to die. The ones that knew what Bellepheros and his alchemists did to them and refused to suffer it. *Ah Li, still a few secrets I haven't told you ...*

She glared at him. 'Now you're smiling. What have I done wrong?'

'Nothing. Other thoughts.'

'Well you're having far too many of those today for my liking, but go on then.'

Bellepheros laughed. 'I wish I could. But in short: how much simpler the world would be if it was governed by the likes of you and I, with care for one another and cautious eyes turned firmly toward the future instead of by greedy lords eyeing one another with suspicion, forever looking for their own secret advantage.'

'Don't be so sure. We both have our own secrets too, eh?' She raised a sharp eyebrow at him. 'There. Have I done well?' She had the coat on now. Buckles down on the side, under the arm. He'd never seen it done that way but there was a sense to it. Joints were always weak points. This way the arm would protect it. He looked Li up and down. With the buckles pulled tight, the dragon-scale fitted her like a second skin. A little too tight in places and a little too long, but Li was a touch stockier than Zafir and not as tall.

'It's magnificent. Zafir will be … content.'

'*Content?* She'd better be a sight more than *content*!' The enchantress picked up the bulky part of the armour, the part that looked like the shed skin of some armoured animal. Overlapping plates of glass and gold shaped like diamonds, thin as anything, arranged to mimic a dragon's scales and as flexible as the true dragon-scale beneath. She lifted it over her head and the plates cascaded down her front and back, over her shoulders and down the upper parts of her arms. They glittered as they caught the light. In the sun they'd be glorious, perhaps blinding. 'And now what do you think?'

'I think I've never seen its like or its equal, Li. You've made it look like dragon-scale.' He nodded, approving. 'It's the most elegant rider's armour I've ever seen. No one in my land could have made something like this. You've made it for riding dragons and for nothing else – our armour isn't normally made that way but her Holiness will understand. She will, I think, very much appreciate its purity of purpose. She won't let you see, of course, but she'll delight in this gift. I thank you, Chay-Liang of Hingwal Taktse, on her behalf. It is magnificent.' He grinned.

Li shook her head. 'It will turn most arrows and it will turn fire and lightning.' She started to strap on the arm guards. 'A little help with this? They're awkward.'

Bellepheros stepped close and reached around her. 'Then make them easier if you can. A rider must arm and mount alone or they're not worthy of their dragon. Zafir will hold it against you if the armour demands more hands than her own. In fact she probably won't wear it.'

'Our knights are dressed by others.' Liang laughed as Bellepheros's fingers fumbled with buckles plated in gold. 'Most of us are, in fact. Well, those for whom tradition and form and the matter of appearance are important. Not us enchanters. *We* dress ourselves.'

Bellepheros snorted. 'Hard to imagine an alchemist with time for such niceties. Most days we fall asleep in our day clothes and then wake up the next day and carry on as we were.'

'I'd noticed.' She was using her teasing voice. She held her arms out wide as he did up the last of the straps and then stepped away.

'It *is* quicker and it *does* save time.'

Li snorted. 'I know, I know, and we both know I'm no better. And so what? Does anyone ever notice?'

Bellepheros's voice fell quiet. 'I notice, Li.'

'Oh I'm sure you do, but we both know that's only because you're every bit as bad. I've seen you in the same robes four days in a row with the same stain on the hem.'

'I change them when it gets *too* bad. Don't I?'

She laughed at him with a warmth that sent a pang of sorrow through him. 'You do.' Then she smiled and squeezed his hand. 'So your dragon-rider doesn't mind parading like a bed-slave, but she must dress herself in her own armour? How do I look?'

'Defiance in every breath, Chay-Liang.' Bellepheros looked her up and down, trying to imagine Zafir. 'We're makers and oilers of the machines of the world, you and I. We have little say in their use and their direction. You look magnificent. *You* should be the one on the back of a dragon.'

Li shuddered. 'I think not!' She fumbled around the clutter on her workbench. 'The gauntlets are my best work. Would you change things, Master Alchemist? Would *you* steer your dragons? Gauntlets, gauntlets. And where's the helm? Do I have it?'

'Zafir kept it. And no. Steer my dragons? I'd prefer not.'

'Why? Ah!' She turned back. 'Now with *these* she'll need no help at all.' She was right too: the gauntlets were a marvel. More segmented bands of metal, gold bound to glass once more and wrapped over dragon-scale.

She handed one to Bellepheros and he put it on. They were lined with a fur that kissed his skin, instantly warm but never hot. Pieces of gold exquisitely worked into delicate shapes were welded to the plates of the fingers and thumb. He wondered what they were for until he clenched his fist and his hand became a dragon's head, mouth open, fangs poised, eyes agleam. He let out a little sigh of envy and pleasure. 'It's a self-fulfilling doom, isn't it? Who else would be an alchemist? If not us then who else would do those things that must be done and for little or no reward save the quiet knowledge that the world has not burned for another day?' He held up the gauntlet, fist closed. 'Although if it means I get a pair of these then I might reconsider. They're spectacular, Li. I've never seen their like. Never anything even close.'

Li laughed and struck a pose with the dragon armour wrapped around her. 'You're bleak today. So will this suffice for your mistress who is a slave to fly to our master's war-that-will-not-happen?'

'Bleak? Li, every alchemist is taught this over and over again: we know we can never win, that our task is never done and that one day, whether we like it or not, whatever we do, some rider will ruin everything for which we strive. It already happened once. A long time ago. A few dragons woke because of one stupid rider and it was almost the end of all of us.' *Bleak? When my mistress who is a slave is Zafir? Should I be joyful?*

'Almost? But then *only* almost, Belli.' Li laughed, and her laugh touched him as it always did and gave him a little strength. 'The Picker, of all people, once said this: when those who rule drop our fragile world amid their squabbles, our purpose is to catch it before it smashes. That's what makes an Elemental Man. Think on that, Belli. They are watching out for us.' She cocked her head. 'So? Armour? Good enough? Yes?' She nodded vigorously. 'Say yes now, Belli. With much enthusiasm, if you please.'

Bellepheros bowed and forced himself to smile, for the enchantress had a kind heart and was not like the others he served here. 'It's superb.' He winked. 'As you very well know, my Lady Li. As you very well know.'

62

The Void

The Taiytakei were leaving Aria. All of them. They weren't wanted and never had been, and while that had never bothered them before, the coming of witches made of fire who burned their ships was making the place uncomfortable. Perhaps it reminded them too much of dragons, but in the meantime, as they packed their chests, they were happy to take every slave or sailor they could get.

Tuuran was already at sea with them by the time he learned all that. Going to exactly where he wasn't quite sure, but at least it was the right realm. He thought maybe they were heading for Dhar Thosis. The glass sliver given to him by the Elemental Man had seen to that.

'Ah well.' He stood at the stern with Crazy Mad beside him, watching the waves churn below. The salt wind across his face felt good. Free, even if they were back as they'd been six months earlier. No one had said anything, but they had their swords, their stolen leathers and boots, and they were the swords, armour and boots of Taiytakei sword-slaves and so that's what they were. 'You know what they do to slaves who run away, right?' he said. 'They send Elemental Men to hunt them down.' Although now he'd seen one it seemed a bit of a waste, and there didn't seem to be all that many Elemental Men about, and he'd heard an awful lot of stories of slaves running away.

'Yeh? The men who turn into wind and water and fire?' Crazy Mad shook his head. He didn't believe a word of it, but then Crazy had gone all suspicious ever since Tuuran had sorted out their ship. All *How did you do that?* and it didn't help that the Taiytakei were being friendly as anything.

'I've seen it.'

Crazy leaned over the edge of the ship and spat. Gulls circled over their wake. Crazy Mad hated gulls and he always had. 'Just don't like them,' he said when Tuuran asked, but it still seemed strange for a sailor to have such a thing about gulls. Crazy had shrugged at that too. 'Not so strange when you know they're the eyes of the devil who cut a piece out of your soul.'

He was eyeing them now. Tuuran yawned. 'Your warlocks sound strange. All this nonsense. Our old blood-mages were a much more straightforward lot. Just wanted to take a few virgins and bleed them dry, make themselves the odd monster or two and rip a few good-hearted nobles apart. Not that we've had any blood-mages, not for a very long time, not real ones.' He stretched, frowning for a moment inside, remembering the alchemist Bellepheros and suddenly not as sure of that as he might have been. But those days were gone and he'd never be going back and so there wasn't much point dwelling on it, was there? 'You can throw in the good-hearted nobles while you're at it. Probably the virgins too.' He sniggered at his own joke and then slapped Crazy Mad on the back. 'Got some sailor's gossip for you, my friend: the real Bloody Judge, they say he's in the Dominion now. The Sun King's ... I don't know what. The night-skins would call him a kwen. General, I suppose. Done well for himself by the sound of it.'

'*I'm* the real Bloody Judge.' Crazy Mad didn't look at him or raise his voice. He sounded more as if he was trying to convince himself than Tuuran.

'You should find him. Have it out between you.'

'No. Not now, not yet.' Crazy Mad drew his arm back and threw a stone at one of the gulls. It flew out of his hand like a bolt from a ballista, straight and true. Tuuran had never met anyone who could down a seagull with a stone like Crazy could. Didn't think he ever would either. 'It's the warlocks I want. The ones who came out to the middle of the ocean. They were looking for me. I want to know why. I want to know what they did.' Being on the move was making Crazy Mad pickier with his questions. The further they sailed, the more he scratched at his memories like an old scab. 'I told you – I met him once just after it happened. I went looking for the warlock who did it and I found the other me. And that's what he was. When I looked him in the eye, it was me in there. And I think he knew it too before he sent me off to be a slave.' Berren let out a heavy sigh. 'So no. I need to know what they did. I need to know how it can be undone.'

The wind was picking up. Tuuran pitched backwards as the ship ploughed into a particularly big wave. The sea was getting choppy. They'd been out for days and the storm-dark was close. Tuuran wasn't sure how he knew. He couldn't see it on the grey horizon yet, but maybe after enough times you got a feel for these things. Maybe the Taiytakei sailors knew and so he knew too. A sailor's instinct.

'The one who came looking. The one called Vallas. The one with the knife with a handle made of gold and filled with stars. He's the one I want and his knife too. Whatever he did, that knife can undo it.'

Tuuran looked Crazy up and down. 'They say your Bloody Judge carries a knife like that.' Maybe it would just be easier to tell Crazy Mad about the Watcher's glass sliver and being sent to keep an eye on him and a lookout for the grey dead too while he was at it. It wasn't like he was supposed to be doing anything that he hadn't been going to do anyway.

'I did – I mean *he* does. Now. They're twins.'

'I like your stories, Crazy.' Tuuran hacked up a mouthful of phlegm and spat on the deck. 'They get more grand and more ridiculous every day but they never quite fall apart. You'll tell me you're a lost prince next.'

'I was mistaken for one once. Will that do you? And what's wrong with spitting over the side like the rest of us? The deck-swabbing slaves upset you?'

Tuuran laughed. 'Because I'm a slave, Crazy Mad, and so are you.' He turned and swept his hand over the ship. '*This* is our prison. *That* out there,' he jerked his thumb at the sea, 'that's free-dom. That's where I want to be. This? This I just want to see burn. A dragon would be nice.'

'You could have stayed in Deephaven. You didn't have to come.'

'Could have.' Tuuran shrugged. 'Didn't want to. Never been much of one for my own company night after night.' He shoved Crazy Mad, almost knocking him over the rail and into the sea, then grabbed him at the last minute and slapped him on the arm. 'Need someone to push about, you see.'

'Arsehole!'

'Ach!' Tuuran let go. 'You can do so much better than *that*.'

'Where are we going?'

'Dhar Thosis, I think. Wherever the Taiytakei choose to take us. Or Xican, maybe?'

'Vallas Kuy, big man. He in Xican?'

Tuuran threw back his head. 'And how would I know that? How many worlds will you search before you find him? You, the ignorant sail-slave. Dhar Thosis is the place to start. We can get a ship there from Xican if we must.' He shrugged. 'That much I can manage for you, but if I were you I'd go looking for the man who's strutting about with my name.'

Crazy Mad looked at him balefully. 'How many worlds are there? How many do I have to search? Because I will, Tuuran. All of them. Until I find him.' And Tuuran had no doubt that he meant it.

That night the ship turned towards a line in the distance that was the storm-dark. The air grew thick and the wind howled and swirled, unsure of its own direction. Lightning raked the horizon. Night-black clouds roiled as far as Tuuran could see, thicker and thicker as the ship aimed for their heart. Always the same. And as the sky grew so dark that the moon and the stars were lost, the Taiytakei banished everyone below, as they always did.

'I've seen it,' he said to Crazy Mad and the other slaves as they sat in the darkness with just a few lamps to light their faces while the ship pitched. 'The lightning turns purple. The stars and the sun and the moon go out.' The storm grew worse. Wood creaked and popped. Slaves wailed and moaned, but not Tuuran and not Crazy Mad either.

'I've crossed it before too, you know.'

No one else was listening. The other sail-slaves in the hold clung to one another, clutched at whatever they could reach as the ship lurched and heaved. The lamps fell over. One by one they rolled across the wooden planks and snuffed themselves out. Tuuran grabbed the last before it died. The ship crashed up and down, lashed and ripped by the wind and the waves. Tuuran and Crazy Mad wedged themselves against a wall, side by side against the pitch and roll of the ship. Tuuran clutched Crazy's arm. Crazy

Mad's eyes gleamed. Almost glowed. 'And then, when you think the ship is about to fall apart ...'

'Let go, you daft bastard!' shouted Crazy over the noise of the ship and the storm outside, and then the abrupt stillness of the storm's heart hit them. It knocked the words out of Tuuran's mouth. There was silence for a moment and then Crazy arched his spine and tipped back his head and his eyes turned luminous silver like the moon. They lit up the hold and he screamed, and Tuuran could hear the other slaves in the hold screaming too, and then something terrible and vast swept into his head and hurled him away. *Dragons! Filling the sky. Hundreds! Thousands! The air black with them and thick with their cries flying to war ...*

'MINE!'

Men arrayed under the sun, light gleaming from silver so bright it blinded. Massed among spires so high they scratched the clouds, flawless white stone ...

'MINE!'

And in the darkness of the night the silver light of the moon shone down, hard and violent, and it burned and he clenched his fist and he would not bow, not ever, not even to the god that had made him, not now because he knew, he KNEW what lay beneath and behind and beyond.

'Go away!' For a moment he was Tuuran again but the words sounded like they weren't his. Like they came from Crazy Mad. 'Leave me *alone*!'

The vision went as suddenly as it came. Tuuran caught his breath. The ship was lurching as though the storm had never broken and Crazy Mad was staring at the ceiling, eyes bright and gleaming silver-white. Tuuran slapped him – hard – and the light slowly faded. Crazy rolled his head, looked about as though he didn't quite know where he was and then shook himself. Tuuran grabbed him. 'What in the fire of the Flame was that?'

Crazy Mad shrugged as though this sort of thing happened all the time and was hardly worth mentioning. 'I see things sometimes. From the other man's life. The one who used to have this face. Skyrie.'

'The one who lived on the edge of a swamp somewhere? Some swamp!' Impossible to see in the darkness now, but Tuuran could sense the other sail-slaves shrinking away from them. Some were still wailing and moaning. He could hear others muttering under their breath, little mantras and prayers as the storm hurled the ship to and fro. Cautiously he lifted his lamp and peered at Crazy Mad's face. Crazy squinted and peered back.

'Strange things happen when you cross the storm-dark, right? People see things. What I see is a man standing over me in robes the colour of moonlight, with a face one half ruined, scarred ragged by disease or fire and with one blind eye, milky white. Happened the last times too, ever since … *I am the Bringer of Endings.* That's what he says. Every time.' For a moment Crazy Mad didn't sound either crazy or mad. Just scared. And Tuuran must have sounded it too. 'What is it, big man?'

'Your eyes,' said Tuuran. 'They went silver. Pure solid silver and they glowed. *That* didn't happen the last time we crossed the storm-dark.' He took a deep breath and let it out between his teeth. Now he'd seen it again there was no pretending about the other time any more. 'It's not the first time. When the grey dead came. After they were gone and I hauled you out the water. Same thing.'

Crazy Mad grabbed him. 'I need to find who did this to me. I need to find Vallas Kuy!' And Tuuran thought, *Yes, Crazy Mad, you probably do.*

They reached land within a week, quick for a crossing of the storm-dark. They were sailing with other ships now, until the whole flotilla anchored together off a cluster of mountain islands draped in a thick carpet of green, deeper and darker than Tuuran had ever seen. The ships lowered boats for fresh food and water, and Tuuran and Crazy Mad went with them to a gleaming beach, a small curve of white sand squeezed between two jagged fingers of black rock. A few dozen yards from the sea the sand gave way to a wall of trees and plants tumbling on top of each other for precious sunlight. Distant shrieks and hoots echoed across the water, but none held Tuuran's ear for long.

Three mountains, not great or grand or even particularly tall but sheer and sharp, rose from the green heart of the island. Each had a tower on top. They seemed small from this distance but two of them caught the sun in a shower of colour, and Tuuran knew, because he'd heard the stories, that they were carved of solid diamond.

63

Hatchling Disease

A dozen glasships dragged the floating eyrie deeper and deeper into the desert. The dunes beneath them were lifeless and after a while, to Chay-Liang, they all looked the same. For a long time no other glasships came. Chrias Kwen was back again but no others, no return of any of the Vespinese. Chrias, she knew from overhearing things that she wasn't supposed to, was preparing to go away to Xican to gather his fleet and then to ... She wasn't sure. It wasn't her business. To the dragon realms to speed the hunt for another rider-slave so that this one could meet the fate she so deserved? But surely that hunt was already well under way. No, this was something else. The Great Sea Council, after two hundred years, was finally going to burn out the runaways of Bom Tark, and Baros Tsen's dragon was going to be their tool. And after that, Aria and its witch. It shouldn't trouble her, she told herself. The slaves in Bom Tark were probably murderers and rapists and thieves else why run away? And this other realm? Far away. The Great Sea Council was only doing what was needed to preserve their way of life. *Her* way of life. But it did trouble her. No one deserved to be set upon by that monster and the murderously deranged slave who sat on its back. And Belli was no help at all. *I'm a slave. Would you burn me too if I ran away? And what do you think you are to anyone from another realm if not a witch?*

Right now, however, those were Tsen's troubles because she had quite enough of her own. The dragon disease again, which was why she was standing out in the yard along with every other Taiytakei, every slave, every single person who lived in Baros Tsen's eyrie. They were crowded together in a great big arc, all of them together, pressing themselves back as far away from the ever-looming presence of the dragon as they could. They were staring at the dozen slaves caged at the dragon's feet. Those found to be infected would be fed to the dragon. Liang supposed it was as good a way as any to dispose of the problem, and Tsen was doing it openly, a grand display for all the slaves and for his own men too. *If you get the disease, this is what will happen to you. If you get this disease you will not be able to hide it. There is no cure. There are no exceptions. Do not get it. No one will leave until the eyrie has been cleared.* He said his piece and then the dragon leaned down with the rider-slave Zafir on its back and picked up the cage between its claws. The slaves inside screamed, tumbling over one another, tangling together as the dragon lifted the cage and eyed it, turning it. *She's enjoying this*, Liang thought, and for a moment she wondered how easy it would be to make a little device on the dragon bitch's helm to make her head explode when no one was looking. Very easy, that was the answer. Very easy indeed.

She watched the alchemist's eyes. He didn't like this either. He was watching the cage now, but as Tsen had said his piece his eyes hadn't been on the t'varr at all. He'd been watching Chrias Kwen. She wondered why. *I am missing something?* And maybe she was. There were clues to be had in the slaves screaming in their cage. All bar one of them were women. It didn't seem likely that the one male slave in there with them had spread it to all the rest. So someone else, and almost certainly a man. She didn't know the ins and outs of the slave hierarchy terribly well, but Tsen would. He'd have worked it out already, who the carrier was. One of the kwen's soldiers? And that made sense, since soldiers were generally stupid and didn't understand anything they couldn't hit, and the ones with the kwen came and went and didn't understand how the eyrie worked at all.

The dragon turned. Its tail swept across the dragon yard and there were more screams. Then it climbed onto the eyrie wall and launched itself into the air. Liang raised an eyebrow. She took Belli's hands in her own and forced him to look at her. His skin was pallid and there were dark lines under his eyes. 'How long, Belli? I need to know how long before I can tell Tsen we've found everyone who has the disease.'

Bellepheros closed his eyes. 'A month, perhaps, before it begins to show. Among the Scales it was quicker but they're exposed every day so that was to be expected.'

'This isn't over, is it? These are just the first.'

The alchemist shook his head. 'It always spreads, despite my efforts to hold it back. There are others here who carry it. A few of your people. I know who they are.'

'Soldiers?'

He looked a bit surprised, then nodded. 'Two so far. Tsen knows. They'll never be allowed to leave now. But I'm certain there are more in whom the disease has yet to show itself. How did you know?'

'When did you last sleep, Belli?'

'I slept last night.'

'You dozed on your couch. When did you last sleep a full night in your bed?'

He turned away from her. Around the eyrie all eyes in the assembled crowd were following the dragon. 'Tell Baros Tsen T'Varr that no one may leave the eyrie for another month at least. After that, for the month that follows, I will inspect any who must depart for sign of the disease. I should be able to see it by then. Really, everyone here or everyone who ever has been should keep to themselves for half a year to be sure.'

'Half a year?' Chay-Liang laughed. 'I'll tell our t'varr but I can't be sure to make him listen.' The dragon was circling high over the eyrie now, still clutching the cage in its claws. Higher and higher, and then it simply crushed the cage in the air above them. Little specks began to fall. They were too high for Liang to see their flailing arms and legs or to hear their screams but she found she could imagine them clearly enough. The dragon tucked in its wings and dived after them, snapping them up one after the other.

'Couldn't you simply have made them into more Scales, Belli? Did they have to die?'

'I could. I have no need of any more, but I could. Don't underestimate the Hatchling Disease, Li. It's a slow and insidious killer that will grip half an eyrie before it even reveals itself. Entire cities have died of it because it's never seen until it's already spread far and wide. All who live here need to understand that. Tsen's right to set an example. He's right to make everyone afraid to their very bones. A dozen men or women lost is a sadness, a tragedy, but a small one. If the disease spreads though the eyrie, I'll do what I can to contain it. But if it ever gets out, Li, you have no alchemists, no resistance, no defences, nothing. It will savage your cities. Your sailors will carry it, unknowing, across to other lands. You can see that dragon, Li, but you cannot see the Statue Plague. No, Tsen's right to do this, although he shouldn't have let the dragon eat them. He's reminded it that we're food.'

'Did it have to be so cruel?' The dragon was coming closer. Falling like an arrow, guiding itself with twitches of its tail. As the last few slaves fell past the eyrie towards the desert below and the dragon rocketed after them, Liang glimpsed Zafir. She was pressed down hard on the dragon's back, dressed in the dragon armour Liang had made for her.

Belli shrugged. 'All *I* said to Tsen was *not* to let the dragon eat them.' He shook his head. 'Her Holiness may have suggested otherwise. Still ...' He looked out over the crowd in the dragon yard. They were still silent. Stunned. 'You can't deny it's put his message in their heads. Her line always did have a flair for the dramatic when it came to spilling blood.'

Liang stared out over the desert. The dragon was somewhere underneath them now. She shook her head. 'And all this because some idiot soldier took a Scales to their bed? Wouldn't that person be the first to show the disease? And why? Why would anyone do that? They were told, all of them. You could hardly have been more clear!'

'I wonder that myself.' And from the way he looked at her she knew he wondered something else too. 'I don't think it was from a Scales. They're all men, and for that very reason. The slaves with the disease are almost all women. If a soldier caught it from the Scales and then spread it, it would be a soldier who was both very busy and had uncommon tastes. Besides, the Scales all deny it.'

'So did the slaves we just fed to a dragon.'

'They had the disease, Li. There's no doubt of that.' He shook his head. 'No. It definitely came from one of the kwen's soldiers. I suspect more than one.'

'If it wasn't from a Scales then how did that soldier have it in the first place?'

Belli looked away. 'An injured Scales, bleeding perhaps. We've had a few of those. A smear on a man's hand just before he eats, perhaps that could do it.' He didn't sound or look convinced; in fact he sounded as though he was making up stories to hide something he already knew perfectly well. 'Perhaps someone has come too close to a new hatchling or one of the tools used to clean it. Although I've taken even more care than usual about such things.' He sighed. 'Perhaps it doesn't matter. It *will* happen, now and then. As well to get the first outbreak over with. What matters is that it never gets off this eyrie. No one who has it can leave.'

The dragon rose from the desert and landed on the eyrie walls with a spreading of wings and a thunderclap of wind. It licked its lips. Zafir released herself from her harness, dismounted and walked towards Liang. She carried her helm under her arm and came with a swagger, her short slave-cut hair rising in sweaty spikes as she ran a hand through it. She seemed filled with an energy that dragged men's eyes after her like slaves on a leash. Even Liang could feel it, the tension and the pent-up possibilities that raged, barely contained, around the dragon-queen when she came back down from the sky.

'Your craftsmanship is superb, Lady Enchantress.' Zafir gave her a tiny bow with only the slightest edge of mockery and walked away. Liang silently swore. She knew she despised this woman, knew she was right to, but still, here and now, it had felt as though the sun had come out from the clouds to shine on her for a moment before casting her back into shadow.

'Poison,' she muttered to herself, quietly enough that Belli wouldn't hear. 'That would do it.'

A handful of slaves climbed over the battlements that night and lowered themselves to the desert floor in a cage suspended from one of the cranes on the eyrie rim. Slaves with the disease that Bellepheros had missed, preferring to take their chances with the desert than with a dragon. The alchemist shook his head when he heard.

'Well, you can understand it,' Liang said to him.

'There's no shame to being eaten by a dragon.' He only looked sad. 'Better than having your joints slowly seize one after the other until you can't move, until your skin is as hard as stone and you can't even breathe any more.' Not that they'd last that long in the desert sun but Tsen sent the dragon to find them anyway. Liang and Belli watched it fly and then they walked among the eyrie slaves, Bellepheros poking and prodding yet again at the soft parts of their skin. They talked of deserts as they worked. She told him of the Godspike and the Queverra. He spoke of his own home, of the Desert of Sand and Stone and the Plains of Ancestors. Of a people he called the Syuss who seemed to Liang like their own desert tribes but who had dragons too. 'The desert around Bloodsalt was the worst. Worse than this.'

The dragon came back. By the end of the day they'd found four more slaves with the first signs of the disease. This time Tsen had them thrown quietly over the side in the middle of the night. Liang wasn't sleeping anyway any more so she came up to watch. She listened to the screams as they went over the edge one after the other. Afterwards she went to Belli to wake him up because she'd realised she knew the answer. When she reached his room though he was already up, pacing back and forth.

'It was her, wasn't it? *She's* got the disease too, hasn't she? Just like you have it. *She's* how those two soldiers got it. Not some Scales.'

Belli shrugged and nodded and didn't know for sure, but yes, he certainly thought so, and he told her what the kwen's men had done and how Zafir had taken away all his cures and how he'd quietly been making more.

Over the next few days the alchemist tirelessly inspected slave after slave while Liang looked for the first inevitable victims among the Taiytakei. Slave or Taiytakei, the alchemist gave them potions and promised them long and happy lives if only they would drink it daily. Tsen was more ruthless. He waited a few days until the epidemic seemed to have stopped, and then the Taiytakei who had it all vanished one night. Liang never knew what he'd done to them. Thrown them off the edge, she supposed. At least they weren't fed to the dragon. She asked about the two soldiers but found they'd gone over the side too, a few days back with their throats cut open. Liang had wondered, until she heard that, whether the story Bellepheros had told her was the truth or whether the rider-slave had made it up, but when she cornered Chrias Kwen himself and he spat at her and demanded to know how she dared to ask such questions, she saw shame under the mask of outrage, or was it even fear? And so the slave Zafir hadn't been lying; and though it was another reason to be rid of her, it was hard to despise her quite so much after that. After that, Liang wasn't sure what she was supposed to feel about anything any more.

At last a cluster of glasships drifted in across the endless blue sky. The desert was starting to change now, growing a little more life to it. In the distance Liang could see a ragged line of hills. She had no idea where she was. Somewhere to the north and to the west, she supposed. Not far from the Godspike, though too distant to see it even from the height of the eyrie. She wondered idly whether the dragon and its rider had ventured that far, whether they'd found it and stopped and stared in wonder at something that would make even them seem small.

Chrias Kwen and most of the other Taiytakei with colourful robes and ornate feathered cloaks and long braided hair left the next day, carried away with the glasships. The eyrie stopped, hovering above the naked stone of the earth. Belli stood beside her as the glasships floated away. He rubbed his chin where one of the Taiytakei soldiers had hit him.

'They shouldn't have been allowed to go.' Saying that once too often to Tsen was what had earned him his bruise.

'A t'varr does not command a kwen,' Liang said, and they stood in silence a while until the glasships were specks in the distance. She looked at Belli when she thought he wasn't looking back. Watched his face as it gradually changed from strain and fatigue to something else. As that little frown she'd come to love crept over his eyes, the one that said he was thinking. They were slowly breaking him. She'd seen that in the last few weeks. The dragons and then the rider and then everything Tsen wanted, all of that had been more than enough; and now the disease. They were grinding their only alchemist away, piece by piece, and yet he still had a spark in him. She smiled and would have hugged him if hugging a slave hadn't been wholly disgraceful, and then she thought of the moment when the Regrettable Man had ripped open his throat and she'd been sure for a few seconds that he was dead. How that had felt. It seemed so long ago now. 'Come to me, Belli. When you need help.' She took his hand and squeezed. No one would see that. 'There's only so much either of us can do, but we *will* do it.'

He turned to her, and there was that spark still bright in his eyes and the frown, deep enough to have made its way into a question at last. 'Your glasships in Khalishtor drew power from black stone towers,' he said. 'You said they need to after every journey. How do they draw their power here?'

'From the eyrie. They draw it from the stone on which we stand.'

'And from where does the eyrie draw *its* power? What keeps it up?'

Liang shrugged. 'We have no idea. Not the least shred of one.'

'So this might simply fall out of the sky at any moment?' He laughed. 'That might be a blessing.'

Liang laughed with him. 'It hasn't fallen for the last hundred years so why would it fall now? A glasship will fly for a few days before it fails. Baros Tsen's eyrie is something else. Something older and greater than us.'

They stood together. Dragons could fly without rest for ... Bellepheros said he didn't know and Zafir had said the same. Longer than any rider could last, certainly. They might get hungry and they might get angry and they would grow hotter and hotter from the effort until they caught alight and burned from the inside, but they never actually tired.

'The Silver Kings,' Belli said quietly, as much to himself as to her. 'We have their relics too, here and there.' He straightened himself. 'Is it coming, then? This war you said would never be allowed to happen? That's where they're going, isn't it? And the dragon will fly to fight beside them.'

Liang didn't answer that. She didn't need to. It was hard keeping secrets in a place like the eyrie where everyone lived on top of everyone else and all of them in the shadow of Zafir and the terrible dragon to whom slave and master alike were nothing but food. '*Something* is coming,' she said eventually. 'I don't know what. I still can't believe Tsen would allow it.'

Belli shook his head. 'Ach! We had our speakers and you see how they become.'

He left her then to make the last preparations for the dragon to fly. To listen to Zafir chide and mock and berate him. To suffer it in silence and bow and call her *Holiness*, as he always did.

'You could be rid of her,' said Liang softly in his ear as the last day came close. 'She takes your potions every day. I've seen her. So does the dragon. You could be rid of both of them. It would be so easy.' Bringing the dragon and its rider into their world had been a mistake. She saw it now. It was clear as glass if you stepped back and looked, and Belli had been telling them exactly the same from the very first day. But Quai'Shu was mad, Jima Hsian hadn't come to the eyrie for weeks, the kwen was a kwen and even Tsen, who was a better man, even *he* wouldn't believe the danger until the damage was irrevocably done.

Belli looked at her and smiled a sad old smile and there just might have been tears in his eyes. 'I am a preserver of life, Li, not a taker. When a man puts aside what's good in him to serve a cause, often it seems to me that he later forgets where he put it.'

'Then I will do it. Show me how.'

Belli shook his head. 'You're an enchantress, Li. You don't need me to show you anything. Kill this war, Li, but with words, not blood. Otherwise that's how we become as they are; and you're so much better than that.'

She could have kissed him.

64

The Diamond Isles

'Oh, for the love of the Flame!' Tuuran grabbed hold of Crazy
Mad and shook him, almost slapping him, banging his head against
the hard sailcloth of his hammock. 'How's a man supposed to get
some sleep? Pity me, slave, Berren, Crowntaker, whoever you are!
Mercy! I beg you!'

Crazy Mad was breathing hard, heart racing. He snarled something obscene. Tuuran backed away. Crazy Mad and his demons,
and they were getting worse.

'You're doing it again!' *Watch him. You will be rewarded.* And
he'd wondered why an Elemental Man was interested in some far-
off slave, but not any more.

'Doing what?'

'Your eyes. Silver and glowing. *That.*' Tuuran took another step
away and shook his head. 'Every bloody night since we got here.'
One hand reached for his sword, thinking on its own without
checking with the rest of him, but his blade was where it belonged,
wrapped up inside their travel chest and wasn't to be had. Just
as well. 'Which one was it tonight?' Half the time Crazy didn't
remember, just looked blank and then laid into Tuuran for waking him up; but ever since they'd crossed the storm-dark and come
to these islands, Crazy had tossed and turned at night. Dreams
or memories, Tuuran wasn't sure which, but they were relentless
things that never left him.

'The silver man with the spear. That one.'

Ah. *That* one. Men of silver. Dragons and fire. White towers of
stone that touched the sky. An endless sea of silver. And always
always the same at the end, arms raised high amid a sea of destruction, calling up the powers of gods-knew-what while a man made
of silver rushed at him with a spear made of the same held aloft,
and then falling and falling with some great *thing* wrapped around

him that Crazy Mad couldn't begin to describe. The dream that made his eyes light up like lamps while the rest of him writhed in his hammock like a skewered snake. The sort of dreams Tuuran didn't want anywhere near him, and it wasn't made any better by the fact that the silver man and his spear sounded exactly like the Silver King and the Adamantine Spear of the speakers even though Crazy had never once seen a dragon or been to the dragon realms. He'd probably only even heard of the Silver King and the spear in bits and pieces from Tuuran's own mouth.

The light in Crazy Mad's eyes faded. Tuuran watched until it was gone. Then, only then, he slowly relaxed. 'You have a problem,' he muttered.

'I told you what happened to me.' Crazy Mad still looked like he might punch someone. Tuuran could take a punch or two if he had to, but these days, with Crazy Mad, you never quite knew what it would turn into. Or what Tuuran feared it *might* turn into.

'No, you have a problem in that you have to share a cabin with me and I get surly round the edges when I don't get my sleep. Go do your shouting somewhere else before I throw you in the sea for a second time.' Tuuran yawned and rubbed his eyes and shambled back to his hammock. 'Go on! Go up on deck. It's warm. Dawn soon anyway.' When Crazy Mad flipped him a dirty finger and climbed back into his hammock, Tuuran tipped him back onto the floor. 'I'm not bloody joking. All bloody night, the worst you've ever been and I've had enough. So you can piss off and bother someone else for a bit and let me sleep, and I tell you, if that's the way you're going to be now, you and I are going our separate ways. There's not a lot I won't do for a man but I draw the line when it comes to not getting my shut-eye.'

'Eat my shit!' Crazy Mad got up and staggered through the door. Tuuran clambered into his hammock and lay there, staring wide-eyed and awake at the planking overhead. After a bit he sighed and followed. No telling what a madman might do. Best to keep an eye on him.

He found Crazy in the middle of the ship's deck under the mast, lying flat on his back and staring up at the cloudless sky and the stars. He looked as though he was trying to count them. They had different stars here, not the ones Tuuran knew from his home.

Different stars wherever they went, whenever they crossed the storm-dark. Or … mostly different. Here and there he saw a few familiar constellations. The Dragon. Hadn't seen that one since he'd been taken from his own land. He'd pointed it out to Crazy Mad on their first night by the Diamond Isles, and the Swan and the Harp and the Ship. He'd pointed to the Adamantine Spear too but Crazy had called it something else, the Earthspear, though they both liked Tuuran's name for it better. And then Crazy Mad had pointed to others, constellations Tuuran had never seen. The Mooncrown rising off to port. The Knife and the Twins and the Sea Serpent. The Torch and the Archer.

High among all those stars the silver light of the half moon bathed the ocean waves. It seemed to call out, soothing and peaceful and seductive, but it made him wary too, and he found his eyes would look elsewhere almost of their own will. Too bright, perhaps. He closed them. And then he must have fallen asleep because the next thing he knew the sun was up and the sky was bright and the ship was full of life and they were getting ready to leave at last. He jumped to his feet, slammed by a moment of panic, but Crazy Mad was sitting right there beside him where he'd been in the night. He looked calm now.

'Didn't want to, you know, trouble your sleep.' He grinned.

'Dreams left you alone up here, did they?'

Crazy Mad shrugged. 'Must have. Don't remember. What I remember is the moon singing to me.'

Tuuran shook his head. He looked over the water at the three peaks of the Diamond Isles. 'I've heard of the sorcerers who live here. Silver like the moon.' It gave him an odd feeling to think of it. Awe and yearning all at once. Men like the Silver King, only that couldn't possibly be who they were because the Silver King was dead and he'd only ever been one man, not three. Maybe that was why Crazy Mad got his dreams so bad here, them being so close.

Crazy wrinkled his nose. 'You about to go all religious on me again?' Crazy Mad could do with a good punch sometimes.

'Mock away, short man. I'll dip your head into the sea until you see whatever god it is that *you* worship if you like. *You* haven't seen a dragon. Imagine them as big as these ships, wings that fill the sky, fire belching from their mouths, sweeping the land and cleansing it of men. My ancestors lived in caves, in holes, always in the dark or deep in the Raksheh forest. They were burned and eaten. We were food until the Silver King came to us. Some say he was a man, some say he was a god, but I tell you he was not fully either; he was both, half one and half the other. There's stories that he was made of liquid silver, or if you prefer it then the silver was armour that sprang from his skin at his beck and call and beneath was a man so pale he was a ghost, with hair as white as snow and eyes like fresh blood. Whatever he was, he was the Silver King. He came to us with the Adamantine Spear and called the dragons to him and bound them to his spell. He taught the first alchemists how to make the dragons serve men. And then he left us. Some say killed by blood-mages, some that he left for who-knows-where. The place the Taiytakei call Xibaiya perhaps, or even the moon and the silver colour it wears now is his. I don't know about that, but that the Silver King came and tamed the dragons? Of that I'm certain. You'll not find a man, woman or child of my land who doesn't know this story.'

'Yeh, but *story*, Tuuran,' muttered Crazy Mad. 'You said it yourself. *Story*.'

'And yet here you are, dreaming of him while up in those towers dwell the moon sorcerers who might just be his children. So mock away, puny one, so I have a reason to feed you to the sharks I've seen circling the ship these nights while I've been *not sleeping*. Perhaps they'd prefer a juicier and less bony morsel with a little meat on him but I doubt they'll be picky.' Crazy Mad laughed, but he did it carefully and said nothing more while Tuuran's eyes bored into him. Eventually Tuuran went back to staring at the islands. 'I wish I could climb up there to see them. What a marvel that would be. To tell my children I walked among gods.'

'You don't have any children.'

'And how would you know that?' Tuuran chuckled and a big fat smile full of memories grew over his face. 'I was an Adamantine Man before I was taken and I can promise you that Adamantine Men father many sons. And I'll father plenty more and I'll still be fathering them when my hair turns white and my teeth fall out and you –' he poked Crazy Mad sharply in the ribs '– skinny man, are too withered and weak to raise your talking head, never mind the other one!'

Crazy Mad snorted. Tuuran stared up at the mountains. He

hadn't seen it before, but one of the three diamond spires was splintered and broken.

'Some of the soldiers I fought with used to call me dark-skin,' Crazy Mad muttered. 'Then I'm surrounded by Taiytakei and suddenly I'm pale-skin. Be nice to be back in a place where it doesn't matter.'

'Should have stayed in Deephaven then.' Tuuran bared his teeth and grinned at the sea. 'Used to have other slaves call me out for my skin, or for my nose, or for the way I talked, or just for where I was from. Didn't bother me much. Adamantine Men learn better. You live a few years in the Guard and then even being an oar-slave is like taking a bit of a rest. But then it came to me that it *should* bother me.' He clenched his fists and smiled at them one after the other. 'So then it stopped. That was easy. There was an oar-master who had it in for me until he vanished one night. I think he fell into the sea while no one was looking. Maybe because someone hit him round the head with a boathook. No one was ever sure though, because the slave who got blamed for it said it wasn't him right up to when they hanged him. Odd, that sail-slave being another one who gave me trouble too.' He bared his teeth at Crazy Mad. 'Funny how things work out sometimes, eh?'

'Hilarious.'

They left the Diamond Isles behind that day, and – thank the Great Flame – Crazy Mad's dreams too; and after a week at sea more ships joined them, three at first and then the next day another six and then another three. When they sighted land there were more, day after day until they were an armada of more than a hundred. There were no slave galleys here either, only sharp-prowed ships that crossed the oceans.

'Only one thing a fleet like this can mean.' Tuuran cracked his knuckles. 'Listen to it. Listen to the sailors at their talk. Listen to the tension. Listen to the whispering of the wind and the hungry knives it brings. We're going to war, my friend. About time too.'

'They can do whatever they like as long as they take me to Dhar Thosis.'

Tuuran shook his head. 'You and your pus-filled wound. You are who you are, Crazy Mad. Even if you find your warlock, all he can do is tell you the same.'

65

Beneath the Skin

Zafir rode Diamond Eye high and far. Alone and alive and free to be the woman of her deepest heart, the one beneath the masks and the disguises and the armour and the pretence. Savage and small. In this world Diamond Eye was the most alive creature she'd ever found, even among his own kind. He flew for her as no other dragon ever had, as if they fed off each other's desires.

The glasships dragged Baros Tsen's floating eyrie ever further until there was nothing to see even from the heights at which she flew, nothing to the horizon but endless sand and burning rock; and still they dragged the eyrie further and each day her dragon flew. There was nothing in the desert for either of them. The camels and cattle that had been hoisted into the eyrie and filled the dragon yard were enough for the hatchlings and the men and women of the Taiytakei but for a full-grown dragon? No. So she went as the whim took her, looking for food, hundreds of miles sometimes, and when they found a herd of something that moved and ran they burned it to embers and feasted together, alone save for the Elemental Man lest they forget they were still slaves tethered by chains to T'Varr Tsen. Bellepheros said that the dragons interfered with the Elemental Man's power. Zafir watched carefully and saw he was right, and what a delicious truth it was to watch the assassin suffer and strain.

Each day after she landed the alchemist was waiting for her with his Scales. The air around the eyrie sang with tension. She saw it as clearly as she saw the violet lightning that sprang from the underside of the eyrie whenever she flew low and close beside it.

'Don't fly Diamond Eye to war for them, Holiness. Tell them no. Defy them, I beg you.'

He'd cornered her today, among the hatchlings where none of the Taiytakei would come close. Perhaps the Elemental Man was secretly listening but he was desperate enough not to care. She smiled at him and let him see in her face that *she* didn't care either. 'They are my enemies, Bellepheros, all of them, and I'll have not one drop of pity for any of them. They should be yours too.' She looked him in the eye until he turned away. 'I don't care one whit how many Taiytakei burn. The more the better.' The only pity was that Chrias Kwen had gone. Would he understand what she'd done to him? He'd seen it in two of the men he'd had with him. It must have crossed his mind. It must have started by now, after all this time, the first little signs, but the Statue Plague was a slow and unpredictable killer. She'd hoped, when he'd come back, to see it on him, but no, and now he'd gone again but she could still imagine him somewhere far away, staring at the strange patches of hard rough skin that he couldn't understand, rubbing himself with creams and ointments and wondering why they wouldn't go away. *For your arrogance. For killing one of my own slaves simply to show me that you could. A shame not to watch you die, slowly and in pain as your skin turns to stone. To show you that I could.*

The alchemist shrugged his shoulders. 'I try not to think of it, Holiness. Those who fall with a spear in their belly and a sword in their hand might be said to deserve their end. But many will die who do not. I know what you do when you fly him.'

'He must eat,' she hissed, 'and they are all my enemy, every walking man in this world save you.'

'And the slaves who are *not* Taiytakei? You see them here and there. Not many on the eyrie, perhaps, but in Khalishtor you saw them. Slaves taken from other lands. Slaves taken from our own, Holiness. Outsiders perhaps, taken by the King of the Crags and carried to Furymouth in his slave cages. What of them?'

'I will free them and they'll be mine.'

Bellepheros laughed bitterly. 'I've heard this Bom Tark is a town full of nothing else yet that's what they will have you burn!'

She smiled at that and shook her head. She'd heard the same, but all her instincts told her otherwise. 'Perhaps I'll bring their glasships down instead and lead the slaves in this eyrie to revolt.' They both knew she wouldn't.

'And the Taiytakei slaves, Holiness? Will you free *them* and make them yours too?'

'I will.'

'But they are the same as the men from the desert! The ones you burned.'

So he knew about that. And she'd gone out of her way since then not to strike down the desert men she found but to fly on and look for lesser prey, even though Diamond Eye begged her to dive and burn and chase these little ones whose fear was so deliciously sharp. 'The ones I burned that one day were not slaves, alchemist. And, slaves or not, a dragon must still eat.' She turned away. *My Vioros would have held his tongue better than you.* 'I remind you of your own words, Bellepheros. After the dragons your duty is to me, not to them. Certainly not to your enchantress.' He bristled at that. *Good.*

'Yes, Holiness.'

She turned away and out of the corner of her eye she saw him bow deeply and as he should to a speaker of the nine realms, but there was rebellion in his voice nowadays. So be it. If anything it hardened her resolve. She turned back to him and stepped in closer, close enough to feel his warmth, put two fingertips on his lips while the other hand snaked around his throat. When she spoke they were so close that her lips almost touched him. Nevertheless her words were so quiet that he had to strain to hear them.

'If you die then the dragons will wake and we will all burn and anything I would do is as nothing. Is that not so, Master Alchemist?'

'Yes, Holiness.' But he didn't move and his head was still bowed and that simply wasn't good enough. She lifted his chin so he had nowhere to look but right at her.

'I do not want to lose you, alchemist, but that is what will happen if you leave me no choice. Do you understand me?'

'Holiness!' There. Some shock on his face at last. About time he understood this was no silly game she was playing, nor him either, him and his eyrie which he'd so obligingly built for the men who'd made him into a slave. She let him go and bared her teeth at him.

'I will if I have to, Bellepheros. I will be a slave for a time if that's what I must do to survive but I will not stay one. Not for any of you. I'll die a statue if I must but I *will* die free. The disease will not kill me so quickly that I won't see the land of ash this world will become.' She meant it. She always had, had never pretended anything else, but the alchemist had never quite believed. His eyes said that now he did. She had him then. She saw it inside him. He was still hers, even though he knew what that must mean, even if he hated it. *The kwen is my Tyan, withered and dying, and Tsen will be my Hyram, who will see what is to come and will do anything, anything at all, to find another way. And then once again we'll see who is slave to whom.* 'Jehal did murder my mother, you know. It was him, with his own hand, and you alchemists with your truth-smoke never found him out. And in time we went to war, he and I, but not over that.' She left him there, among his hatchlings.

The Taiytakei came for her that night. Black-cloaks. *You'll be ready at dawn. You will fly your dragon and you will burn Bom Tark.* Orders given to her as though she was some lowly rider to be sent on errands by her eyrie master. As though she was a slave.

Bom Tark. The name had come now and then, always with a roll of the eyes or a hiss of disdain. A place full of slaves that no one would mourn when she and Diamond Eye burned it to ash. Shrin Chrias Kwen was on his way there, taking the bulk of Tsen's fleet, or so the Taiytakei would have her believe. She didn't know why. To watch? To take away those who were worth saving? To see if she'd be tempted into burning him to ash too? But she wouldn't. Not that she hadn't thought about it but she wouldn't, not yet. Perhaps Tsen would be pleased and surprised at that, or perhaps disappointed. She couldn't tell.

But really? A city full of helpless slaves? She couldn't quite believe in it. There was something else to this. There had to be. A demonstration of power, that's what they wanted although they never came out and said so. Of what a dragon could truly do and with as little consequence as could be managed. A city of helpless slaves? What did that prove beyond what they'd already seen? It *was*, after all, a dragon.

She rose long before dawn, as eager as a girl in her first flushes. She let Myst and Onyx wash her and oil her and then sent them away and dressed herself in her dragon armour alone. It was, she would quietly admit to no one but herself, the finest armour that any rider had ever worn and she was grateful for that. Still a slave; but on Diamond Eye's back and dressed as the dragon-queen she would forget for a while. And maybe she *would* turn on them after all and smash their glasships out of the skies, and burn their ships and crush them and grind their embers until the Elemental Man found a way to get close enough to kill her. Which he quickly would, but it would be worth it.

The black-cloaks walked her across the dragon yard, but not to Diamond Eye. Instead they guided her to the golden egg of one of the glasships towing the eyrie. They led her inside and then they left and the ramp closed behind her and she was alone with Baros Tsen and another man, another kwen by the look of him but not one of Tsen's. He stood behind Tsen, strangely close.

'I've seen you before,' she said.

The kwen ignored her, but she had and now she remembered who he was. The kwen from the city in the mountains. And something about Tsen was different today. He had a gleam in his eye, a nastiness to his smile that she hadn't seen before.

'What have you done to Shrin Chrias Kwen?' he asked her.

66

Fireships, Golems and Dragons

A Taiytakei in glass and gold ran through the sword-slaves' dormitory on the deck below. 'Up up up!' he screamed. 'Everyone up on deck!' The first glimmers of dawn lit the sky. Tuuran had his armour on in a flash, the best of what they'd been able to salvage from the slave galley after the Fire Witch had burned their masters: decent brightly coloured brigandine coat, steel greaves, vambraces and pouldrons. Not a perfect set by any means, not like the dragon-scale he'd once worn as an Adamantine Man and certainly not like the layers of sunsteel mail that Crazy Mad spoke of with wistful sighs. Plenty of gaps and joints for a canny blade or a lucky arrow, but it was what he had and it would have to do. He pulled a Taiytakei helm over his head. Now *that* was a fine piece, a plain open-faced steel helm but with a visor made of gold-tinged glass. Crazy had laughed when he'd brought it out of one of the slave galley cabins, right up until Tuuran had taken the helm and slammed it with a spiked club – one of the ashgars that the Taiytakei soldiers were so fond of. Instead of shattering into a thousand shards, the glass hadn't even cracked. *That* had shut him up.

'Better than steel,' Tuuran had said. They'd found three and kept them quietly to themselves. One each and one sold in Deephaven, that and a lightning wand, the last treasures from the men who'd made slaves of them for all those years. Crazy Mad had found some wizard – that was what he *said* he was, at least – and come away with a pocket full of gold. Lately Tuuran had come to wondering whether Crazy Mad could have come away with a great deal more, but that was wasted now. The helm was gone. A world away.

He lowered the gold-glass over his eyes, marvelling as he did every time at the clarity of it, how much he could still see with a visor over his face. Far away the rising sun lurked below the horizon, lighting up the distant burning clouds. It took Tuuran a moment to realise that the flames across the sea were no illusion of the dawn. Among the armada of ships headed to the shore, many were on fire. The ones at the front. He sniffed the air. He could smell the smoke. *Why?* There were more ships than he remembered from the day before. A lot more.

The wind. In a flash he understood. The wind was taking the burning ships straight at the land. They were fireships. That war he'd been longing for? Here it was at long last. A thing to make him smile like a man's first sight of the sun after years below decks.

Inside Baros Tsen's golden gondola Zafir's face froze. She squirmed. The other kwen was watching her fiercely, an odd look on him. 'Made him look a fool,' she said.

'He hates you with a passion.' Tsen smiled. He'd smiled a lot when she'd first come here, she remembered that, but it had become a rare thing these days. 'One day I would like to know why, but it's no matter for now. You need to know that where we were once rivals, our interests have aligned one more. Perhaps only for a while, but you are *my* slave, and Shrin Chrias Kwen is my ally, and you will respect him for that.'

Zafir snorted. 'I will consider it.'

Tsen got up from his throne and stood in front of her. When she was barefoot they were eye to eye. In her armoured boots she looked down on him but it didn't seem to trouble him. He ran a hand over the gold-glass scales, nodding his head, muttering approval, then stepped back and looked at her and cocked his head. 'Think of this task as repayment for the gift I have given you.' Suddenly, unexpectedly, he beamed at her and clapped his hands. 'So, slave! What do you know of Bom Tark? Have my lesser kwens told you what you will see? How you should reach it?'

Under her armour, beneath the glorious glass and gold scales that made her feel more a queen than anything the dragon realms had ever given her, Zafir shrugged and shook her head. 'A city of runaway slaves, that's all I've heard. Whispers say you wish it burned. It's by the sea. I suppose someone will point me in a direction and I will fly as I'm told, and when I reach the ocean I'll look for this city and I'll burn it down. That's all I know and all I wish to.' She frowned. 'Baros Tsen T'Varr, is this truly a city of helpless slaves? If it is, I wonder what exactly you hope to prove. It sounds absurdly easy. Dispiriting, I might even say. I'm almost insulted.'

Tsen's smile grew even wider, like a cat grinning at a cornered mouse, and it felt odd for a moment until she realised that it wasn't for her, it was for the man behind him who couldn't see what was on his face. 'Mai'Choiro Kwen, perhaps you would be good enough to point the way out to my slave. Tell her exactly what it is you want burned. For my part I have nothing more to say.' And, very deliberately, Baros Tsen T'Varr walked to the window of his golden gondola and stared outside at the dragon and put his hands over his ears.

The kwen from the mountain city glared at Tsen's back. Then he glared at Zafir, which only made her smirk, and that made him growl and grind his teeth and Zafir had to wonder if all kwens were the same and all so easy to goad. But she held her tongue and forced the smirk away and cocked her head. 'Well?'

Mai'Choro Kwen, if that was really who he was, raised one hand and pointed through the gondola window that faced across the desert towards the rising sun. 'That way. And you are not to fly to Bom Tark. You will be told otherwise when you leave, but this is the way for you to fly. I command it.' He waved his hand and kept pointing as though she was some sort of idiot. 'That way. Do you understand? No matter what anyone else says. Towards the sun. You should begin as you are told outside, but when you are no longer in sight of us, turn toward the sun. When you reach the sea you will find a city there. It has three islands. One of them is very tall. From the sky, if you are high, you will see it from many miles away. The attack will begin tomorrow at dawn.' He lowered his hand. 'Where I say you are to go, you will find far more than slaves ranged against you.' And he told her of a city by the sea and of its defences, of black-powder cannon and the Enchanters' Needles where the glasships would be, the island fortress with its lightning cannon and its rockets and its stone throwers. He told her there would be ships filled with sword-slaves to take the city streets led by the kwen who hated her. He told her where those soldiers would falter in their advance and why and how he wished her to help them and he told her of the sea titans and how nothing could be done about them. 'Leave them alone. They cannot be harmed and so the fleet and the sword-slaves will simply have to do the best they can around them. Otherwise you are to clear the way for them to the palace. Do you understand.'

Understanding and obeying, she thought, were two very different things. But she nodded because the kwen had been clear enough.

'Repeat your instructions, slave, so we are clear.'

She did. When she was done, Tsen turned to her from his window and nodded. 'Now you may go, slave. Take your dragon and do as you have been told.'

Zafir blinked and then stared. Tsen was *lying* to her. He'd hardly said a word but the gleam on his face was one she saw in the mirror often enough. She wouldn't question it, not now, not here, but he was deceiving her. Somewhere lay a deadly trap.

She cocked her head. Narrowed her eyes, searching for any clue and finding nothing. 'As you wish,' she said. *A trap for whom?*

'The Watcher will be with you, always.' Maybe he was still lying, but this time she thought not.

She bowed, the first one she'd ever given him. 'Then I will be wary.' She touched her armour. 'I thank you for this gift, Baros Tsen T'Varr.'

A Taiytakei in glass and gold tugged his shoulder. 'Go! Make fire shields!' He shoved Tuuran towards the starboard side of the ship where a dozen sword-slaves were already building a screen of wooden boards covered in sea-soaked hide. Sail-slaves lowered buckets into the sea and hauled them up again, throwing water over the decks as fast as they could. Handcarts lined with bamboo tubes sat behind the screens, draped in sodden sailcloth. Tuuran cracked his knuckles and let out a deep sigh and smiled. Rockets.

'Someone's happy.' Crazy Mad sniffed and wrinkled his nose. 'So this is it, is it? Bom Tark? Wake me up when we're done.'

'Fire.' Tuuran dragged Crazy Mad towards the shields. 'I saw it once when two Dominion ships tried to run down a sloop I was on. The Taiytakei set about them with rockets. A hundred all at once, and even if only a handful of them hit their mark those two ships were ablaze from stem to stern before they knew what had hit them.' He shivered and revelled in the memory as he picked up the next piece of wood and began hammering it into place.

'You have a thing for fire, don't you?' Crazy Mad shook his head but he was smiling. Tuuran grinned at him.

'You know, mostly I'm happy because I got a decent night's sleep for once.' He glared, then moved along around a pair of sword-slaves already working on the next section of the shield wall and stopped again, hands on hips, grinning at the sea. 'This is what an Adamantine Man is made for!' He looked around. Two massive pinnacles of stone rose out of the waters ahead of them. A thread seemed to join them, glittering in the rising sun. He frowned. 'I thought Bom Tark was just a bunch of slaves in huts.' In the grey pre-dawn gloom he couldn't see too much, just a few lights high up in the sky, some more ahead of them and on the port side distant across the water, and the fireships. Through the haze and the drifting smoke maybe he could see the silhouettes of other ships too, anchored not much further ahead. Maybe the shore and maybe an island to the other side.

The ship turned. He felt a shudder. The oar-slaves getting to work below decks adding their own strength to the wind. Shouts urged them onward. The ship turned again. They were going fast now in the wake of the fireships. Sparks and flames flared through the haze ahead. More ships were waiting for them, these new ones helpless at anchor, looming out of the smoke. Tuuran saw a fireship drift into the side of a towering galley. The flames leaped from one ship to the other as though driven by sorcery; a moment later the galley was ablaze and adrift. Their own ship lurched and turned again. A Taiytakei soldier covered in golden armour ran down from the sterncastle. 'Ready rockets!' They powered through the spreading smoke, the wind filling their sails and the oar-slaves driving as hard as they could. This one time they would be unchained and they knew it, free to race ashore after the sword-slaves and the sail-slaves before them to plunder as they pleased, and Tuuran felt their urgency. *Turn the slaves on one another*, yes, he'd seen the Taiytakei do that enough times before.

He spat on the deck. Fireships and rockets. A lot of trouble for a bunch of runaway slaves.

*

Zafir left the gondola as she was asked and walked round the walls of the eyrie to Diamond Eye. She took her time, pacing out the steps, pondering what Tsen could be thinking. A dozen soldiers fell in around her as she came close to the dragon. One of them, a kwen for one of Tsen's seconds, pointed across the desert. 'That's the way to Bom Tark,' he said. 'Keep on until you reach the sea.'

It wasn't the way the kwen from the mountains had shown her at all, but she took note of it anyway. A whole city full of runaway slaves? She could hardly ignore a thing like *that*.

Other fireships struck home. The water filled with men from the burning ships and galleys splashing and struggling. Those who could swim were making for the shore. The rest waved and shouted and screamed and disappeared under the water, appeared and waved and screamed again and then vanished once and for all. Patches of smoke blotted them out then wafted away again to reveal just waves. They'd drown, all of them, and Tuuran cursed himself for never learning to swim. Not that swimming would do any good in so much armour.

The ship turned again, steering so close through the burning wreckage wrought by the fireships that they grazed the side of one burning galley, then hard the other way. For a moment they lost their wind and the sails fell slack. Someone bellowed frantic orders while the heat of the flames from the galley washed over them. The ship turned again. Without thinking, Tuuran ran across the decks and started pulling on ropes that some sail-slave should have worked. His head was full of songs, of dragons and of fire. *This* was what an Adamantine Man was for!

'What the bloody moon are we doing?' shouted someone. The ship heeled as the wind caught the sails again. Below him the oars were straining. A fireship floated past, one of their own, crippled and adrift and close enough for Tuuran to feel the heat from it even through his visor. He couldn't help but stare. There were *crew* on the fireship. In the midst of the flames he could see them, bulky black creatures. The heat must have been enough to melt flesh, yet they worked calmly, steering the burning ships towards their targets.

Golems. Stoneguard from Xican.

Someone was yelling. At him, he realised. 'Never mind them, slave! Get us turned!' Then they were past and in open water again and Tuuran laughed. He felt dizzy with the madness of the fire, the thrill and the fury of the fight, even if this was only the start where all a man could do was stand his ground and hope not to die. Far ahead the first fireships were already ploughing into the docks.

'This isn't Bom Tark!' Laughter surged out of him. Those spires? That bridge? Distant stars of glasshships in the air? 'Renegade slaves my arse! This isn't Bom Tark at all!'

The dragon slave left. The gondola sealed behind her. Mai'Choiro Kwen stepped carefully away from Baros Tsen's throne.

'Will she do what is asked of her, T'Varr?'

'She will relish it.' Tsen closed his eyes and shook his head.

'She'd better, T'Varr, after what your dragon has cost us. Lord Shonda will find a place for you after this. You know of course that your house is ruined.' He snorted. 'Not that it wasn't already.'

Tsen kept on shaking his head. He laughed the broken laugh of the beaten. 'I know that *one* of our houses is ruined. Perhaps we both are. I certainly know that you understand exactly what we've done this hour.'

'What *you* have done, Tsen T'Varr. *I* was never here.' Mai'Choiro Kwen left, striding away so full of himself and sure that he was right, the way kwens always were. When he was gone and the gondola was sealed once more, Baros Tsen T'Varr slowly went back to the window and watched the dragon fly away. The slave was taking her time. It surprised him. He'd thought she'd be more eager.

'Well. You heard all that, didn't you?' he said as the dragon dwindled in the sky.

The Watcher appeared beside him and bowed. 'Of course.'

'I'd quite like to have Mai'Choiro cut into bits and fed to the little dragons. But better you do it in the Kabulingnor. Let his blood touch Shonda's feet and then make it clear. All debts are paid between us and this will go no further. A renegade kwen who would have seen Vespinarr itself destroyed has been removed. We thank Lord Shonda for his generous gift. Go and find Chrias first, however. Mai'Choiro reached him through Elesxian. Stop him before he throws what's left of our fleet against Senxian. I don't say kill him, but please do stop him.'

The Watcher bowed. 'And the dragon?'

Tsen took a deep breath and let out a heavy sigh. The dragon was a dot in the distance now. He watched it until it was gone. 'Well, you can't stop the dragon, can you? So you'll have to stop the rider. She's a slave and she will do as she is told and if she doesn't then we'll just have to find another one.' He sighed. 'Come back to me when it's done. And you'd better send the alchemist to me first. If you have to leave a dragon to wander alone with no rider, let us hope he knows what to do.'

'Rockets!' Bright streaks arced from inside the city, exploding in brilliant light high overhead. Tuuran watched them. He couldn't stop laughing, even when a moment later more followed, and then more, raining into the ships and the sea around him. Boulders crashed into the water ahead as the ship turned to face the land. One hit a fireship. The decks exploded, the keel snapped in two and the ship broke apart, scattering flaming debris across the water. Burning splinters rained across the decks of Tuuran's ship. Someone screamed. Tuuran caught a blur of flames and rushing movement out of the corner of his eye but when he turned to look, whoever it was had already gone over the side and into the water. Patches of the sea around them were burning as though the water itself was aflame. No ordinary fire. The ship had speed again now, racing at a shallow angle to the wind behind them. Over the noise of the fighting and the fire he heard the oar master below, screaming at his slaves.

'Ready rockets!'

'Hoy! Crazy Mad! Berren! Skyrie! Bloody Judge or whatever you are today! Where are you?'

Lights flashed on the island behind them followed by the distant thunder of lightning cannon; and then the sky lit up as more rockets came, hundreds and hundreds streaking from the shore towards the half of the fleet that had turned towards the island and hundreds more streaking back. As they landed the whole sea seemed to catch fire and Tuuran was glad his own ship had gone a different way. He found Crazy Mad at last, doing the sensible thing and hiding behind the fire shield. Tuuran shook him and pulled him out, pointing at the islands around them. 'See! Look!'

'What?' Crazy Mad was hopping up and down in front of him, cringing at the sky as more rockets flew overhead. 'See what?' A thunderclap split the air. Tuuran jumped and turned to look but there was nothing. Then it came again, a jagged bolt of lightning from the island. It struck a ship, lighting it up in a blinding moment of white. Its decks shattered, the ship vanished back into the murk.

'That.' He pointed to the islands and to the black stone monolith rising out of the sea and the golden towers that topped it. 'I heard the dark-skins talking! That's the Kraitu's Bones!' It towered over them, taller by far than the cliffs of Xican, right up to the sky, reaching for the clouds. Beneath it fire swept over the water, driven by the wind. Glorious.

'What about it?' Another barrage of boulders and fireballs flew out from the city. They were well within range of the rockets now.

'The Palace of Roses.' Tuuran cringed and then laughed again as a rocket flew across the deck above his head.

'So?' Crazy Mad almost dragged him down. 'Khrozus! And you say *I'm* the crazy one.'

Tuuran just laughed and laughed. 'Do you realise where we are? No, you don't!' He could see the shoreline clearly now, lit up by all the fires. They were still too far away to see if there were men out on the dockside to defend it, but there would be. They'd be Taiytakei.

'So how about you tell me!' Crazy Mad winced as something too fast to see zipped through the air between them.

'Dhar Thosis, Crazy. This is Dhar Thosis. Where you wanted to be. I told you I'd get us here! Didn't I tell you that?'

Crazy Mad's smile was as wide as the sea. His eyes lit up a brilliant gleaming silver.

After the Watcher was gone, Baros Tsen T'Varr walked slowly over to the little hatch, always locked from the outside, to where the gondola pilot was when the glasship flew. A golem, a mindless automaton that just did what it was told. Usually.

He opened it. 'You can come out now, Chay-Liang.'

67

Purpose

The dragon called Silence waited beside That Which Came Before long after the little one was gone. It toyed with seeing whether it could catch another but soon lost its appetite for such games. Once had been amusing; again was dull. Its attention wandered. It had been here in Xibaiya for a long time now, far longer than its usual passage. The thought came that perhaps it was putting off returning to the realms of the living. Perhaps it was waiting for the silver ones who had sent it here to find other matters to occupy their minds. Perhaps, perhaps, perhaps …

Perhaps it was afraid?

Silence wasn't sure why it should wonder such a thing. Dragons had no notion of fear for themselves, nor any reason for one. A dragon was immortal until the end of creation as far as it knew, although the end of creation *was* fumbling mindlessly right there in front of it. Perhaps immortality was not as stark a thing as it had once seemed.

Afraid?

Dragons understood fear. They understood it perfectly. They devoured it in their prey but dragons were not afraid.

Perhaps there was some need to show this.

The dragon called Silence left the Nothing where it was, creeping and unravelling, and went in search of an egg. There were fewer to be had than before, far fewer but still enough. Most of them were in the places that it remembered. A few were somewhere far away from the rest.

It chose the few.

I am Silence. I come, world of the living, awake and alert and filled with what I know.

And hungry. Always hungry.

The Sea Lord

68

Sail, Fight, Freedom

The air shook with the *whoosh* of rocket after rocket being fired from the carts on the decks. Berren blinked and watched them fly, hunched down, hands over his ears. A boulder crashed into the water a hundred feet to the side of the ship, shooting a plume of water into the air. A few seconds later a fine smear of spray misted his visor. Absently he wiped it away, still watching the rocket trails arcing towards the city. There were more in the air now, a whole skyful of them coming back the other way. Another hurled boulder hit the ship in front of them, shattering its stern in a shower of wood and splinters. Pieces of the vessel drifted away as its mast toppled and crashed into the waves. He hardly noticed. Just stared, hypnotised by the rockets. They seemed to move so slowly and the brightest of them didn't seem to be moving at all, just getting bigger and bigger ...

'Down.' Tuuran threw them both to the deck. The rocket slammed into the front of the ship and exploded in a fireball. Slaves and Taiytakei alike rushed forward with buckets of water while flames shot up the ropes and bit into the deck and foresails. The ship turned sharply, grinding past the sinking carcass of one of its companions, and started to lose way. Men thrashing in the water screamed for help as they drifted past. The splintering cracks of snapping oars rose over the shouts and the roar of the fire and the booms and thunderclaps behind them.

Berren drew his sword and sighed for the moonsteel blade he'd once had, a sword that someone else now carried in his name. It was priceless. Only one place in all of the worlds made moonsteel, and that was in Aria. Black as night, yet now and then the steel would shimmer with silvery moonlight and sometimes he even saw the moon itself shining inside the sword. It cut through mundane mail as easily it cut through flesh and bone and it never lost its edge. The enchanted blades of the Ice Witch, an irreplaceable gift from the Sun King for services he'd once rendered and now he had this: a plain ordinary blade, duller than he would have liked, yet another reminder of the life the warlocks had taken away from him. If they were here in this city, somehow he'd find them. He'd make them tell him what they'd done and why, and how to make it back the way it was, and then he'd cut out their sordid black hearts.

Another ship powered past in clear water. Others were coming out of the lightening sky. Dozens more were wallowing, adrift and ablaze. Ships from the armada, ships that had been caught at anchor in the harbour. Distant fire glowed ahead through the mist and the clouds of smoke drifting across the sea; the shore itself was lost now, hidden in the haze. The air reeked of black powder, burning his nose. For a moment the noise of the rockets stopped, the sudden quiet punctured now and then by the splash of a boulder striking the water. They were moving again, picking up speed. Sail-slaves with buckets of seawater ran back and forth putting out the last of the fires and hurling the bodies of the dead over the side. Booms and rumbling thunder echoed across the waves from behind. The smoke grew thicker. They were getting close.

'Swords! Archers!' More and more Taiytakei appeared on the deck now, armed and armoured for battle. Slaves too. Suddenly, weapons were everywhere. The ship heeled. 'Lines and grapples!' Berren thought he saw a flickering light in the smoke. Then another and maybe an outline. Something tall and dark. A mast. They turned hard again and yes, he was right: out of the smoke came the shape of a second ship. There were shouts across the water as the two glided towards each other. For a moment no one seemed sure whether the other ship was one of their own or an enemy, then a storm of fire arrows rained down on them. Even as the archers were still shooting, the ships came together. He felt it through his feet. Not a crashing blow but a glancing, grinding, oar-snapping impact. An arrow hit his helmet and glanced off, staggering him sideways. Another hit his brigandine coat, winding him. It hung limply from the leather, stopped by the metal underneath. He looked at the sword in his hand again. A short stabbing weapon, the sort he'd learned to use long ago in Deephaven. The sort his thief-taker master had once had. *What would you make of me now,*

Master Sy? All those years you spent hunting after the man who took your kingdom, and now here I am embarked upon the same, far away from home just like you were, chasing after warlocks as you once did. But it's not a kingdom I'm after.

'Grapples! Lines!' The enemy were so close he could almost reach out and touch them. Men on both sides screamed as arrows found their marks, as archers fell from the rigging. Berren slid his sword back into its scabbard and crouched behind the fire shield and checked his weapons one last time. Sword on one side, a ravensbeak on the other – a small hammer-and-pick thing for finding the joints in men with too much armour for a blade. There were spears on offer and javelins and crossbows, but crossbows were slow and heavy and spears were no weapon for fighting in city streets. He'd seen other things too, fire globes like the ones the Prince of War had used half a lifetime ago to reclaim his kingdom. Staves made of glass and gold that Tuuran said would shoot lightning like the wands the galley slavers had carried. Black rods that neither of them understood, but such devices worked only for the Taiytakei, not for sword-slaves who might steal them and run away. Or worse, turn them on their masters.

'Sword-slaves!' Tuuran raised his axe. Berren had no idea where he had found it, but it was enormous and having it seemed to make the big man happy. The ships were bound together now by a dozen grapples. Fists punched the air. 'Sail! Fight! Freedom! No quarter!'

Sword-slaves and Taiytakei alike swarmed over the side. As they did, another group of Taiytakei dumped a heavy chest in the middle of the deck and kicked it open. More weapons. 'All slaves are sword-slaves today,' shouted a Taiytakei solder. He picked up a couple of spiked cudgels and pressed them into the hands of the two nearest sail-slaves as Berren ran past. 'You fight!' he bellowed. 'Sail! Fight! Freedom! Fight or die!'

'Sword-slaves!'

Men rushed to the chest. On the deck of the other ship Tuuran was already laying about him with his axe. Berren grabbed a rope and swung across, dropped, rolled sideways and fetched up against the body of a fallen Taiytakei in glass and gold plates. Around him, slaves too slow or too stupid to do anything but gawk were cut down. A battle madness was growing inside him as it always did, a hunger he had no choice but to embrace.

A man fell out of the rigging above him, stuck by a dozen arrows. The enemy were scattering, some bolting below decks to hide or beg for mercy, others leaping over the side towards the shore. Sword-slaves and sail-slaves and even oar-slaves were swarming across, filled with greed and killing lust, hands clenched around their knives. Most of them had no armour at all, like most of the sailors that lay dead around the deck. Berren scurried across the ship and peered over the other side. Arrows came from the shore, thudding among them, fired blind perhaps but no less dangerous for it. Bolts of lightning came with them, shattering the air with their thunderclap roar, striking the hull, the mast. He saw one catch a hapless sail-slave, hurling him away in a stink of ozone and crisping skin. The smoke had thinned enough for Berren to see the docks. The ship they'd taken was moored to one end of a long floating wooden jetty that reached to the shore. At the far end soldiers were waiting for them, crouched behind huge metal shields. A dozen bulky black creatures stood around them, motionless. They were the shape of a man but half again as tall and as broad as two. Now and then an arrow struck one of them and stuck, quivering, but they seemed not to notice.

Golems. Tuuran had told him all about the Taiytakei and their golems but he'd never seen one before; even Tuuran had only seen them from a distance.

The Taiytakei with the golden armour strode out into the middle of the deck and raised his lightning staff. He screamed at them all again, 'Sail! Fight! Freedom! No quarter.' The words were ringing from his mouth when an arrow struck him in the side of the head, hard enough to stagger him as it ricocheted off his helm and away across the water. A crack of lightning followed, the thunderclap making them all cower and cringe, but the Taiytakei stood unmoved while his glass and gold armour crackled and sparked. Berren was breathing hard now, full of the fight. The air was rotten with the stench of rocket smoke. He crouched beside Tuuran, trying to damp down the battle madness.

'I don't think—'

The Taiytakei with the golden armour levelled his staff at the shore. He let off a bolt of lightning that left Berren's ears ringing. He could hardly hear a thing now but he didn't need to. 'No quarter!' Tuuran's eyes were mad. With sail-slaves and Taiytakei solders at his heels he launched himself towards the enemy; and as he did, Berren fell to his own madness and followed.

69

Desert Twilight

'Kwens like you will no longer be needed when I'm done.'

Zafir smiled at the kwen who was showing her the direction to fly, then pulled down the glass visor on her perfect helm. She climbed the ladder to Diamond Eye's back and buckled and strapped herself into the dragon's harness. They leaped together from the eyrie walls, dragon and rider, and rose towards the desert sky. She took one look along the line of the rising sun and then flew the way the kwen had pointed, urging Diamond Eye up high, on and on until the sky was a deep burning blue and the horizon sun was fierce and relentless and the eyrie nothing but a violet-shrouded speck lost in the haze of the ruddy ochre ground below. When she was sure no one would see her she turned east, the way Tsen's other kwen had wanted her to go. She had no idea why Tsen had given her a different place to fly to and could hardly have cared less. She was on the back of Diamond Eye. She was alive. For a time nothing else mattered.

The miles passed. Up so high she had no sense of the distance, no feel for the change of the ground far below. She felt only the wind, the push of it against her, and revelled in the perfect sight of the enchanter's visor. A dragon-queen, first and last and always. In the hours that passed up in that thin bright sky she lived the months before the Taiytakei had taken her all over again, slowly stepping through them, looking for the mistakes she must have made, the little signs and signals of all the betrayals and failures that had later come. When she didn't find them she made them up. A little word here that she'd never questioned but had meant more than it seemed. A look. A glance. A twitch of the lips. Wasted effort and she knew it, but she couldn't help herself. It was better than going back any further, to the Pinnacles and to the princess locked away in the tiny lightless room, more afraid of what would happen when that door finally opened than of anything else in the world.

The sun shifted. It rose to its zenith and began to sink. The pressure in her bladder grew. She ignored it as long as she could. Dragon-riders learned these things. No water before a flight. Starve yourself. Drink little and often when thirsty. She had skins of water beside her, a saddlebag full of them for the blistering desert heat, yet she touched them as rarely as she could. When she lifted the visor to drink, the wind in her face made her weep. Some riders arranged their harnesses to allow them to stand up and piss in the wind and go on but Diamond Eye had been saddled for war, for battling King Jehal over the Pinnacles or over the Adamantine Palace, and no such thoughts had been in his rider's mind back then.

She flew as long as she could and came down only because she had to. By then the light was failing, the sun dipping close to the horizon behind her, a ball of angry orange fire. How long had they flown? Most of a day. She'd pay for it tomorrow, legs and hips and back stiff and full of aches.

The ground was still a hazy tan blur, passing leisurely beneath them. Diamond Eye had flown for hundreds of miles in a single straight line and yet they were still in the desert. How far did it go? It had changed, though. She saw that as they came lower. Not quite the arid lifeless place where the eyrie had been; there was more to the earth now than rock and sand. A great plain of dirty brown stone, scarred with dried-up riverbeds and littered with thorn trees clinging to whatever life they could find. Huge slabs of rock lay scattered about, flat-topped and a hundred feet high with crumbling craggy cliffs. Mesas like the ones at the edge of the Maze, the lifeless carved canyons of stone with their rivers which rushed from the lush peaks of the Purple Spur not a hundred miles from the Adamantine Palace that had once been hers. The land there had been like this, broken, not quite lifeless, not quite dead and dry but so close it barely seemed to matter. No one lived in these places. Except in the world she'd come from that hadn't been true. The Red Riders had lived in the Maze. They'd made it their home, there and the Spur, a constant thorn in her side, and Jehal had told her and told her and told her to deal with them until finally he'd done it himself and taken their dragons to add to his own. Was that the moment he'd turned against her?

And why was she thinking of him so much today? But she knew the answer. Because he'd betrayed her, and the last thing she'd seen on Baros Tsen T'Varr's face had been that same look. That not-quite-hidden gleam of a knife, drawn and sharp, glittering deep in his eye.

She picked one of the smaller towers of stone, a place where no one could possibly be alive. Diamond Eye glided down among the thorns and the arid earth. A cloud of dust rose around them, choking her as he flapped his wings, angry to be brought to earth. Never mind how many hours he'd flown, he wanted more, always wanted more. He was as fresh and eager and hungry as he'd been when they'd left. More, more, more; always the way with dragons but here in this place Diamond Eye's hunger was greater than any dragon she'd ever known. They were dangerous things, dragons and their urges. They bled into their riders – the want, the hunger and the anger, the urge to fly and to burn, to smash and to crush. Thoughts bled the other way too. A rider had to be careful. She'd learned to control her feelings, especially in an eyrie with a hundred of the monsters around. Calm, always calm, never angry and most certainly never *ever* afraid. But it was harder in the air with the dragon's own desires constantly nibbling at the edges of her thoughts, and when it came to a battle no rider lasted long. They caved in, one after the other, to the fury, to the lust, to the madness. If she'd known that before Evenspire – if she'd truly *understood* it – she might have done things differently. But she hadn't, and so things had gone as they did, and Jehal had taken the chance that she'd given him.

She climbed from Diamond Eye's back, taking a skin of water down with her, and began to strip off her armour. In the eyrie she'd worn it as though it was tawdry and tattered. There had been eyes on her then, Taiytakei eyes, and she was the dragon-queen, haughty and imperious and filled with disdain for anything they could offer. Now she could be a child, gawping with awe at each piece, at the exquisiteness of the glass and the gold, of the construction so far beyond anything the smiths of the Silver City could ever have made. Beautiful. Almost the most glorious piece of craftsmanship she'd ever seen. Almost, except for …

She stopped. Someone else was with them. Not that she could

hear or see them but someone was, nonetheless. The dragon felt a presence and so she felt it too. Diamond Eye was casting his eyes around, thinking how hungry he was. Wary, Zafir put the last piece of her armour down and looked about. She wasn't afraid – it was hard to be afraid with Diamond Eye beside her, his hunger pulsing out in waves through her thoughts. But cautious neverthe-less, given who it must be and the look in Tsen's eye when she'd left him. 'Watcher, you should show yourself before my dragon eats you.'

The Watcher appeared a little way away. He walked towards her slowly and carefully, and sat down cross-legged, keeping a respectful distance. 'Your dragon will not eat me, slave,' he said. 'You are admiring the work of our enchantress. They are very fine pieces. Baros Tsen wastes her talents by keeping her at work in the eyrie. They would fetch a fine price and he could use the money.'

A flush of anger washed through her. She'd been seen after all, after being so careful in the eyrie. By one of *them*. Diamond Eye bared his teeth and hissed behind her. Maybe she *should* let him eat the Elemental Man. But the Watcher was too quick. He'd vanish and then appear again behind her with his knife and that would be that. 'I *am* impressed,' she said at last. 'And curious to know how they were constructed. But they are not the best pieces I have seen.' Which was true. In the Pinnacles, deep under the Octagon and past the Hall of Mirages, there were the mysterious treasures the Silver King had wrought and left behind, carefully put away where no blood-mage or alchemist would ever be allowed to wake them up again; compared to those even the exquisite craft of Bellepheros's enchantress seemed dull.

'You are not flying the way you were told.' The Watcher looked at her.

'Is that so?' She smiled and took a few steps away from the armour laid out around her, back towards Diamond Eye until she was standing almost beneath him. 'If it is then you've taken a very long time to point that out. Do you intend to remain here for the night, Elemental Man?'

'I do not.'

Zafir stared at him, half-tempted to let him see the subtle signs and signals just to see if he'd bite. But she let the temptation go.

He wouldn't. He wasn't the kwen, nor any of the kwen's men. She wouldn't snare this one so easily, at least, not *that* way.

His face was stony. He stared at her and said nothing.

'Well if you have nothing to say, killer, you will excuse me, but I've spent a very long day on the back of Diamond Eye and have only just touched the earth. Avert your eyes if you will.' Not that she cared. She turned her back on him and walked another few steps until she was fully beneath the bulk of the dragon, stripped away the dragon-scale leggings, lifted the short soft skirt beneath and squatted. The relief was so sharp that she let out a little sigh of pleasure. When she was done she walked back and knelt across from the Elemental Man, picked up the skin of water she'd brought down from Diamond Eye's back and drank deeply. 'Is that why you're here? Did you come to tell me that I'm going the wrong way?'

Back the way she'd come, back towards the distant eyrie, the setting sun in the clear sky turned the desert and its mesas into islands in a lake of fire. The Elemental Man watched her drink for a while. 'Did Baros Tsen tell you to do this?' he asked.

Zafir paused. Delicious water trickled down the skin of her throat. 'I'm *his* slave, killer, not yours. Ask *him*.'

The Watcher shook his head. 'I do not need to.'

'Then why ask me?' She finished off the water and rummaged in her knapsack for something to eat. 'Are there Elemental Women as well as Elemental Men?'

'There are not. We are eunuchs.'

Which perhaps explained a lot. 'How disappointing for you.'

'It is a small loss compared to the powers we learn. One that is barely noticed.'

'But how can you know if you don't know what you're missing?'

The Watcher snorted and Zafir couldn't tell whether he was laughing or merely disgusted by the thought. 'The temptation of our nature is strong enough. More would be ill advised. If such things are of so much interest to you, the Righteous Men who live in the depthless caverns beneath the Konsidar are able to change their shape at will. They are not as we are but they are born of a similar seed. They are masters of flesh and bone and they can adjust themselves with considerable fluidity when the need arises.

Or the desire. Very few know this truth that I have shared with you, even among the Taiytakei. Enjoy it a while, while you can.'

Zafir let out a scornful laugh. 'Shall I suppose that you've shared this with me to spare yourself my further interest, imagining somehow that you had it?' She shook her head. 'But you did not. So have no fear of me, elemental eunuch.' The knapsack offered her dry flatbread, hard enough to make axeheads, and salted meat. Linxia meat probably. Both made her grateful she still had all her teeth, and annoyed that she'd left the rest of the water on the dragon's back. 'Will you be a gentleman for me, Watcher? Vanish yourself to the back of my dragon and retrieve another skin of water for me?'

'I will not.'

Something in his voice was off. Not only disdain and disgust but something else. 'Because I am a slave?' But it wasn't that. He was afraid of the dragon. She climbed up herself, took her time over it, found another skin of water and took a third to be sure and tossed them both down to the earth. Stripped to her underclothes, the air still felt warm but it was cooling. The sun was setting and the stars were beginning to show and the desert air was cold at nights. Not that she'd notice, sleeping beside the living furnace that was Diamond Eye. 'Why are you here then, Elemental Man, if not to stare at my strange pale body and let your eyes wander over it, not sure whether it attracts or repels you – yes, I've seen enough of that. It's very hard not to notice these things and it tires me to the bone. But not from you, which makes your company a touch more welcome than otherwise. Nor from Baros Tsen, for that matter – is he a eunuch too?'

The Watcher snorted. 'You are not like Taiytakei women. Or men for that matter. You are tasteless and repellent.'

Zafir laughed. 'How refreshingly honest of you!' Diamond Eye shifted and growled. 'But that's not what your kwen thinks, nor half his soldiers, or does it merely make them hate themselves all the more? That they cannot control their lust for such a degenerate slave as I?' She reined in the flash of anger and with it her tongue. 'Tsen's tastes lie elsewhere, then? Forgive a slave for wanting to please her master.'

The Watcher shook his head. 'I have never been to your land. I am glad of that if all of your kind are like you. Baros Tsen T'Varr sips his apple wine and sings songs to himself and is happy and that is all. If there were a vice then I would know. You cannot hide from an Elemental Man.'

The last words had a bitterness to them. He didn't say anything more. Then he rose abruptly, snapped a stick from an almost-dead thorn tree and began to draw in the dirt.

'Mai'Choiro Kwen told you where to fly. I saw and I heard his words. The city you will find is not Bom Tark. It is Dhar Thosis, seat of Senxian of the thirteen sea lords, and he is likely present.' He drew a line in the dirt and then three islands and told her their names – Vul Tara, Dul Matha and the Eye of the Sea Goddess – just as Mai'Choiro Kwen had done. He told her, word for word, what the kwen had said so she could have no doubt that he'd been there too. He told her in a voice that was ruthless and fatally cold, a voice that said, quietly and without mercy or remorse, that she would die here on this stone on this night in the desert. When he was done, he looked her in the eye. 'Sea Lord Shonda of Vespinarr is the most powerful man in the world. If he cannot hide his secrets, how will you hide yours? I know what you are doing, slave.'

She met his eye. 'Then stop me.'

The Elemental Man drew a blade from his belt. Or rather, he drew the hilt of a blade with an edge too thin for Zafir to see. 'Quai'Shu took loans that Tsen cannot repay. The other sea lords circle like sharks to devour his fleet.' He stood up. 'Stop you? That is what Baros Tsen T'Varr has asked of me. I wondered, with the truth before you, if it would make a difference. But, like the monster you fly, you are what you are. I hope you die slowly and badly, slave. I do not wish you well and I will not give you a quick and easy death.' He turned his back on her. 'When you are gone, Tsen will have to let his alchemist poison your monster. It is better for all this way.'

'I am a slave, killer,' she said. 'Let me go. Let us all go. Back to my palace. Back as it was. I would be content with that.'

'No,' he said softly without looking back. 'No, I do not believe you would.'

He vanished. Zafir dived for Diamond Eye, to be as close as she could to the dragon. Too slow, always too slow when the enemy was an Elemental Man, and yet she saw him coming through the air, a haze of wind that rushed and then slowed and faded into being a man again, a rictus face of furious strain. Zafir crouched under Diamond Eye's bulk, hissing at him, 'Come on! Kill me then! That's all there ever is, isn't there?'

He was breathing hard. She could feel Diamond Eye restless above her, peering down between his feet, trying to see. The Elemental Man screwed up his face and shimmered, half faded and then slipped back to solid flesh again. Zafir snarled. She reached for a knife she didn't have, and that was that. He was going to kill her. The old way.

He stepped towards her. Cautious, although surely he could see she was helpless. She stood to meet him. Quivering not with fear but with despair. She had to blink hard to keep the tears from her eyes. *No pity for pretty little Zafir.* She touched a hand to her breast. 'My heart is here, killer. What's left of it. Strike true.'

'Think of it as a mercy,' he said, and maybe he was right. Maybe that's what it was, but she'd never know because he only took one more step before the tip of Diamond Eye's tail flew like a spear out of the gloom behind him. It impaled him like the bolt of a scorpion and threw him through the air to land broken at her feet. And at the very last, as he lay dying, he didn't even move. Just screwed up his face as if he were trying to shift to another form and couldn't. Zafir stepped back. Diamond Eye lifted up one massive foot, stamped the Elemental Man flat and stared at her. She started to laugh. She was right underneath him and so his head was upside down. He looked faintly ridiculous.

'No.' She closed her eyes. 'No mercy for Zafir. Never that.' She looked up at the dragon. 'But you? You don't even know what that is, do you? Mercy?' She looked down again as Diamond Eye lifted his foot. 'And he was probably right. Have I ever been content? I don't think I have.'

For a long time afterwards she stared at the smear that was all that was left of the Elemental Man. She drank and ate and looked and wondered. Later she picked up his knife with its invisible blade and gingerly slipped its scabbard out from the mess that was the rest of him. When she was done, she curled up tight beside Diamond Eye. 'You stopped him, didn't you? You made his magic not work. I don't understand. Did he think you wouldn't keep me safe?' She nestled closer to the dragon's uncaring warmth. 'Watch over me, Diamond Eye. He's right. We are what we are.'

She fell asleep, and her dreams were as they always were when she slept beside a dragon. Furious and filled with fire.

70

Death From Above

Tuuran charged as another barrage of rockets fizzed out of the city from not far behind the docks. He hit the enemy hard. If the waiting soldiers had had bows he'd have been dead and so would most of the rest of them. But they didn't and so he crashed into them axe first like a wild boar into a band of novice hunters, tossing them this way and that. As Crazy Mad and the rest came on behind him, more rockets shrieked in from the sea. They exploded, fire scouring the far end of the docks in a chorus of screams. From the corner of his eye he saw a man run and dive into the water, on fire from head to toe, but that was only a moment, a flash of something else between the arcs of death he flung before him. The soldiers in his way were sword-slaves, armoured in a hodgepodge of whatever had come to hand, some in nothing but leathers, others in mismatched pieces of steel. His axe battered them aside, cutting limbs and spraying blood through the air. *This* was what an Adamantine Man was made for. *This* was what it meant! He howled as his eyes searched for the men he most wanted to kill, Taiytakei in their glass and gold.

More rockets hissed and shrieked back and forth from city to sea. The sword-slaves turned and fled from his axe but the golems were another matter, hulking brutes of black rubbery skin, terrible enough almost to quell the battle madness but Tuuran was having none of it. 'Are you dragons?' he screamed at them. Behind the screams and the clash of swords and the dull thumps of bursting fireballs and the roar of flames and the distant booms and thunderclaps, a deep rhythmic pulsing was building, louder and louder. 'Are you? Because that's what I was made to kill.' He ducked under a clumsy swipe and split a golem in half with his axe, ripping open its belly. It fell apart and lost its shape like an overripe fruit and now Crazy Mad and the sword-slaves who'd followed him surged forward again. He felled another …

A rocket howled out of the air and struck one of the golems, spitting it. It stood there for a moment, reeling, and then exploded. Tuuran stumbled back, blinded by the flash, only the gold-glass helm saving his eyes from the flames. All around him men staggered and screamed and clutched their faces. There was a terrible smell of burning tar. When he blinked the brightness away, another of the golems was standing right in front of him. It had a wooden beam in its hands. It swung. He ducked easily underneath and inside its reach. They were large, too large to be men, but they were slow and had no notion of how to fight. He hacked at the golem, slashing it open. Black goo oozed from the wound. A substitute for slaves and cranes, that's what they were. Enchanted creatures for loading and unloading ships in the harbour and little use for anything else. Beside him Crazy Mad stabbed and cut.

'Get away from the shore! Get away! Into the streets! Quick!' They'd broken through at the end of the jetty. More attackers were dashing past them. Out in the dawn smoke over the jetties other ships loomed. Wood snapped and splintered. Lightning flashed and thundered back and forth. The Taiytakei with the golden armour was urging them on and now he had others around him, more of the night-skins in their shimmering colours and their cloaks of bright feathers. They had short stabbing swords at their sides, their black rods too, but in their hands were the lightning wands, cracking and fizzing thunderbolts all around them. They carried shields, huge things of glass and gold, and spiked ashgars over their backs. Up and down the shore among the handful of ships that had rammed the jetties, smoke lay over a sea full of bobbing boats, oars straining furiously for the land. The throbbing noise was louder. Across the waves flashes and booms surrounded the island that the fleet had passed in the pre-dawn twilight as they'd lit their first fireships. Within the smoke the water was ablaze with misty glowing shapes, burning hulks and wreckage and pools of fire that floated and seemed to burn the very water itself. The sun had cracked the horizon far out to sea, shining straight though the carnage and the haze, throwing everything into silhouette. Tuuran could see all three of the islands now. The one they'd passed was low and shrouded in smoke while bolts of lightning flared like the sun, one and then another and another. The middle of the three islands, the tallest, must have been a mile away across the sea and he still had to tip his head back to look at the top of it. A great column of rock, sheer sides rising out of the water. With the rising sun behind it, its top glowed with golden fire. The third sloped up from the sea to the meet the cliffs of the second. A bridge crossed the chasm between, gleaming in the dawn with a dazzling fiery gold.

The golems were falling one by one. They fought without thought, swinging their clubs at any who came within range. The stabbing swords and spears of the sword-slaves wounded their rubbery skin, but Tuuran, with his axe and quick feet, he was the one to finish them, fast enough to get in close and split them apart before their clubs could shatter him. They were slow, too slow to be much danger to a man with his eyes open and his wits sharp. 'Next!' He sliced the legs from one and buried the head of his axe into the side of another. 'And again! More! Harder! Give me something that can *fight*!'

'Move! Clear the shore!' The ships out in the water were turning, those that weren't broken or shattered burning wrecks. 'Get away! Get away!' He had no idea who was shouting. He hacked at another golem's leg and it staggered. One heaved its club at him. He ducked and it struck the first golem in the face, splitting it open. The crippled golem sagged to the ground, black liquid pooling around it. Another rocket exploded on the dockside and then a whole string of them rained down, falling on the end of the jetty and on the ship he and Crazy Mad had stormed; and on their own ship too, engulfing everything in a storm of fire. Tuuran staggered away, overwhelmed by noise and light and the heat. *So much for our passage back.* The golems pressed forward. He saw a sword-slave picked up and ripped in two, another hit by a club so hard that it took his head off his shoulders, a third batted out to sea like a ball in a game of circle-running.

A Taiytakei pushed past him and ran right in among the golems. He was clutching one of their black rods. Every golem he touched immediately froze. The work of a few moments and they were like statues. When he was done, the Taiytakei grabbed Tuuran, pushing him away from the sea and into the lee of a low stone wall.

'Move, slave! Get away from the shore!' He was looking up. When Tuuran followed his gaze, he saw glasships floating down from the upper parts of the city. They didn't carry golden eggs beneath them this time; instead it seemed they had great balls of fire.

'Up there!' The Taiytakei pointed across the sea to the abyss between the two islands and the bridge that crossed it. 'Take your men and lead them up there. Across the Bridge of Eternity to the Eye of the Sea Goddess and keep going up. To the Kraitu's Bones! Keep away from open spaces. The glasships are coming. Sail! Fight! Freedom! No quarter!' He slapped Tuuran's shoulder.

'I don't have any ...' *I don't have any men* he wanted to say, but the Taiytakei had already run off. For another moment Tuuran looked at the islands and the bridge between them. *There? We have to get there? They'll bring it down and we'll never get across.* But then again that was where the palace was, and palaces meant the best looting. He grinned to himself and looked about for Crazy Mad and then remembered another thing the Taiytakei had said.

Glasships.

They were closer and lower now, and the golden rim of the nearest was glowing. Further out to sea more were coming from the top of the Kraitu's Bones. They were too far away to see clearly but with the sun behind them they were like little stars, six of them, then seven, then eight.

The rims of the ones floating in from the upper city glowed brighter and brighter, a searing light almost beyond white with the slightest taint of blue. The unbearable brilliance of lightning. His skin prickled. His hair tinged. Lightning cannon ...

Shit!

The air exploded. Tuuran fell to his knees, clutching his ears. He couldn't hear any more. He could barely see. Half the docks were simply gone. Smoke rose from the golems, the ones that hadn't been blown apart. The sword-slaves who'd been in the open were all gone too, vanished utterly. Maybe some had followed him to shelter before the glasship fired. Maybe. The next glasship was starting to glow. He crouched down, huddled against a wall, curled up tight in a ball, hands over his ears and covering his face. The thunderclap ripped right through him. It came at him through the ground; it came at him through the wall, tipping him sideways and sending him sprawling; it came at him through his ears, leaving them screaming, and through his bones to pick him up from the inside and shake him as though he was made of rags.

This ... is not ... how it will end. I am Adamantine!

Another thunderclap. A burning ship exploded into splinters. Pieces of wood and crumbs of stone showered around him. The wall thumped him. There was a noise that wasn't quite the roaring aftermath of thunder. He staggered to his feet.

A voice. He turned and there was Crazy Mad, blinking rapidly, mouth agape, staring up at the sky, pointing and mumbling.

'What?' Tuuran could barely hear his own shout. Pointing at the glasships? *Seen those already, you daft bastard!*

'Loud!' bellowed Crazy Mad. He grinned the grin of a madman lost to the mania that drove him. 'Look!' And did his eyes gleam with a touch of silver or was that just the fire and the lightning and Tuuran's own frayed edges? Crazy was pointing up towards the glasships.

Tuuran shrugged him off. 'We've got to run. No time for your shit!'

'Run where?'

'Where? Away, you dumb slave. Anywhere.' A thunderclap almost threw him off his feet as another ship exploded. He pulled at Crazy Mad, hauling him away from the docks, but Crazy was dragging him a different way. He was still pointing up at the glasships. 'Look! Holy sun! What in Xibaiya is that?'

Tuuran didn't want to look. Looking at the glasships made him feel small and helpless, but something in Crazy Mad's voice made him do it anyway. Behind and above the glasships he caught a glimpse of something much faster, something with wings and fangs and claws and fire coming down on them from above, but that couldn't be right because the Taiytakei didn't have dragons; and then he couldn't be sure of anything any more because the nearest of the glasships had almost reached the docks, and the burning globe of fire that hung beneath it began to fall, and he couldn't do anything but watch it come down towards them.

'Oh ... crap!' He dropped. He pressed himself against a wall and curled up into a ball again, hauling Crazy Mad down while the world exploded around them.

71

Snake Dance

She always rested well sleeping beside a dragon. Sleeping alone was the worst. She never quite relaxed. Alone you never quite knew who would come, silent and creeping into your room, and slide into your bed and clamp their hands all over you. Alone she slept with one eye open. To not be alone was one of the reasons she used to take as many lovers as she did. It was why Myst and Onyx stayed beside her in the eyrie, so she could sleep without her ears picking constantly at the silence. Lovers wanted things too though, and even when she gave herself willingly, in the end they all betrayed her. Dragons were different. Dragons had a purity to them. A singleness of intent and no pretence of being anything other than what they were. Kept dull, they were a part of her own will. Diamond Eye's unsleeping eyes watched over her, and so she slept well.

She woke before dawn. The desert air was cold now, the stars bright pinpricks in their thousands in the clear sky. She watched them for a while, searching for anything familiar. Some of the constellations she'd learned as a child were there but all in odd places, clustered around the horizon if they shone at all. Many had simply vanished in this strange alien world.

'Where are we, old friend?' Diamond Eye was calmer in the nights than he was in the day. Stupid really, to talk to a dragon. She had no illusions about what he was: a monster who'd eat her without a thought if ever the alchemists and their potions lost their grip on him. But then that *was* how a dragon-queen should meet her end, eaten by her own mount. That was *her* way, far better that than being a slave. 'I could let you go,' she said. 'I could send you to fly away, on and on until you find the sea and then sink down beneath the waves where they'll never find you, and stay there still and quiet until you wake up and rise again and wreak vengeance for us both. Shall I?'

She put the Taiytakei armour on one piece at a time as she whispered to him, enjoying again each little miracle. If the Taiytakei had offered her marvels such as this back when she'd been speaker, this and not their tawdry farscopes which merely gave her headaches, perhaps she might have bargained with them from her Adamantine throne and freely given them the dragons they desired. But they hadn't. They'd taken what they wanted and now they'd suffer for it.

'I am what I am.' She climbed onto Diamond Eye's back, buckled herself into the harness and looked down one last time at the stain that had been the Elemental Man. The Watcher was right about that. Right about her in so many ways. 'I am what I am, for aren't we all?' And as she leaned forward, Diamond Eye turned and cocked his head and bared his teeth, and if she hadn't known better, she'd have sworn he was smiling. Her eyes sparkled. 'Now they burn, my deathbringer. As many as we can before they bring us down so they will never *ever* do this again.' And then when that didn't seem to be enough, she threw back her head and screamed at the dark and empty sky, 'I am Zafir! Do you hear? I am a dragon-queen!' And Diamond Eye took to the sky and roared up high into the air and surged on towards the sea and whatever awaited them.

They reached it as the sun began to rise. She felt the changes in the air, the moisture and the warmth; then lower she tasted the salt, and there was the sea and then, in the distance, flashes of light far off to one side, miles away but she knew what they were. Lightning. So she turned toward them and surged on, and as the dawn light split the desert from the sky, there it was, the city of Dhar Thosis as the kwen from the mountains had described it, three islands and its curving shore and two of the three islands rising like mountains from the waves. Sun-bright lightning lit up the morning twilight in flashes, flickering around the furthest of the three. The pitch-dark sea burned with a thousand fires and the sky above it filled with fizzing orange streaks. Rockets.

She urged Diamond Eye on. They would take this city from the desert and from the sky. No one would see them. Not until it was too late.

Thunder rumbled, a distant shake of the air. Another flash

came, from over the city this time. Closer. Diamond Eye banked and rolled, and she saw the glasships floating over the city, a cluster of little brightnesses drifting across the sky beneath her towards the sea and the broken and burning ships that littered the shore. The glasship rims lit up one by one, light pulsing around them, brighter and brighter until each one let loose with a brilliant flash and a clap of thunder and ship after ship exploded into pieces.

Those, my dragon. Start with those. Diamond Eye heard her and tucked in his wings and dived towards them, and as he did she heard him sing, as dragons sometimes did, murmuring to themselves at the joy of being unleashed for war. The song curled around and writhed inside her and she embraced it and took it to be her own, and they were gone, both of them, lost to the hunger and the rage. With her dragon she fell upon the glasships, belching fire, though both of them knew that fire would be no use against these monsters made by men, these creatures of glass and gold – and so it came to tooth and claw and the lash of the tail. And if the enemy saw them coming then there was nothing they could do but hang helplessly in the sky and hurl their lightning.

Diamond Eye hammered into the first and slashed and bit at the glass and the gold discs at the heart of the ship, shattering and bending and ripping until the glasship began to fall; but the dragon spread his wings and held it in his talons, strained to lift it higher and then hurled the ship towards another. The two smashed together and exploded into shards while Diamond Eye stormed at the rest, slashing at them with his tail, swooping and soaring as their gold rims glowed with white-hot light and the air prickled and scratched; and as the hail of lightning began, Zafir saw something bright and burning fall. It vanished into the gloom of the streets below and the city beneath bloomed into a sweeping lake of fire. Her heart sang. Joy. Not hers, but Diamond Eye's.

72

Fire

Tuuran didn't see where the fire bomb landed. Couldn't have been far away. Two streets, maybe. The very air shook. He felt the wall beside him quiver and begin to tip.

'Run!' He pulled at Crazy Mad but Crazy had felt it too and was already up and moving. Ahead the street suddenly filled with flames, a burning cloud blooming fast towards them. The buildings were all coming down. Stone smashed into the road. Tuuran cringed and turned his back as the fire washed over them, wishing for the dragon-scale he'd had long ago. Crazy Mad did the same, tucking his head between his arms and his hands under his armpits. The fireball flashed by, a short sudden scorch and then gone.

'Weak!' Tuuran yanked Crazy Mad away. 'At the end of its reach. Lucky for us.' The air shook from another thunderbolt and then another, each one rattling the litter of rubble and stone around them. He didn't see where they struck. 'We need cover! We need shields!' More booms of lightning overhead, a whole string of them, and with each one the savaged streets shook. Yet more stone juddered loose from already broken walls and fell around them. As he and Crazy Mad ran, Tuuran turned to look up. 'Holy Flame!'

He threw himself flat as a tumbling glasship spun out of the sky and smashed into the city ahead. It exploded into slivers of glass that flew like scorpion bolts. A splinter shattered off his armoured shoulder and a piece as long as a horse fizzed over his head, then glittering daggers showered around him, pinging off his helmet and rattling over his back. He winced. He was feeling the burns from the fire now. Skin burns, nothing deep, but they stung like he'd been whipped. The backs of his hands, the backs of his legs. The back of his neck, that was the worst.

He hauled himself up again and then stopped, transfixed. Everything around him was smashed. The wide stone-paved street was covered in debris, littered with destruction. The buildings either side, whatever they'd once been, their thick stone walls had been ripped apart and tumbled and their roofs were simply gone, disintegrated by fire and lightning. Above him, the glasships were falling one by one and there *was* a dragon among them. They were throwing lightning at it but the dragon was too fast and too agile. It was a big one too, huge, bigger even than the glasships when it stretched out its wings, with claws like lances and a head filled with teeth like scimitars. As the dragon leaped away from one stricken glasship and passed another, it lashed with its massive tail, smashing the ship to pieces. Tuuran watched as it shattered another and then jumped onto the last of them. It opened its mouth and fire poured out, on and on and on until even Tuuran on the ground could feel the air turning hot. The glasship shuddered and then started to fall. Its glass heart was glowing a dull throbbing red and there were drops of bright golden rain in the air. It came down behind the buildings shattered by the fire bomb and the tortured ground shook again. The monster shrieked. For a moment, as it turned, Tuuran caught a glimpse of a rider on its back.

He was grinning like an idiot. He knew it but he couldn't help it. *A dragon!* 'See, Crazy Mad? See that! That's what they made me to fight! A dragon! Flame, but isn't that a sight to make your heart sing?' A decade, more or less, since he'd seen one, and the feeling was like warm cream and honey.

Crazy Mad snorted. 'Yeh, but whose side's it on?' Somewhere nearby but out of sight another explosion shook them; and then pieces of burned wood showered across the street and the hot dry air filled with a rolling cloud of choking smoke. Tuuran ran straight on, Crazy Mad keeping up beside him. He didn't know where he was going but for now any direction away from the fire would do. Now and then he glanced back at the sky, looking for the dragon.

Once they got out of the docks, the destruction was less. Most of the houses, shops, temples, guild houses, whatever they were, were still intact. They crossed a small square. In the smoke and the half-light Tuuran saw people moving on the street ahead of them but couldn't tell whether they were Taiytakei or slaves. Mostly they were stumbling about dazed or else simply staring at the sky; some were running. Tuuran didn't stop but he kept glancing over his shoulder, couldn't help himself. They were away from the fires now but more flames were rising from deeper in the city. The rockets, perhaps, or the fallen glasships. They'd blown apart into glowing pieces as they crashed, setting fire to everything they touched. The golden rain he'd seen really was gold, melted by the dragon's breath. He caught a glimpse of the monster as it swept low across the city, dousing the docks with more flame, pouring fire out of its mouth in an endless stream.

Crazy Mad shook his head. 'So if it's with us, why is it burning where we were?'

Tuuran laughed. 'It's a dragon. It's not *with* anyone. It's got a rider, though. *He* might be.'

'That's still the docks done for. How we going to leave?' *Leave?* Tuuran hadn't even thought about that.

The dragon shot out across the sea, low enough to skim the waves with its claws, and Tuuran lost sight of it. He shrugged. Anyone still by the waterside had been dead long before the dragon came. The glasships had seen to that with their lightning. 'And it'll burn the ships. All of them probably, ours and theirs. Dragons hate ships.' He pulled Crazy Mad into a narrow alley and stopped to catch his breath. His lungs felt raw from the smoke and the heat. 'So here we are, Berren Crowntaker Bloody Judge Skyrie. Leave? We only just got here. The place you wanted to be, for which you can thank me later. Now how do you propose to find these war-locks of yours?'

Crazy Mad smirked and pushed him. 'Thank you? You had no idea this was where those ships would be heading!'

Tuuran grinned back. 'Well if that's so, Mister Crazy Bloody Judge then you'd best thank me for being so bloody lucky!' His grin faded. Not so lucky if you lived here. Here, away from the worst, people were standing at their windows full of disbelief, but that wouldn't last when they saw what was coming. They'd be on the street soon, running – should be doing that right now if they had any sense, fleeing for the safety of the hills, although there was no safety there, not from a dragon. Stay and hide until the fighting was all done, that was probably best, unless the dragon decided to remain and burn every house until the stones cracked.

You couldn't be sure it wouldn't. *No quarter!* The Taiytakei had shouted that a lot. They were here to wipe out this whole city then, were they? Every man, woman and child killed and every building burned to ash? Was that how the Taiytakei fought one another? He had no idea. As far as he'd been able to make out, mostly they did their fighting by getting other people to do it for them and putting wagers on the outcome.

'The warlock,' said Crazy Mad. 'Vallas Kuy. He's here. I can almost taste him in the air.'

'Daft bugger! All I taste is smoke and ash. So where is he?'

Crazy Mad shrugged. Tuuran laughed. There was no way Crazy Mad was going to find *anyone*, not in the middle of a battle, not when he didn't know where to look. 'Good luck with that, then.' He walked down the alley into a small yard and climbed a pile of empty crates up onto a roof. Crazy Mad watched him and smiled.

'Takes me back to Deephaven. Before I was the Bloody Judge. When I was a thief I did this sort of thing all the time.'

'What? Burn cities to the ground?'

'No, you ox, *this*!' He scrambled up from window to rooftop as though it was the easiest thing in the world, vaulting past Tuuran. 'Gods but you're so slow, big man.'

They stood side by side for a minute watching the city burn. Smoke blew over them, thick and acrid. Here and there amid the flames were scars where whole streets had been smashed by the fire bombs or by the dragon or the falling glasships. Tuuran reckoned it didn't much matter which if you were underneath. He could see broken glasship skeletons, a few of them, some of their great discs still intact and sticking up high above the ruins. He swept his arm over the destruction and then out to sea where a hundred ships were burning. The dragon was out there. He could see it by the bright columns of fire that lit up now and then inside the pall of smoke. They *moved* like a dragon, sweeping through the air. 'This.' He grinned. 'I came here for *this*.'

'Well, good for you.' Crazy Mad rolled his eyes. 'Now that you've got it, you can help me hunt warlocks. *If* you don't mind, though don't let it stop you from a good bit of smashing and looting and burning, of course.' As they watched, another stream of rockets shot out from deep in the city, arcing towards the sea. Tuuran squinted. There were still lots of little boats riding the waves to the shore. The rockets landed among them. Crazy Mad squinted up and down the coast. 'Do they have fishermen here?'

'It's a city by the sea so it'd be pretty strange if they didn't.' Tuuran shrugged and looked back to where the dragon had gone now, to the island with its flashes of lightning. 'Over there, maybe?'

Crazy Mad stood up. He started pacing, talking to himself. 'Like he was in Tethis. Like Saffran Kuy. Except Saffran lived by the river, not with the fishermen. The fish for his army of little spies were brought to him. Sun and moon! He has to be here somewhere, and we have to find him.'

'Got any sense, he'll be long gone.' Tuuran turned his back to the dying city. 'Me? I'll help you look if you like. I just want to kill me some of those night-skin slaver bastards while I'm at it and I'll be happy.' He looked further along the curve of the shore and traced the route the Taiytakei at the docks had told him with his fingertip. Another half a mile to the first bridge and the nearest of the three islands. The Eye of the Sea Goddess, was it? Then up and up to a sheer pinnacle hundreds of feet above the waves, gleaming towers clustered around its crown. Another bridge, the one he'd seen so clearly from the docks. Then the last pillar of rock with its glittering palace and its towers of glass and gold. His finger stopped and pointed. 'There,' he said. 'That's where I'm going. If I was a blood-mage or a death-mage or a whatever it is you're looking for and I was stupid enough to still be here in the first place, that's where I'd be. With the kings and lords of this city. Safest place, if there's a safe place to be had at all.' He grinned. 'Well, safe until the likes of us get up there.'

Crazy Mad didn't even blink. 'Then that's where we're going.'

'Good!' Tuuran rubbed his hands. 'Should be a lot of fighting to get up there, I reckon.' And yes, it helped that that was where the Taiytakei lords would be waiting to meet his axe and where all the gold would be afterwards, and what more could an Adamantine Man ask than to sack the palace of one of the kings who'd bound him into slavery? Yes, up there would do very nicely, and if you were looking for a crazy mage while you were at it, well, why not? He jumped back down to the alley, axe over his shoulder, short stabbing sword in his hand, the way it always used to be long ago, and jogged off towards the shore, humming to himself with Crazy Mad running beside him.

73

Lightning

Diamond Eye plunged among the glasships. Lightning shattered the air above Zafir, beside her, all around her. Noise deafening, light blinding, yet Diamond Eye jinked and dived and rose and rolled between the thunderbolts. The air smelled of fire and sorcery, the burning tang that sometimes rose from the depths of her old palace where the Silver King had made his miracles. One bolt struck Diamond Eye's wing. Sparks arced along its length. They rippled over the dragon's scales and crackled across her armour; for a moment the wing fell limp and Diamond Eye tipped sideways and plunged, but only for a moment before he recovered and powered up again. The glowing golden rims of the glasships brightened to fire once more but they were too slow. Diamond Eye tore through them, in among them, tooth and claw and tail and fire, smashing and shattering them. One loosed a lightning bolt as he raced above it. Zafir felt the straps of her harness creak and groan as the dragon wheeled and landed on the glasship's back. He tore at its golden heart and let loose a torrent of fire until the glass glowed red and the gold began to melt, until the heat was unbearable even through the dragon-scale lining of her armour and her face was as red as a cherry and the sweat ran off her in rivers. Parts of the harness began to smoulder. She was almost weeping, begging him to stop before he cooked her alive and yet he wouldn't, he simply *wouldn't*. She felt his rage at these ships-that-flew, all-consuming, burning her on the inside as his flames scorched her without.

A bolt of lightning hit the glasship. She felt the shudder. More sparks ran over Diamond Eye's scales and then another thunderclap. She felt her skin prickle.

Stop! But he wouldn't, and she almost fainted from the heat until at last the glasship shuddered and began to slide out of the air. Diamond Eye let it go. Zafir watched it tip and plunge into the burning city. It hit the ground and exploded in a shower of smashing glass and twisted gold. Diamond Eye powered up again, wings shovelling the air with such force that the wind itself almost screamed in pain. He aimed for the next.

'Smash it! Smash it!' Zafir howled. She had to open her visor, *had* to, so the rush of wind could cool her face and her head, because otherwise she was going to melt like the glasship gold. 'Smash it! Tooth and claw!' More fire now and she'd be scorched to the bone, but Diamond Eye shot underneath the next glasship. Its rim shone with a ferocious white light, lightning ready to be unleashed. He lashed it with his tail and the glass disc cracked. Lightning flashed and danced down Diamond Eye's scales. A white aura shivered and crackled over Zafir's armour. Every hair stood on end. Her skin tingled and her heart fluttered as the gold amid the glass began to glow and little sparks flicked from her fingers into the dragon's back. Diamond Eye twitched. For a moment he froze in the middle of the air and began to fall again, but then his wings moved once more and the stolen lightning arced back and the glasship's core exploded. Shards flew like arrows, peppering Zafir, rattling against her. She felt the sting of something on her cheek where she'd left her visor open. Behind them the glasship broke in two and fell out of the sky. She watched it go. It had a bright glowing fireball hanging underneath it, and she watched that too as it hit the ground and burst into an inferno. She had enough wits at least to close her visor before the wave of scorched air came and threw them upward, dragon and rider both, as the glasship's remains vanished into the flames. Diamond Eye snarled and dived at the next and then the next, one by one until the last of the glasships fell. The glasships were the Taiytakei's terror. They would come with their fire bombs and their lightning cannon and destroy everything in their path – like dragons – but for dragons they were easy prey. A dragon was worse and now they knew it. She'd given Tsen what he'd wanted all along – a demonstration of a dragon's power – and she wished he was here to see it, to beg her to stop so she could tell him that she'd barely even started.

She let Diamond Eye have his way and swoop lower. Where the glasships had fallen the city was ablaze beyond hope, but he wanted more. She closed her eyes and leaned into him, pressing herself against his scales to avoid the scorching choking wind as he flew through it and burned whatever was left to burn. *Hungry!* His urge to feed wrapped around a vicious gleeful joy, the frenzy of the burning shattering thing she'd allowed him to become.

'Ships.' When she had him out over the sea she let him burn those too, but she kept him away from the little boats bouncing on the waves with their cringing soldiers. A part of her hardly cared – *Let them all burn* – but that was an animal part. The cunning in her said no, let the soldiers reach the shore, let them live and let them fight and wait until the end and be the ruin of them all when they think it's done. So she burned whatever was in her path and left the rest alone, and set her dragon towards the island lit up with flashes and thunderclaps where there would be a battle worthy of them, where more ships clustered, burning and adrift. A large four-master reared out of the waves, sails still intact. A flag flew from its mast and Zafir wondered if perhaps *all* of the ships had flown flags to show for whom they fought. It hadn't occurred to her. In a dragon war you knew the dragons from your own eyrie, all of them by sight. You knew your friends and your allies and anyone else was the enemy. And it wasn't so much that the riders knew, it was the dragons – *they* knew.

Diamond Eye tucked in his wings and arrowed for the ship. *They are all the enemy.* Her own thought, but he latched on to it with a crushing hunger. Dragons and ships. Oil and water.

'No.' Her voice was hard and sharp. There were no reins to pull on with a dragon, no ropes to turn its head. The alchemists had once explained it to her as a crude sort of telepathy, and then she'd seen it for herself, not so crude at all when the dragon was free of the alchemists' potions, but for those under their sway, the years of training and conditioning to obey meant that they simply knew what their rider wanted and they did it.

Diamond Eye still arrowed for the ship.

'Stop!'

They had always, *always* obeyed her, even Diamond Eye, but in this world he'd become different. He was right on the edge of her control, had been from the first moment she'd sat on his back. She winced and leaned forward to press herself into his scales again.

He was exhilarating and terrifying both at once. *Why? Why have you changed?*

He took the ship from the stern, flaring his wings and crashing into the mizzenmast and snapping it like a twig. Zafir made herself as small as she could. Diamond Eye ploughed on, smashing through the next two masts and into the centre of the deck, splintering the wood beneath. He powered up again, clutching at the ship with his claws as if trying to tear it clear out of the water. The screams of the sailors fought with the cracking of wood and then Diamond Eye shrieked and let go and soared away again as the ship pitched sideways. As the dragon flew up he bent his head between his legs, throwing Zafir forward so she was hanging helpless from the saddle, and poured fire over the receding deck.

Stop!

He lashed the bows with his tail as he passed. The top half of the last mast cartwheeled into the air. *Stop? No.*

Yes! Zafir stared at the island ahead. A hundred ships sat in the water, half of them on fire, some no more than shattered hulks. Rockets flew to and fro. Bright flashes of lightning arced over the waves, and with each one another ship exploded. She screamed at him, her words ripped away by the howling wind. 'There! Go there! Tooth and claw! Tail and Fire!' The ship they left behind was listing. Sinking. Was that where Shrin Chrias Kwen had been? She wasn't sure what answer she wanted to that. Crushed and burned by a dragon would be a fitting end but she'd already made him another, slower and more painful and more delicious by far. Let him die in slow agony, knowing he'd brought it on himself. Not glorious battle-death.

There were boats in the water, soldiers and oarsmen struggling through the waves to the shore. Fires raged across the island too, in and among its fortresses. More glasships were drifting from the top of the Kraitu's Bones, the spike of stone with a palace on its crown that reminded her of the Pinnacles, of her home. She'd go there last of all, she decided. When all else was done and she could work slowly and at her leisure. She fought for breath, sought for a calm to push away the urges that threatened to devour her. *The glasships first. Then the island.* That's what the kwen from the mountains had said might destroy her and so she faced them, head on, to see. She urged Diamond Eye lower. Soldiers were fighting in the streets. Metal tubes pointed in clusters up into the air around thick walls, the black-powder cannon that fired stone shot to shatter any glasship that came too close. She wasn't sure what they might do to a dragon. 'Those!' She pictured them in her head. 'Keep away from them.'

But she knew at once that she should have learned from the ship. Diamond Eye did exactly the opposite, turned and arrowed straight at them, as though he'd heard her clearly but had made his own decision. The largest of the fortresses sprawled before them, batteries and batteries of rockets with Taiytakei soldiers racing back and forth. Four glass and gold lightning cannon pivoted towards her, one from each corner and each with a hedgehog of black-powder tubes pointing into the air. Diamond Eye soared across the walls and straight over the middle of it all. He unleashed a torrent of fire, sweeping his head back and forth. Men screamed and burned and ran, flames all around them.

An explosion rocked Diamond Eye. Rockets fired off at random, flinging themselves up into the air, some of them arcing away across the sea, others across the land, some straight over Zafir's head. Diamond Eye dived through them and turned, banking into the first lightning cannon. He did the same as he had to the ship, crashing into it with his bulk as hard and fast as he possibly could, wings flared, claws outstretched, tail whipping in front of him as he came down. Zafir, on his back, the last to arrive, small and helpless. The stone embrasures holding the cannon shattered. Glass exploded, metal toppled and fell. Diamond Eye tipped forward and stood still for a moment amid the ruin. He threw up his head and shrieked, the unmistakable challenge she knew so well, then turned slowly, head low to the ground, and poured fire over the remains. Cases of black powder fizzed and burned and exploded. Wooden shrapnel and fragments of stone peppered the dragon's side. Stones and splinters pinged off Zafir's armour. Something hit her hard on the arm and one gold-glass vambrace cracked. In the midst of the chaos, with the dragon's inferno around her, the broken piece of armour filled her with outrage. Or maybe it was simply the dragon's hunger and for an instant that her guard was down for it to slip inside, but either way Diamond Eye took that moment and devoured it. He didn't launch himself back into the air this time but ran across the open ground inside the fortress walls, crushing everything in his path and setting light to anything that wasn't already aflame. It reminded her of Evenspire, of the Palace of Paths burning under the onslaught of a hundred dragons, the heat and the flames and the smoke.

And that went well, didn't it just? Get back into the air, my death-bringer! But he wasn't hers any more, not now, and she couldn't help a glance up back over her head for the other dragons and the great betrayal coming down from the skies to rip her off his back and tear her to pieces; and with that glance she felt another surge of rage at Jehal for what he'd done to her. It seared through her and left her as helpless as a child, all reason finally crushed by Diamond Eye's overwhelming hunger. She wanted to smash and destroy everything, to slaughter every single last one of these men who'd made her a slave.

They closed on the next cannon. She couldn't see it through the flames Diamond Eye was already pouring towards it, running on his back legs as if about to spread his wings and fly, head held high so his fire would have its greatest reach. The whole cluster exploded. Pieces of stone and metal the size of horses flew into the air in whirling arcs of smoke. The metal cannon spun skyward and fizzed like fireworks. A wall of scorched air hit them both, and if Diamond Eye hadn't been her shield it might have torn her to pieces. It lifted the dragon up off his feet and threw him back, all fifty tons of him. The world spun around her and she was flying, hanging upside down, hard stone and a litter of burning debris scattered beneath her and the unstoppable mass of a dragon falling from above. She was about to be crushed between them but at the last Diamond Eye twisted. Did he remember she was there? Or was he simply doing what any animal would do and trying to land on his feet? She'd never know, but it saved her. He came down sideways, hard and heavy, and slid across the stone. The impact savaged and rattled her every bone. Something in her back wrenched and twisted. The pain and the fear were enough to make her cry out but the harness held. She clung to Diamond Eye's scales so tightly that she might easily have snapped her own fingers.

They ground to a stop. For a moment she hung helpless, and

then with a sudden jerk Diamond Eye righted himself. The blast had flattened half the fortress, blowing the fires out and scattering burning pieces up into the air like blossom in a gale. She watched as three burning globes fell out of the sky and hit the ground and bloomed into balls of fire, but there was nothing left to burn. There was no one moving any more. Zafir felt the dragon's puzzlement. For a moment he didn't know what to do.

Her skin tingled. The air around them fizzed. Her thoughts became muddled. She didn't quite know where she was any more, or who, or why ...

The lightning from the third tower hit Diamond Eye squarely in the face. Zafir caught a flash of light so bright that it left her momentarily blind and a thunderclap so loud that her ears screamed. She couldn't see and she couldn't hear. Diamond Eye fell limp beneath her. The rage and the hunger and the fury all vanished at once. Suddenly she couldn't feel his presence at all.

The room. The locked room. Wrapped in darkness. Fear of the light. That was all she was. It took her with it and the world went black.

74

The Titans

There wasn't much fighting left to be had by the time Tuuran and Berren reached the sea again. Hundreds of sword-slaves, thousands maybe, had come ashore from their little boats. No one had stopped them and now Tuuran and Crazy Mad passed them running the other way, heading deeper into Dhar Thosis and away from the sea and the spreading fires. *No quarter* – they'd all had that shouted at them until their ears were ringing. They were sword-slaves, bred to the lash at the oars of a galley but strong enough to have survived; and now here they were, let loose on the very people who'd enslaved them. They would not be kind. The roaming gangs had hungry faces and violent eyes. They looked Tuuran and Crazy Mad up and down, saw the colour of their skin and the swords and armour they wore and passed on with a nod and a growl. Closer to the shore, as the gangs thinned, houses burned, sometimes with men and women still inside and knots of sword-slaves at the doors with spears, laughing and poking them back into the flames. They passed bodies in the streets, Taiytakei torn from their beds and hurled out of their houses and ripped to pieces. Crazy Mad didn't like it but Tuuran couldn't have cared less. They deserved it for what they did, all of them.

They passed a half-dozen sword-slaves dragging a pair of screaming women into an alley. The slaves had already left one body behind them, too small to be a grown man.

'This isn't how an army should behave,' Crazy Mad muttered.

Tuuran laughed at him. 'This isn't an army, madman! This is a horde. A mob. Besides, war is war. Victory is to crush your enemy so utterly they can never stand against you again. Annihilate them if you can.'

Crazy Mad scowled back at him. 'No. Victory is to be better than what you overthrow.'

'Ha! Then slavers or not, I think you're on the wrong side of this battle.' For a fraction of a moment, Tuuran hesitated and remembered the girl from the Pinnacles. It had been right, what he'd done, and was this any different? But then he shook his head and walked on. It *was* different. The Taiytakei were his enemies, all of them.

Berren stopped. The big man was right. Not that he *cared*, but he *was* right, and the Bloody Judge would never have let it be like this, and the screaming from the alley wouldn't let him go. He stopped and turned back, letting Tuuran walk on without him. The body left on the street was a Taiytakei, a boy no more than about ten. He'd had his throat cut.

He drew his sword. The Bloody Judge in him wanted to run into the alley, rush the sword-slaves and cut them to pieces. Kill maybe three of them before the rest could gather their wits. But he held the killing fury back. The alley was so narrow they wouldn't be able to surround him. He had a sword and good armour, and for all their numbers they had neither; so he came up on them and drew his sword across the alley wall hard enough to make sparks and get their attention. It was dark, shielded from the dawn light across the water, and the air was hazy with smoke from the fires around the docks. The sword-slaves had one of the women pinned against a wall, the other forced down on her knees. The women looked small and helpless. 'Stop!'

The nearest sword-slave faced him down. 'Piss off.' He peered. 'You could almost be one of them.'

'But I'm not, and I'm telling you to leave these women be.'

'Or what?'

'Or I'll kill you, that's what.' Berren opened his arms to them. Daring them.

The sword-slave spat and drew himself up. 'There's plenty more. Go find your own.'

The fury came so quickly it took him by surprise. He let out a roar of rage and lifted his sword, but the fury brought something with it this time, something from deep down. Something that wasn't his, that had been left behind when the warlocks had ripped him from the battlefield and consigned him to the pit under

Tethis. He wasn't quite sure what happened after that but the sword-slaves were gone and the alley was empty except for the two women, screaming as though they'd been set on fire. A fine cloud swirled around them all, black ash that must have blown in from the docks. Berren took a step towards the nearer woman. She cried out and shrank down the wall, blubbering, *Please please please*.

'I'll not hurt you. You should run. Run hard and run far. If anyone chases you, look for narrow places where big men in armour will be slow. Or high places where heavy men will fall or dark places where you can't be seen.' The first rules a Shipwrights' boy learned. He was surprised he remembered, but he was wasting his breath. The girl was lost to her fear. For some reason she seemed more afraid of him than she'd been of the sword-slaves.

'*There* you are,' grunted Tuuran from the mouth of the alley. 'Now what?' Berren turned. Tuuran was frowning at the two women. 'I thought you didn't approve of this sort ...' He stopped and stared. Then he looked at the women again. His voice became strangely calm and quiet. 'You two, you should probably go now.' Tuuran took a step back himself. 'Run. Go! Shoo! Quick!'

Berren stared at the big man. He heard the two women run out of the alley and away. 'What?'

'You're doing that thing again.'

'What thing?'

'That silver eyes thing. Weren't there some of our comrades here just now?'

'They ran away.'

Tuuran sniffed the air and took another step back. 'Right ...'

'Well, they didn't just vanish into thin air.'

The big man shook his head as he turned away. 'Really? And exactly how sure are you about that?'

Berren glanced back down the alley. The two Taiytakei women were gone. The black ash was settling on the ground and on his armour. It was greasy and it smelled bad.

'You stink of burned man.' Tuuran strode out of the alley and whatever had happened there back towards the sea. Fast. To be away from Crazy Mad too, but Crazy ran after him.

'Burned man? What does that mean?'

'Means exactly what I said: you stink of burned man. Everything here stinks of burned man. You think I don't know the smell?' He tapped his nose. 'Land of dragons, remember?' They turned a corner and he could see the sea again, right there in front of him. 'So. Those men ...' He stopped.

Shapes were rising from the waves past the breaking surf. Stone giants with craggy features were breaching the water and heading for the shore. There were still boats coming in, the last stragglers. He watched as one of the creatures from the sea picked a boat up, tossed it into the air and smashed it to pieces.

'Now there's a thing.' *Flame! Now what?* Tall as a house they were. Even Crazy Mad had stopped, frozen by the sight. The last gangs of sword-slaves were racing away from the sea, screaming and waving their arms and pointing back to the giants as if Tuuran might somehow not have seen them. And they had the right of it, he decided: running seemed like a fine idea. He turned and shot down another street, shouting over his shoulder at Crazy, 'They had people made of stone in Xican. Where I was for a bit when they took me away. They called them golems so I suppose those things are golems too, only ... bigger. Big golems. Really, really fucking big.' He was talking to himself and he knew it, but sometimes talking a thing out was the only way to deal with it.

He kept running, heading for where he thought the first bridge was. Debris littered the roads again here. The windows over the streets were all smashed and broken glass crunched under his boots. Doors had been kicked in and houses were burning from the inside. Broken pieces of Taiytakei rockets lay scattered about. There was no movement except the odd soldier from the ships picking through the ruins. The tide of sword-slaves had already swept through this quarter of the city and everyone had either fled or was dead or hiding.

Crazy Mad slowed and then stopped, a weird look on his face as though he'd been taken by a sudden urge to go inside a house and find out, in the middle of the city's death, what these people who'd taken him for a slave were like. To see how they lived. Tuuran shook him and pulled him on, pointing back the way they'd come. 'You want to wait for those stone things while they climb out of the sea or shall we keep moving?'

Crazy Mad shrugged. 'Depends whose side they're on, doesn't it?'

'Did you want to go and tap them on the foot and ask?'

They passed more bodies as they closed on the bridge. Taiytakei at first, men and women pulled from their houses and beaten and butchered. They caught up with the last of the looters, a group of sword-slaves carrying bulging sacks. Tuuran shouted at them to draw their swords and head for the bridge. They shook their heads and laughed at him. Disappointments, all of them, but he couldn't really hold it against them.

In a small square they passed a pile of corpses, a hundred or more thrown together and set on fire. Here and there Tuuran saw furtive faces staring at him from the shadows. City folk trapped by the roaming looters. The attacking Taiytakei had set their slaves loose on the city. *No quarter! Do your worst. Take what you will.* And after years of pent-up fury the slaves had become savage animals. These men would never forget and they'd never be slaves again, any of them. And the Taiytakei would know that ...

It hit him then: there wouldn't be any ships coming to take them away. That was why all he'd seen so far were sword-slaves. The Taiytakei were holding back. They would sweep the city when it was all done and put down every slave they found, no matter for whom they'd fought. Or maybe they'd use their dragon. The dragon would be perfect.

Bastards!

The bodies changed. They passed more dead sword-slaves now, some riddled with arrows, others with scorch marks on their skin, and then even a few Taiytakei soldiers with their swords and armour stripped away. They were close to the bridge, three wide spans of gold-glass sitting on squat black piers and lined with a hodgepodge of huts and tiny houses. Towers on each pier rose above the main spans. At the far end another lone tower frowned over the sea. The din of fighting wafted across and flashes of lightning burst from the bridge and arced over the water. Three giant stone golems lumbering through the waves were heading for the bridge.

'So. These golems, then,' grumbled Crazy Mad. 'Worked out whose side they're on yet or do I need to go and ask after all?'

Tuuran scowled at him. 'Let's just get to the bridge before they do.'

75
Vul Tara

Zafir opened her eyes. She hung sideways out of Diamond Eye's harness. The air smelled strange. Sharp and bitter. For a moment she couldn't remember who or where she was. For that moment she was in a dark room and something was coming, something terrible that turned the pit of her stomach cold and made her want to be sick with fear. She gasped for each breath.

The air filled with distant sounds. Booms. Thunder. She could smell smoke. *Evenspire. I'm at Evenspire!* The memory was like a knife. She jerked up and looked behind her, searching for the dragons that would come like rockets through the cloud, diving down at her Onyx to tear her to shreds, only it wasn't her on Onyx's back but one of her riders; and then Jehal would come and he'd be coming to save her, only he wasn't and it was the great betrayal ...

No dragons. And the sky was a dull and cloudless blue, tinged with wafts of grey and brown smoke.

Not Evenspire.

Diamond Eye wasn't moving. For some reason no one was running across the burning stone yard to finish her. She fumbled for the harness straps and undid them one by one, still on the edge of panic. She'd been here before. *Sinking in the water. About to drown. A man made of silver. Haven't you forgotten something?*

Her mind was playing tricks on her. Her head felt full of wool. Everything was unfamiliar. *Where in the realms ... ?* She pulled the last buckle loose and fell off Diamond Eye's back hard onto the scorched stone. Not the realms. And she was the Taiytakei's dragon-riding slave and they'd sent her to war and someone had hit her with lightning. Her armour was splintered. When she sat up to look at it, much of the glass was crazed with cracks. The gold was smeared here and there as though it had started to melt. Which wasn't possible. Was it?

She laughed. *And I'm still alive. A dragon-queen !* And then the laughter wanted to become tears because Diamond Eye still didn't move, and without a dragon what was she? Nothing; and so now they'd kill her, or else they'd dress her in a whore's silks and perfumes and pass her around among themselves, a novelty for their amusement.

Her legs were shaking. However hard she tried they wouldn't quite be still, but she managed to stand. She still had the bladeless knife she'd taken from the Watcher. No, they'd not have her again. Never.

Across the open yard, among the burning pieces of whatever this fortress had been, men were moving. They ran quickly from one piece of cover to another. She wondered why, and then streaks of bright orange fizzed overhead and landed in a crazy pattern around the far end of the fortress and exploded in balls of fire. A few fell closer. Zafir stood and watched. Flames washed over her but her dragon-scale kept them at bay.

The visor on her beautiful perfect helm was cracked. *What do I do now?* Without a dragon she was pointless. She stumbled to Diamond Eye's side. He was hot, the exertion of the battle making his scales burn. She could smell the scorching of the leather in his harness. 'Wake up! Be alive!' She beat on his scales with her fists. *You can't be dead. You can't! I won't allow it! WAKE UP!* But dragons didn't sleep, not really. They didn't do a lot of things that other creatures did. They didn't breathe.

Diamond Eye twitched. 'Wake up! Wake up!' Furious hammering against the dragon's hide. Pointless. He wouldn't even feel her. And yet perhaps he did, for as she screamed at him he lurched and raised his head and rolled to his feet, and she felt such a wave of relief and joy and …

Fury!

The force of it knocked her back. She stumbled and fell. Diamond Eye bared his teeth. His eyes burned and such a rage filled her head that she screamed, the only way to let even a part of it escape. *The towers! The towers!* She tried to turn her head towards the place from where the lightning had come but she could barely even move as the dragon's fury crushed all other thought like a tidal wave. Diamond Eye threw himself into the air without her.

The tower where the lightning cannon stood was glowing again, white hot. He crossed half the distance before it fired and a second bolt of lightning struck him, this time in the chest. Zafir closed her eyes and screamed at the noise and at the dragon's rage and pain as his wings faltered and he smashed to the ground again, twitching and writhing. Wings and claws and tail lashed and struggled, pulverising everything around him, wood and stone and metal alike. Then violent joy burst in her as he staggered to his feet and launched himself forward a second time. The tower was already glowing again, but not yet as brightly as before.

Another thunderbolt, another blinding light, this from the other surviving tower. Diamond Eye shrieked and went down yet again. Zafir clutched her hands to her head. He was colossal inside her, crushing everything else, pain and rage and rage and pain drenching every corner of every thought.

In the locked room, in the dark, with the fear and the dread and the pain to come …

The dragon lurched to his feet once more. Three giant strides. He had his head down this time, mantling his wings to cover himself. The first tower fired again. More screaming pain and furious rage. Zafir fell to her knees. A desire burst inside her. A hunger. An understanding. Diamond Eye moved suddenly this time. Not straight for the tower of the lightning cannon but behind it, with a surge of speed that made Zafir gasp. *Yes!* The second cannon fired and missed and then Diamond Eye fell upon the first, ripping it apart, savaging the metal tubes that pointed to the sky. He tore one loose, held it in his foreclaws, reared up and hurled it at the last tower, smashing it into dazzling crackling sparking shards. The burning white of the growing lightning flickered and died. Sparks ran across the stones. Now Diamond Eye launched himself into the air and fire flooded from his mouth to douse the first tower. Bright flashes popped and crackled inside it. Zafir sat and watched, stricken with awe. *Burn them! Burn them!'*

Diamond Eye left the first tower a molten heap of slag and moved to the second. From somewhere close a barrage of rockets streaked towards him. A dozen of them struck, bathing him in fire. Zafir laughed and she felt the dragon laugh too. *Fire? You think to touch me with fire?*

When the second tower was red and molten and dripping, Diamond Eye flew free, up and down the fortress and all around it, burning and burning, drenching it all with a fire that never stopped. He flew across the island and burned the houses and the streets and the trees and the people, and what wouldn't burn he smashed with claw and tail. When the island was nothing but flames he flew out to sea and burned the ships, all of them, every single one, with no thought to whether they were friend or foe, for now everything was the enemy. Zafir watched it all, too weak to move. A sense of completeness filled her as if the dragon had shown her, finally, something she'd been struggling to see for half her life.

The last ship burned and Diamond Eye vanished under the sea, and the waves churned and boiled and steam rose from the water. When he finally came back to her, he was still blistering. She wondered perhaps if he'd been saving her for last, but he landed before her and bowed his head to let her climb onto his back once more. Half the mounting ladder was gone, the ropes burned away. She paused for a moment, wondering what to do, but he lowered himself to the ground and lay flat. Pieces of harness hung loose, scorched ends dangling in the air, but they made their saddles well in the eyries of the Silver City. She found a hanging rope, the leg-breaker she'd refused to use this time, and hauled herself onto his back. With slow deliberate motions she found the buckles and the straps, the ones that had survived, and fastened herself to him.

'We'll need a new harness for you,' she whispered when she was done. Half of it was ruined but there was still enough to hold. They were whole again, both of them, and Diamond Eye felt it too. He lifted himself up and began to run, slow loping strides as though this time, at last, there was no hurry. *We are one.* Was that *her* thought? His? Both of them? She didn't know and didn't care. The dragon stretched out his wings and took to the air, circling leisurely over the island. It was burning, all of it, the sea aflame with blazing ships. Everything looked blurred and it took her a moment to realise why. She was crying. Weeping with relief and weeping for joy.

You make me whole.

The dragon had changed something inside her – the old wound – and for the first time she could remember, she wasn't afraid any more.

76

The Bridge of Eternity

A clutch of sword-slaves spilled into the street ahead, running as though they were on fire, scattering this way and that. Tuuran skittered to a stop as two men in glass and gold on fast glass sleds chased after them. The riders headed for the bridge. Lightning flashed from their wands and tiny claps of thunder followed; men screamed and fell, one after another. More sword-slaves burst out of hiding and ran the other way, straight at Tuuran and Crazy Mad and then past them. They were screaming in fear. Tuuran spat. 'Outsiders.'

Crazy grabbed him and pulled him into the shadows of a smashed-in doorway. The riders had turned their sleds. They were coming back. 'Let them pass.'

It was almost too tempting when there were some Taiytakei to kill at last, but Crazy Mad held him firm and Tuuran just growled. They sped past, standing on their discs of gold-glass, leaning into to the wind. It would have been so easy to run out and haul one of them down. 'Come on then, you slaving bastards.' But the riders didn't see them in the shadows. They raced on after the fleeing slaves, their wands full of white-hot glow. Tuuran watched them go. Probably best. The last slave he'd seen hit by wand lightning had been hurled like a doll. He hadn't just been dead, he'd looked like he'd been burned by a dragon. 'Just a little thing,' he muttered as Crazy Mad let him go. 'But I'm just wondering whose side they were on.'

Crazy Mad shrugged as if it was obvious. 'Well, clearly not ours.'

'Thing is, I don't think we've got one any more.'

A snort of derision came back at him. 'Thing is, big man, I never thought we did.' Crazy had his fierce face again, all resolute and faraway like he was when his eyes went funny. Tuuran backed away. The street was empty again.

'Right. Night-skins are gone.' He ran quickly for the bridge. Couldn't be thinking about Crazy Mad and what he was or wasn't. Thoughts like that were too difficult. Had no place on a battlefield. No, no, no … because Flame be damned but for a moment back there in that alley he'd been afraid. An Adamantine Man and he'd been afraid and that simply wasn't good enough.

He cast a wary eye over his shoulder. The sea titans were still wading through the water towards the bridge.

The Silver King? A half-god who'd been dead for half a thousand years? And anyway the Silver King hadn't had silver eyes. Everything else but not his eyes, if Tuuran had got the stories right. Blood-red, they said.

So, what then? What have you got inside you? Do I really want to know?

Another gang of sword-slaves came running from the end of the street. Something else to think about – that was good. Then a series of whistling screams overhead. Tuuran grabbed Crazy Mad and smashed in a door. The building shook as they vanished inside, walls quivering, clouds of dust rattling out of them. The flat crump of an explosion rolled through.

'Rockets again.' Crazy squatted in a corner. 'Getting sick of them, I am.'

'And there I was, starting to miss them.' Tuuran pressed himself against a wall. As his ears stopped ringing he heard other sounds, sword-slaves calling to each other and then running and screaming and cracks of lightning. He waited until they were all gone and then peered back through the shattered door. The bridge was quiet now, silent and still. Distant shouts of burning and looting echoed across the water. A haze of smoke drifted over the sea, making the Eye of the Sea Goddess blur at the edges. He poked his foot at the dust on the floor. Hadn't quite been true what he'd said about everything smelling of burned flesh. Just in the alley, amid the haze of greasy black ash.

He wrinkled his nose. *Don't think about it.* 'Come on! Best we get to the bridge before those stone monsters do.' He didn't wait. Didn't want to. Didn't want to even look at Crazy Mad in case he started glowing again. The Silver King was gone and he had to keep telling himself that. Just a story. Certainly wouldn't come back as some short-arse dark-skin slave, would he? *Idiot! Stop even thinking such drivel!* He ran between fires fresh from the last salvo of rockets and didn't look back. The streets and even the beach were covered in rubble. Burned-out ships floated lopsided in the water close by or beached in the shallows. The last of the fireships. A shriek tore the air across the sea – the dragon again. Tuuran scrambled into the shattered remains of another building and found himself a good solid piece of cover.

'I thought you said it was on *our* side.' Crazy Mad skittered down beside him, sliding on pieces of fractured masonry.

'I did. But it's a dragon and you should never trust them, nor their riders.'

The dragon landed on the back of the furthest of the giant stone golems and tried to lift it out of the water, claws screeching on stone, tail lashing the sea and sending columns of spray into the air. The other two giants were almost at the bridge. Tuuran shook his head. *Why do this when I could walk away? Because some slave master said so? Because that's where Crazy Mad wants to go? Just to smash stuff and scar a few pretty night-skin faces? Because I can't think of anything better to do? Come on, Tuuran, what the Flame are you doing here?*

Crazy Mad sidled closer, watching as the giant and the dragon toppled backwards together under the waves. 'How *do* you kill dragons, Tuuran? If that really is what you were made for?'

Tuuran laughed. 'We drink a poison that kills them. Then we make them so angry that they eat us.'

'Funny man. And really?'

'Really exactly like I said, *slave*. You've seen one now. You think you're going to wander up to something like that with a piece of steel and do anything useful?' He cringed as yet another volley of rockets screamed overhead, arcing out towards the stone giants in the sea, exploding around them. *And what was that about? Who are they even firing at? Do they even know any more, any of them?* Didn't matter though. Chaos was chaos, and while everyone was looking at the dragon and the golems they wouldn't be looking at *him*, so Tuuran lunged to his feet and ran out of the house across the beach, through shallow water and over fine muddy sand which sucked at his boots and tried to tear them off. *Talking to myself. I*

579

don't even know which one of us is the crazy one any more. I'll be as bad as he is by the end of this.

There were Taiytakei soldiers running from the city towards them, but before they drew close a rocket flashed out of nowhere and exploded in their midst, wrapping them in a ball of fire, and then another and another. A building burst in front of him, flinging shards of stone through the air. Tuuran swore and staggered and turned his back as they peppered him, thumping and pinging off his armour. Crazy Mad pointed towards the sea. The nearest giant was almost at the bridge. In the shallows the water only reached its knees. It towered over the narrow stone streets.

'Look at the bodies.' Tuuran wrinkled his nose. They were at the edge of the bridge now, looking for a way up, and the dead were everywhere. Mostly Taiytakei, not the gangs of sword-slaves they had met looting the city. They had gold-glass armour and scorch marks on them. He ran on, hugging the wall. Not that that would save him if he was in the wrong place when the next rocket came in. They ran up a set of steps onto the golden bridge itself and he stopped there for a moment, gathering his courage. That was when he saw the back of Crazy Mad's armour. There was a hole in it. He poked his finger through, touching the skin of Crazy's back.

'You've got a hole,' he said, and he turned Crazy Mad around and poked another finger through a second hole at the front. 'And another one.' He wiggled both his fingertips. 'In one side and out the other, but on you? Not a mark. Why aren't you dead?' Crazy Mad only shrugged, not what Tuuran wanted at all. He shivered. 'Isul Aieha,' he whispered. *Silver King.* But that couldn't be. Couldn't possibly be. And maybe those holes were ... something else. Maybe they'd been there all along and he'd just never noticed. Maybe.

Crazy Mad rolled his eyes and pulled away. He vaulted up to the bridge and started to run, fast like there was a wind driving him. Tuuran took another breath and looked around him. The dead lay scattered about like litter after a summer festival, scorched and burned by fire and lightning. Sword-slaves and Taiytakei alike. Crazy Mad just kept going, across the open killing ground of the bridge, hurdling the bodies strewn over the road. Tuuran watched him. 'Have to hand it to you, Crazy. Whoever you are and whatever you are, you can certainly run.'

Gawping. Never useful. When Crazy Mad reached the other side and no one had tried to kill him – yet – Tuuran tore after him as fast as his legs would go.

77

Men of Stone

The kwen from the mountains had told her that nothing could be done about them. They would surely destroy her if she strayed too close. *They will cleanse the bridges. Leave them alone.* He hadn't told the dragon though, or else Diamond Eye hadn't been listening.

She wasn't sure which of them saw the creatures in the water first. They seemed like more boats perhaps, but with bigger wakes than their size deserved. Diamond Eye veered towards them at once but she turned him away, up towards the tallest of the three islands, the sheer-walled peak of Dul Matha if she remembered the name aright. More glasships waited there. They were high, drifting across the water towards the city, floating apart as if they didn't know quite what to do.

Lightning. She'd felt it from the ones over the city and seen the way the rims of their outer discs would glow and burn with a light brighter and whiter than the sun before they fired. Now she knew what it would do to her dragon. To plunge helpless to the sea from such a height would be death for her, even if Diamond Eye survived. So she reigned him in and forced him to hold his hunger in check. They would not fly fast and straight at these, not like they did before. This time she stayed away and circled higher until she was far up above them, and *then* she let Diamond Eye have his way. He fell from the sky like a stone, striking the first like a meteor, disintegrating it into a shower of glass and gold and then arrowed on straight at the sea to spread his wings and skim the waves and turn and rise and strike again.

And that was when he saw the creatures in the water for what they truly were, and this time when she told him to rise, he refused. They weren't boats. She saw that as they came closer. They were men, or giants with the shape of men, with craggy features of the same dark stone as the Dul Matha and long ropes of seaweed draped from their head and their shoulders. They were walking with all but their heads and shoulders lost beneath the waves so she couldn't be sure how large they were, but they were as tall as a barn at the very least.

Leave them! But Diamond Eye would not. He landed on the back of the first of them and snarled. Claws screeched on stone as he tried to lift it out of the water, wings tearing at the air, tail lashing the sea and sending great showers of spray over them all. Where the water touched his scales it steamed. The two monsters shook and Diamond Eye flapped his wings, striving for balance. He twisted his neck towards the giant's face, hurling Zafir forward against the buckles of her harness, knocking the wind out of her.

Let it go! You can't!

What were they? Books hidden in the secret places of the Pinnacles where she'd grown up had had pictures of things like this, and of something the same but much, much greater, something that made even a dragon look tiny. Books the alchemists always coveted but were never allowed to see. But if these creations had a name, she'd never known it.

Leave them! Up! Fly up!

The stone monster toppled backwards into the sea taking Diamond Eye with it. The waves slammed into her side and then she was under the water, beneath the dragon with the giant on top of both of them.

No! Diamond Eye writhed beneath her. Dragons didn't breathe. Dragons could live under water for days if they wanted to. Dragons didn't care … *But I can't.* There was no struggling this time, no cutting herself free. She didn't even try. Her lungs began to spasm, demanding that she take a breath. The rippling daylight far above flashed orange and bright. Fireballs hot and fierce in the air but the water was black and cold and dark. She closed her eyes. She wasn't afraid, not any more. Focused her mind. *Just. Let. Go!*

And then Diamond Eye was free and he surged upwards. She burst out of the water and gasped and gulped at the air. The dragon spread his wings and towered out of the sea, half of him still under, but his head and claws and wings were out of the waves, and so was she. Steam rose all around them. Diamond Eye's wings pulled at the air, harder and harder, but they weren't moving as the stone monster anchored them to the seabed. Then at last Diamond Eye burst up out of the water in a cloud of mist and spray.

He had the stone monster of the sea in his claws. *How* many tons of stone? And he knew what to do, and this time there was no stopping him, no desire to even try. She understood, without quite knowing how, that he'd done this before in another time and in another life. Long ago, before the Silver King had come, he'd fought this battle once before and won. She felt it in him.

He rose slowly and painfully, sinking down again before each upward beat of his wings, but he still climbed and the giant made of stone still hung from his claws. High above the top of Dul Matha he let it go, soared up, turned and arrowed down again, following the stone titan as it fell until it struck the jagged rocks at the bottom of Dul Matha and exploded into pieces and a gleeful satisfaction poured though dragon and rider both. He crashed into the waves and dragged her beneath the water again, but now she simply closed her eyes and waited. He was too hot. The cold of the water would stop him from burning on the inside, and she knew, as certainly as she could, that he wouldn't hurt her, that he would remember her enough to see she didn't drown. And so it was; and they rose together and swam for a while until the heat inside him eased and he pulled himself back into the sky.

He plucked the second giant out of the water like a sea eagle taking a fish. And because he could, when he soared once again high up above the pinnacle of the Kraitu's Bones, this time he dived and hurled it into one of the glasships and smashed them both.

78

Shields of Glass and Gold

Berren, Crazy Mad, the Bloody Judge, Skyrie. More names than he needed, a different man born each day, but this was war, and war was what had birthed the Bloody Judge, and so in the here and now that was who he was. He raced across the three arches of the bridge and on, through smudges of thick smoke, leaping over dead sword-slaves and Taiytakei soldiers alike. Tiny elegant huts lined both sides of the bridge, miniature shops and workshops blocking the view to the sea. All of them were wrecked and ruined by lightning now, and in the gaps between them he saw the rising sun of the morning on one side and the stone monsters on the other. *Spawn of the Kraitu and the Red Banatch.* He didn't know how, but he knew that's what they were.

The first of them was getting close, yet what spurred him on more was the look he'd seen in Tuuran's eye. It frightened him, that look. He'd seen it before on the faces of men across the world. Belief. Fanatical belief. And that wasn't Tuuran. Tuuran believed in Tuuran and that was that. That look in his eyes didn't belong.

He reached the other end of the bridge and slowed as he emerged into the open. Tall and handsome buildings had once lined a wide paved road. They were broken shells now, filled with smoke and rubble that spilled out of them like the guts of a man with his belly sliced open. The bodies scattered about here were sword-slaves again, charred and burned.

Tuuran caught up with him. 'More rockets, eh?' The stubby glass and gold tower at the end of the bridge had been shattered from within. Only the side facing back across the water remained. The first stone giant reached the bridge, and Berren watched as it stopped and raised its fists and brought them down. The ground trembled as the centre of the bridge dissolved into dust and glittering fragments. Tuuran looked forlornly back. 'There were enough dead night-skins back there to find ourselves at least *some* armour that fitted.' He gave Berren a nervous up-and-down glance. 'Something without a hole in it, you know? That gold and glass stuff they have that stops the lightning.'

The streets were ghostly empty past the destruction at the end of the bridge, abandoned, the only sounds the cries of fighting wafting down from higher up the island. Tall stone walls lined the road ahead. They were peppered with grand entrances festooned with bright banners in reds and yellows and vivid greens. Colourful signs hung overhead. Merchants for rich folk. Traders bringing in exotica that no one else had a use for or could afford. There was surely money here, yet there were no signs of looting. Nothing was on fire, nothing broken, no murdered men or screaming women. The quiet was almost eerie. The sword-slaves hadn't been this way or else somehow they'd been kept in check. Here and there Berren saw furtive faces at windows.

Tuuran dragged him into a doorway and pushed him into the shadows. A shape flashed through the sky. 'Dragon.' He made a sign, the warding against evil that Berren had seen so many times on the slave galleys. When it passed they ran on. 'You sure you going to find what you're looking for up here?'

Sure? How could he be sure? But where else was there to look? 'This is where the Taiytakei soldiers came, right? The rest ...' He frowned. The rest had been a ruse, a distraction. The destruction of a whole city in a whirl of fire and hell – but this, *this* was what the fleet had come for. For the palace they'd seen from across the sea.

He heard shouts up ahead that grew louder as they ran on, interrupted now and then by cracks of lightning. The street spilled them into a square. Berren slowed. There were Taiytakei ahead, soldiers, the sort that carried lightning wands. On the far side of the square the road ran between two stone bell towers and started to rise, climbing the island towards the golden towers at the top. A little way beyond the towers a barricade barred the way. Now and then lightning flashed out from it, but the Taiytakei in the square had golden shields and it splashed off them and crackled harmlessly into the stone underfoot. A few sword-slaves cowered in helpless clusters under whatever cover they could find, but nearly all the soldiers were armoured in glass and gold. They were running back and forth and yelling at each other, looking for a way to outflank the barricade. They kept looking up too. Pointing. Another glasship was drifting down from the peak with a bright burning orb hung beneath it. More fire.

Something whizzed past Berren's head and smacked into the stone behind him. An oversized crossbow bolt. Almost a small javelin.

'Scorpion.' Tuuran wrinkled his nose. 'Baby one. We used to have little ones that two men could carry between them. Not much use against a dragon.' He scurried along the side of the square and into an alley – anywhere not to be out in the open – and sat on his haunches against a wall. He yawned and stretched as if making himself comfortable. 'Since we seem to have caught up with the fighting, I say we sit and wait for the night-skins to finish killing each other.'

'No.' Berren kicked Tuuran back to his feet. 'We're not staying here.' He raced back into the square, across it, jinking and weaving towards the bell towers. Sitting and waiting was … No, he didn't want that. From the towers he'd be able to see whatever there was to see. Something to tell him where to go.

'Crazy Mad, you daft turd!' The big man stayed with him though. Berren sprinted for the door at the base of the nearer tower. Shouts rang out from among the Taiytakei. Lightning flared and roared and cracked. A flash blinded Berren but he was still running. Something thumped into his arm, spinning him round. He staggered, facing the wrong way for a moment, almost falling until Tuuran scooped him up, screaming his head off, and hurled them both through the open door at the bottom of the tower. They slid across a dusty wooden floor and thumped to a stop.

'Crazy Mad! I knew that was going to be your name the moment I saw you. Daft as a Scales! Flame, I don't even know which lot was trying to kill us. Both of them, I think.' Tuuran was blinking. He looked at himself and patted his chest as though faintly surprised not to be bleeding. Then he rummaged in his knapsack and pulled out two fire-globes burning a bright orange. The tips from two Taiytakei rockets. 'So who gets these, then? The ones we came to kill or the ones stabbing us in the back? *You* choose!'

'You had those in there all the time?'

'Since the ship.' Tuuran frowned and then his face split into a great big stupid guilty-looking grin. 'What?'

'One slip, you even lean too hard against that wall, and boom! You know that, right?'

Tuuran sounded almost hurt. 'I'm an Adamantine Man, sword-slave. Adamantine Men don't *slip*. I keep telling you that.'

'You just threw us both across the floor!'

The big man ignored him. He poked at Berren's arm, at where whatever it was had hit him. The bottom part of his left pouldron was bent and mangled. It pressed uncomfortably against him. When Berren took it off and looked at himself, he was barely even scratched. 'That was lucky,' he muttered.

'Luck?' Tuuran jabbed a finger into the hole in the brigandine over Berren's chest. 'Luck? Maybe or maybe not. But still, that's what you wear them for right? Me, I'm just going to stand behind you from now on. And duck because you're a short-arse.' Tuuran loped up the steps that spiralled to the roof of the tower, past little landings with a tiny door on each one. Berren counted twenty and then they were pushing on a trapdoor and standing up in the open beside a huge bell. The Taiytakei were spread out in the square below. They could simply toss the fire-globes in their midst. He looked down at the barricade and its Taiytakei defenders, hunkered down behind carts and wagons and sacks and their shields. From up here they all looked the same. Tiny people in glittering gold. Past the barricade the road climbed further. As the island grew steeper it began to zigzag. The palaces and castles up there were built into the bedrock, dozens of little clusters of glass and gold bursting from the black stone like mountain flowers.

'Don't touch the bell, eh?' he said. He could see the scorpion things Tuuran had meant lined up behind the barricade. Six or seven of them.

'Oh, we won't be here that long.' Tuuran weighed a fire-globe in his hand and threw it. It arced over the street and shattered directly behind the barricade, exploding in a ball of fire. By then he'd thrown the second as well. A touch further, perfect for catching the Taiytakei reeling away from the first explosion. The soldiers in the square saw their chance and surged forward behind their shields. Bolts of lightning danced back and forth and then the two sides were on each other, still flickering with lightning, their spiked ashgars swinging. More Taiytakei rushed at the barricade, swarming over it with a few ragged bands of sword-slaves whipped in their wake.

A flash of light and a crack of lightning rattled the tower. Stone splinters showered around Berren's head. He turned and ran, the two of them leaping down the stairs as fast as they could. Back in the square the air stank of lightning. Soldiers swarmed past, running for the road, pushing them on, a sudden horde of sword-slaves. Berren stooped to pick up a discarded shield. Curved glass lined with gold.

'Not much use when a man comes at you with an axe,' Tuuran grunted.

'It stops the lightning, though.'

The big man paused. He nodded and picked one up for himself, then hauled Berren out of the surge of soldiers and into a doorway. He had the strange look on his face again. That gleam of hunger he always got when there was fighting to be had, but something else as well. Reverence, perhaps. Awe. Berren tried to pull away.

'Oi! I got warlocks to kill and I need them alive long enough to answer a question or two first. Fat lot of use it is if I just find a corpse.' He pulled harder. This time Tuuran let him go. 'Anyway, I'd have thought you'd want to be one of the first across that bridge up there, yelling like a mad thing.'

Tuuran was grinning. 'Oh I do, Crazy, it's just—'

There was an explosion. The air was suddenly full of glass, spears of it flying thick and fast through the air, and stones big enough to squash a man's head like a melon. Soldiers fell around Berren, scythed down, speared and lifted clean off their feet; and then a wall of searing fire and howling wind almost threw him into the air. Hands grabbed him. Tuuran again, yanking him out of the way of the stones and the flying glass. The ground trembled, a rhythmic pounding. 'Sun and moon! What was that?'

Tuuran's face was full of savage joy. 'What I was trying to tell you. That glasship we saw from the square? The dragon brought it down. Blew it to pieces. Learn to keep an eye on the sky, eh, Crazy?' As Berren started to rise Tuuran pushed him down again, hard this time. 'Wait! You feel that?' The pounding through the ground. Berren nodded. 'That's the golem that smashed the bridge.' He nodded back to the square and then up towards the island's peak. 'Stone monster one way, dragon the other. This is where we hide, Crazy Mad or whatever-you-are, and stay the Flame out of their way.' He gripped Berren tight as though afraid he'd run off. 'Fight like that, you don't want to be near it, my friend.'

Berren crouched beside him. Tuuran probably had a point. 'What was it you called me back before we crossed the bridge. Issle Ayer or something?'

'Isul Aieha.' The tension in Tuuran's face was sharp enough to cut.

'So what's that then?'

'I told you. Dragons once roamed free where I come from. Isul Aieha was the Silver King. He tamed them and showed the first alchemists how to master them.' The trembling in the ground was getting worse. Berren peered out of their hiding place. Stones and shattered shards flew past his face. The stone giant was crossing the square. 'Still don't know whose side those are on.'

'Not ours.' Berren was sure of that. 'Go on. Tell me about this Silver King while we're sitting on our arses. What happened to him?'

'There were alchemists who followed a different path. Blood-mages.' For a moment Tuuran's voice turned sour. 'Not so much difference between them as I used to think. Anyway. The Silver King wrought sorceries that would make everything you've seen here seem dull and plain. Yet in the end the blood-mages still tore him down.' A barrage of rocks and lightning flew down the street. The sea titan was closer. Hurled stones pinged off its legs and exploded into shrapnel. Lightning crackled over it. It barely seemed to notice. Tuuran winced and shrank back into the wall. 'They ripped him to pieces. They tore out his soul and shared it among themselves. An alchemist once told me that he had the Silver King's own blood in his veins.' He shrugged. 'There's other stories as say the Silver King simply had enough. They say he made a tomb for himself, the Black Mausoleum, and took himself away to it to rest and rise when he was needed again. Bullshit, if you ask me. What sort of idiot would do a thing like that?'

There was something odd in Tuuran's tone, something very off, but Berren was too busy watching the rock monster to pay much attention to anything else. 'I think we should—'

A shape fell out of the sky, huge and dark against the morning sun. The dragon. It plummeted down and flared its wings, and the next thing Berren knew he was flying through the air as though a great hand had picked him up and thrown him away while a wind like a hurricane ripped at his skin. When he picked himself up again the dragon was rising into the air, the rock monster hanging from its talons. 'Sun and moon!'

'Do you remember them?' asked Tuuran.

'What?'

'Do you remember them? The dragons?'

'*What?*' Berren snorted and shook his head and laughed. 'Don't be daft. No dragons where I come from – even *you* know that.' He peered around the street. The dragon flew up high over the island and then tucked in its wings and fell, arrowing towards the glass towers around the peak. At the very last it let the stone giant go and spread its wings. The air thundered and groaned, and even from so far away the shock was enough to stagger him; and then the ground roared and squirmed and shook as the golem smashed into the island. Berren almost fell, and then the air was full of flying stones again. The walls either side of him trembled and cracked. The bells in the towers clanged and the towers themselves groaned and started to sag. A third of the way up the nearer one a great split opened. Berren clutched his head and dropped, crouching against the wall behind him. The air still roared and now it was warm and then hot, hot enough to hurt his lungs. Tuuran took hold of him. They huddled together, making themselves as small as they could.

'They're in your dreams, Crazy. I know they're there, and don't you try and pretend they're not!'

With a long rumble the tower fell. The air tasted of hot broken stone. Chunks of tortured masonry shattered around them. Grit and gravel fell like rain. As the shaking stopped and the roaring fell away, a haze of choking white dust swept over everything. Berren peered back into the street. No one was throwing stones any more. Where the defenders had been there was only a huge crater scattered with rubble, half lost in haze now. From what he could see almost everything from where he was right to the bridge up on the peak had been smashed to ruin. The dragon sat in the middle of it, a shape in the smoke and the dust. Here and there handfuls of figures were moving further up the slope. Not many. A small miracle that anyone at all was left alive. As Berren stared, the dragon spread its wings and leaped into the sky, churning whorls of smoke twisting in its wake. Tuuran stood at his shoulder. 'Do you see now why the Adamantine Men have no fear? When *that* is the enemy and you have learned to face it, what else is there?'

Berren couldn't take his eyes off the monster.

Do you remember them?

He was the orphan boy from Shipwrights' in the city of Deephaven and the warlock Saffran Kuy had just told him his future. *Dragons for one of you. Queens for both!*

He was Skyrie, a nothing farm boy from the edge of a swamp. *Don't be daft. No dragons where I come from!*

But he was something else too, and he *did* remember them because he'd made them. Forged them out of the souls of fallen half-gods and skinned them with his own will.

They're in your dreams.

Yes, and the air was black with them, thick with their cries, flying to war to burn the enemy once and for all. In their thousands, arrayed under the sun, the light gleaming from their scales so bright it blinded, massed among flawless white stone spires that scratched the clouds in the sky; and then in the darkness of the night the silver light of the moon shone down, hard and violent and it burned, and he clenched his fist but he would not bow, not ever, not even to the god that had made him because he knew, he *knew* what lay beneath and behind and beyond.

Isul Aieha? 'He carried a spear, did he?' he asked without really knowing why.

Tuuran nodded and there was that wary look back on his face in a flash. 'Yes.'

Isul Aieha? That's not who I am. But I do remember you, and by another name too. I call you Worldbreaker.

79

Burn

Diamond Eye was beyond her reach once more. He smashed another of the stone giants from the sea into the ground with such force that the world shook, and even while Zafir was trying to find her breath he flared his wings and she was crushed against his scales yet again. Her armour was falling apart now, pieces breaking off with every dive and every turn.

She coughed, choking on the dust and the smoke that filled the wind. But there was something else, something in the air. From the very first day she'd flown with him from Baros Tsen's eyrie, Diamond Eye had been different, a frenzy inside him unlike any dragon she'd ever ridden before, but now there was something even more. He sensed prey, like a hunting dog catching the scent of a rabbit, bright and fresh and close, and yet he couldn't find it. She'd never known a dragon be so wanton. He drew her in with his abandon.

Another dragon?

Diamond Eye leaped into the air and soared away again, out over the sea without waiting for her command. His frustration seeped into her. Something was here. Something that meant more than she did. He was dulled by Bellepheros's alchemy and couldn't think but he was trying so very hard to remember something. But *what?*

She nudged him towards the last of the glasships and let him vent his rage, punching straight through the fragile heart of the first, lashing at another which tilted and spiralled away. A thunderbolt sundered the air and he reared and caught the lightning between his claws. Pain and rage seared into them both as sparks cracked over his scales but Diamond Eye devoured it, fed on the fury and shattered the glasship into a jagged rain that fell like spears onto the swarming battle below. He powered beneath another too low to reach the discs and so he snatched at the fragile gondola instead, tore it away and hurled it across the sky to plunge into the distant speckled sea. Nothing was enough. When the last glasship fell he turned back towards the golden bridge that joined the two islands. He flew under and then over it and around and around, oblivious to the battle that raged across it until Zafir almost screamed, 'Burn! Burn them!'

Another glasship came, this one with a ball of fire hung beneath it. Diamond Eye tore it down and hurled a murder of glass and flames into the seething ground below. He turned his eye to the last stone giant, shaking the earth as it walked, crushing the dead beneath it. Turned away again. *Somewhere near!* Whatever the dragon was looking for was close, but he couldn't find it.

A chance. 'The stone man then!' howled Zafir.

Diamond Eye wheeled. With white burning towers of rage he fell on the last giant and snatched it up, pulled himself high and then dived, slamming the creature into the mass of towers and fighting Taiytakei and then followed it down, shrieking and burning, tail whipping in fury to tear down everything around him. And then on, half leaping, half flying in great bounds up the steepening sides of the island until he was in among the towers of glass and gold that grew together like a giant copse of gleaming trees. He barrelled into them, cracking and tearing until he brought them down, one by one crashing in shattered shards to the earth.

'Enough! *Enough!*' He'd forgotten she was there again. A spike of glass tore a great rent in his wing but Diamond Eye barely noticed. A broken splinter struck a hand's breadth from where Zafir clung to his back, driving deep through his scales.

'Stop!' She summoned all that she was. *I am the dragon-queen and you are mine to command. Enough, my deathbringer. ENOUGH!*

Enough? He rose, reluctant and sulking, spiralling back into the air. Torn and slashed by the glass, a trail of blood dripped behind him, a scorching red rain. His heat was burning her even through the dragon-scale between them, and so Zafir coaxed him away between the islands, down into the cooling sea. Clouds of salty steam billowed around them. She looked at the savaged city, at the devastation the dragon had wrought, yet felt nothing but more madness and rage. *Enough?* Never enough. And he was a dragon;

and dragons did not tire.

He rose from the sea, hers again for a moment, and she flew him high towards the palace now. The Palace of Roses they called it, a last cluster of towers on a single pinnacle of rock that reminded her of home. A glittering glass bridge reached across from the lower island. The road beyond wound up through three rings of stone walls, each with a gatehouse, and then to a small forest of dazzling towers. Each of the three towers at its heart was as tall again as the Tower of Air that had once been hers; around those stood six more, arranged in a ring and joined together by a curtain wall of golden glass. Out further still rose three black monoliths, the enchanters' power stones for their glasships.

'Burn it.' She spoke calmly now, for this moment while Diamond Eye was hers again. 'Burn it all.'

They started with the bridge. Dozens, maybe hundreds, of Taiytakei were advancing through the rubble at its lower end. Others were waiting behind barricades at the far side to meet them with stones and arrows and lightning. Diamond Eye burned them until they were gone and everything was ash. Then on to the first gatehouse, pouring flame over the stone until it cracked in the heat. A lash of the tail and the gates flew apart. At the second the Taiytakei were already scattering. She let Diamond Eye burn them and then land among them, sweeping the ground clean, battering them high into the air or plucking them from the earth and devouring them. A few turned their lightning wands on her as the dragon came but their tiny bolts were little more than an insect's sting. One struck her in the arm. Sparks ran over her armour, cracked and battered, but she felt nothing and then Diamond Eye's fire incinerated them. When he was done he stepped between them, eating the charred remains.

The third gatehouse was empty and abandoned by the time she reached it. She passed it by. On to the palace itself. The way it was built reminded her of the Crown of the Sea Lords in Khalishtor and the thought made her smile. *Show them what a dragon can do.* Tsen had asked for that, so they would understand how much they had to fear. And she would oblige them. The Taiytakei across this blighted world would understand *her*. What *she* could do, the dragon-queen. *And we are but one. Think, my deathbringer, think what we would do to them if we flew in our hordes!* From her throne in the Adamantine Palace the Taiytakei had seemed distant, barely even there, a perpetual splinter in her finger but nothing more. Now she knew them better. And weren't there other realms too? Places she'd never seen. Places of which she'd never even heard until they'd taken her as their slave. And no dragons in any of them. Waiting to be plucked.

Look at us, Diamond Eye! Look at what we are! Nothing stood between the dragons and their desires but their riders and the alchemists, and *they* were all beholden to *her*, the speaker of the nine realms, and all she had to do was find a way to return. And then? No more Councils of Kings and Queens eyeing one another across a table, constantly seeking some advantage and always achieving nothing. Worlds waited, there to be taken! They could build an empire like Vishmir had done but unimaginably greater! An empire to put even these slavers to shame.

She turned Diamond Eye towards the gleaming spires of the sea lord's palace and set about their destruction. There would be a way. Somehow she would find it.

80

The Man in Grey

Tuuran watched, crouched beside their broken wall, keeping Crazy Mad's head pressed down. In the haze of dust and smoke, amid the ruined stone and the shattered glass, the dragon took to the sky at last. The air fell quiet and still, and then he heard sporadic shouts from off among the broken streets. He waited, eyes following the Taiytakei soldiers who'd survived the destruction of the sea titan as they scrambled through the debris, skirting spatters of still-liquid gold, the dull red glow of molten glass, the stones cracked and steaming by the dragon's heat. He watched them climb the switchbacks of the road towards the near end of the Divine Bridge, the thread of gold across the abyss to the Palace of Roses. Crazy Mad kept trying to get up and Tuuran kept pulling him down.

'Stupid slave! Wait! Let the night-skins kill each other.' He looked up, trying to spot the dragon, but for the moment it was gone and so he waited, watching until the shouts moved on and the Taiytakei soldiers were all safely away. Finally he let Crazy Mad go and they started up the last part of the hill. The road to the island peak was littered with broken stone and shards of gold-glass. The walls from the little palaces around the top of the island were cracked and broken, the towers of glass and gold mostly smashed and toppled. Here and there in the few that still stood he saw people. Madmen. Idiots. Just staring numbly when the dragon might come back at any moment. *Why don't you run, you daft buggers?* He shivered. Towers were meant to be made of stone. A man shouldn't be able to look right through a castle's walls at its innards and find people looking back at him.

There were dead Taiytakei scattered where the dragon had been. Limp broken things, arms and legs twisted, their armour smashed to scattered pieces. That was dragons for you. There was something to be said for a good strong coat of steel and leather. It

597

might not do much for the lightning that came out of the Taiytakei batons; it might scorch and burn when people started throwing fire-globes about, but at least it didn't break. He crunched over the litter of golden glass. The sound was pleasing. Dead night-skins. The sound of dead slavers.

He saw the dragon again, storming up from the sea with water showering off its back and wings and a trail of steam behind it. He grabbed Crazy Mad and pulled him down, but the dragon flew high over their heads and off to the far end of the bridge this time. A distant shock of flame rumbled through the air, that old familiar sound that made his heart skip a beat.

The bridge drew him on, but when he got there he had to stop and marvel, just for a moment, even though there was still a dragon on the other side who might just smash it to bits. It was made of gold-glass over a skeleton of iron. The sun shone through its walls, through its steeply sloping roof and the delicate ornamentation carved at its peak. Below his feet lay glass as clear as water and then the island fell away towards the sea, a sheer craggy drop so great that the waves crashing against the cliffs far below seemed like mere ripples. The air smelled of fire, of scorched skin and burned hair.

A distant boom shook the earth. Tuuran stared down.

'Trouble with heights? And you a sail-slave?' Crazy Mad pushed past him. Tuuran didn't move. Bodies lay strewn over the bridge. Some of them had been shot. Crossbows, by the look of it, big ones with bolts as long as his forearm. There were sword-slaves scorched by lightning too, but fire had done most of the work here. Dragon fire. He took a deep breath. *One step at a time. Just enjoy the view.*

'I can hold your hand if you want.' Crazy Mad laughed and pushed on.

'Another word out of you, slave, and you can hold my axe with your skull! I'm a sail-slave. I was climbing ropes and masts when you were still hiding up your mother's skirts!' Looking up. Looking straight ahead. Anywhere, really, as long as it wasn't down. Looking at the dragon, except the dragon had vanished again in among the towers and walls of the palace, and he saw it only in flashes and glimpses.

'Run, you lazy slave!' yelled Crazy Mad from the other end. 'I thought you Adamantine Men weren't afraid of anything!'

He walked faster. Still couldn't look down. Ropes, ladders, masts, rigging, any of those, even in a howling wind and a thrashing storm, they were home. Easy. Even with the alchemist, flying on the glass disc up to the Palace of Leaves. But this? Standing on what looked like nothing at all over an abyss of stone and water ...

Halfway across the bridge a part of the roof had been staved in, nothing left but smashed iron bones. Chunks of glass lay scattered about. Somehow that made it easier. And then more bodies. The dragon. It had burned these so hard that the gold in their armour was smeared where it had melted. At the far side Crazy Mad was on his haunches, crouched beside something. An arm poked out from between pieces of broken stone, a strip of skin as pale as a ghost. Tuuran thought it must be covered in dust but then he saw the tattoos. Sharp shapes writhing through each other across the skin. The tattoos of the grey dead men. Crazy Mad looked up at him and Tuuran had to turn away. 'You're doing the eyes again.'

'They're here!' The hunger in Crazy's voice was a frightful thing, like the insatiable hunger of a dragon. He pulled at the stones, tearing them away from the body underneath. When they got the corpse out, Crazy Mad turned him over. The bodies lying in the open were black and charred for the most part, brittle as charcoal where their armour hadn't shielded them, but the stones must have covered the warlock from the worst of the fire. His belly and face were pale. The tattoos on his arms ran up to his neck. The fragments of robe hanging in tatters around him were grey. No question as to what he was.

'Is that him?' Tuuran made himself look. 'The one you're after?'

'No.' Crazy Mad sat there staring. He looked strangely content. 'But now I know they're here.'

Zafir made Diamond Eye fly between the outer towers and leave them be. Forced him straight for the inner ones, the tallest, and there she let him loose on the first one they passed, tooth and claw and tail, splintering great chunks of gold and glass from its side. Pieces fell into the open yard below among the milling Taiytakei and their slaves and exploded in a hail of deadly spears and knives.

Screams echoed beneath her and joy surged inside – from Diamond Eye but also her own.

Clusters of black-powder cannon. She saw them now, around the outer ring, close to each of the three black needles of the enchanters' monoliths. More lightning too perhaps, although she spotted none of the rings of brilliant light she'd seen around the cannon on the fortress by the sea. She turned Diamond Eye towards them. They were moving, trying to bear on her, but they were uselessly slow, like the cannon that Tsen had shown her on the eyrie. Weapons to fire on glasships, clumsy and worthless against a dragon. Diamond Eye flew to the first and tore the cannon to pieces with his claws, hurling the metal tubes at the black monolith beside them, cracking it. Zafir laughed madly.

'Burn them!' she screamed into the wind and urged Diamond Eye on to the next. 'Burn them!' There was no lightning here. Lightning didn't work against glasships, and what else could fly so high? 'Burn them!' They reached the next cluster of cannon. Fire raged out of the dragon all along the walls, up and over the metal and the stone, and then the wall blew apart beneath them and a mighty hand lifted them up, dragon and all. It tossed them into the air and she felt Diamond Eye convulse with pain, peppered by stones and shards of glass like scorpion bolts. Pain and then more rage and he banked and rolled and dived at the offending ground. Another explosion, smaller than the first. The dragon skimmed the wreckage, smashing the skeleton of iron beneath the glass and pouring flames into the gaping wound. Fire bloomed inside another piece of wall and burst through it like a fist through paper. More glass flew. The Taiytakei were little figures, running and screaming, frantic like ants. Anything to get away. The flying glass tore them to pieces before her eyes. It ripped them open and tore their limbs and sliced off their heads.

A piece hit her in the face, right between the eyes like a stone from a sling.

Tuuran and Crazy Mad passed the first gatehouse, which reeked with the stink of hot stone and burned flesh. There were bodies, dozens of them. Taiytakei soldiers dead at their posts, their armour melted on them by the dragon's fire. Tuuran glanced at them and smiled. Dead slavers! A thing to make hearts sing. People were running the other way now, eyes mad with terror, fleeing from the palace of their unassailable sea lord. Slaves. A few were pale-skinned folk from the dragon lands or perhaps the little kingdoms and the northern edge of the Dominion. Mostly they were darker, Crazy Mad colour from the heart of the Dominion or the southern coast of Aria. There were Taiytakei too, slaves holding their hands high as they fled so that anyone who cared could see the brands they carried. Tuuran ignored them. Slaves were slaves and he had no grief with them, whatever skin they wore.

The second gatehouse was empty. The road beyond was gouged, stone slabs ripped out of the ground in great long slashes. The dragon. Bloody limbs, spiked clubs, shields, batons: all lay strewn about amid streaks of sticky blood. More and more slaves ran past. A few here and there stooped to pick up discarded weapons. At the third a gang of sail-slaves had armed themselves from the fallen Taiytakei. They held up their hands to show their brands and Tuuran held up his own and they nodded to one another. They had a Taiytakei and they were killing him, slowly and with a great deal of relish. If it wasn't for Crazy Mad Tuuran might have stopped to join them.

An explosion shook the ground. Up around the edge of the palace a fireball bloomed and rose into the air. He saw the dragon, saw it lurch and then turn and vanish behind the higher walls. He could smell smoke again, drifting in on the breeze. The stream of slaves fleeing the palace became thicker. There were fights, short and sharp and vicious. Slaves of all colours beating down Taiytakei soldiers, swallowing them with their weight of numbers, tearing off their armour and pulling away their helms and battering them bloody. Lightning spat left and right. It was madness. Chaos. Whether the Taiytakei were attackers or those defending the palace, Tuuran had no idea. The slaves didn't much care.

And there, running straight at him with panic on his face, was one of the men he'd seen on the ship. The tall grey dead man, Crazy Mad's Vallas Kuy, and Crazy had seen him too. The warlock was slow, old and feeble among the young muscle of the escaping slaves. His skin was as pale as the moon and his grey robes fluttered around his feet. Crazy Mad moved into his path; he took off his helm with slow and deliberate care, but the grey dead man was too busy running to look at faces. Vallas the warlock skittered sideways, eyes fixed on the road and his only escape from the dragon, and then at the very last his gaze flicked to Crazy Mad's face and flicked away again. And then flicked back.

Crazy Mad caught hold of him, eyes gleaming. Tuuran stopped to watch.

81

Who Am I?

'Vallas Kuy!'

'You!' The grey dead man gaped. For a moment he looked truly afraid.

'Me. Do you remember me, Vallas? Do you remember me from Tethis? Do you remember Gelisya and Syannis? Do you remember what your brother did to me?' Crazy Mad threw Vallas to the ground, both oblivious to the slaves streaming past, the running battles, the shouting and the screaming and the cracks of lightning. Tuuran craned his neck to scan the sky, looking out for the dragon, but his ears were firmly with Crazy Mad. 'Do you? Do you remember? Get up!'

Vallas rose slowly and unsteadily to his feet, still gaping at Crazy Mad as though he'd seen a ghost. 'You,' he whispered. 'Why are you here? *How* are you here?' The earth shivered and Tuuran cringed as another explosion rocked the Kraitu's Bones. The fleeing slaves had an urgent terror to them. For a moment Vallas stared at Tuuran instead. 'And you! I knew we weren't wrong.'

'Get on your knees, soap maker!' Vallas shook his head. The fear was leaving his eyes and a venom taking its place. From behind the palace the dragon soared high into the sky. The air crackled with energy as it shrieked its victory. Tuuran looked around for shelter. Crazy Mad pointed his sword at Vallas. 'What did you do to me? Who am I? What did you *do*?'

The dragon was going berserk: screaming, burning, smashing, throwing itself against the three great towers of glass and gold, lashing them with its tail, tearing at them with its claws. There was no telling when it might come their way, but when it did – *if* it did – it was clearly long past paying attention to things like who it was supposed to burn and who it wasn't. It would kill them all. 'Oi! Crazy! We don't have time for this. Not in the open.'

Neither of them heard. The grey dead man drew a knife from inside his robes, one with a blade like a cleaver and a hilt of solid gold with a pattern of stars that looked like an eye. It distracted Tuuran for a moment. It was the knife he'd seen before, that time he'd thrown Crazy Mad into the sea. *The* knife. Crazy Mad had talked about it enough after all.

A deep groaning splintering trembled the air. The first of the palace towers crazed with cracks, bent and began to topple. The dragon turned towards them. Tuuran took a step closer. 'Crazy Mad! Whoever you are! We need to—'

Vallas clutched the knife. 'Go, Crowntaker! Be about your work. You have no hold on me, not while I have this. It will crush even *your* soul.' He backed away behind the knife, black shadows beginning to swirl around him.

'Best you drop it then.' Tuuran's axe flashed and the grey dead man didn't have a hand any more. The knife clattered to the stones. Tuuran pointed to the palace and glared at Crazy Mad. 'Not here! Big fucking dragon make big fucking fire!'

But Crazy Mad was staring at the severed stump; and then Tuuran stared too. No blood came from the wound, only wisps of black shadow. The warlock drew back his lips, bared his teeth and howled then pointed. The shadows flew from around him like daggers towards Tuuran's throat.

The stone snapped her head back. Pain shot through her neck, up into her skull and down her spine. She reeled and blinked and then pitched forward as Diamond Eye powered for the sky again. She couldn't see. Her head spun. No, she *could* see, but everything was a blur, just formless light. The dragon wheeled and turned. A shape flashed past.

The visor. The glass in her beautiful visor had crazed. She put a hand to her head to hinge it up and crunching brittle crumbs fell down her face and over her fingers. There was blood on her gauntlet. Hers. Her head throbbed and her neck squealed whenever she moved it, but at least she could see. They were between the great towers at the centre of the palace, Diamond Eye lashing at them with his tail as they passed through, sending more giant shards of shattered glass plunging to the ground, and then they were through and he arrowed for the last cluster of black-powder cannon.

'No fire! No fire!' But Diamond Eye was too lost in his fury to hear. Zafir pulled the visor down again and pressed herself forward, turning her head away, ignoring the howl of pain from her neck. *Broken? No, it can't be.* Diamond Eye shuddered, breathing fire over whatever took his fancy as Zafir cringed on his back. The air shook. Heat washed over her. He turned and tore back into the sky and wheeled for the towers again. She barely had time to think before he crashed into one, gripping at it with all his claws. Glass shrieked and cracked as he tried to cling on, whipping his tail back and forth, striking the tower beneath him again and again. They slid down, pieces of gold-glass flaking away around them, a rain of deadly spears; and then they were falling backwards with half the tower coming down on top of them. Pieces clattered off Diamond Eye's scales, off Zafir's already cracked armour, and then the dragon rolled and spread his wings and they were away as the tower fell. A massive piece of debris struck another of the towers near the bottom. Glass exploded up and down the length of it, overwhelmed by the strain, and that too began to fall. Through the pain and the fury and the fatigue and the terror, Diamond Eye's joy surged into her.

'Down,' she whispered, exhausted, finished but exultant. 'Down. Enough.'

The dragon turned. He cocked his head as if listening for something he could barely hear. And then, for once, he did as she commanded.

Berren snatched the knife off the road. As the shadows ripped at Tuuran he buried its blade into the warlock's chest, right where his black heart should have been. He felt no resistance at all, as though Vallas was made of nothing more than smoke, but he wasn't surprised. He'd done this before. Dismay stretched across the warlock's face and a pulse of fire swept down Berren's arm. His vision filled with ghostly faces. He could see Vallas before him, doubled, one figure made of skin and bone and the other a shimmering ghost of something else. He saw two Tuurans, two of everyone, of each slave who ran past them, staring at these mad men who'd chosen here and now of all places to fight while the palace above them burned and was torn to pieces by a monster. The ghost shapes filled his vision and howled in his ears, and inside the second Vallas he could see the web of the warlock's soul, an endless tangle of threads like a spider's web wrapped within itself, exactly as he'd seen his own once before.

Tell the knife! Make it your promise. And then cut, Berren, cut! Half a lifetime ago Vallas's brother Saffran had held this knife – this one or its twin, Berren had never known which was which. He'd put it into Berren's hand and made Berren drive it into himself and see his own soul, displayed just like this. He'd made Berren make three little cuts, snip, snip, snip. *Three little slices. You! Obey! Me!* Saffran Kuy had made Berren into his slave on that day; and though Tasahre had saved him, the hold had remained, and even after Saffran was gone there was still the hole of what he'd cut away, and Berren knew without knowing how that that hole had something to do with what Vallas and the last of his warlocks had done to him in Tethis.

And now he'd find the answers. Saffran was dead, killed by the same knife. Berren remembered every moment of that day in Deephaven with perfect clarity and now he made three little cuts of his own, and with each cut the knife sliced a little piece of Vallas away. *Three little slices. You! Obey! Me!* He pulled the Starknife away from the warlock and held him fast. 'Let him go!'

The shadow serpents faded. Tuuran dropped to his knees, gasping and clutching his neck. Berren gripped Vallas by the throat. 'You tell me now, warlock, you tell me what you did in Tethis. What spell you put on me and then you tell me how it can be undone!'

The warlock let out a hacking laugh in Berren's face. 'The spell should have pulled the Bloody Judge out of his body and put him in yours, and Skyrie the other way with the thing he carries inside him. That was the spell we put on you but it didn't work.'

Berren's fingers tightened around the warlock's throat. 'Didn't work? You *liar*! How is it undone?'

Vallas Kuy howled with glee. 'There is no *undone*. It *failed*. The Bloody Judge stayed exactly where he was. He remains still stamping his swords up and down the Dominion, bringing our brothers to their ends one by one, filled with the Sun King's favour.'

'No! It did *not* fail. *I* am Berren Crowntaker! *I* am the Bloody Judge!'

'I don't know what you are but you still carry what Skyrie carried. What's left of him is in you and I am glad to have found you again.' He held out a hand. 'Come, brother. I've spent years seeking you out. Come, and we'll see what's to be done.'

'*Don't lie to me!*' Berren couldn't stop himself from screaming and something changed in the warlock's face. The laughing faded. Vallas was looking at Berren eye to eye now, a slow fear filling him, and in the warlock's eyes Berren could see the reflection of his own. They were silver. Bright burning silver. Vallas tried to pull away.

'See! See! We brought you back! We did!'

'Brought *who* back? Who am I, warlock? Who am I? What *thing* is it that I carry?'

Vallas struggled some more, his face sucking in on itself. 'You are Skyrie!'

'No, warlock, I am not. No riddles, or I swear I'll cut you to pieces.'

'You already have, Skyrie.'

Berren drove the knife into Vallas again. Now when he saw the web of the warlock's soul, he saw that the strands were unravelling, snapping and falling slowly apart, whole chunks splitting away and fading to nothing. 'What are you doing, warlock? What's happening.'

'I'm dying, Skyrie. You have killed me.'

'No! Not this knife. This knife doesn't cut flesh and I haven't even started on your soul. Stop it!' And he was sure it was true, nothing more than he'd once done to himself. 'Stop it! I command you!'

'I don't even know how,' Vallas sneered, and then his eyes rolled back. 'Goodbye, Skyrie.'

'Don't you dare die! Not before you tell me!' Berren dived inside the warlock's memories and found them filled with a small bitter man from the marshes that Kuy had found nursing a grudge – Skyrie, so easily turned with a few sweet lies against the Bloody Judge. Flashes of the Dark Queen Gelisya, of Tethis, of spells and incantations, of potions. Desperation as the Bloody Judge drew closer. Kuy's last grand scheme. Skyrie for the Bloody Judge in their last stand, and yes, it was all as Kuy said and he truly believed they'd failed.

'You ask me who you are, Skyrie, but that's not the question. The question is what?' The last strands slipped through each other.

He dug deeper. There was another. A man with one eye ... Gleefully Berren seized on that one fleeting memory. No, not *Kuy's* grand scheme. Someone else! The man with the half-ruined face. And then with the web of the warlock's soul laid before him and the golden knife to guide him, Berren slowly began to see the cuts and the stitches, the delicate reshaping that had been done, even as it unravelled again before him, and it turned out that Kuy was just a puppet after all, strings pulled without him even knowing it. A masterwork of slavery to make even the most jaded Taiytakei coo with envy. Owned mind and soul by the man with the ruined face and the one blind eye. 'Him! Who is he?' Cutting and cutting, ripping Kuy apart as he searched for answers amid the collapsing memories before they were gone. Tearing them from the dying warlock's thoughts.

Saffran Kuy's last apprentice. The one his eyes would never see.

'Where is he? How do I find him? What's his name?'

Aria, Skyrie, where the Ice Witch keeps him in a gilded cage but doesn't know what he is or what he can do, what he brings and what he hides. He gave you a gift, Skyrie, one that not even she knows.

'Gift? What gift?'

Vallas faded. His eyes closed. When Berren let him go he fell limp to the street. Tuuran was looking from Berren to the warlock and back. He shifted uneasily. 'You're doing that eye thing again,' he grumbled, and then he lifted his axe and cut off the warlock's head.

'He was already dead,' murmured Berren. *What am I? What gift?*

'Well then, now he's even more dead.' Tuuran poked at the warlock with his foot. He kept glancing up at the ruined palace.

Something inside me? Was that Kuy playing with him, taunting him to the end? Berren turned and stared back down the street towards the glass and gold bridge and the island of castles and the city of Dhar Thosis beyond, filled with flames and wrapped in smoke. Vallas hadn't lied. He'd seen it in his dreams right from the very start. *At the water's edge, eyes filled with tears and the stars winking out one by one. Dying but he wanted to live, wanted it so badly he'd do anything at all; and there he was, the man in the hooded robes the colour of moonlight, with the silver-white face, one half ruined, scarred ragged by disease or fire, and one blind milky-white eye.*

'Are you death?'

'*I am the Bringer of Endings. Let me in.*'

And he had.

Berren staggered away from the dead warlock, from Tuuran, from the wrecked and burning towers of the palace. *That was someone else. Not me! I'm Berren! The Bloody Judge. That's who I am!*

'Hey.' Tuuran put a hand on his shoulder, slowly turning him back towards the shattered palace. 'You found your warlock and there's a rampaging dragon smashing and burning and doing what dragons do. Can we go now?'

Berren shook his head and stared at his feet. Go? Go where? He'd come for answers and despite everything he'd actually found Vallas, and after all that the warlock had given him almost nothing. 'I have to go back to Deephaven. I have to go home.'

'Good for you!' Tuuran clapped a hand on Berren's back and started off up the road towards the palace. 'I might come too. Still reckon there's a great big fight brewing back there.'

The flood of fleeing slaves had become a trickle. Berren stared at the warlock lying on the stones. 'Well, where are you going *now* then?'

Tuuran turned and grinned. 'The dragon's come down. Shame to come all this way not to see who's on the back of it, eh?' He shrugged. 'Besides, there *is* that small matter of a palace full of night-skin lords and all their treasure. Might be some fun to be had there, I'd say.'

Berren followed him because he couldn't think of anything better to do with himself. *Sure. Stand in front of a dragon. Why not?*

82

Who I Am

Diamond Eye circled the stumps of the two broken towers. The third still stood, a great chunk smashed out of one corner, a maw of jagged glass teeth tinged with gold. The ground was a litter of glittering pieces like a sea of diamonds, and among them lay the bodies of men and women, slaves and soldiers, Taiytakei and others fleeing as the towers came down on them. Zafir felt the dragon's satisfaction. She felt her own. No remorse, not a shred of it, not even the idea of it. *Slavers. You brought this on yourselves.*

There were Taiytakei soldiers still alive. She saw them hiding in the shadows, cowering behind piles of rubble, watching the dragon to see what it would do. Soldiers from the ships to cheer and wave their swords at what she'd done perhaps, or soldiers from the palace, the last few defenders, too afraid to run. She didn't care. She was done. Whoever they were, they'd take away what they'd seen and spread it like fire through dry summer grass.

'Down!'

Diamond Eye fell out of the air, wings tucked in and gathering all the speed he could. The wind wrenched at her, straining to pull her out of the saddle, but the harness was a good one and held fast even after all it had suffered. Bellepheros and his glass-worker woman, the enchantress, they would make her a new one. Tsen would see to it once he understood what she and her dragon could do. The world would change now, and for a while Tsen would be the engine of that change.

Until she was done with him.

She closed her eyes. The wind tugged at the skin of her cheeks, at her lips. As Diamond Eye shifted beneath her to open his wings, she leaned forward to press herself against him. He stopped almost dead in the air a few feet above the ground. The force crushed her, and the wind of his wings lifted and hurled the litter of broken glass into a storm of razor edges that cut through the air. He landed, head held high and twitching from side to side in silent challenge. If there were enemies waiting then Diamond Eye would know. Dragons did that. They felt your thoughts. There was nowhere to hide. They'd know you were there and they'd read your mind, and if you meant harm to their riders then they'd feel it before you even knew it yourself, and you'd burn.

Dragons. Glorious. Terrible.

She fumbled for the buckles on her helm that held it to her shoulders and tugged them apart. One fell to pieces in her fingers. A shame. Such beautiful armour all ruined now except the dragon-scale that lay beneath. The helm's visor was a maze of cracks only held together by whatever force went into a Taiytakei enchanter's art. The golden dragon curled across the crest was scarred, marked by flying stones and glass. For a moment she thought about throwing it away. Riding without a helm was like riding naked, free and open to the wind and with a frisson of danger, but she still had to cross the desert again, back to Tsen's eyrie, and that was a long way to go with the howling wind in your face.

If that's where I choose to go. Zafir thought about that for a bit, then put the helm carefully down beside her and reached for a skin of water. She was filthy, drenched in sweat, sticky-skinned, bloody-faced and thirsty. You didn't notice when you flew. Hunger and thirst fell away, lost in the ecstasy of the dragon. When you landed, it all came back. She tipped almost all the first skin over her head, running her other hand through her hair and over her face, washing off the salt and the blood, then drank a mouthful.

She wasn't alone. Two men were creeping towards her, cautious and afraid but coming closer nevertheless, flitting from one pile of rubble to another, hoping not to be seen. Futile. Diamond Eye felt them so she knew they were there. And Diamond Eye was hungry.

'No,' she whispered. 'No more fire. Let them see us. Let them drink us in, us and what we have done.'

Diamond Eye rumbled. Zafir undid enough straps to get out of the saddle and stand up high on his back. She looked around her one more time. Smoke and flames poured from broken holes in the outer palace. Five of the six lesser towers still stood but the sixth was a jagged stump. She didn't even remember doing that. Bodies lay blasted against the walls by the wind of Diamond Eye's landing, jumbled among the chunks of stone and iron and broken glass.

'Sea Lords of the Taiytakei?' She threw back her head and laughed. 'Do you see me, lords of the sea? You think you are the masters of the world, but you are not. You will learn to fear. You will learn to beg. You will plead and none of it will save you. Not from me. For I am Zafir! I am the dragon-queen ! Do you hear me?'

She waited. If there were Elemental Men here then they would come. If they had a way to touch her, she would only know as they appeared at her back and slit open her naked throat.

Die slowly and badly, slave. I do not wish you well. The words of the Watcher as he'd prepared to kill her.

'But it was you who died,' she whispered. 'I killed you and I have your knife. And as you say, I am what I am.'

There were no Elemental Men. The two soldiers who now came towards her openly were sword-slaves, bared arms held high to show their brands.

Mad. Mad mad mad, but Berren followed anyway. He tucked the warlock's knife into his belt and gripped his sword and then wondered what, exactly, was the point. The dragon was enormous. Obviously it had been *big*, it had to be *big*. He'd seen it flying through the air, seen it smash the glasships over the docks. He'd seen it over the sea against the ships and he'd seen it over the island and over the palace. He'd seen the rider on its back, a mere speck against its bulk. He'd seen it lift up a giant made of stone and as tall as a barn and carry it high into the air and smash it on the rocks below. All these things. But on the ground with its neck and its tail stretched out, it was simply enormous. As long as a ship, maybe longer. And what was a sword going to do against something like that? Like the big man said: nothing. Not even annoy it. It scared him witless. A true monster that would eat him and barely notice. And yet ... What was the eagerness he felt as he followed Tuuran, picking their way through the daggers of broken glass and the flayed bodies?

Madness. Had to be.

*

Tuuran passed through huddled groups of Taiytakei dead, their armour battered and their bright cloaks ragged and scorched. They smelled of burned feathers. They'd been fierce and proud and terrible once, glorious and regal, but now he looked at their faces and saw the wide eyes, the terror and the blank incomprehension. They hadn't known what to do, any of them, and all the armour, all that gleaming glass and gold and all those bright colours, their shields and their batons that hurled lightning and their wicked spiked ashgars, all of those fell away to nothing and they were just men as scared as a virgin oar-slave. It made him want to laugh. Laugh at them for their mad pride, laugh at Crazy Mad for thinking he was any better, at himself for refusing to be scared of even a hundred-foot monster made of fangs and fire that tore cities apart for fun. Or of a man whose eyes turned silver, for that matter.

The dragon lowered its head to the ground as if to look at them, and that only made it seem even bigger. Its eyes were the size of a man's head and slitted like a snake's. Its teeth protruded from its jaws, bone swords. There were great tears in its wings and gashes through its scales. Blood ran down its flanks and dripped onto its claws and onto the rubble beneath, but it had *won*, and victory poured out of it in waves, for *that* was all that mattered. It stared at them, unblinking, as if to ask what in the name of the Great Flame they thought they were doing. Then it cocked its head and rubbed it against the ground. Laughing at them, if monsters could laugh. Tuuran bared his teeth and laughed right back. He lifted his axe over his head and held it in both hands.

'I am Tuuran, dragon-rider,' he roared. 'And I am Adamantine.'

The two men came right up to Diamond Eye's head. Zafir was about to ask them who they were when Diamond Eye did the strangest thing. He cocked his head to one side and rubbed it against the ground. Zafir blinked. It was a rare gesture. She'd seen it among her dragons when they fought one another for mates but she'd never once seen it used to a human. It was submission.

'Stop it!' she hissed. 'Get up!'

The big one grinned at the dragon and lifted his axe over his head. 'I am Tuuran,' he roared. 'And I am Adamantine.'

She frowned and stared at him because something about his

voice was familiar. It was the first voice she'd heard from her own land for months that wasn't Bellepheros. Maybe that was it. An Adamantine Man sworn to serve the speaker of the nine realms.

Slowly she climbed down from Diamond Eye's back. Slowly because half the harness was missing and because she was starting to feel how everything hurt, how much a toll this battle had taken on both of them. The dragon's wounds looked terrible but they wouldn't slow him. They'd heal, and so would she.

When she was on the ground, Diamond Eye lazily lifted his head. The Adamantine Man stood still and impassive, towering over her, patient and not afraid at all, the way an Adamantine Man should be. The other had something about him, something that had caught Diamond Eye's interest. Not another guardsman – his skin was too dark, he was too short and he didn't carry an axe, and yet … It was the sensation she'd had before, a scent of something. *What is it, my deathbringer? What is it about him?*

The Adamantine Man wasn't moving. He waited patiently. *Are there any more of you?* Her heart beat a little faster. She took off her gauntlet and held out her hand, the one that still wore the Speaker's Ring.

'I am Zafir,' she said. 'Queen of the Silver City. Speaker of the nine realms. Come closer.'

The dragon was watching him. Not Tuuran, not anything else, but *him*. He could feel it and he could barely move. Its rider whispered something. The dragon lifted its head but its eyes never left him. And, sun and moon, it struck him to the heart, the most fearful thing he'd ever seen or would ever see again, vast and made of death, and most of him wanted to quiver and empty his bladder and his bowels and fall sobbing to his shaking knees and beg and sob for a mercy that simply didn't exist. And yet he didn't. And he *ought* to be terrified but he wasn't. He felt almost … proud, and it was a pride that didn't belong to him, but came from the thing he carried inside. Fearless and fiery. Like seeing a long-lost son grown strong and powerful and master of the world around him.

That was what scared him far more than this monster.

The rider climbed down, stiff and awkward, and Berren could see how much pain she was in. But she was proud too, and she had a strength in her face. Her short hair was plastered to her pale skin. There were cuts on her face and streaks of blood but she wore them well. Her armour was battered and cracked and broken. A proper soldier. The Bloody Judge in him approved. And when she stood in front of Tuuran, no matter how the big man dwarfed her, she looked him in the eye without hesitation and held out her hand.

'Come closer!' The rider spoke with the same accent as Tuuran.

Tuuran stared at her hand and then he fell to his knees, bowed and pressed both his head and the shaft of his axe to the ground. He was shaking. All his poise was suddenly gone.

'Speaker of the nine what?' Berren muttered. 'I know we don't see many women, but—'

The big man was on him in a snarling blur of speed: 'You come from Aria? Well, slave, this is *my* empress, and you will still your tongue or I will cut it out, despite all that has passed between us!' The rider watched them both, unmoved. Amused perhaps. She certainly wasn't afraid, but then why would anyone be afraid who had a monster like that at their back? Berren held up his hands. Old words came back to haunt him, knocking him off balance. *Dragons for one of you. Queens for both! An empress!*

The rider ignored Berren and kept her eyes on Tuuran. 'I've heard your name, Tuuran of the Adamantine Guard. You served the alchemist Bellepheros. You served him well, with your blood and your heart, and perhaps better than he in his turn served you.' Her voice was strong and proud. 'Will you serve me, your speaker, in this land?'

Tuuran dropped to his knees again and pressed his head against the broken flagstones. 'From birth to death, Holiness. Nothing more, nothing less.'

She was a slave. The understanding hit Berren like a rock between the eyes. A slave from the same land as Tuuran, with the same accent and the same pale skin. But a slave on the back of a dragon. A slave who'd thrown down the palace of a sea lord!

Her eyes shifted. She was looking at him now. 'And you? What is *your* name, sword-slave?'

'Berren,' he said without a moment of doubt. 'I'm Berren Crowntaker. Berren the Bloody Judge of Tethis.'

83

Blood

The holy queen of the Silver City asked him questions about places and people and realms and armies which felt like they belonged to another life, and Tuuran answered them. Beside him, Crazy Mad stared at the rider and the dragon stared back. At Crazy Mad and only him and nowhere else, and its eyes were intense and intelligent and filled with questions. The queen never said, but Tuuran understood. Despite what she was, despite the dragon she rode, she was a slave. A prisoner of the Taiytakei like all the rest of them, and he was but one man, and there was no great army come for her.

It took most of the time they talked before Tuuran realised that they'd met once before. She was the girl from the Pinnacles, the one who'd stabbed a man to death, the one for whom he'd kept silent and had been sold as a slave. He wondered if she remembered him. Probably not, he supposed. *After all, we soldiers all look the same, don't we?* He found it didn't much bother him. Here she was, proud and a queen and on the back of a dragon and furiously alive. It made him smile. He'd done something good then, once long ago.

When they were done she did the strangest thing. The speaker of the nine realms took his hand, the one that held his axe, and touched it to her lips.

'Go,' she said. 'Find your way back to me.'

She turned away and climbed into the dragon's harness and Tuuran retreated into the rubble, pulling Crazy with him. The dragon spread its wings. It stared at Crazy Mad one last time and then began to run, and the wind of its ascent showered them with stones and broken shards as big as a man's fist. Tuuran watched them fly, staring long after the dragon was gone, a distant speck vanished into the horizon over the burning city and the desert beyond.

'I understand,' he said when he finally tore his eyes away. He nodded to himself. 'I understand why I'm here. Why my fate sold me into slavery. It's for her. I have served my speaker. I will serve her again.'

'Well, you do that,' snapped Crazy Mad. 'I have to go back and find the man who made Vallas do what he did. I have to find out who he is and what I am.' He seemed out of sorts now the dragon was gone, but at least his eyes were his own. Normal and human. 'How? How am I supposed to do that?'

'Every man has his own destiny.' Tuuran could almost read Crazy's thoughts. Whatever he said, a part of Crazy wanted to follow the dragon and the woman who rode it as well. To find out who she was and why dragons filled his dreams. Wasn't hard to see. After all, didn't everyone?

Crazy Mad stared out into the sky where the dragon had gone. 'Thanks for that, big man. Something a bit more helpful next time, eh?'

Out around the towers Taiytakei soldiers were stirring again. The dragon was gone but the invaders still had business, finishing this city and its lord. Some were already picking their way into the stumps of the ruined towers. There was no fighting any more, just a smashed-up palace full of ... *stuff*.

Tuuran offered Crazy Mad his hand. 'Come on, slave! You can ponder your existence later when your pockets are stuffed with some rich bastard's silver.' When Crazy Mad waved him away, Tuuran shrugged. 'Well, I'll be sure to loot something nice for you, eh? Don't get left with nothing, Crazy.' He picked up his shield and trotted away to disappear among the ruins.

When he was gone, Berren Crowntaker, the Bloody Judge of Tethis, sat alone together with the last little voice of someone who had once been called Skyrie, listening to the far-off crash of the waves and the crying of the gulls. Listening but not watching, because his eyes were staring into their own reflection in the blade of a gold-hilted knife. The knife that severed souls. The knife that could cut pieces of people away. And he was wondering what it was that he carried inside him.

What did they do to you, Skyrie?

*

When the dragon came back, the hatchlings shrieked and screamed and flapped their wings, straining at their chains, clamouring its victory. Baros Tsen watched it land. He made a show of being slow and not very interested as he ambled across the eyrie to look. It was damaged, bloody scars streaked across its belly and its flanks, but there was a savage joy in the way it held itself. The rider was much the same. He watched her slide off the monster's back and stagger as if half dead, pulling off her armour piece by piece and letting it fall as she walked. She moved awkwardly, held her head gingerly, and he could see bloody scars on her face and the bruises around them. He smelled her before she reached him. She stank. Yet she had the same look about her as the dragon: gleeful and filled with a fierce pride. He couldn't bring himself to look at her. She was only a slave, after all. A slave he'd thought to be dead by now. He could correct that mistake and have her killed right here and now. *Should*, really, but he had to know what had happened first, how it really was. 'The slaves of Bom Tark are no more?' he asked, aware of any ears that might be near.

She looked him in the eye, unblinking. Smiling. 'I flew as I was asked, Baros Tsen T'Varr. I found a city and I tore it to pieces. There were ships too. I'm afraid most of them are gone. There was no resistance of any great consequence.' Arrogance dripped from every word and gesture.

Tsen forced himself to look at her. 'Destroyed? All of it?'

The smile didn't change but the gleam in her eyes brightened. 'Oh yes, Master Tsen. All of it. Every part a shattered smoking ruin. I doubt many survived at all.'

'Then you have done well, slave.' He waved her away, and waved at the air as well, hoping the smell of her would quickly follow. Turned his back. So the Watcher had betrayed him? The Elemental Man had allowed Dhar Thosis to die? It was against everything for which the Watcher and his kind stood and yet they'd let it happen, and so Sea Lord Shonda had been their advocate all along, not their adversary as Tsen had thought. A terrible thing had been done and the world would think that *he* had ordered it. A savagery not seen across the Takei'Tarr for hundreds of years.

He closed his eyes. Someone would die for this, but he had something even the Watcher hadn't known. A second witness to the truth. Chay-Liang. *And now what? Turn the eyrie back towards Khalishtor? Abase myself in front of the lords and navigators and give them the truth and Chay-Liang's word and demand that the Elemental Men explain themselves? Or ... Or perhaps not.* He smiled. Now *there* was a thought. He would enter the Crown of the Sea Lords, yes, but not to abase himself. There would be uproar. They would demand his head and the destruction of his house, the dismantling of his fleet. He would be passive, sorrowful, head bowed. *Yes,* he would say. *It is a terrible thing that Shrin Chrias Kwen has done. And yes, when I am sea lord then he will be caught and he will be punished and every memory and trace of him erased. Of course. And yes, when I am sea lord then reparations will be made and Xican will make every effort to restore Sea Lord Senxian's heirs to their glory.* And the outrage would continue, for he might as well have turned to them all to tell them where to stick it and thumbed his nose in their faces, but then he would hold up his hand. *Aria,* he would say. *Something must be done. Here is that something.* And the Crown of the Sea Lords would shake at his words and he would lead them out onto their balconies, each one to their own Path of Words, and they would all stare at the dragon perched atop the Crown and their outrage would fall silent and they would choke on it. He'd send the dragon away, and whatever it was they wanted done to Aria and its Ice Witch, he would do it for them. And they would pay; and his t'varrs would talk to other t'varrs about extended lines of credit and cancellations of loans and the remains of his fleet would be saved and Quai'Shu's dream with it, and all would be well, and he would get away with it because *he* hadn't done this. He would get away with it because the Elemental Men had permitted Dhar Thosis to die. Because this was *their* design in the end, not his ...

The smell hadn't gone away. The dragon-rider slave was still there. He almost struck her, the first time he would ever have raised a hand to anyone. She deserved it after what she'd done, but then he saw what she had in her hands. The hilt of a knife, and he saw *which* hilt of *which* knife. And it wasn't that the knife didn't have a blade, only that it was so thin that he couldn't see it. And he realised then that the Elemental Men hadn't permitted anything at all and that he was utterly and completely ruined. He closed his eyes. *And what were you thinking, stupid T'Varr? That was the dream of a kwen. It would never have worked. Someone would simply have killed you.*

'You tried to murder me,' she said and tucked away the bladeless knife once more. He couldn't answer. 'As you see, I require a bath.' The same smile, exactly as it had been since she'd landed. 'And your ear, or I will burn your whole world black. Do you understand me?'

She didn't wait for him. She strode off, limping, and he followed, for what else could he do? All the way through the spiralling white-lit tunnels of his eyrie to his most private sacred space, the baths he'd built at the eyrie's heart. She shrugged off her dragon-scale and slipped off her shift at the edge of the waters and never looked round, only raised a hand to beckon him to join her. He closed the door behind them and watched her step in, wincing at the water's heat. Other men might have looked past her ugly pale skin and her muscular arms and legs and her hard curves with no softness in them at all, past her bruises and her scars and the streaks of dried blood. When Tsen looked at her he felt … nothing. He ought to be feeling outrage and fear and disgust, that was what he *ought* to be feeling. And maybe some dread, and he *ought* to be calling his black-cloaks to have her killed and thrown off the edge of the eyrie for what she'd done, but what did it matter when they were already both as good as dead? At least this time she didn't try to flaunt herself. Today her eyes were hard. The pretence of anything tender was gone. She was, at last, her true self.

He followed her into the water and poured a glass of apple wine for each of them. She took hers from him in silence.

'We are alone,' he told her. 'Truly alone. No one else will hear. You have my ear as you asked, slave. Speak then, for when you are done I will very likely have you killed.'

She looked at him long and hard through the steam from the hot water that caressed his skin. He sipped slowly, savouring the exquisite taste of his wine. No sense in not enjoying it. He wondered how long it would be before the news of what he'd done to Dhar Thosis reached anywhere that mattered? Days? A few weeks? And then the killers would come. How long depended on whether any glassships had escaped. Perhaps she could tell him that.

'What happened to my Elemental Man?' he asked when she didn't speak.

'*Your* Elemental Man? Perhaps he had a name, once?' Then she shrugged and let out a tinkling laugh. 'He tried to stop me from carrying out your orders. What else could I do?'

'*You* killed him?'

She shook her head. 'Diamond Eye killed him. *I* could kill *you*, though. Right now if it suited me. I could snap your neck.' She said it in such a matter-of-fact way that he almost believed she meant it. It got to him, the pointlessness of such a threat now.

'If that is your intent then go ahead, slave. Shall we go together? We may as well. The Elemental Men will wipe us from the very memory of the world itself for what you've done.'

A slight smile curled her lips. 'For what *I've* done.' Beside the bath the decanter of apple wine sat in a brass bowl of iced water on a small stone pedestal. She reached across him and took it, filled her cup and then smashed the decanter on the bath's marble rim. She picked up a shard of glass and ran it across the palm of her hand. Blood dripped into the water. Tsen tried not flinch; not that he was particularly afraid but simply from the sight of her. She was a savage, and her blood and her nakedness tied his insides in knots. He forced himself to be still. 'I want my freedom, Baros Tsen T'Varr.' Blood dripped from her fingertips and splashed into her wine. Tsen winced again. Such a waste. 'Are you not clever enough to give it to me?' She stretched out her arms and her legs. Bruises from the battle of Dhar Thosis stained her pale skin. 'I knew another man like you once. He was almost as cunning but not quite. *Much* better between the silk though.'

'I am not interested in your sex, slave.'

'I know.' She laughed again. 'And I'm thankful for that, and so should you be, because if you *were* interested, then by now I'd have opened your throat. I'd be bathing in your cooling blood, waiting for your soldiers to burst through the door to finish me. Call me slave again and I may yet do so. My name is Zafir. I am mistress of the Silver City and speaker for the dragon-kings and dragon-queens of my realms. We both know you didn't mean me to destroy that city. So now set your mind to sending me back where I came from, and I will set mine and my dragon to aiding you. I trust you're clever enough to do *that*, at least? You may keep the alchemist if you must but I want the Adamantine Man who once served him. You should find him easily enough. He was in Dhar Thosis too, so I imagine he's now with your kwen if your kwen survived the battle.'

'Chrias?' For a moment Tsen looked at her hard. 'I happen to know that he did. We have ways, he and I.' He watched for any reaction. Irritation or annoyance, perhaps, but if there was a flicker of anything, it was glee. 'Would you like to see him?'

Zafir shook her head, although he saw the instant of hesitation. 'Give me what I want or I will find another who will. Your friends from the mountains, perhaps?'

For a moment Tsen ignored her. He reached over the edge of the bath to the pedestal with its brass bowl, reached into the water and flipped all the ice out to the floor, then dipped his middle finger into it. 'Quai'Shu had an enchanter bind us all together, years ago.' He held up his other hand and raised his little finger. 'Jima Hsian, though Jima was quick to find a way around it.' Then his first finger. 'Bronzehand. Come. See.' The water in the bowl was already shimmering. 'We may see through one another's eyes as and when we wish, unless precautions are taken. Many sea lords bind their kin and their kwens and hsians and t'varrs together like this.' He watched the water in the bowl. 'Most of the time we keep each other blind, but not today.' Through the kwen's own eyes he saw Chrias in a gloomy room, staring at the soft skin on the inside of his arm, the place where slaves were branded. Staring and staring and rubbing at something. By the look of things he'd already rubbed it raw, or else it was a burn from the fighting in Dhar Thosis. Hard to tell. He glanced at the dragon slave but she made no move to see for herself. When he looked back into the water, Chrias was walking through a door and then along a passage, following one of his black-cloaks. They were at sea, on board a ship. He waited long enough for Chrias to get up to the deck and look about and see that land was nowhere in sight. 'I wonder what he's up to. Running as far and fast as he can with a hold full of Shonda's silver if he has any sense.' He shook his head and pulled his finger out of the water. 'I will consider your proposal, Dragon-Queen.'

Zafir smiled and sighed. 'To life and its potency.' She raised her glass and then saw that his was empty, leaned across and tipped some wine from her own into his. Tsen forced himself to smile back.

'To life, Dragon-Queen, although I am bewildered by the idea that either of us may cling to it for much longer.'

The wine was tainted by her blood and it would spoil the taste. He pretended not to notice as he lifted the glass. The smile on her face stayed exactly as it was, fixed in place.

'I'm glad Shrin Chrias Kwen wasn't killed,' she said. 'And you may keep that middle finger. I'm so looking forward to watching him die.'

84

A Crack of Light

She watched Baros Tsen T'Varr lift his glass. He was looking at her as he did it. She raised her own and then hesitated and didn't quite know why. Shrin Chrias Kwen would die, slowly and in agony, knowing that she had killed him. Tsen would see it all happen and know that without her the same fate was his. All he had to do was drink. It was perfect.

And yet she hesitated.

She couldn't get the Adamantine Man out her of head. Hadn't been able to ever since she'd left Dhar Thosis. There were some who said with little sneers in their voices that the Speaker's Guard were all the same, that they couldn't be told apart except by themselves and that that was exactly how it should be. There was nothing in the way the one in Dhar Thosis had moved to make Zafir think she'd seen him before, but she remembered his voice as though she'd heard it only yesterday.

Leave her be, you fat prick!

The Pinnacles. His knife. And though it had made no difference, he'd never said that it had been her, not him, who'd murdered her mother's consort; and for that she'd sent him to Furymouth to be a slave. She'd done it to save him. And now here he was.

Dragons were uncaring and hostile and utterly ruthless. They were monsters that devoured anything they found to be weak. She'd long ago grown to learn that their riders were the same. Worse because they had to be. Everyone around her. Her as well. The monsters made them what they were. They had no choice. None.

Baros Tsen touched his glass to his lips.

Bellepheros watched the dragon-queen's return. He watched where she went and he watched as Baros Tsen T'Varr followed her down into the eyrie, and he saw the horror and the utter disbelief on the t'varr's face. Then he went back to his study. Each step felt heavier than the last. He sat at his desk and held his head in his hands for a long time. He picked up the bottle of liquid silver that he'd brought with him all the way from Furymouth. He looked at it, felt the weight of it. It was the poison that Quai'Shu had given to one of the princes of the dragon realms so that he might murder his rivals. It was subtle and it killed slowly. Its fumes in the air brought on a madness, but in such a gradual way that no one ever saw until the venom had saturated the bones and the organs of its victim and corroded them from the inside.

He stared at it. *I am not like them. I cannot be. I fight with words. Only words.*

But he still didn't put the bottle down.

Zafir lurched suddenly forward and slapped the glass out of Tsen's hand. They stared at one another, each as surprised as the other. Then she turned quickly and climbed from the water, throwing on her shift. She stooped and picked up the bladeless knife of the Elemental Man.

'The Adamantine Man who served our alchemist,' she said again, and her voice was twisted and choked. 'By whatever gods you believe in, find him. Bring him here! And when you do, you fall on your knees, Baros Tsen T'Varr, and you thank him. You thank him as though you owe him your life. Because you do.'

Then she was gone and Tsen had no idea what had just happened. None at all.

Liang stood in the yard watching the dragon. It was acutely restless, fidgeting and turning and flapping its wings and curling and uncurling its tail and its neck. Now and then it plucked a piece of debris out of its scales. Its discomfort rolled through her, turbulent and disquieting, and she almost didn't see Belli hurrying across the yard towards the tunnels where the Scales lived. When she did, she waved at him, and when he pretended not to see her, she ran, robes flapping around her feet, until she caught him. He was flushed and out of breath and his face was stricken with anguish. He kept shaking his head, even before she started to speak.

'What's wrong with the ...' *What's wrong with the dragon?* she was about to ask, but her eyes were drawn to his clenched fist and the bottle he was trying to hide within it. She looked at it long and hard and then looked him in the eye. His head fell. He started to shake. It took her a moment to realise it but he was sobbing. She touched his arm and held out her hand. 'That is not who you are, Belli,' she whispered. 'You are a builder, a maker, a healer, an architect. Give it to me. You are not a poisoner. You are not a murderer. Leave that to others.'

Wordlessly he gave her the bottle. Her fingers closed over it. It was heavy.

'Stay here.' She clasped his hand in her own. 'Stay, Belli. Just stay.'

He nodded and she walked briskly away, across to the walls and climbed them and then threw the vial of silver poison hard and far, away over the edge of the eyrie to be lost in the desert sands far below. When she came back, he was where she'd left him. She took his hands and then, when that didn't seem to be enough, embraced him and held him tightly. 'I'm sorry,' she said because after all she'd been the one to put the idea into his head. 'I'm so sorry.'

She held him until his weeping stopped, and then they stood apart and looked over at the dragon. 'What's wrong with it?' she asked.

He shook his head. 'Zafir must be more wounded than she seemed.' Then he shrugged. 'He feels his rider's anguish.'

Zafir walked as quickly as she could away from Baros Tsen and his bath, as fast as her pride would let her, back to her own little room. She was shaking. Everything the dragon had given her was gone. She curled up in a corner against the walls, holding Myst and Onyx tight to her, covering herself in their comfort and their warmth.

'No pity for pretty little Zafir,' she murmured and touched a hand to her breast. 'My heart is here. What's left of it. When they come, make them strike true.'

Epilogue

They Just
Come Back Again

The eggs were waiting for it, a cluster of them alone and far away from the others. The dragon Silence felt their call. Urgent skin that begged for the spark of life.

Afraid?

Dragons were not afraid.

The dragon chose one and slipped inside the waiting flesh as a man might slip on an old shoe. The sensation was a familiar comfort, yet always new. Every skin was different. *What colours will I be? Will my tail be long? My neck? How many fangs shall I have?* All these things a new discovery with each hatching. Another joy the little ones had taken away.

It eased into its new flesh like a ghost and opened its brand-new eyes still inside the egg. The urge to smash its way to freedom was strong but it let its senses roam instead, searching for sorcery, searching for thoughts. Things to which the little ones were blind.

It found much of both, and so it stayed quiet and looked at all the things in the strange and wonderful place where it would be born that was filled with alien thoughts and a very few that felt oddly familiar, and with many sorceries that were strange and fresh and one that was colossal and overwhelming and as ancient as the dragon itself. Something made before its first ever dawn.

It looked at all these things and chose its time with care. There were men with ropes and chains always watching. It slid inside their thoughts and sang songs of faraway dreams that lulled them, but they were clever and careful and the alchemist who watched over them was wise to such trickery. So it waited, hidden in its egg, day after day after day, until a change came – more men with more sorceries – and chaos and killing erupted around and above it and the watchers finally looked away. Then it bunched its muscles and clenched its claws; it built the fire inside it as high as its new body would allow, and when it was as ready as it could be, it burst its shell apart and leaped and spread its wings, and the last few men with their chains were too slow and frightened to reach it and it was free. It burst into a night full of thunder and lightning and little ones' screams as they died.

I am Silence, the dragon whispered amid the chaos around it, *and I am hungry.*

Acknowledgements

With thanks to Simon Spanton, devourer of unnecessary prologues, who asked for dragons and got more than he bargained for. To Marcus Gipps for his editorial work and Gillian Redfearn for saying Some Useful Things. To the copy-editors and proofreaders, whose names I've rarely known. To Stephen Youll for his gorgeous covers. To Jon Weir, who wanted more Zafir.

With thanks to all the people who read *A Memory of Flames* and talked about it and were open and honest about what they liked and what they didn't. You have told me what to keep and you have told me what might be made better, and *Dragon-Queen* is a different book from the one it might have been because of you. Don't let it go to your heads, mind.

It's still very true that none of this would have happened without the trust and faith of the same special few as last time. Thank you again. Thank you to lovers of dragons everywhere. Thank you to all the alchemists out there. Thank *you*, for reading this.

To any who want to explore the world of the dragons for its own sake, you can do so at the online gazetteer at www.stephendeas. com/gazetteer. There are other goodies there from time to time too.

Lastly, if you liked this book, please say so. Loudly and to lots of people.